A Turning

Rocelia Kinsman

Book One, Unexpected Journeys Series

Copyright Rocelia Kinsman, 2022
roceliakinsman@gmail.com
All rights reserved under the International & Pan-American Copyright Conventions. No part of this work may be reproduced or transmitted in any form or by any means, electronic or mechanical, including photocopying or recording, or by any information or retrieval system, except in the case of brief quotations embodied in reviews and certain other non-commercial uses permitted by copyright law, without the permission in writing from the author.
The characters in this book, with the exception of historical public figures, are entirely fictional. Any resemblance to actual persons living or dead is entirely coincidental.
First Edition 2023
ISBN: 9798372594579

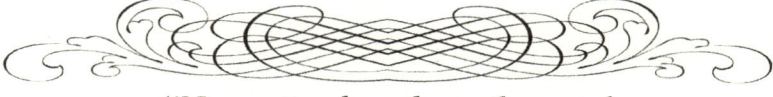

*"No matter how long the road,
there comes a turning."*

Part One

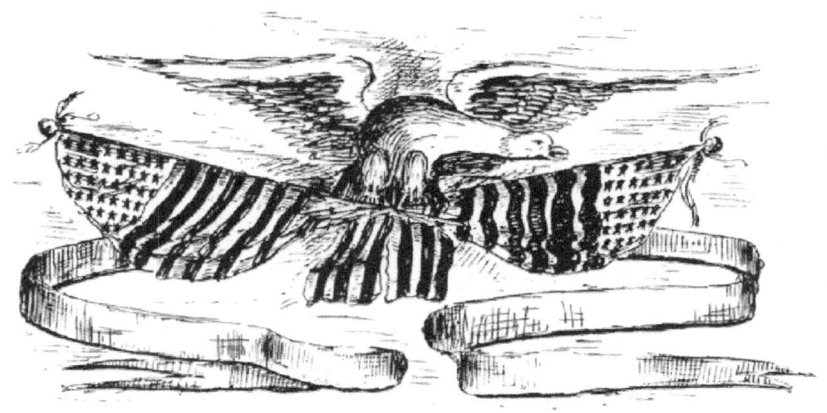

1863

Chapter 1

It was bound to blow up sooner or later. For the past month, his father had been tamping resentment like gunpowder into his cold clay pipe. He felt the pinch in his lungs, spiders of sweat down his back. He had quick-marched halfway up Knotts Hill. Why had the Maker of All given some men an inexhaustible store of energy born of wrath, yet stinted others? Rolling his tongue around, he coughed several times to bring saliva into his throat: usually he had too much of the stuff and now he had too little.

The other officers in his company had daily loaded him with their canteens, knowing he had a skill for finding water, if for little that was martial. He knew this hill: small streams covered the hillside in springtime, and there'd been a hard rain in the forenoon. He traveled off the path for a time following the sound of a brook. There. Tossing aside his hat, he rinsed his hands, then dropped flat onto the stream's bank and shoveled water into his mouth until the coldness of it exceeded his thirst and made him fear another bout of neuralgia. That last siege had kept him a-bed for a day; this weather was too fine to waste under bedclothes.

Continuing his climb, he reached the main path, and halted by an outcropping of boulders. One of the rocks, shaped like a bed, and decorated with painted slogans, was a popular lover's destination. He wondered if "bed rock" had indeed proved as firm a foundation for love as the couples desired. He himself had enjoyed here a few kisses—but little more—stolen from Hattie Caldwell just two years ago. He sat down, hands flat on the sun-warmed stone.

'No chance of that again,' he thought, sure that no woman would welcome him into her bed, except perhaps a whore, and a

short-sighted one at that. The binding-cloth of despair, familiar from his days of convalescence, cocooned him again. Time, they said, time will heal everything. Another platitudinous piece of bunkum. He contemplated his fate until his buttocks grew numb, then slid off the rock and opened his eye to the sun's dazzle.

"I could live up here," he mumbled," all summer and into the fall, if need be. The wild man of Knott's Hill." Retrieving his hat, he stood and began the climb to the hill's summit to survey the full extent of his proposed domain.

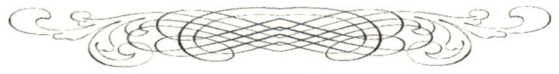

Maggie pushed aside her sketch paper as her employer appeared in the kitchen doorway. "Yes, ma'am, I will," she said automatically.

Mrs. Wilkin thrust her begrimed forefinger close to Maggie's face. "Just look at this smut."

"I'll clean the lamp chimneys now," Maggie replied.

Mrs. Wilkin shook her finger to reinforce her point, then held the offending member far away from her neat garments. "That was thy forenoon task."

"I been polishing the tea spoons," Maggie said.

"For half an hour or more?" Mrs. Wilkin clucked her tongue. "And what is this?" She tapped Maggie's drawing, leaving a sooty mark. "Child," she went on, "Thy scribblings will not put bread on thy table nor money in thy purse. Finish thy duty first. How many times have I told thee that since thou came here?" *At least a thousand times,* Maggie thought, *but surely, you think a thousand and one will work the charm.*

"Many a-time," Mrs. Wilkin said.

"Yes, ma'am."

Her employer frowned. "And we should do our duty cheerfully."

"Yes, I know. But did you see the sky? That's why I forgot the lamps."

A skyward glance out the window that morning had undone Maggie's dutiful intentions - for she had seen there phalanxes of wind-driven clouds, the color of pewter and slate, shadowing a bruised blue sky. The towering masses had advanced until their center was attacked and run through by swords of sunlight. Celestial blue captured part of the field, and then prevailed, as the clouds rumbled a retreat. She had seen the realm where archangels battled: it was a promise, a warning.

"It was stormy, but now it has passed over," Mrs. Wilkin said.

"Oh, 'twas beautiful!" Maggie had no words to explain how her hands had itched to capture on paper the light and the dark magnificence and the space in which they'd clashed; and how her soul had been fed by the sight.

"That is no reason to waste thy time dreaming over it. This is thy afternoon off, but since thou has shirked thy duty I cannot let thee go until all thy work is done. Thy laziness harms thee too."

Half an hour later, Maggie had finished cleaning and filling the lamps, and was back at the kitchen table, polishing. Mrs. Wilkin, watching again, was reflected on the round bowl of the spoon.

Maggie said, "Och, ma'am, I'm almost done. May I go now, if you please, and I'll finish them later, I promise."

"Promises must be kept," Mrs. Wilkin said.

"Yes, ma'am," Maggie called back as she hooked her sunbonnet on her finger and closed the back door. *Free, I'm free! And far away from thee.*

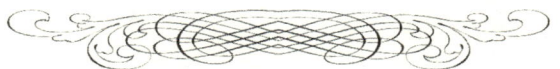

The consistent habits Maggie had admired in her Quaker employers when she joined them at the age of thirteen constricted her now like an outgrown corset. When she first joined the household their discussions of morality and social reform were rich with meaning - but now their talk was background noise in her life, like insects humming. She stopped to rest for a moment, wiping sweat from her upper lip, then leaned her forearms on the split rail fence, enjoying the smell of meadow grass. She wished to carry it back in her bonnet to push the scent of sour dishwater, and old, closed rooms from her nostrils. A grasshopper whirred up, surprising her as it jumped past her arm.

Her father used to catch them for her to look at, and when they stained his hands, he would chide them for "spitting tobacco." She ducked through a hole where a fence rail had fallen, but then glared at the cow patties spotting the meadow. And, wasn't there a bull pastured nearby? At the fearsome prospect, she lost her desire to cross the meadow. *Where does this path go? I never been up that way.* She came back through the fence, put on her sunbonnet and followed the track away from the house, seeking a prettier view.

Halfway up Knott's Hill, she stopped at a place where boulders gathered like men at a tavern: some were huddled together as if sharing stories, but one or two remained aloof. She ignored the flat rock marked with visitors' initials. Pulling up her skirts, she climbed upon the largest rock, and danced a little jig of triumph.

It put her in mind of the St. Patrick's Day frolic a year ago, when three men had danced with her and followed her as avidly as bees to the flowers. The gray-beard, Dooley, told her he meant to marry her; but he was drunk. Next Paddy Molloy, nearer her own age, but florid and pimply and much too forward, had pressed upon her a birthday kiss, pushing his tongue into her mouth.

But last, best! Seamus Corcoran read the newspapers and spoke so stirringly on Irish independence. Rory, all the folks called him, because his hair and beard shone red like banked coals in a grate. His eyes were merry, daring, and perhaps a little mad. He had snatched her away from the odious Molloy and whirled her in the dance. When Rory essayed a kiss, she'd made only a mild protest; yet he'd stopped, apologized, and caressed her cheek so sweetly it had left her longing for the kiss she'd spurned.

This year's birthday had been far from grand: Corcoran waltzed about with two grinning girls attached to him like cockleburrs. Dull Dooley was Maggie's only suitor. She climbed down from the rock and resumed the path, stopping at the stream bank to drink. Her hands and teeth tingling from the cold water, she walked on—wondering why marriage was the only choice a girl could make in life. *Is it a choice, then, if you have no choice? Maybe Da will come back soon and take me with him.*

She reached the popular observation spot at the summit, which was unpopulated today except by half a dozen small birds. Most of the factories strung along the river were in view—as well as the church spire down in Millville and the farm fields in Vinton Center. She held up both hands to frame aspects, as Da had taught her; trying to memorize what she saw so that she could sketch it later. An immoderate thrill of melancholy touched her. *Will this be all I ever see?* She wheeled away from the summit's wooden platform and picked her way through a stand of brush. Turning to flick a bug off her shoulder, Maggie saw two young birch trees leaning at the same angle and looking satisfyingly odd, like a pointing hand. She followed the birches' direction, and found a mossy clearing in the thicket, close to the hill's slope. The slope was clad in a tangle of greenery as thick as matted hair, threaded with brown tree trunks and muddy scars. Siena and umber, she thought, remembering the watercolors in a paint box she'd admired at the store.

With her toe, she poked the trunk of a huge tree which had fallen parallel to the edge of the slope. *A grandfather tree,* she thought, seating herself where two of its branches welcomed her in a stiff-armed embrace. *Da, where are you now? Do you ever think of me?* She had no answer. Finally, she imagined him thriving, too busy to write. She stretched and yawned, at peace.

A sound like running water trickled into her consciousness. She saw pebbles dancing down the slope. Next, she heard a loud mournful creak, an instant before the tree groaned like a dying man, as she was deafened by thunder. She had no time to glance at the skies, for the clamor was in her and beneath her as the tree lurched forward down the slope—tolerating its human cargo for only a moment before pitching it aside.

He reached the peak of the hill but did not climb the stairs to the platform. He could see much of the town below, with a horse and buggy bumbling beetle-like through the main street. His father's house lay beyond the curve of the hill, but the roof of the shed was visible like a speck of lint on the shoulder of a green suit. He recalled an evening, years ago, when he had last escaped the house and found a perch on the roof of the shed: there, he had watched the house until the lamp in his father's study was extinguished; waited until the last light went out, before creeping with a cat's night-eyes into his bed.

A sudden thunderous noise made him duck, and hunch in a crouch, arms over his head, glancing backward in the direction of the enemy's fire. Then, remembering where he was, he got up and moved in the direction of the sound, curious to find the source of the erstwhile "cannon shot." Past the leaning birches he saw in a clearing a huge scar of black earth.

"Landslide," he muttered. This was by far the steepest section of the hill. He heard another odd sound, soft but insistent. Was it a bird? No, a cat squalling: it sounded like a baby. He found an area where the ground appeared solid; peering over the lip of the slope, he whistled at the sight of the big tree that had gashed a road of destruction as it traveled down the bluff.

Is that the creature? A brown and white heap with limbs lay off to the side, nearly beneath another fallen tree. He squinted at it. A fawn? Then the thing moved, and he recognized with shock that it was human, and still alive. As the human, a girl, cried again, he looked about wildly as if a rope, or a winch, would appear merely by his summoning. He thought to run for aid—the place was deserted today, and it would take him an hour to bring anyone back. That big tree, that's a bad one! It was balanced precariously, and she was nearly beneath it now.

Above and far to the left of where the girl lay, the slope inclined more moderately and was ringed with sturdy young trees. Straight down would not work, he would have to angle across the slope. Damn the mud! He examined the terrain for handholds, his mind seizing and rejecting possibilities, then unfastened his braces, leaving them still buttoned behind, and tucking the loose ends into the front of his trousers. Whispering a curse, he began a painstaking descent, his brain free of any conscious thought: focused instead on each step, each grab, each belly crawl and rump slide. Along the way his hat fell off. He heard it skitter down the slope but chose not to watch it descend.

At the approach closest to the girl, the hill cut away sharply. He moved sideways, his front against the slope, until he was a few feet above her. He confirmed his first glance: the tree had broken her fall, but its black trunk rested on a small hillock of mud and wet brush. The tree would shift and crush her if he disturbed its ground by approaching any closer.

He secured the front of his suspenders to a stump, then tested the hold.

"Hello! Can you hear me?"

The girl raised her head.

"Hang on tight. Don't move for a minute." He inched over, his footholds reduced to toe holds, until he could reach out an arm towards her. "Can you stretch? Slowly! And take my arm."

Gibbering animal sounds, she scrabbled to him, caught hold of his arm with strength born of terror and clung to his shoulder and side. The force of her move swung him out of his toeholds. He banged hard on his right side and arm into the slope, and slid a little, but the suspenders and a tangle of pricker bush kept them from going far. The big tree creaked and slithered with a sucking noise to a new gully ten yards from them.

"Get up on my back," he hissed to the girl. He felt her do so, as he regained his footing, and crept cautiously back to the side until he could lean against the stump and rest. Fumbling with his left hand, he wiped dirt from his face, and opened his right eye. All right. Thank God. He unfastened the suspenders from their mooring; spat grit out of his mouth. After shifting the girl's weight and tucking one of her arms to his side, to prevent her choking him, he set off on the upward journey. His world reduced again to handholds, calculated angles, this vine, that exposed root, slippery footholds, that branch, straining muscles. Near to failure, his strength spent, he prayed himself and his burden to the ring of saplings, and with murderous grunts and sobs up over the lip of the slope and onto the promised land.

He endured a timeless blur of gasping, and quivering guts. He sneezed hard, spraying mud. The left side of his face was still pressed against the earth: he lifted his head, sneezed again. Eventually he felt able to release his passionate embrace of the yard of dirt and leaf mold that he'd won with such labor, and crawl on his hands and knees further from the slope's edge to a level mossy area. He sat up and recovered his senses.

The girl had crept up this far already and lay curled in a ball, shaking and swiping at her eyes with one hand, the other still clutching the ground. He staggered to his feet, crashed a short way into the brush, relieved himself, then returned to the mossy seat. The girl's shaking had subsided. She too seemed to become aware of the call of nature and went forward into the brush, got to her feet and began to raise her skirt. He turned his face away. Presently she fumbled her way back and sat. Her hands and arms were bleeding from scratches, as was one leg.

"Are you all right?" he croaked.

She looked at him. Her eyes widened, and she screamed.

"Mother of God," she gasped, "You're hurt!" She was staring at the left side of his face. He turned his body away from her.

Maggie, immersed in shock, babbled again "You're hurt!" and plucked around her in search of a bandage. She wrung her dress in her hands, then noticed that the dress was bloody - but there was no blood on him. She puzzled at the appearance of his injuries. All those gashes were pink, not red. A dim image from her memory began to take shape.

She exclaimed with relief "Oh, I know! You were hurt in the war." Her voice resounded oddly in her ears, as if she was talking with her head in a tin pail. "Mary and Joseph! I thought it just happened down there." He didn't answer, just looked at her for a moment.

"That's why I screamed," Maggie added, feeling it was silly to have to say such an obvious thing. He remained quiet. Was he hard of hearing? "I didn't mean anything by it," she said, loudly. She longed to reassure him, but it was a lie to say he looked all right. The left side of his face was raked by wide, raw ridges that looked as if worms had burrowed beneath the skin. His left eye was white, blind, in a narrowed socket. The bridge of his nose was marked by a furrow. His mouth drooped on the left side, and half of his upper lip bore a large angry swelling as if a hundred bees had stung him in the same place. He was hairy where the livid scars did not intrude.

"I didn't mean a thing, at all!" Maggie shouted. "Except I was afraid you got hurt. I mean that you just got hurt, just now, on the hill."

He glanced at her and muttered. "I'm not deaf."

He doesn't believe me, she thought, *He saved me, we're alive! But I've ruined it, I've ruined him.* As if her heart itself had burst in penance, she was wrenched with sobs. She felt again the shuddering that had overtaken her when she had reached safe ground. Like someone newly dead come to purgatory, she counted each burst of breath, marveled at the solid grip of her hands upon her knees, felt the burn of each cut and the taste of tears—as proofs of a changed but now certain existence.

He shifted, trying to ease his griping shoulder, and watched the girl quiver and moan. She wore a plain dun-colored work dress and boy's brogans, scuffed at the toes. Someone's hired help, by the look of her—a foolish screamer and hardly worth his bother. Her screech had cut through him: it capped the debate with his father with irrefutable proof. It was a hell of a thing: to be proved right in such an awful matter. The girl's weeping continued, heartfelt. He was rather sorry he had deemed her foolish: it was not her fault that his face looked like the devil. He had no idea what to say to her.

Maggie's crying ended as abruptly as it had begun. She sat up, wiped her streaming eyes on her forearms, and blew her nose loudly on the hem of her dress. She felt thick-headed, thick-tongued, wholly shamed. She watched a crow fly from one tree to another. She brushed an ant off her skirt. The sun was hot on her shoulders and head. She rubbed her nose. Then she remembered something.

"I know you," she said, "you're Eleanor's brother."

"Eleanor! How do you know Eleanor?" he asked.

"At school, when she was there," she said, "We were friends at school."

The words amazed him. His sister was usually bright and loving within the family, but when forced to step outside the house or yard she became rigid with fear, open-eyed but blind to those around her. "Seeing ghosts..." Kate called it, always as unnerved as he by Eleanor's blankness.

Eleanor had been tutored at home until she was eleven years old, when their father was named to the Board of School Visitors. He then heard the gossip that he had previously been spared: heard people wonder aloud about his daughter, about why no one ever glimpsed her and why she would not attend the school he oversaw. Wasn't it good enough for her? For him? The rumor reached him that Eleanor was said to be "not quite right in the head." Anxious to disprove the gossip, he forced her to attend the local grammar school. The anguished child ceased speaking. Their father gave her a slate to write on and he himself for a time walked her to school. He told her that she would get used to it; he told everyone that she was far too shy but would soon get over it. Both of his assertions were proved false.

Maggie watched this man's reactions with interest. When Eleanor had arrived at school, the children had echoed their parents' gossip. Maggie was just as curious as the others, though she had no one to gossip with. She had wondered at the time if Eleanor had seen the faerie world that Maggie's mother described so vividly. Had the faeries struck the child dumb so that she could not tell any secrets? The faery-folk in Ireland weren't all that pleasant as neighbors anyhow; according to her mother, they'd as soon play you a trick as do you a good turn. Then if you forgot to appease them, or trespassed into their territory, you'd be very sorry. Is that so, Da? she often asked, but he usually shrugged, saying it was the country people who knew those tales, and he himself was in Dublin from the time he was a boy and his mother had hired him out.

There is something wrong with Eleanor, the children whispered. The schoolmaster shared their opinion. He banished young Miss Whitfield to the back row of desks, nearest the naughty boys, assigning her the Irish girl as seatmate at the shared desk. During the first hour of the school day, Maggie dropped her slate pencil. She bent her head down as far as she could, almost slipping from her seat while trying to look into Eleanor's downcast eyes. Would they look different (dreaming, or glittering, or wise?) because they'd seen into the faery-world? What she saw were apprehensive child's eyes, a bit lighter blue than her own, but otherwise commonplace. Maggie made a funny face and was rewarded by a lift of Eleanor's eyebrows and an evanescent smile.

"Yes," he said. "I believe I do remember. You were the little girl she sat next to."

She nodded and said: "And you walked her home sometimes, when you weren't at the high school."

"Yes, I did. I'm sorry, I've forgotten your name."

As if you ever knew it! Maggie thought, but was pleased by his good manners. "Maggie," she said.

"Maggie," he repeated, then smiled at her with the un-scarred side of his face. "Well, you certainly did her a favor, being her friend at school."

Maggie shrugged. "Truth to tell, she did me a favor being my friend, for I had very few at that place. Most of them had their noses stuck up so far in the air, they could hardly see a body. I hope she is well? Oh, good. Please tell her you saw Maggie O'Shaughnessy. I work at Mr. Merritt's now."

He understood why his parents had not invited "Eleanor's friend" to their home during their schooldays. He thought of the Irish, on the whole, as a big, lumpy, red-headed race, but Maggie was short, slim, and dark haired. She did not have much of a brogue in her voice either.

"I shall tell her. I'm Edward Whitfield," he said. "Pleased to meet you, Miss O'Shaughnessy. You'll forgive me if I don't tip my hat to you, but I tipped it already, right down the hill! And it's gone for good."

Maggie gaped at him, then whooped a huge laugh. "Tip your

hat!" she chortled. After a few rusty snorts, Whitfield joined her in laughter.

When they paused for breath, Maggie croaked "Tip your hat!" and her voice sounded so funny that it set them off laughing again. *Jesus, Mary and Joseph,* she thought, *here I am laughing my fool head off not ten feet from where I almost died!* "Oh, I can't hardly breathe," she said. She longed to cling to the laughter, but her head had begun to throb. As she pushed her hair back, a shock of pain stopped her hands.

"You've got quite a goose egg there on your forehead," Mr. Whitfield remarked, as he brushed dirt from his clothes. He wiped his eyes and face with a handkerchief. Maggie noticed that some of the scratches on her hands and arms were still seeping blood. She looked away, afraid she would faint.

"Well." He labored to his feet, then offered her a hand up.

Maggie froze. Seeing his hand above her, she saw it again as it had appeared to her while she clung to the slope. "You saved me. Mother of God." She shivered all over, whispered: "I owe you my life."

He was startled. All the customary facile responses would dishonor the girl's intensity. Finally, he said, "Don't cry." This last was more of a plea than a command. "Save your tears. It's a devil of a long way home."

She quivered like a dog shaking water from its coat, took his hand and struggled to her feet. One of her ankles buckled and he steadied her.

"You've hurt your leg," he said. "You'll have to lean against me. Yes, this side please." He gestured with his left arm. "The other's not working. Between the two of us we hardly make a whole person." This awkward comment had the effect of distracting Maggie from her frightened contemplation of the wound on her leg.

"Better half a loaf than none at all," she said, and fit herself to him the best she could. It took them a few minutes to work out a shuffling, swaying rhythm to begin the long journey.

I can't do this. It hurts. Everything hurts, Maggie thought, *It's much too far. Blessed Mary, help me.* She could not recall the prayers she'd learned as a child, nor the last time she had been to Mass. She began to fear that she would die and prayed frantically that her lack of churchgoing would not be held against her at her Judgement.

A sudden grunt of pain broke her imaginings. She glanced at him. His upper lip and chin were dripping with what she thought at first was perspiration but then realized was saliva leaking from the damaged side of his mouth. She closed her eyes in sympathy. Then she stopped, overwhelmed with her need to tell him things she did not know how to say.

"What?" he said irritably. "Do you need to rest already?"

"I forgot to say thank you," she murmured.

He was annoyed at the distraction of her gratitude, at the requirement to accept it politely, while the task at hand, getting home, consumed all his resources. "I'm glad I was there," he said, hoping she would accept this and not ask him for more. He wiped his mouth on his sleeve. "Come along now. Can you? We've got a ways to go."

It had been nearly an hour's walk, in a healthy state, to climb the path up Knott's Hill. He wondered if they could make it back to town and what he would do if she failed. His right shoulder and swollen wrist throbbed. The pain worried him. How could he work if his hand was disabled. Then he worried at the slow progress they were making. He searched for whatever near shade he could find, and insisted they rest often.

Sunset came, and the day waned to twilight. He was exhausted, thirsty, and in pain. "You look peaked," he said. "Time to rest again."

"No," she panted, "if we stop now, I won't be able to get up again." He began to protest, but the look on her face shut him up. She seemed to be drawing on some reserve of nervous energy, or courage; he had no notion of how long it might last.

They did not stop or speak again for the rest of their journey into the darkening countryside. Maggie lasted, hobbling in step with him, until they were met by a lantern-lit buggy on the outskirts of town. Then she fainted, the weight of her body nearly taking him down with her.

Chapter 2

The sun woke Ned again. Despite the opium he'd taken in the night, pain in his shoulder and wrist had awakened him twice; and now the blasted light was battering his head. He and his bed were damp with sweat. He creaked to his feet, feeling nearly as old as the hill he had cheated of its prey. He stripped off his underwear with some difficulty and washed his face with his left hand, then rinsed his mouth and brushed his teeth. He fumbled for his partial denture on the washstand and slipped it into the left side of his mouth. *If I get a glass eye,* he thought, *I can leave pieces of myself all over the house.*

After donning trousers and an old loose shirt, he sat down on the bed, aching from these modest exertions, then ventured slowly down the back stairs.

"Who's there? A rat too big for the traps, I see. I was wondering just when you'd creep down here," Judge Whitfield said from the kitchen doorway. "You've missed your dinner. Your mother assumed you were at death's door."

"She needn't worry," Ned replied.

The judge frowned, and impatiently motioned Mrs. Whitfield back into the dining room. He pulled out a chair at the kitchen table, and told Ned to sit down.

"Well, you shot off like a jackrabbit Sunday when I asked how you've been occupying yourself," he began, "Your aimless wandering has made you something of a hero, in saving that girl, but it must end. You're well now, and you need useful employment."

Ned stared at the table, seeking the perfect negative rejoinder; he did not want to begin another fruitless set-to. "I'm not well. "

The judge said: "Nonsense. You're speaking clearly now, when you set your mind to it. All that dentistry I paid for has had a good effect. And otherwise, the doctor says you've healed well. You're certainly well enough for some clerking. Don't shake your head at me! We'll take care not to strain your eyesight."

"The eye is not the problem."

"Then what is the problem?"

Ned snorted. "You think I should get better on a timetable—your timetable. Well, this train's late. Someone's pulled up all of the track."

"That's enough of that talk, Edward." The judge slapped his hand on the table. "Other men have been injured in this war, hurt badly...lost an arm or a leg. Or come home in a coffin."

"Don't you think I know that! Jesus, I saw them! All the men, all the...in...in the...the s- sunken road..." Ned stammered before his throat blocked up. *They go so fast, faster than a blink,* he thought, *they're there, the ones you knew, then they're gone. All that's left...* His shoulders twitched in a shiver. *Those gobbets of flesh spilling like slops from a bucket.* The memory of it filled his mind, more vivid now than the sight of it then when he was a cogwheel too hotly caught in the machinery of battle to waste time in conscious thought.

"There is no cause to use profanity," his father said coldly. "Under any circumstances."

Ned muttered an apology.

"As I attempted to tell you on Sunday, I had a word with Charles Mix the other day. He needs a law clerk and I told him you would more than fit the bill, now that you are recovered," the judge said.

"Mix is a good fellow," Ned conceded, "But I dispute your opinion that I am fully recovered. I am not."

"Just how do you intend to earn your keep—answer me that. Every man needs to earn his keep," the judge sputtered.

"Of course," Ned said in exasperation. "But not in a law office! It's all very well that I can speak now, but what good is gibberish delivered with perfect enunciation? I daresay that Mix does not want a man who can't think properly."

"Gibberish? You exaggerate, as always. You have an excellent mind."

"Not anymore," Ned said.

"Of course you do!" his father asserted, "You are well now. These are paltry objections. I won't accept them. No son of mine ought to have a single objection to choosing useful work over aimless idleness."

"Father. Look at me! I look like the devil himself."

"Pah! You need only visit the barber and wear your best suit. Mix is no simpering woman, swayed by appearances," the judge said, then set the keystone in the arch of his conviction: "What matters is what you do."

Beset by frustration, Ned combed his fingers through his beard, his hair. "Pardon me, you are right, of course, you are always right. You have no need to read entrails, everyone's path is clear to you. Lest a man stray, like Zeus with his thunderbolts you will set that sorry fellow on the straight and narrow or fry him."

The judge sat back and said with icy distaste: "Keep a civil tongue in your head. I've been holding back in consideration of your infirmity, but no longer, by heaven, now that you're back to your old tricks, mocking me with what you think passes for wit. You never learn, do you? With all your brains, you never learn..."

For some reason, this observation, among the shale-slide of the judge's insults, was the one that tripped Ned. "I don't know," he said in despair. "I don't know anymore. It's all gone."

"What is gone?"

Ned closed his eye, shook his head. After a few moments, the blood stopped thudding in his ears. He refused to look at his father.

"You have all that you ever had. What is wrong with you?" his father asked again.

"I wish to heaven I knew," Ned replied. "At present, the opium is playing havoc with my brain."

"Ha, then you'll do without it," the judge pronounced.

The opium or my brain? Ned wondered.

The judge went on. "I'll tell Mix you'll call upon him this week."

Ned shook his head again.

Mr. Whitfield mulled this over in silence, then said: "I can hardly credit that you intend to keep 'to home' like your sister, for the rest of your days!"

"That's outrageous!" Ned shouted, "For God's sake, you know nothing about how I've been trying to come back...to find my way back..."

"Very well," the judge interrupted, "Get a hold of yourself and call upon Mix this week."

"I'm no coward," Ned retorted.

"That remains to be seen," his father said.

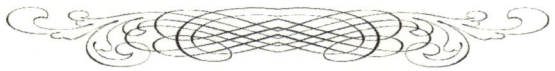

During Monday's daylight hours, Maggie's consciousness returned reluctantly from its haven of laudanum-induced stupor. She asked for more of the drug. Mrs. Wilkin told her there was no more, the doctor had left enough only for the first night, so she would have to be a brave girl and soon would feel better.

"It hurts!" Maggie told Mr. Merritt when he came to her bedroom to see how she was doing.

"Thou are safe now," he said.

She shrank away from the fear that shared her bed; pulled her blankets to her chin, shuddering beneath them: then, too hot, she thrust them away.

"Thou had quite a fall," Mr. Merritt said.

She blurted the story, finding it hard to describe well the shocking noise of the sliding tree; the sudden, horrifying drop; the collision. In the telling, her stomach heaved, causing her to gag and spit into the bedside basin.

"Thou are safe now," Merritt repeated gently.

"No! It hurts," she said. Admitting pain seemed less shameful than allowing him to know how frightened she was. *I nearly died,* she thought.

"It will pass," he replied.

She did not sleep until hours after dark.

"Wake up, child. Here is thy breakfast," said Mrs. Wilkin on Tuesday morning.

"I was dreaming about my Da," Maggie answered. She sat up and ate a spoonful of the porridge. It was as tepid and gray as the rain spatting against the windowpane. I may be believing Da's all right, she thought, I may think I know it, but accidents happen. He would not know if I was hurt, nor would I if he was. She drank the tea in a few gulps, grimacing as if it was bile, but she rejected the porridge. She turned her face away from Mrs. Wilkin's questions. *Things go wrong, after all,* she thought. "Leave me alone," she muttered.

Her employers stayed away from her all afternoon. She stewed in anguish until she felt as if all the meat had fallen from her bones; then she braced herself upright in bed and listened to the rain. Boredom slid into the room. When Mr. Merritt puffed up the stairs with her supper, Maggie launched at him like a newly-hatched flea upon the first warm-blooded creature to blunder into its path. "Talk to me!" she entreated.

"Will thou eat thy supper?"

Maggie nodded. He sat in an old Windsor chair, a little way from her bed. Comforted by his presence and by the occasional creak of the chair accompanying his murmured comments, Maggie retold her story. This time her stomach remained settled. Shortly after he left with her supper dishes, she slept.

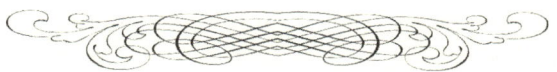

Tuesday was born in a torrent. Ned surveyed the dark gray sky and felt strangely pleased. He took a cold bath. After breakfast, he donned an oilskin hat and buttoned his raincoat over his sling, then plunged out into the rain like a ship mastering a choppy sea. The factory workers had already been rung into the gates following the breakfast bell, and few other residents were out in the rain. He slogged along, making good time, but slowed near the town's main business block.

Yardley the barber was an artless sycophant who–lacking wit–the chasm with simpering enthusiasm. Even if the barber's shop was empty, his trade in gossip was greater than his skills with the razor, and with what relish would he seize upon the judge's son and rat-tat-tat the tale of this visitor (poor fellow, such a sight!) to all and sundry like a telegraph machine?

Ned turned into the closest alleyway. The rain had lulled for a while, but now it increased in tempo. He ducked into a doorway and simmered for a time in this meagre refuge. *I can't do it,* he thought, *I can't start with Yardley.* He fingered the coins in his pocket: yes, he had enough to buy some peppermints–a peace offering for his mother–before returning home. The baker and confectioner's shop was not likely to have many customers on such a rainy morning. With any luck, he'd face only a quick transaction with the clerk. Near the alley's end a lamp glowed in the window of a shop that was empty the last time he'd been downtown. Over its door was a crudely daubed sign: "J. Creasey. Barber." The scissors painted on the sign more closely resembled a heron's head than a barber's tool. He had not heard of this barber before. He squinted through the window glass as he slopped through a puddle in front of the shop. The barber was a black man. How on earth did the man find customers so close to Yardley's territory? Ned walked by, staring at the lamp-lit window until rain seeped under his collar and down his neck. He turned back toward Creasey's shop.

The barber was grooming the hair of another black man who sat in an armchair facing the other direction. He looked up from his work as Ned entered, then hastened to the door, his expression wary. "Yes?"

"I need a haircut, maybe a shave too," Ned said. As he took off his hat, it dripped onto the rag rug laid inside the door, adding its pattern of drops to the dark spots on the rug caused by the rest of his clothing.

The barber looked him up and down. Then he said: "Mr. Yardley's barber shop is just around the corner."

"I know that," Ned replied.

The barber still eyed him. Ned caught sight of his own down-at-heel boots. Perhaps the man thought he couldn't pay. Ned fumbled open his raincoat and dug his left hand into his trouser pocket, coming up with a handful of coins which he held out for the barber to see. "How much?" he asked.

"Coat hook's over there," the barber said.

Ned shrugged the raincoat off his right shoulder and past the sling, then slid his other arm out, catching the coat before it hit the floor.

Creasey left his customer. "Let me hang those up for you, sir," he said apologetically, "Have a seat. Won't be but a few minutes wait."

Ned sat down in one of the straight chairs lining the wall and cooled off a bit. The room itself was clean. It held little furniture: three side chairs, a deal table holding the barber's supplies, a small heating stove, a washstand and towel rack, and the carpeted box the barber was standing upon to work on the tall man's face. The old-fashioned wall paneling was newly white-washed. Over the simple mantel hung a plain mirror. The mantel held only a japanned lamp and a few smooth oval seashells, shining brown and purple.

There was nothing here to read, a gross oversight on the barber's part. Ned pondered his wet socks and the nature of respect, as he listened to Creasey's conversation with the customer he called Billy. The two men talked about high prices, and discussed the method Billy had used to repair a broken baggage cart.

Billy glanced at Ned, then said to the barber: "You still set on army life, Joe?"

"Guess I am," Creasey affirmed. "I could join up in Massachusetts, they got a colored regiment a-going now. But I was born in this state. I'm waiting to see if Connecticut will recruit a regiment."

"Huh," Billy said.

"My grandpa says I could follow the army as a barber, and make some good money that way," Creasey responded, "But like I told him, sometimes when you got a bone to pick with someone, fighting's the only way to settle it. This thing, anyhow."

Billy nodded.

"Scissors ain't much of a weapon," said the barber with some bitterness. He massaged hair oil into Billy's scalp. "The way I see it is this. The Union's doing its all-fired best, but if the war keeps on awhile, the way it's going, they're going to need more men. I can't figure why they mean to draft all these white fellows who are kicking about it, when they could have thousands of us to fight –and we'd fight like the devil–just for the asking!"

"It never made sense to me," Billy agreed glumly.

"When they start up a regiment here, I'm off, quicker'n you can blink," Creasey said, as he removed the cloth drape from Billy's shoulders.

"Your Minnie ain't going to like that one bit," Billy said.

Creasey frowned. "I know it."

"Well, I'll see you, Joe. Good day."

Creasey swept up around the chair. "Ready for you, sir."

As Ned sat down in the barber chair, he was unsettled by the sight of a stranger's face in the mirror. He almost turned to see who was behind him before recognizing the visage as his own. Creasey arranged the toweling to drape him.

"So, you saw some action in this war," Creasey said, "Which regiment, sir, if you don't mind me asking."

"The 14th."

The barber nodded solemnly.

Ned went on, grateful that the man was not making a fuss over him. "It was Fredericksburg. A rebel artillery shell exploded near me."

"Uh huh. I heard some about Fredericksburg. That was a bad time," Creasey said. He stood for a moment in silence, then took his scissors from his apron pocket. "Could you pick your head up a little, sir?" Ned did so, looking at Creasey, who he deemed a prettier sight than the reflection in the mirror.

The barber shook his head, and tutted. "That still hurt you?"

Ned gestured from his left eye down to his mouth. "Sometimes here." He touched his forehead and scalp. "But not here."

Still the barber hesitated.

"Don't worry," Ned joked. "I'm not lousy."

"Well, sir, I wasn't suggesting such a thing...not at all," Creasey protested.

Ned went on: "Jeff Davis' cavalry, that's what they called them, the body lice anyhow. You may have heard that they're so common among the rebels that they say the little pests are stamped C.S.A. on the back so soldiers know they're secesh government issue. I never saw any stamped USA, but I swear, those rebel parasites had no qualms about fraternizing with the enemy!"

Creasey laughed, then moved behind Ned, yet still did not cut, though Ned could see the scissors poised.

"Not much you can do, heigh?" Ned muttered.

"Sure I can, sir. Meaning no offense to Mr. Yardley, I do a better job than he does, no doubt about it. I've seen his work. I'm just taking some time to think on the best way to do this, and that shave you mentioned, I'm thinking about that too. Your hair is straight. How did you wear it before the war, sir, a little longer and pomade it back, or did you wear it short?"

"Shorter, no pomade. Nor hair oil. I don't like it," Ned said. "But do whatever you please."

"Yes, sir."

Ned planned his letter to Charles Mix, drafting and rejecting numerous versions, as cut hair fell onto the cloth draping him. Mix was his father's former law partner, and a good man: fair, intelligent, a no-nonsense sort. Ned still had the handsome volume of Homer's *Odyssey*, Chapman's translation, that Mix had given to him on New

Year's Day ten years ago.

"Take a look at this, sir. See if it's to your liking."

Ned looked at his reflection. "Much better!" he said. Now that it was gone, he realized that the long hair he had grown to hide his flaws had actually intensified his wild appearance. The hermit of Knott's Hill, indeed.

He said: "It's too bad you're intending to enlist. I'll be losing a good barber." Ned saw Creasey's smile in the mirror.

The barber put his comb and scissors into his apron pocket and walked around to face his customer. "A shave, huh," he said. "Could you pick up your chin a little?" Creasey stared at the left side of Ned's face, then frowned. "Mmh, mmh, mmh. I can't shave you, sir, not on that left side. As good as I am, I'd be sure to nick you 'cause of those scars; and if I managed to shave you clean somehow on that side, you'd have to come down here every day or two for me to shave you again. Unless you'd want to try it yourself. It's a tricky thing."

"No indeed," Ned replied.

"I can trim up those chin whiskers though."

"Yes."

It seemed to Ned to take a very long time, especially with his neck extended at an awkward angle. Finally, the barber said: "Done. You can sit easy." Ned sat up and rubbed his neck, as the barber brushed hair off the drape.

"I can trim your moustache too, both sides, I think," Creasey said. "I want you to sing out if I hurt you, otherwise keep as still as you can."

The barber began on Ned's right side, while Ned thought about Odysseus: until—distracted by the snap of the scissors moving closer to the damaged swelling on his lip—he stiffened and held his breath. He stared at the cracks in the ceiling, and finally sighed when Creasey announced that the job was finished. As the barber removed the drape, Ned was again pleased by the results of the man's labor. He looked better with the thinned, if asymmetrical, mustache: and the close-trimmed beard, while it did not hide the scars extending up from his jawline, did accentuate the strength of what his father proudly called "the Whitfield chin."

"Capital," Ned said. "Where'd you learn to make a silk purse out of a sow's ear?"

Creasey smiled. "My grandfather had a stand in Hartford, I

apprenticed with him." He took the broom and began to sweep around the chair.

"Ha," Ned exclaimed, "That's why your name seemed familiar–a Mr. Creasey had a stand near Main Street in Hartford, near the Green. I used to go to him when I was a student at the college."

"You've been to his stand, maybe I've seen you there, Mr...?"

"Whitfield."

Creasey paused for a moment then went on abstractedly: "Yes, my grandpa asked me to take on his stand, because, you know, he's getting on in years, but I set up here instead. Followed a young lady I'm courting, in fact, and waiting to see if I could go into the army and fight."

Ned nodded. He pulled several coins from his pocket and counted out what he guessed was double the man's fee. He placed them in Creasey's hand, saying: "I don't know your prices."

"Thank you." Creasey handed back two of the coins to Ned, "This is too much."

"Well, I'd like you to have it," Ned responded, "You did a good job."

"No sir," Creasey said firmly, "Veteran's discount."

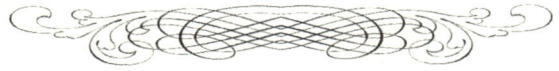

Despite the crick in his neck and the increasing ache in his wrist and shoulder, Ned was content as he went out into the drizzle and ambled toward the confectioner's. *Won't Mother be surprised,* he thought, *By golly, I look as pretty as a picture.* Inspired, he turned back down the alley to Main Street and walked two blocks to Dunn's Photograph Gallery. He climbed the three flights of stairs without panting, proud of how his stamina had returned, glad that his miles of walking since the spring thaw had paid off. The gallery door was open and he could see Dunn's blond head bent over a table of photograph mats.

"Good morning, George," Ned said.

Dunn startled, and when he looked up his mouth dropped open. "Who's there..."

"It's me, Ned."

"Oh my God," Dunn squawked. "Ned Whitfield? You're

supposed to be in a sickbed." He banged into the worktable, rushing to meet Ned at the door. "You scared the devil out of me. Jesus! What did they do to your face! Damned secesh. Hope they all burn in hell. I hope you gave it to them good." He clapped Ned on the shoulder. "I heard you were awful sick, Ned. I even heard you were dead!"

"You heard wrong."

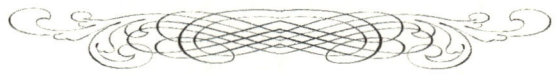

The nightmare began as a comforting dream. She was traveling through the green, sun-waxed meadow; she knew she was in Ireland, headed for her mother's home. A little girl appeared in the path, saying she was lost. Maggie took her up: the child was very light in her arms, and so pretty. Afraid that the sun would burn the child, she carried the girl to an empty cottage and sat her on the hearth. The flowers just outside the hedge were as plump and brightly colored as ripe fruit, so she picked some to feed to the girl; but when she returned to the cottage, the child was fading from sight. The girl whispered to herself then vanished into the wall. Suddenly Maggie's mother was there. "The hunger took her," she said, "Ye should not have left her alone."

Maggie awoke to daybreak. She shivered and rearranged her covers. "Did children starve?" she had once asked her Da after Mrs. Leary had talked about the Great Hunger. "Your family back in Ireland—they didn't starve, did they? It couldn't be." His expression had frightened her more than his words: "Don't you be worryin' about such things."

She rolled out of bed, testing her sore leg. It held her weight. She washed up as best she could, then limped downstairs. She sat at the breakfast table, and ate dutifully, each mouthful seasoned with guilt.

"I don't know how much longer I can 'do' for thee!" Mrs. Wilkin chided. Maggie did not answer right away. The dream still clung like cobwebs to the inside of her skull. She stared at Mrs. Wilkin's bent posture and gnarled hands—and recognized for the first time that the snappishness in the woman's face stood sentry over any expression of physical pain. *Poor thing. I shouldn't like to be old and hurt this way every day,* Maggie thought. *Besides, if I sit in bed another minute I'll go mad.* She cleared the table, and filled the dishpan. Mrs. Wilkin thanked her with nothing more than silence, which Maggie took as a blessing.

Later, she paused while sweeping dust out of the back door. Rapt at the splendor of the sunset, she put aside the broom, and breathed deeply. The evening air tasted as sweet as new cider. *I'm here, here to see it!* Joy burst within her like popped corn bursting from its shell. Her sleep that night was peace itself.

She unwrapped the bandaging from her sore leg on Thursday morning. *It don't look better. Will it scar?* she thought, examining her face in the looking glass. The bump was still there on her forehead. *Why do they say bruises are black and blue? Mine are purple and yellow.*

She cleaned the ashes out of the kitchen stove, built up the fire, and carried hot water to her employers' bedchambers, then washed herself.

"It's high time for breakfast!" Mrs. Wilkin said as Maggie limped back into the kitchen. "Soon we shall be back to rights again." Peering into the egg basket, she thrust it at Maggie.

Maggie scattered corn in the yard for the chickens, then raided the hens' nests. With five eggs in the basket, she hobbled to the barn door and leaned against it. *Back to rights?* The longer she thought about it, the less she believed it was true. As Maggie prepared breakfast, she ignored Mrs. Wilkin's comments.

"Are thou feeling ill?"

"No, ma'am."

"Why are thou acting this way, and giving me sass?"

Have I said a word to you at all, you cross old thing, Maggie thought as she sliced the bread, *Will I never find even one to hear me truly?*

At table, Mr. Merritt told them that he had gone yesterday to visit the Judge at his home, and had chanced upon young Mr. Whitfield. Maggie leaned forward, almost putting her elbow into her plate. "How is he? Is his arm broken? Is he feeling better?"

"Thou ought not to worry—he seems to be mending well. Young people do. He had some sort of bandage round his shoulder, but he told me that nothing was broken."

"Thank the Lord! I was afraid he'd been hurt awfully bad and it would be all my fault and I would never, ever forgive myself!"

"Calm thyself," Mrs. Wilkin said, "Thou ought never to have

done such a dangerous thing, so the poor fellow would not have been hurt at all. Thou had no reason at all to go up there."

"I wanted to see something new," Maggie murmured. "What did he say?"

"Well, he asked about thee." Merritt nodded at Maggie's happy "oh my," "and he inquired if thou were on the mend. I told him I was pleased to report that thou are healing nicely, under Mrs. Wilkin's care. And he remembered my little bookstore. As a matter of fact, he asked about a book that I used to have, perhaps I still have it, I shall have to look. It's that history of the exploration of Africa by, oh goodness, I can't think of the name. I do know it. It is Spencer, or Sparkins..."

"Spurgeon's History of Africa," Maggie said.

"Spurgeon! Has thou read it, Maggie?"

"Yes, I've read most every book you have here and most you had in your bookstore which didn't sell, save Isaac Newton. I couldn't get through that one."

"We still have far too many books," Mrs. Wilkin said.

"No!" Maggie blurted.

Mr. Merritt smiled at her. "In my opinion, one can never have too many books."

"What else did he say, sir?"

"We spoke about the prospects of the Negroes now that Emancipation has been proclaimed. He told me about his sister who is teaching down in the South at Washington..."

"Eleanor?" Maggie interrupted.

"He called her Kate."

"Did you see Eleanor, his sister Eleanor?"

"No, I did not. I had forgotten that there is another sister."

"Thy breakfast is getting cold, Homer, and thou will get dyspepsia," Mrs. Wilkin commented.

"Now that I think on it, there was another girl. I thought she had passed on," Mr. Merritt said.

"No," Maggie said. *I'd surely like to see her,* she thought. She chewed on her cold eggs and crumbled a piece of dry bread into powder.

Chapter 3

As Ned stepped out the back door, morning mist hung in the air: thick in places like long sheets laid on a low clothesline, and elsewhere, like a gauze bandage, obscuring all except the dark bulk of the sheds and stable.

"Will you look at Malabar's right hind hoof for me? He seemed to be favoring it yesterday," Eleanor said.

Her brother did not answer. He stood still on the back step surveying the yard.

"Ned?"

"Mmm."

"What are you looking at?" She moved closer. "What are you looking for?"

"Huh?"

"Every time you come out of doors you look around, just like that, as if you expect to see something."

"I do?"

"Yes. It's as if you're watching for someone…"

He said: "I guess it's a habit I got into in the army. We were always watching the sky, trying to predict the weather." He expected Eleanor to continue on her way after this reassurance, but she remained next to him, staring into the mist. Then she shivered.

"There's no one here, Elly," he added, "I suppose I thought I was back in camp and officer of the guard again."

"I don't know," Eleanor said gravely. She whistled for the family dog, and when Dance trotted to her side, she went down the steps. "I shouldn't like to be a Southern girl right now." She followed Dance into the fog.

"Nor I!" Ned said in falsetto, but his sister did not respond to the joke. He supposed that the fog bothered her, just as the night did.

He wandered to the stable and absently completed his chores, using his left hand to feed and haul water for the horses. He would muck out the stalls later. He checked Malabar's hooves, as Eleanor had asked, but saw nothing amiss. He stroked the black pony's neck, and watched as the barn cat cleaned herself then arched her back and stretched her limbs luxuriantly. "The days aren't so bad," he remarked to the cat. He missed his liquor in the evening, though - missed its calming companionship in his bedchamber.

Dance barked himself into a frenzy nearby, continuing until Eleanor scolded him twice. *Ah, the hounds of hell,* Ned thought, recalling an article he had read about the Italian poet Dante's work, *The Inferno.* He had not been surprised to learn that a Catholic from the Middle Ages imagined Hell as vividly as the Puritans had, but had been impressed by the variety of tortures the Papist had described for all those "sinners in the hands of an angry God" that Jonathan Edwards had prophesied would slip into the pit of fire. As he remembered Dante's evocation, there was a reprobate in one of the circles of Hell who was chased endlessly by snarling hounds. That was the damned one's penalty, but what was his sin? Ned was proud of his power of recall—especially as to literary allusions: but he couldn't remember which transgressions Dante had said merited that punishment. He wiped his hands on his trousers.

The squanderers! He remembered that the hunted man had during life wasted the bounty he received as soon as it came into his hands, and still sought more. The picture haunted Ned: the frantic run, the heart-stopping concealment: all efforts useless as the sinner was, for eternity, caught by the jaws which hungered for him.

The pony shifted his weight, pressing Ned against the stall, and jarring his sore arm; he pushed the animal aside with his hip. "You're getting too fat, old fellow." He wondered why Eleanor asked what he was looking at. What could he see in the fog, anyhow? The cat curled herself up and blinked at him.

It came to him then that since his health had returned, he had been scanning the horizon watching for the next calamity, the event that would finish him off. Eleanor was right. *Still officer of the guard, by God, but I'm safe, and whole...* He balked at the word "whole." Yet he knew that most men in his regiment would give their eyeteeth to be where he was now. Guilt tip-toed into his mind.

Home in one piece, he thought, and able to work.

"Confound it," he said aloud. The cat closed her eyes and fell asleep.

After breakfast, Ned remained at the table. Cushioning his sore wrist on a stack of napkins, he wrote two letters. The first, short and formal, was to the company captain in his former regiment. The second, similarly short but less formal, he addressed to Henry Barton.

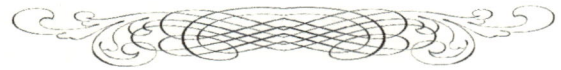

"Yep, I've made up my mind. I'm going to enlist," George Dunn asserted.

Ned looked up from his contemplation of the placid sky and confectionary clouds mirrored on the lake's surface. "Is that so?"

George quit rowing and pulled in the oars. "I'll likely get drafted anyway. I ain't got $300 to pay a substitute and hell will freeze over before my Pa or uncle hand over that much to save my skin. There ain't a patriotic bone in their bodies."

"I wish you good luck. Will you close the gallery?"

"I expect I will," Dunn glowered. "Uncle ain't goin' to like it."

Ned responded. "You have the only photographic gallery in town, but that won't last long when some ambitious fellow hears that you've shut your door. How will you support yourself when you get back?"

"I'm jiggered if I know!" George put out the oars and rowed hard for a while until he tired and stopped, panting. They were now close to the island.

"You're no help..." he remarked.

"I'll spell you for a while if you want, but I can't take it as fast as you have. My shoulder still isn't sound," Ned answered.

"Aw, you're too slow anyway. Every time we came up here you'd be dawdling, lookin' around at the dragonflies or the turtles or something else nobody gives a good goldarn about," George said. "So what can I do with the gallery while I'm gone?"

Ned shrugged.

George said, "I just figured you'd think of something." His tone was slightly accusing.

"I'm flattered. Very well, I'm thinking," Ned responded,

although he hadn't been thinking all day, but instead had allowed his thoughts to float as aimlessly as the drifting rowboat.

"What about that new fellow, your assistant, can't he take on the studio while you're gone?" he asked.

"Naw. Jack seems to know the work, developing the plates and such but he ain't as good at posing folks as I am, and they just don't like him much."

"Can't you ask your uncle if there's a likely fellow who's worked with him?"

George jerked the oars and thumped his feet excitedly until the rowboat rocked.

"Say now, I know a fellow who trained with my uncle in the biz and has nothin' to do and could use a job."

"No, Georgie," Ned cautioned.

George laughed. "You're the man to take on the gallery while I'm off fighting."

"Hold your horses. I'm supposed to start reading law with Mix."

"Why, didn't you tell me, not an hour ago, that you didn't want to read law?" George scoffed, "You said your father's got your nose to the grindstone about it so you're aiming to tell him to go hang."

"Well," Ned disliked being characterized as contrary. "I didn't quite say that. I just don't think I'd be good at it."

"Haw! Oh, yup, Mr. Head-of-the class...sure, you'd be a dunce," George chided, "There's the way to get his goat—tell him you want to run my gallery! If there's anyone deserves to be shown up, it's him, the old tyrant."

"I won't dispute that I could read law, but I don't believe that I want to be a lawyer," Ned went on.

"Then what's the point?" George said scornfully.

Ned opened his mouth to argue, then closed it. *What, indeed,* he thought, *very lazy thinking! Convalescence has left me with half a brain.* He feared falling short now, in the one area in which he had always excelled and did not relish being pressed into competition in the arena of law with his father—that grizzled gladiator. "You must be bored to death. I would be," Kate had written him recently. "You must find something to occupy your mind." He pondered this as he wiped sweat off his forehead. His fingers bumped against his eyepatch.

"You're forgetting something," he broke in. "My one eye."

"Aw, pull my other leg! If you can read law, you can take a picture."

Ned gestured to his face, "George. Think about it. If your customers don't like Jack, what are they going to think of me and this mess."

"Your face don't matter," George bluffed. "It's theirs they're always worried about. Believe me, I know. Y'ain't going to be in front of the camera anyhow. You'll be behind it."

"I can't keep my head under the black cloth all the time!" Ned said.

"Jack can handle the customers. You just take the pictures," George insisted.

"I don't know," Ned replied.

"Whyn't you just say no, and not beat around the bush!" George said, then grabbed the oars and began rowing again. He took them halfway around the island and then slipped the boat onto a small spit of sand between two large boulders. Ned pulled off his boots and socks and hopped out to pull the boat ashore. He unloaded their lunch while George climbed onto the larger boulder.

"Hey, don't shy your boots at me," Ned warned as another boot went past his head, followed by a sock. He caught the second sock. "Stink balls," he remarked. "They need a good washing." He dangled the sock over the lake.

"Don't do it, I'll toss you in there," George threatened.

Ned dropped the sock onto the sand, then climbed up on the rock where George lay in the sun. "Are you hungry yet?" he asked. George shook his head. They sat for a long time. Ned yawned. His nights were crammed with frantic dreams from which he awoke with the feeling that he had forgotten to complete a vital task.

"Say, it's hot for May, ain't it." George sat up and removed his shirt, then tapped his sunburned nose. "I was up on the roof for not more'n an hour yesterday! You can see I been in the darkroom too much."

"I've been out walking miles every day since the Spring thaw," Ned responded, "And climbing. Getting my strength back."

George grinned. "I could still beat you."

Ned gestured to his sore shoulder then said, "If you're so all-fired hot, maybe you should go for a swim." He saw his friend eye the water with apprehension. "Unless you're afraid…" he added.

"I ain't. But it's too cold. I know it is. Too early in the season. A body would freeze."

"How do you know?" Ned made a quick decision, took off his eye patch and stood up to peel off his shirt and trousers. "Well, I'm going in, and you can stay here and bake if you like."

George shrugged.

"I dare you," Ned said.

"I ain't afraid of a little cold water!" George retorted.

A few minutes later they stood naked at the edge of the water.

"So, how is your family?" Ned asked.

George snickered, "Ho! You mean Betsy? Your sweetheart…? don't deny it. She's worn out and that husband of hers, he's a sorry excuse for a man. You were the best of a bad lot, my friend, and she had high hopes until your father scotched that little 'bill and coo'."

Ned looked up into his friend's mocking face, then grabbed him and hauled him into the water. The shock of the cold made them both gasp, and George dropped his defenses. As he pulled away, Ned yanked him off-balance, ducked his head under the water, and then let him go. While George coughed up water, cursed, and swung out at him, Ned swam away: the cold powering his body like steam firing a piston. He stopped, treading water, and looked back for his pursuer, but George had already retreated and was now shivering on shore.

"What's the matter with you, can't take a joke?" he bellowed at Ned. "You tried to drown me, you little piss-ant!"

"I did not," Ned countered. He tried to keep his teeth from clacking together. His sore shoulder twinged as he swam closer. His feet touched bottom. "You forgot, Georgie. I'm faster than you, always have been and always will be."

"No, you're just a slippery little rat, always have been. Come on, Ned," George wheedled.

"Unh-unh. You'll duck me. You're just waiting for your chance."

"I won't," George said, "if you say you'll take on the job at the gallery."

"You're a hard man," Ned replied. He had already made his decision and it had nothing to do with the cold water. He raced out of the lake.

George whooped: "Who's the sharp one now!" as he pummelled Ned's back. Both men climbed onto the sun-warmed rock and huddled under their jackets until they were dry enough to get dressed.

George said, "Uncle will be mighty pleased to hear the news."

"There'll be hell to pay with my father," Ned replied.

Dunn's smile dimmed. "Yep. Let's eat."

"You get enough food in the army? I hear it's pretty bad," George said.

"Most of the time. It depends on your commander, on your supply lines, how bad the roads are, how many men along the line are stealing or substituting horse for beef, and how much you can forage or buy from the sutler."

"Thunder, you're a joker," George said.

"I'm not. You won't starve, though. You'll get your salt-pork, beans, and hardtack," Ned replied.

"What's hardtack?"

Ned smiled. "Let me tell you about hardtack. One time, I heard my corporal talking to one of the men. 'Reynolds,' says he, shaking his head, 'I bit into something soft in my hardtack today.' 'Tch, tch,' Private Reynolds says back to him, 'Yup, sir, I ain't surprised. I bet it was a weevil, eh?' The corporal says, 'No, by God, it was a ten-penny nail!'" George blinked then furrowed his brow. Ned waited.

"Oh! Haw! That's a good one!" George laughed. "I'll be a good soldier. Once I get the hang of it." *After some officer puts a rein on your temper,* Ned thought.

"Some boys, though, some of them show the white feather, don't they?" George went on, "When all the shooting starts, they want to skedaddle, don't they, but I won't. You didn't and Rob..." He stopped short.

"Rob held his ground at Antietam!" The words were as bitter as vomit in Ned's mouth.

"Congestive chill took him, I heard," George said in a whisper.

"Typhoid," Ned responded. A sliver of pain cut him, just a taste of the grief that had overwhelmed him as Rob McKay lay dying.

"By God," George said.

They were silent for a long time.

"I'll come into town and you can give me a tour of the place," Ned said, "then I'll see what I need, and find out about your arrangements for supplies. I'd like some written agreement, of course. We need to discuss whether I'll be getting wages or some sort of share of the profits, maybe both."

"What do you mean, maybe both?" George protested, "And ain't a handshake between friends good enough for you?"

"I prefer to have everything set out clearly with no questions, and the best way to do that is on a piece of paper."

George looked at him in disgust: "Written agreement, now there's a lawyer talking. What a load of shit. I'm glad you ain't going to be a lawyer. I'd have to stick a pin in you just to keep you from puffing up with hot air."

Ned grinned, picked up George's socks and tossed them into the lake.

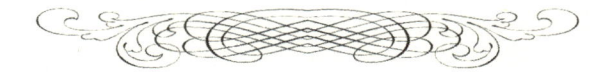

"Ned, look! Read this!" Eleanor said, thrusting the local weekly newspaper at him, while his mother beamed and nodded.

"What drivel, 'daring rescue': it sounds like something out of one of Beadle's dime novels," he said, after he had read it. When the editor spoke to him earlier in the week, Ned had assumed the paper would print its customary two or three sentence summation: such as it did for farming, business and manufacturing news, fires and accidents, marriages, and deaths.

"I'm glad to read it!" Mrs. Whitfield said. "You never told us what happened."

"I'll tell you, but first let's eat. I'm perishing." Seated at the kitchen table they ate a simple meal while he recounted the story as it had happened.

"What did the girl say when you got to the top?" Eleanor asked.

After she screamed? Ned thought. "The girl?" he said aloud. "Eleanor, it was Maggie O'Shaughnessy. She says she was your friend at school. Guess I forgot to tell you."

"It was M-Maggie!? My Maggie?" Eleanor said.

"Didn't you see her the night we got back, and Doctor Green

came?"

"No! When I saw that you weren't going to die, I hid upstairs."

"My goodness, what a remarkable coincidence," Mrs. Whitfield said, "The very same girl? I believe I do remember you telling me about her once or twice, Elly. She sat next to you?"

Eleanor tucked her arms close to her body, her expression grave. "Yes. Maggie never laughed at me." Mrs. Whitfield closed her eyes.

"She put John's shoes on the ant hill," Eleanor continued, as her face lost some of its shadow, "He was a very bad boy. He called me names. He made fun of all the girls." She shivered. "He pushed Maggie into the mud. But when he took off his shoes to play snap the whip, Maggie put jam in them and put them on an ant hill."

"Ha! First-rate. I hope they bit him good," Ned declared.

"How ingenious," Mrs. Whitfield said.

"Oh, he was so angry!" Eleanor said, "But I couldn't laugh, or he might know who did it. He never thought of Maggie or me, but he thrashed one of the boys. One of the other mean boys, and said he was lying!"

"Well, I'm glad that I hauled her off the hill, now that I know that," Ned announced.

"But how did she look?" Eleanor said with concern. "Will she recover, like the newspaper says?"

"I expect so. She had a gash on her leg, bruises, scratches and such. Actually, she was lucky she wasn't hurt worse."

"I wish I'd known that it was her. I could've helped..." Eleanor said.

"She was played out that night, just as I was. I'm not sure that she'd even have known you."

"Oh." Eleanor drooped with disappointment.

"It's a wonder," Mrs. Whitfield said, "that you were able not only to get her out of danger, but then all that way to the road, and both of you injured." Her voice grew shaky. "The good Lord was watching over you again." She stood up and began to clear the dishes from the table.

This past year has been hard on her, Ned thought. "All's well that ends well," he said.

Dance, who was laying at Eleanor's feet, gave out a whining sigh.

"My sentiments exactly!" Mrs. Whitfield said from the sink. The dog sat up and poked his head onto Eleanor's lap. She scooped the remains of her meal into his dish, saying: "But she did remember me, on the hill? Was she very frightened about falling down so far? What did she say, what did she say exactly? Tell me." He told her all that he could recall of the conversation, beginning with the moment that Maggie recognized him. Mrs. Whitfield listened from her post at the sink; when he finished, she surprised him with a hug and a kiss on his head, before she resumed clearing dishes.

Eleanor retrieved the newspaper and re-read it as Ned watched. "You told it much better," she said. "But...I do wish I could hear what Maggie would say."

In the sitting room after supper, Ned offered to play backgammon with his sister.

"Do you mean it? Father will be home soon. I thought you wouldn't want to stay."

"You're right, maybe I'll go upstairs. No, I ought to read some more Parsons. Say, if I slip insensate with boredom off my chair, will you have Dance wake me?"

"I suppose," she replied. "Why are you reading it, if it is so boring? Would you like to read my new Victor Hugo instead?" Ned shook his head, yawning.

"Parsons?" Mrs. Whitfield said. "That's one of your father's books, isn't it?" Tonight, she was not reading, but knitting socks for soldiers.

"Yes. How'd you know that? It's too bad you haven't read it: you could give me a summary and save me the trouble of wading through it."

"*Parsons on Contracts*. I have dipped into it, so don't be so mocking. It's certainly not a book I'd choose for entertainment."

Ned heard the question in her voice but did not yet want to satisfy her curiosity. "I just thought I'd take a look at it," he said. He drowsed in the armchair until Dance got up, gave a short bark, then squeezed under Eleanor's chair with his nose against her heels. The judge blew in, reporting on his meeting as he settled into the larger armchair. He lit the lamp on the side table.

"Where's my pipe? Who is this stranger in our sitting room?"

Ned stretched. "Eleanor took in another stray."

"Where have you been today? How have you been occupying yourself?"

Ned stifled a sarcastic answer. "I went up to the lake with George Dunn for the day."

"He's a ruffian," the judge declared, "the less you have to do with him, the better. Yardley did a good job on you. Who did you see when you were there?"

"As a matter of fact, I didn't go to Yardley. I have a new barber. Mr. Creasey." Ned gave a brief account of his visit there.

"An hour at Yardley's is worth seven social calls when it comes to hearing what folks are about," the judge said. "You'll go back if I hear that you're missed."

"That's not likely," Ned answered.

The judge took up his pipe. "When do you intend to call upon Mr. Mix? You will get quite a reception, thanks to that newspaper article. You're the talk of the town."

"Mm. I figured that you put that story in the editor's ear," Ned said.

"There is no harm in spreading news that bolsters a man's good reputation," the judge said.

"Daring rescue!" Ned scoffed "If you look at the situation logically, I only did what I had to do; it was more a matter of necessity than any…"

The judge interrupted: "Pah. You think too much, that's your problem. I'll wager you weren't thinking when you set off down that hill to save the girl. You saw what needed to be done and you did it."

"On the contrary, I stopped to calculate the best way to reach her," Ned objected.

"That's not what I mean. It's ridiculous to squander such a fine opportunity to show boldness and blow your own horn. I swear this war would be over if General McClellan had done more of that."

Ned said sardonically: "If we'd heard any more horn blowing from Little Mac, we'd all have been deaf. He did that boldly, if nothing else. However, someone else will have to blow my horn: with this lip I can barely whistle, much less blow."

"I don't want to hear another word from you on what you cannot do!" the judge commanded.

"I was joking, for heaven's sake," Ned muttered.

"Not another word!"

Ned shrugged and re-opened his book.

"I think Ned was very brave," Eleanor said.

"And I agree," Mrs. Whitfield added.

"That's my point. Everyone in town ought to know it," the judge said. Ned scratched his cheek, keeping his eye on the book. Drivel or not, he planned to save the newspaper article in his long-neglected diary.

"That being understood," the judge went on, "you owe me an answer to my question, Edward. What do you intend to do about Mix's offer?"

"I'm seeing him Thursday afternoon," Ned answered. Mrs. Whitfield's teeth gleamed for an instant in the lamplight.

The judge puffed his pipe. "You ought to have to done it sooner."

Ned yawned again and stood up. "Good night."

"Oh, no you don't. Sit down. When you see Mix on Thursday, what do you intend to say?"

"Pardon me. I had understood it was common practice to discuss the gist of a conversation after it has happened," Ned retorted.

"I asked you a simple question. I didn't ask for a saucy remark."

Perhaps it was better to beard the lion in his den. "I'll come to your study Thursday night and report in, sir," Ned replied, "In scrupulous detail."

The judge leaned back in his chair and resumed his smoking. "That suits me," he said.

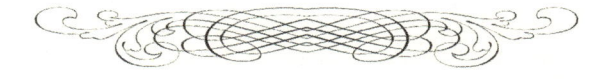

"Goodness, child. What is wrong with thee today?" said Mrs. Wilkin, as Maggie wrung her scorched apron under the pump. "Did the cinders burn thy dress too?"

"No. That old stove. The devil take it!"

"Maggie, do not blame the devil nor the stove for thy own careless ways. I suppose thou blamed the slop bucket for spilling this morning, too, when it was full to overflowing due to thy forgetfulness."

"Didn't I clean it all up, every bit, and leave the floor neat as a pin?" Maggie muttered. Yet it was true that she had dithered from task to task all morning.

"That apron is a sight. It's fit only for the rag bag now. Take it off. Thou cannot wear such a thing."

"What does it matter?" Maggie pouted. "No one ever sees me anyway."

"It matters not who sees thee, for a clean and neat dress is necessary to show respect for God and thyself."

"I suppose somebody will see me someday," Maggie mumbled. She couldn't imagine who it would be. Her employers never entertained. She wondered if Eleanor remembered her from six years back. She was sorry she had missed the opportunity to ask Mr. Whitfield more about his sister.

"I'll turn the fabric and patch it and it will look as good as new," she told her employer.

"We shall have to make do," Mrs. Wilkin replied, glaring at the apron, then snapped: "The sitting room is dusty!"

Dusting the sitting room was one of Maggie's few enjoyable chores: after sweeping cobwebs out of the corners, and wiping down the furniture, it was her habit to read a page (sometimes a chapter), chosen at random, of every book she dusted. She took *Pilgrim's Progress* from the shelf, and wiped it down but did not open the cover. *I ought to go to Mass,* she thought. Surely the Lord was due a proper thank-you for deliverance from death. Though the Catholic church was only a mile or two away, her sore leg would make the walk there harder than usual. Maggie re-shelved the book. Perhaps she'd go instead to see her Mam. She longed to hug her mother, sit in her lap and be comforted. Ah, you're too big a girl for that now, she reminded herself.

The morning sun shone into the room from the east window. Maggie watched the dust motes floating in the light. She wished her own thoughts were as free–not plodding in a circle, each treading on the heels of the one before it.

"Well, Maggie. Good day to thee," Homer Merritt said.

"Good day."

Merritt sat at the old desk and took up his account book, squinting at the pages worriedly, then rubbed his eyes. "Maggie, I have been hoping that our circumstances would improve." He sighed. "Child, when money is tight, we all need to be thrifty."

"It was an accident!" Maggie protested, gesturing to her apron. "I'll mend it, I promise."

"I know, I am not speaking of that. It's that washerwoman we pay. I don't know how much longer we can afford that expense.

It may be—I hope not—but it may be that thou will have to take on some of that wash."

"What?"

"Now, now. Don't trouble thyself. It is not yet definite that the task will fall to thee."

Maggie dusted on. "Och, Mr. Merritt, Mrs. Leary needs every bit she earns by doing our wash! My Mam's been friends with her forever."

Ever since she could remember, her mother, and then Rose as well, had laundered other people's wash, for pay. Mrs. O'Shaughnessy had shouted her little daughter away from danger: "Mind the fire! Ye'll burn to crisp. Mind the boilers! Ye'll scald yerself." One of the neighbor's children had perished in that way, or so she was often told. When Maggie was older, she was pressed into service to watch her baby nephews, while the women did the wash. Sometimes, they put her at the rinse kettle, and sometimes, at scrubbing out stains. Worst of all was the washing: up and down endlessly with the wash stick, until your arms were about to fall off—or the wringing, horribly heavy and you daren't let it touch the ground: she hated every bit of it. If either woman was in a temper, Maggie was scolded for being "too wee" or "too slow." When she was ten years old, they trusted her with simple starching, and by the time she was twelve, with some ironing. Maggie rubbed the small burn scar on her left wrist.

At dinner, Merritt picked at his food, while Maggie tried to swallow her own annoyance and pity. He stopped her from clearing away his half-eaten meal: "No, child. Leave it. Waste not, want not." She took the other dishes to the kitchen and scraped and scrubbed them with unnecessary vigor, drenching the scorched apron. The still-healing scratches on her hands stung a bit when exposed to the soapy water, so she lifted them out of the tub for a rest. She was admiring the airy splendor of an escaping soap bubble when someone rang the front door bell. She dried her hands, but by the time she reached the hall, Merritt had admitted the visitor: a rather short and burly man in his fifties. He had strong features, a decided hump in his nose and luxuriant gray beard mixed with auburn. He was well-dressed: obviously a gentleman. Maggie lingered curiously until banished by a glare from Mrs. Wilkin. From the kitchen, Maggie could hear little of the conversation. She eyed the kitchen door, seeking some chore that would take her within earshot. It sounded as if he was leaving. She ran to the hall in time to see the front door close.

"Maggie, see what Judge Whitfield has brought us." Mr. Merritt said.

"That was the judge?" Maggie exclaimed.

"There is an article here." Mr. Merritt waved a newspaper at her.

"What has happened? Is the war over?"

"Would that it were! Here, I shall read it to thee," Merritt said, feeling his pockets for his reading glasses.

"VINTON NEWS./A Fall From Knott's Hill, Daring Rescue.
         Saturday, May ____
News has reached this office regarding a daring rescue accomplished on Sunday last by Mr. Edward S. Whitfield, the son of Judge Whitfield of Millville in Vinton. Edward Whitfield, until last winter a lieutenant in the 14th Connecticut Volunteers, was exploring a rarely-traversed section of Knott's Hill when he discovered Mr. Homer Merritt's hired girl had fallen down the slope at the easternmost face of the hill. The site of her fall is not far from the popular viewing and picnic spot, yet it is a place of the steepest declivity, where the soil only thinly covers the underlying rocky bluff.

It is presumed that the area was rendered particularly unstable that day due to the heavy rains which had occurred in the morning; and that the girl had lost her footing while crossing some mossy ground. Mr. Whitfield recognized that the girl had fallen beneath a large tree trunk, which rested on the slope, and that the fallen tree could at any time shift and crush the poor girl. Having thus no time to seek assistance, Mr. Whitfield bravely climbed down the bluff, risking his own life to retrieve the unfortunate girl, and carried her to safety and thence down the Knott's Hill path until they met Mr. Josiah Edgeworth, who tendered them valuable assistance by conveying Mr. Whitfield and the injured girl to Judge Whitfield's residence and then continuing on to notify Doctor Green that his services were needed.

When asked to give an account of his heroic actions Mr. Whitfield said that anyone would do the same when faced by the circumstances. His modesty marks him as a true gentleman. Mr. Whitfield's feat is all the more remarkable as he has just spent the winter convalescing from wounds honorably received in the service of the Union. The girl is expected to recover fully from her injuries."

"Has thou ever seen the like, Maggie? The judge told us he has bought a dozen copies of the paper to send to his relations and friends. Did thou ever think that thy name would be printed in the newspaper? Goodness me."

"But," Maggie said resignedly, "...my name, 'tisn't there at all. I'm just the hired girl."

"And so thou are," Mrs. Wilkin said, as if to settle the matter. The old woman's comment pricked Maggie's pride like a nettle trapped in her clothing.

"Shall I cut it out for thee anyway, child?" Merritt asked.

"Yes," she mumbled, "I'll save it to show to my Mam. May I read it myself?"

"Has thou finished thy work?" said Mrs. Wilkin.

"Just about."

Mr. Merritt handed over the newspaper. Maggie read the article once quickly, then re-read it. The second time, her attention lingered on the facts. *I didn't know about that tree, that it could crush me,* she thought. She had thought only about being unable to climb back up. Whatever happened to Maggie O'Shaughnessy, they would have wondered. No one would ever think to look for her up on Knott's Hill. Kidnapped, they would have said; or would they think she'd just run off? And all the while she'd have been dead on the hill, for the worms...

"I still can't believe it. What if he hadn't been there!" she said aloud.

"That will teach thee to mend thy ways," Mrs. Wilkin said.

"Yes, ma'am." Maggie folded the newspaper. "'twill, surely."

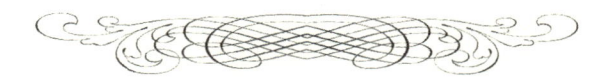

On Sunday morning, halfway on her walk to church, Maggie's leg began to hurt, so she sat down by the side of the road to rest. A wagon appeared over the lip of the hill. She clambered to her feet and walked on, glancing back at the slowly advancing vehicle. Perhaps she could pay the driver with the money she had brought for the church collection. She waved, patted down her hair, adjusted her bonnet. As luck would have it, the driver was Rory Corcoran, and among his passengers were folks she knew: Mr. Hurley, Mr. Dooley, Annie Mulrooney, and Agnes Donnelly. They were headed for Mass: Maggie thought this coincidence almost miraculous, as they squeezed her aboard.

During Mass, she enjoyed the somnolent rolling sound of the Latin. Deo gratias, thanks be to God, she repeated to herself, partially discharging her debt of gratitude. As her interest waned, she admired Corcoran's sleeping profile.

After the service, Corcoran offered her a ride to her brother's house. Ignoring Annie's grumbling, he put Maggie on the front seat next to him.

"Did you mean to walk all the way to church with that gimpy leg? What were you thinking, girl?" he asked Maggie.

"I thought God would provide being as how I was going to Mass," Maggie replied truthfully.

"Ha." He repeated her remark for the others to hear, then chortled: "God may provide, but 'tis Seamus Corcoran who delivers!" The wagon's passengers erupted in laughter.

"You're so clever, Rory," Annie gushed, just as Maggie opened her mouth to say the same thing. Ignoring Annie's comment, Corcoran maintained his attention on Maggie. She lost her ready smile after she heard his topic.

He said: "What were you doing up on Knott's Hill so's you'd be falling down it?"

"Well, just like it said in the newspaper," Maggie mumbled. She did not dare look up.

He was silent for a moment, then said in a joking tone: "You couldn't have waited for one of us to take you up the hill and fetch you when you fell? You went up with some nose-in-the-air Yank and let him do the job?"

"I didn't ever go up with him!" Maggie protested, shocked at his implication. "And I didn't mean to fall at all, 'twas awful!"

Annie Mulrooney said: "No girl ever goes up Knott's Hill by herself."

Speak for yourself, Mulrooney, Maggie thought. Her face burned as if someone held a lit coal to it.

"Pull your claws in, Annie," Rory said. One of the men snickered.

"Leave her be, Annie," Agnes Donnelly added.

Corcoran nudged Maggie. She looked up to see him grinning at her. "'twas a good thing, all round that you fell. You're no bigger than a half-pint after all, and he could fetch you up without breaking a sweat. Just think if it'd been Fi Sullivan or another woman I know…Mercy, I pity the man, he'd rupture hisself hoisting her out. And Yank or no, that's a hard thing!" His audience found this comical, except for the self-conscious Maggie and Annie (a plump and buxom girl) who clicked her tongue in annoyance at Corcoran's joke.

"Maggie, you ain't laughing," he said in a mild tone. Maggie gazed at him imploringly. He smiled at her. "I'd go down to fetch up a pretty girl like you no matter her size."

"Oh my," Maggie whispered, feeling much better.

As Rory lifted her from the wagon with flattering care, Maggie pondered again the mixture of sharp and sweet that formed his character. She hoped that Rose was watching from the window to see this small honor.

After Maggie thanked him, he said with a wink, "Nothing at all, Miss O'Shaughnessy."

"She's gimpy. Carry her all the way," Hurley smirked.

Rory clucked his tongue. Maggie quickly limped to the front door of her brother's row house under her own power.

"Foran!" Corcoran shouted. "Get out here, you slug-a-bed. If you can't stir yourself to go to Mass, you heathen—come out and see who I picked up along the road."

Rose Foran flung the door open. "Ah, Maggie." She gave Maggie a one-armed hug as little Mary whined, balanced on her mother's hip. Rose moved on to banter with the men in the wagon. The house was stuffy and smelled of dust, onions, and bacon, with more than a whiff of the privy out back.

"Maggie," Frank said, pulling on his shirt. "How're you faring?"

"Well enough," Maggie said. "Where's Mam?"

"Out the back with the boys."

Maggie asked her standard question: "How is she today?"

Frank shrugged. "Not bad."

"That's a blessing."

"That's Corcoran out there blathering, is it?" she heard Frank say behind her.

Coming from the dark doorway, the sunlight in the yard made Maggie squint. The sight of her mother made her sigh. Mrs. O'Shaughnessy had draped a piece of torn shawl around her shoulders. Today her gray hair was neatly done up, but adorned with a black feather. She had pushed her sleeves up to her armpits, exposing her red arms, which moved in rhythm as her grandson marched around the yard beating time on a bucket.

"Are you a drummer boy, Denny?" Maggie said, then captured her mother in a quick embrace.

"I am," Maggie's nephew said. "I'm goin' to join the sojers. Like Uncle Mike."

"No!" Maggie said to her mother. "Has Michael enlisted?"

Her mother nodded. "He's sayin' he will to get his bounty money. Or hire as a substitute. Three hundred dollars is nothin' to turn yer nose up at, he says. And Frank's heard the government will be doin' a draft and make the men go."

Although Mikey rarely started a fight (so far as Maggie knew) he had never hesitated to join a scrap. His raggedy right ear testified to his readiness: he'd lost parts of it to Paddy Molloy, exacting one of Molloy's teeth in payment. She was not close to her half-brother, who was eight years her senior. Yet she was unhappy to think that he might be going away, to be wounded, or worse.

"Mam, this is bad news. I'd be worried sick," she said.

"Whissht. Mayhap they'll teach him a thing or two, in th'army," her mother said without conviction. She plucked at her scrap of a shawl. Rose and Mary joined them.

"Come here, mavourneen," Mrs. O'Shaughnessy called to the baby, but the child ran to grab the sticks from her brother's hands. A brief struggle ensued. The boy was stronger, and the little girl ended up on her buttocks in the dirt. She looked at her mother with a cry. Finding no ally there, she got up and began to follow one of the chickens scratching in the yard.

"Michael's going to enlist?" Maggie asked her sister-in-law.

" 'Tisn't a sure thing yet," Rose said.

Maggie shook her head. She pulled an old stool away from the side of the house and sat down. "My leg still hurts," she said to her mother.

Her mother looked at her blankly. "Have ye got a boil?"

"Didn't Frank or Rose tell you what happened?" Maggie asked, then hurried on. "I fell down the cliff on Knott's Hill and almost died."

Mrs. O'Shaughnessy gasped. "God's honest truth?"

"Mr. Corcoran brung the newspaper yestiddy and read it to us, when ye was out with Mrs. Leary. But ye look well enough now, Maggie," Rose put in.

"How'd ye fall?" Mrs. O'Shaughnessy looked her daughter over. "Ye need to take care where ye're steppin', girl. Good Lord preserve ye." *I might never have seen her again,* Maggie thought. Swept forward on a surge of emotion she rose from the stool and hugged her mother a second time.

"Now, what's all this..." her mother said. Maggie did not let go until she had mastered her tears.

"Don't worry yerself," Mrs. O'Shaughnessy said. As Maggie wiped her eyes, her mother smiled. "Ye're a good girl."

Maggie savored the words as she sank back onto the stool. "Do you want to see the place that's hurt?" She unloosed her garter and rolled the stocking down.

"Mercy," Mrs. O'Shaughnessy said.

"I was in bed two days," Maggie murmured.

"It sounds like heaven to me," Rose sniffed. "The only time I'm abed that long is when I have a baby."

"God forbid, she didn't dock yer wages with ye being laid up, did she?" asked Mrs. O'Shaughnessy. Maggie nodded morosely. Her mother frowned.

"Criminee!" Rose spat out. "And the church wasn't slow to be taking yer last bit." Every cent of the wages she gave to Rose went for Mrs. O'Shaughnessy's upkeep. Maggie tried to give it all to her sister-in-law, every week, only rarely saving aside a bit for herself to buy toothpowder or a hat ribbon or a sweet.

"I had to, Rose. What would they think of me if I put nothing on the plate for the poor?"

"There's no need at all for ye to put in yer last little bit, an' with yer wages docked too!" Rose groused.

"Just think though, Rosie," Maggie said with a forced grin as well as a quaver in her voice, "how much of my wages you'd lose if I died?"

Mrs. O'Shaughnessy interrupted sharply, "Don't be temptin' the devil."

Rose shook her head. "Yer always full of queer notions, Maggie. What a thing to say!"

Maggie's face flushed. She ducked her head lower so that Rose would not see. Finally she muttered: "If the wagon's not gone yet, I suppose they'll take me back to Merritt's now."

"No, no. It couldn't be helped, I suppose, ye takin' a fall," Rose said.

"What about yer dinner then, girl? Ye must have some dinner: ye'll waste away. Bide awhile." Mrs. O'Shaughnessy said.

"I'd not turn anyone away hungry," Rose harrumphed.

"I'll stay then." Maggie displayed her injury to the children.

"Hurtee," Mary said, but Denny and Patrick remained unimpressed. Maggie rolled up her stocking and refastened her garter: unhappy she'd made such a fuss over the wound and unhappy that no one else had.

Mrs. O'Shaughnessy had resumed her seat in the patch of shade near the building: she looked to be daydreaming as she watched the children. Maggie was relieved that her mother was sober. The coming of spring seemed to have wrought a change in that aspect of her behavior—for the time being, anyway. There's trouble aplenty, Maggie told herself. No need to make more for everyone. She yelled at Dennis to stay away from the clean laundry drying on the lines, then followed Rose into the house to help with dinner.

Chapter 4

"Yep, Jack knows the business inside and out," George Dunn said as he sat in his office chair smoking a cigar. "He's my right-hand man."

He's your only man, Ned thought. He'd put more stock in Dunn's compliments if the subject of them wasn't present, grinning and accepting the praise as his just due. Jack Rossiter had shadowed both men during the tour of the photograph studio: crowding them in the darkroom, puttering nervously around the supply room, squinting under the roof skylights where sunlight struck the glass negatives and sensitized paper married in dozens of printing frames. He had fiddled with the sleeves of his fancy jacket as Ned examined the box camera. Yet, other than one or two ill-disguised smirks while Ned re-familiarized himself with the chemistry of the sensitizing and developing baths, Rossiter had ignored his new employer.

"Well, thank you kindly, Mr. Dunn," Rossiter said," I expect I could run the place myself, mebbe with just a boy to help out a bit." He paused. "I'll surely miss you, yes, indeed, but you're doing a fine thing. If it wasn't for my weak chest, I'd be joining you, that's a fact."

Here Rossiter fastened Ned with an earnest look. While in the army, Ned had not envied the regimental surgeon his job of sorting out the shirkers from the genuinely sick. Puffing on the mellow cigar, he decided to give Rossiter the benefit of the doubt, for now.

"That's quite an encomium, George," Ned put in.

"That's good, right?" said George, then grinned at Rossiter. "You have to watch him, Jack, he's a college man, you know, and reading law to boot."

"You exaggerate, Georgie," Ned said. "I know as well as anyone what it takes to run a successful photograph studio and it has nothing to do with reading Thucydides. It takes good business sense, steady hands and a good eye–especially a good eye. I've been accustomed to two of them, I'll admit, but I guess one will suffice."

Dunn's assistant frowned. "Well, I'll take charge of everything, Mr. Whitfield. You needn't do a thing. Suppose you want to…rest your eye, you needn't give it a second thought. Yes indeed, you can count on me. Mr. Dunn's leaving you in good hands."

"I'm starved," George announced, "I mean to fatten up afore I face Uncle Sam's beans and crackers. Ned, what do you say to dinner at the hotel? Jack, you come along too. We'll have a drink to toast the new partners, eh?"

"Oh no, thank you kindly, Mr. Dunn," Jack replied. "But I've got far too much to do here. We've got that big order of cartes de visite to be pasted up and matted."

George persisted. "Aw, no, come along, Jack. Join us and wet your whistle."

"No sir, you two go on."

"Well, you'll join me for a round before I go off to the battlefield, won't you Jack?"

"Oh yes indeed, Mr. Dunn, I wouldn't miss that for all the tea in China." Jack pulled his mustache around a simpering smile.

Ned snuffed out his cigar on the sole of his boot and tossed the stub into the nearby spittoon. He still had qualms about portions of his agreement with Dunn, so he was glad that Rossiter would stay behind. The discussion with George could well become contentious - Dunn was a contentious sort of fellow. He wondered whether it was better to engage George on the disputed topics while they were sober or wait until Dunn was well-liquored.

George pitched his cigar butt into the spittoon where it sizzled for a moment. He stood up and made a show of feeling all his pockets. "I'm a little short…Guess I'll have to take something out of the cash box."

Rossiter whipped around from where he was working. "No! No, Mr. Dunn, how about I give you a loan?"

"Jack, you're a prize," George said.

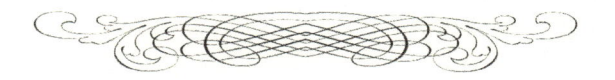

All through the forenoon and on through dinner, Maggie was bent on capturing the angel. A visitor in last night's dream, it beckoned from her imagination as she completed her chores. Mr. Merritt went away to read after the meal, and Mrs. Wilkin's morning ardor for improvement was doused by the afternoon's warmth. She soon nodded and snored in her rocking chair.

Happy for once in the close air and stillness, Maggie drew. The angel came slowly to a likeness on paper; it did not match the vision Maggie remembered—and the wings posed a difficulty. How did angels' wings look? She did not recall if the dream angel had wings, nor if it was male or female: she simply knew it was an angel. Hers on paper was female, wingless. Maggie tapped her pencil on her teeth. Not bird wings, 'twouldn't be right. She left the problem behind, and imagined the man opposite the angel. Just as in the dream, he was kneeling, in profile, looking up at the one who blessed him.

What does she have to give him? Nothing came to mind. Maggie drew the angel's draped garment. With that change, the celestial visitor now resembled an allegorical figure, like Justice, or Lady Liberty, or The Union. The very thing! She added stripes to the garment, and stars to the figure's mantle. The lady is the Union, she decided, so the man must be a soldier. She sketched the kneeling man's clothes, glad that she hadn't imagined him as a Renaissance noble, or a knight–such pictures were more romantic, surely, but awfully hard to draw. She laid down her pencil and rubbed out a kink in her neck. She looked at the stove, the dishrags, the floor-cloth, and found no inspiration there, then held out her own hands just as the Lady Union might, and studied their appearance. A shiver touched her unexpectedly.

"Oh!" A different vision filled her eyes then: grabbing the pencil, she sketched behind the man and woman a forested hill with a path up one side. In the woman's hands she drew a scroll. On the scroll she lettered "Roll of Honor", then more ornately, "VALOR." She delineated the kneeling man's features, squinting as she strove to remember them. *I'll ink it tonight. And put the dedication at the bottom margin.* She tapped her fingertips on her apron, surveying her creation with satisfaction: glad that the woman retained in her posture and joyous expression most of the dream angel's blessed aura, and the man looked appropriately honored.

Will he be, I wonder? Maggie frowned. *Well, I won't know anyway. I won't be there when he gets the mail.* She clamped her teeth as a worse thought came to her: Mrs. Wilkin would insist on folding the fine, large picture into eighths to fit the small envelopes she bought. The fold lines would cut across the Union's face—and Mr. Whitfield's too. *I won't let her fold it. I'll roll it, that'll do it no harm,* she thought, *and I'll have someone deliver it rolled. Yes. No! Mercy, that's it—I'll deliver it myself.*

"The mail's here," Ned called to his mother in the kitchen. "There's nothing from Kate. You have a couple of letters." He dropped the mail on the sitting room table and fled to his room to doff his suit jacket. He changed his shirt, and his collar; tied on a looser cravat, and donned his third-best vest. As he came into the kitchen, he heard his mother laugh out loud: "Well, my stars…"

"What is it, Mother? Share the joke."

"It's a very quaint note from Mrs. Wilkin. Mr. Merritt is an old Quaker gentleman, an acquaintance of your father's. Mrs. Wilkin is his sister-in-law who lives at his home."

"Ah, a woman with no 'merit' attached to her name," Ned put in.

Mrs. Whitfield shook her head a little at the pun, and went on: "First, Mrs. Wilkin begs my indulgence…let's see, her hired girl Maggie has prepared, and here I quote: *'a token of gratitude of her own making for Mr. Whitfield, which would be damaged if mailed.'* She says they would like to deliver it to me at my convenience."

"Oh!" Eleanor said.

"Blast," said Ned at the same time, "She already thanked me. And Mr. Merritt did too, for that matter." His mother's amusement stopped his protests.

"Look," Mrs. Whitfield went on. "It's written in a lovely hand." He glanced at the letter. "Yes. A remarkably firm hand for an elderly lady. Didn't Mr. Merritt say she suffered from rheumatism? I wonder if he wrote it."

Eleanor put in, "I'm sure Maggie wrote it. She was the best

scholar in our form at school, when I was there." Then, seeing her mother's questioning expression, Eleanor said firmly: "She was."

"I believe you, kitten," Mrs. Whitfield said, after a moment.

"A token of her own making?" Ned said. "I hope to heaven it's not some dreadful schoolgirl poem or a felt pen-wiper—I couldn't keep a straight face. You had better accept this token for me, Mother."

"I suppose I..." Mrs. Whitfield began.

"Maggie draws very nice pictures. She made some for me," Eleanor interrupted, "I would so like to see her again! Oh, I'm sorry, Mama. Go on."

"Truly, Elly? Would you sit in the parlor with us?" Mrs. Whitfield said in surprise.

"I'd watch," Eleanor replied. "Don't snigger, Ned. I would watch!"

Mrs. Whitfield smiled widely. "I was going to say that it would be most ungracious for Ned to refuse to accept delivery of a token of gratitude from anyone, even such a girl. I think it's only good manners for him to accept it in person."

"Then I guess I can make a token appearance," he parried.

"Oh, indeed," His mother replied.

"Do you think it's a picture?" Ned asked his sister.

Eleanor nodded. He continued his teasing: "But what if it's awful and I have to pretend I'm pleased to have it? Father's the politician, not me. She's your acquaintance, El, maybe you could accept it on my behalf." He waited for his sister's customary nervous denial, but she kept her eager smile.

"I couldn't accept it, since it's meant for you; but I would watch!" she said.

"Very well," Mrs. Whitfield said. Beaming at her daughter, she folded the letter. "Then I shall invite them here. Let's see. A Wednesday is best, when Daniel is in court at Hebron. After dinner, I think. Three o'clock. I shall have to look at the calendar." She bustled off.

"You'll watch in the parlor when she brings this thing over? Not peeking over the stairwell? You're pulling my leg," Ned said to his sister.

Eleanor said: "Not I."

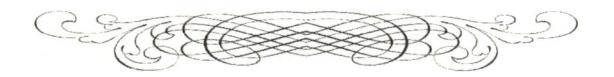

"'tis a wonder, Bridget! Look how fast it goes," Maggie remarked as she fed the cloth of her new skirt under the needle of the sewing machine. "Mm," Bridget intoned, intent upon basting tucks into a shirtwaist, reducing its generous size to fit Maggie's smaller bosom. She finished her task and looked around uneasily. "I never bin in a Protestant church. Ain't it a queer looking place."

"We're in the back rooms, not the church part of church. This is where they have their Sabbath School, and the Ladies Sewing Society of the Congregationals sews for our soldiers and the poor folks and for the Negroes down south."

"It's not a sin to be here, then?"

Maggie looked up from the machine. "Don't be a goose."

"Shouldn't we be asking Father Kelly just to be sure?"

"Bridey, for mercy's sake! You're not going to this church, not to Mass, to a service, I mean—you're just in it, like a market or any other place. Don't be making up new sins that are hardly worth the name. Oh, bless me, Father, I have sinned: I went into a Congregational church and sewed," Maggie huffed.

"But Maggie, we're not sewing for soldiers or poor children. We're sewing for you."

"I'm sewing. You're jawing," Maggie replied amiably.

Bridget smiled a little. "But won't you have to pay them for the use of the machine?"

"Not a penny. I told Mrs. Moore I'd sew a day for the Aid Society on my next afternoon off, if she'd let me use the machine today."

"How'd you get to acquainted with a Yankee lady, to ask her such a thing?" Bridget said over the click-clack of the machine's treadle, "Is she one of the folks your Mam washes for?"

"Look, half done already. Hand me the scissors. Mrs. Moore was midwife for Rose when Mary was born and that was a day I was home, thank the Lord, for my mam was in a conniption; and I helped Mrs. Moore and so we struck up an acquaintance, for Mary took her time in coming." Bridget sucked in her breath. "You helped! You never told me!"

"Faith, Bridey, it didn't bear repeating. What a muss." Maggie hunched her shoulders.

"What was it like?" Bridget whispered.

"All those brothers and sisters at home and you never saw one being born?"

Bridget shook her head.

" 'twas horrid," Maggie said.

"Ah, but the babies are so dear. I'd like to have one," Bridget asserted. She often cared for young children, for pay, while their mothers hired out as laundresses or day maids.

"Are you mad?" Maggie exclaimed.

"No, I would indeed. Though I have to find a husband first."

Maggie stroked the cloth. "It's not the babies that are so bad, they're sweet, but the getting of them! Ugh." Bridget looked puzzled.

"Is that waist finished?" Maggie asked to distract her friend.

Bridget held up the shirtwaist. "Try it now." She helped Maggie slip into the blouse. Then she fingered the cloth Maggie was seaming on the machine. "Look, Maggie. This cloth has a faded stripe."

"Yes, that's why I got it so cheap. I'll hide it in a fold or put on some braid."

"Why have you got so much? It must have cost you two weeks wages."

"I'm needing a lot, for I'll have a hoop skirt to put it over," said Maggie."

"A hoop skirt! How could you ever get such a thing?"

Maggie looked away. "I borrowed it from Mrs. Sullivan, along with the waist and the jacket you're basting." She winced as her friend's surprise turned into scolding.

"Oh, Maggie. Mr. Dooley says he's heard she entertains men in her room." Horror and fascination warred in Bridget's expression. "And all the while her poor husband is away following the army. People will talk about you!"

"Mr. Dooley," Maggie protested. "He's heard such, he's heard so. He likes his gossip, don't he? How does he know she entertains men?"

"Mr. Dooley knows a great many things!"

Maggie knew her friend fancied the older man. "Mr. Dooley's a good fellow," she replied apologetically. "I've heard those stories too. But Mrs. Sullivan dresses so well, and I was desperate for something pretty to wear. You know Mrs. Wilkin is so stingy with clothes, and Quaker-plain to boot, I would look like nothing more than a little brown wren in what she gives me."

"But a hoop skirt. She won't ever let you wear it. Will she?"

"I don't know," Maggie muttered. "But 'tis a pretty waist and jacket, Bridey, surely? And I'll have dress gloves and a ribbon belt as well."

"Begorrah, all that? Why would Mrs. Sullivan let you have all those things?"

"She's never been in a rich Yankee's house, says she, and she's mad to know what's in there, so I promised to sketch the furniture for her and tell her all that I saw."

"I never…" Bridget said in disbelief.

Amused by her friend's reaction, Maggie bragged, "She told me that there was no reason why one of us shouldn't look fine when we visit a rich Yankee."

"I'm glad it ain't me," was Bridget's heartfelt response.

Maggie felt the first tendril of doubt uncurl in her mind. She donned the jacket to top the shirtwaist, and stood still while Bridget pinned and tucked.

"Well, no one I know has ever had such a month as you, Mag," Bridget said, "You falling down the hill and then you was saved by a handsome Yankee. Mr. Dooley says Rory Corcoran was just a bit put out."

"He's not handsome!" Maggie protested, as if answering Rory in person. "He's awfully scarred, from the war. All up one side of his face."

"Oh, is he then? I'll have to tell Mr. Dooley."

Maggie added: "But he's very brave. Terribly brave."

Bridget nodded. "Well, 'tis a grand thing that you'll have something fine to wear." As Maggie thanked her for helping, Bridget shrugged happily. " 'tis a wonder Mrs. Wilkin didn't stop your going. My mam says Rose says Quakers are awful queer."

"Mr. Merritt was a lamb," Maggie said, "and even when Mrs. Wilkin was about to set her face against it, he said I must go, and that she'd go with me. Truth to tell, I think she's just as curious to see a Judge's parlor as Mrs. Sullivan is."

"But Quakers don't hold with fancy things, so you said," Bridget put in.

"Whisst, Bridey, so I did, and so they don't, but a woman's a woman, for all that. She wants to have a look around just as much as

I do, so she can turn up her nose at it, if nothing else."

"I never," Bridget repeated contemplatively.

Maggie grinned. "Well, if curiosity kills this cat, satisfaction will bring her back."

Chapter 5

Confident of her splendid appearance, yet uncertain about how to act, Maggie listened to Mrs. Wilkin's advice during the ride to the Whitfield house. She wished that they could arrive in something fancier than Mr. Park's buckboard wagon.

"Mr. Merritt is acquainted with Judge Whitfield, of course. The judge is a power in the county Republican party," Mrs. Wilkin said.

"But he won't be there, will he?" Maggie said nervously. She thought she could manage well enough with Mrs. Whitfield, but meeting a judge was a daunting prospect.

"I expect not. But we shall see…Thou must keep a quiet tongue and act properly." Maggie nodded. They rode in silence the rest of the way.

The Whitfield house was rather large: built in the "Greek" style fashionable some twenty years before Maggie was born. She compared it in her mind's eye with the mill owners' homes in which her mother had worked sporadically as a laundress. *Tisn't as grand as some I've seen,* she thought. White pillars supported the triangular fronted overhang roof. The remainder of the house was brick painted the color of buttermilk. The path to the front door was softened by a small but charming flower garden. Maggie noticed that some of the window frames on the side of the house needed painting. *Ha, it ain't all perfect then.*

Mrs. Wilkin marched to the front door; Maggie lagged behind. "Pull that doorbell or we shall be late," said Mrs. Wilkin. Through the row of small glass panes alongside the door, Maggie watched the doorbell bounce. Its jangle rang through her. She tucked her gloved hands one inside the other. They heard a dog barking inside and muffled voices, then a gray-haired woman opened the door, introduced herself as Mrs. Whitfield, and welcomed them inside. Maggie admired Mrs. Whitfield's dress, worn over a crinoline. The garment's printed cotton fabric in rose and deep green on white set off her pale coloring well. *Where's Eleanor?* Maggie thought.

Mrs. Whitfield ushered them into the front parlor. The slatted shutters were closed, leaving the room dim and slightly cooler than the hall. Maggie looked around as she sat down: sinuous upholstered furniture, bright floral carpet, oddly patterned wallpaper, and most everything decorated in red. Too much red entirely, Maggie told herself. At a warning sound from Mrs. Wilkin, she turned to focus on the hostess, who was asking if they would like some refreshments.

"Lemonade!" Maggie said, "if you please."

Mrs. Whitfield smiled. "Lemonade it is. Mrs. Wilkin, what would you like?"

"Whatever thou are serving will do me fine," Mrs. Wilkin said. Mrs. Whitfield left them.

"Maggie," Mrs. Wilkin whispered.

"What?"

"It is not polite to press thy hostess for something she may not have."

"Oh. But I do like lemonade," Maggie whispered back.

"Hush."

Och, I've done it wrong already. Maggie brooded for a minute, then patted the upholstered seat of her chair. It was so comfortable that she had a little difficulty sitting up primly. She longed to stand up and peer at the appealing landscape painting hung next to the fireplace. She moved the small cloth purse containing her drawing and fingered the roll of paper through the fabric. "Where's her hired girl?" she wondered aloud. "They must have one, because they're rich, maybe she's taken sick. Ain't it hot in here?"

"Calm thyself," Mrs. Wilkin said.

Mrs. Whitfield returned, followed by her son, who carried a tray of food and drink. Maggie automatically stood up to help serve, but hearing a stifled sound from Mrs. Wilkin, she sat down again. She watched Edward Whitfield with interest. "Your arm is better!" she blurted.

He laid down the tray on a table near the sofa and smiled at her. She saw with delight that he was as surprised at her looks as she had hoped he'd be.

Mrs. Whitfield introduced him to Mrs. Wilkin and then said: "And Miss O'Shaughnessy. I know you two have already met." Maggie liked the humor in her voice and ventured a smile of appreciation.

"Under much less auspicious circumstances," he remarked. "Miss O'Shaughnessy. I'm glad to see you looking so well."

"And you!" Maggie replied. The sling Homer Merritt had mentioned was gone. Mr. Whitfield was wearing a well-cut light summer suit, and his brown hair and beard were now neatly trimmed. Over his left eye he wore a black patch which Maggie thought looked quite dashing.

"Do I pass inspection?" he said, with a military salute. Maggie blushed and dropped her gaze to the carpet.

"Edward," Mrs. Whitfield said. Then to her guests, she added: "I'm afraid that military language is now a fixture of Edward's speech. The family still hears 'Fall in!' and 'As you were', and our dinnertime is 'mess'—Of all things! and for our meals we 'draw rations'. Edward, would you pass the cakes, please."

He did so, not seeming in the least abashed; offering Maggie the tray with a flourish. *Ooh. Silver. How pretty,* she thought, *I'll tell Mrs. Sullivan.* Maggie noted that when he sat down, he angled his body to present the right side of his face to the ladies. She carefully sipped and nibbled at the refreshments, listening as Mrs. Whitfield covered acceptable topics such as the weather, and mutual acquaintances. Edward Whitfield seemed content to eat and drink and said not a word. Mrs. Wilkin had told Maggie that only certain things could be discussed politely during such a social call, and that young ladies ought not to speak unless spoken to. *How can I ask about Eleanor? I wonder if she's ill,* Maggie thought. As she saw Edward Whitfield take another jam cake—she counted it as his fourth—she felt confident enough to say: "The jam cakes are exquisitely delicious."

"I'm glad you like them. Would you care for another?" Mrs. Whitfield replied.

"Yes. Thank you." Mr. Whitfield passed her the tray without comment. Mrs. Wilkin praised the cakes faintly, then brightened and said, "My husband—that is my second husband, Mr. Wilkin—I am twice a widow—always said good plain food, well cooked, is a treasure." Maggie swallowed a sigh as Mrs. Wilkin began to propound on this favored topic. Mr. Whitfield flicked the crumbs on his plate with his finger, pushing them all to the center and then scattering them to the sides.

When Mrs. Wilkin paused for breath, he said: "My sister writes to us that the contrabands–no, I mis-speak, they are freedmen now–eat whatever they can catch or forage. She told us that a fellow teacher was invited to supper one night at a student's house and saw on her plate a crisply roasted creature about so big," he held his hands 8 inches apart, "with little paws and the remains of a long, skinny tail."

"A squirrel?" Maggie said.

Mrs. Whitfield shook her head at her son. She said: "We hear that living conditions are improving, but of course, the freedmen must eat whatever they can obtain from the government or from...their surroundings."

"Was it a rat, then?" Maggie breathed. Mrs. Wilkin and Mrs. Whitfield did not hear her, or perhaps pretended not to.

Edward Whitfield remarked: "Roasted squirrel is a delicacy in some parts of the country." Then, clearly amused by Maggie's relieved expression, he added: "A rare delicacy, I would wager, in a hungry land." Squirrel or rat? Maggie did not dare question him further, for Mrs. Whitfield seemed most uncomfortable with the topic.

Mrs. Wilkin said: "Mr. Merritt told me that thy sister is doing a wonderful work, teaching in the South. Many of the Friends support that work."

"So many former slaves have come into Washington during the last few years. My daughter has seen extreme poverty there. Some of her stories are very troubling," Mrs. Whitfield replied.

"Sometimes what little they have gets stolen," her son added, "Kate tells us that she saw some ruffians trying to take away an old colored woman's little bit of rice and "salt horse"—and that perhaps was all she would have to live on for days."

"I have heard of many sorry things the rebels are doing," Mrs. Wilkin agreed, "War is indeed a terrible corruption."

Whitfield scowled. "These men were Union troops, I'm ashamed to say. Harassing the woman for no good reason. And thievery is the least of their transgressions. The newspaper reports…" "Are quite upsetting and not something I care to discuss at the moment," Mrs. Whitfield interrupted.

"I would have punished them soundly if they'd been under my command," Edward muttered.

"You have a very brave family," Maggie said to Mrs. Whitfield.

"Thank you, Miss O'Shaughnessy." Her hostess appeared genuinely pleased by the compliment.

'Tis now or never, Maggie thought, taking the sketch from her bag. *If he laughs, I'll die.*

"I have something," she said. "Something I made, just a little token, but I mean it as a way to thank Mr. Whitfield…for everything, I'm thinking." She stood up and thrust the sketch into his hands. "What is this?" he said. "Just a picture," Maggie said, as she sank back onto her chair and tried to compose herself.

To her dismay, he unrolled the drawing, said "Good heaven!" and read her dedication aloud: "*Presented to Mr. E. Whitfield. A Token in remembrance of his heroic deed. By a most sincerely grateful M. O'S. 1863.*" She closed her eyes.

"May I see it?" she heard Mrs. Whitfield say. "Oh, my, isn't that clever?"

"It's first rate," Mr. Whitfield agreed.

Maggie opened her eyes.

"You drew this?" he asked. She nodded; when she dared look up, he smiled at her. "Thank you. This is very good. I think it's the nicest tribute I've ever received."

"I do admire anyone who can draw," said Mrs. Whitfield. "I can't draw a straight line."

"My father is a painter. He was, I mean," Maggie said with pleasure. "He's gone out West."

"He was a coach painter at Hicks & Denmore's carriage works," Mrs. Wilkin announced disparagingly. "And gone west without a single word to his family."

"But he…" Maggie began, shocked by Mrs. Wilkin's spite. "He didn't mean to." There was no way to explain it. She covered her mouth and blinked to battle the tears.

A deserter, eh? What a shame, Ned thought. Irked at Mrs. Wilkin's comment, he said: "Artistic talent is a God-given attribute, wouldn't you agree, ma'am? And a coach painter's work may certainly be as moving as that of a member of the National Academy of Design."

"I suppose so," Mrs. Wilkin murmured. His mother smiled at him; better yet, so did Maggie. Her eyes are very blue, he thought. He rolled up the drawing and fingered the silk ribbon. He realized he was proud of her: as proud as if she'd been one of the soldiers under his command who'd successfully learned a new drill.

The thought came to him, as it had not on Knott's Hill, that he was responsible for her continued existence. How close she had come, they had come, to being snuffed out. He glanced at her, and was rewarded by another heartfelt smile. He decided that she was worthy of the effort he'd put into saving her.

With a start, he heard his mother speaking to him. "Pardon me. What did you say?" he asked.

"Would you like some more lemonade?" she repeated.

Ned looked around for his glass, then saw that he was holding it. He couldn't remember picking it up. "No, thank you."

Maggie was deeply contented that her rescuer had appreciated her token and turned Mrs. Wilkin's criticism away. It was wonderfully pleasant, too, to lounge on a soft chair, doing nothing. She heard a snuffling sound. She turned toward the door and saw it open, as a dog's snout poked inside. A girl's voice whispered, "Dance! No!" and the dog's nose disappeared.

"Eleanor?" Maggie said, then jumped up, hastily putting aside her plate and glass. She threw open the parlor door. "Eleanor?" The young woman attempting to pull the dog away from the parlor looked at her apprehensively. *Still shy,* Maggie thought.

She said: "It's me, Maggie. I've grown up some and you too. It's so good to see you again! Faith, what a pretty dog. May I pet him? Is it a boy or a girl? What's his name?" The dog wagged its tail and seemed eager to greet her. Eleanor released her hold on the dog's collar. Maggie held out her hands for the dog to sniff, and then stroked his black and white coat and soft ears. "But here I am talking on, just as I used to do," she said. "Sometimes I talk too much, but only when I don't know what to say."

"Oh." Eleanor's mouth quirked. "His name is Dance."

"I thought that's what I heard. I'm pleased to meet you, Dance." The dog put his paw into Maggie's hand. "Oh, he's smart! You're such a handsome boy." When she stopped petting him for a moment, Dance pushed his nose into her hand. "You're lucky to have a dog. Mrs. Wilkin would never stand for it. She's the old

Quaker lady I work for; she's in the parlor." Dance left her and trotted down the hall toward the parlor. Maggie turned and saw Mr. Whitfield stoop to intercept the dog. He scratched Dance's ears.

"There's just one other lady in there, El. Would you...?" He gestured to the parlor.

Eleanor shook her head. "Dance. Come." The dog returned to her.

"Perhaps Miss O'Shaughnessy might like to see your garden, or your other pets—after we are done in there." This he said in an offhanded, casual manner.

"I surely would!" Maggie said, then remembered her manners. "If you don't mind."

Eleanor kissed Dance's head, nodded to Maggie. "I'll be in the back garden." She pulled the dog away down the hall.

"I don't want to go in," Maggie said to Mr. Whitfield. "Is she angry at me?"

"Eleanor?" he said with surprise, "Not at all."

"Not her!" Maggie jabbed a finger toward the parlor, "Her."

He made a disdainful noise. "Twice-A-Widow Wilkin." He raised an eyebrow at her snickering, but as he stepped aside, he commented: "Eleanor is glad to see you. She's just being shy."

Receiving offers to tour the garden from both her hostess and host flattered Mrs. Wilkin sufficiently to ensure that she and Maggie "will stay just a bit longer." Maggie made her escape as soon as she could and trotted to the back garden ahead of the others. Dance barked a greeting. Eleanor hung back, but smiled. Maggie exclaimed over all the flowers, caressing and naming those she knew, and questioning Eleanor about the unfamiliar ones.

As Mrs. Whitfield and Mrs. Wilkin came into view, she said to Maggie: "Would you like to see a surprise?" Maggie and Dance followed, as Eleanor darted away. She led them into the dim recesses of the stable, which smelled of sweet hay and warm horses.

"This is Greylock's stall. Father has him today. And this is my pony's stall. His name is Malabar: he's out in the pasture now. And here's the surprise." Eleanor pointed to a box at the back of an empty stall. "Kittens!" Maggie cooed.

The dog hesitated outside the stall door. "Mama cat's scratched him more than once," Eleanor said. "Now he's learnt his lesson." Maggie was less interested in the animals, than in the change they effected in her friend's manner. Eleanor was at ease, seated regally in the presence of her subjects in this little kingdom, stroking the mother cat's ears.

"Oh, bother," Maggie said, "if I had my own dress on I could sit down with you." As Eleanor looked at her curiously, Maggie went on: "This jacket's borrowed, you see, and must be returned as good as new. And the skirt is new."

"Oh, I see. Are they from your sister, Nora, the one you told me about when we were in school?"

"Goodness, no. Nora's way down in Bridgeport now and she has nothing as fine as this. I almost had a hoop skirt too," Maggie said, "'twould have looked grand, I think. Mrs. Sullivan lent it to me, and I did so want to wear it, but all I was able to do was try it."

Eleanor nodded, but said in a puzzled voice. "They're so awfully wide. I never care to wear one. I think it would just get in my way."

Maggie laughed. "Oh, my, yes! I had a terrible time with Mrs. Sullivan's. First, it was so long, we had to tack the waistband up to here," she gestured to her ribcage just below her breasts, "and hem it before it was short enough for me to wear. And we pulled it and turned it and pinned and pinned. Rose kept sticking me. I think it was an accident."

"Is Rose your sister too?" Eleanor asked.

"No, my brother Frank's wife," Maggie said, remembering Rose's grumbling comments: "Sure as you're born, they'll say you're putting on airs." And then, after all, Mrs. Wilkin had forbidden the crinoline, nearly outlawing the ribbon belt, too: "I don't want thee looking like anything but the good, modest girl we've brought thou up to be."

"I suppose it didn't fit," Eleanor said, "for you don't have it now."

"Well, yes, it did, after a bit of work. But then I had to learn to sit down in it, too. Ha, ha! When I sat down the edge flew up like this! It nearly hit my chin. And that made me laugh." Eleanor smiled, so Maggie sailed on: "Though Rose couldn't see a bit of fun in it, and was as cross as two sticks, Frank was about to die with laughing, and he don't laugh much. And he said…Oh, Eleanor, the next part isn't polite, so I oughtn't to say."

"Do go on," Eleanor said.

"'Maggie,' says Frank, 'you'd better make sure your drawers are clean because you'll be giving them a fine show!'"

"Ooh, he said that?" Eleanor looked suitably shocked.

"He did. I jumped right up in a tizzy, and tried to walk about instead. The silly hoop was swaying like a tree in the wind, this way and that. First it knocked over little Mary's chair, then I caught it on the table leg and then," Maggie lowered her voice dramatically, "It almost knocked down Rose's best china plate from the shelf, and that the only one she has left without a chip."

Eleanor had begun giggling and could only shake her head in reply.

"To be sure, I was having none of that. I took myself out of doors and walked about the yard," Maggie minced around the stall, "And I was doing pretty well. When all of a sudden…" She paused.

"What happened?" Eleanor said.

"Here I am walking about so nicely; then I feel something sharp at my ankles, ow! And I say to myself, 'could it be part of this contraption has sprung loose to jab me?' But, what's that?" Maggie clucked and squawked. "I lift up my skirt and out comes one of our chickens."

Eleanor giggled, then said: "Look, Dance is laughing too." The dog stood in the stall doorway, jaws open and tail wagging. She stood up, brushing straw from her dress. She and Maggie left the stall and patted Dance. "Do you remember those pictures that you used to draw for me on my slate at school?"

"You remember those old scratches?" Maggie said happily.

Eleanor smiled. "They were awfully good. No one in my family draws. When you drew the schoolmaster I knew who it was right away. It's too bad you had to rub it out so quickly."

"After I put the horns and tail on him, mercy, yes!"

"I wish I could draw. I do a little embroidery, like most girls, and fine sewing. That's all."

"But I'd rather sew than cook," Maggie replied. "Cooking is so plain, it's the same every day. At least at Mr. Merritt's."

"Oh, not here," Eleanor said. "Mother is a very good cook, and she's teaching me quite a lot. I made the jam cakes today."

"You did? I liked them." Maggie smirked. "I expect your brother did too. He ate four of them."

"Sometimes he forgets his manners," Eleanor said.

"Yes," Maggie said, thinking of the story he had told about the rat (or was it a squirrel?) The poor Negroes starved just the same as the poor Irish. She could not imagine eating a rat. "Well, maybe he was hungry, just like Denny."

As she told Eleanor about her nephews and niece, Dance sniffed at Maggie's shoes. "Well, Dance, do you like my new shoes?" She hiked up her skirt a little to show them off.

Eleanor said: "I do. I've not seen any like them before."

"And you won't. I made them."

"You made them? How?"

"I embroidered the uppers on canvas, like Berlin work for slippers—but I made up the design myself. And the soles are pasteboard, glued and stitched." She took one shoe off and held it out for Eleanor to examine. "You see why I can't walk on them too long. They'll wear right through." She re-donned the shoe.

"Oh no, here he is," Eleanor said, looking over Maggie's shoulder. "It can't be time for them to go! They just got here," she said to her brother.

"Not immediately," Mr. Whitfield replied.

Eleanor brightened. "Look Ned, Maggie didn't buy her shoes, she made them."

"Pardon me?"

"She made her own shoes. They're quite pretty, too."

"I wasn't aware we had a shoemaker in our company..." he began.

"Here. I'll show you," said Maggie with pride. She moved closer to him, removed one of her shoes and placed it in his hand, then pointed out how she had constructed it.

Ned paid only scant attention to the mechanics of her explanation. The shoe was warm from her foot and it sat lightly in his hand. He watched her balancing on one foot, her stockinged toes resting atop the foot she stood on. *What a surprising girl,* he thought.

"I see your artistic talents extend beyond ink and paper," he said aloud.

"Oh, thank you!" As Maggie reached for her shoe, he held it away from her. "When I came in," he said, "I thought you two were playing 'Who's got the slipper'."

Eleanor laughed in recognition, but Maggie looked confused. "It's a game," Eleanor explained, outlining the rules and laying out the forfeits required of those who lost the competition.

"I'm the forfeit master, and I've got your slipper," he said. "Before I'll release it, you have to pay a forfeit. Like...hmm...like kissing Dance." Eleanor said: "But I do that all the time."

Maggie arched her eyebrows. "That's not much of a forfeit then, for I know a woman or two as well who would not mind kissing a handsome dog."

And surprisingly quick-witted, he thought. Feeling again a bit of the proprietary pride he'd experienced in the parlor, he bowed and returned her shoe.

"Maggie!" Mrs. Wilkin's querulous voice was unwelcome.

"No, Ned!" Eleanor protested. "Maggie didn't see my birds yet, or Malabar, or my rabbit."

"Maybe another time," he said. Realizing there would be no further visits, he avoided his sister's eyes. Maggie looked at him with an odd expression he couldn't fathom, and he looked away from her.

"Must you go so soon?" Eleanor asked the old woman.

Mrs. Whitfield hesitated for a moment before she said, "Mrs. Wilkin, may I introduce my daughter Eleanor."

"I am pleased to make thy acquaintance, Miss Whitfield." Eleanor stared at her blankly. Ned cleared his throat.

"Oh. How do you do," Eleanor mumbled, and then, louder: "Dance. Come."

"Have you two girls had a nice visit?" Mrs. Whitfield said.

"Yes!" Eleanor asserted, but with despair already filling her voice. She hovered for a moment in what was apparently meant as a goodbye curtsey to Mrs. Wilkin, then walked away with Dance.

"Goodbye," Maggie called mournfully after her, "thank you for showing me the kittens."

Mrs. Wilkin blinked and looked around as if seeking an explanation. Receiving none, she settled her shoulders and announced: "Well, now we must take our leave. We thank thee again, Mrs. Whitfield, Mr. Whitfield, for thy hospitality."

"It was our pleasure," Mrs. Whitfield murmured.

Ned made a polite comment to Mrs. Wilkin along the lines of the one she had offered. He intended to do the same for the O'Shaughnessy girl, but the look on her face stopped him.

"You're so kind," she said to Mrs. Whitfield, her voice brimming with tears. She ducked her head for a moment and struggled for control, then said in a choked voice: "Mr. Whitfield…I …expect I will not see you. Thank you…again, for…for…" She was unable to finish.

"Perfectly all right, you're welcome of course," he replied.

She left without a further word. Mrs. Wilkin murmured a final goodbye, then stalked after her employee. Ned and his mother watched them disappear around the corner of the house.

"Oh dear. Poor Elly," Mrs. Whitfield said. "You talked to them, did they get along well?"

"Like a house afire," he said.

"I thought I heard Elly laughing."

He nodded. "She was quite merry until I appeared to say it was time to go."

"If only your father wasn't so opposed to the Irish, so..."

"Pigheaded?" Ned supplied. "Think about it, Mother. I agree that it's unacceptable to fraternize with the Irish. But, good heaven! seeing this girl once in a while is hardly going to ruin Eleanor's social standing."

His mother stared after their departed guests.

"Will she grow out of it, Mama, like Father says?" Ned was doubtful.

Mrs. Whitfield shuddered. "She <u>must</u>...my poor darling girl."

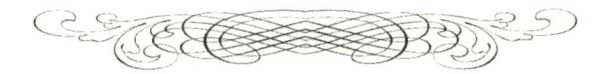

Ned sprawled on the sofa, again attempting to read *Parsons on Contracts*, but longing for supper, when Dance wandered into the sitting room, signalling Eleanor's return. He marked his place in the book and placed it atop the others on the table, then followed Dance into the kitchen.

Eleanor checked the soup simmering on the stove. Mrs. Whitfield stood before a fresh loaf of bread, knife at the ready, and wiped her perspiring face. "Let me do that, Mother." He took the knife from her hand.

Mrs. Whitfield sat down and fanned herself, saying "We were just discussing our guests. Miss O'Shaughnessy looked far different than the night she was brought here."

"Yes," he said, eyeing the slice of bread that he had just cut. It was wider on one end than the other.

His mother said, "I confess I was surprised to see that she was dressed rather fashionably: I didn't think that servants had the means to do that, especially in a household like Mr. Merritt's. She made quite an effort with her dress, didn't she?"

"Oh yes!" Eleanor said. "She cleaned up pretty well," he responded. Good, that slice is straight.

"I liked that pretty hat she wore," Eleanor said, "with the flowers all around it."

"Um hm," he muttered. He remembered the blue eyes under the hat's edge more than the hat itself.

Eleanor giggled, "Ned, have you ever seen Martha dressed like that?"

"I don't notice what Martha wears," he muttered.

"I think that Maggie went to great pains to dress so nicely," Mrs. Whitfield commented. "She has a good skill with the needle. Don't you think so, Ned?"

He ate a scrap of bread that had fallen from the crust, and said: "When have I ever expressed a particle of interest in ladies' fashions?"

"One Whitfield cares not a whit what she wears?" Mrs. Whitfield said with a smile.

"Ha. Very clever, Mother."

"I'm sure that Maggie decorated her hat," Eleanor said, "and she made her shoes too."

"Yes. The pretty shoes," Ned put in.

"Ah, you noticed those, and I did not," Mrs. Whitfield said to him. *She's in rare form tonight,* he thought. Eleanor told her mother about the embroidered shoes and then continued gaily: "And I know where she got the jacket and the waist and the belt and she made her dress, and she borrowed a hoop, but Mrs. Wilkin said no. She told me such a story about that hoop! But I can't tell you now, Mama, not in front of Ned."

"I could turn my back..." he offered.

"Very clever, Edward," his mother said, mimicking his earlier tone.

"No, no, it's a secret!" Eleanor said with glee, "I'll tell you later, Mama. You'll laugh. Maggie's very comical. I didn't know her, she looked so grown up—compared to before. But once we started to talk, I knew she was the same girl."

"Grown up? She's your age, though, isn't she? Sixteen or seventeen?" Mrs. Whitfield said.

"Just the same, except she has her birthday before mine," Eleanor said with animation.

"Yes, your birthday's coming soon, I'd forgotten. Seventeen, my goodness," Mrs. Whitfield said.

Ned arranged the bread on a tray. "What do you want for your birthday, El?" he asked.

"A friend," Eleanor said, smiling at them both.

Ned saw his mother blink rapidly, then drop her gaze, smile gone. He loaded cold ham and bread onto the tray, grabbed the pickle jar and carried them to the dining room. As he returned, he heard Eleanor say: "Dance liked Maggie."

"Yes, he did," Mrs. Whitfield replied.

"Mama," Eleanor said, "Didn't you think she was awfully pleasant? When I listen at the door to the ladies who come to call on you, they are not half as pleasant as Maggie."

"I suppose she seems a pleasant girl, considering her... upbringing," Mrs. Whitfield said.

"Ned, didn't you think she was awfully pleasant? She made you laugh," Eleanor pressed on.

Surprised that his sister was still pursuing the topic, he glanced at his mother, then said truthfully: "I think she's jolly."

Eleanor smiled at him with gratitude, then fiddled with her collar, looking down at her feet. "For my birthday, do you think, just for that day, she could come again? If no other ladies knew: if Papa knew it was just for my birthday?"

Mrs. Whitfield grimaced. "Elly..."

"Mama, please! Just for a little while, that's all I want...It's all I want for my birthday."

"I don't know, kitten. You know how Papa feels about folks of a lower class, and the Irish, well, it just is **not** acceptable," Mrs. Whitfield said with reluctance.

Ned recalled seeing the two girls with their heads together, examining Maggie's shoe. "Perhaps she could come on a day that you never take callers, in the afternoon of a day Father's in court," he suggested.

"Oh! Yes, please, Mama," Eleanor repeated.

"Wouldn't you like a party?" Mrs. Whitfield countered. "We could invite one or two nice girls. I'm sure you would like them, and..."

"But could Maggie come too?"

Mrs. Whitfield did not answer.

Eleanor pressed her lips together, her eyes apprehensive. "I don't know anyone. They wouldn't like me! They did not when I was at that school. Please, may I just have Maggie for now, because I know her and she knows me and we'd have such fun, and maybe… one girl some other time?"

"I suppose we can try," Mrs. Whitfield said uncertainly, then looked as if she'd like to take it back.

"Oh, marvellous! Thank you, Mama!" Eleanor gestured with the soup spoon, spraying drops onto the sizzling stove and onto the wall. Dance leapt up and licked the spots on the wall.

"I think we ought to make ice cream," Ned added, handing his sister a wet rag to wipe the stove.

"Oh, yes! Maggie would love it. Could we, Mama?"

Mrs. Whitfield wore an abstracted half-smile. "I suppose so."

"We don't need ice cream, or cake, Mama. That is a lot of extra work for you, with Martha away, and a visit will be lovely. Truly," Eleanor said.

"Don't worry about that, darling," Mrs. Whitfield said, "I can have a cake sent from the bakery, if need be. I don't like to drop my standards, but I'll admit you and I have been worked to a frazzle since Martha left. Ned, since you clamored for ice cream, you shall have to pay with your labor to crank the freezer. Elly, Ned forgot the butter dish. Would you take it in to the dining room for me? Take Dance with you; it isn't good for him to lick the wall like that."

Mrs. Whitfield turned to her son with a frown, as Eleanor left: "What was I to do? I had no choice! It was all she wanted, and she asks for so little."

"What's the harm in one visit?" Ned said.

"You didn't help matters, saying the girl was jolly."

"Well, she is," he said.

"But your father won't be!"

"When has he ever been jolly?" Ned retorted.

"This worries me," Mrs. Whitfield said, "What if he hears about it! I hope that this is a way to introduce some appropriate girls…Ah, Elly, is the soup ready? Your father will be home soon."

Chapter 6

"There's someone here asking for you, Mr. Whitfield. Says he's a friend of yours," Jack Rossiter called through the darkroom door.

"I'm just about finished. Hold on." The other voice outside the darkroom was familiar. Henry Barton was the last man Ned had expected to visit Millville. A recent graduate of Yale College, Barton did not often stray far from city streets—or city amusements.

Ned burst out of the darkroom door, blinking in the sudden brightness. "This is a surprise, Henry," he said. His friend's welcoming smile changed in an instant to dismay.

"Ho," George said, "You ain't seen him since the secesh got to him, eh? Yup, I hardly knew him myself when I first saw him."

In the nearly ten years that Barton had been a friend, no matter the circumstances or company, Henry kept his wits and parlayed his uncommon charm to good effect. He had always been Ned's model in all situations: but now the model gentleman was speechless, as he rudely stared. Aware of Rossiter's smirk, Ned peeled off the protective over-sleeves he wore in the darkroom, and barked an order: "It's time you checked those printing frames. That sun is strong today." Rossiter stared at him coolly, then at a nod from George, left.

Ned went on. "Henry, I guess you had a craving for country air. How did you know where to find me?"

Barton replied: "I stopped to hire a carriage at the livery stable and asked the way to your residence. The owner said that I would find you here."

"George, this is Henry Barton. Henry - George Dunn. He's the proprietor of this establishment."

"I'm the proprietor for now, until I have to go to camp," George said, "Ned's going to take on my gallery while I'm gone. Yup. I'm aiming to enlist."

"You're a patriot, sir. He's taking on the gallery, is he?" Barton responded. He commented favorably on the furniture, then said: "Mr. Dunn, would you allow me to take your new partner away for a while? I have some business to discuss with him."

"I suppose," George replied, "You ain't in the photograph business, are you?"

"Ha. You are a sharp fellow. No, I am not in any trade," Henry said.

"Then I guess you can have him."

Before they left, Barton complimented Rossiter on the cut of his suit (a particularly flashy outfit) and asked for the name of his tailor. It was a throw-away lie, casually uttered by the immaculately attired Yale man. As they left the building, Henry moved ahead to look into the street.

"Which is your carriage?" Ned asked. He had no reply. Ned cooled his heels in the doorway. "You're welcome to dinner at my house. I'm sure my parents would like to meet you." They tipped their hats to a passing lady and gentleman.

"I take it you're not hungry," Ned stated.

Henry faced him. "I've lost my appetite, strange to relate. I need a drink." "Henry..." Barton held up his hand. "A <u>drink</u>." "There's a bar at the hotel a ways up, across the park." Ned said.

Barton stopped walking and stood in Ned's way. "Jesus Christ, Whitfield, why didn't you warn me? When I got your letter, you wrote me that you were well."

"I am well," Ned said, but without any resolve, "Even if my phiz is a gone goose."

"I was sure you'd get shot," Henry broke in, "That's why I told you that you were a fool to go."

"I wish..." Ned said aloud, and then refused to say the rest. He wondered whether he should make a joke of it. Finally, he said: "That's all water under the bridge now." His friend merely snorted.

"Say, Henry, I took half your advice. I'm a free man. Hattie Caldwell is gone."

"Mirabile dictu! This is good news," Barton said, smiling for the first time. "Congratulations. That was a narrow escape." They walked side by side.

"I presume she threw you over," Henry commented.

Ned contemplated putting a different shine on the matter—he would have tried to bluff George—but Henry would not hesitate to challenge a weak rejoinder. "She just saved me the trouble," he retorted.

Henry laughed. "And you intend to stay with that story? No matter, it's still good news. What a cold fish she is. I trust you are not harboring any misplaced sentimental opinions about the woman." Ned shook his head.

"Good," Henry went on, "You're such a boy when it comes to these things. I will grant you that she was rather clever. What a waste in a woman! Don't start, I know you disagree with me. You played the game of celebrating her intellect rather than her other attributes–not that she had many worthy of praise, and she liked that. I shall have to try that angle if I meet a woman who clamors for it. You played it rather well, actually. I just never understood why. When did the happy event occur?

Ned waved the question away. He could not describe how he had hoped to encourage his fiancée: with the news that he was recovering vision in his right eye; how he would soon be able to speak more clearly as his mouth healed; how he was now able to take care of his own bodily needs without assistance. On the day of the debacle, he was clean, and clothed, neatly bandaged and seated upright in the parlor with a slate to write on. Even so, (Eleanor told him) Hattie had fainted three times. Once: understandable; twice: a bit much; and three times? Hattie Caldwell had less fortitude and common decency than his little sister, who had been a faithful visitor at his bedside and had seen far worse. It was just as well that Hattie broke the engagement: he had reconsidered his impulsive offer of marriage a month or two before his final battle. Her letters had been infrequent; and the sharp wit of her complaints—delivered with pretty expressions in person—lost their appeal on the page.

"After you came back?" Henry said, and with a scowl went on: "It's a pity she cares so little for society. If she had any such aspirations, I'd see to it that she failed. Failed miserably and publicly." He paused, then said: "I believe several drinks are in order!"

"Perhaps an entire bottle," Ned replied. "Or one for you and one for me. Wait, I take that back. One drink will satisfy me."

"One? When did you ever stop at one? Don't tell me you've

signed the pledge," Henry joked.

"I promised that I'd reduce my consumption," Ned answered.

Henry replied: "Come now. To hell with the old man - that was always your favorite toast."

"I'm working today, remember? I work for a living."

"Bosh, Whitfield," Henry scoffed, "not that tired old plebian jibe again. You're hardly a galley slave."

Ned said: "No, I mean it. I promised my mother."

"Ah. That estimable lady who sent you such excellent letters at school," Henry said. Barton contemplated this as they reached the edge of the park. He said, "It's hell having a conscience, it must be."

"You wouldn't know, so you needn't worry. Remember our debates about Dionysius?" Ned answered. Barton walked on without a response, then said: "Perhaps Dionysius sometimes wonders at Apollo…."

"Harry, you surprise me. Did you take Ethics at Yale?" Ned joked, "I shouldn't like my conscience to be a Boswell to your Samuel Johnson. I shouldn't relish doing the work of two men on one wage." He nudged Henry with his boot.

"Hallo. Don't touch the merchandise. I paid a lot for this suit, and it'll be ruined by all this country mud," Barton said.

"The same as New Haven mud, Yalie."

"Quickly done, Ned, if somewhat pedestrian."

"You know I've always been quick on my feet," Ned retorted. "And there's the Eagle Hotel, just ahead."

"Welcome back," Henry said.

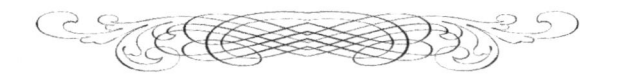

In his letter, Captain Merrill professed himself gratified to hear that Ned was alive, albeit disabled. After briefly reporting news of comrades in the 14th Connecticut Infantry, Merrill wrote that the regiment would welcome George Dunn and any other man Whitfield recommended. The captain admitted that while the men might come down hard at first on "green" recruits, they would not revile them. That treatment was reserved for the upcoming substitutes and draftees: *'An ignorant, wretched, and sorry lot they will undoubtedly be,'* Merrill predicted. Ned wrote a reply—more legible than his initial letter—and posted it, after passing the recruitment information to George Dunn. Dunn thereupon disappeared from the gallery for the day, giving no excuse, leaving Ned and Jack Rossiter in uneasy proximity.

"Father, I'm taking Greylock for a ride," Ned announced as the family finished Sunday dinner. The judge grunted.

Mrs. Whitfield said: "There are some things I need you to do for me tomorrow, Ned, since Martha is coming back."

"Yes, Mother. Make a list, and I'll look it over later." He grabbed his father's musket, saddled Greylock, and lit out for a ride. The ride restored his good humor, but the target practice soured it. He checked the target after his final shot. It had gone wide, like the others. The Judge was an enthusiastic game bird hunter who had always insisted that Ned join him in the pursuit. What the son lacked in fervor for the hunt, he usually made up for in precision at the kill—earning himself a temporary reprieve from his father's criticism. Now that was gone too.

It had been in the back of his mind–prior to his promises to Mr. Mix and to George Dunn–to re-enlist. Captain Merrill's use of the word "disabled" was troubling; this failed target practice confirmed the suitability of the epithet. If he joined again, what duty could he perform, except to marshal bedpans with others in the invalid corps, the inVALid corps? And what had he accomplished in his five and a half months in the army? Miles of marching, a skirmish or two, a few prisoners taken, one Pyrrhic victory in Maryland, and then it was all blown up, with so little of the job done.

The following morning did nothing to make him happy with the realization that Millville and home life were to be his lot. Move the furniture in Martha's chamber, fix that loose rung on her chair, sweep out the ceiling corners, set the mousetraps, patch the crack in the wall, then paint: his mother's list was long.

In contrast, her advice was short and pointed: "Do try to be on your best behavior, Edward. It is hard to find good American help these days, especially as honest as Martha."

"Come now, you're not happy to have her back, the tyrant in petticoats," he said.

Mrs. Whitfield made a face. "She suits your father, and therefore she suits me. As she must."

"If Father will not hire an Irish girl, how about a German girl? There must be some good German girl in town," Ned went on.

"You know that he will only accept American help. And I've

had to offer her an increase in wages."

"I'm surprised you didn't offer her my firstborn child as tribute," he remarked.

"Eddie, that's the other thing I meant to say…"

"You did offer her my firstborn child?" he interrupted.

"Your jokes," his mother continued, "you know Martha thinks them unseemly."

"What right does she have to dictate my conversation?" Ned began, and when his mother sighed, he went on with what he considered extreme forbearance. "God forbid that I would offend Martha's sensibilities, but whose house is this anyway?"

"Your father's," Mrs. Whitfield said tightly.

"But it has been so peaceful here without her," Ned said.

His mother gave him a slight smile. "Well, yes, it has. But Elly and I cannot do everything. We're tired. At least spare Martha the worst of your puns."

"The worst of my puns?"

"I'm teasing; in fact, I'm glad to hear them again, after such a long time," Mrs. Whitfield said.

"You may regret you said that," he said.

His mother squeezed his arm, now smiling widely. "Never!"

Chapter 7

"So, Maggie, have you had any of your visions?" Maggie came back from her daydream and looked at her brother. "What?"

"Those spells you get when you see things going to happen," Michael said. "Have you had any about me?"

"No, not a one," she said.

"Faith, I'm glad to hear that. You've never had a good one."

"Yes, I did!" Maggie began, but her mother's voice rolled over hers.

"Born on the saint's day, and with a caul over her head, she was. She'il have the second sight, said Mrs. Monahan, and she dropped to her knees right there by the bed and blessed herself, so Pen told me."

"Pen," Michael broke in, disgusted. "There's a question for you, Mag. With all your second sight, how come you didn't know your father was going to run out and leave Mam behind without so much as a by your leave?"

"Ah, Mike, don't start her..." Frank cautioned. Rose put a restraining hand on her mother-in-law's arm.

"Four years now and not a word from the scurvy dog! Ye would not treat a dog so bad as he's done me. Don't a poor dog get the scraps at least!" Mrs. O'Shaughnessy shouted. She covered her face with her apron.

"I'm here still, Mam," Maggie said over her mother's moans.

"There, there," Rose said. And to Michael, "D'ye see what ye've done?"

Michael mumbled something inaudible then said: "Don't take on so, Mam."

"I do have good visions, Mikey, you're wrong to say I don't," Maggie put in. "I knew Rose and Frank would marry the very first day I saw her, when I was just a little girl."

"Get along with ye," Rose said, yet she was clearly pleased. "And ye told me you'd say a prayer for my baby boy, before I even knew myself I was carryin' Patrick." Patrick fastened his aunt with a questioning look and began to speak, but Maggie shook her head at him and he wisely shut his mouth.

Mrs. O'Shaughnessy dropped her apron and wiped her eyes with the back of her hand. "My boy," she said, reaching toward Michael. "Ye'll keep safe in this war if yer sister has no visions." *But I don't cause the harm,* Maggie thought. She had always been a little afraid of that, and of the visions themselves. Temporarily united by worry, the adult members of the family sat contemplating Michael's future.

"Sullivan's done all right. He's well, still, two years in. And Malloy's brother, he ain't even bin sick," Michael said finally. "And I'll get my bounty, buy me some fine land up in Illinoy."

"Ye take care, ye mind yerself," Mrs. O'Shaughnessy said.

"Never you worry, Mam. Nobody's ever licked me, remember."

"Nobody's licked him!" Denny echoed.

"Whissht," his uncle replied. "The war won't last long, not with all the men goin' in now. And we'll stop losing battles."

"Like at Fredericksburg, where poor Mr. Whitfield was hurt," Maggie added. "I hope they'll be no more of those."

"Who's he?" Michael asked.

"That Yankee gent who got Maggie off of Knott's Hill when she fell down," Rose answered, "Didn't Frank tell ye?"

"Maggie is friends with his sister," Frank said.

"From school," Maggie said.

Michael laughed. "Hoo, hoo! Ain't we grand now? They've got some greenbacks lying about, I'll bet." Maggie shrugged.

"She's bin to the Judge's house, that's how grand she is," Rose said.

"Hold on, Mag, ain't that the girl who's touched?" Michael pointed to his head.

"She is not!" Maggie protested. "Not a bit. She's just very shy. She always has been, since I knew her at school."

"Huh." He had already lost interest.

"How much does the army pay?" Mrs. O'Shaughnessy asked. Michael frowned. "Why?"

" 'tis a simple question!" his mother shouted.

"You won't be needing any of that. You have Maggie's wage," Michael replied.

" 'Tis hardly enough to keep body and soul together," Mrs. O'Shaughnessy grumped.

"Ain't I given you the money I win when the gents bet on my games? And what do you do with that?" he said, "You use it to no good purpose."

She knew well what he referred to so darkly, and retorted: "Ah, yer baseball. 'Tis a boy's game ye're playin'."

Michael scowled, then said: "This boy'll just keep the money, then, keep it all. Or give it to Agnes; she'd not turn her nose up at it."

Rose interrupted before Mrs. O'Shaughnessy could reply. "Ye'll be takin' Aggie out West with ye, then, Michael. Ye must. She's bin waiting so long."

"It could be." Michael begrudged a small smile.

Rose grinned, and said to her husband, "I told ye so." Then, to Michael: "Have ye set the day?"

"Criminee, Rose! I'm goin' off to war!"

"Ah, marry her now, Mikey. She's waited so long. It must be five years."

"And she'll wait a bit longer, won't she, until I get back, then we'll marry and off we'll go."

Maggie sat up straight: going west had been the topic of her earlier daydream. "I could go with you and Aggie, out west," she said.

Her brother said: "What? You! You're just a little bit of a thing. You'll not go west with me. You couldn't even work at the mill without falling into the machines."

"That's not fair," Maggie mumbled.

Rose stepped in on her behalf. "Now, Mikey, she's older now. Not the little slip she was at thirteen, half-starving herself because her Da went away."

"I have to go with you," Maggie pleaded.

Michael said: "Oh you do, do you? And why is that?"

"I... have to," was all Maggie could say. Her brother's critical gaze weakened her resolve, and she looked away.

"Sweet mother of God!" Michael snorted. "I'll bet I know why - you think to find your father out there. You're mad, girl. In the great wide West!" He laughed in disbelief.

"I'm not mad," Maggie choked, thudding her heels against the chair rung.

"She misses him, is all," Mrs. O'Shaughnessy said.

Michael said: "Misses him…that's one thing, but thinking she could find him? She's taken leave of her senses."

"Leave her be, Mike," Frank said.

"I liked Pen too, back when," Michael went on, "But no one could find him out there, not without some idea where he might be. Show some sense, Maggie."

I know that, Maggie thought, *But I must go, I have to try. I don't want to die here never having gone further than Vinton Center.*

"We've not moved," Michael went on, "he knows where we are. I don't know why, but he gave the back of his hand to you and Mam, and now he's likely…"

"Whissht!" Rose interrupted.

Dead, Maggie thought. "No, he's not," she said.

"But he's gone," Michael said impatiently. "So. If you're still wanting to go out west in a year, find yourself a husband and go out with him, or you and him join us, but don't go looking for Pen. You'll never find him until he wants to be found." *I won't cry in front of him. I won't give him the satisfaction,* Maggie told herself.

Dennis squirmed in his chair. "Paddy says the Injuns got Maggie's Da."

"Shut your gob!" Patrick said.

Michael said in a softer voice: "All the Donnellys say you'll be married soon enough, Mag." *That again,* Maggie thought. *In a pig's eye!* "Aggie says you're a pretty little thing. And you are, I suppose, if you don't let it go to your head," Michael continued.

"Dooley's looking for a wife," Frank said. Maggie stared at her lap. "Wasn't he after talkin' marriage to you last year?" he added.

Maggie cleared her throat. "No. "

"Bridget McGee wants to marry him," Rose said.

"Does she now?" Frank remarked.

Rose nodded, then said to Maggie: "Rory Corcoran, then."

"Well," Maggie replied. *He would not be so bad,* she thought. Her mood lifted slightly. Rose laughed in a knowing way.

"Ain't he courting Annie Mulrooney?" Frank said.

Mrs. O'Shaughnessy snorted. "That one will never settle down till he's old and gray."

"I thought he was courting Nan Quinn," Michael said.

"And Sheila who was at the dance in March, and any other girl who takes his fancy," Maggie put in pertly, to show her brother that she wasn't such a goose as he thought, and that she didn't care for Rory, anyway. Not much.

"I heard he has a sweetheart in Hartford. He goes there once a month," Michael said.

"No, some relation of his lives there, and Dooley says she's got a galloping consumption," Frank answered.

"Corcoran's got no relations that I know of," Mrs. O'Shaughnessy said.

"Poor Rory," Maggie said with concern.

"Don't set your sights on that one," Michael said.

If I even wanted him, he'd court me too, Maggie thought.

"Ned, put that dictionary away please," Mrs. Whitfield said, just as the judge arrived at the breakfast table.

"I had it out so I could read you the reference we talked about last night. About Reverend Story," he said.

"You know the rule, no books at the table," Mrs. Whitfield said absently.

"Why would he be in the dictionary?" Eleanor asked.

"He's not. I called him Reverend Stentor..."

"To his face?" Eleanor interrupted with some alarm. The judge made a noise deep in his throat.

"Don't be a goose," Ned replied, "And not to his face, for heaven's sake. It's not insulting. Not particularly."

"It couldn't have been to his face, because you never go to church," the judge rumbled, "You are a Sabbath-breaker."

Mrs. Whitfield said: "Read me the reference, and then put the book away."

He opened the dictionary to the place he had marked: '*Stentorian, meaning very loud. After Stentor, a Greek herald in the Trojan War, described in the Iliad as having the voice of fifty men.*' I thought it an apt description of our storied reverend."

Eleanor said, "I see! It's true. He is very loud."

"How do you know?" Ned's question came out more rudely than he had intended.

"Edward," Mrs. Whitfield said with quiet warning. He shrugged an apology to his sister, who did not seem offended.

She said: "I heard him when he came here to pray for your recovery, when you first came home, and you were so sick."

Ned did not like to think that anyone outside his family and nurse had seen him when he was helpless. He stared into the dictionary. *'Stercorous, 'Of, containing, like, or having the nature of dung.' Just the thing,* he thought.

"I heard him through the door," Eleanor continued. "And through the floor, and the walls, undoubtedly. Elly, you've proved my point," Ned said.

"Yes, Reverend Story does have a…carrying voice," Mrs. Whitfield commented, "Quite appropriate for a minister, and not unlike your Father's, and your own."

"You're chaffing me," Ned replied, "I'm not shrill like Story; I don't blat and blast like a train whistle! Now that I think of it, I'll bet that's why Alice Story had cotton wool in her ears so often when she was in school, her ears were ringing."

"Ned, for shame," Mrs. Whitfield said with good humor. "The poor little thing had ear problems because of her chronic catarrh."

"Now there's a sick and pitiful Story," Ned began. Eleanor breathed a giggle.

"The poor thing," Martha commented, shaking her head. Mrs. Whitfield covered her mouth, but her eyes were merry.

"What do you have to be so jolly about this morning?" the judge grumped to his son, while contemplating his ham and eggs as if they too had offended him.

"I don't know," Ned lied. As he returned the dictionary to the sitting room, he revelled in the truth that he had not revealed: for the first time since he had been wounded, nothing itched, throbbed, jabbed—not even the troublesome denture. Lacking the sobering counterweight of pain, he felt like a boy let out early from school on a glorious day.

"Have some muffins, sir. You know what they say, feed a cold, starve a fever," Martha urged.

Judge Whitfield said, "I don't feel well. I'm taking Judge Griswold's court today because he's ill. I should be a-bed myself." Martha excused herself from the table as Ned sat down.

That boarding house, he thought, *it didn't look bad.* "I was contemplating taking a room in town nearer the photograph gallery," he said.

"No," Eleanor said in a plaintive tone. "You must stay here. If you live in town, you'll be gone from here all the time."

Causa principalis, he thought. He damped his glee to answer her: "It's not that far away. Not as far as Virginia. Or Washington."

The family's concern about Kate had come to a crisis point just a few days earlier as rumors spread from the panicked capitol city that rebel troops were in Hagerstown, Maryland and raiding farms as far north in Union territory as Chambersburg, Pennsylvania. General Hooker was said to be in command of the Union Army of the Potomac. This news reassured a few but incensed others, who had no confidence in the man since the federal army's defeat at Chancellorsville. Six-month militia regiments had been called up from surrounding states to defend northern territory, and the governor of Pennsylvania had pleaded for help to defend his state against attack.

The judge and Ned had been ready to make the long journey south to retrieve Kate, until a reassuring telegram from Cyrus Whitfield made them drop their travel plans. They would wait and see if the Army of the Potomac would take any action—and hope that the Union action would be effective. However, Kate did not frighten easily; and Ned thought they might have had to bind and gag her and throw her like baggage into their conveyance once he and the Judge arrived to rescue her.

Eleanor frowned as she offered the plate of fried potatoes to her father.

"No, none of that for me," the Judge said, "Didn't I just say that I don't feel well, didn't I make that clear? That's a fine 'good morning', upsetting your mother at breakfast."

Ned looked up: yes, that last comment was directed at him. "I beg your pardon?" he said, but his father simply glared, so Ned glanced at his mother. Adjudging her not upset but bewildered, he replied: "I didn't intend to make light of the situation in Washington, sir."

The Judge said: "Here, don't try to play innocent with me.

That may work with her, but not with me. Moving out, you'd like that—to have a place in town, right under our noses, at a cheap boarding house. You know what people would say, they'd say there's contention in our family."

Ah, there's the rub, Ned thought. "The Eagle Hotel is respectable," he countered.

"For travelers and men without kin in town," the judge said. He sipped his coffee and said: "You'll stay here."

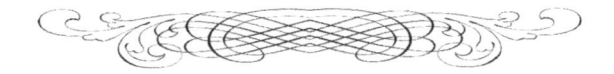

When they entered the study that evening, the judge said: "Sit down," and he lit the lamp. Ned sat, blinking at the bright flame and shading his eye with his hand. "First of all, moving out...I forbid you to mention that again," the judge said.

Ned began: "I'm of age now... "

"That propriety demands you remain here, I suppose is not reason enough for you," his father interrupted, "Until you marry or find a position out of town you stay here, you know that. And I know your aim: all this talk about moving out is calculated to annoy me—but it worries your mother."

"She needn't worry anymore."

"Huh. Your say-so: oh, glorious day, there's proof to take to the bank," Mr. Whitfield pronounced. "And speaking of the bank, that's my topic. You and your jokes about visiting the dentist—who do you think pays the man? Why do you think we no longer have our second horse, or why Jacob was let go after so many years of service, leaving all the burden of the stable care on me."

"I've been taking care of that," Ned put in.

"...and of the garden on your poor little sister," his father went on, "and whatever shiftless boy we can afford to hire? I equipped you for the army; and then sent you whatever money I could every time you asked. And then I paid the bills! From the dentist, the doctor, the oculist, and Sam's wages to nurse you. I vow there is not a medical man in Vinton or Hartford that I don't owe money to."

Thoughts muddled, Ned replied: "I'm not ungrateful. I... wasn't aware of all the money."

"Well, now you are." There was pleasure in the judge's

voice. "With your superior brain, it's odd you didn't figure it out. But since you are of age now, as you are so fond of pointing out, it is high time for you to learn something you never learned in college: the hard task of paying your debts." His father gave him a few minutes to chew on that comment.

"I have no debts. My debts, wait, do you expect me to…pay you for all those things, all of that?" Ned sputtered.

The judge said: "I would not ask you to repay me for the expenses of your medical care. Those were my duty to pay as a loyal supporter of the Union."

Ned closed his eye. "I already paid that debt with my pound of flesh." The lamp wick hissed. He slipped his handkerchief out of his pocket and held it against his mouth. His facial muscles tired after a day of talking, and his lower lip was numb on the left side, failing to dam the saliva.

The judge said: "Pray remain with the topic at hand. I was speaking in monetary terms. You read the newspaper: it must have come to your attention that prices are sky-high. Flour, meat, clothing, coal—they all cost twice what they did last year, but my income hasn't increased."

"Not enough people dying?" Ned murmured. It was an old joke. Probate judges received no stipend, but were paid from estate fees, and were remunerated certain standard amounts for facilitating adoptions, commitments, and conservator-ships.

The judge ignored the comment and blew his nose. "If you have money enough to bandy jokes about residing at a boarding house, or good heaven, the Eagle Hotel! then put that money to good use and pay me board. It would make a start in paying off your debts which are now mine." Ned glanced at his father. "And not a word of this to your mother," the judge muttered, "No need to worry her further."

"How much?" Ned mumbled through the handkerchief. He loosened his necktie and ran his finger down under his collar. The judge named a figure for room and board.

"Very well. But I meant the debt that I supposedly… that I owe you for, for equipping or medical costs. My board ought to count toward reducing that amount," Ned said hotly.

"Ought to?" said the judge, "You have no say in this matter. But I'm a fair man, so I will allow it count in part."

"Fair? Half! Half would be the most equitable, sir. Give me a chance to get established. Be reasonable," Ned pleaded.

"You're in no position to bargain," the judge said. It seemed indisputable. "Good night," his father dismissed him.

"There's no chance of that now," Ned replied bitterly, substituting this utterance for the storm of profanity trapped behind his teeth.

Squinting in the sun, Ned climbed to the gallery's roof top. A glance at the printing frames proved Rossiter was right: the images were still faint. He sat down on the roof ridge to wait, thinking about home, and the army. That was one good thing about the military: there were a variety of ways to punish insubordination. He had used a few of them on the men under his command; and he thought it a pity that he lacked that power in civilian life. Rossiter would certainly benefit from a week's duty policing the latrines; and the judge deserved to be bucked and gagged. The doors to the Eagle Hotel shone in Ned's imagination like the pearly gates of Paradise.

He stood up and stretched, looking at the view. Across the street, the livery stable sat low and dark, a crooked tooth in the neat line of shops. The brick bank's symmetrical columned façade exuded to the passing citizens a comforting stability. Behind him were back yards, sheds, fences, small alleys, privies. Beyond them was the river and its sluice-ways channeling water to power the racketing mills. There was no beauty in any of it: yet, seeing it without distracting pain, blessed to be able to see at all—he found it beautiful. He resolved to borrow Alonzo Dunn's large-plate camera and bring it up to the roof on a clear morning. He would photograph both sides of the street, scenic or not. Someone would buy the views: local pride ought not to be underestimated. One must always pay pride its due.

Chapter 8

"I'm glad Mrs. Moore is here for your party," Maggie said. *And nobody else,* she thought. She had not relished the prospect of facing a phalanx of grandly dressed young ladies looking down their noses at her.

"I am, too," Eleanor replied. "She and Mama have been friends for a long time—ever since I was a little girl. I did not know that you were acquainted with her."

Maggie said: "I'd promised to help the Ladies Aid Society at the Congregational, because Mrs. Moore was so good as to let me use their sewing machine to sew this dress, so I went over on fifth-day, I mean Thursday, afternoon to help. She was kind, for she told me what to do and showed me how to do it. Not like some of the others!"

"What happened?" Eleanor asked, seeing Maggie's obvious displeasure.

"Do you know a Mrs. Eller?" Maggie asked.

"I've heard the name. She's a member of the Second Congregational Church; that's Mama's and Papa's church too." Eleanor paused and said softly. "I've never met her of course."

Maggie frowned and said: "Well, I suppose she's a very important lady."

Eleanor thought for a moment. "I have heard Papa say that her husband is part owner of a manufactory–I've forgotten which one. Was she there at the Ladies Aid Society?" At Maggie's nod, Eleanor said: "I've heard Mama say that Mrs. Eller is rather opinionated. Oh! I think she is the lady that Ned calls Mrs. Carpington Highnostril."

Maggie grinned. "'tis a perfect name for her. She complained that my sorting was wrong and said that someone else now must do it all over again, but I had to wash all the soiled clothes that folks had given for the poor. Now wouldn't you think that if a lady gave clothes for the poor, she'd be washing them first. She tells me to take them to her house to wash. 'It's right on the park,' says she, 'the finest one on the street!'"

Eleanor's mouth made an "O".

"How am I to get them there, then?' I asked her. 'D'you have a barrow to carry them over?' But she laughed right in my face and called me a foolish girl."

"How horribly rude of her. How did she expect you to carry it all?"

"I made two big bundles inside the sheets and tied them with twine and dragged them to her house, once I found it. And it wasn't the finest one on the street, neither. I hope it don't upset your Mama, me talking of Mrs. Eller that way?"

Eleanor glanced around. "It doesn't matter. It's just us here." Maggie liked the sound of that phrase. She said with a smile: "To my way of thinking, Mrs. Eller looks like a sow. She must get it from the Highnostril side of the family." Over Eleanor's snickers, she crowed: "Och, Faith, I just remembered. A sow indeed, just like the one chased my father."

"He was chased by a pig?" said Eleanor.

"Usually 'tis men who chase pigs, but this time 'twas the other way round entirely. You don't keep a pig, do you?" she asked.

"Goodness no," Eleanor replied. "You're so comical, Maggie. Papa would never allow such a thing! We get our meat every day from the butcher's delivery wagon."

Every day, wouldn't Denny and Patrick like that, Maggie thought. Rose bought from the wagon once a week, usually bacon, or salt pork or corned beef that she soaked and re-soaked to make them palatable.

She said: "Oh, but you know how big they can be, pigs, near as big as a door, some of them, full-grown. You'd not believe such a creature could move fast, would you? But they can. And thereby hangs my tale..." She crooked her pinky finger and inscribed a spiral in the air. Eleanor giggled in anticipation.

"This pig in my story was an old sow who was as mean as the very devil. Seeing her piglets sold off from her for years, that's what made her mean, so my Mam says."

"I should think so," Eleanor remarked.

Maggie nodded. "But that's the way of things. One spring when I was just a baby, this old sow charged Mr. Flaherty when he came to fetch one he'd sold off to Mr. Dooley. Flaherty swore he'd butcher her, but then he had second thoughts. Well, says he to himself, I'll keep one of the girls from this litter and raise it myself. As soon as the daughter's grown enough to farrow, I'll butcher that old one."

Maggie wagged her forefinger. "The boys round about teased the sow something awful. I'm sorry to say my brother Michael was one of them. He was about eight years old, I'm thinking, when it happened. One Sunday, he went missing just when Mam needed him for a chore. She called out for him, and Da did too, but nary a sign of him was to be found…"

"Children should always stay close to their parents," Eleanor broke in with an alarmed expression.

"Well, let me tell you," Maggie said, "my Da said, I wonder if he's gone to pester Flaherty's sow, since we told him not to. And Mam said, Go, Pen, and fetch him quick. She'll murther him and eat him up!" Here, Maggie smiled reassuringly at Eleanor. "So, Da hurried over to Flaherty's. And wouldn't you know, there was Michael walking on top of the fence around the pig sty!"

"Oh no," Eleanor murmured.

"Oh, yes, the great fool. Da shouted to him to get down, but Mikey lost his footing just then and fell headfirst into the…" Maggie caught herself just in time. She'd been about to say "into the shite," as her mother and father always told the story. "Into the muck."

"No!" Eleanor exclaimed. Maggie nodded. "The old sow was resting in her wallow in the shade, but when Mikey fell in, she picked her head up and snorted." Maggie imitated the sound, and Eleanor blinked. "Who's this in my sty? Then Da jumped the fence to get Michael out and that made the old thing madder still. Come to get my babies, have ye? And she hauled herself up out of the mud, with all the piglets squealing to beat the band. EEEE, EEE!" Dance barked sharply at this sound.

"My Da threw Mike back over the fence and was climbing over the top himself, when didn't he hear her snorting and grunting right behind him, so near he could feel her hot breath upon him. And that old she-devil crashed into the fence, just missed his foot by an inch, and sent him flying into the barnyard. Then she broke right through."

Maggie took a breath, and continued: "Thanks be to God, Michael had climbed up onto the corncrib, but as soon as Da got to his feet that old thing went at him, so he took to his heels, as fast as he could go. That pig, says he, och, like a mad thing she chased him out of Flaherty's place, with her piglets following behind making a terrible racket, and down the lane to where we lived."

Dance nosed Eleanor, but she pushed him aside.

"Pig! my Da hollered, Pig loose! Mad pig! Everyone scattered and hid behind their doors or up on the fence tops, even the men, after she rushed at them. So there they were, the whole big, brave lot of them, and didn't she stop and give them the eye, as if to say, will you look at yourselves, then."

Eleanor laughed. "I've read that pigs are very smart."

"So smart," Maggie agreed, "that she took her time rooting around Donnelly's garden, and whenever anyone tried to run her off, she'd just give out with a loud grunt, and off they'd run. When she'd had her fill, she marched off with her piglets right back to her sty, where Flaherty found her not an hour later. And Mikey still in the corn crib. If he ever teased an animal again, I never heard of it."
Eleanor smiled widely. "And that's the moral of the story."

Dance looked expectantly back and forth between the two girls. "Come, Dance," Maggie said, and patted him. "Oh, what's this stuck in your coat?"

"Ha," Eleanor gurgled, "Paint. Oh, my goodness, I have a story too, a chasing story. You won't believe it! The same thing just happened to Ned."

"He was chased by a pig?" Maggie said.

"No, no," Eleanor talked fast around her laughter, "By a nest of hornets."

"Ow." Maggie winced. "Is he all right?

"A few stings. Settle down, Dance! It happened last week. Father was upset..." Eleanor hesitated. "Ned promised he would paint the window frames on the east side of the house. But I'd seen some hornets flying up by the roof, my window's on that side, so I told him to be careful. When he went up on the ladder to scrape the old paint off none of them bothered him. I suppose he thought he was safe, but once he had mixed up a bucket of paint..."

"Uh oh," Maggie murmured.

"He's particular about it being just so. He got up on the ladder and was painting, when one of them fell in the bucket and it made a lot of noise there before it drowned. All of a sudden they came at him like a rainstorm, he said, lots of them! He said the buzzing sounded like the bullets do when they fly in battle."

"Truly?" Maggie shivered. She'd never imagined how bullets sounded.

"Well, I was in the kitchen with Mother and Martha. We were putting up strawberry jam, and it's such a chore, the kitchen gets awfully hot when you cook the berries down, and we were very busy. We heard Ned shouting. I thought Dance had gotten loose and run away! Then there was a big clatter, oh my, we jumped, it startled us so. Mama was going out to see what all the commotion was when Ned came in so quickly, he almost knocked her down; and he was slapping all around him with his hat, and he slammed the door. Shut the windows, shut the windows! he said, and he was covered in paint."

"He never was!" Maggie said, trying to contain her laughter.

"Oh yes he was," Eleanor replied earnestly. "We shut the windows and killed a few hornets that got in, then we saw paint all over the floor. What a mess–but he looked so funny! He...he..." Eleanor paused for breath. "He went down the ladder so fast that it tipped over, paint and all. And of course, Dance got in it."

Eleanor continued giggling as Maggie crowed: "I'll bet there were tracks all the way to the door. I can just see him, what a picture... Actually, what a picture it would make. I could draw it."

"Could you? Like the one you brought for my birthday gift?" Eleanor took Maggie's cartoon from the table and looked it over again. The cartoon was titled "Dangers of Fashion." In it Maggie had sketched Eleanor and Dance firmly planted on the ground while enduring a stiff breeze, while she herself—adorned with a huge hoop skirt—was blown nearly parallel to the earth while clinging to a tree. Each figure had a word or two of caption: Eleanor was saying Goodness me, Maggie was crying Help, while Dance added a quizzical woof.

"Mama has a lap desk in the sitting room," Eleanor offered.

"Grand," Maggie said. The girls were met at the back door by Mrs. Whitfield, who listened with amusement to Eleanor's hurried story, and then suggested that the girls stay outside for now while the rain held off. "Has Maggie seen your pets?" she asked.

"No, I forgot," Eleanor said. She took Maggie's hand and pulled her gently along. "Wait 'till you see."

"I've never felt anything so soft." Maggie said while stroking the rabbit's fur. "How did you ever get so many pets?"

"Oh, because I love them so! My orange tabby was first, she died last winter. Then Uncle Cyrus brought me my pony for a birthday gift when I was eight," Eleanor said.

"Do you think you'll get another pet today?" Maggie asked.

"Not this time. I'm having this party instead. I've never had a real party before."

"Neither have I," Maggie said.

Eleanor put the rabbit back into its hutch. "When we go inside I'll show you Castor and Pollux, my canaries."

"What queer names!"

"It's from Greek mythology. Castor and Pollux were twins."

"Who's your favorite pet? I'm thinking it must be Dance."

"Oh yes." Eleanor agreed gravely. "I don't know what I would do without him." The dog came over to them and poked his nose into Eleanor's hand.

"He surely knows his name," Maggie commented.

"He got his name from Ned, too."

"I wondered about that. 'Tis a comical name."

"Well, for a little while I called him Dash, like Queen Victoria's dog," Eleanor said. Maggie wrinkled her nose.

"When he was a puppy, he was such a rascal. He chewed up one of Papa's slippers and stole the other one too. When we finally caught him after quite a long chase, Ned said 'you've led us on a merry dance!'" Eleanor smiled at the memory. "Since we had to chase him every day, the naughty pup, that became his name."

Dance woofed and wagged his tail at someone behind Maggie. "Good day, Miss O'Shaughnessy," Edward Whitfield said. "El, it is time for ice cream."

"Already?" Eleanor asked.

He flexed his fingers. "I've been cranking the freezer in double-quick time."

He noted that Miss O'Shaughnessy was wearing her straw hat. Today it was decorated with fresh flowers, from the Whitfields' garden, perhaps. Eleanor had a few of the same twined in her hair. He had never seen her do such a thing before. The shoes that barely showed beneath the hem of Maggie's calico skirt were neither the battered brogans nor the colorfully embroidered slippers that his mother had teased him about.

"Not wearing your fancy shoes today?" he remarked to her as he walked them toward the house. As soon as the comment left his mouth he remembered that it was impolite for a man to remark on any aspect of a lady's clothing, unless it was to compliment her general appearance.

"No, not today." She stopped and pushed her skirt aside slightly as if for confirmation. "The soles on those are too thin entirely. They could never take the walking; they'd wear right through." The creases in the black leather and the worn areas of the flimsy canvas uppers of her shoes were covered in road dust.

"You walked here? Great guns, that's quite a march for a young lady," Ned said, again without thinking. Maggie looked embarrassed. He went on: "Actually, I like to walk too. It has a very salutary effect on one's health."

"So they say," Maggie replied. *She'd photograph well,* he thought.

"You walked all that way to see me?" Eleanor asked Maggie in a wondering tone.

"Faith, I was happy to!"

He was glad to see Eleanor's answering smile. He hoped for his sister's sake that Maggie's reply had been sincere.

"And I walked uphill from downtown, Elly, in honor of your birthday," he said, as they neared the porch.

"Uphill, in honor of me? I am honored," Eleanor teased in return, "But you knew there'd be ice cream and cake here at the end of your journey, and Maggie didn't."

"Man does not live by bread alone," he said.

Maggie sat alone in the Whitfield's parlor, listening to the rain. She longed to examine the landscape painting, and peek at the titles of the books on the corner table, but instead she kept her hands folded in her lap. *What if someone came in and discovered me playing at Paul Pry,* she worried.

"I see you have a piano," she said as Eleanor returned from wherever she had gone to secure Dance. The dog had caused his mistress some embarrassment by whining outside the dining room door as the small party of five ate cake and ice cream. "Do you play?" Maggie asked.

"Yes, I play it often. Actually, not so often now."

"Would you play something for me, please? I've never heard a piano."

Now she had Eleanor's full attention. "What? Truly, never?"

"Truly," Maggie said, "There's a fiddler who plays at our dances. And I've heard the German brass band, of course, and our neighbor plays the tin whistle and the drum and the jews harp, but no piano."

"You have attended dances?" Eleanor said wistfully.

"Yes, it's jolly. I love to dance," Maggie responded. "I just remembered, one time a fellow came on St. Patrick's day and he played the bagpipes. But I've never known a soul who could play a piano."

Eleanor said: "Sir Walter Scott writes so romantically of the bagpipes. I've never heard them played; I should *so* like to. Do they sound haunting, as Scott says?"

Maggie pondered this. "They sound a little queer at first, like a groaning kind of wind, but when the piper gets a-going, then they sound grand."

"I could play *Annie Laurie* for you." Eleanor removed the decorative shawl covering the piano and dug through her sheet music. Maggie gathered up one that had slithered to the floor. The page looked like a message in an exotic code, and the word "code" was printed on the last page, but spelled wrong, 'coda'. She said: "How queer it looks on paper, all that music. How do you ever sort out what it means and how to play?"

"May I see that one, please? Yes, this is a rather difficult piece, especially all those chords for the left hand." Eleanor pointed to the lower staff, which—unlike the top staff (ants swarming on the page to Maggie's eyes)—was dense with dots in vertical rows. Maggie thought they looked like dried apple slices strung on cords.

"But once you learn the scales, then it's all much simpler," Eleanor went on.

"Scales," Maggie repeated, understanding the word in its context, but still picturing a weighing device. "It don't sound simple at all. Not to me."

Eleanor was eager to play teacher. "Here's a scale in the key of C." She played it for Maggie. "And here's a D", she played the note and pointed to the page, "And here's another. They're always on the fourth line, at least in the treble clef and when it's not a high D or low D above or below the staff."

Maggie nodded, thoroughly confused. When Eleanor began to play a rollicking air, Maggie was enthralled by the sound of the piano and by her hostess' expertise.

"Oh no," she protested when Eleanor stopped suddenly. "What's the matter?"

Eleanor's mouth was drawn down in disappointment. "Can't you hear how awful it sounds? It's terribly out of tune."

"But it makes so many sounds at once, I never knew that. And how your fingers danced! You played so quickly, it was like they were chasing each other back and forth."

"I never thought of that," Eleanor said, momentarily mollified. "But truly, Maggie, it hurts my ears. Kate would be upset if she heard it sounding so dreadful."

"Does Kate play the piano, too?"

"Yes. And she sings beautifully! I wish you could have heard her when she and Ned sang duets." Eleanor looked away, then swept the music off the piano into the music stand and closed the instrument.

"I don't sing well," Maggie confessed. "I sound like...a chickadee. A chickadee with catarrh." She let out with a tiny, birdlike cough to demonstrate. It had the desired effect, for Eleanor smiled. "Your sister sounds like a very interesting person," Maggie added.

"She is indeed. If you only knew! I wish you could meet her." Eleanor sighed. She covered the piano with the shawl and replaced the lamp. Maggie pointed at the photograph album on the table. "Do you have a picture of her that I could see?"

Eleanor met this suggestion with enthusiasm and soon she and Maggie were seated side by side looking through the album. A strong-featured young woman with a mass of wavy hair and smiling eyes, Kate had a look of mischief and willfulness that did not vary in any of her pictures.

Maggie pointed to a young man in officer's uniform whose carte-de-visite was placed next to one of Kate's. "Who is this nice-looking fellow?"

"That's Will," Eleanor said. Is there another brother, then?

Maggie wondered, but hesitated to ask, for Eleanor now looked sad. *Oh, no. He's passed on.*

"When he enlisted, he gave me Dance, so I'd have a friend while he was away in the army," Eleanor murmured, "I was never afraid of Will." Her eyes pled with Maggie to understand. *Never afraid,* Maggie thought. She said: "He's a rare fine man, then, and very kind, to give you such a gift."

"He's Ned's friend. Was his, And mine. And Kate's fiancé." Eleanor lapsed into a brooding trance. *She's seeing it all again, just as 'twas.* Maggie felt the sadness lap toward her like ripples spreading on a pond.

She looked down with blurred eyes at the man in uniform on the album page: another soldier gone. "He's in heaven now," she said. She waited sympathetically: glad that she had not yet lost a family member to death. (Knock wood.) She hoped that Michael would be safe. "Helping all the new souls," she continued softly.

"Yes," Eleanor said, in an easier voice. She stroked Will's image, then turned the page, to reveal more photographs of soldiers.

"Which one is Mr. Whitfield?" Maggie asked.

"What? Oh. Ned..." Eleanor pointed out a picture of a slim, clean-shaven youth, who looked uncomfortable and faintly ridiculous in his formal uniform. "That's him. He despised that hat, he said it looked like something from a Punch and Judy show."

Maggie snickered, then sobered as she examined his face. *I've only known him scarred,* she thought. It was a decent face, thin, long-nosed, a good forehead and chin, but on the whole, rather bland. He did not resemble his older sister.

"This one is better," Eleanor said, gesturing to a carte-de-visite on the opposite page.

Someone had penciled a caption below the image: Last picture. *But 'twasn't his last,* Maggie thought, *he's still alive.* She wondered if they had feared he would not survive. Perhaps it meant only that he would never again pose for a picture, no matter how hearty the state of his health. He had a beard and mustache in the second picture, and the officer's dress hat was replaced by a forage cap. The dress gloves were gone; one hand rested on the hilt of his sword. Maggie thought he looked a bit fierce, and unhappy. Though he had undeniably been a much better-looking man prior to his injury, she preferred looking at him in person. She groped for something to say when Eleanor looked at her curiously.

"Um," Maggie said, "I have a picture of my father. Just one, but it's precious to me."

"How lovely. I think you said his name was Ben, is that right? in the story you told about the pig who chased him."

"No. Pen. Pen is his nickname. They called him that because he used to help our neighbors who couldn't read and write. He'd write letters for them and such." Maggie remembered watching him over his shoulder. "He worked at the carriage makers, as a painter. No one could paint such a fine stripe as he, so the foreman said." She recalled that sometimes men no one recognized would appear at the O'Shaughnessys'. Her mother did not ask them if they'd have some tea. Her father did not chat with them. He made the best lamp blaze, then took his pen, and ink, sealing wax, and paper tied in a blue wrapper from the locked tin box. He sent her off to bed or to the kitchen with her mother. She had seen once, when she peeked, that the paper he wrote upon was printed. What's the name, then? her Da had asked a tall man, just before her Mam pulled her away from the door.

Shortly before he left, she had asked him why these strangers came to him in particular, didn't they have other friends who could help them read and write? He told her that he was doing them a favor, but her mam said, more like doing a favor for their master, Harrigan. Da had shushed her. 'Who's that man?' Maggie asked. A friend from home, her father answered, looking as bleak as February. 'No friend to you!' Mam had yelled. Da had shouted back, then had snapped at his daughter: 'And don't you be asking about things that don't concern you…'

Maggie said: "He took along my picture with him when he left. And I have the one of him."

"I'm so glad he has your picture," Eleanor murmured, "And you, his. It's less lonely that way." After a moment or two, she added: "Would you like to see a picture of me?"

Maggie answered. "I surely would." Eleanor jumped up. "I'll go and fetch it from the sitting room. Oh, and Mama's lap desk too."

Maggie was indeed glad that her father had taken her picture with him, one of the few things he removed from the house. She had never told anyone what he left behind: a tiny note for her, hastily scrawled in pencil, then tucked in her shoe, which had said only: *My darling girl—be good. Tk care of Mam. If I cd stay to watch you grow I would. Impt.! Burn this paper–tell no one.* She thought he had brushed a kiss across her forehead as she lay half-asleep. Maggie had burned the tiny slip and kept the secret of its brief existence: even when her mother's grief had tempted her to tell.

When Eleanor returned with a rosewood lap desk, she sat next to Maggie, raised the desk's hinged top, and put three small black cases on Maggie's lap. Maggie opened the top one: a daguerreotype depicting a girl about six years old seated in an upholstered chair with her arms around two younger boys. One boy was seated on her lap and one was next to her. The two wore matching short dresses decorated in braid, the customary style for boys under the age of three or four. They looked to be about the same age, although one was a little taller than the other.

"Are they twins?" Maggie asked.

"Yes, that's Kate and Ned and Dan. He died before I was born."

"What a shame! He's such a sweet little fellow." And he was, sitting wide-eyed on his sister's lap, looking at the camera with the beginning of a pout on his lips. He held a carved, spotted toy horse in his own lap. His brother was looking above and away from the camera, and his mouth was open. One hand was blurred as if he had moved it to point. In his other hand, his toy horse dangled by its leg, temporarily forgotten.

Maggie was amused. "What do you think he was looking at?" she asked, pointing to little Ned.

"I'm sure I have no idea," Eleanor said dismissively, and pulled the second case open, "But look!"

This was the largest daguerreotype of the three. In the center was a very pretty toddler with a headful of blond ringlets. Her expression was serious but untroubled. She was standing on a chair but leaning slightly into her older sister standing behind. Confident Kate with her wavy, darker hair caught in a ribbon fillet, had placed a protective hand on the baby's shoulder. Young Edward, now clad in a short-trousered suit, stood close to each, by the side of Eleanor's chair—looking at the camera this time, but with the same alert, interested air he'd displayed as a baby.

Maggie thought it a charming picture, not only in its composition and clarity, but also in the way that it had captured the characteristic expressions of the three children.

"Oh, my, look at your curls. I do think you were the prettiest baby I've ever seen."

"Thank you," Eleanor responded, "It's Mama's favorite. I don't mean to brag. Kate says I am vain about my hair."

Maggie shook her head. "My garters, if I had curls like yours, you'd never see me in a hat bigger than a teacup!"

Eleanor giggled.

"You're lucky you'll never have to scorch yourself with a curling iron. Ugh, what a stink. I nearly fried my forehead the last time I tried to give my hair a curl," Maggie said as she opened the last daguerreotype case.

It was a stark, strong image: Kate and Edward posed together, photographed from the waist up. Kate was now close to the age when she'd put her hair up and let her skirts down to announce she was a young lady. Her expression was, for the first time in all the pictures Maggie had seen, not just properly serious for the camera, but truly grave. Edward was dressed in a dark jacket, white shirt, and dark necktie. Mouth set in a line, he gazed at the camera intensely, his eyes darker than his sober clothing. Maggie would have considered it a mourning picture, except that Kate was dressed in light colors and Edward had no black band of crape on his arm. She looked uncertainly at Eleanor.

"I brought that one to show you because it was taken by Mr. Augustus Washington. He was a Negro photographer in Hartford who was rather famous, and Papa said all the best people thought very highly of him."

"I see," Maggie said, but she was struck with the change in the two children, and the sudden disappearance from the photograph studio–indeed, from all congress with society–of the third child, now her friend.

"Well," she said, "Well, I liked seeing your picture. Thank you kindly for showing me all of these. And I just had an idea for the one I'll draw for you."

Using the materials Eleanor provided, Maggie sketched for a while. After a time, she stopped, and pulled at her lower lip, vaguely dissatisfied with her work. "What is that you are holding, Eleanor? Is it clay?"

"No, it's an India rubber eraser which Papa just bought in Hartford. I thought you might like to use it to erase some pencil marks."

Maggie thanked her and rubbed the eraser in an unobtrusive spot. It did its job well. Inspired by this new power to undo, she looked critically at her cartoon. The top panel, lettered Before the Battle, showed a man on a ladder with a bucket of paint in his hand, and a nest of hornets above his head. In the middle panel, Attack!—the man slapped his hat at a line of hornets. In the last panel, the man stood in a pool of paint, behind a door, while the insects gathered on the other side of the barrier. She had titled this panel Foiled! She decided the hornets in the middle were too small. They could as well be flies, for all that, she thought.

She poised the eraser over the panel, as Eleanor went to the window. "Still raining. I hope it stops before supper time, so that you can get home safe and dry. But it's only three o'clock now. That's good."

Maggie sketched a larger hornet, stinger pointed like a bayonet, in the foreground of the middle panel. Eleanor sat down again, watching her friend draw.

"No, it's still not right," Maggie murmured.

"But I like that big hornet. You've made him look so disagreeable," Eleanor said. Maggie drew a kepi on the large hornet's head, then erased the cap's bill. She held up the eraser. "This is the most wonderful thing," she said as she re-drew the cap, penciling "C.S.A." in miniature letters on the kepi. "Now it's done."

Eleanor surveyed the drawing with a smile. The sketch sagged into her lap as the parlor door opened. "What is it?" she said anxiously as Edward came in. "It can't be time for Maggie to go."

"Pardon me for intruding, ladies. No, but it's time for a smoke. I just came in to get a match." He waggled a cigar between his fingers.

"Good," Eleanor said with relief, then: "You had better not light that in here. You know Mama doesn't allow it; and there are plenty of matches in the kitchen."

"Very well, I confess that I was curious to see what you two were doing here in the 'sanctum sanctorum.'" His last two words came out in a bass whisper. Maggie giggled.

Eleanor allowed a reluctant smile. "I was showing Maggie the photograph album."

"Ah, a subject dear to my heart," Whitfield said, "Did Eleanor tell you about my new venture?"

"Yes, it sounds grand."

"The most magnificent photograph establishment in town. I hope you'll come and 'get your image captured'. Our ferrotypes are quite inexpensive," he said.

"I'd like to sometime," Maggie said, "But I was thinking..." She rolled the eraser between her fingers. "D'you know how much one of these erasers costs?"

"No, I don't. Ask me about a photograph and I can tell you. But I could ask Morton if you like. Say, Elly what have you got there? Another work of art?"

Eleanor held it back. "I told Maggie about the hornets."

Edward looked embarrassed. "Huh." He stowed the cigar in his suit coat pocket and took the drawing from his sister. He looked it over, smiled.

"Isn't it comical?" Eleanor said.

"Ah yes, but quite a blow, no, a sting, to my dignity." He handed the drawing to Maggie. "I pride myself on always maintaining a sense of decorum." His arch tone belied the words.

How does he put up just one brow like that? Maggie wondered, *mine always go as a pair.* "Do you?" she said.

"Indubitably," he replied.

"In-doo-ba?" Maggie said.

He removed the cigar from his pocket and flourished it. "Indubitably. Without a doubt." Eleanor shook her head in tolerant disagreement.

"Is that so?" Maggie asked merrily.

"Yes. In fact, not to put too fine a point on the matter, one could say that dignity is my middle name." He nodded, straight faced.

Maggie said: "But dignity starts with the letter D, not S, and you have an S in the middle of your initials. What does the S stand for, then?"

"It stands for Seeley—Mother's maiden name," he answered.

"Oh!" Eleanor burst out, giggling wildly. "Oh, I know! Ned, with the way you've been behaving, S stands for Silly!" She covered her mouth and quivered with laughter.

"Eleanor, Eleanor, tch, tch. You astonish me," he said.

"I caught you out, for once!" Eleanor said gleefully.

"Such unseemly jocularity, and such an unwarranted insult, silly." He hid his mouth, but his uncovered eye held an amused expression. He looked down at the floor for a moment, then held up the cigar like an exclamation point, and said: "Here now, gals. This won't dew. I'll have no laughing in my class, not a particle. Dew yew hear me?"

"Mr. Bullard!" Maggie said. She stared as the nasal twang of the schoolmaster's voice emanated from Whitfield's mouth.

"Yew, miss," he said, pointing the cigar at Maggie. "Dew yew want a taste of the switch acrost yer knuckles? Say now, dew yew?" He wrinkled his nose as if sniffing a putrid odor and thrust out his lower lip just as the teacher used to do.

Eleanor let out a yelp of nervous laughter. "Don't, Ned, don't...it's too much like him."

"How do you do that?" Maggie asked. "That's grand." She applauded.

Whitfield dropped the persona and bowed. "Thank you. That's my party piece." He turned to the fireplace mantel and moved aside the bric-a-brac, muttering: "Matches." Then he turned back and said: "Would you like to hear a declamation? I know some dandy ones."

"No," Eleanor protested, "Get a match from the kitchen, for heaven's sake, and go and have your smoke."

"You're my witness, Miss O'Shaughnessy," Whitfield responded, "You heard her: rejecting the edifying art of declamation and in its place, encouraging the vice of tobacco use."

"I did not! It is a horrid habit!" Eleanor exclaimed.

Edward grinned. "Ah ha, here they are. I think I'll take the whole box with me. It's damp out on the porch. Goodbye, ladies."

"Goodbye," Maggie said cheerily, and after he had left the room, she remarked to Eleanor: "I didn't know he was so comical."

"He isn't usually. Since he came home, he hasn't been. Not for a while."

Eleanor's disconcerted expression confirmed Maggie's guess that Edward Whitfield had been showing off for the guest's benefit. The idea tickled her. She said: "It must have been the ice cream that sweetened his disposition."

Chapter 9

Alone, separated from his regiment, he followed the creek north as night descended. Soon he would have to cross over, like it or not: but where was the water shallow enough to ford safely? At the sound of hooves and the grunt of a winded horse, he turned away from the creek. A mounted Union officer appeared, pointing with his sword. He recognized the pose, if not the man. 'Oh, Jesus. It's him. Tell him!' He tried to shout a warning, frantically grabbing his throat—but remained voiceless. A heartbeat later, the shell burst. He opened his eyes and looked upon the horrible thing that remained. "No!" The creek's rush was muted by someone's gasping, close by. Everything was black. 'I'm blind!' His body shook; he flailed his arms: one hand struck something hard.

Ow. Alive. Home. Not blind. No, it was just a moonless night. He could hear rain splashing his bedroom window. He fumbled for the bottle, but felt only air, bedclothes, the bedstead, and dust. He sat up abruptly, pulse pounding. Someone was near.

The black shape snuffled and whimpered.

"Dance," Ned slumped down, wiping saliva from his mouth and chin. He pushed the dog away. "Go on, you." The dog moved up along the bedside, huffing on Ned's face, then thrust his tongue inquiringly against Ned's ear. "Get out of here," he mumbled.

The door to his room creaked open. Dance left the bed with a subdued woof.

"Who goes there?"

"It's me," Eleanor whispered.

"What d'you want, El?" Ned readjusted the towel that covered his pillow.

"Are you all right?"

"Uh-huh."

"I heard you shout. Did you have that nightmare again, the one where you say 'no'?"

Who ever says yes in a nightmare? he wondered. "Mm," he said.

"The man with the top of his head gone," Eleanor said. "That awful one!"

"How'd you know?" He raised his head in surprise.

"You had it when you were sick, too, a few times, and you wrote that on the slate after I asked you what it was about."

Uncomfortable with the sympathy in his sister's voice, he muttered: "Sorry I woke you. Go back to bed."

"You didn't wake me, I was awake. I can't sleep anyway." This was nothing new.

"Well, let me sleep," he grumbled. Dance poked his head onto Ned's arm and sighed a dog sigh.

"I'm always afraid to go back to sleep after I've had a nightmare," Eleanor confessed.

He agreed, but he was damned if he was going to admit it to her. "Everyone has nightmares. There's no reason to worry about them."

"Yes, I do. All the time."

He kept silent, hoping she wouldn't elaborate.

"I have one that comes over and over, always the same..." she whispered in that child's voice that always spooked him when it issued from her. *God, not now,* he thought and groaned aloud.

"Does your head hurt? Would you like a drink?" Eleanor said in her normal voice, with concern.

"Yeh, I need a drink."

"Shall I get you some water?"

"Whiskey and water is what I need."

"Ned!" Eleanor hissed, "I hope you haven't hidden ardent spirits here in your room again! You mustn't, not any more. Mama would be so upset."

"Ardent spirits? How quaint. I only wish. No ardent spirits, you little goose. Just ghosts! Ha." He thought of the dream officer's shattered head and shivered. "Ghosts who will never drink. Teetotaling ghosts. The only sort Father allows in the house."

"Oh, Ned."

"Joke, Elly."

She sighed, sounding rather like Dance had. Then she said: "If you have a headache and can't sleep, drink is not the answer. But I have some laudanum, if you need some."

"What? Where'd you get that?"

"Mama got it for me when you were sick and I wasn't sleeping at all. Now I'm better. I have some left because I didn't like to take it: it made me sleep too hard, and then I couldn't hear you when you needed me or Mama needed me and...I wouldn't be ready if...if someone came...I wouldn't be awake to know, and the nightmare I have, that's what happens, the thing comes so suddenly." The old fear suffused her voice.

"It's just a dream, El. Dreams aren't real. You're all right. Do you hear me?"

"Yes." She wanted to believe him.

"No one could ever get in here without Dance barking up a storm," Ned said.

"Oh. Yes, he would bark."

"Try to sleep, now."

"I don't think I can."

"Try."

Eleanor was quiet. Ned listened for her weeping. Hearing none, he said: "Dance. Go give Elly a kiss." The dog left the bed again. Then Ned heard his sister say: "No, pup. Go give Ned a goodnight kiss." For once obedient, Dance did as he was told.

"Ugh. Dog breath," Ned said. He thought he heard her laugh, a sound as faint as a feather falling. The dog padded away.

"Goodnight," Ned called as his door whimpered shut.

Rossiter brought a married couple into the room where Ned stood behind the camera, and sat them down, fixed their heads in the restraint, told them to look at the camera; then disappeared into the darkroom. Ned waited for the prepared negatives. He checked his watch: five minutes. They waited. Ten minutes, eleven: he could no longer tolerate standing by the customers in silence, feeling in his own joints the strain of their frozen positions. He stepped forward out of the shadow.

"Pardon me, ma'am, if you would lower your chin a little, please. Yes, that's fine. Just pretend you're in your own sitting room, and not here waiting for us. And sir, if you'd sit back, and kindly fold your hands in your lap. Thank you."

The wife tittered. Her husband humphed, then said: "Well, you aren't as bad-looking as that other fellow said you'd be."

"Oh? Oh. Yes. It's a war wound," Ned said.

The woman murmured something sympathetic. The man wiped his forehead with his handkerchief, replaced it in his pocket and refolded his hands. "Yep. My nephew's serving in the 21st regiment volunteers. I declare, it's hot in here, under that big winder." He pointed to the skylight.

In the succeeding days, Ned experimentally introduced himself to customers as they entered the camera area. Some were relieved, as the first couple had been; some were pitying, and spoke to him as if he was still an invalid. Some were elaborately polite. At least one was terrified—a toddler who screamed at the sight of him, upon which its mother glared at him and threatened to leave. Rossiter came forward then, feigning distress, as Ned retreated to the darkroom.

In the afternoon following the "baby scare" Rossiter ushered in a trio of uncertain children and their equally dubious parents, then disappeared. The smallest child, a girl, stared at Ned in fright, and grabbed for her mother's skirt. Her brother plucked at his mother's sleeve as well.

"My face looks strange, doesn't it?" Ned said to the boy. "It does not look like your Papa's or yours, or your brother's." The girl's eyes were big. She reminded him of Eleanor.

"I used to be a soldier, before I started taking pictures. Have you ever seen a soldier?" Ned asked her.

The girl shook her head. "Lots of 'em," her brother said.

"Yes, ma'am. That's a good pose. Sir, can you move your older boy a little closer to your right arm. Thank you. I'll be ready to take your picture in just a moment." Ned called for Jack to hurry in with the prepared glass plates.

"I wonder if any of you children have ever fallen down at play? Did you ever get a cut on your knee, or bump your head?" Ned asked. The two brothers nodded.

Ned went on. "So you know that the cuts and the bumps get better and then they don't hurt anymore." The older brother sneered;

but Ned had the attention of the two younger children, and the parents as well.

"I got hurt when I was a soldier. When it got better, it left all these lines on my face." He said, tracing one with his forefinger, into the hollow where the swell of his left cheek should be. "But they don't hurt me now, and they don't hurt anyone else, so you need not be afraid of them. This eye over here got hurt too, so the doctor told me to cover it up. This other one is fine. It can see that this little girl has on new shoes today."

The girl put one foot out for display.

"Look at that," Ned said to her, "How pretty."

"What do you say to the nice gentleman, Naomi?" Mrs. Grafton prompted. The girl made a curtsy, charming Ned and her entire family. The parents then agreed to his suggestion that after taking the family in one picture, the children should be photographed together, followed by the parents as a couple.

Ned accomplished the work quickly while the good mood held. He sent Jack into the darkroom with the exposed plates, then pointed the group toward the office. He intended to mark the sale in the ledger, but first paused to wipe the camera's lens. When he arrived at the office, Dunn glared at him. "Mrs. Grafton here was just telling me that she heard Mrs. Fuller's little girl had her picture taken for free, last week, because the girl behaved so nicely."

"And mine were as good as gold today, so why shouldn't one of my pictures be free of charge?" Mrs. Grafton put in.

"Well...ah...that was my mistake, you see, Mrs. Grafton," Ned replied, "I'm new here, and I didn't realize that Mr. Dunn has a policy against free photographs, which of course, makes perfect sense. I certainly agree that your children behaved splendidly. Umm...Actually, I'd like to offer them the gift of some sweet biscuits from Foster's Bakery, with your permission of course." As the children clamored, he untied the packet of biscuits he had purchased that morning as a treat for himself and Eleanor.

Mr. Grafton was sufficiently pleased with his brood to announce that he'd buy a new photograph album when they returned later in the week to see their finished pictures. Ned swept up crumbs as the family departed. He could hear George and Jack talking as they returned to the office.

"Giving away pictures, that's bad business."

"Yes indeed, Mr. Dunn. Bad business. You see how fast

word gets around and then all the customers expect favors," Rossiter said.

"How do you expect me to make any money that way," George grumped at Ned.

"Why don't you take it out of my **pay**?" Ned responded. He had received very little money so far for the hours of work in the gallery.

"It's coming, didn't I tell you, so hold your horses," George asserted. Ned shrugged.

"No more free offers," George went on.

"I heard you the first time, George."

Dunn said: "I sure hope they buy that red velvet album. I've been trying to move that out of here for months."

"Micah Park told me that the rebels are invading the North! Another one of his tall tales..." Maggie told Mr. Merritt, expecting him to laugh along with her.

"I am afraid it is true, this time. A goodly portion of the Southern army is trying to cross into Pennsylvania," Merritt replied.

"Into Philadelphia? Where the Friends live?"

"No, no, the rebels are farther west, out in the country near the Maryland border. But it is nothing for thee to worry about. I believe our army will turn them away."

"They must! How did they let them get so far? I wish we subscribed to a newspaper!" Mrs. Wilkin entered the room and sniffed at Maggie's comment. "An illustrated newspaper would be grand," Maggie persisted, "with engravings and maps."

"We cannot afford such a thing," Mrs. Wilkin said.

"I read the newspapers yesterday at Morton's," Mr. Merritt told Maggie, "Mr. Morton says that two regiments alone contain more men than live here in Millville; and there are dozens of regiments that will fight. Some of our soldiers are marching up from Virginia to help defend Pennsylvania."

"Homer, mind thy words. Does thou interest thyself in this war fever? It is not our way," Mrs. Wilkin chided.

"I do not need thy reminder, Jemima."

"The people who live there will have to leave, or they might get hurt," Maggie went on, "Like the ones down South when our army went into their towns: they must have been awful frightened! But I don't know why I should worry about them, since they started all this trouble."

"War is a terrible evil," Mrs. Wilkin said. Mr. Merritt remained silent.

"Why is the war going so badly? Why is it lasting so long? Why haven't we won it yet?"

"Such questions, Maggie!" Mr. Merritt said.

"My brother has enlisted," Maggie replied.

"Oh my. The one with young children?"

"No, not Frank. Michael. He's not married yet, although he is engaged to be married, I think. What I wonder is why didn't we just let the South leave, why did we have to go to war at all?"

"The great evil of slavery!" Mr. Merritt exclaimed, "We ought not to have that pernicious disease in our country at all, and we cannot let it spread further!"

"No, we can't," she said hastily "but some folks don't care about that, although they surely ought to, but they don't, so why are they being forced to fight?"

"Ah me, I expect thou are speaking of the conscription law. A very bad idea, that one, to my way of thinking. The government is over-reaching its powers," Mr. Merritt said.

"Yes! Why must fathers and husbands be made to go, when they're needed here to support their families?"

"They ought not," Mrs. Wilkin asserted.

"They say it is all for the Union, but isn't that so broken now 'twill do no good to try to mend it?" Maggie went on.

Merritt sighed sadly. "We began as one nation not even a hundred years ago. Many of our heroes in the war for independence were from the South, including our great president Washington. How he would mourn to see what is happening today." "Dreadful!" Mrs. Wilkin said.

"But think, Maggie," Mr. Merritt said, "George Washington would not let his fellow citizens crown him king. He knew the dangers of that. Now that the South has left our Union, what is there to stop its leaders from falling under the influence of some foreign king in the future. Then we would have hostile, slave-holding foreign countries right by our side, and surrounding our nation's capitol."

ever thought of that," Maggie said, "The president would ape, and the folks who live there, like Eleanor's sister. And who would get the Western states, the rebels or us? What would the people there do?"

"If the Union is preserved, thy questions will not matter…" Mr. Merritt began.

Mrs. Wilkin said: "Homer, I think thou <u>does</u> need my reminder."

"Discussing a concern does not mean that I favor a violent solution, Jemima," he replied testily.

Mrs. Wilkin held her peace for a while, then remarked: "That pile of mending in thy workbasket is not getting any smaller, Maggie, while thou sit idle."

Maggie took up her mending and sewed for a few minutes. Then she said: "Mr. Merritt, I was wondering about something else, not the war, but when the war began, there was a big to-do in the mills, and some men lost their jobs. Frank almost did. But now they're building new manufactories, and railroad tracks into town. And I'm not sorry, mind you, but d'you think it means good times for a while yet?"

"Where is thy brother employed?"

"Springhill Company."

Merritt said: "Ah, yes, they manufacture satinet. When the Southern states seceded, factories all over the state had trouble obtaining cotton. I expect that Springhill's found a new source now. Millville is fortunate, for many of our manufactories make wool products and there is no shortage of wool." He rubbed his belly and grimaced, then went on: "All of the manufactories here are now producing goods for the Army: uniforms, and blankets, harness, paper; my, my, it seems that as the war continues, our state's prosperity increases. 'Good times' thou call them, but I think not. They also cost us dearly."

"Thou cannot expect a child to understand such things, Homer." Mrs. Wilkin shook her head.

Maggie said: "Oh, but I do! Because the money comes from war—the Friends believe 'tis like the thirty pieces of silver Judas got; even if he'd used it to help someone, it would still do no good because it came of such a bad thing."

"True indeed," Mr. Merritt replied.

Tainted though it was, Maggie felt that the money might do

some good if it made its way into wages for her family and friends so they had roofs over their heads, and enough to eat. Though the jobs seemed more secure for now, she had heard that the factory hands had seen no increase in their pay, even as prices rose and rose for food, kindling, coal, and clothes for the growing children. She pondered the meaning of "prosperity" as she re-threaded her needle and knotted the thread.

So many Northern men had volunteered to fight, to risk their lives. Some, surely, did it to preserve the Union, and end the evil of slavery. So many had died! She knew that saints could praise God even in the midst of horrible torture, and thus be guaranteed Salvation; but when it came to volunteering to die for the sake of others' immortal souls? She thought only the Savior Himself was capable of that. Him, and maybe a few others, like missionary priests. Although he did not strike her as the missionary sort, nor the adventurous sort, Mr. Whitfield had gone to war. It certainly must have been to help free the slaves: his own sister now taught the freed women and children. Michael had no such engine driving him. Maggie said a prayer for her brother, then amended it to implore God to bring all of them home safely, the zealous and good, the indifferent and bad: all alike in peril.

Chapter 10

"Merciful heaven!" Mrs. Whitfield clutched Ned's arm nervously, as firecrackers exploded in the road not far from their front door. "That startled me."

"Me too," Ned admitted. For an instant, he had thought the crackers were musket fire.

"Who are those boys?" she said as a cluster of youths trotted away. "I hate this day. Will you be back soon?

"I don't know. Goodbye, Mother."

"Be careful!"

"Let's go," he said, squeezing in next to his father in the chaise. They were both glad to leave the tense household, where Eleanor huddled in her bedroom, terrified; and where her mother fretted over old fears. He felt a moment of guilt for abandoning them, but quickly rejected the thought: what was the use, when he had no solution to the problem?

He and his father sought release by joining the crowds: the judge in Vinton and Ned in Hartford. The father would surround himself with men: assess them, glad-hand, grant and accept favors, cement alliances or renew grudges; then he would make a speech. The son would observe humanity, and this time–having lost his prior facial anonymity–would undoubtedly be observed in return. He had no plan except to meet George Dunn at the Vinton railroad depot, and later, Henry Barton at the racetrack, and see where the day led him.

"You've bin to Hartford then, Maggie, have you?" Bridget asked.

"Yes, Da took me once when I was a little girl." Maggie remembered that he took her along with him to see an important man. Her father had cautioned her to hold his hand the whole time and to be a good girl and keep quiet, and she had. That was the day that she had had her (so far one and only) photograph taken. She wore a new frock, which her mother had cut down and made over from a boy's dress. Green plaid, it was—and Mrs. O'Shaughnessy had added ribbon to it. Maggie remembered stroking the ribbons and feeling like a queen. But her old shoes had pinched something awful.

"I never bin," Bridget said.

" 'Twill be grand!" Maggie said.

"And it's all thanks to you, Mr. Dooley," Bridget simpered. "Tell me about the fireworks again, will you?" Dooley scratched his chin whiskers, then indulgently explained for the second time that morning what fireworks were, and that they were free for everyone to see, being out in the open; and how the railroad company had added special cars, lots of them, to the train, which was running as late as midnight: the stagecoach ran late as well, to get folks back to Millville from Vinton station.

"I'll be needing your money now, Maggie," he said, "Och, will ye look at that crush in the ticket line. You ladies stay right here and don't move." She handed over her money. Mr. Dooley was paying for Bridget's ticket, as he had invited her especially. Maggie was glad to see Mr. Dooley's and Bridget's little romance going so well. Dooley had never again mentioned to Maggie his drunken pledge of marriage on her sixteenth birthday: she hoped he had forgotten it entirely, for he was a good man and a good match for her friend, although he was forty years old and homely, to boot. *I like a different sort of fellow,* Maggie thought. She shrieked as someone grabbed at her from behind and held fast. Looking back, she saw a familiar grinning face.

"Rory Corcoran!" Maggie pulled away from his hands with an embarrassed laugh. "You scared me half to death. Bridey, why didn't you tell me he was there?"

"Well, I could hardly have seen him in this crowd then, could I, Maggie? He crept in so quiet."

"Good morning, ladies. Seeing someone off, are you?" Corcoran said.

"No, we're going to Hartford for the fireworks! Maggie is so excited," Bridget said.

"I spy a new suit of clothes, Mr. Corcoran," Maggie said.

" 'tis, and the best quality. Feel those goods." He put his arm close to her, and she lightly touched the fabric. "That's not enough to tell the quality," he said, brushing his arm against hers.

" 'tis a fine suit," Maggie said.

Corcoran sighed and dropped his arm. "It can't be you two girls are going off to Hartford all alone."

"No indeed. Mr. Dooley's kindly said he'd escort us," Bridget replied.

"Ha. He never said a word to me about it, the sly dog. Wanted you all to himself." Bridget giggled, but Corcoran was looking at Maggie. "We'll come along with you and form a party." Annie Mulrooney emerged from behind Corcoran, with Mr. Hurley on her heels.

"You look ever so handsome," Annie said, stroking Corcoran's arm, then fastening her hand on his forearm. The way he placed his hand over Annie's made Maggie turn away.

But not half an hour later, it was Maggie he handed into the train, and Maggie he sat next to.

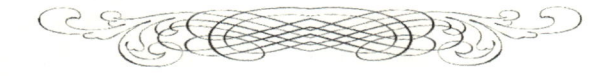

George Dunn made a rude noise and glowered in disgust: "Uncle's got the notion to haul his camera up onto a roof and take a picture of the balloon ascension. He's going to need every hand he can get. Even my Pa will be there, if he can bear to leave his child bride and his new brat for more than ten minutes." Ned had not met John Dunn's new wife, who was only 22 years old. Yet he, like George, was repulsed by the thought that not only had she married a man old enough to be her father—her stepson was old enough to have fathered "the new brat" himself.

"I'll never make a fool of myself like that over a girl," George proclaimed. "Well, anyhow, to my mind this balloon picture is a waste of time, but you know Uncle: he's bound to try it."

When Ned and George arrived in Hartford, they parted ways at the station, agreeing to meet an hour later at Alonzo Dunn's photograph studio. Ned intended to buy a lager beer at one of the stands, but the size of the crowd was daunting. Inspired by a different idea, he cut away from the crush lining Main Street, and walked toward the telegraph office. There was a clump of men there, five or six deep, near the counter.

"What is the news from Gettysburg?" he asked an elderly man at the back of the line. The man looked at him, took a second look, then looked away.

"If you're seeking news of a friend or relation, you're out of luck, I'm afraid," the man remarked to his own dusty shoes. He gestured toward the clerks. "They've just told us they have no list of casualties yet. They are waiting for official reports."

"General Reynolds was killed, I heard," Ned answered.

"Yes, I believe so."

"That's a shame. Any news of the 14th Connecticut?"

"There is no word yet," the old man replied. Some of the surrounding men examined Ned.

"I'm sure they're in the thick of it, though," said a man wearing a tall top hat.

"Is that your regiment, young man?" a middle-aged man queried.

"Yes, sir. It was, until I took this face wound at Fredericksburg." Ned kept his voice diffident. He heard a couple of murmurs in response.

The top-hatted man said: "Well, this battle was Fredericksburg turned inside out! The rebels are in retreat, and this is our victory, pure and simple."

"A great and glorious victory," the elderly man put in.

"Hurrah!" Ned shouted, unable to contain the visceral joy that surged through him. He slammed his fist into his palm. "At last. Now there's cause to celebrate." Their murmurs and laughter followed as he ran to the door.

"Pardon me." He dodged past an entering tradesman and dashed back toward the beer stands. He would think of the wounded later, and hope he knew none of the dead. For now, though, victory! The sweetest word in the dictionary.

As he waited for his beer, another inspiration took him out of the line and back into the crowd. *Why pay for beer when I can have free lemonade and gingerbread at Aunt Caroline's*, he thought. An hour later, he arrived at Dunn's Gallery. His aunt, uncle, and cousins had greeted his sudden appearance with wonder, and happy tears.

Lazarus raised from the dead, Ned thought, sure that he would not get the same reaction from Alonzo Dunn.

"Good day, Mr. Dunn."

"There you are." Dunn stared, but when his survey was complete, he took Ned's hand and shook it. "Welcome back. It's men like you who are saving this Union, although why we want those Rebs back, I'll never know. "

He went on: "It's good for me to know someone with a head on his shoulders will be keeping Georgie's place while he does his duty. I've got an upper story window on Ford Street, overlooking the park. George told you, eh? With any luck, we'll get a good picture of the balloons. If the weather holds. We're going to get the camera over there soon and set it out the window. We'll tie it down if we have to. If we've got someone out on the window ledge to keep her steady and take off the lens cap and put it back on my count, so much the better."

"I can do that," Ned offered.

"Not afraid of heights, are you? This window is on the third floor."

"No, sir."

"Good. George, you stay back here for the developing after we've taken our pictures. Your Pa will be here soon. Si will run the plates over, and then back to you. Be ready! Ned and I will stay with the camera. It's too bad I can't photograph the tightrope walker. That would sell."

"I'd like to see that fellow," George put in.

"Well, go up on the roof and see him. He's starting at the Main Street bridge in half an hour. I'll call for you when I need you."

"Come on, Ned," George said.

"You go along, I want to talk to Ned," Alonzo said. George hesitated, then went off.

"Boy, you've got to stop George from spending all his bounty money on these tarnal soldier geegaws! Patent drinking cups and brass whigmaliries–he should be using it to pay his debts," Alonzo Dunn said brusquely.

"What debts?" Ned asked.

Dunn snorted. "He owes money to his suppliers; he's a horse's ass when it comes to keeping his books properly. He goes through paper and silver nitrate and hypo like a green apprentice. He owes me money, too. I can't carry his studio much longer. That's not to say, mind you, that I won't give you a month or two to get on your feet over there."

"Well, thank you. I...had no idea that the place was in such a state," Ned replied, beginning to worry.

"I didn't think you did. A word to the wise, eh? You can break even, anyhow, if you can get him to part with his bounty."

"But hasn't his father spoken to him, or have you..."

"He's riled at Johnny for not paying for a substitute for him and riled at me too. Though why he should think it is any of my duty, I don't know! So, do what you can, will you? There's a good fellow." Alonzo Dunn turned and barked an order to young Simon, then said: "Let's go see that Frenchman walk on air."

Maggie had never seen so many people in one place at one time before: not at the Vinton Independence Day parade, not on Election Day, not even at the great Union rally after the war began. She pressed her arms to her sides, making herself as small as she could, grateful that Dooley, Corcoran, and Hurley had formed a protective wedge in front of the three women. Bridget looked nervous; but Maggie rather liked the feeling of being just a particle in the body of humanity.

The six of them advanced, in piecemeal fashion, away from the Hartford train station and toward Main Street. Surrounded on every side by men taller than her by half a foot or more, there was yet much for Maggie to see: the occasional skirl of summer-hued crinolined skirts; the bobbing of sun umbrellas, men's hats, ladies' colorful bonnets and parasols; the variety of beards, mustaches, and whiskers—some as wispy as feathers, some as thick as felted wool. Her other senses were awhirl in sorting smells, and listening to the calling of vendors and the bits of conversation floating by like so many twigs in a creek.

"Bridey, look at that. Did you hear him? Oh, look!" Maggie exclaimed every other minute, until Mr. Dooley laughed and Bridget said: "Whissht, Maggie."

Annie sputtered: "They'll think we're a crop of country hayseeds, Maggie, sure as you're born—if you don't stop gawking and slowing us down."

"I beg your pardon, Miss Mulrooney!" Maggie answered in a hoity-toity voice.

"Now, girls," Corcoran said, "No fighting, do you hear? You leave that to me and Hurley here." As they moved on, Maggie kept quiet. In her head, however, she echoed "*look*" and vowed to remember it all—all the better to capture the day on paper later. Nearing Main Street, they heard the tootling of a band.

"It's the firemen's parade," Dooley said.

"I can't see anything," said Maggie. "I'm too short."

Overhearing her, Corcoran said: "There's too many in the way, entirely. All I can see is the tops of the hose carts and some plumes on the horses."

Maggie coughed, then sneezed. Had the crowds not obscured her view, the dust kicked up by the parade itself would have. Although she now did not like heights, she envied the boys who had climbed up the lamp posts to get a good look at the marchers.

"They ought to wet down the road before the parade," Dooley said.

"Keep moving," Corcoran commanded. He directed them in and out of the clots of parade-goers like a mariner undoing a knot. Close to the dam over the Hog River they struck a snag, where the foot traffic entered a bottleneck in the narrow street. Corcoran sought an outlet, in vain. After voicing his opinion of the delay, he began to tell them a story about the shipping and packing crew at the Rock Mill. A sudden commotion towards the rear of the queue stopped his yarn.

"What's happening?" Dooley said. "I'll find out," Corcoran replied, squeezing away from them, back toward the noise.

Maggie fanned herself, then glanced at Annie's perspiring face. *She's as red as a beet,* Maggie thought, *I hope I don't look that bad.* A short time later, Hurley, craning his neck, reported: "There's a young fellow climbing up the dam, trying to get ahead of everyone."

"He should wait his turn. Who does he think he is?" Bridget protested. Shouting commenced behind them. *Irish voices,* Maggie thought. Through the crook in a man's arm, she saw a man tumble off the dam and into the water below. Dooley saw it too: "Ha! look at that. There he goes, into the drink."

A buzz, and then the choppy dit-dit of mirth moved through

the crowd, which pressed back and to the side, to look down at the river. Maggie peeked around a thin man. She watched the water and was relieved to see the young man floundering on the surface. He struggled to the riverbank, where he shouted and shook his fist up at the people in line. Most of them jeered in return. A young woman nearby shook her head, harrumphing at his bad language.

"Irish ruffians," Maggie heard a man proclaim.

Five minutes later, a ragged ripple of cheers accompanied Corcoran as he maneuvered his way back toward his friends. His hat was scuffed and dusty, his vest hiked up above his waist, his cravat was awry, and his new suit skewed in the shoulders. He laughed a huge laugh as he returned to them. "That blaguard won't be jumping the line again soon—not ahead of me!"

"Ain't you on holiday, boyo?" Hurley joked. "Why're you still unloading bales, then?"

"Not bales, Matt. Just tippin' out a load of rubbish, is all!" Both men laughed, as Bridey and Dooley joined them, while Annie oohed and ah'd in admiration. The crowd began to inch forward. Maggie tucked a stray lock of hair back into the hairpin.

"Step aside, Bridey," she heard, and looked up to see Corcoran at her side. "Well, then, Miss Maggie, what did you think of that?"

"I'm glad the man wasn't hurt," Maggie answered.

Corcoran snorted. Maggie touched his arm for a moment and continued: "And I'm glad you taught him a lesson!"

"All right, Ned, get out there. Good heaven, boy, what are you doing? You'll fall—keep a leg inside. There you are. Steady now. Get that rope up there." Alonzo Dunn issued orders until the bulky box camera was arranged to his satisfaction behind and partly on the ledge of the open window. Ned had found a perch on the ledge and sat, ready to remove the lens cap at Dunn's command. "They're still laying the gas pipe to fill the balloons," Ned commented to the men in the room.

Alonzo peered over the camera edge. "Are you set there?"

"Yes, sir. First rate."

"You won't fall out of bed, eh?" Dunn said, then chuckled.

While watching the French tightrope walker lay full length on the rope, which had swayed a little in the breeze, Ned had dryly remarked: "He's never afraid of falling out of bed."

"Not a chance," Ned responded, "And I'm enjoying the view." Just as he said it, he looked down to admire a young woman passing below. Her bosom was generous in size, and her neckline was rather low, so that he had a clear look at the cleavage between her breasts. She was with a man in a flashy checked suit who stopped and removed his hat, revealing a head of red hair. After wiping sweat from his forehead, he replaced his hat, spoke to a shorter man wearing a workman's cap, then had a word with a slim girl wearing a bonnet jauntily decorated with red, white, and blue ribbons. Ned reluctantly took his eyes from the big-breasted woman and turned his attention back to Alonzo Dunn.

He watched the activities around the two large observation balloons, now beginning to be inflated. People in the crowd were searching for places to view the action. A father boosted a child onto his shoulders. Way to the side, hidden in an alley (although clearly in view to Ned) the red-headed checked suit man was kissing and fondling the buxom woman and appeared to actually have a hand inside her bodice. Ned observed this scene with ardent interest, until Dunn peppered him again with commands and questions. He helped adjust the position of the camera, holding a steadying hand on its edge. When he looked back toward the alley, the "loving couple" had disappeared. He wondered if they had ducked behind a shed to continue their activities. The crowds by the shops had all advanced further into the park, leaving behind the girl with the red, white, and blue decorated bonnet. She peered into a shop window, as if transfixed by something there.

What would it be like, Maggie thought, admiring the paint boxes in the bookstore window, *to have that all to yourself, so many colors filling your eyes—surely one for every color in nature - and fine brushes galore?* "Think about the background," her father had told her more than once, "for how you fill it is just as important as what you put up front." She stared at the sketchbooks, imagining such a stack of clean, fine paper under her command, ready for filling.

Some of the books were as big as her lap. Maggie rubbed her fingers together. She turned away from the window unwillingly, believing she felt Bridey's impatient gaze. But Bridget wasn't there.

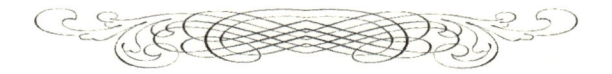

"I will," Ned told Dunn, as he looked down at the girl again. She turned from the window and appeared to realize that she had been left behind. She walked a little way up and down the street, searching, then returned to the shop step and stood on tiptoe, hands behind her back, scanning the crowds. Something about her was familiar.

"No, not yet," he told Alonzo Dunn. "That rotund fellow is still making a speech." He watched the lost girl, hoping she stayed put. There were some rough men in the crowd, and she would fare better if she did not wander among them. The sound of applause drifted over to him.

"The speech is done. The aerialists are going over to the baskets. Yes, I think they're ready," Ned told Alonzo, then looked back down at the street. The older man he had seen the girl with earlier was headed down the street in her direction, although he was still a block away.

"Get ready," Alonzo commanded. The bunting fluttered in the breeze. Ned forgot the girl as he watched the aerialists climb into the baskets. He described each action out loud for Alonzo, aware that Dunn was viewing the same proceeding upside-down through the camera's view-piece. He reached out, ready to remove the lens cap.

"Now!" Dunn shouted.

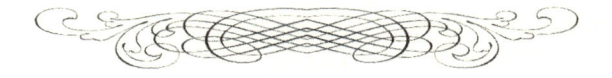

'Twasn't so bad if it made Mr. Dooley the hero,' Maggie thought. She hadn't minded his scolding; indeed, it was less severe than the one she had given herself. They had missed the balloon ascension ceremony but were able to see both "The Constitution" and "The Stars and Stripes" aloft. As they rejoined Bridget and Mr. Hurley, Bridget made much of Dooley and gave him a paper of roasted nuts

she had bought at a stand. Mr. Dooley was good enough to share them with Maggie. Annie and Rory found them soon thereafter.

"What happened to you?" Bridget asked. "Were you lost? Maggie got lost, but Mr. Dooley found her."

"You stay with us, Maggie. Here, give me a bit of that shade," Corcoran said. He seemed in very good spirits and did not chide her. Annie was redder than ever. She sat down close to him with a self-satisfied expression. Maggie sat down next to Bridget but facing the crowd. She watched them for a while, then unpinned her notepad and pencil stub from their pocket just under the waistband of her skirt. She drew a rough outline of the park, showing the two balloons aloft in the distance.

"What are ye drawing? Me and Rory?" Annie asked.

"No. Whatever takes my eye," Maggie said.

"Just like Pen. Remember, Des?" Corcoran said lazily.

"I do," Mr. Dooley replied. Maggie beamed as she went back to her sketch.

After a time, Corcoran said: "How'd ye get lost, then?"

"I was looking in a shop window and I didn't see that Bridey had moved on."

"Some pretty bonnets must have caught your eye," said Corcoran

"Next time, you hold onto Bridget, and don't be wanderin' off," Dooley put in.

"Oh, 'twasn't bonnets," Bridget added. "'twas books. An't I right, Maggie?"

"Not this time. 'Twas a paintbox, and paper. I was looking for erasers, too, but I didn't see a one."

"What're those?" Annie asked. Maggie explained. "Why do you care about such queer things?" Annie said derisively.

"Ah, no harm if she likes to draw," Rory put in before Maggie could reply. "Better than having her nose in a book. It'll pass anyway, once she's got a man and children."

The fine feeling caused by Mr. Corcoran's earlier compliment was obliterated by his last two comments. "No," Maggie said.

"It's just that you'll be too busy then by far, Maggie," Bridget placated.

Annie delivered her words with rich condescension: "What, are ye goin' to marry a rich man and have a girl or two in yer place so ye don't lift a finger? Like a lady! And no time at all fer yer own husband and children? No, she's too busy scratching on paper or reading bad books. 'Tis a crying shame. Some would say such a one as that thinks she's better than the rest of us."

"I never said such a thing!" Maggie asserted, then turned away, her cheeks hot. She heard the fabric of Corcoran's vest brush against the bark of the tree as he straightened up from his slumped position at Annie's side.

"Begorrah," he said humorously. "The kitten has a temper."

"They all do," Dooley remarked.

"I don't think I'm better than anyone else. I never said such a thing," Maggie insisted in embarrassment. She wanted to say that she was smarter by half or more than Annie Mulrooney, but held her tongue.

Corcoran chuckled. "Will you look at that now? D'you know, Des, they say if you stroke a cat the right way when they're all puffed up like that after a fight, you can gentle them right down. I've a mind to try it on this one." That made Maggie look at him. She was about to tell him he better not try it, but, warmed by his grin, she giggled instead.

"Kittens scratch too, Mr. Corcoran, though their claws are small," she said.

"Ah, but it's such a pleasant little hurt, and then they're sweet again."

"Only if they like the hand that's petting them," Maggie said pertly. She smiled at him sidelong over her shoulder in response to his delighted laugh.

"I'm thirsty, Rory," Annie said. "Are you, dear?" He stretched and stood up. "Let's go get a beer." He nudged Hurley to wake him. Maggie stowed her pad and pencil, and the party moved off. Now he ambled, allowing the people around him to set the pace. Maggie yawned.

"Everyone's had the same fine notion," Dooley muttered. Corcoran whispered something to Annie, then he left. The rest of them stopped, with many others, to watch the aerialist drop a little dog from the basket. The dog was fitted with a parachute. Everyone speculated as to where it would fall. So many people were looking up that forward movement was impossible. The dog landed safely amid applause and cheers. *I'll have to tell Eleanor,* Maggie thought.

The crowd began to move again. Dooley pulled the girls

aside into an area where an obstruction caused the pedestrians to eddy around them. Hurley stopped sky watching and went ahead to talk to someone out in the crowd. Soon Maggie noticed that Hurley's acquaintance, a man with a voluminous gray mustache and an air of self-importance, was staring at her. It was not in a pleasant, puzzled way as if he thought he knew her, nor in the leering way Hurley had; but a steady gaze as if she were an expensive item he'd purchased that he was no longer happy with. He said something to Hurley, who looked at her, and gestured toward the women. Maggie looked down and away. A glance at Annie and Bridget confirmed that they were watching the exchange but were not concerned.

"Maggie O'Shaughnessy," Hurley said at that moment. Thinking he'd called her, she looked up and saw him smile unpleasantly. The other man smiled too: nodded, and kept nodding. Maggie stepped backward, and took Bridey's arm. "Och, what's wrong with you?" Bridget said.

"Shy," Maggie muttered.

The man came to them and tipped his hat. "Good day, ladies. My friend, Mr. Hurley, tells me that you have travelled here all the way from Vinton, for the very first time. Faith, I told him, there is nothing so pretty as a country girl. I was so taken, my dears, with your fresh beauty that I begged him for an introduction, and I am hoping you'll not think me too forward for asking."

Maggie felt slightly sick at her stomach: she had no idea why.

Bridget tittered. Annie gave him a close-mouthed smile (for her teeth were none too good and she did not like to show them).

"Ah, Mr. Hurley," the man said impatiently. Hurley hurried to his side. Out of the corner of her eye, Maggie saw Dooley back away and disappear.

"Ladies, this is Mr. Harrigan. Mr. Harrigan, this here's Bridget McGee."

Bridget dropped a curtsey. "Pleased to meet you, sir."

Harrigan nodded to her. "The pleasure is mine." Hurley introduced Annie Mulrooney, who gave out a hearty: "How d'ye do, Mr. Harrigan."

Harrigan kissed her hand. "A charming girl..." he said. Annie beamed in response, forgetting her bad teeth.

"And Maggie O'Shaughnessy," Hurley finished, with the usual sneer in his voice. Since Maggie had put her hands behind her back, the man could not kiss her hand in greeting.

She said: "How do you do, sir." He fixed her with that same strange gaze, nodding in the way he had before. At that instant Maggie remembered that she had heard his name before, in her mother's scornful epithet, and her father's words: him that used to be a friend.

A bit of her recollection must have shown in her expression, for Harrigan said: "Haven't we met before, Miss O'Shaughnessy? I believe we have." Maggie opened her mouth to deny it, but had no time to do so, for Corcoran came back just then, elbowing his way through the crowd.

"Well, Mr. Harrigan," Corcoran's voice was overly loud and his smile was false. "Fancy meeting you here." They reminded Maggie of two dogs on neutral turf, facing off but not quite ready to snarl.

"Seamus, boyo. This is a lucky throw. I need to have a word with you: a bit of business has come up. I've been looking for you. I ought to have known you'd be about anywhere there are lovely young ladies." Harrigan winked at them.

Corcoran's smile hardened on his face. He said, with exaggerated regret: "You'd take me away from these beauties, then, would you, Harrigan? On a matter of business...And while I'm after enjoying my holiday?"

"It can't be helped. My apologies, ladies. I hope you'll have a fine day and come back soon again to grace our city." Harrigan bowed to them and strode away. When he realized Rory was not following, Harrigan stopped and, not bothering to face his intended hearer, said: "Have I not made my meaning clear enough, Mr. Corcoran?" Anger passed over Corcoran's face like a flicker of heat lightning. Then he resumed the tight false smile. "I won't be but a minute," he replied. "Des. Take care of the girls for me."

Dooley had reappeared from out of the crowd. He nodded. Corcoran caught Maggie's look of concern, and the nasty smile vanished for an instant, before it froze on his face again as he stalked away.

"Mr. Dooley," Maggie said, "Who is he, this Mr. Harrigan?"

"Why?" Annie said sarcastically, "Set your cap for him too, have you? You'd have no luck with him. He's an important man."

"How do you know?" Maggie asked, with interest.

"I can tell," Annie said.

"Does Mr. Corcoran work for him?" Bridget queried.

Annie sniffed. "Don't be stupid, Bridey, he works for Mr. Maxon at Rock Mill. But I'll wager…" She looked around, then said in a loud whisper: "that Mr. Harrigan has something to do with the Fenians."

"That's enough of that gossip, girls," Dooley said. "If we don't get along to the stands now, we'll never get a drop to drink. Maggie, don't be strayin'. "

"Where's Mr. Hurley?" Maggie asked.

Dooley wiped his forehead with the back of his hand. "He'll turn up."

"Mr. Harrigan seemed like a nice-spoken fellow," Bridget remarked, looking curiously at Maggie. "Why were you so shy?"

"He's nobody I want to be knowing," Maggie answered.

Bridget was used to Maggie's mysterious pronouncements, but Dooley gave Maggie an odd look. As Bridget and Annie moved ahead, Maggie hung back a little, and said to him: "Nor did my father, I think."

Dooley startled, then pulled his whiskers. "You just keep that to yourself, Maggie. That's a good girl."

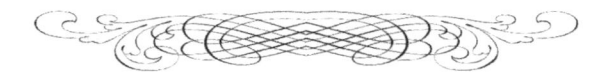

"Why did you bet on the mare, Whitfield? She was new to the field and a long shot to win," Henry said. "I liked her name, Kate May," Ned answered.

Barton clucked his tongue. "Sentimentality may win you friends, but not wagers. You ought to have put your money on the favorite, as I did—and placed a larger wager. Fortune favors the bold."

"As Horace instructs us. No, it was Ovid," Ned remarked absently. "I think Fortune favors the favorite." He thought it was as true of Henry (betting aside) as of the chestnut stallion who had won the harness racing matches that day, three out of three. "No, wait, a favorite is by definition presumed to be favored, by talent, or circumstances, or consensus, so…" He put down his drink. "Whew. Whiskey favors circular reasoning."

"Forget the semantics. You always tangle yourself in semantics when you're drinking: that, or Shakespeare, and you always end up talking only to yourself."

Ned considered this jab. "At least then I'm assured of an intelligent audience."

"That's an old one," Barton sniffed. "But it is amusing to hear you when you catch yourself talking in circles, or when you butcher the Bard."

"Butcher? Selective quotations... merely that," Ned mumbled.

Henry said: "You're slowing down. Are you, by chance, intoxicated?"

"Intoxicated, but not drunk," Ned chortled. "Did you know that the Army's court-martial rules define ten degrees of drunkenness that are, umm," he groped for the word, "actionable?"

Barton reacted with interest. "Et mentior!"

"No, I'm not stretching the truth this time. I..."

"That confirms my worst suspicions," Henry interrupted. "How could those bureaucratic blockheads presume to define such a thing with exactitude: ten degrees!"

"I swear it's true. Hold on, I'm trying to remember them all. Umm - one is 'in liquor but not drunk', and another is 'intoxicated but not drunk.'"

Barton shook his head in amused wonder.

"Then there's, um, 'drunk but not too drunk for duty.'"

"Ha! That gives me confidence in our country's defenders."

"And the worst is staggering drunk, I think. No, no, it's beastly drunk."

Barton laughed in disbelief.

George Dunn put in his opinion. "No sir. You're either drunk or you ain't, that's all there is to it."

"This is incredible," Henry said to Ned. "Ten degrees. And just how did you come by such familiarity with the rules of court martial? Were you some sort of judge: what a pretty irony, eh?"

"God forbid. No, that would fall to a higher-ranking officer."

"I can't believe that you were called on the carpet for anything yourself."

"Well, you're wrong, Henry. I was. Though not for drunkenness."

Henry sat back. "You? I can't credit that. For what, if I may ask?"

Ned hiccupped. "For questioning an order from a superior

officer. And when I say superior, I refer to his rank only, for the fellow was otherwise a jackass of the tenth degree. God almighty, yes. Biggars was his name. Captain Biggars. A contemptible blowhard. No one respected him. With good cause."

Ned sipped his whiskey. "It happened when we were still in camp here in Connecticut, drilling. We were about to have a visit from some important personage, so I was ordered to form a detail to police the camp's streets. George, you haven't seen a camp. The tents are put up in rows, and the ground between the rows and around the camp, as to the mess hall, or the surgeon's, or the parade ground, are called streets. Policing means a good tidying-up. Of course, that's right in my line." He stopped as George muttered something, then went on: "The corporal and one of our sergeants set the men to work and they soon had everything looking dandy so I went off to report to Biggars. I found him in the shade, with his servant peeling apple slices for him. Yes, well you may laugh, Henry!"

Ned stood up, swaying slightly, and saluted Barton. "'Sir, the camp has been policed. 'I'm sure it's not clean enough for our visitors, I've never seen a filthier place,' says he, 'have you swept the streets?' Now, mind you, these are dirt streets, not stone, not macadam, nor boardwalks. 'We swept out the tents and disposed of all rubbish, and the manure on the streets, sir,' I said. 'Have you swept the streets!' he says. So I thought, that's a good joke; I didn't know he had a speck of wit in him. 'No sir,' say I. He says: 'Sweep the streets. That's an order. Send those men out to do a proper job.'"

"Good God," Henry said.

"I still thought he was joking, so I said: 'May I dismiss the men, sir?' It was quite a hot day, and the men had been working for hours. The jackass practically burst his buttons off his coat and says to me: 'You ignorant puppy!'" Ned laughed, although it had been far from funny at the time.

'You most certainly may not dismiss the men, said he, when the job is not completed.' I didn't like to be insulted in front of the servant, so I said 'It is completed.' And he stands up, pointing at me so! with his damned apple, Ha, ha, hold on." Ned's laughter stopped the story for a moment. "Oh Lord. And he says 'Are you questioning my order, Lieutenant?' 'Yes, sir,' I say, and that was my mistake. As soon as it was out of my mouth, I changed it to, 'No, sir. With all respect, sir, if you'd come and take a look…' Ah, too late! A second lieutenant was passing by, slow as molasses, and taking this all in. Biggars says to him: 'You heard that, Lieutenant!' and he drops his apple and stomps around like a baby having a conniption fit."

"Asshole," George interjected.

Ned barely controlled his snickering. "The second lieutenant looks at me, as if to say, this one's crazier than a bedbug, then he just salutes Biggars, because he doesn't know what else to do. 'That's an order, Biggars yells at me, Sweep the streets, immediately!' I saluted him and marched off, wondering what in thunder to do next. The men were still standing, at ease, but in the sun. I took Corporal Hawley aside and told him what had happened. He had about the same response as you did, Georgie, but he's a canny fellow. He says to the men, 'Lieutenant Whitfield's orders are to fall out for a quarter hour, then report back here for further orders from Captain Biggars.' Hawley was taking it off my back."

"Good man," Henry said.

"I'd tell that damn' fool of a captain where to put his damn' fool order!" George said.

"If you have such a notion when you're in the army, you'd better keep it to yourself or you'll end up with your pay docked, or worse," Ned replied.

"Just for talking?" George squawked.

"For insubordination to an officer," Ned said. "Anyhow, where was I, oh yes, Hawley and the sergeant scared up more brooms, and the men assembled and got Biggars' orders: sweep the streets. There was a little wind kicking up just then, blowing southerly towards the officer's tents, so I gave them one more order. I told them to start just here, with the wind at their backs and sweep those streets heading towards the south."

Henry laughed. "Whitfield, that's capital!"

Ned said: "Their brooms stirred up a dust storm, George. And the wind blew it into the officers' area, see?"

George whooped in enlightenment. "Old Bugger's tent, too?"

"Yes indeed. And what I'd hoped for happened: Captain Merrill got a mouthful of dust and saw the men sweeping the streets like Irish maids, and immediately ordered them to stop. Then he came at me, madder than a wet hen. I told him about my orders from Captain Biggars. Merrill took care of it from there."

"Is that idiot Biggars still in command?" Barton asked.

"No, he's not. He quit about a week before we saw any

fighting." Henry snorted. "Bravo."

George said: "What makes these assholes, these <u>officers</u>, think they're better than anyone else, that's what I'd like to know. Just because they've got the money to buy a commission, like your Pa did for you." He gulped his whiskey. "Answer me that," he said to Ned.

"I don't like the sound of that, Dunn," Henry said.

"He's drunk, Henry, that's all," Ned said.

"Yep, we been friends a long time, me and Ned. Longer than you, Barton, I'll bet. I've known him from a boy," George retorted.

"You say the man is drunk, Lieutenant? To what degree?" Henry said.

Ned considered this. "I'd say drunk and disorderly."

"Hunh? I ain't disorderly. Hell's bells, Barton, I never said he was a asshole." George jerked his thumb at Ned. "Even if his Pa bought him a commission, Ned wouldn't give out damned fool orders."

"That clarifies matters," Ned put in. "Say, Henry, what was that song of Horace's, about the Sabine jug of wine? You ought to know, Yalie: that awful translation about time wasting?"

Barton grimaced. "You and your Horace. I much prefer the vernacular. Why do you remember all that nonsense now that you're out of school and have no earthly use for it?"

"I have a retentive memory," Ned let out a dignified belch.

"You spent far too much time at the books," Henry said.

"I've got it," Ned shouted. "Something, something...I've lost the first stanza, but then it goes:

> Draw, my Thaliarchus, from the Sabine jug of wine.
> The rest leave to the gods who still
> The...(something....fierce? or something...) wind,
> And to tomorrow's store of good
> Or Evil give no mind.
> Whatever day your fortune grants,
> That day mark up for gain,
> And in your youthful bloom do not
> The sweet amours disdain.
> Now on... on the land...no, something...
> The shades descend...

Damn. I've forgotten the rest. It's something to do with kissing a maid."

Barton smirked. "Ah yes, Horace's well-known 'Something, something Song'. A most inspiring rendition, too."

"Well, if you'd give me a little time, I could come up with…" Ned began.

"That's a fine idea, yep," George broke in. "Kissing. Yep."

Barton took a cigar from the box, eyed it, then returned it with a smile. "Most inspiring. I say we pay a social call, gentlemen, a little visit to Mrs. Campbell's."

"Does she keep a tavern?" George asked.

"You can have a drink there, yes, but it's a private club," Henry replied, "There is a place to play billiards downstairs, isn't that right, Whitfield? and then a gentleman can go upstairs and play an altogether different game with his stick and balls."

"The next time you criticize my puns, Henry, I intend to remind you of that one," Ned remarked.

Barton said: "She has a new girl she's reserved just for me."

"Huh?" Dunn frowned foggily.

Ned waited for Barton to exercise his sarcasm: when it was not forthcoming, he went on: "It's a house of ill repute."

"What? You're pulling my leg, ain't you? It's a bawdy house?" George exclaimed. Henry looked at Dunn in mild perplexity, as if he was speaking a foreign language.

"Yes, George," Ned answered.

"Shoot! Wouldn't I like to go," George said. "How much does it cost?"

Ned winced. "George, you don't ask about money."

"Why not? They ain't giving it away, are they?"

Henry interceded, now amused. "My treat, for a veteran soldier and a recruit. Consider it my modest offering to assist the Union cause."

"Mrs. Campbell will never have you back," Ned muttered to Henry. He watched as the meaning of Henry's offer filtered into George's inebriated mind.

"Whoooeee! Thank you kindly, Barton." George rolled out of his chair, and ecstatically pumped Barton's hand. "I'm ready." He stumbled over Ned's feet. "Say, why the long face? Have another drink. Here…"

"No. No more. I'll get maudlin," Ned said.

"What?"

"Lachrymose."

"Huh?"

"Melancholy."

"Oh." Dunn shrugged. "When can we go?"

"As soon as Whitfield is ready," Henry said.

Ned drained his glass in two gulps. He had the sensation of disassociating from his body. *A treat indeed,* he thought, *as soon as my head clears a bit.* Then it came to him dimly that this offer posed a problem. *You're scared,* floated into his head. *Am not,* he told himself. *I satisfied her, what's her name, quite well last time. That fellow died at Fredericksburg,* the cynical voice whispered. *No, he didn't, by God. I could do it again,* his libido asserted. His groin prickled at the memories: those transports! That praise! *But you were whole then,* the voice persisted, *and praise was what you were meant to hear. Mrs. Campbell wants repeat customers.* No, it couldn't be: his mind backed away from that prospect. Henry maintained that women were easily understood, and their transparent needs easily met. In contrast, Ned believed them to be as complex as any man: as he himself.

He shook his head. "No, thank you, Henry," he heard himself say with polite regret, as if passing up another drink.

Barton hesitated. "We'll do it some other time." His disappointment was clear in his tone. Ned was too drunk to care much.

"No!" George roared. "Come on Ned, that again, for Christ's sake! Jesus, these gals ain't going to be looking at your face, that ain't the business end. Even if they do, they got to do it with you, that's what you're paying them for."

"See here, Dunn…" Henry began.

"I can speak for myself, Henry," Ned said, then let sarcasm speak for him. "Eloquently and cogently expressed, as always, George."

"You and your god-damned big words!"

"You and your god-damned big mouth," Ned said hotly. "You go. Henry, take him - he's going to war. He deserves it." *That and a dose of the clap,* he thought.

"If that's what you want," Henry responded, after he'd spent a moment studying them both. *It's not what I want!* Ned thought. "Yes," he said to Barton, "I'll find my own way home.

Chapter 11

Supper, two days after the military draft began in Hartford, was a tense affair at the Whitfield's. The judge ate little and his family less. During the meal, he fixed each of them, in turn, with a prolonged formidable gaze. Ned wondered as to its cause: try as he might, he could think of nothing he'd done wrong recently. The evening had cooled: the family would normally gather on the veranda. Tonight, the judge, rather than joining them there or disappearing to his study, insisted they all accompany him to the sitting room. Eleanor tried to leave, pleading a headache. Although she had successfully employed the excuse in the past, the Judge instead told her, "I'll have none of that." He pointed her toward the back parlor.

Ned stood where he could watch everyone. Mrs. Whitfield sat with bowed head, hands pressed together in her lap, as if in prayer. Eleanor moved about the room, with Dance at her side, eventually relegating herself to a far corner.

The judge sat down and leaned forward in his chair. "Would you like to know what the infernal Irish have been up to in New York? Rioting, mayhem, the murder of innocent men, cold-blooded beating and killing of women and children!" He pawed for his spectacles, jammed them on, and read from the newspaper:

> *The mob attacked negroes without mercy wherever found, and it is said that at least a dozen were killed, while a large number were badly beaten and their places of residence destroyed. The crowning act of the infuriated mob was the demoniac act of setting fire to (over the heads of the terrified and screaming children) an Orphan Asylum. Seventy-five of the provost guard arrived at noon,*

and on being drawn up, were quickly surrounded by the mob, who stoned them. One of the soldiers was nearly torn to pieces, and thrown over a precipice, when the body was stoned until half buried. Soon after a squad of police, arrived, but were driven off, one of them being torn to pieces and kicked to a jelly.

"Dear God," Mrs. Whitfield whispered. *The war has come to the streets,* Ned thought, too shocked to speak.
Judge Whitfield gave out an angry sigh. "Eleanor, you are silent again. Have you no defense for your Irish friends, like that stupid little Biddy you had the misfortune of sitting by in school?"

"Come now," Ned growled, "How...

"Stay out of this, Edward," the judge interrupted. "Eleanor," he said loudly, jabbing the newspaper at her. "Do you read anything besides bad novels, do you even read the newspaper? No, of course not, it would be too much for your delicate feelings to bear." Eleanor shuddered as if she had the palsy. "You can't stay wrapped in swaddling clothes any longer," the judge went on, "Your mother's had free rein with you for too long, far too long. I won't allow it. Do you hear me!" The dog tensed and made a low sound deep in his throat.

"Don't you dare growl at me, you worthless cur!" the judge shouted. The dog barked an alert. Eleanor opened her eyes, murmured to Dance, calming him with a firm movement of her hand, and grasped his collar tightly.

The judge said: "You cry about a baby bird that's fallen from the nest, but you have no tears to shed for these innocent people beaten to death and burned alive by your friends!"

Eleanor choked out: "They're evil...not...my friends."

"I'm glad to hear that you still have a Christian conscience," the judge's words were benign, but his voice was freighted with scornful disdain. "Albeit you do nothing to help others and persist in being a Sabbath-breaker like your brother."

"I want...I wish to go with Mama to church..." Eleanor said.

"Then do so!" the Judge shouted.

At this Eleanor wept, clutching Dance, who keened a dirge for her. Ned clenched his teeth: any move he made to aid his sister, the judge would seize as proof of collusion, as he always did, and apply to her further torment. Mrs. Whitfield sat as still as stone.

Mr. Whitfield tossed the newspaper aside and folded his

arms. "Is there ever a day that goes by in this house without you crying about something? Get a hold of yourself. You're not an infant anymore." He pulled his handkerchief from his pocket and thrust it at his daughter, making a show of his impatience. "Blow your nose." Eleanor did so.

"And shut up that infernal dog." She twisted the cloth in her hands and took several deep breaths, then hushed the dog. He gave out a final whimper before quieting. She pulled him closer still, and put both her hands on him, closing her eyes again, whispering to herself.

"Your mother befriends the oddest people—she would be the talk of the town if most of them did not chalk it up to Christian charity, thank heaven," the judge went on, "I've heard whispers about Kate's teaching work, that she allows blacks to call upon her! By Jove, they had better not say such a thing to my face, I would soon set them straight on that matter. As if her uncle or I would countenance such a thing. While there may be some decent Negroes, my family does not fraternize with them. The Irish are worse, there is not a speck of decency in any of them." Eleanor shook her head slightly.

The judge said, "Don't you know that you could have visitors every day, even if you never stirred from the house? You could have dozens of friends—good American girls, just for the asking. If you had even a particle of sense, and more of a woman's heart, you would go out to help your mother with her war charity work, even if you did not attend the frolics that most girls your age pine for. Go out, hah! I guess I'll never live to see the day." His face darkened further. "People never speak of you in my presence anymore. I expect they've forgotten you exist. But I suppose that's better than saying you are feeble-minded. Don't think I haven't heard that."

Eleanor's eyes flew open and she let out a weird, convulsive cry, then screeched: "No!" She covered her ears and ran from the room; with Dance nearly tripping her up in his simultaneous desire to protect her and flee with her.

"Come back here." Her father pursued her. Ned followed, but he was not swift enough. The judge grasped her arm, twisted it, kicked at the dog. Eleanor slumped to the floor in a heap. Ned grabbed the dog's collar, dragged him to the kitchen and shut the door. Through the dog's scratching and yelping, he heard his father say to Eleanor: "Do not defy me!" She scrabbled away from him on all fours.

"Leave her alone," Ned said. "For God's sake!"

"You ought to be ashamed," the judge said to his daughter. Eleanor covered her head as if to protect it from a blow. "What in God's name is wrong with you?" She struggled to her feet and ran for the stairs. "Go!" her father yelled belatedly, "Get out of my sight." Ned stood between his father and the staircase. His father pulled down his waistcoat, sweating. "She was being impudent."

"That's no reason to haul her around like baggage. You hurt her," Ned countered angrily.

"I did not hurt her," the judge responded. "And don't you dare to chide me!' Ned bowed his head, obeisance to a dangerous lord. "That dog's barking will be the death of him yet!" the judge said.

"I'll take him outside," Ned said.

"See to it," the judge ordered and returned to the sitting room to excoriate his wife. As Ned tied on Dance's leash in the kitchen, he heard his father say: "Now you see what happens when you indulge your children. You always have, and you never see the harm it causes."

"Harm!" Ned said incredulously and pulled the dog outdoors. When he returned to the sitting room, his father was gone.

Mrs. Whitfield stood staring at the floor, white-faced. When she saw him, she asked in a strained voice: "The dog?"

"Safely tied in the stable," Ned responded.

His mother closed her eyes and sobbed, once. Ned patted her arm ineffectually and offered her one of his clean handkerchiefs. She wiped her eyes and nose. "I'm sorry," she mumbled.

"For what? Good God, Mama! That was one devil of a blow-up." He lowered his voice. "He's gone mad."

She looked drawn and nauseous in the dim light.

He went on, "Mama, don't blame yourself. You look ill. You ought to go to bed."

"No!" She shuddered and sank into a chair. "I can't be...I can't...until he gets out of this state he's in. So cruel, did he hurt her? He did!"

"No," Ned replied. "He took her arm, but she... she was afraid for Dance, I guess. It was the riots, Mother, that's the cause, otherwise he just would have... I don't know, criticized, or said the usual things, as he began."

She said: "I can't bear thinking of those poor people and how they died! They must have been terrified before the end came. It is so horrid, so evil."

"That's so," Ned agreed bleakly, "It's unconscionable. Mob rule. A mob is a creature with a mind of its own. No, 'mind' isn't the right word: a creature of mindless will." He remembered when the men of his regiment had been pushed so far by exhaustion and hunger that they nearly grew mutinous. He continued: "The poor Negroes are always the targets of every idiot's bad humor."

He thought for a moment. "No one wants the draft, but I wouldn't be surprised if it was Southern sympathizers who incited this gang to riot."

Mrs. Whitfield stirred in her chair. "There were riots against the Papists by Americans in Philadelphia when you and Dan were babies. And against the abolitionists. How I hate the violence!"

"The devil seeks his own in every age and country," Ned replied. Quiet settled over the room. A moth that had found its way inside fluttered in erratic circles around the side lamp.

"I haven't seen him go at her like that in a while. Like he did before I went to live with Aunt Caroline. But that was a long time ago," he said. "Well..." He took a step away from her, gazed at the door. "Guess I'll go to bed."

Her response was barely audible. "Poor Elly...."

"Yes. It's d...utterly unfair," he agreed, "especially when she has just found someone to bring her out of her shell. One or two visits from a little girl–no one pays such things any attention. It has no effect on anyone's social standing. I don't know why he cares so deeply about what folks say."

"My poor little lamb. Losing her one bit of happiness." Mrs. Whitfield pressed the handkerchief against her eyes. Ned longed to escape, but his mother looked so unlike herself, that he sat down next to her instead. She immediately took his hand. Hers was cold.

He sat without speaking, in bondage, until he had an idea: "If the family is so concerned about people seeing some Irish girl being "received" as a caller, thunder, if I were Elly, I'd visit with the girl in the orchard or someplace no one would see. El walks out to the very edge of our property with Dance, so it would do no harm to the family's precious reputation if she visited with the girl out there."

"No, not again..." Mrs. Whitfield said.

"Come now, Mama. I'm just thinking like a lawyer.

Wouldn't Father be proud? Ha. The higher good is served when an unjust law is changed, and if it cannot be changed, then cautiously circumvented. If Elly will keep the girl out of the house, it will not harm his reputation. I say she could still see her friend, by hook or crook."

"It's too devious," his mother said.

"But if the cause is right, I say it's justified," Ned replied.

"All of us would suffer if he found out," she said, anger edging the fear from her voice.

"You're right, there's that." Ned sat back and closed his burning right eye.

After a time, she said: "It's such a shame that this girl is so unsuitable. I mean nothing against her personally, she seems a good girl, and rather sweet. But…"

"So, your sticking point is that she's Irish, not that she's just a hired girl," Ned mumbled.

His mother said: "Good heaven, yes. I don't care particularly about those distinctions, as you know. If I hadn't gone to school-teaching, I'd still be on the farm myself. If it was up to me, yes, I'd indulge Eleanor, as your father says, indulge! The poor child has little enough to bring her joy! I would like her to have a friend, even if the girl wasn't from a 'good Millville family.'"

Ned opened his eye, glanced at his mother's scowl, took her measure. "So, allow her to see Maggie outdoors," he repeated, "And if she would visit here with some young ladies, take some callers when you do, that would appease him for a while."

"Be reasonable, Eddy," she said tartly. "She is much too frightened to greet callers. It is not that simple. Eleanor is different."

"Tell me something new," Ned said, "She might not be so frightened of the young ladies as of Father and she might not be so frightened if she got what she wanted, for once in her life. Why don't you ask her?"

His mother dropped her head, rubbed her eyes. He waited, brushed lint from his trousers, yawned, then stood up. She suddenly sat straight in her chair. "We cannot live this way," she muttered, then said: "Let her cry for a while. Then you go and talk to her."

"Me? Why? I have nothing to say."

"Yes, you do," she said firmly. "And she may listen more readily to you. Tell her about your solution, meeting outdoors. If you truly think that it will help her more than harm her. She can decide for herself. I don't know any more, I don't know what to do with him. Or with her."

Ned said uncomfortably. "Well, neither do I. She certainly doesn't listen to logic when it comes to getting out and about. Besides, I just thought it was a good suggestion: I didn't say it was a solution."

His mother said in a soft voice, "I just can't bear to leave her with no hope. I'm afraid she will get as bad as she was before..." Ned avoided his mother's pleading gaze. "Kate will be home soon," he said.

"Do talk to Elly tomorrow," she repeated.

He gave up. "Very well, but I wish you'd wait until Katie gets home and recruit her."

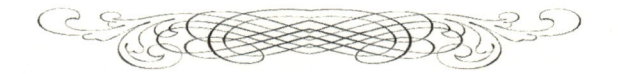

Fourth of July pictures rolled in her hand, Maggie was startled by a voice which called her name. As she neared the Whitfield house, her friend came from behind a bush, and right into the road. "What?" Maggie said in alarm, for Eleanor looked grim and frightened.

"No, come first, hurry, please!" Eleanor said. She led Maggie behind the bushes and back toward the big tree at the edge of the orchard, out of sight of the house.

"It's the worst thing," she said, leaning against the tree, panting a little.

Maggie said: "Is everyone all right? Where's Dance?"

"I tied him in the stable," Eleanor said, "Here, in the newspaper, read this. Right here."

Half an hour later, nearly as confused and frantic as she had been when her father left, Maggie trudged toward Frank's house. She caressed her abdomen protectively, as it threatened a second bout of nausea. The first had come after she had read about the horrors wrought by the mob in New York. *It can't be. It can't be true,* she thought. And so she had said to Eleanor when her stomach righted itself. Something came to mind now that had not occurred to her when she was with her friend: how did anyone know it was an Irish mob, for the newspaper did not say so, did it now? She glanced down to where she held the paper between her fingers like a chunk of rotting meat. *I'll read it again when I get to Frank's.*

"Some of the boys were talking about it at the tavern the other night," Frank remarked after Maggie had read the article aloud and asked him how anyone knew it was an Irish mob. "They were saying it was a shame, as I say, a dirty shame, but Hurley said 'And so what if they were every man, woman, and child Irish?' 'Treat a man like a dog,' says he, 'and he'll rise up someday and bite you.'"

"Wicked devils…" Mrs. O'Shaughnessy muttered.

Frank went on: "And when Dooley said it was a terrible thing they did, Corcoran, he said 'What did the damn Yanks think might be happenin', when they treat ours no better than dirt under their feet, and tell us now we must go and fight their battles for them down South? I'll do no such thing,' he says, 'no such thing for the Yanks nor the woollyheads. I have no quarrel with the South,' says he."

"But it's wrong to hurt the…" Maggie tried again.

Frank spoke over her, "And I'm thinkin' Corcoran is right. We have no need of the Southron, now do we? Couldn't they take themselves off wherever they please, and I'd not lose a minute's sleep over it."

"Mam! He's stealin' my dinner!" Patrick yelled, whacking his brother on the head.

"Here, Paddy, take my potato. I'm not hungry," Maggie said, handing it over.

"Mam! He's kicking me," Denny said.

"Shut yer gob," Mrs. O'Shaughnessy said, "Keep yer hands and feet to yerself, the both of you."

Rose said, "We've every right to be angry, when you think on it. Mother of God, wives and children can starve, for all the Yanks care, while our poor men have their freedom taken from them, and get put in the way of harm, not their own choosing. That's a crime, surely!"

"Ah, now, Rosie…" Frank began, while Maggie said simultaneously, "Rose, they killed those men!"

"Well, I'm not saying that was right," Rose relented. "Hear me, boys, that was wrong, that was, killing the soldiers and the guard."

"And the negroes," Maggie said.

"And the negroes too, I suppose," Rose said, "'Tis a sin, how far they took it. Still, Maggie, 'tis unfair, the way we've been treated, and in this, the Yanks are no better than the English were."

Frank added: "Hurley says the Yanks will starve out their own kind in those Southron cities, just as quick as the English starved us: all to get rid of the trouble and keep a penny in their pockets."

"Criminee, he blathers about the poor starved ones, don't he, Saint Hurley—when he hisself was here eating praties in America from the time he was a boy!" Mrs. O'Shaughnessy said spitefully. "And ye'll not soon see him taking a place in the Army, like our Michael, now will ye? He's paid some doctor in Hartford to say he's unfit."

Frank shrugged. "I'd have paid for one for our Mikey to stay out of it if I could." Although Frank was the sole support of a wife and three children, he could not have obtained an exemption from the draft on that account. Since his brother had enlisted, however, the Vinton draft committee had winked, and granted Frank an exemption as sole support of an aged parent.

"I get down on my knees every night and thank the good Lord, and you boys should too, that your Da don't have to go," Rose remarked with high feeling. "And we'll pray every night for Michael to come home safe."

As Mary whined, Frank took her onto his lap: "Whissht, darlin'."

"Can I have your carrots, then, Aunt Maggie, since y'aint eating them?" Denny ventured.

"Little beggar," Patrick muttered.

As Maggie passed the boiled carrot over to her nephew, she said: "I still can't believe it. How could anyone burn up the home of those Negro children–little innocent ones like Mary–and kill..." She put her face in her hands, too distressed to worry about what the family thought of her weakness.

"Ah, don't take on so, Maggie. It's surely a sad thing, a very sad thing, but you're too tenderhearted, entirely," Rose said. Mary boohooed a little but quieted as her father put a drop of honey into his teacup and gave her a sip.

"'Tis a sorry thing, this hate. All this hate. 'Tis the work of the devil," Mrs. O'Shaughnessy said.

"You're right, Mam," Frank said. Then: "There, Mag. It didn't happen here, did it now, and we'd none of us ever do such a wicked thing, so put it out of your mind, there's a good girl. 'Tis all in God's hands." He stood up and slid the child off his lap. As he removed the newspaper from Maggie's place, he said: "This is fit only for burning. I'll put it in the stove."

"No," Rose said, "Put it by the back door so's we can use it in the privy."

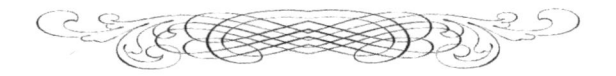

"If I were thou, Miss, I'd be knitting socks for the poor, not sitting idle," Mrs. Wilkin said. It was the first word anyone had spoken for an hour or more.

"I was thinking about..." Maggie began, then subsided, sure that Mrs. Wilkin would rail against the Irish mob if she'd learned of its ghastly work. "Nothing," she said, "Yes, I ought to be knitting socks."

"It's too late to begin now. It's time we were abed. Homer?"

Mr. Merritt stirred slightly. He had an open book in his lap, but he had not turned a page in several minutes. "I'll be along presently, Jemima."

Maggie returned to her painful, repetitious thoughts.

Mr. Merritt sighed. "I have not slept much of late."

"The Quakers, the Friends, I mean, they believe there is a seed for good in every man," Maggie said urgently, "But how can they, when some men are so evil? There must be a demon who takes them over and makes them mad and do mad things. It must be!"

"Maggie, what has upset thee so?"

"I saw a newspaper..." she faltered, "about what happened in New York. Did you hear?"

Mr. Merritt put down his book. He looked very old. His armchair creaked as he sat back. "I heard it at Morton's today," he replied. Maggie watched him, dreading his pronouncement of guilt. He remained silent, staring at the far corner of the room, meditative, troubled.

"It is the darkest time," he said finally, "The light is waiting to shine in us, the truth to cleanse us and make us see aright, but we heed it not. Men have closed their ears and their eyes—sealed them tightly. Their souls are blinded, they blind themselves and huddle in the dark. The time of trial..." His voice weakened and stopped.

"I'm sorry! I'm so sorry," Maggie said. She knew he did not blame her, but she groped to apologize for the Irish—and perhaps for all humanity. She blew her nose once, and again.

"There is that of God in every man," Homer Merritt said in a stronger voice, "I do believe it still. For the light can never be extinguished entirely: the truth lives in some, as long as man breathes on the earth. There are some now who follow their concerns to aid their fellows; they act on the truth, giving up all possessions, their safety, all they have, to do the work of good. Sit still now Maggie and calm thyself. Wait in silence for God to speak."

That is what they do in Quaker meeting, Maggie thought. Although she had no rosary in her hands, Maggie repeated prayers in her mind, until she found a small measure of peace. "I will not treat anyone badly or ever harm them. I can do that," she said aloud.

Merritt said: "Yes, Maggie. Follow the Truth."

Chapter 12

Ned held the glass negative up to the red glow of the darkroom light. It had good density, it was clear, and the sitter posed well: it would make a good photograph. He placed the developed plate, the last from that morning's sessions, on the drying rack. Outside the door he heard Jack arguing with someone. He opened the door to listen.

"Yer not Mr. Whitfield, then, are you?"

"I most certainly am not," Jack snarled.

"I thought I'd be seein' him, as he's the boss."

"Mr. Dunn is the proprietor, but he's not here," Rossiter said loudly.

"I come to have my picture took," the man said.

Jack said: "Of course you did; we don't run a hat shop here. We don't sell on credit, and we don't barter with folks with little worth having. If you want your picture taken, you'd better have good coin."

"Coin? Y'can't get coin these days," the customer said.

"The prices are posted over there. If you can't read, I'll tell you what they are," Rossiter's voice was drenched with disdain.

"I kin read! I went to school, same's you." The workman in the reception area balled his fists.

Ned broke in. "I heard someone ask for me."

"Yer the one, then," the man said. He grimaced. "So, you'll take only coin?"

"No, we'll take currency as well," Ned replied.

"Stamps is what I got. "

"They're legal tender. We'll take them," Ned said, over Rossiter's sound of protest.

Now the customer's stare showed a twitch of recognition; and although the man's looks were unremarkable, Ned thought he remembered seeing the fellow once before. Of course, Millville was a small place.

"Ain't I seen you at a baseball game," the man said.

"That's right. I remember you. You're a thrower," Ned answered.

"That I am," the man agreed.

"A good thrower," Ned continued, "You lost me some money on a wager, though, with that arm of yours."

The laborer took this as a compliment. "You just placed yer wager on the wrong team, is all," he said.

"I won't make that mistake at the next match," Ned commented.

The man grimaced again. "Well, that's the thing…yer out yer money, for good; for you won't be seein' me in the game no more. I've jined the army. That's why I'm here for my picture."

"I'm always glad to meet a man who supports the Union. What's your name?" Ned held out his hand for a shake.

The man tucked his hat under his arm and shook Ned's hand. "Name's Foran."

"When you learn to shoot as well as you throw the ball, Mr. Foran, the Union will have a good soldier," Ned said.

Foran nodded his thanks. "You was in it, so I heard," he said, "So I see. You seen the elephant, certainly." Ned recognized the popular expression used to describe going into one's first battle. He nodded.

"And what's he like?" Foran's question was free of apprehension or bravado. He appeared merely curious.

"Have you ever seen a real elephant, or a picture of one in a book?" Ned asked.

Foran blinked. "I seen one at the circus parade when I was a boy."

Ned went on: "So you know how they look. There's a Hindoo story about five blind men who met an elephant and were asked to describe the beast. Have you heard that one?"

Foran shook his head.

"The first blind man stood by the elephant's long nose and felt it all over." Ned mimed the action. "Ah ha, he exclaimed, an elephant is like a snake. "

" 'tisn't at all," Foran said with a laugh.

"The second blind man stood by the elephant's ear and felt around. He said: I declare, an elephant is like a large fan."

"Ha!" Foran said, nodding.

"No, indeed, said the third man, an elephant is like the trunk of a tree. Where do you imagine he stood?"

"The leg," Foran said immediately.

"Just so. The fourth man touched the elephant's side and leaned against it, then he told them all that an elephant is like a brick wall. And the last man held the very tip of the elephant's tail. He said: No, you're mistaken, every one of you, an elephant is very like a rope. "

Foran said: "And they was none of them right."

"Ah, but each of them correctly described what he experienced," Ned responded.

"That they did," Foran said. He went on, not unkindly: "This elephant you seen, he was a big one, surely. But here y'are now, runnin' a shop, so you beat him after all."

Ned moved over to the display case. "Now, as to your picture, Mr. Foran, would you like a ferrotype or a carte-de-visite?" He held up a sample of each.

"Why's this one so dark?" Foran pointed to the ferrotype.

"It's a photograph on black lacquered metal," Ned replied, "Ferrotypes are very sturdy, they travel well. A lot of the soldiers carry them. You can get four for twenty-five cents."

"Four pictures? For the same money? Do I have to come here four times to get them took?" Foran asked.

"Ignorant...." Rossiter mumbled.

"No, indeed," Ned said loudly, "You can have it all done today, in just a few minutes, ten or so. Mr. Rossiter will go and prepare the plate."

Foran addressed his comment to Ned. "I need to get back to work, is all."

"Of course. Come this way."

"Four pictures for one price is good," Foran remarked as they entered the camera area. "My sister told me to come and get my picture took so's I could give it to my Agnes. She's the gal I'm goin' to marry. You know her."

Ned showed him where to sit and adjusted the head restraint. "I beg your pardon, I don't believe I am acquainted with any young lady named Agnes."

Foran sat down, peering backward nervously at the apparatus. "No, not Ag. You know my sister."

"I don't recall being introduced to a Miss Foran," Ned said.

"Not Foran. O'Shaughnessy. Maggie. You got her down off the hill, so she says."

Ned smiled. "Yes, I am acquainted with Miss O'Shaughnessy." Jack Rossiter came in as Ned said this. The assistant stood by the camera, looking like he had downed poison.

"She told me to come and ask for Mr. Whitfield, for he's a gentleman," Foran said pointedly to Rossiter.

"Very gracious of her," Ned said, "So, Mr. Foran, look over here at my hand. I'll be counting off the seconds, please remain still until I tell you that you can move."

As Jack removed the plate holder from the camera, Foran spoke up once more. "I'll be sending Agnes and her sisters over here too, now I've bin here, and seeing as how you can get four pictures for one price."

Rossiter leaned close to Ned and muttered: "You'll drive away all the decent customers if you let more of this trash in here."

"Just do your job!" Ned hissed in a whisper.

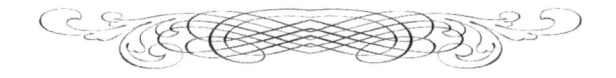

"We'll have a good talk tonight in bed. I want to walk in the garden alone for a while," Ned heard Kate say to their younger sister as he returned from the stable. He cleaned his boots on the scraper set near the back door, then sat down on the steps to enjoy the cooler air. He closed his overworked eye to rest it, then snapped it open again when Kate, quite close by, called his name. "Come and walk with me. And tell me all the news."

"Mother and Father and El have told you all the news already," he said as he joined her.

"They told me their news, yes, I feel stuffed to the gills. But you and I haven't had a good 'turn to' for a long time." As she walked, Kate pinched off and discarded flowers that were past their bloom.

"I have been busy, but I ought to have penned you a line or two," Ned apologized.

"Getting a letter is lovely, you know that from when you were in the army. Mother's I like especially, but it's not the same as being together. I just about fainted when you came to the station to collect me. I was…"

"Yes, I am a sight," Ned interrupted.

"Stop it." Kate whacked him on the arm. "You were a sight for sore eyes! You look so much better than the last time I saw you, so well and hearty again."

Ned smiled and prepared a retort but Kate intercepted it. "No, I <u>mean</u> it. Don't tease me." She sniffed, busied herself with the flowers for a moment. "You'd better not, you beast. I was about to say that it's so good to hear your voice again too, but if you don't behave, I'll take it all back."

"It's good to hear your voice again, too. No, I'm sincere," Ned responded, "And I am, as God is my witness! Extremely glad to be off the sick roll, finally."

"Yes," Kate said with a tremble in her voice, "We all are so glad…" She let the tears fall, then pulled a handkerchief out of her sleeve and shook her head.

He said: "Only a passing shower? When you were a little, remember? you told me you liked to taste your tears and I laughed myself silly."

Kate chuckled and blew her nose. "But I think I've tasted too many tears in this past year. It's just that there is so much need, and so little I can do…And there's so much to do!"

He remembered Maggie's awed remark about a brave family and said: "You're doing good work. I'll grant you the right to let out a howl now and then." He sang a line from *Hard Times Come Again No More*, then told her about Dunn's enlistment, and about the photograph gallery, ending with a brief summation of his arrangement with Charles Mix.

"But what about the exciting rescue?" Kate asked.

He said: "I expect you've heard it already from Elly or Father. He's the one who had it put in the newspaper."

"Of course he had it put in the paper, you ninny! He's proud of you."

"A rare event," Ned replied.

"For any of us," Kate agreed.

"It was nothing more than good fortune," he went on, "Good timing, actually…"

"Nonsense," Kate put in.

"Well," he said, "How do you like this? I am a remarkable fellow. A prince among men. As brave as a lion."

"A reluctant lion, you mean," she retorted.

Ned smiled. "A pretty turn of phrase. I like it. No, better yet, listen: not a reluctant lion, but reluctant to be lionized!"

"Very well, Mr. Full of Fun. You won't hear a word about it—just accept the praise!" Kate said.

He snickered. "No. I'll tell you why. I'm afraid if too many young ladies hear of it, they'll be flinging themselves off of Knott's Hill in droves, and where would I be then, hey? In a pickle. Think of it, a veritable horde of damsels in distress."

Kate smiled. "How very like Sir Walter Scott!" "Verily," Ned replied.

"Ow," Kate said, then: "Elly told me about it: that the girl you rescued is the same girl who befriended her at school. She had quite a lot to say about it, in fact. She's very taken with this Maggie."

Ned hesitated, then asked: "Did she tell you about the big blow-up with Father?"

"She did. She still looks quite peaked, don't you think?"

"It was a bad one, Katie."

Kate frowned deeply. "Why does he...well, I am sure it was. That's why I was so surprised when she told me she took Papa's newspaper off his table and sneaked away to talk to this girl about the riots."

"I didn't know that!" he said, "Hang it, why did she bring up the riots? Who would guess that some little Biddy from Millville was the secret ringleader. Why must all the Irish be tarred with the same brush? Some good Irishmen served in our regiment, like Sergeant..."

Kate talked over him. "Let me finish. Elly said she'd had a talk with Maggie, and they've visited out in the orchard since then."

"Oh, I didn't know that. Good for her," Ned replied.

"And wait till you hear this," Kate continued, "El told me as plain as day that she was angry at Papa... Our little mouse! Angry at Father, that's the hobbyhorse you always ride, but Elly has never let out a peep about such a thing before. She also told me she'd like to find a way to keep seeing Maggie and not have to go behind his back."

Ned snorted. "She may as well have set herself one of the labors of Hercules! He's completely unreasonable. She ought to see her friend. It's not as if she's consorting with criminals. And she's not a child anymore."

"But she's not of age," Kate said. "And more to the point, Father would punish her severely if he found out."

"He did not forbid a visit, not in so many words," Ned countered, "Not in the same way he forbid you from going to Washington, but that didn't stop you."

His sister glowered. "I can manage things quite well," she said, "you know that. But this is Elly. It's a far different situation. I do wonder about this Maggie. Is she good for Eleanor? Eleanor may be seventeen but she's really such an infant, she's shut herself away for so long. I'm concerned that this girl may be a sly, fawning sort, trying to get something for herself."

"Of course not. You've been dealing with government types for too long," Ned responded impatiently.

"Well, what do you think?" Kate asked.

"She's smart. Quick-witted anyhow. She has spent several years with Quakers, and they are a decent sort. She seems truly fond of Eleanor. She has a sense of fun. I think you'd like her," he said.

"I do like her cartoons." Kate smiled. "I'll go along the next time Elly meets her in the orchard and see for myself." It was none of her business; but from her position as eldest child Kate made everything her business. She was often a bossy soul, but sometimes he welcomed her blunt opinions, and was also grateful that she protected with loyal silence all confessions that she had been asked to guard. Everything else a man said was fair game.

She straightened her bodice with ferocity: "Did you hear that Mrs. Warren asked me to speak to the Ladies Freedmen's Aid Society, which of course I will gladly do, and Reverend Millard said what a shame it was that I couldn't address the whole church on the subject. He asked if I could write it out so that he could read it to the congregation!"

"Ouch," Ned said, "Father probably wishes he could have read it to the congregation and then taken credit for it. But did you hear that Anna Dickinson came to Hartford again recently and spoke to a mixed crowd. I would have liked to have heard her."

Kate replied solemnly: "I wouldn't mind emulating Miss Dickinson."

"Mrs. Warren would have the vapors, and Father would disown you," Ned joked.

"Pray do not bring that up again! One never knows when he will follow through on his threats." Kate shook her head. "Poor dear Mrs. Warren. Pooh! Isn't it funny, she's ten years younger than Mama, yet I think of her as an old woman. How different they are. Oh, by the way, Mrs. Warren said she was sorry you weren't able to stop by and visit too."

"I assumed that you needed some time with them alone," Ned replied. Kate was silent. Ned was not eager to meet Will's parents again. They would want to talk about Will, of course, and he could not. Will was that rarest of human beings: a genuinely good man, yet blessedly free of preaching, judging, or cant. It was hard for Ned to imagine how the Warrens coped with the passing of their elder son. *But they're better Christians than I,* he thought.

"Will is in a better place," Kate said finally, in a tight voice. Ned remembered how she had mouthed that phrase over and over again, nodding like a mechanical toy, during Will's funeral. Yet he had seen her two days later collapse on the Whitfield's sitting room floor, screaming in grief and rage while mother and sister hovered ineffectually around her–and brother watched. He had envied her wild grief and knew it would be better could he share the wordless cry. Instead, he had skulked to the rubbish dump with his father's musket and shot at discarded bottles, imagining each was the face of the enemy.

"I don't doubt it," he said aloud, and pulled out his handkerchief.

"No," Kate said, "I'll be alright."

"Oh. It's for my mouth, actually," Ned said, "Since I got shelled, sometimes it springs a leak."

Kate's face wrinkled in concern. "Oh dear! Have you told Doctor Green?"

"Have I told Doctor Green! Come now, Kate." She sighed and began picking flowers. Ned eventually put away the wet handkerchief.

"Better?" she asked.

He nodded and followed her toward the house. "Finished everything on your bill of particulars, have you?" he mocked, "Pumped me dry and now you're done with me?"

She transferred the bouquet to her left hand and gave him a

few hard thumps on the back as they went up the stairs. "So there!" she said happily, "It's so good to be back home."

"To strike me?" Ned grinned. "The truth of the matter is you've offended me so thoroughly for years, that I've got accustomed to it like an old dray horse taking his daily beating."

"Pshaw. You are so insulting." She put the bouquet down and then advanced on him, poking him and tickling his side as he took off his hat.

"What's this? Trying a flanking maneuver on me?" he grabbed her hands. "Stop tickling! Where is your dignity, woman?"

"Dear, dear, I must have left it back on the train," she said.

"About-face! Go and fetch it," Ned commanded.

"Hush, and go and fetch me a glass," she responded.

"A glass of what?" he said.

"For the flowers, you simpleton!" Kate laughed.

Chapter 13

"So, I guess I have you to thank for my increase in business," Joseph Creasey said, "Morton's clerk came by. And a man from the livery stable said you sent him."

"That dirty fellow?" Ned eyed the tobacco stains on the floor with distaste and continued: "I expect he's the one who kept missing your spittoon."

"Yes sir. But I'm obliged to you for sending them on here," Creasey said, "Until harvest Mr. Park don't have much work for me. I've been helping Billy Vickers at the freight depot in Vinton. Billy had some news for me that he heard from a fellow on the train. He says the Republicans are working hard to get state law changed so they can recruit a colored regiment. He says they'll pass it this fall."

"Yes. That's good news, I suppose. Do you still plan to enlist?" Ned asked.

"I do," Creasey replied.

Ned thought for a while, then said quietly: "It's an unfortunate but likely possibility that the monthly salary to the colored soldiers will be less than it is for the men I served with; perhaps as little as $10.00 a month. That's what happened with the 54th Massachusetts. Another example of short-sighted stupidity on the part of state government. I thought you ought to know."

Creasey let out a breath between his teeth in a slow hiss. After a moment he said: "I ain't surprised."

Ned went on: "If a man does the full work, then he has earned the full wage, in my opinion. I think it's shameful to treat any man who risks his neck to save the Union, just as you'd treat a beggar."

"That's right," Creasey said.

"There was an account in one of the Boston newspapers about the 54th Massachusetts' assault on Fort Wagner. The men showed extraordinary courage even though they were green troops. Perhaps you heard?" Ned asked.

"I heard they fought pretty hard, but that's all I heard," Creasey moved around to face Ned, putting his scissors into his apron pocket.

"The attack happened more than a fortnight ago, around the 19th of last month. You know about Fort Sumter, of course?" Creasey nodded.

Ned continued: "Well, Fort Wagner is down in South Carolina; and if our side could capture it, we could mount an assault on Sumter and have an advantageous position over Charleston harbor, which would lead, God willing, to the fall of Charleston itself. That was the objective. The generals had a plan, but it was a bad one, and they hadn't allowed time for their scouts to report on the lay of the land."

He held up his left hand palm-up as he continued: "You see, here's Charleston, where my second finger's curved in. The Union position was down here." He pointed to the side of his hand opposite his thumb. "There are a lot of long islands in the harbor. Fort Wagner's on a peninsula on an outer island facing the Atlantic Ocean." Ned tapped the middle joint of his pinky finger. "That's Fort Wagner. But just above it," he wiggled the tip of that finger, "was a large battery full of fixed guns and moveable artillery."

The barber said. "Mm, mm, that'd cause a ruckus."

Ned nodded. "It certainly did. The 54th led the attack force toward the fort up a narrow beach, as they had the ocean on one side and a big marsh on the other hemming them in." He traced a line up the side of his hand. "So they didn't have much room to form their firing lines. The rebs had set up obstructions in the path to the fort, you know, cut trees and brush all piled up in their way, and even a big ditch full of water."

Creasey shook his head worriedly.

"But the 54th advanced as ordered, taking heavy fire from the fortifications. Their lines broke a few times, but then re-formed and advanced. And once they stormed the fort they knew they couldn't go back. Colonel Shaw was shot and died there on the parapet. Some of his men raised the Stars and Stripes, but they were overrun by secesh. A sergeant in the regiment somehow managed to save the colors and take it to safety, even though he was shot. Some of our white regiments followed on the attack, but they were cut down." Ned faltered, thinking again of Fredericksburg. He stared at the tobacco stains on the floor, then closed his eye.

"But they fought like the dickens," Creasey put in.

Ned opened his eye and said: "Yes. Gallantly." He disliked the way that people overused the word, but in this circumstance, it was apt. "They proved they could do it and do it well. They put the lie to that notion that black men don't make good soldiers."

Creasey's mouth formed a smile, but his eyes remained somber. "Folks have no idear about the truth. Never have."

"Did you know any men in the 54th?" Ned asked.

"I guess I do! A fellow I went to school with, he went to Massachusetts and joined up," Creasey replied.

Ned stared at his shoe tips. Eventually he said: "Have you heard from him?"

"No sir." The barber moved back behind Ned and resumed his work.

After a time, Creasey remarked: "Billy tells me that they're aiming to finish the Providence & Fishkill Railroad spur line up here to Millville by the third week of August. They're a-building that depot mighty fast."

Ned said: "It couldn't be fast enough to suit me. I was marooned at Vinton Center on the Fourth of July after the last stagecoach for Millville left, and I had to travel shanks mare up High Street."

"Billy says the fellows backing the line are going to have a celebration when the first train comes in; gonna bring up lots of important folks from Hartford and show them around. I hear the Governor may even come by."

"I'm sure the Judge will attend," Ned said.

The barber came around the chair to face Ned again. "Say, I was thinking. You told me how you took some pictures of those balloons that went up in Hartford on the Fourth. Maybe you could take a picture of the depot when the train gets here. Then put it in your window so folks could see it."

"Huh. It's a capital idea, Mr. Creasey!" Ned was already figuring out how to photograph the scene. He'd borrow Alonzo Dunn's large camera, and perhaps cut him in on a portion of the sales profits. The finished picture could be displayed in the studio itself, with a card in the window telling people to see it there. Yes, get them up the stairs and into the gallery and then sell them something else.

The depot was less than half a mile from the business district where the gallery was located; Jack could run…Hell's bells, it wasn't likely that Jack Rossiter had ever run anything anywhere; and he was sure to balk at hustling a large glass plate or two through the busy streets: but Rossiter was the hire, not the boss. *I will have to make that distinction clear, again.*

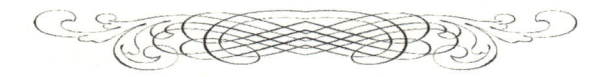

Maggie stared at Michael's back, willing herself to memorize the look of him. At least they had a picture of him, a good likeness; but that was nothing like having him here, nearby, mumbling to Aggie, and shifting from foot to foot as he did when he was ready to be moving on. Agnes was holding up well, but Mam was not. She had followed Michael to the train station with tragic sighs, and now seemed well on her way to an outburst. Maggie looked around her, glad that the other recruits were absorbed with goodbyes to their families. *How few there are here today,* she thought. How different from a year ago, when a hundred men had left from Vinton as the brass band played.

A baby began to screech nearby. An older man handed it off to its mother, but despite her efforts, the child continued to bray without pausing for breath. The man gave a hasty handshake to the blond recruit, then left with the woman and baby.

The recruit tore off his hat and slapped it against his leg, gesturing angrily after the older man.

"For God's sake!" she heard the young man shout; then another holler from the blond recruit, followed by a feminine cry, as a young woman in a fetching bonnet flung herself—not at the recruit—but at the young man with him. Maggie was a bit afraid the lady would crush the infant in her arms, so ardently did she embrace the recruit's companion. As the recruit glared at the woman, the other man disengaged himself from the lady's embrace, pushed her toward the recruit, then left them behind.

"Oh! It's Mr. Whitfield," Maggie said.

"Good day." Ned looked up. The Irishman he had photographed two weeks ago was now standing in his way. Ned scanned the crowd; seeing no sign of the judge, he slowed. "Good day," he said, tipping his hat to the three women accompanying Foran. One he had photographed recently: Foran's sweetheart. He had forgotten her name. Another was Maggie O'Shaughnessy, lacking her usual smile. The last was a wild-eyed older woman, bent over her own pain like one of Macbeth's witches over the cauldron.

Mrs. Whitfield had chosen to wear a veiled bonnet to the train station a year ago, when he left town to go to war. He had never seen her wear it before, or since.

"Well, Mr. Foran. You're assigned to the 14th, aren't you?" he said, "Look for Sergeant Flynn when you reach the regiment. Company D. He's a good fellow. He may remember me."

"I know him. I'll look for him," Foran replied.

"One of our own," the older woman said with approval.

"Do you have any advice for Michael, Mr. Whitfield?" Maggie asked.

He shrugged. "Obey orders. Always carry an extra shirt and socks. And keep your canteen full."

"Full of what?" Foran joked.

"Clean water, if you can find it," Ned replied seriously, "You won't find whiskey in camp. And if you find it elsewhere, and bring it into camp, you may end up in the guardhouse if it's discovered."

"What's this guardhouse? Like a jail?" Foran scoffed.

"Yes. Like a jail. With short rations and hard labor," Ned answered.

Foran blew out a breath, shaking his head, but did not question Ned's statement. After a moment, he said: "D'you hear that, Mam, what this fellow's saying?"

"Ye mind yerself, Michael," his mother said.

"Don't be wagging your head at me," Foran said, "That's something for you to hear, if you take my meaning."

"Whissht, Michael," Maggie said with alarm.

"Holy Mother of God," the old woman wailed, then covered her eyes with her hands.

"I can see the train," Foran's sweetheart said, taking his arm.

"Good luck to you," Ned said as he stepped back to leave, and trod upon a man's foot. The small crowd was edging nearer the platform's rim as the train approached.

"Mr. Whitfield, wait. Please," Maggie called. She left her mother's side. "Tell Eleanor... please, tell Eleanor..." She paused, her voice quavered. "I have a letter for her. I hope that's allowed, because... och, all those things in New York. I'll mail it today."

The train whistle blew. Ned waited, then said: "If you have it with you, I'll deliver it to her. It will save you the stamp." *There's the smile, at last,* he thought.

Maggie pulled a small, folded paper from her sleeve. "Thank you," she said earnestly. He put it in his jacket pocket just as he caught sight of the judge conversing with the recruiting officer a short way down the platform. "Pardon me." Ned elbowed past the obstructing gentleman and left.

Who was that woman that held onto him so tight? Maggie wondered, as she tried to comfort her mother. Perhaps Eleanor would know. If I ever get to see Eleanor again! She wished Michael had not been so harsh to Mam: it was not a proper way to take your leave (though his words were true enough.) Soon he would board the train and be out of their sight: and for how long? She wiped her eyes on her sleeve and struggled to her brother. Reaching around Agnes, she squeezed his hand.

"Michael! I'll miss you. Give Mam a kiss."

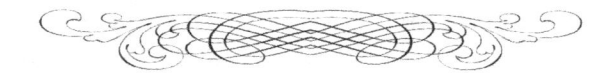

"Good day, Katie. This is a surprise. Jack, this is my sister, Miss Whitfield. Kate, this is Mr. Rossiter."

"This lovely lady is *your* sister?" Rossiter exclaimed. Kate's face took on a mulish look for an instant, then transformed into a set smile. "Yes, indeed, Mr. Rossiter. And he is a favorite of mine." Rossiter bowed slightly and maintained his "best customer" smile, which never reached his eyes.

Her voice became cloying: "I've come to bring him home for a good dinner. He looks thin." She gave Ned a sisterly pat on the ribs. He held her hand to prevent her from tickling him.

"My, my. There's nothing I like to see more than a devoted

sister. My poor dear sister..." Jack hesitated, "Aurelia has passed to her reward, I'm sorry to say."

"I'm sorry to hear that, Jack," Ned said.

"How unfortunate." Kate said, "Mr. Rossiter, I should like to steal my brother away from you for a short time. Would you mind very much watching the establishment? "

"Not at all, not at all."

"Thank you. I'm sure you are most capable."

Rossiter preened. "No doubt about it, Miss Whitfield." Kate took Ned's arm and turned her head to gaze at him devotedly. As she did so, she made an annoyed face, and mouthed the word now.

"It was a pleasure meeting you, Miss Whitfield," Rossiter said, "I hope you'll come back sometime soon, and we'll try to catch all that beauty in a picture, eh?"

"You're too kind. Good day," Kate simpered.

When they reached the sidewalk, she let loose: "Where did you ever find that lout? He doesn't even recognize a cut when it's being delivered. I could have filleted him like a trout and he'd just stand there smiling at me, thinking he was the finest fellow who ever put on trousers!"

Ned laughed. "I inherited him from Georgie. I told you, remember? He's the one I've been complaining about."

"Laws, you have been much too circumspect. And what a liar he is: did you see him trying to make up a name for his dear, departed sister?"

"Uh...yes," Ned replied, although he had, in truth, missed that lie. He looked up and down the street: "Where's your carriage? I thought you and Mother hired one for your calls this afternoon." Kate's expression darkened. "Over there. I told the driver to wait. I must talk to you about what's happened. I forgot you'd have that horrid man there in the gallery."

"No dinner? What has happened? What has Father done?"

"Pray don't stop and pepper me here in the street, keep walking. You'll wait until we've reached the park. My stays are laced so tightly I can't walk and talk at the same time. Don't walk so fast." Ned slowed down, then waited until Kate had ensconced herself on a bench in the shade of a tree in the park, until she had rested. She looked around to see if anyone was passing nearby, then took her handkerchief out of her sleeve.

"I had such an argument with Papa this morning after you

left. It was horrid."

"Why? As bad as the one when you went to Washington?"

"Yes! Oh! I hate it! I hate the things he says."

"Huh," Ned muttered, then went on: "What is this all about? Not Mama!" Kate shook her head. "Good," he said, "Speak. I'm all at sea here."

Kate looked up from her handkerchief. "It... it was...wait..." She composed herself somewhat. "It was, is, so important. That's how I could do it. I just marched in. It was all for Elly."

Ned blinked. "Is she all right?"

"Yes, well, I guess so. I met this Irish Maggie of El's, I thought I could point out to Elly how impossible this is. But then Maggie didn't seem at all bad to me, that first time. But I wasn't sure, so we had a secret picnic last Sunday, the three of us. I couldn't see any harm in her, and of course, it was clear then that Elly adores her, and that Maggie was fond of El. Elly has been just sick with dread that Papa would find out that she was still seeing this girl, and I felt dishonest keeping Elly's secret. You have to admit it is dishonest!" Kate said vehemently, as her brother shook his head.

"I'm studying law. Lawyers admit very little, not without a concession from the other party. Never mind. Go on."

"I don't like to be dishonest! I don't like to hide anything!"

"I know. What happened?" he asked again.

"I sent Mother and El out of the dining room after breakfast, and I, I told him what I'd done and how unfair it was to treat her so..." Kate gulped back a sob. "So truly unfair of him to prevent Elly from seeing a friend, especially as she has seemed so much better, or braver, I guess, lately. Dear heaven! He said such awful...!" She paused to wipe her eyes and blow her nose.

"Oh, the conspiracy his family has against him," Ned commented bitterly, "and how Mother has indulged us and ruined our characters and our futures. That old saw again!"

"Yes, but Ned, I do think it...if we, perhaps if we tried to show respect sometimes, so that Mother wouldn't have to inter..."

Ned broke in, "Respect! We have the right to challenge his pronouncements and appeal his judgments!"

"Stop legalizing," she commanded. At that, he was quelled. He did, on extremely rare occasions, feel sorry for his father; but he was also convinced that the judge (despite his churchgoing) had never practiced the Golden Rule.

"Go on," he said.

"If you'd, either of you, ever give an inch, you'd make it far easier on the rest of us!"

"I give lots of inches!" Ned shot back angrily, then smiled a little at how odd his response sounded. Kate smiled half-heartedly. "Well, Father did too, this time. So there. He will permit Eleanor to continue seeing Maggie."

"I can't believe it. That's first-rate! How did you manage that?"

"Unfortunately, he didn't accept any of my pretty arguments, about how Maggie was brought up with Quakers, and so on, so...I..." she stopped. Ned waited.

"I had to! I had no choice. I told him if he took this away from Eleanor he'd break her...finally break her..." Kate's voice gave out and her last phrase was nearly unintelligible: "and it would be on his head."

Ned paced in front of her as she wept. He stroked his beard and readjusted his eye-patch, remembering Eleanor's account of her nightmare. "Well, it's true," he said.

Kate took some time to respond. "I know. But I didn't want to...have to...say it..."

"No. He'll always make you say it, though."

"Why?" Kate burst out. It was a question she knew had no answer; a question Ned had always asked. Now he stopped his pacing and sat down on the bench next to her, internally proposing, then rejecting, dozens of responses, until he tired of it. He said finally, "At least he agreed with you, after all."

Kate grimaced. The tears had passed. "We compromised."

"Ah ha."

She went on: "First he said Eleanor had his permission to visit Maggie at Homer Merritt's. I know what you're going to say, hush. But," this she added loudly to stave off her brother's next protest, "But I said that he must do better, so, in the end, he agreed that they could visit outdoors in our orchard, out of sight of the road or the house."

"Well. Good. Elly must be glad. And he need not worry about any taint of socializing with a hired girl. But in a few more months she will literally be out in the cold. Let's see how long her visits last then," Ned remarked.

"And I asked his permission to have them write to each other and he gave it," Kate said.

"How gracious," Ned mumbled. She continued: "I think you'll be surprised. Elly has a backbone, everyone forgets that. You must remember how long she'd wait and how patiently she'd wheedle for us to play with her - hours sometimes - until we always broke down and did what she wanted."

"I held out longer than you did," Ned grumped.

"That's a lie, you were the first to give in," Kate sniffed cheerfully, then said: "I just hope Maggie is up to it–it's rather a long walk from Merritt's. She did not look particularly well-fed. But then, she is a working girl." Ned recalled how resolutely the O'Shaughnessy girl had stumbled down the long path from Knott's Hill with him, without a complaint.

He said: "Let's hope so, for Eleanor's sake. Or that Maggie isn't so insulted by this treatment that she'll stay away."

"Good heaven, how silly. You sound as if she is a Topliff. She hasn't any pride," Kate remarked, "Not that sort of pride, I expect. Besides, if she had even thought to take offense, I mended that on Sunday, I'm sure. She drew a picture of me, it's rather flattering."

"I believe you deserve a reward for your valorous conduct. I saw a placard in the Union Hotel advertising ice cream," he said, "I'll treat you." He held out his hand to help her to her feet. "Ice cream before dinner? We're not greedy children anymore," she countered.

"They advertised chocolate ice cream," he said.

"Oh. Oh, dear. I adore chocolate. I ought not to…no, let's go!" she said.

Chapter 14

"President Lincoln has set tomorrow as a day of prayer and remembrance of our gallant soldiers. The shops and mills will be closed," the judge announced, "Reverend Story will be conducting a service. We will all attend to honor Will's memory."

Will and Kate had announced their engagement to the joyous reaction of Whitfields and Warrens alike on New Years Day 1861. Three months later the war began, and Will enlisted. In November of that year, while on cavalry patrol in Virginia, he was killed by a sharpshooter. An undertaker near the camp embalmed Will's body, at his family's expense, and the Warrens had the body shipped north. A grieving stone angel stood upon his grave in a well-groomed cemetery in Hartford.

Eleanor was crying. Still recovering from a full twelve hours of fierce neuralgia during which he had wished himself dead, Ned for once did not scorn her for weeping. He wondered whether she cried for Will or because she could not attend the service.

Hot. The weather was too hot. He could hear the sawing sound of cicadas in the night air. When he was a boy, he had once found clinging to the same tree the perfect but empty forms, shed in their summer molting, of four cicadas. He had collected them in a box, scared his sister with them, been scolded. He had dissected one with great interest, then crunched them underfoot, stomping them in a dance of destruction. Dust thou art, and unto dust thou shall return.

"Th...there's no gravestone for Rob," he muttered. The catch in his throat and the push of tears in his eyes and nose came too fast for him to halt. Will had been an acclaimed favorite of the judge, and true friend to the rest of the family—but Rob McKay was Ned's alone. While Will would cluck his tongue and urge Ned to endorse a gentler view of mankind, and Henry would sneer and urge a harsher one—Robbie would simply laugh and shake his head and let Ned follow a thought wherever it led.

Tall and strong, but plain and painfully awkward, McKay had barely said a dozen words to Ned's family during the ten years they were friends. He was a coffin maker in his father's undertaking establishment, and Ned's refusal to visit that workshop was a standing joke between them. Yet just before they reported to training camp, Ned developed a morbid interest in the casket business, and visited his friend at the shop. Rob fingered a board, planed and sanded until it was a smooth as a baby's cheek, and said: "Promise me that if the rebs get me you'll stow me in the best box we sell." He had ended up in a rough rapidly made pine box, under the sucking Virginia mud.

Ned's mind skittered away from the recollection. He stood up and went to the sitting room mantel, rearranging all of the familiar things placed there: lamp, match holder, Kate's seminary medal, his framed poem about shaving. He did not touch the mantel clock, but moved the china shepherd next to the shepherdess, so close that they could have kissed. *It's too hot in here.* He went to the nearest window and yanked it. It did not move.

"You won't get that one open. It's stuck fast," the judge said. Ned was furious at his ineffectuality. He braced himself and wrenched at the window. With a groan it split from its seam with the sill and opened an inch or two. He rubbed his wrist, then put his fingers out into the tepid trickle of air.

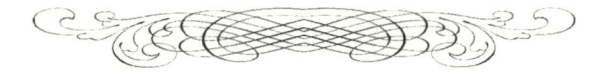

As the final hymn ended at the Second Congregational Church, Ned decided that he had weathered the service well. He had been polite to the interested, the exclaimers, the murmurers, to those who stared. He had not slumbered during the minister's address, nor had he choked up or scowled. He felt that he deserved a rapid and easy escape now that the service had come to a close: but he supposed it wouldn't do to hurry his mother. He nodded to two young ladies who he recognized as grammar school classmates. They were among the few young people at the service. *Wait,* Ned thought, *is that*

Emma whatshername…who told me I was sweet when we were ten?

"Reverend!" the judge boomed. "Good day, sir. An excellent sermon, one of your best! And very affecting…very powerful."

Reverend Story shook the judge's hand, greeted Mrs. Whitfield, then turned the full force of his august personality upon Ned. "Edward. Praise God. It is a blessing to see you with your health restored. The last time we met I prayed for such an outcome as this."

"Good day, sir. Thank you." Ned dulled his mind to the resulting flood of the Reverend's words: aware, as Story undoubtedly was, that the entire congregation could hear this encore sermon. In a low voice, he agreed with the Reverend, that yes, he was fortunate to survive, and yes, blessed was a better word, and yes, he was grateful to God for such a deliverance. When Story said that survival meant that Ned was marked by God for a mission and yea, perhaps as a sign, Ned shrugged, suspicious of the direction the oration was taking.

Story then went on to the parable of Zaccheus from the gospel of Luke. "Among that large crowd that followed Him, it was to the man who sat afar watching from the tree, that Christ reached out and spake. Jesus, our Savior, graced that sinful man's home with His presence, when our Lord and King would have been welcomed in the finest houses of the land. He spake then to Zaccheus, as He speaks to you now, Edward."

That's enough! Ned thought, *just pretend I'm a Pharisee, and go away.* Story went on in the same vein for a minute or two, undoubtedly adding a wrinkle or two to his concerned frown. Ned was staring at the pulpit.

"For many men, the ordeals of war are the trying-forge in which the gold is purified. I hope, I expect, that there has been a transformation of sorts in you, Edward."

You expect? My ass! Ned thought, then said aloud: "With all due respect, sir, no man can experience war and not be transformed. But such a change is, I think, a matter between me and God."

"Yes, indeed, Edward, between you and our Savior. As it should be. But I do hope to see you at services here more frequently, for no man should enter the field of battle without faithful comrades at his side, and properly equipped and armed, don't you agree? This field of battle is for your immortal soul, and we are your comrades, and you will be armed with the word of the Lord."

"Um-hm," Ned muttered, thinking: *Go and peddle that soft-soap to somebody else.*

As the Reverend left, with parting words of comfort to Ned's parents and a parting admonition to him, Ned brushed past his parents, and headed for the church door. He made it to the front steps, before he saw Mrs. Reynolds advancing on him. She was too close to side step. She stopped in his path, stared.

"Good day, Mrs. Reynolds," Ned said, "Have you had any word from Norman?"

"Yes, Edward, good news. He came through the battle at Gettysburg with just a slight wound, thank the good Lord, and he is out of the hospital now and back to his regiment. We've just had a letter from him. I hope... you are keeping well yourself?"

"Yes, thank you." He remembered Norman Reynolds' ghostly white face, from which issued an hysterical tittering right after the shell had blown up behind them. Blown to bits! Reynolds had gasped, punching Ned's arm, It coulda bin us!

"I saved his bacon at Antietam," Ned said, "Did he tell you? I went back in the ranks as we marched to battle, because he and Druckman and Simmons were dawdling in our rear, and I hauled them forward, told them to catch up to our company double-quick. And not three minutes later, a shell exploded in our line of march—precisely where we had been—and killed four men in Company F."

"He wrote to us about it," Mrs. Reynolds said wanly.

"He's a good soldier," Ned went on. "I'm glad to hear he's well." Mrs. Reynolds greeted his parents, then moved on.

Mrs. Whitfield seized his arm. "You never wrote to us about that..." she said. Her face was gray.

"I didn't want to worry you," he answered.

Mr. Morton tipped his hat to them, then began to talk about the victories at Gettysburg and Vicksburg. "The Fourteenth will come home wrapped in glory!" he said.

What's left of it, Ned thought. "We've...They've got some experience under their belts now," he said. "Now it's a veteran corps. We were so green at Antietam that we marched upright into the fields, just as we'd been drilled to do, and men were getting picked off right and left, with hardly a chance to fire—until a veteran officer ordered us to get down." He smiled a little, recalling that Captain Merrill said he could hear Whitfield above all the ruckus, shouting to a private: "Get down! Down, you stupid son of a bitch. That's an order!"

Morton was watching him uncomfortably. Judge Whitfield wore the same expression. *I've said too much,* Ned thought.

Morton said: "Is that where you got wounded?"

"No. At Fredericksburg."

Morton grimaced. "Oh, I heard about that."

Andrew McKay, Junior, chugged toward them. Unlike his brother Rob, he was renowned for his volubility and quick temper. "Ned Whitfield," McKay said.

"Well...uh...good day, Mr. Whitfield. Mrs. Whitfield. Judge," Morton said, and hastened away. McKay moved in close to Ned, took a good look, then backed away and tipped his hat to Mrs. Whitfield, who still had not released her grip on her son's arm.

"Good day, Andrew," Ned said, before guilt spoke up for him, rather than his own customary good sense. "I meant to come and see your mother and father after I got back. I swear I did! But I was sick for a while..."

"Not so sick that you couldn't go into business. I hear you're running Dunn's photograph rooms," McKay said.

"Yes, I've recovered. I wrote to them. But I ought to have...I wanted to come by to tell them...how sorry I am about Rob, you must know that! And what happened..."

McKay apparently saw something in Ned's expression that was more compelling than the stumbling words. He said: "I suppose I oughn't to blame you, but you recruited him. He wouldn't have gone otherwise. He said you were his friend, and he was bound to follow you."

"I know..." Ned muttered.

"I blame the government," McKay said bitterly, "The conditions he wrote us about! No tents in the freezing rain, stolen knapsacks, stolen money, no supplies, bad food and worse water, not fit for pigs to drink!"

The judge raised his hands. "Mr. McKay, hold your temper. You can be very proud of Rob, he did his duty."

"I am proud of him, by heaven! I am..." McKay said, his voice breaking on the last word. His wife murmured something. He found his voice again rapidly. "I'm proud of him but confounded sick of this bungling army with its tinhorn generals who couldn't fight their way out of a paper sack, and a government, a so-called government, which allows its own men to be treated worse than dogs, and no apologist," he flung the term at the judge, "like you, can convince me otherwise!" He tugged at his wife's arm. "Come along, Rachel."

As the judge fulminated about the man's impertinence, Reverend Story greeted Rob's parents and gestured in Ned's direction. Then it was worse than he could have imagined, for Mrs. McKay fell weeping into his mother's arms at the sight of him, and Ned was unable to speak. He stood like a dullard, gazing at the ground. When they told him that they had found Rob's burial site in Virginia, just as Ned had described it, and brought his body home, and had just purchased a stone for Rob's grave, and asked him if he would like to see it at the stone cutter's, he croaked: "No."

"Of course, we would," Mrs. Whitfield said. Following the McKays' equipage, the Whitfields made a silent journey in their carriage.

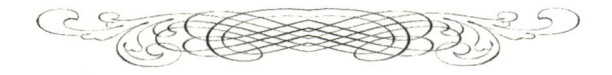

The stone was elegantly formed, clean white. Ned stared at the dates carved on the stone, 1842-1862. That was his own birth year. "Billington did a fine job," Mrs. McKay said.

Ned removed the glove from his right hand and touched the stone. It was pleasantly cool on this humid day, and smooth. He stroked it with his fingertips. *Did you get put in the best box, Rob?* Ned said silently to his friend. He startled: Mrs. McKay was speaking to him.

"I beg your pardon. I didn't hear you," he said.

"Do you think Robbie would have liked it?" She waited for his response anxiously, as if only his good opinion would validate this purchase and her sacrifice.

"Liked it?" Ned's eyes and nose betrayed him. He pulled out his handkerchief and cleared his throat.

"I know that you miss him," Mrs. McKay's croon of sympathy undid him. He covered his face with his hands. *Robbie, where are you?* Ned thought, *you ought to be <u>here</u> telling your mother how you like this gift, or telling her how you'd rather have a fast new horse...You never got your fast horse.*

"He was such a quiet boy," Mrs. McKay said. Ned nodded, and blew his nose then turned to glare in his father's direction.

Making me stew in pious sentiment and other people's misery, he thought, *this is why he dragged me to church.*

He said: "Rob would...It's a beauty. But pardon me, Mrs. McKay. Um. I think my parents are about to take their leave."

"Let me say goodbye to them," she said, "I hope you will not be a stranger, Edward. You are always welcome to come and see us."

"Um. Thank you. Very kind." His parents and Rob's father were discussing some matter with serious expressions. *Another grave conversation,* Ned thought, and almost snickered aloud. He was a little afraid he was losing his mind. He said to them: "Perhaps we should be on our way."

Mrs. Whitfield blinked at him, and the Judge scowled at this blunt comment.

Ned added: "I, uh, thank you for showing me Rob's...It's a mighty fine stone, and I know Rob would be, would have been...um, ah, pleased." This last word came out sounding like a question. The lugubrious McKay bowed slightly and thanked them all for coming.

The judge's glower began as the Whitfields got into their carriage. He held back his comments until they were out of earshot, then he let fly. "I have never seen such poor behavior, Edward. You had no reason to be rude to the McKays simply because you can't be still for more than five minutes."

"At least I'm here to provide you with fertile ground for reform, and not dead in Virginia," Ned retorted.

"That...that's..." the judge began, then finished "...outrageous. And not the point." Ned peeled off his dress gloves, creating a backward and inside-out pair. He shook them out, studied them for a moment, then popped the fingers in and wiped his hands on his handkerchief.

The judge tried again: "I do believe you are the oddest duck ever hatched. I hope you're not taking after those Seeley cousins who went off to join the Shakers. "

"Quack," Ned replied, and smiled a little at his mother's frightened giggle.

"That is an impertinent answer. Deliberately impertinent. When will you leave off these childish tricks?"

"It was meant as a 'gentle answer which turneth away wrath'," Ned said.

"Nothing you ever say is meant as a gentle answer. You

mean to provoke my wrath, you delight in it. You enjoy distressing people and provoking me."

"No, Father, I didn't..."

"Then what possessed you to frighten Mrs. Reynolds with your stories and to tell Morton that you went through a battle groveling on your belly like a whipped dog!"

"I didn't say that!" Ned asserted.

"Pah!" the judge spat out.

"Groveling? Our company would not have had more than a dozen survive Antietam if we hadn't got out of that crossfire. We were ordered to lay down and stay down and we followed orders. My God, not every battle is like the Charge of the Light Brigade! Would you have me lie about what happened?"

The judge was not deterred. "There was no reason, except your own wrong-headed amusement, to describe it so cravenly. When you came home disabled, the Colonel wrote us that you followed orders bravely and did your duty as an officer. Surely you have other, better stories to relate?"

"You've heard the ones about our skirmishes," Ned said.

His father said: "I cannot believe that your behavior at Antietam was shameful. But it's shameful for you to tell such stories."

"Shameful," Ned repeated, trying to ignore the high-pitched sound in his ears, like screaming heard from a distance, "You don't understand."

"Then tell us. You've never said a word to us about the battles. Your letters criticized the general's strategy and complained about the problems of command: but we heard more from you about the cost of your rations and the opinions of your messmates than any descriptions of battle. Tell us—do not subject our neighbors to your ridiculous opinions."

Perhaps such stories, true or not, are better kept to oneself, Ned thought. But how could he concede the point without conceding the debate? "I did my duty," he said.

"Of course you did. No son of mine would do anything less. But now that you can speak, you refuse to. I insist you tell us what went on. If your behavior was dutiful, then you have no reason to hesitate to tell us about it."

Clear in Ned's memory was the conformation of the town of Fredericksburg and the position of the high ground the rebels held.

"Sir, they cannot expect us to take that ground!" he had protested to Captain Merrill.

"Madness," Merrill had muttered in response, "Madness."

"If you had seen," Ned began. *Eye hath not seen, ear hath not heard,* he thought. His right leg began to jitter. The whispery shriek in his ears persisted. He wondered if his parents had ever received the farewell note he had written to them in Fredericksburg, that last night before the battle, when he was sure he was going to die.

What was it like to be dead? Peaceful, they said. The peace that passeth all understanding. But was there any freedom to act? Or did a man let his will and freedom float away as an unwanted burden? He believed it made more sense to allow the dead to be useful in heaven, not have them drift like sailboats on a windless day. He wondered if he would have seen Will Warren, or his own brother Dan, or Rob. Or ended up in Gehenna. He hoped that God would not deny a man (a good man?) entry simply because he sometimes drank, or was not pious. Someone was speaking to him.

"Present, sir," he said automatically.

"Present? I doubt it. I'll wager you haven't heard a single thing I just said," the judge growled.

The panic came unexpectedly, pouring through Ned's body like a swarm of bees erupting from a destroyed hive. His heart jumped and he gasped for breath.

"What's wrong, darling? Are you ill?" Mrs. Whitfield said.

"It's the neuralgia," the judge said.

"Stop the carriage," Mrs. Whitfield said. The judge did so. Ned clambered out, nearly falling. Arms crossed over his chest, he strove to even his breathing.

"Is it neuralgia?" Mrs. Whitfield asked worriedly. He shook his head. It was a return of battle nerves, in the wrong time and place. He took an experimental step. The feel of the road under his feet reassured him slightly. He straightened up, forced his arms to hang down at his sides. Marching had carried him forward then, and must do so now. "I have to walk," he told his parents.

"What is wrong with you? " the judge asked, "What if you have an attack on the road?"

"I'll walk home. It's better."

"What is better? What?" the judge said.

"We'll see you at home, dear," Mrs. Whitfield interrupted.

He set off slowly. Paying no attention to the argument in the carriage, he concentrated on his steps, measuring the ebbing of fear from his body. He was glad to taste the dust the carriage raised when it rattled past him.

Chapter 15

"Good day, Mrs. Moore, I hope I'm not too late with these socks. Have you packed all the things you're sending?" Maggie asked, trying to catch her breath. "Oh, good day, Mrs. Whitfield. It's five pair, I wish I had more for you. I'd started another but only had time to finish the one. I brought it too. I thought you might send it to the hospital for a poor fellow who's lost his leg."

"We will. There are too many boys who now need just one, I'm afraid." Mrs. Moore replied.

"Good day, Maggie," Mrs. Whitfield said, "It was good of Mrs. Wilkin and Mr. Merritt to give you time to bring those over. I hope they are well."

Maggie had slipped out of the kitchen while her employers napped. *They'll find my note,* she thought, *and surely they won't mind, since it's for charity?* "Mr. Merritt's digestion is troubling him a bit," she said.

"What a shame. Perhaps it's just a summer complaint," Mrs. Whitfield said. *'Tisn't likely,* Maggie thought. He'd been up half the night.

"I hope he'll feel a bit better tomorrow," she said, "I'll stay for a while, if you need help packing." She did not fancy walking back home from the church until the perspiration soaking her had dried.

"Come along," Mrs. Moore said. Maggie enjoyed working alongside the two women, despite the heat in the room. Mrs. Eller spent most of her time directing orders at the two laborers loading the packed crates and barrels: Even her sharp voice was flattened under the weight of the damp, oppressive air. When Maggie finally heard thunder in the distance, she almost cheered. She went to the window. If she could just breathe in a little moving air.

One of the men outside began to sing "John Brown's Body" in a reedy tenor. The other man joined in, but changed the words on the refrain: "Loading one-ton barrels with no pulley and no crane, Loading one-ton barrels 'till our backs are all a-pained, Loading one-ton barrels—in the heat and in the rain..." The voice stopped for a moment, while both men laughed. "How are you going to end?" the tenor asked. The other man sang in reply: "Lady Moore goes marching on."

Maggie giggled, glancing quickly around to see if Mrs. Moore had heard them. She was across the room, but Mrs. Whitfield, who was nearby, smiled. She joined Maggie at the window and called outside: "We heard that! Don't laugh at him, 'Lijah, or he'll start on the verses."

"Yes, ma'am," the tenor voice replied

"Get that canvas up, you two," Mrs. Eller said from outdoors. "That rain won't hold off just because you aren't ready for it."

The promised thunderstorm did not arrive, just a steady rain. Maggie would have liked to drench herself in it. She finished inventorying the last container. Mrs. Moore perused the list. "Well done," she said, "I'll have the boys seal this up, and then it will be time for a rest and some iced tea. Can you stay? Or must you return to Merritts'?"

"I'll have a drink, but then I'll be needing to go back, for the walk takes near three-quarters of an hour."

"Heavens, that's right. Have you an umbrella? No? You can't walk in this rain; it doesn't look as if it will let up soon. Well, have Mrs. Eller give you some tea." Mrs. Moore set off on another task. Maggie rapidly downed her tea, watched by Mrs. Eller, until Mrs. Moore, Mrs. Whitfield, and the Reverend's wife arrived.

"Ned will take you home in my chaise, Maggie, whenever you wish to go," Mrs. Moore said.

"I don't want to put him to any trouble," Maggie responded.

"It's no trouble," Mrs. Whitfield said.

When Maggie saw Edward Whitfield she guessed he might have disagreed with his mother. He tipped his hat to her then tumbled wearily out of the driver's seat to help her up into the chaise. The dark perspiration stains on his worn vest and shirt, and the onion-y tang of sweat on his skin confirmed that he was the other laborer who had loaded soldier's aid containers that day.

"Good day," she said, "It's good of you to drive me home."

"Good day." He supported her as she missed the iron step and clumsily plopped onto the chaise seat. He clucked his tongue to the horse, who plodded forward, evidently as dispirited by the rain as the human passengers. She wondered what time it was. What if Mr. Merritt had taken a turn for the worse? Is there anything for supper that would settle his stomach?

Ned kept his eye on the road, hoping he would not be required to make conversation. He knew that this girl liked to chat; there were times he liked that too, but not today. His passenger was silent.

After a while he glanced over at her to see if she had fallen asleep. The skirt of her dress and her petticoats had caught on a loosened tack on the underside of the seat, revealing her left leg. He took in the sight: the slender ankle above the disreputable brogans, the swell of the shapely calf, clad in a darned stocking whose surface was speckled with mud. The tantalizing track of speckles led his eye to the curve behind her knee, but there the sight ended. The brogans were stained with rain and mud. He guessed that her feet were as damp as his; then imagined removing the brogans and peeling off the wet stockings, then moving his hands up those legs.

"Oh mercy!" Maggie said as she saw how high her skirt and petticoats had caught on her left side. She wrenched the layers of cloth from the offending tack and smoothed the fabric down tight to her ankle. "You ought to have told me!"

"What?" he said, "I was just looking at the scenery."

"The scenery," she said, and giggled nervously. It was such a poor excuse. He had indeed been staring at her leg, she'd swear to it.

"Yes," he said in such an earnest tone that she giggled again. Sometimes it was difficult to tell when this gentleman was joking. She decided not to risk a further comment. After five minutes of silence, he said: "The scenery. I think I may have spied there a pretty little calf which escaped its mistress and ventured out on its own."

Maggie was delighted. "Ha!"

He favored her with a dry half-smile, although he still looked straight ahead.

"It escaped because she was so tired, she wasn't paying attention to it. That's why. And you won't see another such today," Maggie said in a light tone. There was another silence. She waited.

"That's a pity," he said.

"Whissht," she said happily, just as she would have to Rory Corcoran.

He looked at her, raised an eyebrow. "What is that noise? Do we have a leaky valve around here somewhere?"

Maggie laughed. "Faith, no! I said hush."

"Thank you for the translation."

"You're welcome."

Those who said Yankees never bantered like the Irish didn't know this fellow well. While his style was different, the underlying pleasure in the game was the same as Corcoran's. Today Mr. Whitfield looked just like many of the men she knew; for he was dressed like a working man in a soft-collared, faded gingham shirt, a worn straw hat, and down-at-heel boots. He could as well be Irish. She thought it was too bad that he wasn't one of their own. It would be fine to have such a pleasant young fellow, squiring her home. And admiring the scenery.

So what if he's not so tall and thick in the shoulders as Mr. Corcoran, she thought. She slid easily into the fantasy: the man driving her home worked at the mill, had a good job, and he liked her well. He intended to make enough money to go West, and he'd eagerly take her with him, for hadn't he as much as said he'd not stir a step without her. Yet he was in no hurry to marry, and that was fine with her. When he laughed at her, it was because she meant him to, and they laughed together.

"I liked your song," she said.

"I beg your pardon?" The polite words delivered in the flat Yankee accent drove a splinter into the skin of her dream. "The song you sang about a-loading one ton barrels in the rain, to the tune of *John Brown's Body*," she said.

"Oh. That." He was pleased. Men were not all that different, on the inside.

"How can you be singing while you're working? Don't you get out of breath?" Maggie asked.

He replied: "No, in fact, sometimes singing helps to regulate one's breathing during strenuous activity. We sometimes started the troops singing while we were marching. It kept us in rhythm and passed the time."

"You sound as if you miss it, a bit," she said after a moment.

He stared at her in surprise: "Miss it? Why on earth would I miss being a rebel target?"

"I didn't mean that, to be sure. I'm not so silly as I seem. I meant your friends, missing being with them," she explained, sure that she had heard some longing in his voice in the way he said 'we'.

"Guess I do miss that," he said. He sat up straight, turned his face from her, and said: "But collegiality–friendship of comrades, that is–hardly balances the privations of camp life and the... possibility of losing such friends."

"Yes," Maggie said somberly, belatedly remembering his friend Will. "I'm sorry I reminded you. I oughtn't to have said it."

Ned tightened the reins and guided the horse around a particularly rutted area of the road. He refused to think about Rob. He supposed he ought to say something polite in response to her apology.

"Such are the perils of war," he remarked. *Bother, that was trite,* he thought. It was a good thing that she was not like Hattie Caldwell, always ready to examine every word and top him in conversation. This girl looked at him as if he was the wisest man on earth. He liked the way that a strand of her dark hair slipped sometimes from the hairpins: Hattie's had never escaped, and Betsy's had fallen in smothering masses upon his face. Although Miss O'Shaughnessy's nose was a little too sharp for perfect beauty, and her hands were work-reddened, he still thought she was a fine-looking girl: in fact, far better in appearance than most females sharing her low station in life. And she had marvelous legs.

"God bless the brave soldiers," she said.

Appeased by her evident sincerity, he smiled at her. "Well said."

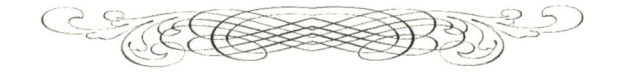

"Whatever aspersions I cast upon your little country town, Whitfield," Henry Barton said, "I now retract. Your hotel serves a top-notch dinner. It's a pity you missed it, dashing about like an

Adams Express team. What on earth were you doing?"

"I was running plates after I took pictures of the train. When I expose the negatives, didn't I explain this before? I must have. The glass is coated with a chemical which has to remain damp while I take the picture, then I have to develop the latent image in the dark room back at the gallery while the coating is still wet."

Henry covered a yawn. "Good Lord. That's too ambitious a project for such a warm day. Why didn't you send out your splendid assistant for the gallop?"

"I preferred to do it myself," Ned replied, "to ensure it was done properly."

Henry shook his head. "I had hoped you would tell me you've already discharged him."

"Not yet."

"Perhaps he's well-connected here; after all, such charming manners, and so well turned out!" Barton said, laughing a little.

Ned snickered. "George hired him."

"Ah, that explains it. The credulous Mr. Dunn."

"The bibulous Mr. Dunn," Ned put in.

"Please don't remind me. I regret his visit to Mrs. Campbell's."

"That will teach you to heed my advice," Ned joked.

Henry frowned.

Ned added: "Did he cause some trouble there? with one of the girls?"

"No, he just puked up all the good liquor I'd served him. Tch, such a waste," Henry said.

"So he didn't rise to the challenge after all?" Ned said sarcastically.

Henry looked at him with appreciation. "No, he was too...ha! once he had unloaded my whiskey outside Mrs. Campbell's back door, then Dunn was done."

"Done brown," Ned said, "Done in."

Barton responded: "Now I understand why you brought him along on the Fourth: you owed him some debt of friendship and he dunned you for payment. You laugh, sir. He is now persona non grata at Mrs. Campbell's, so I trust you won't invite him on future outings."

Ned said: "Actually, he sought my acquaintance when we

first met."

"You've just risen in my estimation," Henry said dryly.

"He tried to thrash me, but I outran him and climbed a tree. I threw an apple at him. I guess he decided I was more useful than I looked, so he scraped an acquaintance. The debt of friendship was that he once saved me from extermination by Sid Nason, the terror of the schoolyard," Ned said.

As a drift of girlish conversation came toward the two men, Barton gestured. "Say, Whitfield, who are those delicious young ladies standing by Mr. Topliff and Mr. Kellogg?"

"Those are the Misses Topliff. Their mama is no doubt within spitting distance and aggressively marriage-minded on their behalf, I warn you."

"No matter. Would you introduce me?"

"If you like. But I thought you said you didn't intend to marry until you're thirty?" Ned commented.

"I don't," Henry answered, "You can put good money on that wager. But they look as if they are worth a sporting chance. I understand a scenic carriage tour is next on the day's agenda. Seeing the lake, or some such thing. Why don't you join us?"

"I'll come along to keep you company," Ned said, covering a yawn. "You won't get much intelligent conversation out of the Topliffs. Perhaps you'd like to come to my house for supper later and meet my mother and sister, and the judge."

"Ah, the judge. I forgot to mention that I met him at dinner today. He had his eye on me as soon as he saw the company I was keeping, and had himself introduced," Henry said as they walked toward the Topliff sisters. "I begin to comprehend your desire to subject yourself to boarding house life. But I should like to make the acquaintance of your estimable mother."

Chapter 16

As Maggie neared the Whitfield place, she removed her sunbonnet and put on her hat, and waited by the oak tree for Eleanor. After several minutes, she left the tree and peeked into the yard. There was no sign of Eleanor or Dance, but Edward Whitfield was hunched by the rabbit's hutch. As she watched he dove quickly beneath it, then backed out with something brown in his arms.

"Good day," Maggie called as she hastened over to him. "Has he got out? Did you catch him?"

"I've got the rascal." Whitfield dropped the rabbit back into its hutch and latched the door, giving it an extra shake. "El rigged up some wire contraption," he gestured to a makeshift wire enclosure nearby on the grass, "so that he could graze. But she didn't sink it deep enough into the ground."

"He dug his way out," Maggie observed.

"Yes, she forgot the peculiar talents of cuniculus," he said.

"What's that?" she asked.

"Cuniculus is the Latin name for rabbit. Genus: rodens. In other words, a burrowing rodent."

"Burrowing, to be sure," she said, "Do you know the Latin for everything, then? Did you learn that at the high school?"

"For the most part, yes. And I studied biological classifications in college, 'though I've forgotten some since then." He bent to examine the wire of the enclosure.

College, of all things! Maggie told herself. She said: "I graduated from the Brick School here in town and I've read all Mr. Merritt's books from his shop that failed. He has a book on birds, with fine illustrations, and one on botany, but he hasn't many scientific books at all, save Isaac Newton. I've read that."

"You've read Newton? Which one of his works?" Whitfield asked.

Oh no, Maggie thought, *now I'm in for it.* She replied: "Well. I tried to read Optics."

"That's an excellent book," he said.

Maggie shrugged. "So they say."

He went on with enthusiasm. "I read it when I was a boy at the academy, and we repeated some of his diffraction and dispersion experiments with prisms. Especially the one proving that white light is comprised of the seven spectral hues."

"Oh." Maggie warmed slightly to the author, if not his writing. "He surely was a great thinker. But I found it hard going, reading Newton. I'm wondering why he didn't just say what he found out and leave it at that."

"But that wasn't his sole intention," Mr. Whitfield replied, "In describing the basis for his experiments as well as demonstrating their results he intended to make them replicable. He doesn't just state his conclusions; he shows how he arrived at those conclusions." Maggie was anxious to prevent him from clucking his tongue at her and commenting that the work was nothing a woman would understand.

She said: "I'll go back and read it again. And now I'm looking at it from a different side, from what you've told me, 'twill seem different to me. If I had a prism, I'd try it myself, I guess."

"Yes, that would illustrate some of his observations clearly. You have no prism anywhere at home? They're common enough, on candelabra," he said.

"Not so common at Mr. Merritt's."

"Of course, pardon me. Perhaps you wouldn't find one in a Quaker home."

Maggie said: "But I'm thinking that you can learn science from a story too, a good story. Like Melville's stories about the South Seas. I learned ever so much and 'twasn't hard going at all."

Whitfield nodded. "Melville is first-rate. He's one of my favorites."

"Mine too," she said with a smile.

"Even so," he went on, "one can't compare Melville to Newton on that basis. However much we may admire his addition of natural history and description to his stories, Melville never set out to write a scientific treatise or propose methods to discover explanations for natural phenomena."

"They're bent to different tasks, d'you mean?"

"Precisely. And each is worthy in his own way."

"That's so!" Maggie said. Pleased with his summation, she did not stifle the questions that bubbled in her. "D'you think that science will find a reason for everything?"

"As to natural phenomena, yes. Have you read Francis Bacon? No? No matter. Bacon said that if men collected a large enough body of observations of any phenomenon, that body of facts would lead to theories accounting for the cause of the phenomenon. So, I believe that there are discoverable explanations for most things, well, natural phenomena in any case," he responded.

"And God meant us to find them out," Maggie said, inspired, "For other things, though, for…for human nature, surely not…"

He scratched at his beard. "Ah, there you have the philosophers' realm. Or the poet's. And since today is the Sabbath, as the judge took pains to remind me this morning, I shall say only that religion instructs us that man will never have answers for every question."

That answer's sour in his mouth, Maggie thought.

"I expect Elly has forgotten the time," he said as he turned away and began to knock dirt back into the hole the rabbit had made. "We had the piano tuned last week and she's probably caught up in playing."

Maggie said: "I'm glad. She'll be so happy to have it sound right again. I'll wait by our tree until she's ready."

"I'll tell her you're here," he said, "or why don't you stand outside the parlor windows, they're open: you can hear her play. And then you can call in at the window and surprise her."

"Am I allowed near the house?" she said.

"Of course," he replied stiffly.

" 'twill be grand to hear her play again. Good day. Oh, wait. Thank you for telling me about rabbits and Isaac Newton. It was ever so interesting."

"My pleasure," he said.

Even had it been the house of a stranger, Maggie would have been enticed to pause by the window to savor the sounds coming from within. The music's sweet bounce and joyful rebound enthralled her: until the barking began. A shadow passed behind the window blinds, then the dog ran around the house and greeted her. Eleanor hurried behind him, trying to manage the sway of her hoop skirt. She grabbed both of Maggie's hands and swung them with delight.

"Oh, Maggie. You won't believe what has happened!"

"What? Get down, Dance. Where-ever did you get that hoop skirt, Elly?"

"I borrowed it from Kate. Come into the garden."

Maggie felt wilted and drab next to her friend, for Eleanor looked like a graceful bellflower, with an elegant wide skirt in pale blue and white. "I thought you didn't like them," she said to Eleanor, "I'm sorry I never got to wear the one I borrowed."

"I like them now," Eleanor said. Maggie sat on the garden bench, but Eleanor remained on her feet, prancing on tip-toe. "It's so exciting, Maggie. You will think I'm playing make believe, but I'm not. It is better than make believe, and it's true!"

"What could have happened?" Maggie asked, playing along, "Is it about the piano being tuned?"

"No, not the piano, although that is marvelous - and that's how it started! Lie down, Dance. Behave yourself." The dog lay down at Maggie's feet and put his head on her shoe, sniffing indignantly.

"It's because I had made a promise to Kate and Mama that I would stay in the parlor on the day we receive callers, AND that's why I was in the parlor when it happened! I truly did not want to do it, but I had to see if I could, you know, for I promised them I would, because of what Kate did for me by talking to Papa about letting me see you."

They had exhausted this topic at their last meeting, so Maggie said only: "She was very kind to help us."

"Yes, promises can't be broken," Eleanor said, "The ladies came, just two of them, thank goodness, and one of them was very quiet. I did very, very well, Mama said."

"That's grand. And you wore your hoop skirt."

"Yes. Oh, I must tell you: the day before, when I told Kate the story about your hoop, she made me practice wearing hers, and especially how to sit down properly. She made me practice for an hour; but I suppose that was all right, because I didn't want to show anyone my drawers, like you did!" Maggie laughed at her friend's expression.

Eleanor went on: "In the evening, we told Papa how well I'd done, and he said I should join Mama and Kate every day that they receive visitors, even if I wouldn't go out with them in the carriage to make calls. He said it was good to see me finally looking and behaving like a young lady. I do try to…be good."

"My garters," Maggie muttered. She hoped she would never have to meet Judge Whitfield. "It's too bad that he didn't just tell you how pretty you looked, as you do today."

Eleanor asked: "Do you think I am pretty? Truly?" Her expression was serious.

"Of course I do!"

Eleanor thought about this for a moment, then smiled with satisfaction. "Well, thank you. I did not mean to fish for a compliment. I needed to know the truth, because of what happened. One does not like to think that one has been the subject of insincere flattery."

"From me? Not from me," Maggie said in confusion.

"No! No. From the man I love!" Eleanor laughed at Maggie's astonishment. "Yes, I have an admirer, and it happened so quickly, but I, oh Maggie, he is the most marvelous person I have ever met. I have never felt this way before. It seems like a dream, but it's better than a dream. I think of him every minute."

"Who?" Maggie burst out, "Tell me. How did it happen? Weren't you shy?"

"I'll tell you." Eleanor sat down gracefully. Her hoop skirt took up much of the bench. "On the day when the train came to Millville, you heard about that, didn't you?"

"From Mr. Merritt," Maggie said.

"That afternoon I decided to wear the hoop again, for more practice, since I knew I must sit with the callers again this week. The man who tuned the piano had come the day before, but I was busy helping Mama and Martha. I played it, and it sounded glorious, and Mama came in to listen, and she told me she did not need any help with supper. She said I should play as long as I pleased. When Dance began to bark, I peeked out the window, but I only saw Ned coming up our drive, so I let Dance out, then I went back to the piano. I was playing a piece I adore." Eleanor stopped, then said in a wondering voice: "I never thought such a thing could happen."

"Tell me," Maggie said again, smiling at Eleanor's expression.

"Well, when I heard Ned in the hall, I called to him to come in and hear how lovely the piano sounded. I played on, and then...oh, dear me! I heard a voice behind me that wasn't Ned's at all: it was Mr. Henry Barton. And he said that when he approached the parlor, he had heard the music of the angels, and when he entered, there was the seraph herself at the instrument." Eleanor paused with a misty smile.

"Truly?" Maggie said. No one had ever admired her so extravagantly.

"I was too surprised to move. He was so handsome, and smiling so beautifully, so kindly, that I suppose I forgot to be shy. No, that's not true, I was shy, but I stayed! Ned was surprised too, he must have thought I would run away, but I didn't. He introduced us, and Mr. Barton bowed to me, and said that his first love was music. It's mine too. Isn't that heavenly, Maggie? He's just like me." Eleanor blushed as she continued: "Then Mr. Barton asked me the name of the piece I had been playing, and I told him it had no name yet, that I had made it up myself. When he heard that I had composed the piece, he...he... oh my..."

"You composed the music?" Maggie thought this as exciting as the news of Mr. Barton.

"Yes, sometimes I do. But do listen to what Mr. Barton said next! He said that I had great talent to add to my beauty and that he felt privileged to make my acquaintance!"

"Holy mother of God!"

Eleanor giggled. "Yes, indeed! And you couldn't be any more surprised than I was. Of course, I would *never* run away, not after he said that. I just wanted to sit and look at him and listen to him speak."

"I never!" Bridey's favorite expression came automatically to Maggie's lips. "Did...did you...did he...how did you ever learn to make up music?"

"I don't know. After I learned how to play the piano, the music just came from my mind, it does that sometimes."

"Like drawing!"

"Yes, I suppose so." Eleanor smiled.

"Why didn't you ever tell me?"

"Oh, we've had so many things to talk about, you know, but not much time. But listen, Mr. Barton stayed for supper, and we had the most marvelous time. I didn't say very...all the things I thought to say, but he must have seen me smiling at him. I hardly stopped smiling, I was so glad just to be with him. He is such a fine gentleman." Maggie readjusted a hairpin and wished it could skewer the envy rising in her.

She said: "You're right, Elly, 'tis so grand - like make believe, or dreaming. What did your sister say?"

"She wasn't there. She's visiting some of her friends, so she does not know. And she mustn't. Only you know, because you're my friend. I'm afraid she'd laugh at me, if I told her," Eleanor said.

"Och, like Rose does," Maggie said in agreement.

"Not to hurt my feelings. But she's had so many beaux and been engaged, I just know she'd laugh, like one does at a puppy playing. I couldn't bear that. Don't tell her, please. I know you don't see Ned, but if you do, don't tell. Don't tell anyone."

"I never would. It's for you to tell whenever you please. But, Elly, how do you know I haven't lots of beaux, like your sister," Maggie teased.

"You have not! Have you? If you have, you never told me."

"No, I haven't. Well, one or two, but I didn't love them, then, did I; though Kevin Foran was the nicest fellow. It was fine when he kissed me."

"He kissed you?" Eleanor responded with alarm. "I shouldn't like that."

"You would, surely! That's the best part of courting, if you like the fellow," Maggie said in surprise.

Eleanor shook her head in dismay. "I saw Will and Kate courting. I used to hide and peek at them. And Ned and Miss Caldwell…" She shuddered.

"What did they do?" Maggie asked breathlessly.

"They held hands, and he'd squeeze her shoulders and they'd kiss."

"Faith, that's not so bad. But who's Miss Caldwell? Is your brother courting her? I haven't heard you speak of her before."

Eleanor waved this question away as if she were batting at an annoying fly. "That engagement is broken."

"Is that so? I thought she might be the young lady who seemed so glad to see him at the Vinton depot. The one that was holding a baby."

"It couldn't be!" Eleanor said.

"The lady I saw gave him a hug, but I think she was seeing

off a recruit, a blond fellow. And she herself had on a very grand bonnet and a frock with ruffles, but the color didn't suit her," Maggie said.

"Oh. Good heaven." Eleanor rolled her eyes. "Betsy Dunn. She's always been very forward."

"Well, there you are," Maggie said with relief. "But you know, Elly, if there's an engagement or the fellow has good intentions, and you love him, then 'tisn't so bad to have a kiss."

"No, Maggie, ladies don't allow a gentleman such liberties, and a gentleman doesn't press for them. One really shouldn't until one is married," Eleanor instructed.

"But engaged then..." Maggie began.

Eleanor went on: "Kate really ought not to have allowed it, I suppose, but sometimes Mama gave her some liberty because the engagement had been announced. I would never allow it until I was married. You can love someone without. Ned told me about the poet Dante, and his beloved Beatrice. Dante only saw her a few times, and they never courted, but he worshiped her all his life and when she died he wrote about her and said she was his angel in heaven. She was his inspiration for his great works."

"I didn't know that." Maggie was glad now that she had not blurted out her stories of kisses, including Kevin's sweet, fumbling attempts. She was interested to hear that real gentlemen did things differently, as they did in books. She hoped for Eleanor's sake that Mr. Barton was like Dante the poet, even if his friend Mr. Whitfield was not. *If I was afraid of people, though, I'd not want them touching me,* Maggie thought. She imagined how unwelcome, how fearsome a kiss would seem in such a world as that. She shivered a little and patted Dance.

Eleanor said: "Mr. Barton does not care for girls who are forward. Papa said that at the celebration dinner for the train, one of the speakers referred to Mr. Barton as the most eligible bachelor in Hartford. Mr. Barton said right away that he is troubled by some very forward girls and that their mothers regrettably encouraged their behavior, but that he did not regard such ladies with favor."

"He's surely a gentleman. When will you see him again?"

Eleanor said earnestly: "After Mr. Barton left, Papa said to Ned why had he kept an illustrious friend such a secret, and that he must be sure to invite Mr. Barton here again soon." She frowned. "Ned is so contrary sometimes."

"I hope he didn't tease you," Maggie said, fearing that he had.

"No. He said Mr. Barton came and went as he pleased. I'm sure that's because he has many business responsibilities."

"Does he own a business, then?"

"Papa asked him that," Eleanor said, suddenly irate. "I thought it was so rude."

"Oh, 'tisn't something to be asking?" Maggie said quickly.

"I didn't mean to say that you were rude, Maggie. Goodness. You would not have gone at him like Papa did."

"And it don't matter what he does for a living, if you love him," Maggie said.

"Of course. It does not matter at all to you or to me, but it does to my father. He was, how did Ned say it…cross-examining poor Mr. Barton. But Mr. Barton answered very graciously." Eleanor would not allow a speck of dust to fall upon the portrait of her knight.

"He sounds perfect," Maggie said, beginning to feel slightly put out.

Eleanor laughed. "Oh, no one is perfect."

"I guess this fellow comes close enough," Maggie replied, "I only wish I could meet such a one."

"I hope you will someday," Eleanor said this with sincerity, but with a flavor of doubt.

But not until I've done some things I want to do, for even with a perfect husband, you dance to his tune, Maggie thought, and this obliterated her envy, and made her grin.

"Whether I do or not, 'tis no matter," she said, "You have, and you're so happy I think you could float up to the treetops, and now you've got the crinoline to carry you away. I know, I'll teach you to dance! Perhaps you'll dance with Mr. Barton sometime: all ladies are allowed to do that, surely. Come along, show me how you can twirl."

Chapter 17

"It's getting on toward supper time," Rossiter announced, "I'll close up for you."

"Not tonight. You go ahead home. I'll be staying late," Ned said, placing a sheaf of bills in the ledger.

"Why? I... ah... I've been careful to finish the work. If I haven't, if there is something I should do, I'll stay and do the job," Rossiter said. He had been offended and combative during Ned's lecture earlier in the week about "proper record-keeping. Perhaps the man had finally learned his lesson.

"My mother's planning a late supper to accommodate the judge, so I may as well stay and poke around here for a while," Ned replied. Rossiter lingered for a moment, clearly intending to say something else.

"Good night, Jack. I'll see you tomorrow." Rossiter grimaced a bizarre smile. After a glance at the clock, he grabbed his hat and rushed out without another word.

What a strange bird, Ned thought, putting a pencil into his pocket. He turned down the gas-lights in the waiting room and locked the office door. Once he'd arrived in the supply area, he regretted not asking Jack to stay: it was another scene of disorder. He began to inventory the room's contents. Occupied in puzzling over the scarcity of silver nitrate, he ignored his growling stomach. The ledger clearly showed payment for three containers of the chemical: counting normal usage, there should be one and a half left on the shelves. Instead, there was a single container there, half empty. He wondered whether Rossiter had broken a container and hidden the evidence. Would that explain the man's nervous behavior? Silver nitrate did not come cheap.

He heard a muffled sound in the waiting room: Jack must have returned: but Rossiter did not call out hello. Ned opened his mouth, but then closed it: the sounds from the front room were stealthy. He stepped quietly to the waiting room's entrance and peered out–watching with alarm as a blocky fellow went to the office door and tried the handle. The intruder next poked around the display table, easing open its drawer and fingering the contents. As the man approached the work-rooms, Ned looked around for a weapon. Rossiter, for once, had hung the pole used to retrieve printing frames in its rightful place in the supply room. Ned grabbed the pole, charging out of the room with a yell. The stranger squawked in fright and ran for the outside door, but Ned got there first and blocked the exit, waving the pole menacingly.

"Let me out!" said the intruder in a quavering and oddly high-pitched voice. *A boy,* Ned thought. Keeping his body between the boy and the door, he turned up the gaslights.

"You'd best let me go, I didn't steal nothin'." Most of the boy's defiant comment lay in the deeper register, yet his voice squeaked on the word 'steal'.

Ned said: "What the devil are you doing here? I should call the constable and have you jailed for breaking and entering, with intent to steal."

"Hoh," the boy said, "I'd like to see you try it." He was taller and stockier than Ned. The potential threat posed by the intruder's size was undermined by his half-hearted expression. "I didn't break nothin'."

"Sit down over there," Ned ordered. The boy stood still, looking at the door. "I could knock you in the head and drag you to the constable. You aren't going anywhere. Sit down."

"Hunh. You couldn't drag me, I guess." Yet the boy sat and looked at Ned for a few seconds then dropped his gaze.

"I know you," Ned went on, "You're one of Eph Fish's brothers. The constable would have no trouble finding you again, even if you managed to skedaddle." A school of Fish was the joking term Ned used to describe the family. All ten children closely resembled each other in size. All had doughy skin and spiky, colorless hair; and even the kindest residents of Millville labeled the family "no-account."

Fish hung his head even lower, but after a moment, looked

up with a smirk. "I know about you. Eph told me how you paid him to get you whiskey and bring it up to your house when you was ailin', right under your Pa's nose, almost, and sometimes of a Sunday too. But that wa'nt anything he told the constable about." Ned, uncertain whether this last was a play for sympathy or a warning, ignored it. "So which Fish are you?"

"Zek," the boy answered, then growled: "I bet the constable would like to hear about your liquor." Not even a warning, a threat. Silence.

Zek shifted in his seat. "But I won't tell, if you let me go." Counter-offer. The boy was not as dull as he appeared.

Smiling at Fish like a mean tomcat, Ned said: "It would be my word against Eph's, if it came to that." Ephraim Fish had first-hand knowledge of both the local and county jails. Ned watched the import of this comment sink into Zek's mind, sinking his shoulders in the process.

"Now, Zek," he said like a schoolteacher, "I want you to tell me why you're here."

"I didn't take nothin', " the boy repeated. Ned allowed the silence to simmer, then expand.

"Well, I didn't. And I didn't break nothin'. The door wa'nt locked, was it. I jist walked in. So whyn't you jist let me go." His plea ended in a treble note.

"I saw you try the office door."

"It ain't a crime to turn a doorknob," Zek retorted.

"What were you looking for? A cash box?"

"No! No stealin'. I ain't stupid. I wa'nt looking for that."

"What were you looking for?"

Zek shrugged coolly, but his face remained worried. "I was jist lookin' around."

Ned thunked the pole end onto the floor. Zek jumped. "Do you think I was born yesterday, Mr. Fish?"

"I was jist lookin' around, that's all!" The boy's panic was real. Ned twirled the pole between his palms, thinking. He suddenly recalled seeing Rossiter in conversation with Zek, and how Jack had shooed the boy away as soon as he realized Ned was watching. *Good God, was it possible…?*

"Who sent you here to look around, Zek? After dark."

Zek opened and closed his mouth several times like his namesake animal, then managed: "Nobody sent me."

"Was it Eph? Is he waiting outside, so he can come in and take what he wants after you've scouted the territory?"

"Not Eph, I swear it! He don't know nothin' about it. I swear he..."

Ned interrupted. "I didn't think so. But somebody put you up to this. Jack Rossiter." Zek gaped, then plucked at his lower lip. His expression answered for him.

"Jack's a friend of yours: I've seen you two talking." Ned went on.

Zek dropped his hand. "No, he ain't. I don't like him a bit. Nobody does."

"I can believe that," Ned said, with a ferocious smile. "How much did he say he'd pay you to look around?" Zek's misery returned. "Say now, this is too bad. I didn't do nothin'. You know that. I didn't do no harm, so... jist let me go now, won't you?"

"No harm? Only because I caught you in time. You were conspiring with Rossiter."

Zek twitched with eagerness to escape. "I wa'nt conspirin' to steal," he protested, "I'll swear on the Bible." He paused and cleared his throat. "It was jist borrowing things, things that Jack oughta had anyway 'cause he's your clerk. He said you're keeping them away from him jist because you're such a piss-ant."

Ned cursed.

"He said that, not me, 'bout you bein' a piss-ant," Zek hurriedly went on. "You two don't get on, he says. He says you don't trust him."

"Ha! I don't, by God!" Ned exclaimed, "the son of a bitch. I'll bet you ten dollars that he wanted you to take the ledger."

"Borrow it, yup. How'd you know that?"

Ned said: "If you tell me the whole story, Zek, I'll let you go."

Zek's response was eager. "All right, he wanted the ledger 'bout the customers who had their pictures took, and some invoices too that he said was folded up in blue paper. He was goin' to look at the book, he says and fix it neat, 'cause the way he did it afore didn't suit you, and then he'd bring it back here in the mornin'. So it was borrowin', see?"

"Invoices?" Ned muttered in confusion.

Zek went on: "Yup. And some blank ones too, out of the drawer, he said. But he didn't tell me which drawer; he says he couldn't fix it durin' the day cause you were bein' a…bein' mighty hard on him about a few mistakes in the ledger and such, and you took the books away from him."

Ned scoffed: "I would not have penalized him for plain errors. I've already let many of those pass."

"You pay him real well," Zek said, "so I bet he was afeared you'd dock him."

"I pay him the same as any clerk in town," Ned replied,

"What do you mean?" Zek looked baffled. "But he's got piles of money. He showed us when he was buying us beer. Says that's how he dresses so dandy."

They stared at each other and came to the same conclusion.

"Damn his hide," Ned mumbled, shocked.

"Holy Hannah! He took money outa the box! So, so, so," Zek's words fell over each other as they rushed out, "I guess Jack didn't want that stuff to fix mistakes, no sir." He slapped his knees. "Don't know why I fell for that soft soap he was peddlin'. Whyn't Jack ever get that old ledger himself, anyhow. He jist wanted to get me in dutch. Eph never liked him, nor Ike neither." Zek swore, then looked glumly at Ned. "He's just bin stealin', and a-thinkin' he could cover it afore you saw what was what. But you figgered it out."

Too slowly! Ned thought, *but I **will** figure out how he did it if it takes me till daybreak. I'll wait for him when he comes in tomorrow.* He whirled and slammed the pole into the door furiously.

"You better fetch the constable. He'll catch him. Kin I go with you?" Zek asked, "I'll tell him all about it, since I didn't do nothin' wrong."

Ned examined the injury he had caused to the door. He said: "The constable. That's useless now. Jack is probably on the train out. And I have no evidence that the bastard stole anything."

"I guess you do! He stole it outa the cash box," Zek said.

"There's no cash missing. He must have done it some other way," Ned said.

"He's runnin' some sort of fiddle on you," Zek opined.

"Of course he is. But I have no proof!" Ned growled in frustration.

"But, but…sure you do, from the ledger," Zek persisted.

"I presume that whatever flim-flam he devised, he kept most of it off the books," Ned said.

"We better go and catch him!" Zek said eagerly.

"I just told you! He's already gone," was Ned's bitter answer. One eye had not sufficed to watch Jack Rossiter closely enough.

"Say, this is too bad." Zek slumped in his chair, then went on: "He said you wa'nt a regular fellow like Mr. Dunn. He told us you had a row cause some Irish came in to get his picture took and he says you wanted him to kiss the man's arse."

"That's a lie," Ned said with venom.

Zek hastened on: "Yep, he's a dirty liar. Besides, you got to be mighty careful 'bout how you serve a customer. Got to be nice as pie, or you lose the business. Y'can't pick and choose."

"What do you know about it?" Ned snarled.

"I used to clerk sometimes for Mr. Markey," Zek said, "at the feed and grain. He says an' I say so too—if a body's got the cash or the credit, or somethin' good to barter, then there's the end of it, you got to treat 'em proper."

"You're smarter than Jack Rossiter will ever be," Ned replied acidly. He propped the pole in the corner and moved away from the door. "Get out of here. Tell Eph he owes me a favor." He rubbed his eye, thought for a moment. "Fetch Mr. Garside."

"He won't believe me, he'll think I'm up to something," Zek protested.

"Tell him I sent you. Go," Ned replied.

Ned walked slowly through the suite of rooms comprising Dunn's Photograph Gallery. All things were now in good order; yet the odor of Jack Rossiter's betrayal lingered there like miasmic fumes. According to Billy Vickers, the last night train to Hartford from Millville depot had left with Rossiter inside it. Garside, the justice of peace, had listened to Ned's aggrieved tale, then explained that Rossiter's embezzlement was a violation of Section 194 of state law, "...if you can spell out your losses in dollars and cents, but I don't know as how you've got enough proof yet on that charge for me to find probable cause. You're better off to swear out a complaint of simple theft of supplies."

Ned had concurred with disgust.

There was cold comfort at home when he finally arrived

there last night. Though his mother and Eleanor had murmured sympathy, Kate said: "I told you so!" Following a short outburst against the thieving clerk, the judge had read out his long list of charges against his son: What good did it do, he said, to waste money on a college education when a clerk could outwit you? Didn't you learn a thing about keeping books when you clerked for your uncle? I told you to study with Mix and let Dunn look after his own business, but since you insisted on taking on the task, why did you leave the fox to guard the hen-house? Where would I be if I allowed such a thing to happen in my court? I taught you better than that: I taught you the importance of good accounting and proper accountability.

He had broken his father's monologue at that point with a question: "Speaking of accounting, sir, isn't it true that you still owe me an accounting regarding some debts we discussed in June?" Like the last turn of a wheel closing a sluice gate, this question ended the pour of the judge's words.

Ned laughed in the empty gallery. It was an inspired comment, he decided, a gem: unpolished, yet valuable for its rare and dazzling effect. What the judge did not know, did not care to know, was that Ned had no intention of leaving a place that suited him so well. He liked the work: that this preference happened to stand in opposition to the Judge's stated opinion was coincidental. Indubitably.

Chapter 18

"It's a fine evening," the judge said with satisfaction, as he sat on the veranda of his home with his family around him. He lit his pipe. "Now, Katie, I want you to stay to home for a while. I declare you've seen more of your friends since you came North than you have of your own relations."

Kate fanned herself languidly. "I've just come back from Grandpa Seeley's. Wouldn't he be surprised to hear you say that he and Aunt Es and Aunt Sue and Uncle Charlie and the cousins are not relations of mine."

"Huh, you could spend a year visiting Seeleys, and still not run out of them. There was no need for you to spend an entire week over at the farm. There's no one of any note in little Fiskdale. So, no more gadding about for you, Miss." He punctuated this opinion with a puff of smoke.

Kate replied: "I spoke to the ladies at the church there and raised donations for the freedmen's cause. That hardly qualifies as 'gadding about.'"

The judge said: "You run the risk of wearing yourself down and taking ill. I will not allow you to go back to that pestiferous sink of a city if you are not perfectly well."

"I am perfectly well. And I'll sleep all day tomorrow if need be. But I am not as tired as Elly. She just can't seem to get to sleep. Did you try drinking hot milk before bedtime, El?" Kate asked.

"I did, but I do dislike…" Eleanor began. The judge broke in: "I'm not concerned about her. You're the one who is going back to an unhealthy place and too much activity. She's not going anywhere."

"Papa," Kate reproved him.

"Of course, Cyrus needs to remain in Washington," the judge went on. "That's his job. Our Navy is vital and so far has been the only effective tool in this war. And young Cy should stay to help out and learn the business. But Lavinia and the children don't belong there when it isn't safe. If there's another alarm about rebel advances on the city, then you will not go back at all."

"We'll see about that," Kate muttered. Her father eyed her, but let the comment pass. As his mother asked about Aunt Esther, Ned watched the setting sun gild the trees in the yard, then he took off his shoes, leaned his chair on its back legs, and rested his head against the wall of the house.

"Speaking of the Republican party, Edward," the judge said, "You must register to vote as soon as you're of age in September. The party needs you."

Ned responded: "Were we speaking of the Republican party? Father, I doubt that the value of my property is high enough to qualify. What is it, one hundred dollars-worth or some such thing? I have no horse, and no worldly goods beyond the clothes on my back, unless you count the value of my gold tooth."

"There are your books. Lord knows, you have enough of those, and your clothing, and your money in the bank."

"What money in the bank?" Ned parried.

"And your sword…" Mr. Whitfield continued.

"Good golly, I am a valuable fellow!"

"You can join me and all the young ladies in the marriage market," Kate said, matching her brother's joking manner.

"Don't jest about that," Mr. Whitfield said to her, "You're barely out of mourning weeds for Will." Kate's fan stopped suddenly. She furled it with a snap, her expression closed as tightly.

"Once you are registered," the judge said to Ned, "If I can pry old Jed Fessenden out of his chair, then you can run for selectman a year from now. In the meantime, I'll find you a minor office and get you elected to it this coming April."

Don't make any plans for me, Ned thought, but decided to keep cool on the matter. He said: "What office—hog reave? Pound keeper? Fence viewer? Actually, I wouldn't mind that one."

"Oh yes, you'd make a good fence viewer: you like to sit on the fence rather than choose up sides. That's your problem." A thunderhead of smoke accompanied the Judge's observation.

Mrs. Whitfield was watching her husband anxiously. For that reason only, Ned remained silent.

After a few moments, he said: "Fence viewer would suit you, Katie, considering how you love to ride."

"It's an absolute disgrace that Mother and I can't vote! Nor run for office—even for the Board of School Visitors," Kate said hotly.

"Nor Mrs. Moore, nor Aunt Caroline," Ned said.

"If I could…" Eleanor began. Once again the Judge spoke over her. "What nonsense! We can't risk giving the vote to women. I shudder to think of adding scores of ignorant Irish slatterns to the voting rolls–what a bargain the Democratic traitors and Copperheads would get then, eh? Getting two votes for the price of one whiskey waved at the drunken husband. You can't tell me that you fancy the prospect of vicious harridans like the ones who stoned soldiers and burned stores in New York voting in a parcel of scoundrels and thieves to govern us!"

Kate rapped her fan on the side of the chair and crossed her arms. "You need not lecture me, Papa! I see enough of the dregs of society in Washington to know full well of what vice and foolishness they are capable. But you forget the legions of educated, moral women who are silenced because they can't vote. Their good influence would more than outweigh the bad elements, but the good women have no voice."

"I agree," Mrs. Whitfield said quietly.

"Hear, hear," Ned said.

"If I could…" Eleanor began again.

"United against me. Not another word from any of you," the Judge announced. Kate's fan tapped repeatedly. The twilight pooled by the porch. Ned set the front chair legs down with a thump and said: "Darn you. Now you'll catch it."

The judge lowered his newspaper. "What did you say?"

"Not you, Father. I was addressing a mosquito," Ned replied. Mr. Whitfield raised his paper again.

"How *does* one address a mosquito?" Mrs. Whitfield said softly.

Ned snickered. "With a crushing embrace." There was silence for several minutes. Dance sighed. Ned waved away the insect (or perhaps there was a pair of them), then chuckled.

"Ode To A Mosquito," he began. His mother and sisters

looked at him expectantly.

"You start, Katie," he said.

"All right. Let me think," she said, "Here: 'The bird on high, the moth, the butterfly
all soundless wing their way…'"

Ned said: 'Evoking awe, awakening fond recall, and mirth.'

"Mirth?" Kate said skeptically.

"Yes, why not? I like it," Ned replied, "Here's my second line: 'But to thee, o lowly skeeter, if I may…' Does anyone care to do the next? Mother? El?"

Mrs. Whitfield said: "Since this is doggerel, I think you should ask Dance to join." Dance lifted his head.

"Mother," Kate said in mock horror.

"He ought to speak—he's known for a wag," Mrs. Whitfield went on, trying not to laugh.

"First rate," Ned commented, while Eleanor giggled.

"This is too much," Kate said, "You're worse than Ned."

"Impossible," Mrs. Whitfield said.

"Dance isn't playing," Eleanor said. "It's back to you, Kate."

"Very well. 'I dub…' No, that won't do…'I grant thee highest fame, for…' "

"Not fame—blame," Ned said.

"Shame," Eleanor said.

"Oh hush. I can't think when you interrupt."

"No, this is better, Kate," Ned put in, 'I grant thee grudging accolades…'

"Now what can I find to rhyme with that?" Kate demanded.

"That's your problem. How about cascades? Or lemonades," Ned suggested, "No? Then I'll end this part: 'I grant thee grudging accolades for thy confounded song—the most annoying sound on earth!' Now you see why I put in mirth."

Kate said: "Pooh. Your meter is all wrong."

Ned continued: 'Thou pluckest man's nerves like fiddle strings…'

"Like the bagpipe's air at Highland flings," Mrs. Whitfield suggested.

"No, Mama. That upsets the rhyming pattern. I'll set it right," Kate said.

"Ha!" the judge shouted, "One of the devils is caught, and they've shot the damned scoundrel! There's more here in the

Courant about that demon Quantrell. Our men are on his trail now: he and his pack of dogs can turn tail but there's nowhere they can hide that we won't run them down! Hanging is too good for them. His wife and children should be shot down in cold blood just the way he butchered 100 innocent men in Kansas."

"No! That's not the answer," Mrs. Whitfield said.

"I know your answer: praying," the judge sneered, "Prayers do nothing to stop a devil like Quantrell."

His wife did not back away, as he had expected. She said: "They stop us from becoming as bad as he is–and worse, if we deliberately kill innocent women and children."

"An eye for an eye, and a tooth for a tooth," the judge quoted to her.

"No! No. That is wrong, and we must move beyond it," Mrs. Whitfield said.

Kate pleaded, "We talked about this just a few days ago, Papa, when you first read us the news about the raids. There's no reason to bring it up again. There's no good solution, as Mama said, except bringing the criminals to justice."

"You're wrong, I just gave you the solution! Destroy them, as they have destroyed others. And by heaven, if I was a few years younger, I'd be out there myself hunting them. They wouldn't escape me," the judge said.

"Vengeance is mine, saith the Lord..." Ned said so quietly that no one heard him. Although he had been briefly seized a few days ago with the notion of re-enlisting to join the search in Missouri for Quantrell, he had reconsidered the impulse in the meantime. There were hundreds of miles of border territory filled with Confederate sympathizers and populated by the extended families of the raiders themselves. The search would be a tremendous effort, requiring as much cunning as Quantrell himself possessed. Ned was not confident that much of that could be found in the Union army leadership. That was the pragmatic answer. And the moral answer? Tonight, he agreed with his mother and Kate.

The judge, having vanquished all (spoken) opposition, folded the newspaper to a different page, creased it and read on, defiant of the disapproving atmosphere around him and the waning light. Eleanor and Dance left silently a moment later. Ned watched with satisfaction as his father contended with a mosquito. The one that inspired Ned's verse had recruited a raiding party.

"I'm going in," the judge announced. A moment after he left, Kate said in a tremulous voice: "Mama, what can I do?"

"What, darling?" Mrs. Whitfield asked.

Kate threw her fan onto the chair. "Never mind," she said, and strode off the veranda. Ned and his mother sat looking at the darkening sky.

"There's never any peace," Mrs. Whitfield said, dispirited.

He stood up. "Guess they won't rest 'till they've taken blood. Come in."

His mother stared dully at the house. "No. I'll stay here awhile longer. I'll risk the bites for a spell of quiet."

As Ned prepared for bed, he heard a knock at his door. "Who goes there?"

"May I come in?" Kate whispered, "Please."

"Hold on." He put his nightshirt on and pressed his upper denture back into place and opened his door. "What's wrong?"

"Hush," she said and came in, closing the door softly behind her. She wore a summer wrapper over her nightgown, and her hair was unpinned. Bouncing, coiling around her face, the hair's vitality mocked her downcast expression. She sat on the edge of his bed, just as she used to do when they were children, and said, without preamble: "I loved him, Ned, you know that, don't you? You know that I did."

"Will?" he said, "Of course you did!"

She went on: "I loved him, just as everyone did. How could any person not love such a man—it came as naturally as breathing, when he was so good, and so...Will-like." At Ned's nod of recognition, she smiled slightly. "And he adored me. That's what... oh, I don't know. He was too good for me! I didn't deserve such a man. I'm a wretch!"

"I've called you names before, but that's not one I'd ever use," he said. Kate did not respond to this, just wiped her eyes, and looked at him piteously. "What's the matter?" he asked, "Do you miss him tonight, Katie, is that what brought this on?"

"No! Yes! That's the trouble," Kate exclaimed, "I don't miss him enough. Or so Father seems to think and so the Warrens act: as if I should spend the rest of my life weeping and carrying on, but I can't! And oh dear Heaven, if he had lived and we'd married I'm afraid we would have argued. He wanted me to be a...like a pastor's wife...no, I can't explain it...and I couldn't do it, Ned! I did it for a while because I loved him, I see that now."

"Did what? I have no idea what you're talking about," Ned put in.

She said: "I pretended to be good, and kind, and gentle, and modest, and just as the Warrens think I ought to be, just as Will thought I ought to be, because I loved him, you must believe me."

"I do," Ned began, then decided to save his breath, for Kate had collapsed into one of her torrential bouts of weeping. She always insisted such storms made her feel better. He thought this incomprehensible but accepted her assertion. He picked at a callus on his writing hand.

In a few moments, she sat up and said in a blurred voice: "Give me a towel."

He tossed her a towel from his washstand. She caught it in one hand, scrubbed at her face, then pounded his mattress repeatedly in what he regarded as a sign that she had moved from tears to action.

"It won't do," she said. He waited, but she did not explain. Finally, she said with defiance: "My life did not end."

He replied: "Of course not. Will would not have wanted you to stop everything, leave everything to…I don't know, mourn his memory. Honor it, yes, but you're doing that by teaching, and organizing, and helping…"

"Yes!" Kate interrupted. "Thank you! But think, truly, would Will have allowed me to do such things if he were here? And even if he was able to allow it, because he'd want to indulge me, how long would he stand it in the face of his family's disapproval. He said he loved my enthusiasm, but he did not like the direction it took." At Ned's surprise, she retorted: "Oh yes. That was the quarrel before he was mustered in. You heard part of it."

"But you two made it up," he asserted.

"Yes. Because I did love him." She dabbed away tears, twisted the towel in her hands as if strangling it.

"Well. Perhaps you might have been able to compromise somehow…" he began.

"Ned," she hissed in disgust, "Don't get mealy-mouthed. I came to talk to you because you were the only one who might see how awful it has been to love him so and to know I could not have married him. Because you loved him, but you know what he was like and what his family is like and since you've come back from the war you have changed so; I hoped you might understand."

He was alarmed by the plea in her voice; by her belief that he could understand, when he felt that he now understood less about life than he had as a boy. He turned away, examined a small stain on his shirt, folded his trousers over a chair. He said: "I knew him as a friend. Guess I wouldn't know him as a fiancé!"

"I can see that you don't care to discuss it," Kate said coldly, and slid off the bed.

Ned turned back. "Hold on. I have an idea what you're saying. I just don't know what you want me to do. How can we remedy…"

"There's no remedy," Kate broke in, "I just wanted someone to know! I couldn't bear it."

"You could tell Mother," he said. Kate considered this. "Yes, I could, now. Now that I've told you. I had just… I was worried that knowing might hurt you, because you were so happy when Will and I announced our engagement."

"Of course I was, he's my friend. And you were so happy. And Will was. Seemed so happy, anyhow." Ned rubbed the bridge of his nose. "But if he didn't suit you… I think you ought to choose someone who suits you." He paused, then went on: "I guess I didn't think of that, with Hattie."

Kate gave this admission a respectful moment of silence, then said wickedly: "She was not the model woman! What did you ever see in her?"

Ned said: "Think you've scored a blow? Well, you haven't." He shrugged. "Guess I liked her because she said I was the only one who ever made her laugh." Kate sighed. Ned picked up the towel, which had fallen on the floor. He shook it out.

"Aren't we a pair," Kate said.

Chapter 19

In the shade of the maple tree, Eleanor put down an old blanket, scolding Dance as she did so: the dog was straining at his leash, dashing one way, then changing direction and tangling himself in Maggie's and Eleanor's skirts. Maggie eluded him for a moment and plopped onto the blanket, fanning herself. It was a long walk from Mr. Merritt's some days. She tried not to think of her employer, suffering in his bed again with stomach pain. *Surely he ought to be seeing the doctor, no matter what he says,* she thought. Merritt had insisted that she take off first-day afternoon as usual, saying: "Every child needs a breath of fresh air now and then." And though she was no longer a child, Maggie had gratefully taken her leave.

  Eleanor's round face was flushed, and her reddish-blond hair frizzed out around her face, not laying in shapely curls as it usually did. Maggie was pleased that her friend turned a becoming pink in the heat, not that nasty, blotchy red that covered Annie's face when she swanned around with Rory Corcoran. Maggie broke a biscuit into portions over the napkin in her lap, then popped them one by one into her mouth, as Eleanor held her biscuit in two hands and nibbled it neatly like a squirrel.

  "Mm. Very good. Did you make them?"

  "Yes. Martha and I. Mama has been so tired, after getting Kate ready to go back to Washington and sending her off. She wanted her to stay longer, so that the unhealthy vapors from the summer air there would have time to clear off, but Uncle Cyrus and Aunt Vinnie had to go back, and Kate said she must go with them: of course, she couldn't travel without an escort." Eleanor frowned as if contemplating an insoluble problem. "I hate it when she goes away."

"You miss her," Maggie said.

"I do. Terribly. Just as you must miss your dear Papa," said Eleanor.

"Mm," Maggie said, rolling onto her side. *Mother of God, I do!* she thought. She awaited the feared questions: Has he written to you? Why not? How do you know he's well? And that's the worst, not knowing. (He couldn't love you, couldn't have ever loved you to have run away so sudden and left you in hard times.) She examined the blanket's weave and watched an ant trundling with a burden across the fabric's edge. She said: "He's in my prayers every night."

"Yes," Eleanor said sympathetically. *Bless you,* Maggie thought. She lay on her back and looked up past the leaves to the clouds above. Soapsuds. A fat sofa. A bowl of plums.

"Is the orchard your father's too?" she asked.

"Yes, all this land is his," Eleanor replied, "Maggie, I do hope your family, your mama and your brother–I hope it does not upset them or make them angry when you miss visiting them on the Sundays you come to see me."

Maggie sat up. "Mercy, no. They would miss me, I guess, if I went far away, but so long as I visit when I can, and send my wages home every week, they don't mind." *Not every family's as close as yours,* she thought, envying her friend, a little.

"I'm glad to hear that. I would not want to cause you any trouble," said Eleanor.

"Ah, you needn't worry. No one at home has a bad temper; well, except Rose, she'd get cross if she needed my help and I wasn't there. And Mam, sometimes, but she never gets cross with me."

"Good," Eleanor said, "I so dislike quarrels, don't you? It's so difficult to know what to do with people who never get along. And then one says cruel things, and the other answers back, and it goes from bad to worse." *Who never gets along in your house, then?* Maggie wondered. She assumed Eleanor was the observer, like she herself was, and not the quarreler. *That father, it must be. And who else? Mother, eldest daughter or son?*

She said: "My nephews quarrel all the time. Frank leaves them to it, but sometimes he says if they don't quit, he'll knock their heads together and knock some sense into them."

Eleanor gasped. "Does he?"

"No," Maggie went on hastily, "he barks with no biting, for

he's never done more than spank them."

Eleanor twirled a curl in her fingers, grimacing. "Adults are too big to spank."

Maggie giggled. "Pity. 'Twould be grand, Elly, if we could give them a licking, or put them in the woodbin without supper when they went at it." She could just see Rose sitting bedraggled and repentant, with bark and dust in her hair.

Eleanor's answering laugh was gleeful. "It would be lovely! I know one or two at home who'd mend their ways as quick as a wink. I'd allow no quarreling in my house, and I'd punish every unkind comment, because that's the way the contention begins."

"Birds in their little nests agree," Maggie quoted. Dance yipped a complaint, covering Eleanor's response. She suggested they take him for a walk.

As they walked, Eleanor told Maggie about a new book she was reading, Victor Hugo's *Les Miserables*. She told Maggie that the title meant "the miserable ones."

Maggie preferred not to hear a word about misery on such a beautiful day, but she asked politely: "And how do you like it?"

"Ever so." Eleanor recounted the tale in such a way that Maggie was interested in spite of herself. Eleanor said: "That's as far as I've read." Maggie frowned: "Oh, bother. How will I know what happens? Will you tell me when you finish it?"

"Of course I will, when I see you next time," Eleanor said with a nod.

Maggie asked: "Why do you think that Inspector is such a hard man? Why does he go on so much about punishing Valjean?"

"It's a mystery to me," Eleanor pronounced, "Men are a mystery."

"Even Mr. Barton?" Maggie put in.

Eleanor thought about this. "I have not seen him again, not yet, although I asked Ned to invite him. I thought I must be careful and ask him just a certain way, you know, or he might wonder why I was asking, but he doesn't pay attention to such things. I suppose Mr. Barton is a mystery, but that is only because I do not know him yet, as we're only newly acquainted."

"Perhaps he won't be a mystery," Maggie responded, "Not all men are. Faith, some of them, it's as easy as pie to know what they're all about."

Eleanor looked doubtful. Dance stopped short, half-sat,

raised his back leg and licked his hindquarters vigorously. Eleanor turned her head away in embarrassment. Then she said: "Where are we?"

"Oh, I don't know," Maggie said.

"We've lost the path," Eleanor said.

"No, we haven't. 'tis just a bit faint here." Maggie looked back. Yes, there it was, rather indistinct in the long grass. "I see it now. Is it time to go back, then?"

"I'm **lost**." Panic suffused Eleanor's voice.

"No, Elly, you're not lost. Not at all. We'll just follow the path back. See, there 'tis." Maggie's reassuring words soughed past like the breeze moving the grass. When she reached out to take her friend's hand, Eleanor shuddered and shrank away.

"What's wrong?" Maggie said.

Eleanor stared at nothing. The warm air could as well have been a January nor'easter, so hard was she frozen in place, and so much did its touch make her shiver. *She's got the frights again,* Maggie thought, recalling a time when Eleanor had been paralyzed in much this way just outside the schoolyard. The dog whined. A bit of the fear touched Maggie. She shivered too and peered at the inoffensive trees, wondering what they hid. Dance whined again. Maggie tentatively touched Eleanor's hand, but it was snatched away as her friend shrieked. The dog barked in response. Eleanor looked through Maggie, eyes wide in horror.

Mother of God, what can I do? Maggie thought. Dance put his front paws on his mistress, who screamed and pushed him away. He howled in earnest, joined by Eleanor's cries.

"Hush!" Maggie shouted, took his leash. "Whissht, Dance. Hush, Eleanor. You're not lost, not a bit. Not while I'm here. We'll lead you back home. You just take Dance's lead, he'll take you home."

Since Eleanor did not move to take the leash, Maggie held on to it: "Come along. Come, Dance. Home." The dog did not move, staring at his mistress. Maggie gave the leash an anxious tug, to no avail. She felt she should run for help but did not dare to leave her friend alone. Perhaps she could rope the dog and girl together with the leash: he would stay, surely, while she went to fetch the others. *Oh mercy, won't they be angry at me for bringing on the spell!* she thought.

She said: "Elly, walk home with me now. Can't you hear

me? Show me you can. Follow me and Dance, we know the way." She had no response. "Oh, do come!" Maggie was close to tears. "Your Mama will wonder where you are, and she'll worry about you."

Eleanor whimpered. "Mama?"

"Yes!" Maggie exclaimed, "Your mama will be looking for you. Come with me now and we'll go right home." Eleanor shivered. Fingers fumbling in haste, Maggie looped the leash around her friend's arm and made a loose knot. She bent down and pulled Dance by his collar.

"Come, doggie. Home," she commanded. Eleanor stumbled after him, now crying. Maggie hustled them forward: afraid that her friend might trip and fall, but more afraid that she would freeze in place again.

"Yes, home," Maggie said, "Your Mama will be waiting, surely. And your canaries and your rabbit, and Malabar too. He needs you to pat him. Didn't you tell me no-one else but you pays attention to him? Who will give him his carrots in the morning, if you don't come home now. And your brother Edward will be waiting there at home too and looking for…"

"Eddie?" Eleanor panted, with a sob.

Maggie said: "Yes. He's there too. Waiting. Just a little ways ahead. We'll be there soon, God willing!"

"Och, I'll tell you a story," Maggie went on desperately, "A good story for the way home, one my Mam told me…about…um, the pookas. They are magical animals, like a horse, sometimes a donkey, or a dog, like Dance, see? And they take up a man who is traveling by night. Take him up, they do, on their backs, and ride off as fast as the wind, then the next morning there he is back home, with quite a tale to tell." She left out the part her mother had told her about the pooka being as black as coal, with red eyes that glowed: "I never knew a one harming a fellow, but b'gor, they'd scare the daylights out of ye," her mother always said.

"Dance is your good magical pooka," Maggie puffed, "who protects you always and brings you back home, no matter where you go." Although the dog was trotting ahead readily, he was panting. Eleanor's sobs were mixed with hard breathing due to their pace, yet Maggie wished they could move faster still.

She said: "And your Mama will want to know what you've been about, and hear how brave you've been, and all about the good pooka brought you home. And...oh, Mother of mercy! There's your Papa's orchard, see? Almost home."

Eleanor lifted her head a little, and said, between gasps. "Mama."

Maggie said: "And there's our tree, and our blanket, where we had our picnic." Eleanor staggered ahead of the dog, who tangled the leash in her legs. She fell head-first onto the blanket. Clutching it, she wept convulsively as Dance climbed on her, trying to lick her face, his whining echoing the sounds she made. Maggie skidded to a halt and collapsed on the grass, taking enormous breaths, overheated and dizzy.

Eleanor moaned something in a child's voice, but all Maggie could make out was 'Mama' and 'woof'; no, it was 'wolf'. Dance looked back at Maggie as if to ask her what to do. She did not even dare to untangle his leash. She inched over to the basket, retrieved a half-full container of ginger beer and gulped it down. She blew her nose on her handkerchief and belched, past caring about politeness. Eleanor's cries slowed and grew soft. Her body shook at every other breath with dry sobs.

"I'm so sorry, Elly," Maggie said fearfully, "Are you all right now? Are you thirsty? Will you have some ginger beer, and then you can go back to your house."

Eleanor sat up. Dance, still entwined with her, licked her face. She looked as if she had been startled awake. Turning her head away from Dance's kisses, she fumbled and tugged at the leash. Once loosed, Dance jumped on her lap, but she pushed him away. Maggie scooted over and caught the leash, pulling Dance to her own lap, while Eleanor examined her own twisted skirt and stockings with concern. Wiping her wet face and nose on her sleeve, she mumbled something Maggie could not hear.

Maggie said: "You seem a bit better now."

"I'm thirsty," Eleanor said in a tiny voice.

Maggie got up, tied Dance's lead to a nearby bush, then brought her friend the remainder of the ginger beer. The container almost slipped out of Eleanor's fingers; so Maggie helped her drink. "Lie down now, rest a bit," Maggie said worriedly. Eleanor lay down. When Maggie picked up the container a moment later, she saw Eleanor's eyes close and her chest rise and fall in the rhythm of sleep. Maggie sat down next to Dance, and leaned against him, petting him with shaking hands.

"What happened, doggie?" she asked. The dog gave her an impenetrable look, which Maggie fancied was sad. He lay down, put his head on her thigh.

Wolf, Eleanor had said. Was it a waking nightmare? Had someone scared Eleanor, when a child, with too-vivid tales of Red Riding Hood and the wolf? Brothers tease their little sisters sometimes, but surely the good-humored young man back at the Whitfield house had never been so cruel. Maggie recalled that he had not even pressed Eleanor to meet Mrs. Wilkin that first day. The father, then. He was the one who forced Eleanor to go to school, though she was so terrified at first that she had trouble holding her water, big girl though she was. But he was not here, he had not frightened his daughter now. It did not dwell at home, then, this unknown fearful thing, but away from home.

Dance was panting. She got up and led him to the water trough at the edge of the horse pasture. The black pony ambled over and he and the dog peaceably drank their fill. She led the dog back to the blanket, but Eleanor slept on. Maggie saw the slant of the sunshine; she began to fret that Eleanor's family would miss her and be angry; or that Mr. Merritt had taken a turn for the worse.

"Eleanor, you have to get up," she said. She allowed Dance to wake the sleeper with his nosing and sloppy tongue. It took a while for Eleanor to rouse herself.

"Oh, Maggie? Goodness. I must have dropped off to sleep. I hope you don't think me rude to nap while you're visiting. My, it must be getting late, look at the sun. Mustn't you go back to Merritt's soon? Now why did I sleep?" Eleanor said. Maggie gathered the ginger beer containers and packed up the basket, then helped Eleanor to fold the blanket. Dance lay at their feet obediently, until they walked slowly back toward the house.

"I don't know why I feel so shaky," Eleanor said.

"Sometimes 'twill happen when you've had a nap," Maggie remarked gently.

"I suppose so. I haven't been sleeping well at night since Katie left. Well, may I send you a note again? Perhaps you might want to go to your family next week, though," Eleanor said, rubbing her eyes.

"Yes, send me a note. I like to get them," Maggie replied.

Eleanor stopped. "Pardon me, I need to blow my nose. I hope I'm not getting a cold in the head." She felt inside one sleeve and then the other. "Now where is my handkerchief? And what have I done to rumple my skirt so. I must have slept all twisted up."

"Sure as you're born," Maggie said.

"I suppose I must use a napkin to blow my nose." Eleanor took one out of the basket. "Ow, how my head hurts. What's wrong, Maggie? You look so worried: it's probably just that I'm coming down with a cold in the head."

"Yes," Maggie said.

"Something happened," Eleanor said next, in a flat peculiar tone. "What."

Maggie said: "We got a bit lost, walking. But we found the path again and came back." She did not like to see the dawning recollection in Eleanor's face. "Not lost at all, truly, just away for a bit, and..."

"What happened. What did I do?" Eleanor interrupted.

"Nothing. We came back," Maggie said.

"Maggie, tell me!" Eleanor said harshly.

"Nothing at all," Maggie protested, "See, you stopped, and you didn't seem to hear me for a bit, like at school that time, but then you came around right as rain and we came back."

Eleanor groaned. "No. And I cried, like a baby. Don't tell me I didn't, I know I did, I can feel it in my nose."

"But I was scared too. I was, truly!" Maggie exclaimed.

"Only frightened of me! What you must think of me..." Eleanor turned away in shame. "I think no such thing. I was scared, I was, scared for you, some, and that you felt so bad..." Maggie pleaded.

Eleanor put the napkin up to hide her face. "Dear God, you must think I'm insane."

"No! I never thought such a thing, not for all the world," Maggie said earnestly, "how could I ever, when you're so good to me; and you're so much better now than you were at school, for you didn't say a word then, not much, and now you're so interesting and we have good talks."

"No," Eleanor said, muffled beneath the napkin.

"Yes, Elly, God's honest truth. Can't you believe me? You must."

"I have to go home," Eleanor said.

Disappointment bit Maggie. "Elly, I'm ever so sorry. But I don't think anything badly of you, never, never. And 'twasn't your fault, just… something that happened…" Dance was the only listener to meet Maggie's gaze.

"I'll go," Maggie sniffled, "Will you write me?"

Eleanor peered around the napkin, swabbed her eyes, nodded, then hauled hard on the dog's leash, and was gone.

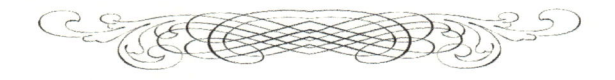

Pleased with the beauty of the day, and the excellence of the ride, Ned unsaddled Greylock, rubbed the horse down, then turned him out into the pasture. He ambled by the stable, intending to sleep in the shade for a while. Sundays were good for only one thing. Yet his conscience made him pause by the door.

"That harness is filthy. Did you allow your men to pass inspection with dirty muskets or tarnished brasses?" the judge had said that morning. Ned fetched rags and oil for the leather, then took the harness off its pegs in the tack room and carried it into the sunshine.

As he worked, peering at a worn section of the reins, he heard Eleanor sobbing. He often avoided her when she was crying, but this weeping had a wrenching quality that disturbed him. The dog whined anxiously from the stable.

"Eleanor," he called out. The sound of crying and the dog's noises stopped abruptly. He went to the stable doorway.

His sister made a soft sound from a heap of straw in the corner. "Papa?"

"No, it's me. What's wrong?"

"Eddie!" Eleanor wailed. Scrambling up from the stable floor, she flung herself into his arms. He was astonished, not at her use of his childhood nickname, but at her embrace. When they were children, she had snuggled with him as readily as she had with her sister, but from the time he had first grown fuzz on his upper lip and his voice had dropped gradually in pitch from alto to bass, she had shunned all physical contact with him, except to stroke his forehead or hold his hand when he was ill. "What's the matter, baby, did you hurt yourself?" he asked with concern.

"I've had such a bad dream," she said against his chest. He began to return the hug, then realized that his hands were covered in dried mud and linseed oil.

"I'm sorry, I've been cleaning Grey's harness and I stink from this stuff." He pulled out his handkerchief, swabbed his hands.

Eleanor shook her head and mumbled: "You smell good, like Greylock."

"That's the first time someone's complimented me by saying that I smell like a horse," he said lightly. She hugged him tighter and sobbed. The dog put his paws on Ned's leg.

"Come now, mouse, what's the matter," he continued, "You must tell me. You look... overheated."

"I h-have a h-headache," she murmured, then interrupted his consoling sound with an angry noise and lifted her wet face. "No! No, I have to st...op being a baby. You've had the neuralgia, which is m..much worse, and you've been in the hospital. I have to stop. Everyone will hate me!"

"Nonsense. Nobody hates you," Ned replied.

Terror distorted her expression. "They'll think I am insane!"

"What? Where on earth did you get that notion, hey? Who's been saying that, Father? You should go in now and rest," Ned urged.

"No. I can't. If Papa sees me... I couldn't bear it," she said.

"So, it is him..." Ned began. When she shook her head, he asked: "What happened?"

She moved away from him and stumbled back to the straw pile and sat down. "I had a horrible dream. I thought I would die. Why am I so queer? There's no wolves here, I know that. How could I be so stupid. Why am I such a baby, and get so frightened?"

Ned wrapped his hands in the handkerchief, rubbed under his fingernails. When he knew he could keep his voice steady he said: "There are no wolves here, of course not. You must go inside now and talk to Mama."

Eleanor pushed Dance aside and got up, pulling hard on Ned's arm. "Please, Eddie, I don't mean to be a baby. You must tell me, you would know, because you worked with Papa. What does he do at the court with the people who are insane? What is 'committed,' is it jail? He makes them go away, doesn't he?"

"Don't say that! This is absurd. Go inside now," he ordered.

She clung to his hand. "No, don't treat me like a baby. Tell me."

Keep cool, or you'll make things worse, he thought. He said: "If you'll get it out of your mind that anyone thinks you're insane, or there's any...ever any chance...You can't think that we'd allow it! If you promise me, you don't believe that anyone would think that, or do that, well, maybe I'll tell you." She looked at him hopelessly. "Promise me, Elly," he repeated. She nodded.

He chose his words with due care. "Well. First of all, it's only an issue if the person is a danger to himself or others. The family has a say in the matter, of course, and someone like Doctor Green. The family tries, finds a safe and pleasant place: you've heard me speak of the Retreat in Hartford? I've walked on their grounds a few times. It's beautiful there, like a first-rate water cure resort."

"Do they ever come back to their families?" she asked.

Good Lord! Don't look so, he thought, and said: "Why? Why do you want to know, El?"

She shook her head.

"Yes of course they come back, when they're better," he said. "It's not a prison. Have you been reading something that's bothered you? More Dickens? Is that what has frightened you so?"

His sister shivered. "No. *Les Miserables*, I've been reading that."

"How appropriate," he said gently, "You look miserable. Go in and lie down. Please, it would make me feel better." He went on, "Think it through, Elly. In this family, if odd behavior was enough to get a person committed, Father would be the first to go! And I'd be second."

No smile, but Eleanor's anguish lessened. "But if someone disobeys?" she said.

He laughed without humor. "Then I'd be committed first." Eleanor wiped her nose. "Poor mouse," he said.

"No!" His sister shuddered. "No, I'm not. And you mustn't tell anyone."

"What do you mean? Of course we must tell Mother."

"No, we mustn't," Eleanor pleaded, "She'll worry, and it won't do any good. Promise me you won't tell anyone."

"I have to," he said.

"No, you do not," she countered.

"I have to," he repeated uncomfortably, surprised by his sister's vehemence. "Come now, El. You must tell... someone. At least write to Katie and tell her."

Eleanor shook her head again. "She's heard it too many

times. Why did this happen now, when I've been trying so hard to be good, for him. And I'm usually well, most of the time, aren't I? But you mustn't tell. He would hate me."

"Father doesn't hate you," Ned said.

Eleanor shivered. "Never mind. I don't know what I'm saying… It's this headache. But you know I have been trying, don't you?"

"Yes, you have," he assured her, "But what'll you say to Mother when she sees you've been crying?" Eleanor shrugged. "I cry all the time. She doesn't even ask me why anymore." The truth of her answer chilled him.

"Go in and rest," he mumbled.

She said: "I'm a baby who never grew up. Just like Papa says."

After a moment, Ned said: "What does he know…"

"There, you see?" Eleanor said harshly. "Give me your solemn oath that you won't tell, or I'll never forgive you. I mean it. It's dreadful enough that it happens to me, but I could not bear if everyone knows how awfully stupid I am. Give me your oath, Ned."

He said: "You have it. But I don't like…"

"You don't have to like it: just keep your promise!" she said, as she left him.

Chapter 20

Ned sat down for the first time since breakfast and closed his eye. Sole proprietorship had certain disadvantages: fully a dozen chores called out to him as he chided himself again for breaking a glass plate negative just before the last customer left. Yes, the damned things could be slippery when wet, but he was no fumble-fingered apprentice. In fact, it was the first one he'd ever dropped. *A good likeness, too,* he thought, *wasted.* He drank from his canteen, then took out his jack-knife and cut up an apple and downed it.

Without a doubt, stemming the insidious bleeding of cash and supplies had improved the gallery's finances—and he had said as much in his recent letter to George Dunn. Dunn had not yet responded: whether this was due to mail delays, troop movement, or anger on George's part, was unknown. There was an additional disadvantage to being asked to study law at the same time one ran a business. He had stayed up late reading his assigned chapter of *The Restatement of Trusts*. Eleanor was up late as well, padding quietly down the hall with Dance, down the stairs, checking the locks on the doors and standing by the windows to peer out and listen.

At the sound of foot-steps coming up the outer stairs to the gallery, he wiped his mouth and straightened his necktie. He left the office to await the customer. He said: "Good afternoon, sir. Oh. Fish."

Zek Fish hesitated just inside the door, then took off his hat. "Good day." He was dressed in a rusty black coat that had undoubtedly descended from some more respectable Fish of days gone by. He was cleaner than usual about the hands and face and had slicked down his unruly hair.

"Are you here for a photograph today?" Ned asked.

"No. Umm. I dunno. Maybe. I'd like to, see, but..."

A customer is a customer, Ned thought. He said: "I may be able to extend you credit. Or barter for your labor. There's some work needed in our garden."

"I ain't exactly here fer a picture. I seen your card in the window downstairs, 'bout needin' a clerk, so that's why I came by." Zek took in Ned's doubtful expression. "But if you want me to get my picture took, I will, I guess."

Although the three men who had inquired about the position had turned it down when they discovered how poorly it paid, Ned was sure someone acceptable would appear eventually. A Fish was not acceptable.

"No, you're too young, Zek. I need someone older," he said.

"Uh-unh. I'm old enough, I'm eighteen...next birthday."

"Fifteen is more likely, despite your size," Ned replied.

"Yup, fifteen, come October," Zek agreed stolidly, "But I clerked fine for Mr. Markey. You ask him if I didn't."

Ned replied: "I regret to say I can't hire you here."

"Aw, why not? You need a clerk, and I kin read and write and cipher. I stayed in school till I was 'leven."

Ned shrugged. "As big as you are, I'm sure you can find work as a laborer on one of the farms, or your father's place." He hesitated to call the Fish homestead a farm, as he had never seen anything growing there.

Zek said: "Naw, I don't wanna do that. I want to learn somethin'. I could learn it fast–picture-takin'."

Subtlety is wasted on a Fish, Ned thought, then said: "Why would I hire someone I could have had charged with trespass and attempted theft?"

"Me?" Zek said incredulously, "I didn't do nothin.' Jack lied to me. I wouldn't do nothin' to harm you, no sir. I felt mighty bad about how he stole from you, and all."

Ned thought this comment was very likely true. "You must know that your brothers' reputations would give anyone pause," he said quietly.

"Aww. Tarnation." A blush mottled Fish's white face like a rash.

"I have nothing against Eph or Ike," Ned went on, "I've known Eph since we were boys. But I wouldn't hire him. I must hire a man I can trust, particularly after dealing with Rossiter."

"Aw, I wouldn't ever steal nothin': jist because Eph does, that don't mean I do," Zek protested, "And, and, guess I'd be stupid to cut any shines when I know you'd be watchin' like a hawk, because of Jack the crook!"

A very good point, Ned thought. He said: "Hauling feed sacks at Markey's is a far different task than handling glass negatives or looking after a lady who suddenly feels faint or does not like the results of her photography session."

"But the other fellows who want the job, they'd have to learn all that, too. They ain't none of 'em worked in a picture room," Zek said, "Sellin' is sellin'."

Perseverantia omnia vincit, Ned thought, *at least one Fish is blessed with common sense.* On an impulse, he said: "Look around and tell me which photograph you like best in this room."

Zek accepted the command readily. "In that case over there, too?"

"Anywhere in the room," Ned replied. Fish took his time, bending to look at the carte-de-visites and melainotypes laid out in the case, then going to peer at the showpiece George had borrowed from Alonzo Dunn's shop: a salt print of an attractive young lady. The photograph was hand colored, handsomely matted, and framed in glossy carved wood with a gilt liner. "I guess that one cost the most," he remarked.

Ned nodded his agreement then added: "Leaving price aside as a consideration, is that your choice?"

Zek responded: "If it don't matter how much it'd sell for, I kind of like that old lady and gent in the card pictures." He took it out of the case and held it up. Ned knew the photograph: it was one he had posed, taken, and developed. He was inordinately proud of it, for he felt it captured the elderly couple's stalwart devotion.

Some of the men under his command had surprised him by displaying hidden abilities when put to the test. He had thought Flynn too pugnacious at first, but the sergeant had turned out to be a good instructor and a just man. Reynolds had begun as a scatterbrained recruit but had ended (at least as far as last December, when Ned's war ended) malleable and resilient, if not steady. Nason had always been an obnoxious fool and likely remained so. *Even if this boy is honest, and trainable,* he thought, *the judge won't allow a Fish in his establishment. His? Not his, by God! It's mine.*

He said: "Anyone who clerks here would need to be clean about his person, and properly dressed. Could you do that? Take pains to smell clean every day, and get yourself a suit that fits?"

Zek said, "I washed up under the pump!"

Ned almost laughed. "You're not so bad today. But you'd have to do even better if you wanted to work for me. The ladies can be very particular. And you need a haircut, I know a barber you can see about that."

Zek's pale eyebrows went up to meet his blond thatch. "Y'mean I got the position?"

Ned said: "Hold your horses. I said IF. Go have a seat and give me awhile to think about this."

Zek replaced the photograph in the glass case. He brushed at the seat of his trousers before seating himself nervously on the velvet armchair. Ned sat on a side chair and pondered. He was sixteen years old when he began clerking at Alonzo Dunn's gallery—always preferring to play with the technical processes of photography, rather than being adept at sales. He had once nearly discarded a photograph that he deemed not good enough to offer; but had been brought up short by Alonzo Dunn who insisted on a different definition of good: anything we can convince the customer to buy. Even if Zek improved his cleanliness, his clothing, his manners, some Millville folks would harrumph at a Fish. The pertinent question remained: After harrumphing, would they buy?

He asked: "Why did Mr. Markey let you go? Did you break something?"

"Nope. His clerk was sick, and I was helpin' out some, but then one of his wife's relations wanted the job," Zek replied, "You kin ask him, he'll tell you!"

"I intend to," Ned said, ignoring Fish's pleased reaction. "If I like what I hear from Mr. Markey, then you can begin training here. Training would be at half the usual wage, and if you break a glass plate, that comes out of your wages. And if you aren't suitable, I'll let you go."

Zek bounced a little in the chair like an excited child. "Yes sir. Guess you won't though!"

A spot of soot and another one there on the baseboard, and there: a shoe-print as plain as day on the dingy wall. While Mrs. Wilkin muttered angrily about the man, now ten minutes gone, who had come to clean the chimneys and stovepipes, Maggie wondered why he had put his shoe against the wall half a yard above the molding. He had not been happy to be called out on a Sunday, and then to be paid for his work with used books and two old china plates. There was a handprint too, and smudges where his hip or buttocks had leaned: he must have had to brace himself against the wall to pull the stovepipe apart. Maggie thought it was lucky that he had come at all. The vision of fighting a fire caused by a dirty chimney or stove frightened her, more so now that Mr. Merritt was sick in his bed.

"Thou must clean this up. And try not to ruin thy clothes," Mrs. Wilkin said.

"With a muss like this, I'd be better off barefooted and scrubbing it wearing only my shimmy. 'Tis far easier to wash skin than clothes," Maggie said.

"Thou'll do no such thing!" Mrs. Wilkin said.

"We're out of washing powder," Maggie said, "Remember, I told you last week."

"As if I have not had enough on my mind!" Mrs. Wilkin snapped, "Use the soft soap."

Enough on your mind, Maggie thought, as the soft soap and hot water smeared the gummy soot stains and made a greater mess, just as she had expected. *I wish he would get better too.* Last night Doctor Green had come and dosed Mr. Merritt with purgatives. In Maggie's opinion, the medicine was worse than the original ill. Mrs. Wilkin had moved the commode next to Merritt's bed, and Maggie had spent time emptying the chamber pot and cleaning up after him much of the morning. She pushed her skirt higher with her elbow and curled her bare toes in the chill air, thinking: *At least soot don't stink.* She was immediately ashamed of her thoughts, remembering how apologetic Mr. Merritt had been about losing control of his bowels, as sick as he was, too, the poor man.

Last week, on her afternoon off, she had gone to visit Mam, for there had been no letter from Eleanor. Maggie had been pleased at her mother's high spirits and had laughed with her for a short time until Rose's disgruntled comments made it clear that Mam's happiness was due to a trip to Sullivan's for a drop or two. Maggie did not have it in her to scold her mother; but Rose had prodded

Frank to do so. When he gave it only a half-hearted attempt, Rose had finished the job as Maggie's peace-making pleas were cut in mid-air by the two sharp-tongued women.

Mam must be feeling low because she's had no word from Mikey, Maggie thought, *What a thing to go so far away from home. I'd not mind that, but I'd not like the fighting. Surely if something had gone wrong with Mike the officers would have written the family. How long did it take for word of such a thing to come back home? I might ask Eleanor,* she thought, *though I ain't had a letter yet. Is she ill? Is she embarrassed about having the frights?* In Maggie's opinion, any embarrassment was unnecessary—didn't everyone have some queer thing they believed or did?

It was the vastness of Eleanor's fear that was puzzling. She had said, we're lost, though they weren't. And she cried about the wolf. Had she lived out West in the woods when she was a girl? Had a real wolf chased her, or threatened her with harm? It did hurt her, Maggie realized, even if it never bit. She would not ask her friend about such a deeply distressing thing, for she did not want Eleanor to go to ground like a rabbit to its hole, hiding for too long, and starving there.

Hearing a quiet groan from Mr. Merritt's chamber, Maggie scratched two words with her fingernail across the gummy soot stains. It would take an hour at least to scrub away the soot; and the afternoon was waning and with it her usual time off. No one had said a word about her leaving and she did not feel that she should ask for anything while there was sickness in the house. Some of the dirty water had dripped from the washrag onto the petticoat rolled nearly to her thighs. *You can't clean properly, can't help anyone, can't even pay proper attention,* she told herself, *you're good for nothing.* She got up to fetch sand and a bristle brush.

Later, when the wall was clean, Maggie prepared beef tea for Mr. Merritt. He would not drink it, despite her wheedling. She fled to the study when he, once again, threw back his covers and rushed for the commode. She put a finger into the spot where Dickens' *Great Expectations* had stood; evidently it had gone home with the chimney sweep. She wished that she could talk about the story with Mr. Merritt, to ask him why Miss Havisham chose to keep her desiccated memories, and why Pip was such a nincompoop.

A slim book had been pushed to the back of the shelf behind the others. Maggie pried it out. *Necessity of Moral Examination: A*

Christian Youth's Companion opened of its own accord, with a little click in its spine, to a chapter entitled: Pride. *I ain't proud,* she thought. She flipped past this chapter, and the next, Disobedience, but stopped short at Indolence. Biblical quotations about indolence were followed by instructional text, which Maggie skipped in favor of the cautionary tales about the tragic consequences that lazy boys (and girls) caused by their negligence. These were so appalling that she read every one, feeling more guilty as she read.

"Maggie! Where are thou? Fetch the clean sheets," Mrs. Wilkin shrilled from Merritt's bedchamber. Maggie did so, then stripped the bed, remade it, put the soiled linen in to soak, stored the un-drunk beef tea in a crock in the pantry, prepared supper for herself and Mrs. Wilkin, and washed up the dishes.

While Mrs. Wilkin dozed in the study, Maggie went to see if Mr. Merritt needed some cheer. He was sleeping, at last. She stood by his bed, worrying: *I don't like his color.* She clutched his arm in fright. Reassured somewhat by the solidity of flesh and bone beneath the linen sleeve, she patted his hand.

"You must get better." She did not whisper the words: she wanted him to hear and pay attention. She pulled the blanket up over his hand, not liking how cold and frail the skin had felt under her fingers. "What would I do without you?" The horrible possibilities besieged her imagination. "Truly, Mr. Merritt. You <u>must</u> get better now!"

Mrs. Wilkin's voice came from the study: "Maggie. Come here. Open the mail," she commanded as Maggie joined her. "We owe money, I've no doubt. We shall have to tell them that Mr. Merritt is ill and wait they must. I'll tell thee what to write and thou must write it for me."

Later, Maggie paused, hearing Mr. Merritt's moaning above the scratch of the pen.

"I'll go see to him," Mrs. Wilkin sighed.

"The next is the last," Maggie said to the old woman's back. But the last letter in the stack was not a bill. She stared at the handwriting and the postmark date in dismay and ran to find Mrs. Wilkin.

"This is from my friend. It came two days ago! Why didn't you tell me?" She shook the letter at Mrs. Wilkin.

"Hush. I've been far too busy," Mrs. Wilkin snapped in a whisper. She shut the door silently.

Maggie urgently whispered her protest. "But she might have asked for me to come today, and I wouldn't have known! She might've waited for me there and thought I didn't care to come. 'Twas my half-day off today and I surely would have gone, but I stayed to help you."

"As well thou must to do thy duty," Mrs. Wilkin said.

"'twasn't right to keep this from me," Maggie said.

"Keep it from thee? I did no such thing! Mind thy tongue," Mrs. Wilkin's voice shrilled.

"Whissht," Maggie warned.

Mrs. Wilkin said: "Thou ought to have gone today, for thou're more trouble here than not! When a girl gets older, she's meant to get steadier, and I have been waiting to see thee do it. Always fretting me to go and see thy friend, and coming home late, and neglecting thy chores!"

Mr. Merritt said something from his chamber. It sounded like a complaint and a plea. Mrs. Wilkin glared at Maggie, beckoned her back to the study. The older woman listened at the study door. "Thou made me wake him, when he needs his sleep."

"I'm sorry," Maggie quavered. The letter in her hand reproached her too. "I didn't mean it. I'd have stayed anyhow because you need me, certainly. But I'd have let Eleanor know I couldn't come."

Mrs. Wilkin eased into her rocking chair, apparently satisfied that her brother-in-law was resting. She settled her shawl around her shoulders and neck, spoke from its shelter like a turtle from inside its shell: "Open thy letter and write thy friend now. Then get to bed. I will sit up with Homer for a time, then I will fetch thou to stay with him 'till morning."

"I'll do whatever you say," Maggie replied, "I want to help."

Mrs. Wilkin opened her mouth to deny this, but then seemed to reconsider the matter. "Least said, soonest mended," she said.

Satisfied with the meager peace offering, Maggie read Eleanor's letter, which was openly apologetic. In the final paragraph Eleanor mentioned an aunt's planned visit and said that could not meet Maggie this week. "Perhaps next Sunday afternoon?" Eleanor wrote, "should you even wish to see me at all." She had left a half-sheet of stationery blank below her signature. Maggie fetched the scissors from her sewing basket and clipped the paper off.

Dear Eleanor, she wrote on it, The good Lord willing, I will see you again soon.

Chapter 21

Ned set the law books down on his instructor's table. "I begin to comprehend Master and Servant," he said, "but I'm tangled up in Conveyances."

Charles Mix yawned. "Before we begin tonight, I have a task for you. At the behest of the Ladies Soldiers' Aid Society, your good mother has written to ask me if I would help a soldier's widow. What is her name, let's see - Carruthers. She hasn't received her widow's pension, so I want you to find out just what is what. I usually charge a small fee to handle such matters, but if you take care of it for me then I can waive the fee for her. Consider it part of your education."

"I remember him. He was a Vinton man in my regiment. Company F, I think," Ned said, "He died at Belle Plain when we were there."

"Was that a large battle?" Mix asked.

Ned replied: "No sir. No battle. He took ill with typhoid, I think, no it was diarrhea. Some men pulled out of it, like I did, and some didn't. He was an English fellow. A wool weaver or some such thing."

Mix said: "Go and pay her a visit and see what documents she has to support her claim. If you think you can expedite the process, then do so." He smiled. "You have connections in Washington, isn't that so?"

"Guess I could think of some," Ned said with humor.

"And I should like you to call upon the Shackelfords," Mix went on. "Phineas Shackelford was severely wounded last December, and his mother says they never received the money promised to disabled soldiers. Goodness knows, they could use it."

"He was in my company," Ned put in, "I didn't know he was hit! Was it Fredericksburg?"

"Yes, the same battle in which you were shot," Mix said with some sympathy.

"Shelled," Ned corrected absently, then: "Phin was a year behind me at the Brick School. Poor fellow. I'll go and see him."

"You're certainly the best man for the job," Mix said.

The next day, Ned spoke to Mrs. Carruthers in a corner of the cramped boarding house kitchen, as the plash and clink of dishwashing accompanied their conversation. She was as thin as a lath and about as handsome, a woman in her late twenties born in the farm country east of Millville. She had married Carruthers (yes, he was English) just a week before he went to camp; remaining in Vinton during his brief military stint. Now she had taken a position as cook in a barely respectable boarding house, as she had no family to rely upon. She did not weep nor complain about her circumstances, nor about her loss, but neither did she smile. However, as Ned left, she thanked him sincerely, saying: "Mebbe now there's some chance to get what I need."

He took the road to the Shackelford's at a slow pace. *Severely wounded. Lost an arm and a leg, perhaps both legs?* he thought. *Why didn't I ask Mix for the particulars? It won't do to arrive ignorant and unprepared.* He greeted Phineas' mother and sister and explained the reason for his visit.

"Call Phin," Mrs. Shackelford told her daughter. To Ned, she remarked: "He's out back splitting kindling."

Isn't blind and kept both arms, at any rate, Ned thought. He heard no thump of a crutch as Phineas came up the back steps into the kitchen. A horrified laugh escaped him as Phineas entered the room and nodded to him in greeting. The man's jaw was almost entirely gone: his mouth was reduced to a pucker like the small puff of fabric created when you pulled the drawstrings tight on a purse. Above this grotesquerie, Shackelford's nose, unscarred, rose prominently like the prow of a ship; and the two sad eyes, with perfect vision, took in Ned's reaction, while the untouched brow furrowed.

"Uh. Uh. Ph-Phin..." Ned stammered finally, mortified. "Phin Shackelford. By heaven, here you are. You made it. I didn't know you were hurt until M-Mix told me just yesterday.

Fredericksburg. Good heaven, one devil of a shell, heigh? I got some too but not as bad." He realized he was babbling. "Well. Anyhow. I came about your pension. Um. So. How are you... faring?" The answering voice was Phin's, but it was small, garbled, incomprehensible.

Ned had no idea what Shackelford had said. When he was a child, he and his sisters used to play a game to see how funny their words sounded when they distorted their faces by pulling their cheeks back tightly or squeezing their mouths with their fingers. But this was no joke for Phineas.

"What's that, Phin?" Mrs. Shackelford said, "Is it about the pension? No? Well? Guess he wants to say he's glad you're well."

"I'm fine," Ned replied, too loudly, "Fine." How was a man so clearly disabled, so marred, capable of asking about a visitor's health? He fumbled for his pencil and paper, then launched into questions, addressing Mrs. Shackelford, supplying half the answers himself from his own recollection of Phineas' service in the regiment. Mrs. Shackelford, however, persisted in repeating some of the questions to Phineas, and waiting patiently while he labored to speak.

Ned pushed the paper and pencil across the table in Phineas' direction. *Write it down, confound it,* he thought. *You can write. How can you bear to live like this? Damned army and their damned delays!* Since Phineas was ignoring the pencil, Ned picked it up again.

What was that sound? Phineas said something and reached over to tap Ned's hand. Ned drew his hand away quickly–dropping the pencil–and looked at the man. It was a mistake: he stared with sick fascination, then said forlornly without thinking: "Phin. God in heaven. Why did this have to happen to you?"

Phineas blinked at him. Thank goodness his eyes had not changed. He wiggled the tiny mouth in a response that Ned heard as a hard "g" sound and a "w" sound. *Go away?* Ned guessed and almost said it aloud.

"It was God's will," Mrs. Shackelford said, while Phineas nodded. Ned gaped at them both. They evidently believed what they said and found some comfort in it. He finally remembered his manners, and replied: "Yes, of course."

"Phin's a great help to me, since his Pa died," Mrs. Shackelford asserted, "Now he's here to see to the crops and the stock, means his brothers can work at the mill." Phineas nodded again. His eyes smiled a little. The sewn-up mouth remained frozen. Admiration for the man filled Ned's mind: it almost pushed aside the horrified sympathy, and the shame he felt at his own ungoverned reactions.

"Yes, indeed," he said, "But you earned a disability pension, Phin, by heaven, you certainly did, and it's a disgrace that you don't have it. I'm here to see what I can do about that. Perhaps the judge can help too. But you'll get it if I have to call on the President himself."

On his way back to the gallery, Ned engaged in a furious imagined parley on Phineas' behalf with a useless Washington bureaucrat. Just as the foe crumbled and began to stamp approval orders, Ned walked into a hitching post and stubbed his toes.

Zek had served two customers in Ned's absence, and painstakingly recounted his conversation with each as Ned sat, still wearing his overcoat, in the velvet armchair.

"So, to summarize, no one wanted a photograph, which is just as well, since I wasn't here, and the lady bought one of our card cases," Ned said.

"Yup," Zek replied, "But I wanted to tell you what they said and all so you know I did right. I cleaned up the storeroom, like you told me. Ain't nothin' out of place here, no sir."

"Mm," Ned said, then shivered. "You did it properly, Zek."

Zek said: "Did you take a chill? You look like you're feelin' poorly."

"No, I'm fine." Ned stroked his jaw from ear to ear, then stirred himself to remove his hat and overcoat and hang them up. He stopped by the mirror and stared at his reflection as if it were a new book to be read.

Later, as he yawned his way into the house for supper, Eleanor handed him a letter from Hawley, of the 14th Connecticut Volunteer Infantry. According to Lieutenant Hawley, George Dunn's silence was not due to sickness, but to periodic enforced visits to the guardhouse. Although George had avoided the most serious crimes such as desertion, assault, or sleeping on guard duty, he had broken nearly every other rule, and neither public humiliation, bucking, gagging, or docked pay, had deterred him. Hawley wrote that the Irishman with the good throwing arm had used it to throw a few punches but had been smart enough to aim them at other enlisted men and not at officers. In Sergeant Flynn's opinion, Foran would make a good soldier once he learned he couldn't shirk in the sick call line. Ned communicated this information, unadorned, to Eleanor so that she could pass it on to Maggie.

"Say, Mother, did I tell you about Joe Creasey?" Ned said, "He's engaged to marry Minnie Park."

"That's good news!" Mrs. Whitfield said, "He's been smitten with her for months; Micah tells me all the gossip when he brings our butter and eggs. I'm glad to hear they've come to an agreement."

Ned went on: "He's going to enlist, he says, so he came to have his picture taken, and hers, of course. She told me they won't marry until the war ends and his military service is complete. Joe didn't look happy at that, but he didn't say a word. Guess she's got him on a short leash."

"A fiancée can have that effect on her future husband," Mrs. Whitfield commented dryly. Ned shrugged but looked up as Eleanor snickered. "What?" he said.

Eleanor closed her eyes, smiling, and cupped her hands to her ears. "I hear a spirit rapping. What's that? She says her initials are H. C."

"Ho. Ho. Ho," Ned said, "I told *her* we had to wait."

"'Oh, Edward, dear boy, promise me we shan't live in Millville, I declare I couldn't bear it!'" Eleanor quoted with a giggle.

"Well, if you wouldn't listen through closed doors..." Ned said.

"I wouldn't know anything interesting," Eleanor said, "Except what I hear from Maggie."

Mrs. Whitfield said: "Minnie Park has faculty: look how she has run that household since her mother died. She'll do fine. But I am sure she'll miss him and worry about him. Engagements in wartime are such a mixed blessing. I hope he'll receive an enlistment bounty?"

"Yes, three hundred dollars, and thirty from the state, but the monthly pay is only $3.00. It's ridiculous," Ned said.

"Three dollars a month is a disgrace," Mrs. Whitfield agreed.

"Miss Park thinks so too," Ned replied, "It's too bad he's going, he's a good fellow, and so much better than Yardley!"

"I expect you'll miss him," Mrs. Whitfield murmured. Ned nodded.

"I wish this war was over," Eleanor said.

Chapter 22

From the maw of the dark house, from worry and witnessed suffering, Maggie was ejected into the fresh whiteness of sun on snow. Mrs. Wilkin had arranged her deliverance: had called her away from her watch at Mr. Merritt's bedside and told her she must rest. *There's no rest anywhere now,* Maggie thought, *not even in bed.* For weeks, she had lived a dim half-life indoors, going out only to dump waste or rubbish, or shake the broom. She could manage no visits elsewhere: she was needed in the house. No visitors came. She couldn't even go out to gather eggs, because the chickens had all been sold or eaten. Through the windows she had watched bright blue October pass, seen the leaves drop and collect around the corners of the house as the wind blew them; and she had seen this November snow-fall, longing to be out in it.

She walked in the main road, staying a dozen yards behind the horse-drawn roller that packed down the snow for easier walking or sleighing. To be sure, Eleanor had written: Come whenever you are able, come and call on me. Could that also mean on a sixth-day afternoon, with no notice? It would have to, for Maggie needed to do more than whisper and wait. Dance's barking heralded her arrival at the Whitfield's. She had just raised her hand to knock at the back door, when Eleanor opened it.

"Maggie! What a surprise. It is so good to see you."

"Good day. I'm sorry I couldn't write to set a time, I didn't know when I'd get leave to come. Can you come out? It's grand weather, all shining, and not so cold," Maggie said, as Dance sniffed and bounced around her in the doorway.

"Of course I can. Just let me get my wraps and tell Mama."

Maggie sat down on the back step. Eleanor came out quickly, hooded, cloaked and mittened. "Let's go and tie Dance out in the stable," she said. "How are you, Maggie? How is Mr. Merritt?"

The choke returned to Maggie's throat. She shook her head. *This is why I came,* she thought, as Eleanor hugged her. The dog nuzzled her leg and danced around her, binding the two girls together with his leash. At the stable they tucked up their skirts and climbed to the hayloft, where they sat, talking in the fragrant half-light until Maggie was able to tell her friend a portion of what had happened at Mr. Merritt's.

"I'm awfully sorry," Eleanor said.

Maggie blew her nose. "I don't know what I'll do."

Eleanor sniffled, looked down at her lap. "I'll help you. If I'm able to. I'll ask Mama. Come down now, and we'll have something hot to drink. You must come in."

"I mustn't," Maggie said.

"Papa's away today. I'll ask Mama. You must get warm, especially as you have such a long walk home."

Maggie made no further protest.

As she gloomed back to Merritt's, chilled by dread rather than by the weather, she wondered why Mrs. Wilkin had not called for help from the Friends at the Meeting she and Mr. Merritt attended before he got so ill. It would do them all good, Mrs. Wilkin not the least, to have her bend a little, to have her ask for and accept aid. *Tis a sin not to,* Maggie thought, *I may be indolent, but she's too proud.* And mean as well, for how else could Mrs. Wilkin find it in her heart to stint on the laudanum Mr. Merritt took for his pain? Maggie always gave him an extra measure when she sat watch by his bedside.

Eleanor had kindly saved some newspapers for her friend. Maggie took one from the basket to read as she walked: perhaps there'd be some news of the 14th so she could imagine where Michael was and what he was doing. She could only hope he was behaving himself now, but it didn't seem likely. She swerved back to the side of the road as the jingle of sleigh bells sounded behind her. There was little war news. Edward Everett Hale and the President had dedicated the new cemetery at Gettysburg.

Squeezed in the dense columns of print was a name she recognized. *The Fenian Brotherhood* headlined the article: *For several years a new political organization has been forming among the Irish population of the United States, calling itself the Fenian Brotherhood, and having for its avowed object the liberation of Ireland from British rule and the establishment of an independent Irish nationality...*"

Annie Mulrooney had mentioned the Fenians, in that annoying way she had. That man Harrigan who'd been "no friend" to Pen O'Shaughnessy was involved, no doubt, and it could be that Mr. Corcoran was too. The article said the organization had met in Chicago with 300 delegates from Ireland, Canada, and the American states, and the body had resolved to liberate Ireland from English domination "*by every honest means which are not in the violation of the Constitution.*" While that phrase was reassuring, why did the Brotherhood "*enjoin upon their young members to learn military tactics*"? Rory Corcoran was not a man to sit in congress and debate independence–he'd toss the opposition headlong into a river as he had the line-jumper on the Fourth of July.

And look at this line of the Brotherhood's resolution: "*that every subject relating to partisan American politics, and to difference in religion, be absolutely and forever excluded from the counsels and deliberations of the F. B.*" Could a Democrat and a Republican, a Prot and a Catholic unite in brotherhood to liberate Ireland? How would they do it?

She folded the newspaper and returned it to the basket, peeking again at the food Mrs. Whitfield had packed inside for Mrs. Wilkin: eggs, roast beef, white bread, jam, a paper cone of butter, half a pie, a small tin of tea. Edward Whitfield had appeared briefly in the kitchen, wearing odd green-glass spectacles: Eleanor said his eye was bothering him. Maggie had seen him drop a paper wrapped cylinder into the basket. Perhaps it was a packet of peppermints. She stopped, put the basket down on the snow, and reached into the bottom of the container.

Written on the packet paper was: "For optics experiment. Hold at horizontal angle to strong direct sunlight." Inside the wrapper was a glass prism, its top third broken off, then filed down so that the broken edge would not cut your fingers. Maggie held the prism up, turning it - but the prism did not split the sunlight into colors; even so, she liked the way the thing shined, and the way the gold sun, white snow, long blue shadows looked like bits of hard candy when seen through the faceted glass.

In Mr. Merritt's house the old-style staircase turned, turned again, and turned back, cramped in against the center chimney, and ended in a short hall leading to the two bed chambers. Maggie sat up sleepily in her bed looking at the faint glow visible through her chamber doorway. She thought it was moonlight, but it moved and brightened. It must be Mrs. Wilkin, coming to bed, with the small lantern's light preceding her. Yes, there was a face at the door, but it was Homer Merritt's, bearing the light in his countenance. Maggie smiled at him. As she blinked, his face disappeared.

Are you well? Come back, she thought. She lurched up to follow him, but the heavy bedclothes were in her way. She pushed off the coverlet and blankets, wincing at the cold.

'Twas a vision, Maggie thought. Wrapped in her shawl, she went down the turning stairs to tell Mrs. Wilkin. Her employer met her joyfully in the narrow front hall. "I was about to fetch thee," she said, "He is gone. God has been merciful."

Maggie shivered in the draft coming in from under the front door. "What?"

Mrs. Wilkin said: "I thank God I was there to hear his last words, which were praise and glory. I have never heard him speak so! Help me to write them down, child, so that I can tell the Friends how the Spirit spoke in him!"

"He can't be gone," Maggie replied stupidly, "I just now saw him, as if he lit his way with a candle. I had a vision."

Mrs. Wilkin's gnarled hand took Maggie's chilled one. "He is now in glory, and at peace. The Spirit must have touched thee too. Come along with me and write down what I say. I must remember it, to tell them all."

Maggie stared at her, then sank down onto the bottom step. "He's dead?" she whispered.

"Yes, Maggie, but thou must not grieve. It is a better land he has gone to. Come down into the study now." Mrs. Wilkin turned away, turned back. "But first, put out the fire in his chamber; no need to waste that wood. At dawn, thou must fetch Minnie Park to help thee lay him out."

Maggie covered her head with the shawl, drawing into the woolen dark: safe from Mrs. Wilkin's words. *I'm still dreaming,* she told herself—and would have believed it if the cold had not seared through her nightgown, setting off a shivering that would not stop.

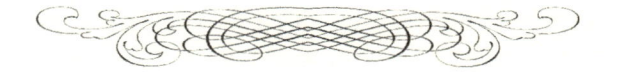

"I've seen a burial at sea, and now I've seen a Quaker funeral, and neither one amounts to a hill of beans," Judge Whitfield opined at the dinner table a few days after Mr. Merritt's death. "They had him in a plain coffin. No procession, just a few Quakers standing in the cold while they put him in the crypt. They would have gone home hungry, if it weren't for the food you sent over, Libby. McKay made nothing on the whole business but the price of a pauper's box."

"Mr. Merritt was a good man," Ned commented.

"He certainly was. It's such a shame," Mrs. Whitfield said.

"He was kind to..." Eleanor murmured, as her father spoke over her: "A good Republican, for all his Quaker ways."

"I remember when he donated all those readers from his store to Kate's school," Mrs. Whitfield said.

"Too many people are dying now!" Eleanor said, then to her brother, "Don't laugh at me."

"I didn't mean to, Elly. It was just the way you said it—as if they offended etiquette by dying without waiting for the proper season."

The judge said: "There's such a thing as being too generous, he had no head for business. Mix tells me there is a lot of debt on this estate; he's not confident that a sale of the property will pay everyone who is owed."

Eleanor looked at her brother and mouthed a silent phrase at him. "What's that, Elly?" he said.

"Maggie didn't get paid," she whispered, then jumped as her father said: "Speak up."

"It's nothing, Papa," she said. Ned sighed.

"Is Merritt's hired girl one of the creditors?"

"I can't believe that there is so little in the estate that it can't pay that small wage," Mrs. Whitfield said.

The judge forked a chunk of turnip into his mouth, then spoke around it: "She'll have to put in her bill and wait in line with everyone else."

"But it's such a small amount, and she relies upon it," Mrs.

Whitfield said.

The judge said: "As Green does on his doctoring fees, as the butcher, the baker, and the candlestick maker do–she can join the crowd clamoring for money owed that they may not get."

"When I clerked for you at the Probate Court, you made it a practice to expedite payments to those who needed them most urgently, especially poor widows, and orphans," Ned put in.

"She's neither a widow nor an orphan," the judge said, then frowned at his daughter: "There is no reason that I ought to favor her claim over others. I can't show favoritism. I never have and I never will."

Patently untrue, Ned thought. The judge stored favors and grudges alike as if they were gold coins: counted them, gazed upon them with affection, spent or hoarded them as the political situation required.

He said: "Yet you do customarily favor the claims of defenseless women, and rightly so! You say that she must be treated like all the others; very well, treat this girl as you do the poor women whose interests you protect. To be consistent…"

"Consistent, my eye! Why are you pressing her cause?" the judge retorted, "If your sister has some complaint to make about my treatment of this servant, then let her tell me. Let her plead the case." He stared at Eleanor who kept her eyes downcast, twining her hands in the hem of the tablecloth.

"That's what lawyers do," Ned said, "advocate for others."

"You're not a lawyer yet! Don't make me laugh," his father said, "I had to force you to go to Mix in the first place, and now you presume to tell me what lawyers do, and hold it over my head?"

Mrs. Whitfield said hastily: "The truth is the girl supports her mother and can ill afford to wait months for her wages for work she has done."

"Hear, hear," Ned muttered. The judge glared at his wife, then his son. He wiped his mouth with his napkin and stood up to go. "Quint's going over there tomorrow to do an inventory. I promise nothing."

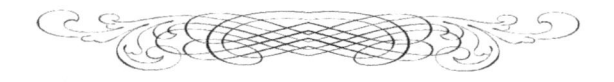

"Those are mine, sir. Those silver spoons belong to me. I

brought them to this house when I came to live here ten years ago," Mrs. Wilkin shrilled. The gray and grumpy man examined one of the spoons. "Those are my initials there. JM, Jemima Merritt. The spoons were gifts to me when I married Abijah," Mrs. Wilkin said.

"You'll have to sign a receipt saying that they're yours," the man remarked.

"The Friends do not swear any oaths…" Mrs. Wilkin began.

Maggie did not wait to hear what else either had to say but left the room and went to her chamber. She pulled her tin treasure box out from under her bed and placed it on the coverlet, then rushed to gather her cloak, brush, hat, fabric flowers, an unfinished letter to Michael and one to Eleanor, and piled them together on the bed. Her hands hovered over the bureau containing her extra chemise, petticoat, nightgown, and drawers. Surely the horrible man would not dare to paw through her underwear? *Och, that one has such a stain,* Maggie thought, folding the offending garment. Though Mr. Merritt and Mrs. Wilkin had supplied them, surely this clothing still belonged to her, who else would want it? She shivered.

Sooner than she expected, Mrs. Wilkin called her downstairs. Maggie penciled a note: "These belong to Maggie O'Shaughnessy" and left it on the pile of her possessions. She worked for an hour under Mrs. Wilkin's and Mr. Quint's direction, then followed him upstairs into the bigger bedchamber and finally into the one she shared with Mrs. Wilkin. He frowned at the pile on the bed and at Maggie's timid words: "I'll sign that paper for you sir, to say those are my things, on the bed there." He went for the tin box, but Maggie seized it first. "That's mine."

"Everything's got to be looked at, girl," Quint said in disgust, "Hand it over."

She clutched it tighter, then fumbled with the box's hasp. The box had been her father's. When the men came that night after he left, they had broken the box's lock, emptied its contents onto the table, and looked through the papers. Not finding what they sought, one of the men hurled the box down, denting the top.

"Here, I'll show you everything that's in it," she said. She took out each of her special things. He barely glanced at her sketches, nor the baby curls tied with twine, nor at the ribbons she'd saved from her best dress, the one she wore when she graduated from grammar school. He took the broken prism from her, unwrapped it, glanced at her as if he had smelled a sour odor, and tossed the glass on the bed. He also took Eleanor's letters. He peered into the envelopes, poked his finger into each, then discarded the letters on the bed.

The cased ambrotype of her father was last in the box. She held it up so that Mr. Quint could see it, but he took the picture, pried the photograph out of its case, smiled acidly at the penny laying therein. "This your beau?" he said.

"'Tis my father!" she exclaimed.

He thumbed the matted glass back into place and handed the ambrotype back to her.

After examining the items on the bed, Mr. Quint reviewed the contents of the chest of drawers; paying little attention to Maggie's underwear but pausing at her blue calico skirt and bodice that were carefully folded in the bottom drawer.

"I made those," Maggie said, "With my money I earned, I made them in May."

Quint sat down on the bed and wrote in his notebook. He took out his penknife and sharpened the pencil, then squinted at the chest of drawers, stood up and reached beneath it, pulling out a dusty book.

"Oh, there it is," Maggie said, happy to see her copy of *Aesop's Fables*. "I been looking for that. It must have slipped down under there."

"Fetch a dust rag," Quint said.

"That book's mine too. Here, I'll wipe it on my apron," Maggie said.

"Yours, you say?" Quint was dubious. "This is an illustrated book, gold stamped calf binding, not pasteboard, it's worth a pretty penny. Got Merritt's bookplate in it too."

"Mr. Merritt gave it to me when I was so sick two winters ago. I had a bad fever, and then I got better, so he said I could have any book I liked, and I picked Aesop. He gave it to me."

Quint frowned at her.

"God's honest truth!" she said.

"Can you prove it?" Quint said.

"He gave it to me, truly!" she insisted.

He said: "This is worth a deal more than all your other traps put together. Unless Mrs. Wilkin can vouch for what you say, I say it's got his bookplate in it, and it belongs to the estate."

Mrs. Wilkin had been nowhere in sight when Mr. Merritt had

smiled at Maggie, patted the book in her hand and told her: "Thou has made a fine choice."

"She wasn't there, but he did give it to me, he did. He said I could have it," Maggie repeated.

Quint shook his head, tucked the book under his arm. "His bookplate. Belongs to the estate."

She had been so dutiful, so careful about her tears, so grimly proud of her fortitude during the past three weeks. In this book that Mr. Merritt had read with her, had laughed, and nodded his head over, his physical presence lingered. She reached for the book, gasping, overcome. She had not wept when his body was laid out, when he was borne to the crypt; now she wailed and wrung her hands. Quint watched her in amazement. He put the book behind his back, grabbed his notebook and pencil and escaped the room.

She got down on the floor, surprised at how the weeping hurt her sides, her throat, her head; at how it shook her just as hard as the power looms shook in the mill, frightening her nearly as much. Putting out her hand, she stretched to touch the place the book had lain.

Chapter 23

"Yuh, we put a notice in the Courant for colorists, right enough, jest Monday of this week, but we had a considerable lot of women come by here and we filled the last position yestiddy forenoon," the clerk at the lithography works said.

"But Mr. Barton told me that you've been selling a deal of the new battle prints, especially now that Christmas and the New Year are in the offing," Ned said.

"Yuh, they're sellin'. But we don't need no more women to color 'em," the clerk replied.

"What about a reserve list?" Ned countered, "You're sure to lose some of the new hires; perhaps this young lady could put her name down in case you have someone take ill and you've need of a replacement. She's an excellent colorist."

The clerk shrugged. "Already got a list as long's your arm."

Ned looked inquiringly at Miss O'Shaughnessy, who shook her head.

"What a shame," Mrs. Whitfield said, "It would have suited you so well, Maggie. As Eleanor said."

Eleanor had first seen the advertisement and suggested the trip; perhaps, Ned thought now, as much to please their mother with the outing as to find a position for her friend.

They took the horse cars back toward the train station, while Mrs. Whitfield pointed out the sights to Maggie. Partway down Main Street, Ned announced: "The next is our stop."

"Why, we're nowhere near the depot," Mrs. Whitfield said.

"No, we're going to make a call at Dunn's," he answered, "I have some photographs I sent to be colored there, I may as well fetch them while we're here."

Alonzo Dunn's female colorist sat in a corner of the gallery adjacent to the reception room, painting photographs with watercolors. After exchanging pleasantries with Mrs. Whitfield, Dunn left the two women with the colorist, and took Ned aside, saying: "Glad to hear you ran that double-dyed scoundrel Rossiter off the property."

"No gladder than I am to be rid of him," Ned said, "You've heard from George?"

Alonzo frowned. "Yep. You?"

"Yes. He'll sort himself out soon, I expect. Most soldiers do," Ned said without expression, then added: "I should have the last of the gallery's debt to you paid off after New Year's Day."

"Figured you would." Dunn nodded his approval. "With that thief's hands off your ledger you'll be all set. Clear profits from now on. I have your pictures about here somewhere."

"They certainly like the colored pictures in Millville. Those are my best sellers," Ned said, then had an inspiration: "Mr. Dunn, I'll bet you could use another colorist. Miss O'Shaughnessy is a good artist, and she's looking for a position right now. I took her over to Kellogg's Lithography but they weren't hiring."

"I might. That's a funny name, ain't it, Oceansee? She German?" Alonzo said.

Ned said: "No. It's O'Shaughnessy, not Oceansee."

"Is that Irish?" Dunn asked.

"Yes. But you ought to see…" Ned began.

Alonzo Dunn shook his head. "Pshaw, Ned, don't waste my time. Is that your mama's new project? She ain't just doing charity for slaves, now she's civilizing the Irish? Well, she's a good Christian woman. So long as your Pa don't object, it's none of my affair. But I can't take on any charity cases."

"She's not a charity case, for heaven's sake, Mr. Dunn," Ned protested, "You ought to see her drawings. If you'd just speak to her, you'd see how much she could offer to your establishment."

"No, my Jane wouldn't stand for it anyhow, working with Irish," Dunn replied.

"She's a pleasant girl. If you could see her work…" Ned quit. It was no use lecturing a fence post.

"Here they are. You had a big order," Dunn said, handing the package to Ned, "and I'm happy to oblige you, but there'll be considerable delay getting yours colored here for the rest of the month."

"It sounds to me as if you ought to hire another colorist," Ned muttered.

"If you think she's so good, why don't you hire her yourself?" Dunn countered.

"Well, I would," Ned answered, "but after the rush is over by New Year's day, my business won't support a colorist full-time; and I doubt she could live on piece-work pay."

"Huh," Dunn said.

"Guess I would hire her, if I could," Ned insisted.

"Guess I'll be getting more packages from Vinton," Alonzo Dunn said with satisfaction.

As Ned rejoined the women, his mother whispered to him: "This young woman says she has a lot of work. Perhaps Mr. Dunn would hire Maggie to help."

"I asked him," he whispered back, "No." He looked at Maggie, who was watching the colorist like a cat watches a mousehole.

"What a shame," Mrs. Whitfield said for a second time. A shame indeed, Ned agreed silently. Although Maggie was untrained, he presumed that once she got the hang of coloring, she would produce finer work than the slapdash jobs Jane turned out. Eleanor said Maggie drew from nature and sometimes copied prints from books or from the illustrated newspapers. What might she be able to do if she had drawing lessons, or the opportunity to see fine art?

"We can see it," he said aloud, to his mother, "I'm taking you ladies to the Wadsworth Atheneum. Hartford has a public art gallery: we may as well employ it to good advantage." He smiled at the way his mother clapped her hands in glee like a little girl, and at the way Maggie stared at him in awe as if he was Apollo personified.

Maggie enjoyed the paintings fully as much as he had expected she would. However, the works he had assumed would interest her she rejected after a brief polite perusal - while she lingered, rapt, before certain works he had hardly noticed. He began to follow her to watch her reactions. She spent only a moment or two before each of John Trumbull's life-size paintings of American colonial battles. Ned thought them masterful works.

"I see you don't care for this one, Maggie," his mother remarked, as they stood before Trumbull's *Quebec-Death of*

Montgomery.

Maggie said: "Oh, the way he put everything in is all right, ma'am. He must have thought about that for a long time. And the funnel clouds he put back there and the gray light up at the front to make you look in the center at the dying General, that's fine. My Da said you could use that white or gray, something different from the background to draw folks' eyes in to what you want them to look at."

"John Ruskin wrote about that," Ned said in surprise, "I read some of his essays in college. About art, do you know them? Perhaps your father did."

Maggie shook her head. "'Twasn't in our reader at school, and Mr. Merritt had nothing by a Ruskin. I don't think Da read those essays; he likely just knew from the painting of things that 'twas a way that worked well."

Ned and his mother stared at the large canvas. "I suppose it is not a true evocation of battle?" she said to her son.

He said: "Now that I examine it, you're right. It's too static, like a tableaux vivant." He searched for the right words but found unsatisfactory substitutes: "Too clean."

" 'Tis a hard task to paint action," Maggie said equably.

"It's not confusing enough," Ned added, "He hasn't caught that. And it lacks the noise of battle. It's a politician's idea of war." *The clean skeleton of war hanging in the glass-front cabinet,* he thought, *with none of the blood and bowels.*

"I see," said Mrs. Whitfield, and Maggie nodded in agreement.

Satisfied by these responses, he ceased following the girl and began to wander on his own. He examined the paintings more critically, remembering fragments of Ruskin's commentary. After a time, he looked at his pocket watch. He had lost sight of his mother and their guest. He hastened into the next room, where Maggie stood in front of Thomas Cole's massive landscape of the Italian countryside. She appeared, finally, to be as impressed by a painting as he was. As he watched, she spent ten minutes motionless before it, smiling slightly.

"Mount Etna, in Sicily. Magnificent, isn't it?" he said.

"Oh yes," she replied ardently.

"It's probably six feet by five and half in size. It must have taken him half a year to complete it," Ned went on.

"To see it all, to sketch it, surely, and then six months more to paint," Maggie said to the picture.

"It looks as if you could walk right into the landscape," Ned said. "I'd like to, although I wouldn't fancy living there, especially when the volcano is active." That comment drew her attention.

"Mt. Etna is a volcano? Still? Is that why he's shown it smoking at the top? I wondered if t'was just a cloud."

Ned replied: "Etna's an active volcano. I believe it erupts about every forty years or so, I can't recall precisely."

"But there's a village right there, at the bottom of the mountain. How can that be when the volcano might erupt any time?" Maggie asked, as if he had some experience of such things, and could give her the answer.

He commented: "I've read that the mountain gives some warning: rumbling, and ash falling, perhaps, so the people there have a chance to escape."

"It didn't in that Pompeii story a long time ago," Maggie said, "How could they live there? I'd worry all the time."

"Most of the residents grow up knowing nothing different," Ned responded, "so I guess it would not seem out of the ordinary for them to live near a smoking mountain. And even if they were not raised there, people are adaptable. They probably don't give it a second thought."

She exclaimed softly, shook her head, her face grave and doubtful. "It would always be there in your mind, the shadow of it. And not knowing…" she said.

He looked at the painting again. Mt. Etna bulked in the background like the bended back of a peasant laborer: the smudges of white smoke hung placidly above its summit, while the Mediterranean curved its gentle blue at the mountain's feet. Upon mountain, sea, and upon the green-clad classical ruins crumbling picturesquely in the foreground, the honeyed sunlight flowed. The scene was peaceful, the view sublime.

What troubled her? Perhaps she was thinking of her employer's recent death, and the loss of her position there. Her expression was desolate. Had she been that fond of Mr. Merritt, as if he were her father? It occurred to him that she might be missing her own father, the deserter. Artist or not, Ned was of the opinion that any man who would leave his own child, especially a child as sweet as this girl must have been, did not deserve the name of father.

"One can grow accustomed to all kinds of odd and difficult circumstances," he remarked, thinking of the army, and hoping to reassure her. She returned from wherever she had gone in her thoughts and gazed at him.

In a pinched voice, almost to herself, she said: "You have."

"I have...pardon me?" he stammered.

"Got used to a bad circumstance," she said.

How long would this last, Ned wondered, this disconcerting about-face: either he was too conscious of his injury, or he forgot it entirely. Those looking at him had a constant reminder. He walked over to stand in front of a muddy still life. He had been wounded in mid-December 1862, a year ago: certainly a year was enough time to heal and move on. After a few moments he resolved to confirm for her that he had become accustomed to his condition, his (how had he phrased it?) odd and difficult circumstance. He turned to do so and made a sound to get her attention, but it was already fixed upon him.

"I will, then," she said, "I will too."

He nodded, several times, yet he was struck by an impulse to take her to the bench outside the door, sit down next to her, and tell her all of it: of how he hated the forced conspicuousness, the infantile drooling, the uncertainty of waiting for the next sudden descent of pain. He wanted to bathe in her sympathy, wanted her tears on his behalf, to cleanse and heal him. He memorized the still life, every drab and receding line.

"Well, here you are," Mrs. Whitfield said by his elbow, startling him. "What is so fascinating about that painting, Ned?"

"Nothing at all," he mumbled.

"Thank you for bringing us here, my dear," his mother said. "I don't know when I've had a better time."

"Are you ready to go?" he asked brusquely.

"Shall we? You're the commander in this journey, so lead and we shall follow. I'm not sure if Miss O'Shaughnessy has seen everything," his mother said.

"It's dinner time and I'm starving," Ned said.

Mrs. Whitfield said: "Very well. We'll go back to the depot."

He announced: "No indeed. I despise that slop they peddle at the station. I'm taking you to the State Street Hotel for dinner."

"How wonderful! You are spoiling me: tomorrow I shall grumble in the kitchen and expect to be fed with a silver spoon," Mrs. Whitfield said with a smile.

"Eat at a hotel?" Maggie asked, "A real eating-house? But I don't have any money."

"It's my treat," he replied, then laughed. Her expression alone was worth the cost of the meal.

The bullying wind and slippery sidewalks slowed the women's steps, but not their excited talk. Mrs. Whitfield, holding Ned's right arm, made steady progress as she talked across him, but Miss O'Shaughnessy (on his left arm) paid little heed to the pedestrian traffic or the condition of the sidewalk. He steered them around a bad patch near the corner of State Street. Two women, hurrying to escape the mush of freezing water and manure thrown up by a passing wagon, struggled to the curb. The lady wearing a brown cloak slipped on the curb, knocking her companion into Mrs. Whitfield. Mrs. Whitfield helped both ladies regain their footing.

"Thank you. Oh! Mrs. Whitfield?" the young lady in the red cloak said. The lady wearing a brown velvet hood lined with gold satin gasped in horror, and stepped backward, almost off the curb.

"Miss Caldwell. I didn't realize it was you," Mrs. Whitfield said.

"Oh goodness. Hattie, it's Mrs. Whitfield!" the red clad Caldwell said.

Maggie strangled an exclamation that was about to sneak from her own lips. That one! She stared at Hattie Caldwell, taking in the expensive but surprisingly drab brown cloak, the flat blond hair, the thin pale visage, now crimson-webbed. Miss Hattie was staring too, at Mr. Whitfield, her mouth open.

The other Miss Caldwell continued in a strained voice: "What a surprise."

Maggie now looked at Edward Whitfield.

"Evidently," he said tightly. He tipped his hat. "Miss Caldwell. And *Miss Caldwell*: It's good to see you looking so well."

Hattie Caldwell mumbled something, then: "No."

After a glance at Maggie, she pulled her arm from her sister's grasp and brushed past them rapidly, sliding a little as she went by.

"Hattie!" The other Miss Caldwell called out, then said apologetically. "Oh dear. She's just rather…you understand. Please excuse me." And she followed her sister.

Whitfield stared after them, his expression unreadable.

"What on earth is wrong with her?" Mrs. Whitfield said severely.

He dropped Maggie's arm and his mother's as well and turned to follow the Caldwells. There ensued an odd tug-of-war as his mother grabbed his arm, he pulled it away, and she seized it with both hands.

"Didn't you see that? She cut me!" he said loudly in annoyed disbelief.

"Edward, mind your voice," his mother said with embarrassment.

"What about her manners?" he retorted just as loudly. Maggie saw a passing lady and gentleman exchange a disapproving look; and a laborer with thick chin whiskers pause to smirk.

"Come along," Mrs. Whitfield said. With an eloquent shrug, he retrieved his arm from his mother's grip, rewrapped his muffler around his neck and lower face, and took both ladies' arms. Maggie sighed, sorry that the party's gaiety had been spoilt by Miss Hattie: the worm in this sweet apple of a day.

The good smells, warmth, and gleaming light at the eating house caught Maggie's attention for a time. Mrs. Whitfield, however, remained in a restrained bad temper as they were shown to a table and seated. Edward Whitfield, bemused, ordered a meal for them, asking Maggie a single perfunctory question: "Do you care for roast beef?" She assented timidly.

After the waiter left, Mrs. Whitfield rearranged her silverware and frowned at the tablecloth, then said: "What possessed her to act like that, the silly little thing! Poor Isabella was mortified."

Edward Whitfield came out of his musings, glanced at Maggie. "Mother, it doesn't merit discussion." His mother heard the warning, and subsided. Edward turned his drinking glass this way and that. Mrs. Whitfield rearranged her silverware again. Then she sat still, her lips pressed in a line.

Maggie looked around at the other diners, to show the Whitfields that she knew the discussion was none of her business. That fat gentleman: wouldn't you think he'd lose a button off his waistcoat, the way his belly pushed at it so. And that lady in the corner has so many patterns in her dress, all the choicest fabrics indeed, but why do they go every which-way? She wished Eleanor was here beside her now (amused and unafraid) to see all these people. No, if she had one wish, it would be for Eleanor to see the Atheneum's paintings. *Mother of God, there's nothing better in the world than that,* she thought.

The arrival of their meal took her from this reverie. There was so much food: beef, potatoes, jellied salad, beets, pickles, and bread looking as soft and white as a new handkerchief. It was served on more plates than she had ever seen for any three people. Ah, is that the fork to use for that, then? She commanded herself to remember every bite so as to tell Eleanor, and Denny—although he would surely say she was making it all up.

Ned sampled each dish: all met with his approval. He paused to cut his serving of beef into small pieces to avoid any mishap with his denture. Maggie thereupon cut her meat into small bites. As he took a drink of cider, he saw Maggie do the same, and wipe her lips after she saw him do that. The girl then turned her attention to his mother. He watched as Maggie alternated bites and observations like a browsing deer wary of attack. He used to make Henry laugh by imitating the mannerisms of people they saw at school or in the street. Wouldn't it be fun to experiment with this girl: if he did something odd like switching his fork from one hand to the other repeatedly, would she copy that?

Catching his gaze upon her, she held her napkin over her mouth, but smiled with her eyes. When he returned the favor, she looked away shyly. She was equally as pretty as any young lady at a ball flirting with him from behind a fan.

Mercy, Maggie thought, *what a sweet smile.* In truth, it was half a smile, as always, for that was all the scars would allow, poor man. *If I could only paint his portrait, paint it true, keep the other scars, so's to show the world what he's done, but give him back his eye and the whole of his mouth, to show what he is.* No one had ever been so good to her as he. The gas-lit room, the full plate, the people surrounding her receded from Maggie's view. She felt shivery, light-headed, glorious; just as she had whenever Kevin Foran came to see her. Maggie frowned now with scorn at the thought of that boy, lovely, yes, but rather simple, silent, tentative, so unlike this man...

"Don't you like your meal, Miss O'Shaughnessy?" he asked. Maggie plummeted back into her chair, into confused response: "What?"

"Your meal. I hope it's satisfactory," he said.

"What, this? This! Oh, no, 'tis grand."

"Good. You were making a face at it," Whitfield said.

He doesn't believe me, she thought. *My garters! Yes he does. He's teasing. Och, maybe not.* She rushed to explain: "'Twasn't that at all! It's Miss Caldwell is a perfect *goose*." Hearing the desperate sincerity in her own voice, Maggie was shocked when Whitfield barked out a belly laugh, and when his mother joined him, less raucously, in the chorus. When they quieted, Maggie said: "I oughtn't to have said it, for I don't know the lady."

Mrs. Whitfield smiled at her, and then at her son, when he said: "Ah. But I do." He leaned toward Maggie a little as if to share a confidence. "You say that you're not acquainted with the lady, Miss O'Shaughnessy, yet you made a most perspicacious observation about her just a moment ago. What else can you tell me about her, from what you saw? And, I beg you, speak frankly this time, and don't hold back out of a sense of decorum."

She saw mischief rising in him like the bubbles in his glass of cider. Mrs. Whitfield did too. So, in deference to that good lady, Maggie simply shook her head. She made a face to show that she indeed had further opinions on the topic of Hattie Caldwell. *That brown and yellow didn't suit her complexion at all,* she thought, *Faith, her eyes looked like boiled gooseberries.* And how could such a smart fellow pick such a ninny? It was nothing more than (like Aesop said) sowing your pearls to the swine. Miss Caldwell must have tricked him, but now he saw her true color. No doubt she had pots of money: that must be it. Mr. Caldwell owned a great house somewhere and a railroad line or two and the families had pushed the match–so luckily broken!

Edward Whitfield said: "Very well. You refrain from comment because you don't know the lady, which is eminently diplomatic behavior. I think you do know the name, however. Ha! You do. Hang it all, Eleanor's been telling tales out of school."

"No!" Maggie protested, "Not so's you'd notice."

"Not so's you'd notice?" He repeated, finding this amusing. He stroked his beard. "I ought to know better; Damon will not malign Pythias." Maggie did not know what he meant. Mrs. Whitfield hurriedly changed the subject to the changes in Hartford since her last visit. Maggie had only to nod at the appropriate times, and could follow her own thoughts: from Eleanor, to paintings, to finding a position, to Damon and what's his name.

At a lull in the conversation, she said: "Oh. I'm thinking that was a Roman story, that one about Damon and um…They were great friends."

"Yes, that's right," said Mrs. Whitfield.

She looked to Mr. Whitfield for approval, but he had fixed her with a speculative gaze, which made her feel warm and light-headed again.

What a shame that this girl was not educated beyond grammar school, he thought. *Despite her position in life, she has sought to learn more. She certainly appears to have the mental capacity to do so. And if you dressed her properly and glossed her manners a little, she would make a good governess, if she wasn't Irish. Or a drawing instructress...or colorist. Perhaps I could give her enough work to sustain her for the next few weeks.*

He was aware that it bothered Eleanor to suppose that Maggie would end up scrubbing grates, and kitchen floors, and laundry: wasting her talents through no fault of her own. Ah, but her name was legion. Fortune was capricious. How many men on the earth were able to do what they were meant to do? Will and Rob had not had the chance, Phin Shackelford had it no longer, Joe Creasey might never have it. And he, himself?

"Wouldn't you agree? Edward?" Mrs. Whitfield said.

"I beg your pardon," Ned said, "What were you saying?"

"I said what a shame it is that there is no intelligence office, no hiring agency in Millville, as there is here in Hartford."

"Yes, however, I was thinking..." Ned began.

"There's a hiring office in Millville," Maggie said, "but I'd no more go there than fly to the moon. I know the fellow who runs it, Mr. Hurley. He hires out the work crews, and that makes him think he's grander than the President, and that he knows enough about hiring girls out to help, when he knows nothing about any such thing. I'll talk to Bridey and Maura Donnelly and Mrs. Leary, and Mrs. Kernan at the boarding house, and they'll find me a better place than ever Mr. Hurley could."

His mother said: "I see. Mrs. Ives from our church asked me how one goes about hiring a girl to help. Her husband will be clerking at the new mill that's being built closer to the lake. She's been married just a year or two and she has a little boy who she has just weaned, and so she had hoped to begin calling on ladies here in town and receiving them one or two afternoons a week. She and Mr. Ives have been living with her relations near Boston, so she is new at setting up housekeeping. If she oughn't to visit the intelligence office, can you recommend how she might proceed?"

Maggie said: "No, ma'am, she mustn't go there. 'tis a rough

place, and the men know nothing: they'll give her some silly little girl who still wants to be home with her Mam, or someone shiftless like Annie Mulrooney."

Mrs. Whitfield said, "Mrs. Ives also mentioned to me that she cannot afford to pay for help but a few hours a day or perhaps a few days a week, so I assumed you would not be interested in the position."

Maggie appeared to consider this for a moment or two: "As she's a friend of yours, this lady, I could see her, if you like, and help her for a bit until she finds someone who suits."

Ned seized his chance, saying: "I was thinking I might hire a colorist at the photograph gallery. I would pay her by the piece. The problem is that I expect we'll have a rush for colored pictures 'till the New Year, but then I can't promise any work after the first of January."

"I could do it!" Maggie said. She put down her fork and placed both hands on the tablecloth, leaned toward him. "I'll do it for as long as you need, if only a month."

"Capital!" he said.

"You could buy the paints and brushes," she put in.

He replied immediately: "Guess I could. And an easel, too." She shook her head: "No, she didn't like it, that girl at Dunn's, and neither would I. I need something flat, maybe with a slanted block underneath and something to rest my hand on."

"I could rig up some sort of working frame to tack the picture in, with a track and moveable dowel as a hand rest." he replied.

She went on: "And you'll be needing a spot in the gallery where I could work, for people like to watch sometimes, and you get a better picture when you can take the colors from a person his own self, in the same light as the photograph. Mr. Dunn wrote the colors on the picture for his colorist, but, mercy! brown means nothing, there's half a dozen browns it could be, d'you see?"

He smiled. "Yes, I see. Like a custom-made portrait. Could you do that?"

"As sure as you're born. I'd just sketch the folks as they sat for you and put in samples of the colors, then use the same to color the photograph. Or if a lady wanted a different color frock that suited better, I could do that."

She's bargaining like a sutler, Ned thought, surprised but not displeased.

"I'll talk to Mrs. Ives too, Mrs. Whitfield, if you like," Maggie went on, "It may be I could help her too, day-maiding or minding her baby or such."

"I think that is a good idea," was the answer.

Ned said: "Well, you ought to come by the gallery, Miss O'Shaughnessy, when you are able to."

"I'll come tomorrow," she said, took her hands from the table, clasped them, and amended: "If that's all right with you?"

"First rate," he said.

Chapter 24

Guessing that the weak December sunlight that greeted him at daybreak might last, Ned opened the gallery barely an hour after dawn. Zek Fish had been watching the weather too: he arrived a few minutes later. The two of them worked together without a word to prepare several large orders for delivery. Trim the picture, paste the back, center it on the cardboard mount, stick it down. Fish left with the finished orders. Ned looked over the photographs yet to be painted, admiring one that was almost completed. He watched the clock.

She came into the gallery apologizing. Pushing back the hood of her cloak, she removed the hairpins holding on her maid's cap: an affectation Ned presumed the Ives' had insisted upon.

"Mrs. Ives wanted me to stay because baby is sick," she said, "but I told her I was needed here."

"We do need you here," he replied, "but if they have sickness in the house, perhaps you'd better go back."

Maggie made a face. "My garters, I'd much rather be here! Baby's cutting some back teeth, 'tis nothing more. They know well enough that you have first claim to my time now; but Mr. Ives don't care a fig for that, for when I was getting my things to go out, he says to me, Come back, Mary, I want my breakfast, when it was layin' there on the table ready for Himself to eat."

"Mary?" Ned said. She was halfway to the coat hooks but turned back to him. "Every servant's Mary to him, so he says."

"Tch. Arrogant fellow," Ned said, "He's from Boston, so perhaps that explains it."

She commented: "I don't see much of him, thank goodness,

so I suppose it don't matter. Besides, he happened to have got it right, for 'tis my name, after all."

"Is it? Your middle name?" he asked.

"No, 'tis Mary Margaret," she said, running the two names together so they sounded like a single long one. For some reason, he liked the sound of it. He waited until she had hung up her cloak and smoothed down her hair; then he picked up the painted carte-de-visite he had admired.

"Mr. Simmons is coming in this morning for his daughter's pictures. It looks as if you've finished that order."

"No, sir. I'm having a bit of trouble. I can't get Miss Simmons right," she said.

"It looks fine to me. How many did she order to be colored?"

"Just the one. And the rest plain."

"Ah, good. I'll mat these now."

"Take the others, but do leave that one for me, if you please. Not five minutes more and I'll have it just right," she said. He kept the colored picture in his hand, remarking "Whoever thinks a faultless piece to see, Thinks what ne'er was, nor is, nor e'er shall be, as Pope says."

"The Pope says that?" she said in surprise.

"Ha, that's a good one! Not your pope. I was quoting Alexander Pope, the poet." A vista of humorous possibility opened before him, in light of her smile. "You know," he began, but the first customer entered. He handed her the picture and left her to her own devices.

Later in the morning, Ned emerged from the darkroom. "These ferrotypes are finished, Zek. Cut them and mat them now, will you? That fellow from the livery stable is coming in to get them." Ned took his task list from his pocket.

"That one," Zek responded, grabbing the shears. "Did ya see him, Miss Shaw? That dirty one? I swow he had horse flop on his vest."

She shook her head with a grimace.

Ned glanced over at her. He said: "I heard of a fellow like that when I was in the army. The company was lined up for inspection, and the private's shirt hadn't seen a washtub for a month or more. 'Private O'Reilly', says the lieutenant. 'Here, yer honor', says O'Reilly with a salute. 'How long do you wear a shirt?' the lieutenant roars at him. O'Reilly looks down at the thing, thinks to himself for a moment, and says: 'About twenty-eight inches, sir!'"

As Zek laughed, Miss Shaw said slyly: "Well, sir, he must be a famous fellow, for didn't I read that same story in the newspaper."

The gallery door opened again. Mr. Whitfield greeted the couple that came in, chatting with them at the door before leading them to the showcase. Another man entered.

"Good day, sir," Maggie heard Zek say.

"Hm. A Fish if ever I saw one," the man said. Maggie looked up at that.

"Yep, sir, you hit the nail on the head," Zek replied, "Kin I interest you in having your picture taken?"

"Yes, you 'kin'," the man answered. "That's my intention, after all." He took off his hat. "Well, look who's here. Good day, Perkins. Mrs. Perkins." Edward Whitfield turned from the showcase, tense, unsmiling.

"Good day, Judge," Mr. Perkins said. Maggie kept her head down, pretending to work, but listening with nervous fascination. The voices advanced, bowed, circled: all present keeping to the semblance of friendship and courtesy. *'Tis all for show,* Maggie thought, even as Judge Whitfield praised the gallery's appearance, and discussed his intention of sending his photograph to his daughter in Washington. Edward Whitfield escorted the Perkins' into the camera area, saying over his shoulder to his father: "Take a seat."

The judge disregarded this directive. Instead, he hung up his coat and hat, then roved the reception area, ending next to her worktable. He said: "I know most everyone in town. I believe we may have met before, Miss...what is your name?" His voice was similar to Edward Whitfield's—dark like roast coffee, but far harsher than his son's.

"Shaw, sir," she said.

"Huh. I think not," he said, "Where are you from?"

Maggie touched the brush to the photograph, stroking the figure's dress, thinking. She said: "I work for Mr. and Mrs. Ives on Lancaster Road, and come here to paint when I can."

"That's not what I asked you, is it?" he said. *No good answer, no escape.* Maggie wet the brush.

"I'm sorry, sir, what? I thought you meant...I'm from here, Millville."

Silence, then: "Born here, were you?"

"Yes, sir."

"Yet I don't know the name, Shaw." That must be what judges did: say a lot of things that didn't really call for an answer but allowed them to be offended if you didn't speak.

"No, sir."

He said: "Some folks move into this town, and out again directly. They never set down any roots. It's a hallmark of the laboring class. Yet they keep their names. I had a German fellow in my court, by the name of Krippenholz. Now there is a name you'd think any man would alter to make it easier on our English tongues, wouldn't you agree?"

"I...I don't know, sir."

"Do you have a strange foreign name that you've altered, Miss Shaw?"

"No sir," she replied.

A huff from him, he was losing patience. The cat's paw came out: tap, tap, reach, snag with a claw. He announced: "I think you do. There's a pack of laborers here in town, hod-carrying, ditch-digging Paddys and Micks, some by the name of O'Shaughnessy. Yes, indeed, that's a name I've heard. Don't you belong to them?" He said it as if she were a stray piglet found wandering near the courthouse.

"Yes sir." Maggie thought this the safest answer.

"Then you assuredly have a foreign name that you've altered," he said.

She said: "No sir. Not at home. Mr. Whitfield calls me Miss Shaw when I'm here."

"Ah." He laughed a little, with no humor. Finally, he said: "Well, that was a pretty little game. And a waste of my time. You know who I am, don't you?"

"No sir. Yes, sir, the Judge, I heard them say," Maggie peeped, "but we never bin introduced." Now she glanced at him and was relieved to see that he was undecided whether she was pert or merely stupid. He abruptly turned his back on her and moved away. For once in her life, she was glad to have been dismissed.

The judge opened the table-top showcase as if he owned it, picking up and examining its contents. Maggie soothed herself by imagining his downfall. How would it come? It must be something to leave him weeping with humiliation. The humble shall be exalted, and the proud ones cast down! Yes, he would watch with amazement as his daughter threw down her shyness, like the cripple had his crutches when the Lord healed him.

Mr. Barton, rich Mr. Barton would propose; and away from this locomotive of a man, Elly would flourish, and dance to the music of her new husband's sweet words. He'd take her away to Hartford with him and keep her safe: how gladly she would go! Her mama would visit of course, and brother, sister, Maggie herself perhaps, but this one—no, he would not be welcome in that fine house. He'd come to know, too late, how he had misjudged his youngest daughter, and then (burning black with secret guilt), he'd take himself down to Washington, leaving Millville in peace.

The Perkins' returned with Zek Fish. Fish blinked at Judge Whitfield, whose hands were still in the showcase as if he meant to gather all its contents into his possession. "Uh," Zek said, "Uh, guess he's ready for you now, sir."

Ned was ready. He had decided to take the offensive. "Where's Mother?" he demanded as his father came into the camera area. "Mrs. Perkins was asking if she's taken ill. I expect they were wondering why you came to be photographed without her."

"Ah," the judge replied, "I'll send her around to you the next time she makes her social calls. Of course I mean to have her photographed. And I needn't explain myself to Myrtie Perkins! I happened to have business with Mix this forenoon, that's why I came by here."

Ned said: "The negatives are already prepared and in the camera. When they dry out, they're worthless. So, sit down." The judge did so. "Here, lean your head back and I'll fix it in the restraint," Ned instructed.

"I won't put my head in that thing. I can sit still. I'm not in my dotage," the judge protested.

"This light isn't as strong as I'd like. You may have to sit for a while," Ned responded.

His father said: "Just take the picture. Mix told me that he and his missus came here to be photographed. He said it was high time to get my picture taken. Here you've been a photographer for six months…"

"Eight months," Ned said, "You haven't come."

The judge continued: "and Mix said it was a case of the cobbler's children going barefoot. I've been busy, but now here I am."

"Yes. But you can't talk while I'm taking your picture." Ned stepped to the camera and put his head under the black cloth, examined his father's upside-down image. "Turn your head a little to the right. All right. Sit back. Yes. Put your chin down. Too much. Up. There." He came out from under the cloth. "Can you at least try for a pleasant expression?"

"I don't like your tone of voice," the judge said. Ned shrugged. "It's a hazard of the picture business. Just think of something pleasant: election to high office, fortune and fame. I guess that'll have to do. Look over here." He took the pictures, then beckoned to Zek:

"Mr. Fish. Take these to the darkroom. You can develop them."

Zek gaped: "Me? Yes sir!"

The judge indeed had not required the head restraint: by force of will, he sat unmoving, implacable. Ned was tempted to make the man wait until he was in a state of rictus.

"I'm finished," he said, after a while. "You can go."

The judge stood up, shook out his shoulders, pulled down his vest. "Shaw!" he said.

Ned thought his father was exclaiming another protest and said: "What's the matter? Got a crick in your neck? That's what the head restraint is designed to prevent."

The judge said: "You didn't tell me you had hired a colorist. I had to hear it from Mix. Miss Shaw: what bunkum, when she's as Irish as Paddy's pig. Who did you hope to deceive by disguising her name? It's just like you to think that changing a word or two changes the facts," the judge said.

"Mutatis mutandi," Ned retorted. "I hire the help I need. If I choose to call my assistant Merlin and my colorist the Queen of Sheba, I'll do it. As long as my ledger shows a profit, what's in a name? I'll bring your pictures home when they've finished printing out. It may be a day or two, depending on the sun."

"Just bear in mind that it's not the first of April, and you haven't fooled me," the judge said.

Chapter 25

Much too boring, Ned thought. He scribbled over the paragraph he had just written, took out his penknife and sharpened his pencil. He had formed the habit of penciling initial drafts when he was in high school, occasionally earning five cents here and ten cents there by composing love letters for others and pruning his fellow students' written class-work. He had revised his wartime letters home as well, for different reasons.

He began again: *You no doubt read about the defeat of our men at Chickamauga and their suffering in the siege of Chattanooga. They were subsisting on half-rations and their horses and mules starved: not for the first time in this war. But the Old Rock of Chickamauga would not budge, saying 'We will hold the town until we starve'. And starve they did, until Gens. Grant and Hooker opened up the supply lines. Who could have imagined that those same men, like the alchemists of old, would turn lead to gold, defeat to victory, as they charged that impossible height at Chattanooga and took Missionary Ridge, shouting all the while, Chickamauga, Chickamauga! their answer to the rebel yell.*

In like fashion, albeit in a less glorious matter, I have risen from starvation in the siege at my gallery, have charged up and taken Profit Ridge—while shouting my battle yell: Rossiter, Rossiter! Yes, several nice turns of phrase there. He continued: *Although I no longer command a company of a hundred soldiers, merely a staff of two, the unprepossessing Fish I landed...*

Ned sucked on the pencil, smiled. Katie would like to hear what Zek had said today. The two of them had worked steadily until 2:00, when he paused to pull his rations out of his haversack, and asked Zek: "Did you eat?"

"Yep, sir," Zek said, then farted loudly.

"Who let that duck in here?" Ned said. Zek giggled, punctuating his merriment with another sound from his posterior.

"Another round from the worthy Bottom. I hope that was all sound and fury, signifying nothing," Ned commented, "That's Shakespeare."

"Hoh! Shakespeare wrote about farting?" Zek asked.

"Ha, yes! One of his lesser known sonnets!" Ned laughed, "Phew. What the devil have you been eating?"

"S-sorry, s-sir. S-s-sausage."

I had to pinch my nose at that one, Ned thought, *before we went on with the Bard.* "Hie thee far from me, thou sibilant varlet."

"I guess that's Shakespeare too, heigh?" Zek said, "Sounds like him: civil ant fartlet."

...the Fish I landed, who today surprised me with his knowledge of Shakespeare, by.... Ned crossed that out. Better to see Katie laugh. He'd tell her the story in person.

...the Fish I landed and the Shaw I... What? Abbreviated? He crossed that out too.

...the Shaw gracing my gallery and distracting...Me. And other men too, he thought. That phrase merits deletion, definitely— even if it was true.

Two days ago, a handsome, red-headed son of Erin came to the gallery. "Where's Whitfield?" the man asked, as if they were fighting words. Ned entered the reception room and identified himself. The man's demeanor changed, but in a way that Ned had rarely seen: the scars elicited a smile from the fellow.

"Fancy that," the Irishman said, "And where's our Maggie today?"

Ned disliked the man's use of the possessive word, disliked the man. "Are you a relation of Miss O'Shaughnessy's?"

The man grinned in response. "I've known her since she was a baby."

Zek took over, extracting the man's name, Corcoran, extolling Miss Shaw's work as a colorist, and touting the low prices of a fine set of cartes-de-visite. Corcoran sat for his photograph as if he was a king: no matter how he was posed, there were no bad angles to his face.

If a camera was a sentient being, Ned thought, *it would*

undoubtedly express a preference for the arrogant, the dramatic, the romantic, and the poseur. Meeker folks, whatever the excellence of their characters, did not often fare well as photographic subjects. He wondered again now if Corcoran was Miss O'Shaughnessy's beau. Perhaps Eleanor would know.

He wrote: *...the Fish I landed, and Miss O'Shaughnessy have proved surprisingly able as clerk and colorist.*

You asked whether I share Mother's opinion that our mouse is doing better these days. I do. She did not flee when presented to my friend Henry B. in August, she meets Mother's callers regularly, and I'm sure you heard that we hosted Uncle Elijah, Aunt Fan, and cousins here for Thanksgiving for the first time, and how well Elly did. Your charge up Judge Ridge this summer was indeed a victory. I promise to make that my last use of the metaphor in this letter. Ned paused and flexed his fingers.

I don't know if you heard about Phineas Shackelford. Most of his jaw was taken off by shrapnel in the shelling at Fredericksburg. He can barely speak. I told Mr. Mix I'd help Phin get his pension for the injuries. I thought it would be an easy matter, considering how badly he was hurt.

A private receives eight dollars a month pension if he is totally disabled, or lesser amounts corresponding to a rating of the severity of his disability. Thus, for example, if a man lost two fingers, he is rated 2/8 disabled and gets two dollars a month. The national pension law passed last year requires the soldier to have his disability rated by a surgeon.

Because Phin is as tough as a knotty tree, he has recovered enough to work his Pa's farm, and so he is not judged disabled, because his eyes and arms and legs function and he is able to work. The law counts as naught the loss of his speech, and the fact that he is now viewed as a grotesquerie. Is it not a ratable disability when a man must eat the pap fed to babies? Not according to our sage lawmakers: he can work, then let him work.

I appealed to Dr. Green...

He paused again. Green had been sympathetic but insisted he could only report the truth of the matter about Shackelford's condition.

Then he had peered at Ned, peered closer, cleared his throat, and said: "Why didn't you call for me when you had your last neuralgia attack?" Ned had muttered that he did not care for the effect of the morphine injections to his face. Green said: "If it keeps up at the rate it has been going, I'd recommend you see a surgeon. There's a fellow I know in New Haven who is an expert in neurology. You may have to get those nerves cut."

Ned contemplatively drew X's through his reference to Green, and wrote instead: *Relate this to Uncle Cy, and ask him if he can recommend someone to intervene for Shackelford at the Pension Office. I will send any information that's needed.*

I've just been called to mess, so I'll close. I shall celebrate this New Year of 1864 in a far better state of mind and body than I entered 1863. I wish you and the Washington Whitfields a healthy, prosperous, and dare we hope, peaceful New Year.

So, the old year's gone. I won't drink to the new one, Maggie thought, regretting the end of her good times at the photograph gallery. "Perhaps one afternoon a week," Mr. Whitfield had told her, "Business is very slow in the winter." The beer in her glass was blood-warm and smelled of dishwater. She moved it aside.

I'm painting, Da! she told her father silently, and 'tis the best time in my life altogether. If only he knew it, could see with his own two eyes how she did. But he knew nothing of it. He knew so little of her now: less even than Mr. snooty Ives. Nearly five years gone! And the last time she had seen him she had been so childish, plaguing him for more of the praise he'd awarded her the day before at the Brick School's graduation exercises. He had looked upon her and smiled, and said, I never thought I'd have so fine a child.

For that first hard year, she was sure it was her Mam made him go—Mam and her bad habits. He had not wanted to, surely, or why would he have put the note in her shoe? But maybe it was those men who had dented the tin box who made him go.

Corcoran yawned and settled himself in a chair by the coal stove. He'd been the object of the New Year gathering's attention for most of the night as he joked, told stories, expounded, advised, argued. Now he was alone, staring meditatively at the stove.

Maggie pulled a side chair next to his. "Tell me about my Da." He regarded her for a while.

He said: "You'd best be thinking of your own future, dear,

and not all this auld lang syne."

"Please Rory, do tell me."

"Ah, leave it be, darlin'. You've something to tell me - why I've not yet had my New Year's kiss from the prettiest girl here." He leaned toward her.

Maggie scooted sideways. "No, you tell me about Da and then you'll have your kiss."

"That's how 'tis, then?" he responded, amused.

"Was he a Fenian Brother?" Maggie asked.

Corcoran sat back in surprise. "How'd you…? Heard some gossip about, have you?"

Maggie said: "Is it a secret, then?"

"Who's tellin' you such things?" he bluffed.

"Annie told me," Maggie said. He glared in Annie's direction.

Maggie added: "And I read about the Fenians in the newspaper, too."

He said: "Ah, did you…and what did it say?"

"About a convention of Irishmen from here and from Canada, and England too, I think, to take any means for Ireland's independence," she answered, "And I'm thinkin' if Da was in it maybe that's why he had to go West."

"What's this, had to… he always said he'd go West, you remember that," he replied.

She said: "That was a joke, for he'd say to Mam, you mind yourself or I'll leave you behind as baggage when I go West." As he shook his head, Maggie went on. "Yes! And if you're about to say he took his leave because he stole money, yes, I know that too. I was a child when he left but not such a baby as all that: thirteen, after all. I know he took some money from the carriage works, but 'twas only his own wages, I heard that too. And I say he didn't go because he took the money, but he took the money so's he could go and go in a hurry."

" 'tis the same thing," Corcoran said.

Maggie scowled at him. "Surely not. Some men came to get a paper out of his writing box after he went, and…"

"That's nothing," he interrupted, "you know he was clerk of the payroll, and had some records of the men working on the building crew, no harm if one of them needed his papers."

Maggie countered: "But he started at the carriage works

when I was a girl, and he didn't keep the payroll once he was there, did he now?"

He shrugged. "I'm thinkin' he kept someone's papers, is all, and they wanted them."

"Who's Mr. Harrigan that we saw on the Fourth of July?" Maggie asked, "Annie said you don't work for him, but that he's an important man. Mam said he was a friend of Da's but then I think they fell out."

"Annie again," he said with annoyance, "You must not take what she says for gospel truth: you know better than that! Work for him, indeed. I don't work for him. All you need to know is he's a big bug over to Hartford, so you mind yourself when you talk about him, and Annie must do the same."

"I'm sorry. It's just that when the strangers came, the ones asking for the box, Mam tried to send them off, but they took up my Da's box without so much as a by your leave, and broke it open right there."

He looked disturbed but merely shrugged again.

Maggie said: "And they looked through all *our* things when they saw what they wanted had gone missing. So, I..." She could hardly say it, for it seemed real again, telling Rory. "He had to go." Corcoran shook his head. He reached for his drink, gulped it down. He seemed to have nothing to say. His silence frightened Maggie in turn, and she called his name in appeal.

"Whissht!" he replied. "You stop all that talk now, or I'll send you home. D'y' not see how they're all looking at you as if you're mad, like they do for your Mam. 'tisn't any harm if they think you're a bit fey, as they do, but you don't want them thinkin' worse of you."

Maggie fought the urge to weep.

"Here now," he said. "Have a sip of this." He gave her his glass and Maggie took in some of the whiskey, its taste as bitter as the apprehension in her heart.

He went on: "That's a good girl. Give us a smile, then. You're a good loyal girl, it does you credit, surely, but that ain't the best way to be sometimes. Och, no tears, no tears, now. Give us a kiss." Although Maggie didn't give it, he took it, and she was warmed by the whiskey and by the rough mouth upon hers.

Part Two

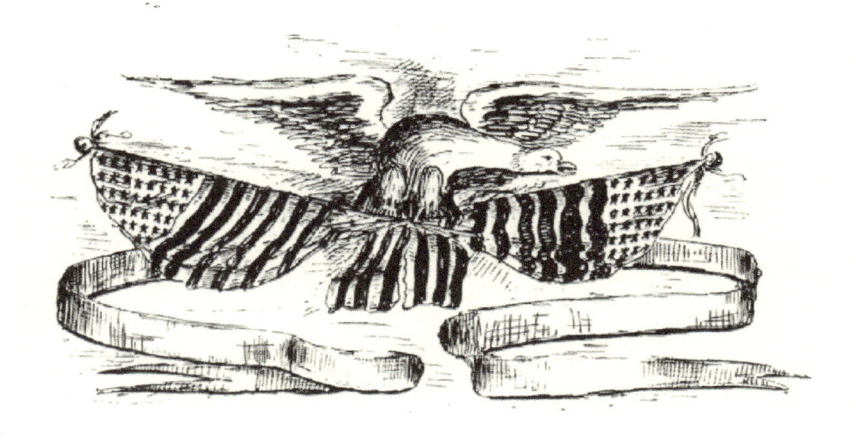

1864 - 1865

Chapter 26

Teasing a stray paintbrush hair from the surface of a baby's cheek she had newly daubed in pink, Maggie did not look up when the customer entered. Heavy tread, no rustle of skirts, a hint of tobacco: male. She successfully captured the tiny hair with the tip of her fingernail, then said to the man: "Would you like me to fetch the clerk, sir?" He said: "There's no hurry." A tall young gentleman, handsomely turned out in a fine overcoat, he removed his hat but kept his brown eyes upon her in a flattering manner. She smiled at him.

"I didn't know that Whitfield had a new ornament in his gallery," the man said. Maggie could feel the blush rising. "I'm just the colorist," she said. "And coloring quite nicely, I see," the customer replied with a smile as he removed his overcoat.

"Oh, hullo," Zek said. "Good day. Didn't hear you come in, sir. Would you like your picture taken today?"

The customer gestured toward the photographs Maggie had just painted. "I might," he said. "These are fine."

"Yep, that colorin' is first-rate, ain't it?" Zek said, "She draws you while you're sittin' for the photograph so she kin put down the colors from life and get the same light we took the picture in. You won't find a better bargain at the price."

Maggie said: "Zek, would you hang up the gentleman's hat and coat."

"S'pose I can," Zek muttered, and took the garments.

The customer went to the mirror and glanced at his reflection with the air of someone who really had no need to look. His custom-tailored suit was as grand as the overcoat. He was just about the best-looking man Maggie had seen, except, *dress Rory Corcoran up in a suit like that and he'd take your breath away*, she thought.

Mr. Whitfield sprang in from the darkroom, apron-clad, vigorously toweling his hands. "Henry," he said, "You do beat all. I never know when you'll turn up. I guess you have more business in town—Topliff business, heigh?"

"I do indeed," the customer said.

"Will you join me for dinner before you call on the Misses T? Zek, take these." Whitfield handed off the apron and towel and rolled down his shirt sleeves.

Henry said: "Thank you. But I should not like to impose on your mother a second time, uninvited." Maggie could not pull her gaze away from the compelling visitor. Without a doubt, this was Eleanor's Mr. Barton.

Mr. Barton said: "I can see that you've made substantial improvements, especially in your adornments–like that pretty new picture in the corner." He cocked his head in Maggie's direction. Maggie smiled, looked at Mr. Whitfield to see how he enjoyed this joke. He seemed perturbed. A moment later, he took an empty gilded frame from the wall and held it up to contain Maggie in his view. "Quite the most admirable frame in the shop, wouldn't you agree, Harry?" he said.

"Mercy," Maggie whispered. The compliment thrilled her.

Mr. Barton laughed. "Indeed."

Whitfield laid the frame carelessly on the display case. "So," he said, "We have a draw on the matter of dinner, but perhaps I can persuade you to have your image captured."

"I'll admit that I am tempted to do it, Ned. If only so that I can sit in the presence of your colorist, Miss…" he paused, so that she could supply her name.

"Shaw," Zek said. Mr. Whitfield was examining something of interest near the ceiling.

Mr. Barton nodded. "Miss Shaw… and watch her work." Maggie picked up her paintbrush uneasily. Nothing wrong in it, surely, but he belongs to Eleanor. Perhaps he spoke so to every girl, as Corcoran did. Maggie looked at Mr. Whitfield, to verify that the remark was simply a jest, despite the rather too interested way Mr. Barton had said it. Her employer was no help, however: he looked like thunder. He coughed and said: "There, you see, you've rendered her speechless. Come into the office and have a cigar while we talk business."

He waved Henry toward the chair, produced cigars and matches, moved the spittoon close to the desk to catch the ashes, lit his cigar, sat on the edge of the desk, stood up again, straightened the ledger, then leaned against the wall. He contemplated his friend.

"I've decided to have my photograph taken," Henry said, "and have your fair colorist do her work upon it. It's a pity that she can't touch the original."

Ned puffed rapidly on the cigar. "Don't," he said, "She's not your sort, Harry."

Henry looked at him in surprise. "Every pretty one is my sort. You know that."

Ned shrugged. "Save a few of them for the rest of us mortals."

Henry peered at him. "Say, do you fancy her yourself?"

"That's not what I meant," Ned replied, "She... My point is, haven't you conquests enough in Hartford to keep you occupied for years to come?"

"Shall I leave the fair country girls to you and your brethren, Whitfield? It seems so. This is encouraging, actually. I thought you'd lost the taste for the hunt."

"I didn't say anything of the kind," Ned protested.

Barton said: "You certainly admired her frame. You're never more serious than when you pun. By God, look at you! I declare you do fancy her, you show all the signs."

"I didn't say that!" Ned repeated.

"You don't have to say it. It's clear. And I see now that she slipped my net the moment you came into the room. That's why she was so bashful. Those blue eyes of hers were fixed on you."

Ned took the cigar from his mouth, feeling slightly dizzy. "Bunkum. Of course she would look to me, I'm her employer."

"You are a dunce," Barton announced with a laugh.

Ned stood in awkward silence, trying to limn the boundaries of the situation.

"She fancies you," Henry said.

"Aw, pull my other leg," Ned sputtered.

Barton was highly entertained. "Come now! You know I can always tell when a woman fancies a fellow; I've seen it often enough."

"Guess not, an ugly skunk like you," Ned said, buying time

to cogitate.

Henry said: "Well. Who is she? Poor but honest country girl, the usual drill? An orphan? Supporting an invalid parent or some such thing?"

"I have no idea," Ned lied, wondering why as he did so. "Aged mother, I think. She's the Ives' hired girl. She's only here one morning and one afternoon a week now."

"That's good. She's needy. And smitten with you. So, the only pertinent question left is her virtue."

"There's no question!" Ned burst out, "No question of that. Good heavens, she's a friend of my sister."

Henry hesitated, then said: "You have my apology. I intended no offense to a family friend."

Ned opened the window and snuffed out his cigar in the snow on the sill. "You didn't have the full particulars," he said.

Henry relaxed, finished smoking his cigar. "Brr, shut that window, will you? Hmm... pretty, poor, love-sick maid, and, heaven forfend, virtuous! You get no benefit at all from the arrangement."

"Love-sick," Ned muttered skeptically, "She's just tenderhearted."

"Perhaps I exaggerate. She has a keen admiration for you at any rate. But it's all a waste, as I assume she is not suitable marriage material." Ned shook his head.

"Ah," Henry went on, "she's the wrong class, certainly. Father or Mother don't approve, a raging Methodist or some such thing?"

"Huh? Yes. No." Ned abruptly decided to be truthful. "She's Irish."

Henry gaped. "Well, I'll be hanged. You know, I thought I detected an accent when she spoke, but I did not place it as a brogue." He stroked his mustache. "A Papist. Too bad, too bad. Poor, virtuous, Irish Catholic. Some big bog-trotter will carry her off sooner rather than later, I expect. Such a pretty little package, too. How dismal."

Ned shivered, and shut the window.

"Well. Cheer up," Henry said, "I have an offer for you. I've been invited to the Topliffs this evening for a chamber concert and program of choral selections in honor of Washington's Birthday. I'm sure there will be dancing and a splendid collation as well. My invitation says that I may bring a guest, so you must come along with me. What do you say?"

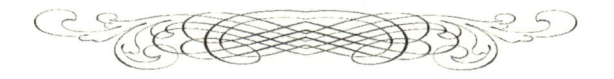

"My grandfather plays the fiddle, and I always wanted to learn it," Mr. Whitfield told Maggie while describing the entertainment at the Topliffs' Washington's Birthday ball. "Do you know what a chamber orchestra is? Two violins…"

"Like a fiddle," Maggie put in.

He nodded. "And the quartet completed with a piano and a violin-cello. That one sounds something like a deep singing voice; it can be very affecting, particularly in a fine piece of music, like that excellent piece by Mozart! That was the best of all." He hummed part of the melody happily, then said: "I wish you could have heard it!"

"Did Eleanor play the piano?" Maggie asked.

"Oh, not there at the party, but yes, she did at home. Henry and I stopped at my house to dress beforehand, and she disappeared. I thought she would not show her face again, but she came downstairs dressed up in a pretty gown and played for Henry and Mother and me."

Maggie clapped her hands. "That's grand! Of course, she ran up to change her clothes, no girl would want to be seen in an everyday dress in front of such a fine gentleman as Mr. Barton!"

"I suppose you're right," Mr. Whitfield said stiffly.

Och, now I've made a mess, Maggie thought, *Help!* "Some say," she said quickly, "fine feathers don't make a fine bird."

"Aesop's Fables," he said.

" 'tis," Maggie agreed, "But meaning nothing against Mr. Barton."

"He's a good fellow, quite humorous as a rule, and indubitably is considered very good-looking by the ladies," Mr. Whitfield shrugged as he turned away from her.

"But," she said, "But some girls do like a mockingbird better!"

"A mockingbird?" he said, turning to look at her. Maggie blushed and nodded.

"Oh," he said, "That's a good one!" Though Maggie could not answer, as he left her side, he sang a line from "Listen to The

Mockingbird," then hummed something sprightly that sounded like more Mozart.

Back for the evening at the Ives' Maggie sang "The Wild Rover" and swung Dickie Ives around and around in her arms until he giggled.

"Kiss your Maggie," she commanded the child.

"No. 'wing!" was the response, so she did it again.

"Here's my precious," Mrs. Ives said from the kitchen doorway.

Maggie put the boy down and he went to his mother. "Pooh, Maggie, his pinafore's all wet and his hands are sticky."

"Yes, ma'am. He made a mess with his bread and milk."

"Well, shan't we clean him up? What would his Papa say, to be greeted like that?" Mrs. Ives queried. From any woman with half a mind to be helpful, Maggie would not have quibbled with the remark; but Mrs. Ives always wrung her hands and never stepped forward to offer anything other than directives disguised as questions.

Maggie replied: "If you'll see to him, ma'am, then I'll be getting Mr. Ives' supper ready for table." Hired simply to watch the child, and clean the house, she had become cook and unwilling recipient of Mrs. Ives' confidences, as well. Mrs. Ives carried her son to the sink. Dickie splashed his hands under the pump's flow, ignoring his mother's scolding, then screeched when she attempted to wash his face with the dishcloth.

"Not that one, it's too dirty altogether. Here, give him to me," Maggie said.

"I suppose I ought to go wash up and wait for Mr. Ives," Mrs. Ives said.

Maggie splashed the baby's hands under the water again, then patted them on his dirty cheeks. "Wash your own face, you." She topped the struggling child off with a wipe from her apron.

"Why does he howl so?" said Mrs. Ives, "The poor duckie has a sore toothies. Perhaps he ought to go to bed. Do you think he's ill?"

"He's two, is all!" Maggie said, "and you choose, ma'am,

baby bathed and bedded, or supper burnt. I can't be tending them both."

"Off we go then, Dickie," Maggie said as she carried him to the back stairwell.

"No up," Dickie said.

"Yes, up," Maggie told him, as in her imagination she ascended in company with a mockingbird while Mozart's violincello sang them up the stairs.

The sickness began with Mr. Ives, late in February. It was a bad one and "nearly carried him off," as Maggie told her Mam. Although young Dickie was spared when his anxious mother sent him to his grandparents, Mrs. Ives and Maggie nursed the master and soon both of them fell ill. Mrs. Moore and Mrs. Whitfield came to help, sending Maggie home to Frank's. There, she shivered, sweated, coughed for almost a week before she came through it. Mam and Denny were sick for a time, but also recovered. Mrs. Ives survived but miscarried her baby.

When Maggie returned to the photograph gallery, Edward Whitfield reported that his mother had been quite ill but fortunately was now on the mend. He had been sick, but not severely so, and Eleanor was unscathed. He did not mention his father.

Due to the coughing sickness and other winter ailments, there had been many deaths in town, more than the usual rate. For a week, Whitfield and Fish photographed the deceased more frequently than the living, while Maggie had little more to do than put a touch of color into faces that would never be pink again.

Zek Fish had passed a long day at Ned's side, running negatives to the gallery from the homes of several residents; yet he balked at the last house, because he knew the youth who lay in cold decorum in that front parlor.

"Go on home," Ned told his assistant, "I will see you tomorrow."

The parlor was exceptionally chilly, the light within it low. Ned opened the drapes and shades and fumbled the glass plate into the camera. Cupping his hands around his mouth to warm them, he tried to ignore the occasional outburst of grief he overheard from an adjoining room. Thank merciful heaven, his mother was better. Thank God Kate was away from Millville and safe. Thank goodness the judge had recovered enough to leave the house daily: he had been a demanding patient. Eleanor had borne that burden well and had managed to keep the household running while Mrs. Whitfield recuperated, and Martha lay on a sickbed.

Back at the gallery, he had a brief moment of satisfaction in the darkroom. The negative was acceptable. He placed it with the others taken that day: five likenesses preserved. He emerged from the darkroom to find that Maggie had stayed and taken on Zek's job of tidying the gallery prior to closing. He thanked her, then told her to go home so she'd reach the Ives' house before dark.

"I'll clean these brushes, then I'll be on my way," she said, "and you must go as well. You're tired, to be sure."

"Yes, I'm played out," he agreed, then took out his pocket notebook. They were running low on...what was it that he had meant to order?

It was to be his last conscious thought for some time: for at that moment the assassin, invisible and silent as a scout, slashed his face. Not satisfied with that first saber cut, the pain of neuralgia attacked him in force. It was a crushing arm that seized him, pinned him close, all the while stabbing him in the cheek, jaw, throat, eye, and turning the knife in the wounds. His body slowly folded under the blows, and he sat hard on the floor. He pulled at his necktie, put up both hands in fisted protest. The pain screamed louder and called with a laugh for its confederates. Pain's toady, nausea, came at once. The sweating creature that was their target curled its body away, panted and made animal noises. One demon sat at the dying animal's head, burning it, raking it with nails, pulling out its hair, the other kicked at the belly. The animal moaned, and this they liked.

"How will we know when you have an attack of neuralgia?" Maggie had asked, when Mr. Whitfield mentioned the possibility to her after he had been out sick from it for a day at the height of the Christmas rush.

"You'll know," he had responded.

And she did, immediately. She watched as Whitfield fell to the floor and writhed there, making terrible noises. Immobilized with horror for several moments, disbelieving, she watched him, and did not scream for Zek until she had found her voice. Fish did not appear. She frantically searched the gallery for him, before recalling that Mr. Whitfield had sent the boy home.

What can I do? she thought.

"There's nothing you can do," Mr. Whitfield had replied to the same question in December.

"There must be," she had protested at the time, and felt the same protest ringing inside her now. She hurried to the gallery door, then stopped, yanking the reins on her runaway panic. She remembered further: he had told them that putting extreme cold or heat against the skin sometimes stopped the neuralgia.

"But I don't recommend pushing my head into a stove," he had joked, and she and Zek had laughed.

She ran to the floor grate where heat rose from the building's coal furnace. No, it was barely warm. Cold? Everything outside was cold, could she drag him to the window? Maggie raced into the office, wrenched open the window there, reached as far out as she dared and broke off icicles, gathering them into her arms.

The animal, having found no surcease, coughed, and grew limp. It did not feel the hands pushing at its arms, and barely noted the new shock of cold. The pain thinned to a thread. But now the fish was out of water and gasping for breath as the fisherman cut open his belly. The fisherman stopped his cutting because there was something too cold at the fish's head.

The moaning stopped. Whitfield's body was still curled however, and he coughed repeatedly. Maggie felt sure that he would vomit. Keeping the icicles pressed to his face, she ignored the burning cold against her left hand, and moved a little out of his way, squatting behind his head. He was gagging and she steeled her own stomach, but the gagging evolved into a slow pant. Slowly, his breathing quieted, and the tell-tale green ebbed from his face, which was yet drenched in sweat. He moved abruptly and struck out with an arm, tipping Maggie out of her crouch.

Why is it so damned hot in here? Ned thought and moved to throw off his bedcovers. His arm struck someone, a girl, who said something to him. *You're in my way, Eleanor,* he thought, *Open the window.* His eye popped open to see a fancy rosette plastered into the ceiling around the gas fixture. He realized he was on the floor and coming out of the neuralgia. He struggled out of his suit jacket, half-sitting, then lay back down as the room swung in circles. He put his hand into a cold wet puddle, drew it out, then put it back in because everything was so hot, and the cool water felt good. He heard Eleanor ask him a question, and he grunted back in annoyance. Wait. He opened the eye again. *Oh, yes. Gallery. Not Eleanor. Maggie.*

Maggie got to her feet, encouraged by his ability to take action to cool off, by his steadier breathing, and by the opened eye, which seemed to see her. She bent over him. "A bit better?" she asked. His eye closed, opened again. His mouth moved as if to say something but all Maggie heard was a tiny hiss. He held up a hand and twirled his forefinger in mimicry of the room spinning.

"You're dizzy, surely. Just rest," she said. But he didn't: taking a deep breath, he pushed himself into a seated position and soon thereafter into a shaky stand. Maggie helped him to the velvet armchair. His left eye was twitching, but it was apparently painless. He fumbled for a handkerchief, rubbed down the right side of his face, but did not touch his left side. He wiped his neck and tugged at his necktie. It was sodden, and too tightly knotted to budge.

"Let me help you," Maggie said.

He held up a hand to halt her, then stood up from the chair, wobbling a little, and moved toward the door out of the gallery.

"Where are you going!" Maggie said.

He wagged a forefinger in warning and added a hissed command: "Stay!"

She waited anxiously at the open door until he made his way back from the water closet down the hall. She pulled a chair toward him and was relieved to see him sit. She handed him his eye-patch and his suit jacket, both of which he restored to their proper places on his person.

"I'll fetch the doctor," she said.

He shook his head. "I'll fetch a carriage from the livery stable, then," she said, but he shook his head again. "Oh you must! You're ill–you can't walk all that way home," she pleaded.

"Can so. G'home."

"No, I won't, 'till I see you're all right," Maggie protested.

" 'm fine."

"You don't look fine!" she said in frustration.

He surprised her with the lift of his eyebrow. "Never do," he said clearly.

"Mercy, no!" Maggie cried, "Don't say such a thing! Jesus, Mary and Joseph!" She loved him so. He looked to her like an angel fallen from heaven, his damp hair a halo, and his left side a-burning, for he had turned to watch Lucifer's fiery descent.

Astonishing, Ned thought, as she took his hand, squeezed it, and told him: "You must never say such a thing." She had tears in her eyes. He closed his own and shook his head again, ready to explain his comment away. She put her fingers gently on the right side of his lips, then he felt her lean toward him, and a kiss as light as a butterfly's touch brushed his head. Her lips were cool and soft. He kept his eye closed: the sensations she created on his hot, half-numb skin were too marvelous to ruin with vision. The light kisses continued: one on his forehead, one on his right brow. He thought he heard her whisper, "Promise me."

Ned sat very still, as if dreaming. Then her hand left his, she stepped away, and said: "Wait here," and when he opened his eye he saw only the back of her cloak going through the door.

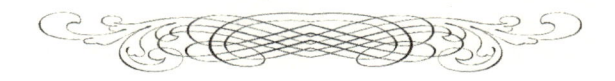

"You'll be all right then won't you," Maggie said to Mrs. Ives, "just sit up here by the fire, 'tis cozy, and now you've got some dinner in you. For I must go out, there's something I forgot at the gallery. I'll just run over and fetch it and come back directly."

"Oh stay here with me, Maggie, I don't feel well, and Mr. Ives won't like it, to have me all alone. Whatever did you leave behind that you can't do a day without?"

Maggie thought: *Left my pride, to be sure. Left my heart... If he's angry over what I did, I'll die.* She replied: "Faith, you won't tell the Mister, I know you won't. You're too good to me, entirely. You rest here, I won't be gone but ten minutes, but I must go."

The ground was covered with new snow. Trickster winds blew Maggie around corners, disappeared until she lowered her hands from her hood, then blew again. Yet she was hot with hurrying, sizzling with doubts. She paused outside the gallery door to gather enough breath to speak; then opened the door and peered in: no customers.

"Hist, Zek, is Mr. Whitfield here?"

"Yup, in the darkroom. You done up your coloring from yesterday? It ain't your day to come by."

"Oh, he's all right then? That's a blessing," she said, "He wasn't well yesterday. He had a spell."

"I was ailin' yesterday, too," Zek said.

" 'twas the neuralgia," Maggie went on.

Zek left the work-table and crossed to the door: "You don't say! What happened? Heigh, Maggie, come in and tell me. He won't. He didn't say a word about it." Zek grabbed the doorknob; Maggie held the knob on her side.

"No, I mustn't," she said. Mr. Whitfield came out of the darkroom. Maggie tried to shut the door, but Zek was pulling in the opposite direction.

"Who's there?" Whitfield asked.

"Miss Shaw," Zek said.

"Why are you keeping her out? Let her come in," Whitfield said.

"I ain't, sir. She's keeping herself out."

"I only came to make sure you were well," Maggie peeped from around the door, "You are, I'm glad, I must go!"

"No, come in. I won't keep you long," Mr. Whitfield said. Maggie came in, sure that she was redder than Annie had ever been at her worst.

"I'm glad you came by, and provided me with an opportunity to thank you," Whitfield continued, "I had an attack of the neuralgia yesterday afternoon, Zek, but fortunately Miss Shaw recalled my instructions about what to do, and because she did, it was a short-lived attack."

"Thank heaven!" Maggie said. He was all right, all was set to rights now, now her heart could stop its jumping.

Mr. Whitfield briefly recounted the event, mercifully making no mention of the liberties she'd taken. He went to the coat rack, took his outer garments in hand, and said: "Zek, put out the Closed card and go get yourself something to eat. Miss Shaw, I was about to head to home for dinner. If you're going back to the Ives', I'll walk you there. It's on my way."

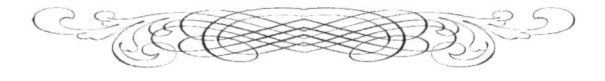

Now that he had her here beside him–just as he had been idly hoping most of the morning–Ned had nothing to say. The same thing happened sometimes during examinations at school: you knew the answers, but something sewed up your tongue. He had not taken her arm. That would not be proper. Another confounded rule: he wanted her arm twined in his, his hand over hers, and her face as near his as it was last evening. "There's quite a wind," he said.

"My, yes," she said.

A weather report, you dolt, he thought, *Next you'll tell her that Spring is right around the corner. Why did she kiss me?* "Am I walking too fast for you?" he asked.

"Just a bit." He slowed his pace. They were away from the main streets now, about two blocks from the Ives house. "Watch that, it's slippery here."

"So 'tis."

"Would you like... perhaps if I took your arm, so you won't slip."

"Yes, thank you," she said, smiling a little, a shy and sidelong glance, yet he was swept in and dowsed by the summer blue of her eyes. He walked quite slowly, glad to feel the slight pressure of her arm on his. Near a large tree, the wind lessened; Ned lagged and stopped.

"I... ah, I did, of course, wish to express my gratitude; you offered me a... a real service, so I thank you for what you did... <u>all</u> that you did," he said.

"All that I did," she said faintly, then: "I didn't ever mean to make free with you, or, or, Mother of Mercy! any such thing." Hellfire and damnation, he was wrong again: she didn't care a bit for him; Henry was wrong, and he was right—she was simply tenderhearted.

He said: "No, no, of course not. You were kind enough to take pity on me."

"No," she said urgently, "'twasn't pity at all, that's just the thing it never was and that's why I did what I did though I surely oughtn't to have."

He said: "Um. Well, regardless, I assure you, I had no objection!" His comment had an excellent effect. The tension left her arm and she smiled with relief. "It was very kind of you," he added. She grimaced and shrugged. Was she disappointed?

Hope rattled his tongue loose. "No, I take it back, Miss Shaw." She looked at him in surprise. He said: "I do have one regret about what occurred."

Och, no! Maggie thought. She studied his face. *Was that something of a smile? Yes, it was.* "Oh?" she said.

He said: "Yes. One regret: that I did not return your kisses."

She had an instant of disbelief, then felt sure, back on solid ground for the first time in months. Her pulse was ticking in her ears, something in her spoke for her: "A man oughtn't to live with regrets. So they say."

He understood the invitation. Slipping his arm from hers, he placed his hands on either side of her head and kissed her, full on the mouth. Kissed her well and truly; not hard-lipped and wet-mouthed like Rory, not like Kevin (soft and hasty, as if scared she would dissolve)–but simply taking a taste, curious, ardent.

Maggie closed her eyes: lost, yes, so glad to be lost. She reached up and put her hands behind his head. *Don't you see, then? This is where I'm meant to be,* she thought. The wind pushed them. He ended the kiss but kept his gloved hands cradling her face. "Mercy," she whispered. He laughed at this his breath warm on her skin. She liked that too.

"I knocked your hat," she said and straightened it back on his head. She saw that his eyes, ah heaven, his eye, and how she longed for the other to be restored to him!—this one remaining was beautiful: not gray at all, as she'd thought, but blue twilight rayed in silver, and the light in it was for her.

Chapter 27

Millville experienced no gentle Spring, as the keen cold and grainy snow lumbered off in a disorderly fashion. For Edward Whitfield, however, the sullen rain was refreshing, the chill illusory, the wind as mighty as his own energy. Because of Maggie, the winter-damaged root within him, long thought dead, was greening.

Now he crushed annoyances as easily as straw beneath his feet; jollied his father with good grace; dove shallowly into his law studies until his imagination drifted back to her. Heretofore forced by the circumstances of his life to drink too long at a trough of stale and bitter water, he believed he had a right to this spring of joy he had discovered, and to the Naiad from whose hands it flowed. He pondered Knott's Hill and Maggie's fall. The very oddity of their pairing as well as the conditions under which it had occurred reassured him that Fortune (or Heaven, if one tacked in that direction) had from the beginning intended Maggie to be his.

There is no studying for this sort of thing, Maggie thought, *nor any book to tell you how grand it ever is.* "When you feel as if his breath is yours as well," she had wanted to say to Eleanor, "and if he catches it, so do you, and when a time is hard for him, so 'tis for you, and when his day is good, you're wanting to dance through yours."

"Your brother," (so she would tell Eleanor as soon as she was given leave to) "has a way of asking a girl's opinion and then paying it heed." Maggie would not reveal how this gave her pause: what if he thought her pert, low, or stupid! He would surely scorn a stupid girl.

" 'tis fine to be admired by the likes of Kevin Foran or Rory Corcoran, even though he has lots of girls on his string, but 'tis a different thing entirely to be truly loved." She would pass that bit of wisdom to Bridget. Maggie sang to herself under her breath, "truly loved." She had sometimes to cross her arms over her chest to calm her heart, for the intensity of the realization made her dizzy, made her wish to draw away, as she was now (since that horrid May day) afraid of heights.

"We must put our trust in General Grant, and in our President," the judge said late in March, as he campaigned for election to the state House of Representatives. "We cannot leave the job half-done."

On Election Day in April, the Republican party won a majority of positions in state government. Judge Whitfield maintained his sinecure as Judge of Probate but was defeated in his campaign for state representative. He blamed his lack of success at the ballot box on the lack of progress on the Southern battlefronts, and opined that the people of the state had no gumption left and that too many were sunshine patriots. Ned presumed that many in the North were, like him, tired of a war that had just passed its third year with so few victories and those few, so costly.

"Heigh ho, Ned," the plump young gentleman chortled, as he entered Dunn's Photograph Rooms, "Do you still like pears?"

"Who was that?" Maggie asked after the gentleman had his picture taken and left the gallery.

"He's an exemplar of the effect of undeserved wealth on a man's character," Ned replied.

"That's Mr. Topliff's son! He owns Eagle Mill," Zek said.

"Why'd he ever ask you if you like pears?" Maggie asked.

"Oh, I know," Zek put in, "Eph told me about it."

"It does not merit discussion," Ned replied.

As he walked her toward "Irish Lanes", she asked Ned: "But DO you like pears?"

He sighed, then said: "I don't suppose you've heard of Mr. Putnam? He used to own the big white house on the way to Knott's Hill."

She replied: "My mam did laundry there sometimes. He had so much linen he only needed a wash once a month."

"That's the fellow," he agreed. "He won prizes every year at the fall harvest fair for the pears from his orchard. They were of the finest kind, and all the boys used to steal them. My friend Rob loved those pears..."

"Was he in the army?" Maggie asked softly.

"He was in the 14th Regiment with me. He died at Belle Plain."

"Oh," she said, after a moment, "I'm so sorry." He opened his mouth, closed it, and walked on in silence. After a time, Maggie patted his arm.

"Mr. Putnam put up a good-sized fence," he went on, "and let loose a mean dog to bite any boy that tried to bite his pears. There we sat on the fence, Sid Topliff, Eph Fish, Georgie Dunn and Rob, and I, with Cerberus, the three-headed dog growling at us."

"That's from the Greek stories," she said.

"Correct. We had a formidable foe. We eyed those pears, we could almost taste them, but there they were beyond our reach. The dilemma of Tantalus, do you know that Greek legend, from school?"

When Maggie shook her head, he continued: "Tantalus' punishment in Hades, was to be hungry and to have the food eternally just beyond his reach. That's the origin of the word, tantalizing... but I digress. Rob was tallest and I thought he could reach the pears if he stretched enough. But he could not do it." He laughed a little. "We were mighty low, I'll tell you. So, I put some thought to it and then told them that I knew a way to make the pears come to us."

"What!" Maggie exclaimed.

"Simple physics," he said, "We got some rope and a big hook from Rob's barn, rigged up a pulley on our side of the fence, then tossed the hook over and pulled a long branch near to our perch on the fence."

"Och, you got to pick them after all," she crowed.

"Not exactly," he countered. "We had been strictly instructed not to pick the pears, and I'd received a switching from my father for doing so before the fence went up, so I told the boys we mustn't pick the pears. Instead, we ate them while they were still on the branches, then we eased the branches back as easy as pie and ran away."

"What a fine cartoon 'twould be. You were so clever," Maggie said.

Ned tapped his forefinger on the side of his head. "As clever as Icarus until he flew too close to the sun. I was sure that Mr. Putnam would assume that a flock of birds had eaten them. And perhaps he might have, except that Sid bragged on it at school in front of Alice Story, who tattled to her father and then my goose was cooked,"

She smiled. " 'twas just a boy's prank!"

"The judge did not see it that way," he said diffidently.

"What about Sid, didn't he get a switching too?" she asked.

"Sid got nothing but a good story," Ned answered, looking none too pleased; so she changed the subject, describing how she had seen a ship wreck picture in the illustrated newspaper.

"I never seen the sea, only in pictures."

He said: "I've been to the shore in Rhode Island. It's like nothing you'll see here inland."

"'twould be grand to see it, I'm thinking," said Maggie, "But I don't think I'd like to go out on it because my mam said being on the sea was like being corked in a pint bottle and shook up until your insides became your outsides."

"Ah, yes, sea sickness," he responded, "I expect she's correct in her description, if she crossed the Atlantic in an old sailing vessel." He paused, looked at her somberly. "Did your mother come here at the time of the famine? I have read a little about it."

"No. Some folks do talk about it, even now, how it was," Maggie said unhappily, "but my Mam came over when she was just 18 and worked in a grand house in Providence and married Mr. Foran over here, so we were all born here, Frank and Nora and Michael; but Rose wasn't, she came over later and so did Mr. Corcoran. Och, poor man, he had a bad time of it. Black '47 so they call it, that's when he came."

"And who is Mr. Corcoran," he asked, "Some relation of yours?"

"Oh. No. He used to board with my Mam and Da when I was a little girl."

"He came to the gallery one time looking for you," Ned said.

She heard the distaste in his voice and spoke up hastily: "He's like a big brother, is all." He slowed his pace; Maggie hoped for a kiss as they neared the big tree. When it was not forthcoming, she said: "My Da came over before I was born. I'm thinking he knew what it was like, the Hunger, but he didn't ever tell me about it. When he came to Millville he met my Mam."

"Mr. Foran having passed to his reward in the interim, I presume?" Ned put in.

"If he hadn't, I'd not be here walking with you!" she said.

"Well, then I have to say that I'm glad the poor fellow shuffled off this mortal coil," he commented.

Maggie smiled. "That's from Shakespeare, sure as you're born."

Chapter 28

As April's snow melt caused freshets in Millville's streams and factory sluice-ways, news came to Connecticut of the massacre of the Negro garrison by Confederate troops at Fort Pillow, Tennessee. The 29th Connecticut, Joe Creasey's regiment, was in South Carolina, not Tennessee; yet if colored troops were captured anywhere, his fate would be the same as that of the unfortunate men at Fort Pillow. Ned could not buff the worry from his mind as he did the dried mud from his boots.

A fortnight later, the Whitfield family read of the Battle of the Wilderness, of wounded soldiers unable to escape from the blazing forest ignited by shot and shell. Ned stared at the fire in the grate that evening. He knelt by it, put his hand out to the painful heat, pulled it back.

In Millville people tilled the soil, ran their businesses, did their spring cleaning, sued their neighbors, and had their photographs taken. A few words about battle news with Billy Vickers or Phin Shackelford were all that Ned could endure.

Beyond a brief lecture to Maggie about Kate's work with freedmen in Washington and an assertion that the value of colored troops had been proved beyond a doubt, he did not speak of the war, or of his worries. Nor did he speak of Maggie to anyone else. He assured himself that the woman he chose was no one's business. He did not intend to give her up; yet he was grateful that politics occupied the judge's attention so fully. Having Maggie was an indulgence, like gorging upon strawberries in season; and was it not fitting to dine exclusively on a sweet that grew in abundance for such a short time?

In early June, the Army of the Potomac engaged the enemy at Cold Harbor in Virginia in a battle worthy of comparison to the Trojan War. When Whitfield, Senior heard of the massive Union casualties, when he accepted the news as fact, he spent the day shaking his head and muttering with discouragement. Ned waited grimly for information about George Dunn; and Maggie waited with prayers to hear of Michael.

Within the week, having apparently channeled this bad news into one of the cisterns of his soul, the judge again urged fortitude to all who would listen and to all who would not. A few days after the Battle of Cold Harbor, the National Union Convention re-nominated Abraham Lincoln for president. Judge Whitfield confidently expressed his certainty that the Rebellion would end in Union victory before the end of the year.

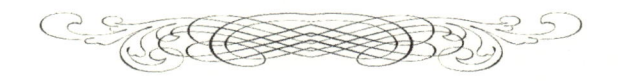

"Is that from Kate?" Ned said. Mrs. Whitfield looked up from the letter, smiling. She said: "She has written more about Major Fariday than her students, and in a complimentary fashion. I wonder..."

"Let me see that letter," he said, reaching for it, but his mother held it away. "Who is this fellow? What regiment?" he asked.

"He was mentioned in her last letter as well. I believe it's one of the New Jersey regiments involved in the defense of Washington. I don't recall exactly. I'll find out more about him from your Aunt Vin. I owe her a letter," Mrs. Whitfield replied, "You can have this as soon as I've finished it. Oh, and I ought to come to your gallery and be photographed. Your father and I. Kate has been asking for a picture."

"First rate, come any time," Ned said, "Father's already been photographed, but he never paid nor came back for the pictures."

"Oh?" his mother said in surprise, "Ah. I didn't know that. Well, perhaps he will soon. I do wish that Elly would come with us. I suppose we'll never have a likeness of her. If only you could bring the gallery here!"

"We live too far away for me to run the plates here and back while they're wet."

"Yes, I understand," she said. She folded the letter with care and handed it to him.

"Maggie could draw a portrait of Elly, I am sure. I'll ask her," he added. Mrs. Whitfield looked at him curiously. "I suppose that her work there and for Mrs. Ives are keeping her well occupied. We have not seen her for several Sundays."

"She's well occupied," Ned agreed and hastened out of the hallway.

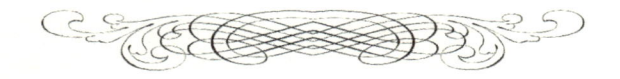

Rory Corcoran stalked into the kitchen, ignoring Rose's greeting. "I hear yer walking out with someone, Maggie," he said. Maggie shrugged. His anger, which would have cowed her in the past, was now just a stone in her shoe: an annoyance to be shaken out as soon as possible.

She retorted: "Without so much as a by your leave. Good day to you Mr. Corcoran. I'm well, thank you for asking."

"Are you walking out with a fellow?"

"Who's been telling you such things!" she said. Corcoran was nonplused by her answer and the outrage with which it was delivered.

"Never you mind," he said, "Are you?"

"Then never you mind!" Maggie turned back to the dish tub and scrubbed at a plate. The surprised silence behind her pleased her.

He tried again: "Paddy Molloy says he saw you and that ugly Yank."

Maggie broke in: "Paddy Molloy! Dirty Molloy, why would you believe a word he says. He's softheaded, and he's been hateful ever since he pawed me at the dance, and I told him he oughtn't to touch me again if he wanted to keep all his fingers." *Mercy,* she thought, *that mauling was nothing like the loving caresses of a true gentleman.* She'd never tell a soul about Ned and the glory of that communion: a true communion of minds, it was. It was hers, hers only, the only secret she had ever kept so well, except for Da's note, but Ned was not a painful, shameful secret. He was the best man in the world, and her salvation. Let them wait until she was married!

"Hurley said so too," Corcoran added. Maggie was crestfallen; she stayed at the tub to hide her face. "Ah, there's another fine one," she replied.

"Says yer walking out with that Yank you work for."

"What's this?" Rose gasped.

"Walking out!" Maggie cried. *I wish it was more than walking out,* she thought, *I wish I was on his arm, in his arms and his only forevermore!* She said aloud: "He walked me home is all."

"Did he touch you?" he roared.

"Here now," Rose said.

Frank came into the kitchen. "What's all this?"

"You take it back!" Maggie screamed at Corcoran. "What kind of a girl do you think I am."

Rory held up his hands. "Whissht, now, I wasn't saying any such thing. Was I? It's just you got to take care with these Yanks, slick as they are, he could turn your head with his money and his ways, not with his looks!" He grinned at Frank and Rose. "Have you clapped eyes on the fellow —one-eyed and ugly as sin."

"He never is!" Maggie said, "'tisn't his fault he got hurt in the war."

He scowled: "There you see, you do like him."

She cast about for an answer: "So I like anyone who's kind to me and pays me to do what I like to do and doesn't order me about or treat me like dirt under his feet."

His scowl faded. "You're an innocent. You don't know what men can be like, so you..."

She spoke over his words: "I know what Molloy and Hurley are like and they're men, though they act like a pair of dogs."

"You watch yerself with that Yank, is all I mean to say."

"You've no right to come in here shouting and accusing me," Maggie pouted, "You're not my brother, nor my father."

He looked as astonished as if his own teeth had jumped out of his mouth and bit him. In an injured tone he said: "Ah, darlin' ain't I known you since you was just a little thing. And your Da told me to take care of you... sure you..."

"When?" Maggie interrupted eagerly, "Did you see him when he left?"

Rory shook his head. "No! What are you saying, girl? Go, begorrah, I would have stopped him, don't you know."

"But if he told you to take care of me..." she persisted.

"Indeed, he did, but 'twas years ago. So I don't want to see you come to harm. Nothing wrong in that, is there, then? 'tis awful hard of you to come at me hotter than the hobs of hell when I just was watching out for you."

"There, y' see, Maggie," Rose announced as if that settled the matter, "What's got into ye?" It suited Maggie's purposes not to go back to the subject. She gave Mr. Corcoran the sidelong smile he liked and said softly: "Aw, get along with you, now."

His smile proved that he believed her, and she had not lied, she just had not blabbed, for once in her life. It was only her Ned, his brilliance, his love, her towering protective love in return that had inspired her words and given her this pulsing fearless heart. *Soon enough, you'll all see what I'm made of, and then you'll see the back of me,* she thought. Och, Rory. A year ago she would have thrilled at this display of his, convinced it was evidence of his love. She would have instantly bowed to his advice, and not only that, thought him wise and doubted her own actions. But now: *he's jealous, and I love a far different man. He would never come like a storm into my house, yelling accusations.*

Corcoran said: "This gent may think he can just take whatever he pleases, but he ain't yet taken the measure of a good girl like this one."

Maggie wrung out the dishcloth and looked at him straight on. "That's so," she said.

Chapter 29

"I told Phin that Congress had voted for a more comprehensive pension system; but the pension office is slower than a snail," Ned said. "And no manner of appeal or filing of forms in triplicate will speed their decision." Maggie shook her head and said: "'tis like that Circumlocution Office."

"Ah yes," Ned said, "Dickens' Little Dorrit. They are exemplars of how not to do it. There is no place in their manual for a definition of this man's suffering. By thunder, if they could only see the man!" He moved away from her, muttering angrily. Maggie shaded her eyes from the sun, sorry she had worn her skimpy straw hat rather than her sunbonnet.

She said: "Can't you take his picture and send it to them?"

"There's an idea. I hadn't thought of that," he turned from his pacing and smiled at her. "My clever girl!" Maggie ducked her head like a dog happy with the petting.

"He may not want to be photographed," he said, scowling, "Understandable. His face is much worse than mine."

"No matter how long the road, there comes a turning," Maggie said earnestly, after a moment or two.

He pondered this. "While one is alive," he said, then tipped his hat back, wiping sweat from his forehead. She wondered if he was thinking of his lost soldier friends, Rob, and Will and that fellow lieutenant who had not survived Fredericksburg.

Ned fanned himself with his hat, muttering: "It's hot as blazes."

"I don't mind it when I'm with you," Maggie said, "'Tis always hot on the Fourth." He did not reply, just kissed her for a long time until she giggled and stepped away. "Och, you take my breath!" He blew gently on the back of her neck, then seized her again and kissed her ear. She shivered and danced away, grinning. "We ought to find some shade," she said.

"There may be rain coming," Ned said, clearly admiring the turn of her waist.

"Mercy, I hope it won't thunderstorm," she said, "My Mam's awful afraid of them. She closes up all the doors and windows and sits and says her rosary, and it makes Rose so cross."

"That is an extreme reaction. I can't tell you how many thunderstorms I've been out in, through no choice of my own," Ned said.

"Mr. Foran was struck by lightning, so that's what made her afraid of it."

"My stars. Was that how he died?"

Maggie shook her head. "Not then. He was burnt some, but he wasn't quite right after that and then he died that winter."

"I see. From the effects of the strike," he commented.

"No, 'twas a bad fever took him." She paused, then said. "I'm thinking something like that gave Elly a fright."

Ned plucked a blossom and examined it. "I suppose she's afraid of lightning. Any sensible person is at least cautious about it."

"Not that. At least I don't think so. Something like a wolf gave her a fright," Maggie said, looking at him with concern.

Don't you dare say a word, the adults had commanded him and Kate, especially him, for he had been a talkative child: anyone who would listen to his prattle would get an earful. But he was also a good boy, then, and did as he was told. "That's absurd," he countered, "You know how she is…shy, she's always been shy, I've never known her otherwise, since she was a baby. At any rate, she has improved considerably since she's grown up and actually, now that I think of it, it has happened since she has known you."

"I surely hope she likes me," Maggie said, "And your mother too, she's such a good lady, I hope she…don't think ill of me…"

Her anxious words burned him. "Good heavens, of course," he replied. He hoped that his true friends would sense the intrinsic excellence of this young woman and overlook her station and unfortunate parentage. And religion: he intended to talk to her about that sometime soon, about conversion. Her own personal Reformation. He smiled a little.

Maggie hugged him. "I hope…" she said but did not finish the thought; instead saying: "I hear thunder."

Ned glanced at the sky. "Yes, look at those thunderheads. There's a storm brewing." He took her hand. "Come along. We have to find shelter. There's no way to outrun this one by heading back to town. We're liable to get a soaking."

Their fast walk (pull me, pull me, Maggie thought, breathless, happy) soon became a dash as the sky heaved warm pebbles of rain. She squeaked: "My hat!"

Then he made a sound and swung her out sideways abruptly nearly taking her off her feet. "There!" They skidded, wet and panting, into the open door of a barn. "Hello," Ned called out. Two cows looked them over and several chickens muttered no welcome, until, as the storm hit directly, bright, dark, terrible, they lowed and cackled in consternation. "We made it just in time," he said.

"Not in time to save my hat," Maggie remarked ruefully, as she untied it and took it off. It was soaked, misshapen, the straw discolored by the rain and one ribbon's blue dye running into the straw. "I must look a sight."

"We both do," he said. She reached out to smooth his wet hair so that it would not drip into his eye.

In a short lull, with only the sound of hard rain, Maggie said: "It will take a long time to get dry."

"I could kiss every drop off your face and then begin on your neck, then your shoulders," he paused suggestively, "and so on…"

"Mr. Whitfield!" Maggie protested, amused. "May I borrow a handkerchief?"

"Of course. How practical. You're dashing my hopes, you know. No, these are soaked too." Simultaneous blue light and a massive clap of thunder made them both jump. The cows and chickens gave voice in alarmed agreement.

"Jesus! That was close," Ned said, "Come away from the door!" Maggie leapt to him. He held her while they watched and listened; he could not hear her heart but only feel it beating under his wrist. He remembered being out in such furious weather, while at war. How had he borne it? He could feel her breathing against his neck, her occasional shudders, and the hard ridges of her corset under the wet fabric of her dress bodice. Timeless, they held each other, waiting out the storm. Gradually the flash and noise lessened.

"Better now?" he asked.

She may not have known what he referred to, but she nodded anyway and added, "When you hold me."

He again found himself distracted from Nature's performance outside by a vision of her breasts, so close, under the corset and layers of cloth. He thought if he might only touch them now, he could die a happy man. He imagined the soft swell of them under his hands, and their ripe tips between his fingers. Catching his breath, he massaged her right shoulder and kissed the knuckles of her left hand which he held in his. She evidently liked it.

After a moment, she said, very quietly: "I'd like you to kiss me."

He did so with eagerness. As the kiss lasted, it became urgent. His groin stirred, reacting to the kiss and her nearness with reassuring strength. It had been such a long time. He pressed against her as hard as he dared, almost molding himself to her body. She broke the long kiss with a shaky sigh and moved her lips along his neck. At that, he pulled her hips against his, closer still.

It was apparently that pressure, and not his hand that had strayed to her bosom, that made Maggie take her mouth from his skin and say: "Ow."

Ned left her embrace, stepping back, then turned away from her in embarrassment.

"What's wrong?" he heard her say. Leaving thunder answered her.

"Uh…" he said. He could not answer truthfully: she was too much of an innocent.

"Did I hurt you?" she asked with concern and some confusion.

A moaning laugh escaped him. "No. Not at all! It's just my trousers are too tight." He did not dare to look at her. He could feel the blush move over his face and settle in to fire his ears.

Maggie only puzzled for a moment. That? That was what had embarrassed him? Well, it was perhaps a bit embarrassing. But rather than the disgust she had felt when confronted with the same evidence of Paddy Malloy's excitement, she was rather proud of herself and also anxious to put Ned at ease. She thought, then said lightly: "Oh, I suppose that's my fault."

Ned looked over his shoulder at her, astonished. She looked down demurely. He said: "Fault…no fault of yours, anyone's, really. Just a matter of cause and effect." He was proud that he was exhibiting self-possession under trying circumstances: that "itch" he couldn't scratch.

"I'm the cause," she said in a warm, forgiving voice.

He grinned at her. "Marvelous girl! Yes."

"I'm sorry if I hurt you." She put her hand on his arm.

He grabbed it as if it was a lifeline and stroked it. "Hurt?" He gave a strangled laugh, "No, no, and no." He couldn't believe that he felt so good: it had never been like this with any other girl. It had always been such a fumbling, earnest business.

"I would never want to hurt you," Maggie said, with an underlying humor.

"You've never hurt me, only made me feel better."

She smiled at him and came forward, then stopped. "I'm thinking we must go home soon."

He said: "No! Not yet. It's still raining. You'll get wet."

"I'm wet to the skin now," she answered.

"I meant...I don't want you to take a chill or become ill. Wait here awhile and dry off." Maggie looked around at the dust and dung underfoot and the cobwebs in the rafters.

"Up in the hayloft," Ned said breathlessly. He had been eyeing it for the past few minutes. "It will be clean up there, and warmer."

"I'm warm already," Maggie said, but she smiled again.

"We really should take off these wet clothes...some of them! And dry off. It's still a steady rain, it won't let up for a while. Not for a long time, I expect. Come along."

She allowed him to pull her toward the hayloft and assist her up the ladder, ahead of him.

As Maggie flopped onto the hay, she realized–from Ned's flushed face–why he had sent her first up the ladder. She smoothed her skirt down. "Enjoying the view, again, sir?" She laughed at his expression.

"Tremendously," he said, then dropped to his knees next to her, in supplication.

She placed her hand flat against his chest. "Will you mind your manners?"

He grinned. "I always do."

"Not always," she teased. He peeled off his jacket, then his vest, tossing them aside, and then unbuttoned his shirt partway. Maggie watched his pulse beating in the hollow of his throat and made her decision.

She said: "You won't...We can't do..."

Ned lay down next to her: "I won't hurt you. I would never hurt you, not for the world. I love you. By God, I do! I won't do anything you don't want. We won't do anything wrong. Please, just let me kiss you."

So, she did: and slid, un-protesting, into the whirlpool.

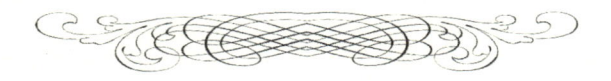

"Maggie, darling, have you come back to earth yet?" he said, gently kissing her forehead and her ear. She released her grasp on the back of his shirt collar and trailed her fingers on his sweaty chest.

"What happened?" she whispered.

Ned laughed. "Haven't you heard of courting and sparking?"

Maggie's mind was still far away, reeling with sensations. "Courting..." she said.

"Sparking," Ned went on, "that was the sparking."

The connection between the whispered giggled stories of her girlfriends and the hot glow still pervading her skin crashed into her brain. "OH! That's it? It's lovely." She knew it was a puny word for such a grand experience.

"Climaxes usually are," Ned said.

He kissed her mouth, and when he stopped, she said: "I did that? Is that the word for it, then?"

He was amused. She thought he looked beautiful smiling down at her. "One word for it, at any rate. Rapture is another. You were marvelous. You are marvelous."

He bent his head to kiss her again, but Maggie stopped his mouth with her hand. "We didn't..." she faltered "but we didn't do...?" She gestured: their clothing was still on, at least in places, but greatly disarranged, and she was happily, acutely aware at this moment of the places where each of them was naked.

"No indeed. There'll be no child from this game."

"You're sure?" she persisted.

"I'm sure," he said firmly.

"Oh good! Now you can kiss me." As he did so, Maggie had another thought. "But what about you? Are you alright?" She thought she had heard that men exploded or something if they didn't get release.

"I'm better than all right. I'm feeling first rate. Insanely happy," he responded.

"Even though you didn't…" Maggie waved her hand again vaguely and he looked puzzled. "Climax?" she mumbled. He hugged her as he laughed. She liked the feeling of his bared chest against her breasts, both slick with perspiration.

"But I did! What, did you think I was twiddling my thumbs and parsing Latin while you were in rapture?" he asked.

"Oh, well. I didn't know, but now I do and I'm glad. And 'tis a fine word for it, rapture!"

"It is," he agreed. This time she kissed him, long and slow. He removed his hand from where it rested, firm and warm, against the skin of her thigh. Maggie sighed.

He fumbled with her underskirt. "I'm the cause of that spot on your petticoat, for which I apologize," he said. She heard him rearranging his trousers.

"Och, it'll wash," Maggie said casually. She enjoyed the way he was admiring her breasts: like a contented puppy about to fall asleep.

He said: "It seems she hangs upon the cheek of night, Like a rich jewel in an Ethiop's ear; Beauty too rich for use, for earth too dear! Did my heart love till now? Forswear it, sight! For I ne'er saw true beauty till this night."

"Shakespeare," Maggie said, "and 'tisn't night."

He replied, "You are the most beautiful woman I have ever seen."

"Such palaver," she said with delight. She pondered his experienced hands and artful caresses. "Tell me, how many have you seen like this?" She held one hand over her breast. Once she had said it, she was sorry, for his smile fled.

"Not as many as you might think," he replied, after a moment.

"I know you've courted, so I thought you might have sparked," Maggie said gently, "being engaged before and all…"

"What? Oh. Yes." Maggie snickered at the tone of his voice and tugged on his beard.

"And how was Miss Caldwell," she whispered. *Did you please her as you did me,* she thought, *worse, you blackguard, did she please you?*

"You are a hundred times, a thousand times more beautiful than she could ever hope to be, and better in every way," he said, and his kiss almost convinced her.

When he paused, she smoothed his hair back, then asked boldly: "But did you…rapture with her?"

"What?"

"Oh, I'm sorry," she began, but he interrupted her with a sound which she at first took as pain or anger (for he had hidden his face on her shoulder) but soon realized was laughter. He laughed so gustily against her skin that she began to giggle too.

"You're tickling me," she said.

Chapter 30

Two weeks later, Maggie climbed the stairs to the photograph gallery on her usual work day, stopping still before the Closed sign on the door. The door was locked. She knocked and called out for Zek but had no answer. She waited for a quarter hour, then set off. Sweating and breathless, she stood on the Whitfield's back step for several minutes before timidly knocking.

A formidable woman she did not recognize peered out the kitchen window, called: "Who is it?"

Maggie stepped back off the stairs and put her hands behind her back. "Maggie," she said, "Here, to...for Eleanor." The woman hushed the dog, disappeared, then held a muffled conversation with someone else. The door remained closed. Finally, Eleanor appeared at an upper story window and pointed toward the orchard. Maggie trudged there, pushing at her dire thoughts with each step.

"The rebels attacked Washington again, and Kate was in danger and there was a terrible battle, and Major Fariday had his leg cut off!" Eleanor said in a tumble as she struggled to keep Dance from tripping her.

"Mother of God! Is she well, did she get away? Did Ned go down to fetch her?" Maggie asked. Eleanor handed off the excited dog to Maggie and sat down in a heap.

"Phew, I was resting when you came, because it is so hot. None of us has slept a moment since we heard the news, it was a telegram from my uncle. Ned has gone to send one back. I hope that she will come home, but she might not because of him."

"Because of him? Ain't he to go and get her?" Maggie asked, relieved that her darling had forgotten her for a good reason.

"Ned? I don't know. I meant Major Fariday. She may stay because he is hurt, though I do very much hope she comes home now. "

"He's the soldier who had his leg cut off? Is he a cousin of yours?"

"No, no cousin, Maggie, how silly!"

"You have such a lot of them, you said," Maggie replied.

Eleanor fanned herself. "Oh, I thought I had told you, but I have not seen you in such a long time. Every time Kate writes to us she says something about Major Fariday. He's in the Army there and a friend of my uncle's and of Mr. Welles and very helpful to her, getting supplies for the school. It is such an awful thing to think of him so badly wounded!"

"Will he live?" Maggie asked.

"He must!" Eleanor said, "We just had a letter from her sent before all this terrible news and she was so happy because he was helping her to plan a gala Sunday School picnic to raise money to build a new school for all the colored children." Maggie shook her head in commiseration, sat down and pulled the dog to lie beside her.

"Will he...who will go to get her? Can't she take the train?"

"Father says the rebels held up a train and boarded it, so she must NOT take a train. I don't know if he or Ned will go down to get her. Father says he is tired of her..." Eleanor stopped.

"Tired of her?" Maggie prompted, very curious.

"I ought not to say," Eleanor went on, "But he was so vexing! He said she had chosen to defy him by staying in Washington, but that is not true. Well, he did write to Uncle Cyrus and tell him to send Kate home, but she does so like to teach and be useful..."

"She's not a child," Maggie said.

"Yes," Eleanor replied, "But I do wish she'd come home."

Maggie studied her friend's drooping head: even the curls seemed wan, dragged down. "I'm sorry," she said, "I've been missing you, Elly."

Eleanor twisted her collar as if that might boost her spirit. "I have missed you too. I am ever so sorry about my birthday party. It would have been so much jollier to have you there. Only two girls came and their mothers and no one nice like Mrs. Moore."

"Your Mr. Barton didn't come, then?" Maggie inquired.

"No. No gentlemen. Well, a boy came, a cousin of one of the

Topliffs, so Father insisted he be invited. He has not even started shaving yet and he only said two words the whole afternoon. I think he agreed to come as a prank, for he stared at me the entire time."

"Because you're pretty," Maggie put in.

Eleanor shook her head. "Well, thank you. I think he stared because he heard I wasn't right in head."

"Faith, no!" Maggie cried.

"I am surprised that his mother allowed him to act so rudely. Mama said she wanted to spank him." Eleanor laughed a little, "And you ought not to say *my* Mr. Barton, Maggie," but she sounded pleased.

"But he is, or by hook or crook he ought to be," Maggie replied, "For you love him."

"I think I do. I miss him, anyhow," Eleanor said softly.

Now I can tell her, Maggie thought, *about my own dear love, if he'd only let me.* Why had he commanded her silence? She wanted to cheer Eleanor with the news that they would soon be sisters. "Someday you'll see him again, surely," she said, "and you needn't mind about my not being at your party: 'twasn't so much missing the party, I was just wishing that I might come to see you again sometime."

"But we do see each other, we would have before this, but you were too busy," Eleanor said.

Maggie spoke without thinking. "Yes, too busy entirely, but I was thinkin', well, 'tis a hard thing to be left standing on the back step like a peddler or a knife-grinder that you don't know from Adam.,"

"Oh?" Eleanor was surprised. "Well, that was Martha. She follows every word of Father's to the letter. I...I thought you understood what Father said. And how Kate had such a time last year, you do remember? convincing him to let us..."

"I know," Maggie broke in, "but couldn't I, I'd like to come in the door sometimes, I mean, to visit in the kitchen or hear you play so nicely on the piano. I'd never hurt any of you, not for all the world, and 'twould do him no harm at all!"

Eleanor shook her head, perplexed. "I should like that very much, you know that. And Mama would not mind, I don't think she would. But you know how Father is."

"But why," Maggie blurted, "What've I ever done to him, so's he treats me that way? Will he never change his mind?"

"I don't know!" Eleanor said, but she shook her head miserably.

"Oh, I did not mean to make you feel sad," Maggie said, "I'm sorry."

"I'm sorry, too," Eleanor said.

"Faith, I oughtn't to have said a word. 'tisn't your fault at all. Not at all." The dog licked Maggie's perspiring hand as if it were a delicious treat. She usually found it amusing; now his tongue swirled her thoughts, stripping the salt that had preserved her confidence.

The judge would not accept her, perhaps hated her, although he did not know her. And, if not her in particular, then he hated her poverty, her religion, or her Irishness, or all of these, perhaps far too many to overcome? Ned must find a way to introduce her to them slowly, as she went for conversion to their church.

How did one become a Prot, was it lessons? Mother of mercy, that had been a short and prickly conversation! She had, of course, agreed to what he said to do. But now, in the licking, in the heat, her doubts became liquid and rained about her. Would this family after all turn their backs on her (not Eleanor, surely)? And Mam, Rose, Frank, Bridey, would they push her away for giving up her faith to the Yanks? It couldn't be, they loved her, surely they did; but not as Ned loved her. Yet she couldn't bear to be the object of anger on both sides, pulp between rollers. *We could go West,* she thought, with a thrust of hope like ice between her teeth.

"Oh, don't be angry with me, Maggie," Eleanor said. Maggie looked up: seemed to see her own face, her doubt and fear, in the face across from hers. Go West? How could they marry and leave? How would she then see this girl beside her, this girl she liked so much, this friend she loved, so nearly a sister?

"Och," she said, with a sob. Eleanor scooted close and put her arms around her friend. "You will still come to see me, won't you? You must!" she said.

Maggie stood up, shaking. "I will. I will. If I can. Any way that I can," she said, wiping her nose on her sleeve and handing Dance's leash to her friend. "But I must go now, Elly."

Go, Maggie told herself, *for you'll tell her everything if you stay, and he'll be angry, and the world will end for you.*

Chapter 31

She bore Phin's visit well, Ned thought. She and Zek had heeded his words of warning, and Shackelford had been well treated and well photographed. It was only after Shackelford left that she had sat with her head down, still and sad. When he began to recount the story about Kate, she said that Eleanor had told her. Several customers arrived at once, and she went to work and spoke to him no more.

Just before noon, he sent Zek home for dinner, then coaxed Maggie from her chair and into the gallery office for kisses. She allowed one, then said: "I've never done such a bad thing before– what we did on the Fourth. You took liberties and I let you. But I thought it meant something more. It does, doesn't it? I mean, that's what people do who are engaged to be married…"

"Married!" he repeated stupidly. *By heaven,* he thought, *that was what Betsy Dunn assumed, too, when I'd done far less with her.* He snorted, and Maggie pulled away from him. He hated witnessing her dawning distress. "This is different!" he said.

"Different from what?" Maggie asked. He had painted himself into a corner. "Different than anything else I have experienced. I thought you enjoyed it," he mumbled. Maggie looked down. "Well…If I did so I did, but…that's neither here nor there."

Ned thought, *I want you all of the time.* He said: "I thought so. I would never force myself on you."

"No! You didn't. But I thought…" She frowned and went on: "No, I didn't think. I didn't think it through, just as you scold Zek to do, but you didn't either!"

Ned would not confess to her his fear at the prospect of the judge's rage and the coming disgrace; he had successfully expelled them from his consciousness for the past months, as he'd sought larger and larger helpings of pleasure.

He said, "Marriage is a very serious matter, and cannot be entered into lightly," then stopped, aware that he sounded as sententious as his father often did.

"I know that!" she retorted, her face flushed.

"Maggie. Please. Let me explain," he said.

"Do," Maggie said faintly, not liking what she was seeing in the turn of his head away from hers.

He was silent for a while, too long for her taste, then he said: "If there was ever anyone that I would want to marry...when I was ready to marry, I mean... it would be you. I expect that neither of us is ready to marry now. Someday, of course, but I'm not, not now, and it has nothing to do with you, with how I feel about you, nothing at all. You're extraordinary." He glanced at her, then looked away, apparently sorry to have made the attempt.

Maggie, stunned, was sure she had misunderstood. "So, so, you just want to wait awhile?" she whispered.

He said: "I...I don't know. I mean to say, when? Good Lord, honestly, I wasn't thinking of marriage, Um, not so...precipitously."

"But how can you not think of it! Like putting your thoughts into boxes, if you close one up does it stay closed until you open it again?" She struggled with this concept, so foreign to her own way: her feelings were like a wash of color that seeped into the paper itself until you covered it with another shade or began on a new sheet altogether.

"What do you mean?" he asked.

She studied his face. It was another factual question. She said: "It seems you watch what you say to me now and it was never so before."

"A man has to watch what he says, or it can be used against him," he replied.

The judge was there with them, for a moment. *But wait,* Maggie thought, *just wait till I convert, it will be different.* She wanted to say to him, Mother of God, it might be my own people will never speak to me again, look what I will do for you!

He went on hesitantly: "I'm not speaking of you, of course, you would never use my words against me. I don't know; It's just that I...I've been so happy having you by my side, these days that we've had." All this was true, Maggie knew it, and he was looking straight at her.

"I have never been so happy in my life," she replied simply. Ned reached for her hand, and she gave it to him. The slender link calmed them both.

"This is what's right," Ned said, "Us, together, like this."

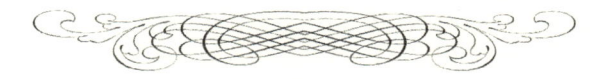

Yes, Ned admitted to his father, he had avoided reading the newspaper recently, for the news was rarely good. You cannot stop the world a-turning, his father had replied, and read aloud (with a hint of glee in confirming his Hobbesian belief that men were evil and life was nasty, poor, brutish and short) the articles about the catastrophe at the Petersburg mine crater. Ned thought it yet another Union disaster: a stupendous example of its officers' stupidity and of needless suffering. But I have been stupid as well, he told himself. It would not do. *If Maggie was a man,* he thought, *I could tell her all the details of the massacre, and she would understand that poor planning leads to a disastrous outcome.*

He wrote *Nr. 1* on the paper laid on the table before him - beginning his draft list of practical points for discussion. It would be difficult for her to take them all in; but she must see what misfortune awaited them if she did not listen to him and agree that head must lead heart in this vital matter. Maggie, lovely innocent, did not comprehend that her class weighed as heavily against her as her Popery. If she was an heiress to a great Spanish fortune, Millville and the judge would find a way, if grudging, to tolerate her and their match.

All "ifs" aside, he thought, *can I keep my position if I marry an Irish servant? Mix might suspend my law studies and no longer permit me to clerk there. Loss of position?* he wrote, feeling sick. Photography might be how he'd make his living. If George returned, he might be willing to take a partner. Good Lord, George as a partner: that would be a trial. Perhaps it was better to look into buying a kit of his own and setting up in another place; but there would be the costs of equipment, supplies, rent, advertising, and then paying board and rent for himself and Maggie, his dental bills, clothing costs. *Christ almighty! What if I'm disabled by neuralgia? What pittance could we live on, and then if a child came...*

Nr. 2, Alternative livelihood, he wrote, *Amt. sufficient to live?* He hoped that they would have enough time for him to plan and prepare; that it would be many months before word got out that they were seeing each other. He had already stressed the importance of this to Maggie. As to income, he knew she would offer to work, but no wife of his was going to take in laundry to support the family. Maybe the Irish did it because they were by and large shiftless, but he believed it reflected badly on the husbands. If she was only a nice Protestant girl from the middle class, fallen on hard times, their climb would be Knott's Hill, not Mount Washington!

His dreams of traveling west, of joining his uncle Benjamin in California were now out of the question. A partnership of two men (someone steady, unlike George) could pool resources and succeed, but a man and wife? No Good heaven, when he began gently, even a little, to lay out all the obstacles, she could not, would not hear the facts, but kept falling back on the same answers: "I love you. We'll find a way. I don't need much. I can work too." She was wonderfully brave and sweet, utterly sincere. She believed in him. He wrote *Nr. 3*, then jabbed the pencil into the number until the paper opened in a small circle. He jabbed again, at the 2, and at the 1, and connected the holes with a penciled line.

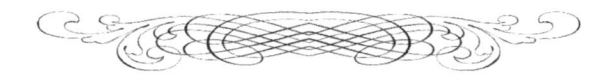

Kate had been home for three weeks, after spending time with her Whitfield grandmother in New Haven and scandalizing that lady by daily visits to the soldiers' hospital. She told her father boldly that she had vowed not to return to Millville until Major Fariday had been discharged to recuperate. Impervious to the judge's harsh words, she announced that the Major was the finest sort of gentleman; that he owned a paper manufactory (so there, Papa!) and was a dear friend and that she had invited him for a visit. Ned was grateful for the diversion and told her so. "It was not for your benefit. I've saved your bacon too many times already. When you meet him, you'll see why." Kate said.

Major Fariday arrived ten minutes early as Ned was scything unruly grass in the front yard. He dropped the tool and stood ready to help the visitor from the rented carriage, but the tall man stepped out on his own with a grunt, aided only by a crutch. "Major Fariday?"

Ned said and gave his own name. Stifling the urge to salute, he held out his hand.

Fariday completed a firm handshake and a rapid but thorough examination of his greeter. "Good day, sir. I have heard quite a lot about you from your sister," he said.

"All good, I hope," Ned replied. Fariday pressed down his mustache with his thumb and forefinger and smiled.

"No? Very well, I insist on equal time for rebuttal," Ned said. Fariday did not hide a wider smile. "Then you shall have it," he replied.

Chapter 32

"It went well, then. That's a blessing," Maggie commented as Ned completed his tale of Fariday's visit.

"He's a good fellow," Ned replied, "The judge rode him back and forth over the same conversational ground and questioned him minutely, but Fariday stood up to it well. He seemed rather amused, but Kate was incensed."

"Och, yes. Because she loves him," Maggie said.

"You weren't there," Ned began.

"I'm thinking she does," Maggie said, "And since he agreed to come again, I'm thinking he's taken with her. Will your father stand in her way, do you think? If he don't approve of the Major?"

"Don't jump ahead in the story, Maggie, there's no talk about anything besides a further visit." As she nodded, Ned rubbed the bridge of his nose. Far better to stay away from any speculation about the judge's actions. He said: "Did I tell you the Major's corking good story about the defense of Washington?"

As she shook her head, he said: "Ah. Well, sit down, and I will."

After the story, they shared a deep kiss, but fumbled apart when Zek entered the office. Maggie fled to her work area. "This is not fodder for gossip, Zek. Keep it to yourself," Ned commanded.

Zek pulled on his lower lip and said: "'Course I will. Ain't I done that already?"

"Already..." Ned repeated, his thoughts tumbling. "What do you mean?"

Zek shrugged nervously. "That you're sweet on her and such." Ned turned away to the window and addressed it with silent curses. He wiped his hands on his vest and sought a response.

Zek took his silence as assent. "Are you courtin' her, for real?"

Panic robbed Ned of his voice.

"She's first-rate, she ain't nothin' like my sisters," Zek commented helpfully.

"I have to...I have an errand. Just keep it to yourself," Ned said as he left.

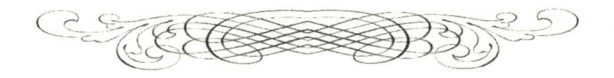

How could I have mixed such a muddy color? Maggie thought and started a new swatch. The gallery door opened. She looked up to see Judge Whitfield. She said: "I'm sorry, sir. Mr. Whitfield is out. He ought to be back soon." *The sooner the better,* she thought. Mercy, how this man frightened her.

"And Fish?" he asked.

"He is delivering pictures," she replied. He closed the gallery door and stood in front of it, staring at her. "That suits me," he said.

Maggie tracked him with her other senses, her eyes remaining on the photograph in front of her, her fingers tight on the brush. She felt him watch her: as before, he was like a cat, mad to have a bird in a fragile cage—mad but patient, reaching a paw out to tap, to test the strength of the wicker, sure of eventual success.

"Tell me, girl, have you set your cap for him?" he said.

No, no, Jesus savior! Not a word! Maggie told herself. But her brain was sluggish, her body cold. She shook her head.

He said: "I've heard it said that the Irish are a clever race. What bunkum. I have not seen such a marvel myself, so I never put any stock in the expression. But with a young fool like my son, it would take no more than pretty ways and an innocent face to turn his head."

Does he know? She put down the paint brush and hunched her shoulders to calm her racketing heart.

He went on: "You've never before been acquainted with any of your betters, I'll wager. And that is as it is meant to be. Keep your cap firmly on that silly little head or toss it at a hod carrier." She did not respond. The man did not stop. "That you've insinuated yourself into an acquaintance with my daughter means nothing. Let me be clear on that point, as well. She will tire of you as she comes out more into society." Maggie made a sound and shook her head again.

The judge ignored her movement. "There is little harm there at any rate, since you'll never cross my threshold."

Silence. Maggie strained to hear any sound of Ned or Zek's return. She prayed for another customer.

The judge said: "As for my son: I say this for your protection. He likes women of a lower class. He likes to make them believe that he is their hero, that he is superior in every way. I trust that he has not led you on?"

No, he loves me, Maggie thought instantly. She knew it as a fact. She shook her head a third time.

The judge said with disgust. "I expect he may if he has not done so yet. Remember, girl, he is your employer, not your hero, despite whatever pretty words he uses to exalt himself before you, so do not allow your imagination to run away with your senses."

He don't exalt himself, he'd never play such a mean game, Maggie thought, *That Betsy Dunn, she was too forward. He'd never lie to me, he just puts his thoughts into boxes and closes the lid but 'tisn't lying. He loves me.* She looked up. She had lost all feeling in her hands; she held them up as if to show him, to stop his words. Her hands fell into her lap. Anguish bright and hard stopped her breath.

"Well. You've been warned," the judge said and took his leave.

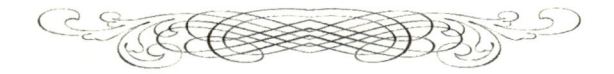

"He's mad entirely, 'tis true!" Maggie wept after repeating to Ned every word the judge had said. She was glad to see how angry her lover was on her behalf, glad to hear the invective he shot at that horrid man. But 'twas ugly, too, she thought, to see this hate in her lover's face.

She reached for his hand, uncertainly, and said the first thing, the worst thing, that came to mind. "Don't leave me!"

"I have no intention of doing that!" he spat out and stalked across the office. She watched him open the window, sweep the sill with his hand, tug at his vest, rearrange the objects on the neat (always ever so tidy) desktop.

"I'm sorry, I'm sorry!" she said.

"Please stop crying," he said, "We are due, overdue in fact, for a discussion of the difficulties. Sit down."

She sat trembling during his lecture. Each point he made fell like a blow: she had not thought of these things, how stupid a girl she was after all, not to realize them and to ease his rocky way a little. As her unquiet mind continued its insults, she recalled an old saying Mrs. Leary had used against Mrs. Sullivan.

She blurted: "Dress a goat in silk, 'tis still a goat, so they say, and that is what your people think of me." *Faith, she thought, am I, am I that goat after all, too ignorant to do nought but chew, never knowing the ways of fine silk?* "But I ain't that to you!" she said aloud.

"Good God, Maggie." Yes, the words had hurt him, she could tell. She loved him with all her heart.

"Good God," he repeated. "Of course not. Where do you come up with these things? It has nothing to do with what I have been discussing!"

"It has everything to do with what you been telling me," Maggie said, "They believe it. If they didn't, once I'd become a Prot that would be that." He shook his head. "And I love you so because you don't believe them," she whispered.

"Certainly not," he replied so truthfully, wearily that she took his hand and kissed it. She said: "I'm sorry, I will be good and I was listening, truly, I heard every word and you are right. I have been so stupid, and I won't be silly anymore. I will do everything that you say."

His answering sigh was deep. He removed his eyepatch and rubbed at his eyes vigorously. "So, that is...that is what we must do," he said, "I will attempt to set a course between Scylla and Charybdis and hope that I am up to the job of navigator."

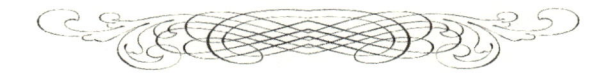

All our talks are painful now, Ned thought as he sweated under the gallery's skylight. He hated their current circumstances as strongly as he loved the girl. Wide-eyed and passionate, Maggie stepped on his heart with her truths and healed it each time with the treasures flowing from her own.

"To be sure," she'd told him just yesterday, "if you marry a mountain girl you marry the mountain. I've met your people and love them all, save one, so someday you must meet mine." He reminded her that he had met her brother Michael, and Corcoran who was like a brother to her. She had blushed adorably.

"Please do think about it, Ned," she said, and had kissed the senses out of him, then repeated, "but we'll do whatever you say."

His body still yearned for hers.

"Congratulations to you both," Ned said, when he could finally get a word in over the noise of Fariday's happy laughter, Kate's and his mother's exclamations, and the dog's shrill barks. He pushed past the stiffly smiling judge to shake the Major's hand.

"I am glad you welcome our news," Fariday said.

"It's first-rate, nothing better. Have you set a wedding date?"

The Major answered: "I must wait for my regimental discharge, and move out of my house in New Jersey, and of course, the ladies must have time to put their heads together and make their plans."

"I expect they've already begun," Ned commented.

"You're in no hurry to marry. No man ever is," the judge said, nodding at the Major.

Fariday replied: "In fact, sir, the sooner the better as far as I am concerned. Your daughter is a remarkable lady and has graced my heart for many months. I could not be happier that she will soon grace my home."

"You strike me as a practical man, Major," the judge said, "There's your new partnership at the envelope manufactory, and a house to rent or build in town, and wedding preparations. I expect we'll keep her here until the big event."

"She is worth the wait," Fariday said, smiling at Kate as she blew her fiancé a kiss.

"Where has Eleanor got to?" the judge asked in annoyance. "She ought to be here."

"She took the dog out. I'll fetch her," Ned said.

He sat on the back step and waited while Eleanor paced in the garden. Finally, she came and sat next to him.

"Is Papa angry?"

"No more than usual. You needn't rush in," he said. His sister was silent. "I like this fellow," he put in.

Eleanor said: "Oh, it's not him. He seems all right. It's just that I wish the one I...oh, I can't explain."

"You'll still have your sister, Elly. She'll be living closer as well." Eleanor nodded morosely.

"Maggie was right. She predicted there would be an engagement," Ned said.

"How is she? I never get to see her anymore. You take up all of her time," Eleanor said.

"I? Ah, the gallery," he replied. Eleanor frowned. "I miss her. I think she's forgotten me. I hope that she isn't angry because Martha made her wait on the back step."

"What do you mean?" he asked.

She recounted the story, then watched curiously as he got to his feet and kicked the boot-scraper. "Goodness, Ned, what has he said now, why are you so angry at him?"

"He has a lot to answer for," he replied.

Chapter 33

The mills had rung their supper bells half an hour ago, sending the laborers home, like cows from the pasture. He did not wish to be late. "Pardon me." Ned advanced, expecting the men to move aside for him; instead, they closed ranks, blocking the path.

"And where might you be goin'?" said the shorter man. The big man whapped a cudgel repeatedly into the palm of his hand. Ned struggled with disbelief. All those stories about unprovoked attacks by Irish roughnecks–true indeed? "Broke his nose. And two of his fingers. He still can't straighten them," the judge would say every time he described the beating a friend had received for the abolitionist cause in upstate New York at the hands of three Irishmen.

Ned stepped back uneasily. Two against one: he did not like the odds. Was it better to head toward one of the houses or back the way he'd come? He did not know this territory as well as he ought: his eye had always been on Maggie and not her surroundings.

The shorter man stepped forward. Now Ned could see something of the man's face. Maggie had told him about a man named Hurley. "He sneers like a cur snarling," she'd said. And where there was Hurley there was: what was the other name she had mentioned? Dooley? No, Dooley was 'near forty,' her friend's suitor. This big fellow was Ned's age. Hurley and… 'Paddy with a face like the man in the moon.' And here he stood, with a weapon. Perhaps this was not a random attack. These men might know him by description, if not sight. Molloy, yes, that was the name. Ned said: "I have no business with you, Hurley. Nor with you, Molloy. Let me pass."

"Wuh, how'd ye know me?" Molloy said with surprise.

"Shut yer gob!" Hurley hissed to his companion.

Ned assumed they were merely trying to frighten him. Nevertheless, he weighed his options. Stupid and drunk were not in Molloy's favor, but the cudgel and his size and strength were. Hurley had retreated back into the shadow: he carried no obvious weapon, but perhaps had a knife hidden away.

"Let me pass," Ned repeated. Molloy laughed and slapped the cudgel faster.

"Come along then," Hurley said. Ned could hear the sneer rather than see it. "Y'don't know the neighborhood, do you then? You might run into some trouble, bein' as it's after dark and all. We don't want you getting lost hereabouts, a gent like you." Molloy chortled. Ned began to worry.

"Come with us, boyo!" Molloy said, "Hee, hee, hee."

"In a pig's eye," Ned replied. A schoolboy's retort! He was not in the schoolyard here, with the school master a howl away. These two were not bluffing: he was alarmed by the size of the cudgel and Molloy's glee. *To hell with them all,* he thought, and stepped back.

Molloy said: "Run along. Hee, hee."

"The devil I will!" Ned snarled, incensed by the word "run."

Molloy cursed, the words garbled. He swayed a little. "Ye run home, ye bastard," Molloy repeated the insult several times, liking the sound of it, "We know why y'here."

"Do you," Ned said.

Molloy thought about this a moment. "Ye can't fool me." He belched loudly. "S'Maggie Shaughnessy. Ye bastard." When Ned did not respond, Molloy went on: "Maggie Shaughnessy, she's Rory's girl, so… get along with ye or I'll be teach' ye lesson."

"And who the devil is Rory?"

"Rory Corcoran," Molloy answered. *The one Maggie has known for ages,* Ned thought.

"Ye stup…stupid…" Molloy said, then stopped, swayed, cogitated.

"Bastard?" Ned said.

Hurley's snorting laugh was swallowed by Molloy's triumphant roar: "Yank!" There was a silence, broken only by a loud fart from Molloy. He giggled at this like a child.

Ned longed for his walking stick: left at home in his

chamber, as it often was. He had purchased it at Henry's suggestion during their high school days, then had hidden the expense from his father and the stick itself from his uncle, for its elegant exterior concealed a stiletto blade attached to the ivory handle. He mentally reviewed the contents of his pockets: Handkerchiefs, pencil, notebook, cigars, matches, a penknife.

He said: "It looks as if we have a stalemate. I might as well have a smoke." He made a show of moving his right hand under his jacket, the left nudging against the fabric and slipping into his trouser pocket to palm the penknife. He took out a cigar and the box of matches, opening and transferring the small knife to his right hand during the outward show of sniffing at, tapping, and lighting the cigar.

"Wh'th'divil...?" Molloy said, as Ned restored the matchbox, concealing the penknife in his sleeve. He puffed a smoke cloud. "Rory Corcoran," he said experimentally.

" 'S right," Molloy obligingly answered, with an obliging tipsy sway.

"Did he send you to waylay me?" Ned asked.

"Whissht," Hurley said to Molloy.

"Ye bastard," Molloy said.

"I believe we've established that already," Ned remarked.

Hurley said: "Think you're fine, then, don't you? A word of advice to you: you don't want to be tangling with the likes of Paddy Molloy." Pleasure mixed with the menace in his voice.

Molloy suddenly bellowed. Ned's stomach twisted. An instant later, Molloy's enraged bulk moved toward him. Go for the eyes, Eph Fish had once told him. Ned dodged, ducked, and felt a breeze as the cudgel whizzed barely over his head, sending his hat on the fly and the cigar to the ground. He slipped out the penknife, nearly dropped it, seized the hilt with his fingertips as if he was about to play a game of mumbletypeg, danced behind Molloy, crashed onto the man's back, grabbed onto what felt like an ear, a nose? and jabbed the penknife home with all the force he could muster. With a roar of pain, Molloy shook him off. Ned stumbled over something hard, fell, but came quickly to his feet, still holding the penknife. As Molloy moved again, Ned pivoted, stumbled a second time. The cudgel! He cried out in relief, bent and seized it in his other hand, ducking at an imagined swipe from Molloy.

"Aagh! Och! Fock'cut me!" Molloy had retreated with his

hands on his face. "Blagard cut me!" he moaned to Hurley.

Hurley went to his companion, pulled the man's hands away with some difficulty, then said: "Idjit! Swingin' your stick like that! Stop yer whinin' and go home. Have yer Mam see to it." Molloy unexpectedly lurched to one side, as Ned jumped to attention with the cudgel, but the Irishman merely bent over and began to retch. Hurley watched this from the shadow. Ned wondered again why no one had come to the windows of the row houses nearby. Were arguments and drunken brawls so common here that they elicited no interest?

"Go home, y'gavoon," Hurley said. The retching sounds ended. Molloy groaned, then staggered off up the path and disappeared into a side alley. Ned took the opportunity to move slowly forward, keeping his eye on Hurley and trying to avoid the area where Molloy had vomited. He retrieved his hat, kicking Molloy's aside.

"Go along yerself then," Hurley said angrily, "You've no right to walk out with one of ours. That the girl's silly enough to be taken in, still gives you no right!"

"Why don't you go back to the shithole you came from?" Ned shouted. "I'll swear out a complaint against you. I intend to charge you with assault."

"You're the one cut Paddy. I niver laid a hand on you."

"Self-defense..." Ned began.

"I tried to give you a word of friendly advice, is all." Hurley stopped short, as a man's face appeared in the window of a house nearby.

"Kiss my arse, Yank," he muttered, then merged into the shadow and down an alley.

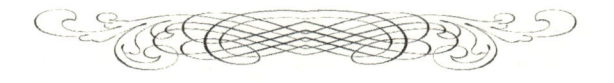

The privy was filthy! Ned had no choice, for his bowels had turned to water. He left one of his handkerchiefs behind as a sacrifice to the god of Irish cleanliness, and made his way slowly to the Foran house, shaken, irresolute, surprised by the depth of animosity aimed at him and now possessing his own soul. Here was the house. He knocked at the door with the cudgel. Maggie's face shone at the window like a vision. *A vision of goodness,* he thought, *if you believe in such beings. A mirage.*

"What's wrong? What's happened?" she said frantically. He shook his head, tolerated a round of prickly introductions, sat in the nearest chair before being asked to.

"He's got Molloy's blackthorn," Mrs. Foran said to her husband, loud enough for him to hear. So he told them the story, unembellished, barely damping his fury, no longer caring what they thought of him.

When he said, "He'd have split my head like a melon if I hadn't ducked," Maggie fainted. He felt only a dim concern. Her sister-in-law splashed her face with water. Her brother aided her to a chair.

"Are you all right?" Ned asked, not leaving his own chair. "Put your head down on your knees." She did so and after a moment lifted her pale face.

"I'm sorry," she whispered to him. He knew her, he knew she was sorry: not for the fainting, but for Molloy, for bringing him here, perhaps (now he hoped it was so) sorry for loving him.

Mrs. O'Shaughnessy scraped a chair away from the table and sat down next to her daughter, regarding him like a wary mother wolf. "The good Lord preserved ye..." she said to Ned but looking at her daughter. The Forans quietly assented, as the little girl, Maggie's niece, pouted with fright and uncertainty.

He said: "Molloy told me that Maggie is Corcoran's girl. Do you think that Corcoran put them up to the attack?"

"No! He'd not do such a thing. What are ye saying?" Rose Foran put in.

"No, 'tisn't likely," Foran added immediately, "Corcoran ain't stupid. They took it on themselves, so they did. Molloy did, being drunk and all."

"I ought to swear out a complaint against him with the justice of the peace. For assault and battery. For attacking me," Ned finished, unsure if they knew the legal definition of either crime. The antipathy in Mrs. Foran's face edged to scorn.

"They'd put him in jail, then?" Foran asked. Ned nodded.

" 'tis where he belongs," Mrs. O'Shaughnessy said. She put her hand over Maggie's arm.

Foran said: "He's fought some of <u>us</u>, but with fists, nought more than that. I'm thinkin' he'd not have gone after a gent if he wasn't drunk; he'd be meanin' to give you a fright is all..."

"Is all," Ned repeated, "He did more than give me a fright. I've been intoxicated myself, but I have never attacked anyone in my life, particularly with no provocation." Maggie made a sound and reached her hand to him across the table. He did not take it, but she did not withdraw it.

Foran shuffled his feet. "His brother's in the army. 'tis only Paddy's wage keeping his mam from the poorhouse."

"Ye'll be keepin' his shillelagh?" Rose said tartly. Ned shrugged. "'tis blackthorn. 'twas his grandfather's. Cursed, so they say, a one who steals it will have only bad luck," she continued.

Superstitious, to boot! Ned thought. Scorn overcame his anger. He stared at Maggie's hand, then laughed shortly. "I already have bad luck," he told Mrs. Foran, "And a tree branch has nothing to do with it. And bad luck for him, for swinging the blasted thing at me. I have stolen nothing. I'll keep it for tonight in case someone else tries to go at me; but I don't intend to keep it as a souvenir, I assure you! I will give it to Mr. Garside for safekeeping."

Rose Foran sniffed in annoyance. "There'll be no one goin' at ye."

"Who's that, then?" Foran asked.

"The justice of the peace," Ned answered with thinly concealed impatience.

"We've had nought to do with him," Foran said, "else I'd have known the name. We have nought to do with any fightin' or trouble."

"Of course," Ned said rather more politely.

A cinder crackled and fell in the stove. On the plate before him, gravy had congealed on the corned beef. Perhaps they would heat it after he had gone. His soldiers would have snapped it up, gray and gristly as it was. "I'm sorry that your meal was ruined," Ned said to the table.

Mrs. O'Shaughnessy and Rose exclaimed. "We're sorrier Molloy went off his head," Mrs. O'Shaughnessy said.

"What will you do?" Foran asked. Ned was muddled. He looked at Maggie then quickly away, scalded by the pain in her eyes.

"About Molloy..." Rose Foran added.

"I don't know," he said. Maggie made a sound like a small animal caught in a hawk's claws.

It can't be, Maggie thought. They had both struggled so hard. She had feared that the great flood of troubles would sweep them both out to sea, but she had never imagined herself alone on a hilltop, not to drown but starve, and to watch as he rowed away! The man who owned her heart stood up and grabbed the cudgel.

"I'm sorry, for..." he said, "I'll take my leave. Good night."

Maggie stopped him as he opened the door; the skin of her hand felt like ashes. "Don't go," she moaned, "I'll never see you again."

"Nonsense," he replied, "Neither of them will try this on me again. I'll be fine. Tuesday. I'll see you Tuesday at the gallery."

"Tomorrow?" she said faintly. Sunday afternoon was their small time together alone.

"I don't know," he said again. He stepped away from her hands clinging to his sleeve and left. She watched him stride away until he was lost to the gloom.

Mrs. O'Shaughnessy reached around her and shut the door, then put her arm around her, tight. The arm was a great weight that wrung the first sob from Maggie. She wailed like a child, beating her hands on the door handle. Her mother enfolded her, put her heavy head on Maggie's, murmuring, "There, there..."

Chapter 34

Early in September, the Whitfields received news of the fall of Atlanta under the onslaught of Union troops. Ned was happy with the news, believing along with his father that this action presaged an ultimate Union victory, yet it meant less to him now that affairs of his own life were following the rebel course: the burning cause was reduced to embers, the path was clouded, defeat inevitable. He saw Maggie at the gallery only. Each time she appeared in the doorway there, his heart rose, then withdrew, damped by her tears. When he had joked that she was a leakier woman than his sister Kate, Maggie had gaped at him in horror, grabbed her cloak and run home. When she returned, he apologized.

"'Twas very bad," she said, "you just don't know. 'Tis too close to the bone." Didn't she know that his bones were aching too? He had stepped softly with her after that. She recognized that and apologized to him. She said: "We've always been easy with each other, you and me, I was glad for that. Now 'tis gone, and I can't bear it." He had gathered her into his embrace, holding her tightly, wanting nothing more than to never let her go.

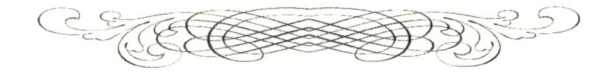

Mrs. Moore frowned at her patient as she dressed the burn on Maggie's hand and the cut on her head. Mrs. Ives and a frightened Dickie hovered behind her. "Tell me how this happened," Mrs. Moore demanded. Maggie had idly wished for something to take her mind off her heartbreak and now she was very sorry. The burn hurt viciously, and still she wondered "will he love me now?"

"'twas a mistake," she said, "I was feeling faint and then down I went."

"Have you been ill, Maggie? Are you eating properly?"

Maggie shook her head, and Mrs. Ives said: "We feed her well."

"But are you eating, Maggie?" Mrs. Moore asked, "You do not look well." Dickie began a tantrum, which Mrs. Ives ignored.

"Take him to bed, if you please," Mrs. Moore commanded.

"What is wrong?" she said to Maggie. "Have you been feeling dizzy of late? Have your monthly courses been regular?"

"No," Maggie said, "Nothing's been regular entirely." Her voice caught and the sobbing began all on its own and would not be stifled. Not knowing why, except that there was no one else to tell, she confessed that she had a love, greater than ever the world had seen, but he could not have her, and she could not have him, and her spirit was broken, and she would never be happy again.

"Who is it?" Mrs. Moore asked. Maggie shook her head. Mrs. Moore understood the gesture as it was meant: the man's name would not be revealed.

"Has he…" Mrs. Moore began, "Is there any way you could be with child?"

Maggie laughed raggedly. "No. No. No such thing, for I ain't done a thing…I ain't done such a thing."

"Have you severed every connection with him?" Mrs. Moore said quietly.

"What? I…I cannot…" Maggie said.

"You must. It will be better for you, in the long run. Only clean breaks heal properly. In time…"

"No!" Maggie wailed, "I never will get over it! He is my life!"

Mrs. Moore was silent. She allowed Maggie to sob, shooed Mrs. Ives away when she returned. She sat and listened as Maggie's cries tapered down, then she lifted Maggie's chin gently. "Think about what I have said, my dear. Go home now, have your mother put you to bed. And come to see me tomorrow. I will show you how to dress that burn so it heals."

Maggie did not sleep long, perhaps she never would again. Half an hour down, then up awake for an hour or more most of the night. She had not appeared at the gallery for her half day's work, but there had been no word from Ned or Zek. They did not need her, they had not wondered nor asked where she was nor how she fared. She could not have him, she could not bear to be near him, she could not bear to be away from him. She would explain that to Mrs. Moore.

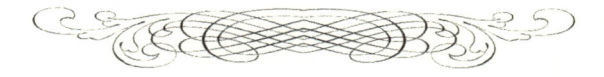

"It just isn't right!" Mrs. Whitfield said angrily. "He promised you a new watch for your 21st birthday, and he ought to have given it to you then."

"It doesn't matter," Ned replied. He thought, *I was promised joy with the woman I love and that is gone.*

"I reminded him last month, but he still has not given it to you," she continued.

"I don't care," he said. He wanted to tell his mother everything that had happened, but he never would. He would tell no-one.

"There's a letter here," Rose said.

Maggie grabbed the letter, then put it on the table in disappointment, seeing Eleanor's handwriting on the envelope. "It's from my friend," she said.

"That stuck-up Yank?" Rose asked angrily. Maggie shook her head and read the letter as Rose peeked fruitlessly at the paper from time to time. The message was a bright thread of comfort in the rusty black of Maggie's days. *Someone cares for me still,* she thought, *at least one. I will not spend another Sunday afternoon, looking and waiting and hoping for him to come to me.* She found a scrap of paper and wrote a quick, left-handed reply.

"I wondered if I would see you again," Ned said with relief when Maggie appeared at the gallery a week later. Her visit with Eleanor had been a sore trial, for Maggie had not liked to confess the secrets she'd kept, her horrible pain. But after all, sister was faithful, if brother was not. She held up her hand, the burn still visible, and told him of falling against the stove. Her heart quivered when he reacted with shock and dismay.

"That's dreadful!" he said, "I did not have any idea you'd been injured!"

"You might have asked about me or sent a note," Maggie said.

He said, "Good God, I am an idiot. I thought Mrs. Ives was keeping you and you had no chance to tell me. Then I wondered if... I would see you again," he said, his expression more than a little wild. She was very glad and very sorry that he had redeemed himself.

She took the book from under her arm and handed it to him. "Here's *The Last Days of Pompeii*," she said.

"Oh, have you finished reading it?" When she shook her head, he said: "Well, keep it, so that you can finish it."

"No, 'tisn't mine. You must have it back," she said.

"I lent it to you, but I meant for you to keep it. So that you can read the entire story," he persisted. She wished she could tell him of her burden of sadness and how she could not bear a single further straw. "Surely they all die anyhow," she said. From the droop of his shoulders, the sudden intake of his breath, she knew that he shared some of that burden.

She said: "Mrs. Moore took care of my burn, and my head, I hit that too."

"Are you all right?" he interrupted.

"My head and hand are, so she says, but I told her I'd lost a man I loved, and I did not say 'twas you, I'm thinkin' she believes it must be an Irishman. I'd never tell and hurt you, not for the world. You know that."

"Yes," he replied.

"She said...she said..." Maggie tried to breathe. "If 'twas never to come to be, then 'tis...a clean break that's needed, she said..." Her nose was running, it was not fair, when she was trying so hard not to cry, he hated crying so. He automatically handed her a handkerchief, staring at her as if she held his fate in her hands. *More the other way 'round,* she thought.

"See, you must see, it comes, 'twill come sometime, like the end of day comes any way, she says…"

"No!" He was stricken. She had more to say but could not say it. "No," he repeated. "Not yet. Not today. I need you. Another month or two."

"So that you can make another plan?" she moaned. He did not reply. "You know my colors," Maggie said dully, "write aquamarine for a dress, and I'll paint it at home until you find another colorist."

"Oh, Maggie. By the almighty, a colorist! I don't give a damn about that. I don't want **you** to leave." He reached for her, but she held her burnt hand against him so that it would hurt her, and she would not stay.

"Oww. Jesus, Mary and Joseph," she said, and let out howls of pain.

"Oh good Lord," he said, "No. Don't do that. Don't hurt yourself." He guided her to a chair, and sat her down, and stood behind her, his hands moving like an anxious vise on her shoulders. They stayed like that until her sobbing slowed. Zek had come into the gallery and stood watching them.

"How much did you hear?" Ned said without interest.

"Nothin'. Not much. I wasn't tryin' to, anyhow. Maggie ain't a-working here? I kin bring her the pictures if you like," Zek said somberly.

"She's not going," Ned replied, his voice thin like an old man's. "Not now."

Maggie stood up. She walked slowly toward the door.

"Say, that's too bad," Zek said, "Whyn't you stay?"

"Stay," Ned said.

Maggie turned and looked at her lost love. "I can't," she said to him, pleading. He stood in his place, tears standing in his eye. "What am I to do?" he said, "What am I to do without you?"

Maggie was so tired. She just wanted to sleep and dream this all right. "I'll always love you," she said and forced her way to the gallery door, wishing after all that she would feel his hands on her, making her stay. There was no sound or movement behind her as she opened the door and escaped.

Chapter 35

Like Rip Van Winkle, Ned wished he could sleep for years and arise, creaky in body, but blessedly past all memory. Eleanor had apparently guessed at all that had happened between him and Maggie. "How could you do such a thing to her!" she had said to him, and he had shouted at her with all the fury pent in his body. So now his sister knew he had not been playing at loving Maggie. It was no consolation. He could not explain to her or anyone else how this loss had torn his soul. He spent his time at the gallery, the law firm, the Lancaster taverns, avoiding his family, especially Elly and her pink-cheeked, pained silences. He was glad that Kate had returned to Washington for a visit: she could not now pierce him with her questions. *I had no choice,* he told Maggie (and now, Eleanor) in his mind, daily. *I had no choice.*

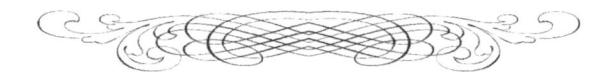

'Tis queer, Maggie thought, early in the morning of a perfect September day, *I can't cry now, though my eyes go to burning. It seems like I'll never get warm.* She believed now that death must be icy; but perhaps there was some good in that long cold sleep. "Oh, I'll ask Ned," she'd always thought, and now she could not. She missed the lessons on everything: what the classical poets wrote about love, why birds sang, how the English class system had prevented the lower classes from bettering their lot, how a piano is put together. She missed the warm voice, the jokes, the set of his shoulders and softness of his hair, the musical interludes, his

enthusiastic response when she said something that caught his interest. The loss of each she experienced as a separate new loss, and so there were hundreds of small rough cuts like being flayed by a grater.

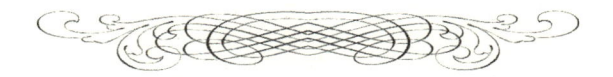

Yes, the money ain't bad, Maggie thought, *but 'twas a mistake to come and live with the Ives.* Clerk or no clerk, God had favored his lowly servant with an even lowlier servant, and this suited Mr. Ives' proud ways. Just yesterday she'd overhead him complain to a visitor about the shiftless Irish. *I'll give you something to crow about,* Maggie thought, and thrust his bawling flesh and blood at him, as his wife wept in dudgeon and dinner burned. Mrs. Ives' indulgence and energy had faded as her belly grew with child again, and she had ceased being Maggie's ally.

Every Sunday morning, the mister and missus went to church, leaving the boy with her, but the moment they arrived for a cold Sunday dinner (he kept the Sabbath strictly now that a promotion at the mill seemed imminent), Maggie was free to go, to wander and weep for Ned, or write a letter to Eleanor, but usually to go to Rose and Frank's and sleep on any bed in sight.

This Sunday the weather was unsettled, and Mrs. Ives the same. Mr. Ives sent her back to bed, then followed Maggie from room to room, watching her.

"Not off to services then?" Maggie finally said, when he had chided Dickie for the fifth time in fifteen minutes.

"Not while Mrs. Ives is ill. You ought to go and tend to her," he said.

"Yes, sir." Maggie mounted the stairs and peeked in at the mistress, who was sleeping. *All she wants is a moment of peace,* Maggie thought, as she tiptoed down the back hall to sit on her bed, the only furnishing in the narrow room.

"Mary," Mr. Ives called up the stairs.

Maggie ran down the back stairs with a scowl. "In the kitchen," she yelled. He came in with Dickie and ordered her to sit the child on the potty. He did not ask about his wife. When Maggie returned, he announced that they must both join him in the sitting room and listen while he read from the Bible. She sat Dickie in his chair but retorted that she had to lay out the dinner.

"Would you like me to take a meal up to Mrs. Ives before I go," Maggie asked.

He said: "Mary, you may not leave us today, while Mrs. Ives is ill. I will give you the full day whenever she is well."

"No, sir, I cannot stay, my family will be waiting for me," Maggie said.

"Well, that is too bad, but you are needed here," he replied shortly. She fled the room before she could tell him what she thought of him, then chopped the cold meat with the biggest knife, enjoying the thunking sound of it against the cutting board, then banged down the stove lid with pleasure. Mr. Ives read the Bible aloud—some passage about patience. She sat wearily on the kitchen floor, leaning her head against the dish cupboard. Was it a sin, she wondered, to wish harm to the man who paid your bed and board?

A firm series of knocks sounded on the back door. Maggie opened it to see Rory grinning at her as if she was a basket full of gold.

"Come along with me, dearie," he said.

"He ain't given me leave," she said, jabbing her thumb back toward the sitting room.

Corcoran came in over the doorstep and shut the door with his elbow. "Leave or no leave," he said, "'tis your afternoon off."

Mr. Ives came into the kitchen. To Maggie, he always looked like an owl ready to urp up the leavings; and never more so than at this moment. "Who are you?" he said.

"I'm here to fetch Maggie," Corcoran said.

"She hasn't yet served dinner, we need her here. Who are you and where do you think you're taking her?"

Rory smiled a long, mean smile. He said: "And who are you to ask what she does and where she goes on her time off?

"She is my servant and a member of my household," Mr. Ives said with umbrage, "and I have the right and duty to protect her morals and ask you any question I please."

Corcoran said: "If you knew Maggie at all you'd know she's a good girl and you've no need to protect her morals. Nor to ask ME any question you please! Get your things Mag, I'm here to fetch you home to dinner."

"You'd better watch your tongue, or you'll cause her to lose her position here," Mr. Ives blustered.

Rory moved from the doorway and close to Mr. Ives, close enough to overshadow the screech owl. "She ain't said a word to you now, has she? She ain't done a thing wrong. And you ain't my boss," he said with menace.

Mr. Ives stepped back half a dozen paces and added one for good measure. "She must be back in time for supper," he said in Corcoran's direction.

Maggie said softly, not hiding her glee: "Mrs. Ives told me she'd put her hand to that, sir, since I ain't had an afternoon off in two weeks. I'll be back soon as I can." She grabbed her cloak and basket from the pantry, and slipped out the back door, holding Rory's hand.

"What a mean, puny bit of work that one is!" Corcoran said just after the door had closed. "I have to get you out of that place, for good and all." He smiled and squeezed her hand, "But I can see to that."

Maggie said: "I'm thinkin' you mustn't get him riled, Rory. Not till I've got a new position. Have you heard of one coming open?"

Corcoran kept smiling. The dimple in his cheek winked at her. "I have. A good one, entirely."

"Och, that's grand! Where is it?" Maggie said.

"Here," he replied. "Right here by me."

Maggie did not let go of his hand. "I am glad you came to walk me home," she said.

"There's the smile, it's been a long time coming," he said. He put his arm around her waist. "Right here by me," he repeated, giving Maggie a shiver—not a sad one, not a sad one, for the first time in many weeks.

Chapter 36

Sharing a patch of late September sunshine and one of Ned's good cigars in the alley behind Mix's office, Davis shuffled his feet and essayed a comment: "What do you think of the new partner?" Ned looked in surprise at the clerk, an assiduous copyist who normally remained invisible in the office and as silent as old dust, then shrugged.

"Yep," Davis went on, "We ain't had a dinner hour in three weeks, young Morton nor I, since he came."

"Nor I," Ned commented, rubbing his belly.

"We don't work fast enough; we don't amount to a hill of beans, so he said," Davis continued. "Did you hear him?" He looked coolly at Ned, but drew at the cigar in rapid, agitated puffs. At Ned's nod, Davis pulled the cigar from his mouth, coughed. "I guess he thinks he'd do it better. I'd like to see him try! But I'd wager he hasn't made a copy since he was a school boy."

"That's a winning wager," Ned said, "Mr. Putnam's family used to own half of the land in Millville before they moved on to even greener pastures."

Davis said: "That's always the way!" He rapidly finished his cigar and returned to his desk.

Ned closed his eye, which felt as if someone had rubbed pepper in it. He had a hangover and had been reading law digests since breakfast seeking an elusive case for Mr. Putnam. He heard a girl laugh in the distance, a light laugh. He launched out of his lean against the building, sure that it was Maggie. He walked to each end of the alley, looking, seeing no-one.

Crinkling in his suit pocket, out of sight but fully on his

mind, was the letter from George Dunn: a rant from beginning to end, an enraged puke of words about the explosion at Petersburg and the battle (more properly termed a disaster for the Union troops) at the Crater. Ned was sickened to imagine himself in George's place–sliding on blood in the crater, folding in among the bodies around him, buried alive. He had kept the letter in his pocket for weeks, knowing he must answer it: but how to answer? He was afraid that even if Dunn returned to Millville, he might have left his sanity behind in that anteroom to Hell.

The assistant copyist, young Morton, put his head out of the back door. "Say, there's two fellows waiting here for you."

The two fellows introduced themselves as Mr. Sullivan and Mr. Cohan. Thankful that both law partners were out of the office, Ned took the men into Putnam's office. As they were seated, Sullivan thrust a packet of papers forward, saying: "The fool's put the law on us, when 'twas his own fault."

Ned sighed. Tolliver Adams, the plaintiff, was well known in the community for his litigious nature: his name appeared on so many documents in Mr. Mix's firm that Ned had jokingly renamed him "Intolerable Adams".

"So," he said, "Mr. Adams is suing you for an injury sustained on the joint premises of your tavern and brewery while he was on the property to buy beer..."

"He's a liar! A lying blackguard!" Cohan asserted.

"And you are business partners?" Ned asked. He had passed by the tavern and the brewery while walking Maggie home. He sometimes frequented low drinking establishments, but never in Millville. Cohan nodded, and Ned went on: "It says here that when Adams came in the evening, let's see, in March of this year, to purchase beer..."

"He's a liar," Sullivan put in.

Ned said: "Mr. Sullivan, I am just reading from the complaint sworn against you and Mr. Cohan. He says the premises were dark, hold on, Mr. Cohan, permit me to finish and then I will hear your perspective on the matter. Premises were unlit and plaintiff opened a door and stumbled against some machinery, falling and injuring himself."

"He was looking for a place to piss, when he could have gone over to Sullivan's in the blink of an eye," Cohan said.

"I beg your pardon?" Ned said.

Sullivan said: "The fellows get off work at the mill, they come down right away to get a growler to take home. Some piss along the lane, o' course, but most of them come to the privy at the tavern."

"So, the tavern has a necessary. Is that path lit in the evening?" Ned asked.

Sullivan replied: "'Tis indeed. There's two lanterns there, and they use it and cross the way to Cohan's to get a growler."

"He come over one night to get his and said he had to piss," Cohan said, "and I told him to go over to Sullivan's, 'tis no more than 10 yards from my place. And we'd broke a path up there in th' snow. He'd no business being in the brew house in the dark…"

"Is there a privy anywhere in or near the brew house?" Ned asked. Cohan said, "Not in the brewery, 'tis on t'other side of my place. 'tis for the men working there, not for the likes of him!"

"Was Mr. Adams familiar with the layout of the property? Was he a new customer?" Ned inquired.

"Tch! Hasn't he been comin' there for years now," Sullivan answered.

Ned glanced through the complaint again. The plaintiff's attorney, Samuel Peasley from Lancaster, had recently hoisted a sign for his business in Millville, trolling for soldier's pension cases, and other "small fish." Mr. Mix characterized the lawyer as an ill-mannered upstart and questioned his ethics. Perhaps Mix would welcome a case, however noisome, against Peasley. He said: "I will have to discuss this matter with Mr. Mix. It is his decision whether or not to represent you in this case."

"He's no leg to stand on," Sullivan said.

"Lyin' through his teeth," Cohan added.

"Presuming you are referring to the plaintiff, that remains to be seen," Ned replied.

Mr. Putnam was openly derisive when Ned described without elaboration the complaint and the defendants. "You ought to have sent them away immediately," he said, "We will not represent a saloon owner."

"Without a hearing?" Ned replied, not as politely as he had intended, "For Mr. Peasley to make his name?"

"That will never happen," Putnam said, "It is a pity that this town permits the sales of spirits." They both looked at Mr. Mix: Putnam with confidence and Ned with curiosity. The senior partner was reading the complaint and Ned's notes and did not favor them with a response until he had finished his perusal.

Mix said: "While I agree with you, Isaac, that this town would be better off dry, Mr. Whitfield raises two interesting issues: First, under the law, was Adams a trespasser in this instance, or a mere licensee, or an invitee? Second, if an invitee, what duty of care, if any, does a proprietor owe to a person who opens a closed, unmarked door apart from the customary business area? The defendants are certainly not to my liking, but neither is Mr. Peasley." He re-folded the document and thrust it at Ned. "Two salient points for you to research, Mr. Whitfield. Report your results to Mr. Putnam and then we will decide whether this is a matter worthy of our effort."

"Yes, sir," Ned said, "And as to the defendants' assertion that Adams had a grudge against them from a prior matter?" Putnam snorted with annoyance.

Mr. Mix said: "Immaterial in this case, and generally, Mr. Whitfield. Facts, sir; do not forget your lessons."

"Yes, sir," Ned replied. *Facts,* he thought, as he put the complaint under his arm and took his notebook from his pocket, *I have ignored them for too long.* He thought again with pity of the facts that George was facing: the constant and inescapable rapid-fire recollection of horrors seen, smelled, felt. Ned was thankful to be far from that; and bare-bone facts, facts alone, would be his salvation.

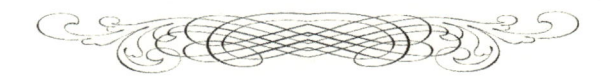

Maggie cleared the dinner table as quickly as she could. After Mr. Ives left, she ushered the missus and Dickie to their respective beds. Thank the Lord neither of them protested, and Dickie was already drowsing with a thumb in his mouth as she left his chamber. Rory would be along soon, on his way back to the mill. She ducked out the back door. There, she could hear him nearby. She peeked around the corner of the house, hoping to surprise him. He had his back to her and was talking to Hurley.

"Why would ye do such a thing?" she heard Hurley ask.

"She's a fine-looking girl," Corcoran said.

"She kisses so fine, she loves so sweet, she makes things

stand that have no feet," Hurley snarked.

Rory laughed. "As sure as you're born." Maggie coughed loudly, then walked to them. Hurley leered at her and took his leave. Corcoran took a kiss from her until Maggie pulled away.

"Mr. Hurley has a hard heart, in my opinion," she said.

Rory turned his head to look down the street. "Keep your friends close, and your enemies closer, so they say."

She hesitated, then said: "I don't like the way he looks at me."

"What way does he look at you?" he said balefully.

She scowled: "Like he thinks I'm no better than I should be."

"He don't know you like I do," he replied, "That's just his way, with all the girls."

"I'm thinking that's why he has no girl of his own," she retorted.

He shook his head a little. "You do have a tongue sometimes."

"Is he Mr. Harrigan's man?" Maggie asked suddenly.

Corcoran gripped her arm. "Harrigan has nought to do with you! I told you that before. Don't be askin' me nor anyone about him. D'you hear me?"

"Ow. I'm sorry, Rory. I won't. I do wonder just because my Da knew him."

He shook his head again and then released his tight hold, as he said: "You know, Maggie, I bin thinking about far more important things. Now, don't make eyes at me, I have, to be sure. Here's God's honest truth in the matter, I'm thirty years old, I never had a family to speak of, as you know, and it's high time I was married and raising boys of my own."

Maggie was surprised at her own fright. She put her head down against his chest, but as he spoke again, she placed her hand on his lips.

"Sweet mother of God, Rory, don't say more now! I've always been fond of you, but I don't even know you, not truly," she babbled in distress. "Whissht and let me say what I have to say. You think you know a fellow and then he turns out far different."

He shouted: "That one! That lyin' bastard! He only wanted one thing from you and threw you out when he didn't get it."

It was far more complicated than that, but Maggie did not go into it. "What about Annie?" was all she could think to say. She kept her eyes down, away from his, for if she looked him full in the face, she would be towed under by the current.

"What about her!" Corcoran said angrily, "She don't own me. If I walked out with her, so I did with others, and now I am with you."

"She says she knows you better than anyone, she can even tell what you'll do every time. How can anyone say such a thing, I'd like to know."

"She said that?!" he fumed.

"Or something like it," Maggie replied. Thinking of Ned's mysteries, shy Kevin, and the incomprehensible behavior of Mr. Barton, she added: "No woman can know a man that well; 'tis a lie to say you can, unless he's stupid."

"She thinks I'm stupid, does she?" Corcoran roared. Although Maggie shook her head, he muttered to himself for a moment, then stared at her, appraising. "You say you don't know me, though I been around since you was a little girl. You don't know me, then, but you'd like to know me better."

She looked at him, so handsome, the compelling green eyes, the confidence, the tenderness in them now. "Yes, I would," she said sincerely; and was pleased, if a little worried, by the touching pleasure she saw there

He smiled: "There's something to that. You need some time to get to know me. That's what courting is for: that and other things... You'd be wanting that at any rate then, Maggie dear, surely?"

She saw the eagerness there, not just physical desire; and how he waited for her response, his usual bravado down several notches. Although she had been transparently honest and honorable with Ned, she had always been tempted to play with the power she had then. What if she had instead given all her power to keeping him? The familiar pain in her soul gave her pause. But this man was here and thought her worthy of his pursuit. Perhaps he loved her. He had been ready to ask her hand in marriage, until she stopped the question.

She raised her eyes to Rory again. "I might, Mr. Corcoran," she replied, giving him her sweetest smile.

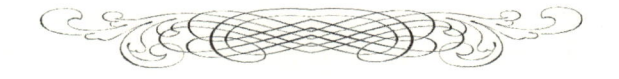

In celebration of the Union victory at Cedar Creek which had occurred a fortnight before, the Judge insisted again on reading to the family his favorite poem, *Phil Sheridan's Ride*:

> *Up from the South at the break of day,*
> *Bringing to Winchester fresh dismay,*
> *The affrighted air with a shudder bore,*
> *Like a herald in haste, to the chieftan's door,*
> *The terrible grumble, and rumble, and roar,*
> *Telling the battle was on once more,*
> *And Sheridan twenty miles away...*

Ned spent the next minute meditating in annoyance on the god-awful rhyming of grumble, rumble and roar, adding to himself, *Quoth the Raven, Nevermore!*

But the Judge went on:

> *He dashed down the line 'mid a storm of huzzas,*
> *And the wave of retreat checked its course there, because*
> *The sight of the master compelled it to pause.*
> *With foam and with dust the black charger was gray;*
> *By the flash of his eye, and the red nostril's play,*
> *He seemed to the whole great army to say,*
> *"I have brought you Sheridan all the way*
> *From Winchester, down to save the day!*
>
> *Hurrah! hurrah for Sheridan!*
> *Hurrah! hurrah for horse and man!*
> *And when their statues are placed on high,*
> *Under the dome of the Union sky,*
> *The American soldier's Temple of Fame:*
> *There with the glorious general's name,*
> *Be it said, in letters bold and bright,*
> *"Here is the steed that saved the day,*
> *By carrying Sheridan into the fight,*
> *From Winchester, twenty miles away!*

"Hurrah," Ned commented sourly as his father finished with a flourish, "Thrice in a week this poem has run, so hurrah, hurrah, for now it's done."

The judge lowered the paper. Ned could feel the glare, although he kept his eye on his law book, and waited.

"Deliberately provocative, as usual," his father said, "and shamelessly scornful of a great poem and a great man."

"A great general, I agree," Ned replied. "I've heard he's Irish in lineage, by the way. But a bad poem: 'huzzahs and because'? It glorifies the horse more than it does the fighting men."

"They were in retreat!" the judge said.

"That is not what I read elsewhere. Wright had them rallied, although Sheridan's appearance certainly helped their morale," Ned retorted, as he warmed his hands by the stove.

The judge folded the newspaper, mulling his next sortie. He said: "You have been in a foul temper for weeks, ever since Kate left. Pray do not inflict it further upon your family."

Since Maggie left, Ned thought. It had been a mistake on his part to stay home this evening, rather than join his convivial drinking companions in Lancaster, with whom he was now on a first-name basis. He spoke without consideration: "Pray do not further inflict that poem upon me."

"That's enough," Mr. Whitfield said through his teeth, "You've no right to make this family miserable with your nasty moods and disgusting comments! Your mother is very concerned about you." Ned was aware of this. He retrieved his law book, said goodnight and left.

In his chamber, he drafted a letter to George, then threw it away, and instead began to draft a heartfelt note to Maggie. He wrote rapidly, telling her that he had never feigned any emotion with her, but had loved her with all his heart, and that his intention was never to hurt or mislead her; that, in truth, she and her actions and her proposed sacrifices had moved him greatly, although he was not worthy of such devotion. He thought he was not worthy of anyone's devotion, but he did not write that down.

Re-reading his draft, he frowned. He rolled the pencil restlessly across the table and back. It dropped to the floor, but he did not pick it up. The letter was much too revealing. If eyes other than hers saw it, he, with not enough money to strike out on his own, would be doomed to remain in that damned sitting room listening to his father spew for years to come. He folded the draft, sealed it in an envelope, locked it in a small wooden box, and replaced the box in its hiding place under a loose baseboard.

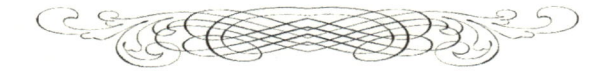

"You're marrying Mr. Dooley!" Maggie repeated with astonishment as her friend Bridget sat before her, bouncing in excitement.

"Thanksgiving Day, for the mill is lettin' all the men out for a holiday—and you were thinkin' you and Rory would be first!" Bridget said and went on to describe where the wedding supper was to be held, what they would eat, and how they would dance: for Mr. Dooley had been so good as to hire the fiddler, and that cousin of his (who had brought his bodhran all the way from Ireland years ago) would be there as well.

When her spool of talk finally ran empty, she accepted the good wishes of Maggie and the Forans and went to visit Agnes Donnelly and tell her the same tales.

"I wasn't thinking I'd be first," Maggie said to her Mam and Rose, "And Mr. Dooley is a good man, but he's so old. And not a bit handsome."

Rose rolled her eyes and commented that Mr. Dooley had a good job and wasn't that the best thing after all.

"'tisn't your time to marry. Not that one," Mrs. O'Shaughnessy said, peering with intent at Maggie.

"What do you mean by that?" Maggie asked. She had always wondered at her mother's comments about Corcoran, and now they bothered her more and more.

Her mother shrugged. "It means what it means," she replied, then went out the back door.

Chapter 37

Ned watched the flames from the torchlights bend, stand straight, twist and bend again, and thought that the wind was more measurable than the affairs of men. In truth, he was more than a little intoxicated and inclined to become unduly rapt by firelight and philosophy. The top of his father's tall smooth hat shone in the firelight: all else was in shadow. Although the Judge's favored candidate, President Lincoln, had been re-elected, his own race for state representative had ended in defeat, so he scowled as he walked in the Republican victory march.

Such flames were burning through the South, as General Sherman marched to the sea. The images troubled Ned: he imagined Millville burning, the contents of homes and stores turned out onto the street, smashed, afire. He had seen a torn and trampled copy of the Federalist Papers in the street in Fredericksburg, as some of the Union soldiers entered the abandoned houses and seized whatever they liked. He had bent to retrieve the book, almost stopped to read it—as if the road during a siege was a gentleman's library! then had tossed it away as tumult rattled around him, resigned to seeing all creation torn and discarded. He turned his back and drank from his hidden flask. He took another drink, restored the flask and re-joined the parade.

Fuzzy-minded, dry-mouthed and slightly late arriving at the office the next day, Ned heard Mr. Mix call out his name.

"I'm sorry sir," Ned said, "I celebrated the President's re-election last night, and I am afraid I lost track of the time this…"

Mix waved away the explanation with a smile. "Your Mr. Shackelford has finally received approval for his disability pension."

"First rate!" Ned said as he scanned the letter Mix had handed to him.

Mix said: "I trust that the others we have pending will have a similar result. Sit down, I would like to review some of your research. I see you found nothing on point in Mr. Putnam's matter on the Eagle Mill's water rights. That's a shame, it is one of his pet causes. I'd like you to take another look."

Nothing is too good for Mr. Putnam, Ned thought sourly. He nodded to Mix and penciled "Find the golden fleece" in his notebook.

After they had reviewed the research, Ned stationed himself by the book shelves. Mr. Mix thrust his head out of his office and said, "Oh, I forgot to tell you. In the matter of Intol... Mr. Tolliver Adams vs. the Irishmen, I've decided we shall represent the defendants, so prepare the papers for Davis, if you please."

"Yes, sir."

Mr. Mix shut his office door, and Mr. Putnam shut his—a bit too quickly, a bit too hard, causing Davis to smile.

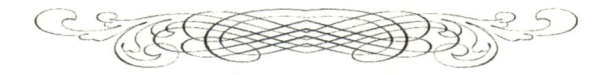

A draft slipped in under the baseboards, quivering the evergreen bridal decorations. *Ah, they do look happy, after all,* Maggie thought, watching Bridget (now Bridey, indeed!) and Mr. Dooley dancing and all smiles at each other, following their wedding supper. As Maggie reached up to steady a garland, she saw Rory watching her.

Not ten minutes ago, her Mam had said to Bridey, "Better an ass that will carry you than a horse that'll throw you," and had nodded meaningfully at Corcoran, managing to offend him and the new Mrs. Dooley both with one blow, and leaving Maggie to make apologies. Bridget had given up nothing in marrying Mr. Dooley; both had gained. Maggie thought of Ned, pondering what he had asked of her.

Mam was now laughing raucously; Maggie tensed and looked around in apprehension, but no one had blinked—they did not mind her, even those not in the same sorry state. Maggie smiled, remembering the wave of small silver fish she had seen once in the mill pond. All the tiny heads and tails had followed along, and the mass of them moved like one great fish: how right, how easy. *For mercy's sake,* she told Edward in her mind, *why must anyone change name, manners, religion, a lilt in the voice, and <u>always</u> be thinking of what was proper to say and to do?*

The fiddler struck up a tune, a favorite of hers. She danced alone in a corner, the beating of the old Irish drum setting her chest a-quiver. *I am not your little Maggie,* she thought, *weak and dreamy, nor meant to wallow alone in dark places. I am quicksilver in the music.* The fiddler took the pace faster, but Maggie kept up. Shaken loose, memory and pain and fear spun out from her and away; and as her hair came down from the pins she jigged on. The crowd stopped now to watch her, this duel between fiddler and moving feet. Smiling fiercely through her exhaustion, heart beating nearly out of her chest, Maggie ended with her arms upraised at the fiddler's last note. She sat down hard, waving to show them she was all right despite her bucketing gasps for breath.

"Give her some air," Rory commanded the folks who surrounded her. He gathered her up and carried her to a chair, petting and praising her as the guests laughed or commented in surprise.

Hurley said: "She's had too much of the ardent! Just like her Mam."

"No, she ain't," Corcoran shot back, "She hardly takes a drop!"

Rory leaned close to Maggie and stroked her hair. "How are you, then?"

She squeaked: "Fine, now."

He whispered: "You're magnificent." He gazed at her, and she knew she had won him: and there would be no hanging back by this one, no view of love as a curlicue maze. Rory Corcoran was not a man who'd try to force a love as big as the world into a shape and size that he'd calculated was "better suited." He held her hand tightly, stroked it.

After she had her drink and rest, he drew her out into the yard—as cold as it was—and pressed her close to him, kissing her frantically. She knew what that hard thing was, like an extra limb, that he also pressed against her.

"I love you, darlin,'" he said. These words and the caresses and the knowledge of their truth started a hot beat in her body. She kissed him in return, matching his desire. *This is what love is meant to be,* she addressed Ned in her thoughts, *I'm sorry you'll never know that, but I shall drink it until I've had my fill.*

"'tis time," he said, "Marry me! 'Tis high time you said yes."
"Yes," she said, "Kiss me!"

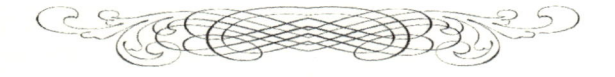

"We must call upon the Topliffs on New Year's Day," the Judge said, "and you shall see your friend Sidney."

"I've been invited to spend the evening before and New Year's Day with Henry Barton," Ned put in, "And I intend to take him up on it."

"Will he come here?" Eleanor asked. Her book slipped from her lap to the floor.

"No, he will be making calls in Hartford," Ned answered.

Mrs. Whitfield shifted uncomfortably in her chair, "What a pity," she murmured.

"I will give you a list of gentlemen with whom I would like a better acquaintance," the judge said, "I expect you to mention me to them and express my best wishes to them for the new year."

Dance could be heard, barking from his exile in the barn. Mrs. Whitfield asked her daughter for help preparing baskets for the poor for Christmas Day.

Eleanor picked up her book and said softly, "Of course."

The judge took up his newspaper and read to them a description of Sherman and his troops burning their way across the state of Georgia, and soon to reach the seaside city of Savannah. He read loudly, and with relish.

"They ought not to burn people's homes!" Eleanor exclaimed, "What will they do, all the ladies whose men are gone away, how will they live with no roof over their heads, and nowhere to turn?"

The judge glared at her. "What has that got to do with anything? As General Sherman has said, they must be made to suffer the retribution for their rebellion."

Ned said: "Elly, the General and the army have been disrupting all of the railroads and supply lines, and their numbers are so strong that there is little the rebels can do to stop them. It is a strategy of war."

"But what about those left behind?" Eleanor murmured.

"You're an ignorant girl," the judge replied, "Shall we

simply back away, shall we basely apologize for setting foot on their territory? They began this war! Good heaven, have some sense!"

Eleanor stared at her book, cheeks and eyes red. After a few moments, she excused herself and left the room.

Left behind. Ned wondered if his sister would ever forgive him for... well, what HAD he done to Maggie? He had only loved her. It was worst in the dawn hours when he lay still, eye closed, wishing himself no longer empty-handed.

"I never thought to have such a stupid child," the judge said suddenly.

His mother spoke up. "She's not stupid! It distresses her, thinking of those suffering."

The judge snorted in disgust. "Didn't you hear what I said!"

Ned shut his ears to the rest of his father's opinions and vowed to buy his sister some new sheet music and a capital new book, full of engraved scenes.

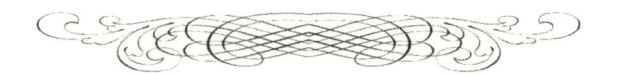

"He's been with me, d'ye hear me, he's been with me!" Annie said. She had come out of a corner as Maggie left the Ives, and charged at Maggie like a whirlwind.

"And now he's courting me. Can't a man change his mind?" Maggie replied.

"Have ye been there at his beck and call like I have?" Annie laughed, but Maggie winced to hear the pain there. Rory was there between them as suddenly as if he'd been conjured from their minds.

"Here now," he said, putting his arm around Maggie and glaring at her rival.

With her eyes red as raw meat and her mouth contorted, "Rory, ye cannot do this," Annie said, quietly, too quietly, so Maggie thought, and she moved closer to him in fright.

"Don't dare to tell me what I can or can't do," he replied to Annie in the same manner. Maggie shivered.

"When we've lain...." Annie began.

"Shut your mouth!" he shouted. "Lies," he said, and then to Maggie, his gaze sidelong, he repeated, "She's lying."

"She is," Maggie asserted loyally.

"Leave us be," he commanded. Annie moaned and reached

for him, but he stepped back from her, pulling Maggie with him: Annie's hand brushed against Maggie's shoulder. Then Annie Mulrooney stood with her hands at her sides, weeping fat tears.

"Keep yer mouth shut, and leave us be," he yelled again over his shoulder.

"Rory! No!" Annie cried.

"Never you mind her, she's not right in the head," he said to Maggie, "I never saw a woman make such a row about nothing. Next week we'll be married, and she'll have nought to do with us ever again."

As he yanked her away, Maggie turned her head back to look at Annie, feeling both superior and sad.

"The poor thing," she said.

Chapter 38

No dancing, and the supper ain't the best, Maggie told herself, *but I could not be happier, could I?* Rory was so handsome, and everyone had admired her new dress (a perfect shade of dove gray) and the armful of fabric flowers she had twined into a ribboned bouquet. And hadn't he bought her the prettiest ring which shined now on her hand? She smiled, surely it was the best day for a wedding, New Year's Day, for only good things lay ahead for her and her new husband. She whispered the word aloud, and Bridget smiled at her. It was just too bad that Mam drank herself sick and disappeared from the party almost before it began. Maggie had drunk more than she usually did, but it only made her pleasantly dizzy.

As the party ended, Frank stood up and awkwardly but sincerely gave her the first blessing of the marriage in the traditional way. Rory bundled her into her warm wraps, passing her around for hugs and kisses from the women. The men nodded to her and clapped him on the back with wide smiles. Her new husband walked her carefully down the icy path to the house he had just rented. They would have boarders arriving the next day, but he said he would not have any in his house on his wedding night.

He lit a lantern, then carried her up the stairs to the tiny bedchamber, just big enough to hold a chest of drawers, and the bed—where her new nightgown rested. Maggie giggled all the way, even as he unwound her from her wraps and went to kissing her. Grinning, he began to remove her clothes, cursing at the hooks and buttons.

"Don't pull so hard, Rory, you'll tear my dress," Maggie said.

"You do it then," he said, "and be quick about it." Maggie did so, shivering, even though the stove was lit. "I'm thinking it's too cold a day to get married," she joked.

"I'll soon warm your arse," he said. He tossed her nightgown onto the chest, turned the bed covers down, took some ragged sacks from under the bedstead and threw them on the sheet.

"What are you doing?" she asked.

"We don't want to dirty the bed, now, do we?" he said. Maggie paused, down to her underwear, bewildered.

He pulled her close, she pushed her hand against his chest, "I must get my nightgown on," she said.

"You'll not be needing that!" he said. Seizing her, holding her close, he ran his hands along her frame, removed the rest of her clothing and his own. His warm skin felt fine, and she began a caress, but he rolled her down onto the bed.

She began to tell him that she was afraid, as he lay upon her and she could hardly take a breath, so heavy was he, so hard did he press her, so hard was he all over. She felt him force her legs apart, heard herself scream in pain and surprise. He mashed his hand onto her lips. She couldn't breathe and stabbed at his hand with her fingernails.

He took it away, and said angrily, "No more noise now, or I'll give you the back of my hand! What's the matter with you, are ye dead down there?" Maggie shook her head, uncertain of what he meant.

"There's a good girl!" he said with a fierce grin, and she relaxed, and raised her arms for an embrace.

He attacked her then. His grunting overpowered her screams of pain, until she went still—simply and purely praying for survival. After a time he shuddered and the grunting stopped.

He rolled off her. "Wasn't that a fine ride, now?" he said. Through her riotous thoughts, a single one came clear: *I've married a madman, I have to get away.*

Rory left the bed, fetched the lamp and pulled down the bed covers. Maggie grabbed them to her, but he wrested them away, telling her to move.

"WHY...?" she began, swabbing her nose, but he shoved her over on the bed and held the lantern to peer at the sacks. Smiling with satisfaction, he gathered up all but one of the sacks and tossed them in a corner.

"Hurley owes me five dollars," he said. Maggie saw dark stains on the sack under her.

"I'm bleeding!" she cried, "You've killed me." She held the covers to her stricken body.

He said: "Have you taken leave of your senses, girl? Did your Mam tell you nothing of what happens when a woman's bedded for the first time?"

Maggie wept into the quilt.

"Here, now, go and clean yourself up," he said in a softer voice, "And when you're done, we'll have a little kiss and go to sleep."

Ned awakened, sure that he had heard a scream. Eleanor? He sat up in bed, fumbled to light the candle, but there was none: this room had gas lights. He was in the guest room at Henry Barton's. He dried his wet chin then turned the towel over on his pillow. Laying back, he rubbed his cold nose, and smelled on his fingers the scent of Mrs. Campbell's woman. Henry had meant well: he had insisted that the surprise visit to Mrs. Campbell's was necessary to cheer Ned and start the New Year on the right foot. Ned had chosen the only woman in the house who appeared wholly unfazed by his appearance. She was round, plump, and a little untidy. When they were both moderately drunk, he told her to undress and pose for him in the lamp-light. He had liked the sight of her bare flesh and been glad to feel her powdered skin against his skin, her warm mound beneath his hands. Yet although they spent considerable time playing at other pleasing games, he was unable to do what he came for, and he left Campbell's shortly after midnight.

Maggie! He had said aloud as the woman attempted to pleasure him. 'No sir, Polly, that's my name,' the woman had replied, with a gusty wine-soaked laugh, 'but you call me whatever you like.' He cupped his hand over his nostrils, inhaled the scent again, then dropped his hand onto the bed covers. *Snares and delusions.* He was no better than Dance sniffing and licking at an empty dish.

He stroked the coverlet—in lieu of Polly's wiry hair, in place of the soft curve of Maggie's cheek, then stirred restlessly, and thrust both hands under the covers to indulge in the vice forbidden to all decent Christian men.

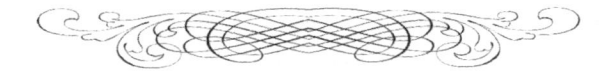

In the pitiless dawn, Maggie was awakened by the mill bells and a grumpy command from her husband to get up and make sure breakfast was ready when the bells rang him home. She staggered into her clothes, washed with icy water: all of it like those nightmares when you wake, but fall back to sleep and into the next bad part of the same story. After he left for the mill, Maggie slowly climbed the stairs, her heart (no less than her insides) sore, empty, desecrated. She packed the clothes he had brought over and placed in the drawer just days before and laid the untouched white nightgown on the bed as a shroud for the death inside her.

The path to Rose's was cold but she walked it quickly: it was her only escape. Her Mam sadly opened the door to her, placed a hand on her shoulder. She led Maggie into the kitchen, then shouted at Rose: "We ought to have told her! Didn't I say so…"

Rose replied frostily: "You dragged your feet, and 'twasn't my place to say such things to her." She looked at Maggie for a moment, then said: "Och, Maggie, 'tisn't the end of the world."

"He hurt me," Maggie murmured, but her pride kept her from crying. Rose tutted in embarrassment, and Mam would not look her way.

"I'm not going back there," Maggie said tightly.

"'twill get better," Rose said, "Ye love him, so ye said, and you'll get used to it and come to like it, to be sure."

Maggie took this thought in, sat with it, turned it around and around. Too tired and ashamed to fight, she nodded.

"Yer Mam will go back there with ye and set the place to rights and help ye cook a bit of food so's Rory will have somethin' when the breakfast bell rings," Rose said.

"That I will," Mrs. O'Shaughnessy said without hesitation, "not for Himself, but for *a thaisce.*" Maggie knew little of the old language of Ireland, but this—*my treasure*—she knew from the heart, so rose from her chair with a weak smile at her mother.

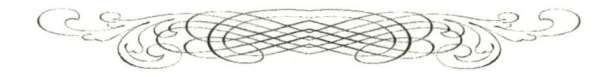

Again at the behest of Mr. Putnam, Ned had missed dinner. At three in the afternoon, Putnam gave him leave and Ned trudged home to forage. Martha was not in the kitchen and there was a sleigh and tethered horse in the front drive. He opened the pie safe and fetched his own dishes and sat at the kitchen table eating rapidly. Through the half-open door, he could hear his mother in the back parlor speaking to Mrs. Moore.

"Well, Abby, I am not surprised to hear it, but I do hope she is happy with him." There was a muffled response from Mrs. Moore. "Yes, she had some notion it might happen, she received a letter just a week ago," his mother said.

He caught only part of Mrs. Moore's response, "…the one she was pining for."

Martha came down the back stairs into the kitchen then and exclaimed, "You gave me a fright, Edward!" The voices from the back parlor stopped; and Martha took pains to point out to him that he had missed his dinner and the pie in the safe was not a fit and proper meal.

Escaping her as soon as he was able, he raced up the stairs, nearly colliding with Eleanor.

"What are you doing here?" Eleanor asked in a frightened voice. He told her that he needed a fresh scarf, and she said, with too much relief: "Oh! Of course." She put both hands behind her back.

"Why?" he said suspiciously, "What's happened?"

"Nothing at all," she said quickly and would not look at him.

Martha's pie was sitting like a lead weight in Ned's stomach. "Something's happened," he muttered, "You look mighty queer." With a sudden pulse of fear, he said: "Have you heard from Maggie?"

Eleanor hesitated in agitation.

"What?" he said, "Is she well? Has she lost her position? You must tell me."

She shook her head with tears in her eyes. "You… I cannot… you told me not to speak of her… don't ask me."

He exclaimed: "I said not to speak of her unless she was in trouble, or ill! Tell me!"

"No, no, she is well!" Eleanor replied frantically. This

stopped him but did not give him any relief.

He said, "Promise me that you will tell me if she is ever injured or… in a bad way."

"Go fetch your scarf," Eleanor said, "She is… well enough, don't worry."

He went into his chamber unsatisfied, yanking open a drawer in the chest. As he left, he stepped upon the loose floorboard and could hear the hidden box shift in place inside the baseboard. 'The one she was pining for,' Mrs. Moore had said. Of whom were they speaking? *Something is wrong,* he thought.

He knocked on Eleanor's door and spoke through the wood, "Something has happened to Maggie. Tell me, Elly, you must." He heard her weeping and banged harder on the door.

Mrs. Whitfield came to the bottom of the stairs, calling: "Edward, what on earth are you doing?"

"Something's wrong," he said, "and she won't tell me."

His mother hastened to Eleanor's chamber and entered, shutting the door. There was some low conversation, then Mrs. Whitfield opened the door, appearing stricken. She told him to come in.

"Maggie is well," she said, "She was married a fortnight ago and is living with her husband near the Rock Mill."

Surely this is not true, Ned thought, *it could not be true.* "She wasted no time!" he said, without thinking. He stood very still, trying to herd his scattered thoughts. The left side of his mouth began to leak, and he fumbled for his handkerchief. "Whose the… who did she marry?" he said finally.

"A Mr. Corcoran," his mother replied.

Blow upon blow, Ned thought. He remembered Hurley's vulpine face and his words: "She's Corcoran's girl." God damn the man! *I meant nothing to her,* he told himself, *it was that cocky Irishman all along.*

"I must go," he said aloud. His mother agreed, looking at him with sympathy, patting his arm. *She knows,* he thought. Pushing back his humiliation, he left.

Head down, he crunched through the snow, heedless of direction. It's all for the best, he reprimanded himself. She did not love me at any rate, she could not have. No one ever will. He stopped and pulled down his scarf to press his handkerchief against his face. Maggie's neighborhood: he passed it every day on his way down town. Perhaps he would see her, confront her. *I must be insane*, he thought. *She must be happy with her new husband. I could have had her; I had her in my hands. And she was so good to me.* It seemed the huddled houses all smelled of bad beef. He spat in the snow and continued his journey.

The following Sunday, he left the house at dawn. Tracking through fresh snow, he headed toward Knotts Hill, imagining himself the first man in creation, wholly alone. What a fine thing: to have no others to bid him to speak, or to be silent; or to tie his heart to theirs. He climbed quickly. The landmarks were so different in winter, many nearly buried.

A laborer, Maggie! Vigorous, surely, but also doubtless proud of his ignorance. He cannot be what you wanted, an intelligent girl like you! How could you swear your heart to me, then give in and marry an opposite as quick as a shot? He stopped at the observation platform to rest. The sky was lowering, and there was little to be seen. From his haversack, he extracted the wine bottle that his mother had hidden behind the wood bin. He drank. The wine was awful, worse than a spring tonic, and having no purgative effect upon him. The cold made his eyes tear, his nose was running.

"Why, Maggie?" he muttered aloud. When she was his, she had acted as if she could live on love alone, with little thought of a livelihood or practicalities. Perhaps she loved the Irishman.

His own amused, superior observations of the foibles of mankind as he hid and watched them—the contrast between his singularity and their commonplace commonality—now mocked him. He stared at the smear of snot on his mitten. *Man is a series of exhalations and vapors,* he thought, *that is all. There is no reality but pain and the release of fluid back to the earth.* He took a swallow of wine, but spat it out, where it marked the snow dark red. Then he poured out the bottle's contents in a circle around himself, a libation to the devil who had married her away, and all the lesser demons who had taken everything from him.

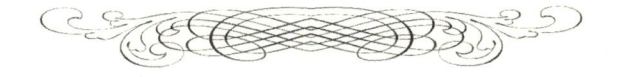

Maggie blessed Bridget and Mr. Dooley again in her thoughts for the chiming shelf clock. Although it was a bit too plain for her taste, it worked well. Each day she hurried through her tasks after feeding the men breakfast, so that she would have an hour to drowse in the chair seated next to the clock whose chime would rouse her to prepare dinner. Rarely was there a spare hour to drowse again before supper must be made and served.

She dreaded the next arrival of laundry day. The men paid Rory extra for cleaning their clothes; the work had taken her the entire day and made her so sore that she could barely move the following forenoon. *Perhaps Mam will come and help,* she thought. Rory must know that she could not do it all on her own! The nice boarder who Corcoran had tossed out of the house a week before had said as much. She rubbed her eyes: she could not break herself of the habit of lying awake nights after Rory slept. It was so quiet then, the only time she ever felt like herself. Sometimes she sneaked from the bed and stared at the winter stars, or wrote a letter to Eleanor, or dreamed about painting again in the gallery, or sat wrapped in a blanket feeling sad.

Last night she took the newspaper from the woodbin and read it. When her husband read it aloud to her, he only read bits and pieces. It had little war news at any rate, unlike the paper that the Whitfields subscribed to. She sensed, and urgently prayed, that the war would end soon. She prayed for Michael's safety, and that her father had not been caught up in the conflict, for wasn't the fighting out West too?

When the war is over, she told herself, all will be well: but only if we can hire the laundry out.

"Ah, here is an invitation addressed to Edward," the judge said, slitting the envelope with his knife.

"Is it from Mr. Barton?" Eleanor asked eagerly.

"Even better, it is from the young misses Topliff," her father said. As he handed it to Ned, he went on: "Don't shake your head! You will go. I need Topliff's vote in April, and he is on the fence. Beyond that, it would do you good to become acquainted with some eligible young ladies."

Ned tossed it on the table, indifferently. He said: "They must be desperate for an unattached male to match the number of females. Tch, the privations of war."

The smoky, seductive taste of good whiskey dripped into Ned's memory. He wanted it now, to bring the jokes back, to help him drowse comfortably through his father's yammering. It was an effort to stay awake during the day, except when he was working, and then an effort to stave off the dreams that woke him at night.

The judge said: "Believe me, you will find a suitable young lady sooner rather than later."

"Mundus vult decipi," Ned replied.

"The world wants to be deceived, eh? Well, I don't," the judge said, "And I never am. You can take my prediction to the bank: you've been working too hard, and there is much to be said for a frolic hosted by the right sort of folks to banish your indigos."

Ned had not heard any good music, except Eleanor's piano, since last year's Washington's Birthday fete, and the weather had been dreary. He was tired of this house, tired of studying, tired of misery. "I did not say I would not attend," he commented.

The judge scowled. "Very well, then. Pray do not bowl us over with your enthusiasm."

Trimmed and pomaded to within an inch of his life by Yardley the barber, in what he growled to his mother "is the very latest style: popinjay!" Ned finished dressing for the Washington's Birthday Ball. Overcoated, hatted, and muffled, he hitched Greylock to the sleigh, and drove off with speed. The horse's hooves threw back clots of snow, and the harness bells jingled cheerily. All the world whizzed by and Ned nearly overshot the entrance to the Topliff's mansion. Nearing the grand house, his high spirits dimmed as he watched the various young ladies, swathed in rich wools and furs, step down from their conveyances. When he pulled up near the door, the servant in charge of the horses looked in the back of the sleigh, and seeing no one, asked who he was.

"Invited guest," Ned replied, hopping out of the vehicle, and heading for the front door.

Mr. and Mrs. Topliff greeted him as soon as the servants had taken his wraps, and then the Misses Topliff advanced upon him, with their usual gasps and twittering about his appearance.

"Mr. Whitfield, so good of you to come, when you have been

SO ill!" the eldest said.

"I do hope you feel able to dance," the middle daughter said. The youngest twitched her skirt without looking at him and told him where the refreshments were.

The last time he had attended such an event was on the heels of Henry Barton. Ned had then been warmly greeted by the girls and his attendance had been a pleasure. On his own this time, he was sorry he had agreed to come, despite the glittering rooms and smell of rich food. He lingered awkwardly near the refreshment table, then wandered over to a corner where a couple of elderly ladies were seated. He put his hands in his pockets, then took them out, and began edging slowly toward the library, where perhaps he could escape until the dancing began.

The middle Topliff girl (Lottie?) caught sight of him and said "There he is!" to her sisters. The misses ushered a young woman towards him.

"Oh, Mr. Whitfield, I would like to introduce you," the eldest said.

"Miss Mountain," the youngest said wickedly, "I'd like you to meet Mr. Whitfield."

As she and her sisters dissolved into giggles, the youngest said, "Oh, Oh, I am so sorry I mis-spoke, Miss Minton!"

The woman who faced him was half a foot taller than he, a massive person, with a head of tightly and plainly coiffed black hair and a pair of blazing brown eyes. She had turned an unbecoming shade of red, clenching her gloved hands. Ned imagined her tossing the little misses against the opposite wall with a wave of her arm.

He said: "I am pleased to make your acquaintance, Miss Minton." He put a slight stress on her correct surname, and added, "I understand that Mr. Minton has had considerable success on his turbine at the Lockett mill. Are you perhaps related?"

Eyes still blazing, she straightened her shoulders and turned her back on the misses. "Yes, he is my father," she replied.

Strategy calls for an immediate retreat, he thought. He asked her, "Would you care for some refreshments?"

"Oh, yes, Miss Moun...Miss Minton, please do!" the youngest girl said, "There is LOTS of your favorite cake!"

Miss Minton lowered her head, but then lifted her chin, took his arm, and said: "Yes, if you please." He escorted her quickly to a quiet corner, seated her, and went to the refreshment table, very glad to have something to do. When he returned, she was holding a beautifully painted fan, hiding most of her face. As he sat at her left side, he offered the plate, and she thanked him, took it, but ate not a bite.

The misses were still in the doorway, the eldest and middle daughter greeting new arrivals, but the youngest looking at him and Miss Minton, and ill concealing her ongoing amusement. Miss Minton did not look in that direction but seemed to be aware nevertheless. Her eyes were wet and she held her fan even higher. Since the girls clearly found him just as risible as this lady, he presumed that he had been expressly invited as Miss Minton's escort: to make an odd couple for the misses' delectation—danged annoying little cats!

"Well, Miss Minton," he said, "Did you know that George Washington said that offensive operations are the surest means of defense?" She looked over her fan at him, and he nodded toward the Topliff girls, then went on: "As we are celebrating his birthday, I believe we might well employ his advice. They appear to enjoy others' discomfort, so perhaps a little play-acting is in order. The more we enjoy ourselves, the less they will." She blinked rapidly but continued her gaze at him, cautiously lowering the fan.

He went on: "I am in earnest but will certainly understand if you do not care to participate in dissembling."

She folded her fan and placed it in her lap. "I apologize, sir. I did not properly hear your name when... they... when we were introduced." She paused, and he supplied his name. She dabbed at her eyes with her handkerchief and sat up in the chair. She towered over him, and he realized that she had been slumping to make herself appear shorter.

She said: "Are you perhaps related to Miss Eleanor Whitfield?"

"Eleanor?" he said with surprise, "Yes, my sister."

"I see," she said, "Well, I doubt that she would remember me, but we were acquainted as children when we attended the Brick School. I hope she is perfectly well?" To the last question she added a look of hesitation.

Another friend from school, Ned thought. "Yes, she is," he replied. She smiled and said nothing, but then dropped her hanky in her lap.

"I have forgotten my manners," she went on, "I am very

pleased to make your acquaintance, Mr. Whitfield. It is good of you to have afforded me something of an escape from our kind hostesses." She raised an eyebrow as she stressed the word "kind."

"Deliver us mortals from that *kind* of hostess," he remarked.

She gave a short, wry laugh. "Do… Do you think perhaps I might call upon Miss Whitfield? Or I should like to leave my calling card."

"She is not much in society," Ned responded carefully, "but I am certain that she would be glad to have you leave your card."

She said: "Your sister was truly kind to me during the short time I was at the Brick School. I generally have been educated at home, but I wished to attend a public school because I had read so much about them."

"Yes, it is quite an experience," he said. She understood his tone of voice and there was a pleasant silence. He said: "Eleanor is just as kind."

"Ah," she replied, "Yes, so I recall. I hope that she will receive my call when it is… convenient for her. I should so like to visit, at least to have the opportunity to thank her for assisting me when I was at school."

"Eleanor has many tales about the Brick School," he said, and told her the story of Maggie's revenge on the boy who pushed her down and stole her lunch pail.

"Oh, they stole mine too!" Miss Minton said uncomfortably, but then laughed aloud, glancing at the three sisters. Ned laughed with her, gesturing with his head toward the foyer.

"Our strategy is succeeding," he said to Miss Minton, "they are none too happy." She took up her fan and fluttered it, laughing more loudly, and reached for a small cake.

"That's the way," he said, "First rate!"

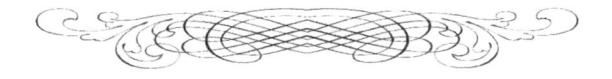

"This place has got too many spiders," Maggie said as calmly as she could, for Rory would not hear her otherwise. They were gathered in the front room, with all the boarders. There was no time alone with her husband, except the nightly "slam and snore." Whatever she had to say was open to all. He did not respond, brooding by the stove.

"Rory," she said again softly, "They drop down out of

nowhere, 'tis every day now. Yesterday, one got down my neck and bit me." *My skin is crawling yet,* she wanted to say, *no inch of it belongs to me anymore.*

"If you ever picked up a broom, they'd not bother you," he muttered.

Why did the tears still come when they were useless to her? He had good reason to be curt, surely; she was foolish to be bothered by things that would frighten a child. And perhaps she did not deserve a kind word now: she was artless, lacking in every way as a cook, a housewife, a wife; or so he said, with silent dudgeon or swift cutting words. Maggie sat as still as she was able to, forcing herself into coolness, making her hands continue to stitch at the tears in McGrath's trousers. He paid for the mending, paid Rory anyhow. She was not sure how much.

The men had celebrated St. Patrick's Day recently. Her birthday, the same day as the Saint's day, had passed without a single word from anyone, but she was glad anyhow, for her husband had finally agreed to have Mrs. Kernan's relations do the boarders' laundry, leaving Maggie to wash only his and her own. It had been a bitter victory on her part, for he had been short with her ever since. She jabbed the needle repeatedly, missing showing her Mam the neat stitches, hearing Rose say, "Have ye finished it already, then?" *See how fast I can sew!* she thought, *that's a thing I do well.*

Now her eyes were closing. She jolted awake and stabbed again at the stiff cloth. Garrity was snoring; they were all a-drowse but Rory. She must finish this mending so McGrath would have trousers tomorrow. She held up the garment with a slight smile to show her husband. "No more holy McGrath," she whispered. He shrugged. Maggie closed the last bit of the tear.

What would it be like to be a spider, she wondered, *was it grand to hide, to swing down from on high and scare folks, or would you be just as frightened as the giant you'd landed on, and scrambling (in the sudden flurry of big hands) for a return to your dark corner?*

In early April, the people of Connecticut received news of the surrender of Confederate General Lee, and "mud season" was transformed into a time of private joy and public celebration. The people of the town spontaneously gathered at the park, the dry goods store, the telegraph office, the train depot, the bank, the churches, in business offices and in homes to cheer, weep with relief, chatter or pray.

On his way to the tavern at the Eagle Hotel, borne along by the throngs, Ned had seen the tall red-headed man with the slight young lady on his arm: Maggie and her husband. He had veered off unhappily, but then told himself the sighting was of no consequence. *What's done is done, and these personal matters are of no import: the war is over!* He found a great crowd of men thronging the bar at the hotel and did not stint his grateful happiness nor his alcoholic consumption.

Less than a week later, the people came forth again and gathered, stunned by the news of President Lincoln's assassination. Struck to the heart, Ned went to church rather than the tavern. Late in that day, he found himself standing at Rob McKay's grave. He tore a branch from a bush, stripping the buds, and dropped them on the grave.

Squatting by the grave with his hand on the stone marker, he said aloud: "It's over." Voice clogged and halting, Ned told Rob that the Union was saved, the President foully murdered and lost to eternity, Captain Merrill killed in battle; and wondered aloud how, how he could live rightly, while bearing the cost of this victory and its losses.

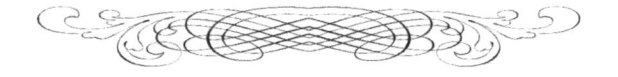

Rory told Maggie only a little of what he had heard at the tavern: he had no liking for Lincoln himself, but the mood was somber. Maggie took to bed early but could not sleep. When Bridget stumbled through the front door after breakfast the next day, teary-eyed, she and Maggie shared a long embrace, and spent a short time together, pinning black ribbon to the collars of their dresses. Maggie wrote a long letter to Eleanor, pining to see her, and drew a picture of the president from an engraving in the newspaper. She was very afraid at the illness that had been creeping into her, as she vomited every morning and could not keep much in her stomach. Was she soon to follow in the same way that Mr. Merritt had passed from the earth?

What did anything about keeping house matter when the entire world had turned upside down?

"What's got into you?" her husband finally asked scornfully, a week after the President's funeral, as Maggie looked again at the newspaper describing the services. "Ye been puking every day now," he scolded, "surely it ain't all due to Lincoln!"

She could see worry mixed with his anger and confessed that the vomiting had begun earlier than that. Cursing about the cost, he told her to see Doctor Green.

Leaving the dinner dishes soaking, Maggie instead went to see Mrs. Moore. Mrs. Moore was full of questions: how much she was eating, how was she was sleeping, were her monthly courses regular, and what was hurting her. At the last question, Maggie gestured toward her bosom. Mrs. Moore shook her head a little, then looked long at Maggie.

"Will I live?" Maggie asked fearfully.

Mrs. Moore said, "Yes, my dear, I've lost very few mothers. You're with child. I thought you had guessed."

Maggie gaped at her. "So soon? It can't be."

"You are not the first woman to say that," Mrs. Moore commented, "You must eat two dry crackers before getting up in the morning, whether you feel hungry or not, and you must make sure to eat something every hour or so, and rest often."

Maggie said: "There's no time to rest, with feeding my husband and the boarders, but I'm sure I will feel better in a day or so."

Mrs. Moore frowned. "Do you have anyone else at home, your mother, or a sister, anyone to help you?"

"I've hired out the boarders' laundry, but I'm thinkin' I do need some help, Mrs. Leary said so too. But I can't ask my husband. Money's awfully tight," Maggie replied.

"With income from four boarders?" Mrs. Moore said skeptically.

Maggie shrugged, feeling she'd already said too much and certainly he would not like her telling their business to anyone; though perhaps the baby would please him. She could not believe there was anything inside her body except all the organs that had been there since she was born. She had seen Rose swell with pregnancy three times and did not view "being with child" with anything but apprehension.

"I believe that you need extra help in your house for a week or more," Mrs. Moore said, "I don't want you to lose this baby from overwork or hyperemesis gravidarum." Maggie looked up with alarm.

Mrs. Moore went on: "I shall come and speak to your husband about what is needed. An unhealthy mother bears an unhealthy child and is at danger herself."

"No!" Maggie interrupted, "He won't like you telling him what to do... I... I will tell him. Surely he'll do what I say now, because of," she stumbled on the next word, not wanting to say it aloud and make it real: "the baby..."

Mrs. Moore again looked long at her patient, finally saying: "Does your husband know how to read, Maggie?"

Maggie said: "Oh yes, very well."

The midwife nodded. "I will write all the instructions out for him, and of course, foremost your need for help at this time. His first responsibility is to protect you and baby from harm, whether money is tight or not. Give him my letter and we will see. Maggie, do promise me that you will call upon me if he does not follow the letter, or if you have any other needs."

"Mercy, yes," Maggie said with relief, "You're so good to me. God bless you." Mrs. Moore was silent. "I promise," Maggie said.

"Come to see me in two months' time," Mrs. Moore said, "Unless you have bleeding, then send for me right away."

Chapter 39

"Look at me, Ned!" Eleanor called out with glee as her brother came down the back steps on a drowsy Sunday afternoon in May. "I'm going riding!" Ned bounded over to the gig, greeted Miss Minton and told his sister that she was a most surprising creature. Taking Dance's leash from Mrs. Whitfield (who looked nearly as excited as her daughter) he waved the young ladies goodbye and took the barking dog to the barn. He consoled the dog by taking it upon his lap and telling all the details from the week's depositions by parties and witnesses in the "wandering pisser" case. His mother came into the barn, marvelling at Eleanor's outing, and how Miss Minton drove her own carriage.

"Elly has told me that she feels safe with her!" Mrs. Whitfield announced to him, "I am so glad that you made her acquaintance in February and that she has called upon us so often." Remembering Maggie banished to the Whitfield's back steps, Ned muttered a yes.

His mother sat next to him on a straw pile and went on: "I had a letter from Katie yesterday. Major Fariday expects to be formally mustered out of his regiment in June, and Katie of course will return with your Uncle Cyrus. They will set the wedding date soon; I expect it will be in August. How we will have a wedding supper in this hot old house, I can't guess. Oh, I meant to tell you: I saw Mrs. Shackelford at church today. Phin has received his pension, he thanks you for that! And he is engaged to be married."

"Mirable dictu," Ned said.

"To Esther Fish, one of Zek's sisters," his mother continued then quieted for his comment.

Everyone is marrying except me, he thought. He said: "And? I know you have more to tell."

"And you will be invited, of course," she said.

"Of course," he said, "You are full of news today. I wondered... has Eleanor heard from Maggie?"

His mother turned away and petted Dance's chest. The dog rolled over on his back. "Yes," she said finally, rubbing the dog's belly so that one of his back legs tapped in a happy rhythm.

Ned was concerned that his mother's tales had come to a full stop. "And she is well?" he prompted her.

She paused again, stopped her work on the dog's belly, and looked down at her hands, saying: "Yes. Mrs. Moore says all is well."

"Mrs. Moore?" he repeated. His mother set her shoulders, stroked the dog's ears. "Yes, she says all is well and Baby is due in December."

As if he was observing from a distant peak, Ned saw himself rise from the straw, brush off his trousers and walk away—out of the barn, down past the orchard, towards the neighbor's fields beyond. Before this moment, his hell had been perpetual November, sere and dry. Now his control, like a wall of dead cornstalks, cracked and powdered before this unborn child's blow.

By the next day, he had deposited the pain into his rapidly narrowing internal vault. With the precise care of an old man, he traveled to Vinton Town Hall, examined each land record, made slow notes, and pristine copies.

There was nothing left to do but go back to Mix's office. Ned's jaw and head ached. Perhaps he could beg off, citing the pain. He needed a rest, darkness, quiet, perhaps a dose of sage tea. Hogwash! He needed a drink.

The last time he visited Vinton Center, there were no taverns on his route to the train station. A German had opened a new one in an old stand, had freshly painted the door, hung a new sign. The man stood in the doorway and invited him in: how often did a taverner ever do such a thing? He entered and drank. He drank until he lost sight of memory, regret, duty, kin.

When Billy Vickers woke him as the train reached the Millville depot, he stiff-marched to Morton's shed, and secreted himself in his favorite spot in the storeroom among the grain sacks. He awoke after dark, cotton-mouthed, crept out of the shed unnoticed and walked to the judge's house. Once there, he circuited the house, identifying the location of each person in the household from the evidence of lamp light in certain windows. Head throbbing, he entered the back door and reached his bed chamber in safety.

He awoke again to a banging on his door, mean light at the window, and then the shock of Dance's cold nose on his face. He got up as usual but was troubled by the blank space in his recall. Only a name repeated in his mind: Keller. Who or what the devil was Keller? The judge had already left for the day. The sight of breakfast turned Ned's stomach. Something bad had occurred at supper last night, no, it must have been at dinner yesterday. Eleanor and his mother were staring at him apprehensively. He had no time to answer their questions or his own. He was late arriving at Mix's office.

"Where are those descriptions of the Topliff parcels?" Davis said urgently. "Mr. Mix's been asking."

"Descriptions?" Ned repeated.

"The title search copies - you went over to the Center yesterday to get them," Davis said.

Ned thought, *'I must have gone to Vinton. I must have copied them. Where are they? At Keller's? Who? Oh, hellfire and damnation, Keller's tavern!'*

"Mr. Whitfield, so good of you to finally make an appearance. Bring in those titles," Charles Mix said from his doorway. Ned grabbed a sheaf of papers from Davis' copy table and followed his employer into the office, shutting the door behind him. Keep cool, he told himself uselessly, as fear took him over.

He said: "I'm sorry, sir, I can't... I don't know... I did copy them yesterday, but I must have left them in Vinton. I'm sorry. I'll go now and get them."

Mix was dumbfounded. "You spent the afternoon in Vinton when we needed you here. And you forgot the copies: it can't be! You never forget anything, you remind us all of our work, every detail of my cases." Ned blurted another apology, as Mix cut him off: "Never mind the excuses. Get yourself on that train or hire a rig if that's faster and fetch those descriptions. The costs are coming out of your pocket this time."

At the end of a miserable trip, Ned was betrayed by Mr. Keller. Jawohl, the tavern keeper had found some papers, and had put them back into Herr Whitfield's pocket; but then Herr Whitfield ran out of money, he was sleeping in the chair, and when the tavern closed, he was very hard to move. Ja, and then the Herr fell out the door, and could hardly walk to the train, so, the papers must have fallen out on the way. Ned cursed as he left and ran to retrace his steps to the train station, even stopped to examine a scrap of paper which blew by. Nothing.

He returned to Mix's office later in the day, bearing hasty and minimally legible copies. Mix took them, frowned at Ned's croaking explanation, and retreated to his office, while Ned collapsed in his own chair, took off his hat, wiped his sweating forehead. Ten minutes later, as Davis looked up worriedly from his copy work, Mix shouted through his office door: "Mr. Whitfield. Come here."

"How the mighty have fallen," Putnam commented as Ned got up.

"Close the door," Mix said. Ned did so, closed his eye, trying to throttle his shrieking nerves.

"What is wrong with you?" Mix asked. Ned shook his head, wordlessly.

Mix said: "Losing those copies was a clerk's mistake, Edward, and a brainless clerk at that! and you have never given me cause to imagine you'd make such an error. Your work has generally been quite competent, although it has suffered of late. I'm sure you agree."

"I... I have no excuse. I made a... I don't know..." Ned said, rubbing his forehead. The tic in his left cheek was jumping; he prayed that it was not a harbinger of neuralgia. He could not bear the thought of ending splayed on Charles Mix's floor, helpless, moaning. Mix was silent for a time. Ned waited in despair: *everything will end now,* he thought, *I will lose my position - all of the study and work of the past two years.*

Mix said: "I think, Ned, that you believe you have hidden your ill health from me. Although you do not complain, I am aware that your injuries were severe and Doctor Green has told me that neuralgia does not heal," he sighed, and continued: "It does not quickly heal."

"Dear heaven," Ned said, waiting for the bad news, his permanent dismissal. Mix looked at him for a moment, then said: "Go home and rest. Be here early tomorrow morning. We have much to do." Ned arose shakily, stunned at his survival, unable to tell the truth. He thanked his employer, then left without a word to the others.

"Good day, Mr. Whitfield! Can you stop a minute. I have something for you," Billy Vickers shouted. Heading for the millrace, Ned had kept to the alleys. He waved the man off and kept walking. Vickers caught up with him. "I have something you left behind. Say, where's your hat?" Ned reached up. His head was bare. He felt his head again, smoothed his hair, began walking again, more slowly.

Vickers fell into step with him. "You were feeling mighty poorly last night. You left some of your legal papers on the train: I only found them today, back in the freight car." He took a roll of papers from his waistcoat and held them out. He glanced at Ned, then went on, "I had you ride home there, because Mr. Garside was in the passenger car, and I didn't think you wanted to see him, not then anyhow. Hope I did right."

Ned looked at him in panic. Public drunken-ness was a statutory violation. *Will he use this against me?*

"You don't remember?" Vickers said. Ned stared at his shoes, envying Vickers' rectitude. He envied the man's clean conscience, even his dark skin that never showed the scarlet evidence of shame. He dug at the dirt alleyway with his heel, mind blank. They'd dug themselves hollows, some of the men, at Sharpsburg, in that field: hollows to hold hips and shoulders and sore arms—anything to burrow further from the flying metal overhead. His heel chipped back and forth. He felt saliva oozing from his mouth, and put his sleeve to his lips, tongued the fabric. The tic that had moved from his cheek to his left eye had slowed to a sluggish beat. He took the roll of papers, but they dropped to the dirt. He slowly picked them up.

Vickers said: "It looks like you're still feeling poorly. Why don't you come to the station with me and sit down for a spell?"

"It..." Ned began, "It's too late now. It's my own damned fault. I'd better go." He walked forward automatically. Vickers held up his hand, although he did not touch Ned, and said: "The station's back this way."

"No," Ned said, "I'll go home. I... I thank you, for... watching out for me last night. You did the right thing. I'm sorry that I gave you cause."

Vickers was silent for what seemed too long, then he said: "Well, sir, you are not the only gentleman I've hauled here in that condition."

Ned felt the constriction in his lungs slide away. He looked at Vickers, not hiding his own relief and said: "Good heaven. I appreciate…deeply appreciate that. All your help, in fact."

"Well, sir," Vickers said with dignity, "that's all right. You've been mighty good to my friend Joe."

Marveling at this second deliverance from disaster in a single day, Ned replied: "He's a good man. And I will not be such a devil of a…such troublesome baggage henceforth. You need not worry further." *How many times have I said that,* he wondered, *said the same to Mother and Father, to friends?*

Vickers nodded, then said: "I hope your health improves."

Chapter 40

As Davis put the Closed sign into Mr. Mix's window, Ned jumped off the steps like a boy. He had heard the song in his ears all morning, singing itself in snatches: When Johnny comes marching home again, Hurrah, Hurrah. He joined the crowds at the station: they were making an excited high-pitched babble, backed up by the blip, blap, tootle of the brass band, readying its triumphal salute to the surviving soldiers from Millville and Vinton from "the Fighting Fourteenth."

The train arrived, the band did its best, but was overcome by the noise from the people. Ned was carried by the crowd, unable to get close to the men stepping down from the train. There was Norman Reynolds. Ned pushed forward, grabbed Reynolds' elbow and shouted: "Welcome back." Reynolds nodded gleefully as his family engulfed their boy.

More soldiers Ned knew came off the train, none could he reach or speak to. Young Morton's cousin went by, and here was Phin Shackelford's brother. Ned turned as best he could, seeing Phin and his new fiancé back in the crush, looking for this boy—now lank and worn—but alive. Joe Creasey would not be on this train: the 21st CT CVI was stationed in Texas and had not yet been mustered out. A hard hand seized Ned's shoulder as a big man with a cannon of a voice sounded: "Lieutenant!"

"Sergeant Flynn!" Ned replied. The man took Ned's hand in both of his own and cranked a handshake as if he was pumping from a deep well. "Our little lieutenant," he said joyfully, "Sure, I thought you was dead. 'tis grand to see you." He released Ned and pulled at the shorter man behind him. "Mikey—see here, here's our

Lieutenant was taken down at Fredericksburg—breathing and big as life."

Michael Foran nodded to Ned, as Flynn went on: "This is the fellow who gave our Tim his own coat, and bought us food at the sutler once when all the boys had nothing to eat." Then he said to Ned: "We were less than 100 left after Fredericksburg. We're the lucky ones!"

"There's my Mam and Aggie," Foran said, moving forward toward his family.

"I'm glad to see you, Sergeant," Ned said to Flynn, "Welcome home. Go to your family." *I'm one of the lucky ones,* he thought. His soul seemed scraped empty since he'd so narrowly ducked disaster after his shameful episode at Keller's Tavern.

A man roared in rage deep in the crowd: George Dunn was off the train, pushing at his sister Betsy. "Where are they?" he bellowed.

The people around him moved away as best they could. Ned began to do the same, but George saw him, thrust Betsy away and charged towards him. "Some welcome, some welcome I get for nearly dying ten times over!" George shouted at Ned. "My family never wrote me a letter, I could be dead and they'd cry more over the cost of a headstone than over me."

Ned opened his mouth to reply, but George had more to say: "That damned sergeant riding me from the first day: drilling, and rules—and what the hell good did that do me in the Crater? I clawed my own way out, no thanks to them, I showed them all what I'm made of, and here I AM, but my own father can't be bothered to shake my hand and bring me home!"

"Welcome home," Ned inserted hastily and offered a handshake, which Dunn did not accept. "Hunh, welcome, that's bunk, that's a lie! I'll bet there ain't even a place left for me to work," George said, "not a red cent left to me since Jack stole my money, and you ain't written me neither."

"Yes, I did and all is well at…" Ned began.

"I want to see my money," George interrupted, "I'm going to take it and get out of this shithole."

"We'll go to the gallery tomorrow," Ned replied.

"Now!" George shouted, "We'll go over there now. To hell with my family." Ned shook his head. "I have to get back to the law office."

George said: "No. I got no patience with you, or anybody in this town. We'll go there now—you owe it to me."

"The devil I do!" Ned said, "You're not in the army any more and neither am I. I won't jump because you say jump. You go ahead to the gallery. Zek will show you all the books, and I will meet you there this evening."

"Zek Fish. Another mistake," George said.

Ned turned his back and threaded his way into the crowd.

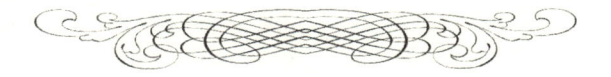

Maggie read Eleanor's letter again by candle light in the kitchen, while the men slept. Each reading made new pictures in her mind of Eleanor's birthday tea: the shining silver service, clear brown tea, pink cakes; a carriage ride on the hillside, deep in the green branches, behind the white horse, orange sun striking your eyes. Mr. Henry Barton was on a European tour now that the war was over. From the few details Eleanor recounted of his letter, Maggie saw visions of stone buildings, winding streets worn by footfalls through hundreds of years, with herself plunged up to her neck into art: room upon room, painting upon painting, marble gods with ancient eyes—all that was bright and beautiful. She did not hear Rory barefoot on the stairs.

"What's that?" he said. Maggie folded the letter and held it in her fist. "Who's that from?" Rory said.

"My friend," Maggie replied.

"Give it to me," he said.

"It's only about a tea party. From my friend Eleanor," Maggie placated.

"Just another Yank, is all she is," Rory said, "She turns your head, that one. Let me see it."

"Mercy, Rory, she's my friend, and it has nought to do with..." Maggie began. He seized the letter and she let it go, fearing he would tear it. He read it through slowly, while Maggie watched mutinously.

"Palaver," he said and tossed it on the table, "I guess it's all right if you don't tell her anything in return."

Maggie put the letter carefully under her hands, smoothing it. "What, tell her all the secrets about the washing, and cooking and the boarders who snore so loud they'd wake the dead? What do you care about that? Can't I have a friend write me a letter? Something that's mine, only mine?"

He broke in: "A friend who's sister to that one, that ugly Yank. Why'd you even have to ask me?"

Maggie gaped at him in horror: "You don't trust me? D'you think I'd ever write to him…or do anything so low, any such thing!"

Rory slapped his hand on the table. "Don't you be coming at me." After a moment, he sat down at the kitchen table, leaned close to her and softly said: "Maggie, there's so few I can trust, I must be sure of you, is all. You, above all, my own wife."

Although dawn was graying the windows, the darkness in this man at the table frightened her. "Rory, tell me, you must trust your friends…" she said.

He pushed back his dishevelled hair. "Not a one."

"Not even Mr. Dooley?" Maggie ventured. Rory stared at her and said nothing.

"Why?" she whispered. He continued to stare at her. She could see him now in the dim light: he was not angry, thank goodness, but not right somehow.

"None," he said finally. "Which is why I must be sure of you."

Mother of God, Maggie wondered, *what is this about: Harrigan or someone else? Or me?* She remembered the bloody sacks on their wedding bed. *I don't know you at all, you're a stranger,* she thought, and her mind whispered to Rory: but can I be sure of YOU? Suddenly guilty, she got up and came to him, taking his hand in hers, and saying what she knew he needed to hear.

"You can be sure of me."

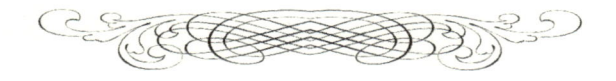

"Lord almighty," Zek said, "A good thing you're here, I'm afeared of **him**!" He paced to the gallery door and opened it, looking down the stairwell. "He ought to be in the mad house. He thinks I'm stealing his money. I showed him the books but he don't believe me!"

"I know, Zek. I have no doubt about you," Ned replied, "It's the war. All he went through: I believe it has left him unhinged."

"Unhinged, heigh? He's as crazy as a loon. Hush! He's a-coming." Zek rushed past Ned into the office and brought out the ledger book as George entered the gallery.

Ned diverted Dunn from a tirade by proving page by page in the ledger that he and Zek had properly accounted for all income and expenses, and maintained a worthy inventory and a modest profit.

"I ought to fire you, anyhow," George said to Zek.

"Why?" Zek said, "He showed you..."

"He showed what a goddamned old schoolteacher he is," George said, seizing the cash box.

"Christ almighty, George! Just hand over my share," Ned shouted, "I'm finished!"

"Your share!" George repeated, turning on him.

"In lieu of salary half the time, our agreement was that I'd share any profit..." Ned began.

George opened the cash box, grabbed a handful of bank notes, bills and coins and flung them onto the floor. "I had a good place here and you ruined it! For all I know, you been stealing from me too! There's your share, you little shit."

Zek stepped forward. "The only one stealing from you was Jack. Mr. Whitfield and I, we ain't taken a thing."

George waved the cash box. "Shut your mouth and get the hell out of here before I bust your head in!"

Zek said, "Whyn't you go down to New Haven and roar at old Jack, 'stead of yelling at Mr. Whitfield and me, when we been trying to keep things a-goin' here and help you out."

"How do you know..." Ned began, while George interrupted. "You and Jack are in this together, to cheat me again. Have you been conniving with him? I'll beat your ass."

Zek shouted, "Not for a minute! I hate that cheater!" Ned moved between the two, shouldering into Dunn to stop the man from advancing.

"Hold off," Ned said to Dunn, and then to Zek "Why did you say that Rossiter is in New Haven?"

"You know Elisha Shackelton? He came here for his picture when the draft started, and now he's back. Says he saw Jack down at the station in New Haven, tryin' to get the soldiers coming home to get their pictures took. Drumming up business for some fellow down there."

"Where is he?" Dunn demanded.

"New Haven!" Zek said, "I jist told you that."

"Did Elisha mention the name of the photograph establishment Jack was touting, or any other information?" Ned asked.

Zek shook his head. "Someone ought to go down and talk to **Jack** about stealing," he muttered, "'stead of saying they're gonna beat MY ass."

After a moment, Dunn quivered to life, saying: "I'll do that." Shifting the cash box under his arm, he jammed his hat back on his head and left the gallery.

Ned removed his eye patch, rubbed his eyes. "Zek. If you need a letter of referral for another position, I will provide it."

Zek said plaintively: "Can't you buy him out and come back here again?" Ned shook his head.

"Guess I'll need a letter then," Zek said, shoving the ledger onto the floor.

Chapter 41

Since the county courts had been abolished by the Connecticut legislature, the civil cases pursued to trial by Charles Mix's law firm were either heard by the Superior Court or tossed willy-nilly into the local justice court together with petty criminal cases. Tolliver Adams versus Sullivan and Cohan was placed upon short notice into the justice court and into the hands of Justice Eller—widely known for his irascibility and rendering of peculiar opinions. Mr. Mix waved away Ned's concerns, saying: "Just keep an eye out for errors of law and assist Mr. Putnam."

A trying day, Ned thought for the third or fourth time in the courtroom, no longer amused at the pun. While Putnam drowsed through the various cases, including several for petty theft, assault, public drunken-ness, Ned watched the proceedings with interest.

He whispered to Mr. Putnam: "Justice Eller has not made the same judgement twice, even when the charges and circumstances are similar."

Putnam whispered back scornfully: "You're green, aren't you? You can't expect much more from justice court. It's his court and his rules."

When Adams v. Sullivan & Cohan came to hearing, the Justice refused to allow as evidence the photographs Ned had taken to demonstrate the short distance from the growler line to the privy behind Sullivan's tavern. Eller sniped as often at Lawyer Peasley for the plaintiff as at Lawyer Putnam for the defense, and sat impatiently through the witnesses' testimony.

Putnam objected to an error of law on Eller's part. Ned caught two additional errors of law, scrawled them on the case file and passed them to Putnam. Putnam objected aloud only to one of the two.

"Do you know how long I have been on the bench? Do you see how **many** cases are on the docket?" Eller snarled at Putnam, who made a mollifying response. Within fifteen minutes of his last command for speed, Justice Eller whacked down the gavel with relish, and ruled that plaintiff Adams had been injured on the brewery property and deserved recompense for his injuries from the defendants. Putnam walked out of the court room immediately, leaving Ned behind to shrug at Lawyer Peasley's mock condolences and Tolliver Adams's beaming spite and to stand with the defendants—alternately counselling and consoling. Cohan was ready to be done with it all; but Sullivan declared them both more than ready to appeal. Ned instructed them to let the law firm know and left them arguing in the hallway.

A tall, thin, top-hatted lawyer who had lost two petty criminal cases that day in front of Eller, nodded to Ned as he passed, saying: "Five errors of law in less than half an hour. I believe that is a new record for the Justice."

Ned paused. "Five?" he said. The tall man pulled on his whiskers in amusement. "That was my count." He gestured toward Sullivan and Cohen. "Will your clients appeal?"

"I don't know," Ned replied.

"Appeal is often a fertile field after this Justice has laid down the manure," the tall man said with a smile. "Good day to you."

As the men clattered out of the house following breakfast, the firecrackers that had awakened them all continued popping. Maggie heaped the breakfast dishes in the sink, balled up the dishcloth in her fist and grinned: Rory and the boarders would be gone until after dark. She did not regret missing the picnic, parades, speeches, or fireworks, as something better awaited: her own Independence Day. She flicked the dishcloth onto the table and stretched. Going back to sleep seemed such a waste, although the weather was muggy and overcast. She climbed the stairs and fetched her tin box from its place under the bed. As she got up from her knees, she felt the little flutter that was Baby. She patted her waist and said aloud: "It's time to draw, little birdy." The soft flutter continued. "I'll teach you, if you like," she said, "when you're out here in the world."

The last time she had stopped to tear down an old posted advertisement in order to use the paper for drawing, Rory had slapped her hand and scolded her: "D'you want folks to think I haven't a cent to my name!"

He had marched her into Morton's and purchased her a packet of paper, half-sheet size, and a new pencil. She smiled and untied the packet's string, pulling her fingers along the paper's surface, then splayed out the papers—so many! She sat down and drew a little of this (birds, a dead fly on the table, the pattern on her calico dress) and a little of that. She removed from the box the cased ambrotype of her father, and said a prayer, then dug underneath the packets of Eleanor's letters and pulled out some old sketches she had done.

There was Mrs. Wilkin at the (horrid) old cook stove, and Mr. Merritt reading. These two made her sad, so she put them aside. Here was Eleanor and Dance, Mam and Denny, and Frank dozing in his chair. Maggie looked through the little notebook and smiled at the sketches she had done of Rory and Mr. Dooley at the park in Hartford. Annie was in the corner of one sketch. What is she doing on this Fourth of July, Maggie wondered uneasily. Rory had not told her where he was going today. Maggie scribbled over Annie's face and felt better.

"If I had an India rubber eraser," she told Baby, "I'd just rub her out." She giggled. "Well, didn't your Da marry me, and you will be our little one..." She decided she had seen enough of the old sketches. The box was still rather full; no, there was a sheet rolled over and taking up more than its share of space. She removed the extra sheet and gave a little moan.

Edward Whitfield, in profile, from his good side: sketched secretly while she worked at the gallery. He looked intent, too dearly familiar for her now to bear the sight of him. She picked up her pencil to scribble him out, dropped the pencil and crumpled up the page instead.

I'll go to bed now, she thought, *No, I'll wash the dishes.* "None of this," she said aloud to Baby. The tears came anyway, and Maggie bent her head onto the table and cried. *I'm trying to be a good wife,* she thought, *I'm trying to do the best I can. Why do I care about that one, he was a traitor, he did not want me. I miss him so.* She reached into her sleeve for her handkerchief, but had none, so she wiped her nose on the sleeve, then wrinkled her nose in distaste: what a dirty habit. *What does it matter anyway,* she thought, *nothing matters. All I want to do is sleep.*

The back door opened, startling her, and Rory came in. "I was thinkin' you'd not be back home till dark," Maggie said.

"I forgot something I promised to a fellow," Rory said, "I left it up in the chamber." He went on, "What are you crying about?"

"Oh no, I'm fine," she replied instantly, "just a bit tired, is all."

"Too tired to wash the dishes," he said, then added "Well, I guess you need a holiday too." She nodded gratefully: "I was drawing a bit on the nice new paper you bought me." A weak breeze came through the window and the crumpled paper dropped to the floor. Maggie seized it.

"What are you drawing, then?" Rory asked,

"There's nothing to draw here." Maggie said: "Oh. Just anything that comes to mind, that's what I draw."

"What's that one in your hand," he said. *No,* she thought, *no.* She said: "Nothing. I just, it was not right, I did not like it, I'll throw it in the stove."

He grabbed her hand. "Show me."

When she did not move, he took the paper from her hand, opened it, "That one!" he shouted.

"No," she said, panicked, "I ha... I hate it, I hate him, 'tis why I crumpled it. It's old, Rory, done a long while ago..."

Her husband's face was terrible. "That devil, that blackguard! You're drawing him! "

"No!" Maggie screeched. He yanked her out of the chair, and she fell against him. He shook her and slapped her face.

Through the sting and shock, she shouted, "No, it was a long time ago!" He grabbed her chin and turned her face to his: "Why are you crying then?"

"Be... because... it's that I hate him," she whimpered, "and I been so tired lately with Baby. I don't know!"

Rory twisted her around and forced her into the chair. "You drew him. And not a single picture of me. Draw me, draw me!"

She scrabbled for a sheet of paper and her pencil. The paper flew to the floor, the pencil dropped there. He scooped both up, pushed the pencil into her hand, took her hand in a tight grip.

"Draw me," he commanded.

"Rory, mercy, no, I can't now, I am too fretty, but I will draw you, I promise!"

"Your promises!" Rory yelled, and swept his arm across the table, knocking the box, paper, Da's picture, down. He pushed the balled-up drawing into her face, crushing her lips, then thrust it into the cookstove. Grabbing the rest of her drawings with two hands, he shook them in her face and put them into the stove.

Maggie leaped up. "No! Those are mine! You've no right to burn them."

"No right," he said coldly, "No right? This is my house. Who puts the bread on your table, the dress on your back, the god damned paper you draw on?"

She sagged against the back of the chair. "They're mine. You've burned my only picture of Mr. Merritt, you've ruined them all, all my things…" She darted past Rory and found her father's picture, the packet of Eleanor's letters, a scrap of ribbon—then ran out the back door with them. She ran as long as she could. Winded, wet with sweat, she leaned against Donnelly's shed, clutching what little she had saved from his wrath. She wrapped her things in a scrap of horse blanket and hid them in the shed.

When she finally dared to creep home, Rory was gone, and the table was empty. Maggie drank two dippers of water, then climbed wearily to the bedchamber. On the bed was her tin box. She opened it suspiciously. Her pencil was inside, atop a neat stack of the new white paper. Knowing that this was all the apology she would get, she moved the box to the chest of drawers and rolled onto the bed, murmuring to Baby.

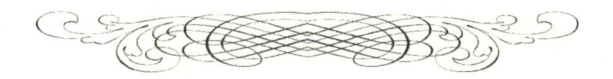

As the Judge argued loudly that the invitation list for the wedding supper must be expanded—after all he was man of importance and many were owed favors, et cetera—his wife and daughter protested and Fariday looked grim.

"I'd like to see the building site for your new house," Ned announced.

Kate looked at her fiancé and replied: "That's a capital idea. Go, Worth, do!"

"Very well, my dear," Fariday said, not bothering to hide his relief.

"What a circus," Ned muttered as he drove the gig onto the main road, "meaning no offense to you and Kate."

Fariday said: "Ho! It appears that the Judge does not wish to offend anybody either, except his own flesh and blood. He is dashed lucky that I have so little family." He shook his head, and grimaced as the carriage wheels hit a rut. He said: "I never thought I'd marry. I can't bear those soft girls, with their heads full of nonsense."

"Well, you've met your match in Kate," Ned said. Fariday's grimace eased slightly.

"So I have," he said. Ned guided the horse around a series of hillocks and holes in the road, then commented: "This street isn't much better than a corduroy road. The 14th built a lot of those."

Fariday said in a tight voice: "Let me tell you: when our 6th corps detail was skirmishing with Early's troops at Fort Stevens, I never for a moment thought that I'd get hit. All those battles before, under worse fire, and I came out with no more than a hole in my hat. Well, that bullet finally found me. When I came to and saw that the all-fired surgeon had cut off my leg, I very nearly crawled out of my bed to choke the life out of him. I scared him like hell, at any rate."

Ned shook his head in sympathy. He said: "They told me later that some country dentist took out all my broken teeth after Fredericksburg, and he was the one who stitched my face. The surgeons were too busy…" They were silent for a time. Ned added: "His wife would have done it a sight better."

Fariday grunted in amused agreement. He said: "Most of the time it feels like my leg is still there. It's burning like the devil right now." Ned nodded.

"There's the lot, just ahead," Fariday said, gesturing to a stand of young trees surrounded by a ramble of old stone wall.

"That will clear nicely," Ned responded, "you'll have a good view of the hills."

"Katie found it," Fariday replied, "And she knows what will suit."

Ned smiled. "Indeed, she does."

The defendants in the wandering pisser case had decided to fund an appeal to the higher court. Ned spent most of the day in the stifling office preparing research and draft language for Mr. Putnam to craft the legal brief. Putnam finally donned his hat: "It is past time for my supper. Close up the place." Ned replaced bookmarks in the pertinent volumes of law, closed and stacked the necessary ones on Putnam's table, and returned the remainder to the book shelves. As he locked the front door and went into the empty street, he turned to look at the Eagle Hotel in the waning light.

A good meal, peace and quiet: none of these were to be his lot today, as his parents had a long list of tasks for him in preparation for the wedding. Neither his mother nor Eleanor had touched the cook stove in days and over-worked Martha slapped down the bare minimum in food at each meal. He thought that feeding and housing a regiment would be easier to plan for than this wedding supper: every evening, discussion and argument about the plans hung over his head like a cracked branch sodden with rain.

"Hist, Ned!" George Dunn said from the alleyway, beckoning for Ned to join him.

"I'm late for supper," Ned began.

George seized Ned's lapels and said: "To hell with your supper. I did it! I found that god-damned skinny little piece of shit." George's breath stank of drink, his eyes were wild, red whirlpools.

Ned pulled away from George's grasp. "Did you take Jack to the jail?"

George laughed. "Better than that. Cooling his heels in a jail's too good for that bastard. I found him and caught him and he squealed like a pig. I wish you coulda heard him." Ned cursed and said apprehensively, "What did you do."

"I beat the crap out of him," Dunn replied with glee shining from his wet face.

"No!" Ned shouted, "You blasted idiot! You ought to have hauled him to the constable."

George's face darkened. "He stole from me! Nobody does that. I ought to have killed him, wish I had."

Ned felt sick. "Good God," he muttered, "Battery is a crime!"

George said: "What the devil r'you talking about? Ain't his stealing a crime? I ain't ever getting my money back—how about that?"

"Where is Jack now?" Ned asked, desperate for time to think. George wiped his face with a grimy sleeve. "Why?" he commanded, "Why'r you asking me."

"There's blood on your shirt," Ned said, "how did you get up here from New Haven—people must have seen you…"

George looked down at his clothing, then over at Ned. "Well, I drove a rig, what'd you think, I flew like a bird? Hey, ain't you glad? I'm the one who tracked him. You did nothing. Nothing! and I got him back for what he done to me."

Ned said: "Good God, you could have killed him!" He belatedly recalled that he might have a duty under the law to report George's attack; he said: "You can't… you ought not to tell **me**….you **must** go to Garside…"

George swore at him, stunned, outraged. Before Ned could martial a further thought, Dunn punched him in the stomach. Ned landed in the dirt, paralyzed, as he tried to breathe, hands on his belly. As Dunn began to kick him, howling curses, Ned curled his body as best he could.

Pain in his thigh, buttocks, forearm; there was blood in his mouth, buzzing in his ears. Keep down, keep down when the bullets are flying. One of his men began to shout. *Get down,* Ned thought, *I'm done for.* Hearing more shouting and the dull thuds of bullets, he reached for a musket. Where in hell was it? A body fell next to his; the man was moaning. He smelled something rank, had the soldier been killed? He opened his eye, moved his arm, lifted his head very slightly.

He was on the street, not the cornfield. His sleeve was covered with horse flop and Morton the shopkeeper rolled in the dirt near him, holding bloody hands to his nose and whimpering. George Dunn was nowhere to be seen. Ned crawled to his hands and knees, but was unable to go further, shivering like a dog for some moments. He dizzily lay down and closed his eyes.

Chapter 42

"One for me," Maggie said, dropping a raspberry in the tin pail, and "one for Baby," as she ate another berry, smacking her lips at the tartness. When she ran from the house on the Fourth of July, she had found the wild berry bush among the brambles behind Donnelly's shed. Now they were ripe, so she was set upon picking enough for two pies. Rory had been a perfect lamb since the Fourth, with nary a scolding.

At her own back door, she peeked into the woodbin. Good, there was an old newspaper; she plucked it from the bin and read the date: only two weeks old. By the clock, she had nearly an hour before preparing supper, so she sat in the kitchen chair and read through the paper. Hurriedly passing by a headline about the desperate conditions that the Union soldiers had suffered at Andersonville prison, she flipped to the back. The inside back page had an entire section torn out. She turned the remnant over and found a short article about a Fenian Convention scheduled in October.

At that, she pushed the paper aside, and stood up to rinse the berries. There was a bit of old maple sugar in the cupboard: she broke the hard lumps and smashed them flat with a spoon, then added them to the berries and began to make the pie crust. As she worked the lard and flour together, she thought that Rory must have torn out an advertisement he wanted to keep. No, she did that sometimes, but he did not. Perhaps it was something he had not wanted her to see? She wiped her hands on her apron and looked through the newspaper again. On the remnant of the last page she spied a small square advising customers that Dunn's Photograph

Gallery would be open only one afternoon a week until further notice. She threw the paper back into the woodbin, heart beating fast. Something was wrong with Ned.

Eleanor's last letter had mentioned nothing but Kate's wedding plans, since Maggie had warned that "Himself" now insisted on reading all correspondence. *How can I find out?* There was, it seemed to her, no safe way to do it: she could not ask Eleanor, for Rory might stop the correspondence; she could not call upon or write to Zek Fish, for he was a male over the age of twelve, hence suspect in her husband's eyes. She could ask Mrs. Moore: but what if word of that got back to Rory? Maggie sighed; surely she owed no allegiance to Edward, a traitor. She finished making the pies, trying to work her fears away, and to make her heart straight again.

The interminable wedding supper was nearly complete: the wedding cake cut and served. The Judge smiled his party smile, glowering only when he looked at his son. The attendance at the supper was lower than expected—perhaps due to the heat, perhaps due to an overabundance of invitations on the Judge's part; or maybe the noteworthy splash that a headline in the weekly newspaper had made: *Vicious Attack Upon Edward Whitfield, Morton's Rescue.* Although Whitfield, Junior, was not the cause of the scandal, the judge had opined at length, privately, that Ned's negligence in allowing a friendship with Dunn and permitting Rossiter's theft had tarred the entire family.

Ned covered a yawn and stared at the plate of cake in his hand. *Better to be in bed, reading about California,* he thought. He replaced the plate on the table, his left arm twinging with the movement. *At least the damned sling is gone,* he thought. Had it still been on his person he feared that the ladies would have pinned it with the flowers that covered the room.

Mrs. Moore said: "Have you lost your appetite, Ned? I am sure that no one would remark if you went upstairs to rest. Those bruises still look angry. You don't look well."

He said: "We are ALL played out. I'll be heartily glad when this circus parade is over."

She peered at him. "Dr. Green is a good man, but he sometimes sees only what is in front of his eyes. When he examined you, did he ask if you have had pain in your chest on the left side and fatigue, and a fluttering of your heart, or diarrhea?"

Ned smiled, "Straight to the point, heigh?" he said, "No, he did not. Why do you ask?"

"And do you have any of those?" Mrs. Moore inquired. *She means well,* he thought, as he picked up the plate and took a bite of cake to prove his hearty appetite.

"I guess so. Sometimes," he admitted, "What does that signify?"

She said: "Some of our veterans of this late conflict have these symptoms: it is a physiological condition that I have been reading about, sometimes called soldier's heart."

"I've been out of the army for three years," Ned countered, "Surely symptoms do not persist that long."

"They may," she said, "and you have recently been under attack again by another soldier that you once considered a friend."

He scowled. "Obviously I was wrong!"

She raised her eyebrows at him and said mildly: "I regret bringing up the subject again. My point is that I heard from his father that George Dunn was subject to rages after he returned. And I am aware from my nursing of mothers, wives, and sisters that some others with soldier's heart have an excessive devotion to spirituous drink…" Ned stiffened, then shrugged.

She went on: "…and some of these men are constantly weary—weary perhaps of life." He nodded, looking at Fariday who was still stoutly masking his pain for the sake of his new wife.

"Rest cures…" Mrs. Moore began, pursed her lips at his laughter, and went on: "are not just for ladies, or a place to be seen by the best people, as your father might insist. There is an excellent one run by Mr. and Mrs. Ames up north of here at Stafford Springs, and I recommend that you consider…"

"I appreciate your concern," Ned interrupted, "but I am far too busy. Truly."

"I seem to recall," she replied, "that Amelia and Charles Mix go to the shore for a week's holiday in late August. And I have heard that Mr. Putnam intends to end the summer season at Saratoga to be in company with the best of marriageable young ladies. Ned, I fear that if you go on as you have, you might lose more time at your position than you can spare. I know that Mr. Mix is concerned about your health."

Ned put the rest of the cake slice in his mouth so that he would not say what he was thinking. "How good of him," he growled, "Certainly I agree with what you said about George: he was not the same man when he got off that train in May. But in my opinion, Mother needs a rest cure, not I."

Mrs. Moore sighed and sipped her wine. "I certainly agree: I wish she had the opportunity. Or any opportunity to rest. But you have the freedom that she does not; and I do believe that she will rest a little easier here if she believes you are…healing."

Ned was silent for a while, then said: "I don't know. I guess I'll think about it."

Mrs. Moore pulled a paper from her purse. "Dear boy. Here are the particulars. I brought this for Libby but she said to give it to you."

He put the cake plate down again, licking a bit of frosting from his thumb, and quickly read the leaflet. "I did not know you had all of the high cards in your hand," he said, "You already played the ace and king, and now the queen is on the table."

She smiled. "You are my favorite," she said, "but don't tell Katie."

They say it is a privilege, Ned wrote to his mother and sister, *to be at a rest cure as fine as the Ames', and I cannot dispute that, but only if one considers cold baths and cold showers, cold soaks and frequent wrapping in wet sheets a privilege. Indisputably, the chaise lounges on the southern porches (where the sunshine lingers, bless us!) are in great demand, but I believe most of us feign deep sleep there to escape the next scheduled wetting.*

He put down his pen. Of course. it would not do to tell them that he had barked at the attendant this morning to drop the blasted sheets, as they might bring on the neuralgia; nor would he relate that he snuck away in the afternoon and bathed in a sheltered part of the spring fed creek, taking his rest cure successfully on the mossy bank and feeling better than he had in many months. *There is the bell ringing us to supper*, he wrote, *the food here cannot hold a candle to*

Mother's, but presumably boring fare eases digestion, and boring company leads to slumber.

After supper, one of the guests—a wan young lady—sat at the piano and played. Ned was drowsing until she began to play a song he knew. He approached the piano, asked the lady's permission to sing. She played the introduction and Ned sang *Her Bright Eyes Haunt Me Still*. He paused for a moment when the phrase repeated in the refrain: seeing Maggie in his imagination. He was disappointed at his faltering voice; surprised she had not yet been banished from his thoughts. A year ago, she had still been in his arms.

It appeared that the young lady at the piano and a few other female guests were touched by the song. He cleared his throat and apologized for the pause. Several guests murmured polite answers, but a man at the back of the parlor said loudly: "Get the fellow some cold water!" A few in the crowd frowned at the tall man who had spoken but others tittered in amusement. Ned grinned in the man's direction and began to sing *Listen to the Mockingbird*, while the game young pianist scrabbled for the sheet music and then played to accompany him. That song too made him think of Maggie, so he returned to his seat as a mother insisted her daughter must also have a turn.

When the evening ended, Ned recognized the man who had made the joke: the lawyer who had been amused by the proceedings in the local justice court. He and Ned greeted each other and made introductions. Ned said: "I discovered the five errors of Justice Eller."

"I thought you might," commented the attorney, Mr. Lang. Ned named them and told the attorney that the defendants would appeal.

"Capital," said Mr. Lang, "Here's my card. Would you let me know when it goes to the higher court? I'll come and take a seat in the court room; your hearing would be a sight more interesting to me than haggles over water rights."

"Of course," Ned replied.

"Who is that fellow who came to justice court with you?" Lang said.

"Mr. Putnam," Ned replied.

"Ah," said Lang, "that explains it. Has Mix taken him on as partner?"

At Ned's nod, Lang went on: "His uncle and his father

owned a lot of property over to Tolland and some in Millville, I hear. So he's a big bug."

Ned laughed. "Like a locust?"

Lang smiled. "No, he's smaller fry: the son of a locust anyway, and he ought to have caught those errors."

Ned said: "I hope the appeal is successful. Mr. Mix has been criticized for taking on a... folks call it a distasteful case."

"People **will** talk," Lang replied, his expression clouded. "Were it not a crime to make a wager in this state, I'd put my money on you. By the by, I liked your songs. I'll tell my sister to come to the parlor tomorrow evening if you promise to sing."

Ned went into his chamber and stood for several moments in the dark, resolving to invite Lang to enjoy the quiet of the mossy creek bed, away from the yammering, the cold soaks, the curious gazes; to keep silence there.

Maggie sneezed hard, turning her head from the stew pot just in time. She pulled a fresh handkerchief from her sleeve, blew her nose. Rory got up to help her bring the stew to the table. The boarders spooned it out on their own, while she sneezed and blew again, then brought the platter of bread to table.

"Och, sit down, Maggie," Rory said.

"I need to go to bed, Rory," Maggie responded, "My head is so stuffed."

"Eat a little first," he said, so she sat down and drank two cups of tea and picked at a ladle full of stew. The men ate quickly and went to the front room or up to bed. Maggie rinsed the dishes and banked the fire in the stove, then loosened her stays and fell in bed, with Baby bumping inside her. When Rory climbed in beside her, he did not pluck at her nightdress, or insist upon "a nice ride," as he usually did, but simply gave her a pat on the back and remained still. Maggie fell asleep with a smile of gratitude.

Rory came in late to supper the following night and answered Maggie's questions with "I had something to see to," and cheerfully downed his meal. That night as well he did not press upon her. The third night the same thing occurred, Rory late to supper, this time looking downcast; with no answer to her questions. In bed, her husband put his arms around her but did not force any congress.

He said, "Just trying to give you a little rest, while you're sick."

Maggie kissed his hand and snuggled against him. "I do love you, Rory," she said impulsively.

He did not reply, and she thought he had fallen asleep, but when Baby kicked against his hand upon her belly, he cleared his throat and said: "You're a good girl."

"This house is falling down around my very ears!" the old woman exclaimed to Ned.

"I expect you'll be more comfortable at Uncle Cyrus..." Ned began.

His grandfather Elbridge Whitfield's widow had a tail wind in her sails and spoke over him: "Oh, it is such a trial to leave my home!"

He nodded, then said to the two men bending to lift a heavy-bottomed sideboard: "Not that one."

"I will need a place for my china," his grandmother insisted.

"I'm sorry, but that is not on Uncle's list," Ned replied, "and I doubt that it would fit into your rooms at his house."

"I must have it. It is the best piece I own," she said.

"Unfortunately, it is much too large," Ned responded.

"It certainly is not," she protested.

He eyed the ponderous piece, which he estimated was nearly the size of a small dock. "It is not on Uncle's list to move," he continued, "but on the sales list."

His grandmother fumed. "Your father always neglects me dreadfully, he always has, but I should have thought my own son would have more respect for my wishes."

"Father sent me in his place," Ned said, "and I am sure Uncle Cyrus and Aunt Lavinia have..."

"Do not mention her name," the old woman interrupted, "She don't want me, it's just her Christian duty. Your mother is far kinder, but your father won't have me." She shook her head and waved away his murmur, then proclaimed: "Where is that foolish girl? I need a cup of tea."

She made her way into the dim hallway, called to Ned, and touched the looking glass hanging there. "This is going with me, no matter what is written on that plague-y list."

He followed her into the kitchen, a dark and sooty spot smelling of potatoes. The hired help was nowhere to be found, so the old dame took up the kettle and some damp, used tea leaves stored in a small crock and made two cups of tea. She sat with difficulty, drank the tepid tea and examined him more thoroughly.

"I am surprised to see you at all," she said, "Your mother feared for your life. And Daniel spent quite a parcel transporting you to New Haven from that place down in the South. I see you take after your mother. Hmm, just as well."

"Thank you," Ned said, regretting again that he had obeyed his father's command (and Mr. Mix's amused agreement) to help his grandmother move. He looked with longing out the window at the bright October sun.

"I blame that woman," she went on, "that horrid woman who bore him. She does not deserve the name of mother! I was more a mother to him than she was. Elbridge said she left her baby for days on end, did your father ever tell you? It's true! that woman gave him to a slattern of a nursemaid, then left him hungry when he was still in skirts, with no one to see to him but an addle-pated girl."

She stared into her teacup. "Oh, laws, your father was wild and headstrong! Did you know he had not a single day of schooling until I married your grandfather? I took them both in hand and made them a good home. He knows all I did for him, he knows it as well as his own name, but now he won't have me in his home! He ought to be ashamed."

"I did not know that," Ned said, "How old was he when you married?"

"Just a boy," she said, taking a gulp of tea, "I can't recollect, he might have been ten or eleven years of age; he was such a scrawny little thing. He was a cabin boy on the coastal packet when your grandfather took him off that ship and presented him to me. That boy was as wild as a wolf. 1820 was the year we were married, Elbridge and I. Everyone who said that I'd be an old maid, had to eat their words. We had one of the finest receptions this city has seen. The mayor and the Governor attended."

As she paused for breath, Ned asked the question he had always wondered about: "How did she die, his mother?"

"What did your mother tell you?" she queried sharply.

"Only that she had drowned," he answered, "How did that happen?"

"Yes, she drowned," the old woman replied, then turned the rudder in her response and announced: "Let them take the sideboard of course, it is too large, but I must have the looking glass. It would have been best for your mother to visit and set this to rights for me, but I suppose she couldn't sway him. Done with your tea?" She gathered his cup, then went to the back door and called for her hired girl.

Ned wondered silently whether the cause of drowning was an accident—a mis-step in the dark near the wharf? If so, his mother would likely have told him the tragic story, unless the Judge had forbidden it. *It may have been suicide,* he thought, *the only sort of drowning that they would not discuss. What had that lost woman been through, and that left-alone boy, as wild as a wolf?* Except for the judge's rages, Ned could not reconcile the unlettered cabin boy with the man who now walked the narrow path of propriety without looking to the right or to the left, with grim satisfaction, but without joy.

Chapter 43

"It can't be," Maggie insisted to everyone who came to see her, "We were just getting on so well." During the hasty fitting for the black dress, she said the same. During the moments that Mr. Dooley broke down when he told her that they'd be needing a closed casket, as Rory's head had been hurt bad, so bad, don't you know, that she mustn't see it, she had said "It can't be," and added: "You're a liar." Mr. Dooley shook his head; he and Frank, and McGrath, the boarder, ill-hid tears behind bent hands and gruff voices.

To all the women fussing around her, Maggie said: "'tisn't true!" even as Mrs. Kernan wailed, Mrs. Leary, Rose and Mam, and Bridget and Aggie bustled morosely and mopped their noses and gave Maggie the kisses and embraces that Rory had only begun to bestow. She sat dazed throughout the funeral Mass. "'twill be all right," she murmured to the little one when he got the hiccups inside her.

When the pallbearers picked up their burden and took it away, Maggie rose to go with the others. The women surrounding her argued among themselves: some contended that she would faint and harm herself and the baby, but old Mrs. Kernan said the baby would grow up mad at any rate for all the tragedy its mother had witnessed, if it wasn't born dead. Frightened nearly out of her wits, Maggie clung to Rose and told them she wanted to go home; but as the procession of females neared the church door, Rory's baby kicked and turned in agitation. Maggie looked up to see Annie Mulrooney standing in her way in the aisle, her face a storm of agony.

She knew him best, Maggie thought, suddenly seeing more

than just what was before her eyes. "You..." she whispered to Annie, then gathering full voice, "You. I've so many questions." Annie shrieked and threw herself at Maggie's feet in a perfect frenzy, while Maggie began to feel very bad, for something awful had happened and the baby was jumping inside her, and if Annie was so full of grief, that meant that Rory was gone. *Not gone West. Och, I'd best sit down.* The roar of the train was in Maggie's ears and its smoke filled her eyes before she sagged to the floor, Annie Mulrooney providing an unexpected soft landing.

The child in her womb now did not move. Maggie was afraid she had killed it by falling down, or by refusing to eat. Rory would be so angry when he found out she had hurt his boy.

"I didn't mean to!" she said, as she cried out the news to Rose. Several of the women ushered her to the bed-chamber. They felt her belly, whispered, plied her with hot tea, and sent one of the children to fetch Mrs. Moore. When Mrs. Moore arrived, the baby rolled and kicked inside Maggie. *Blessed is the fruit of thy womb,* Maggie thought, *just like in the prayer.* Mrs. Moore examined her and put her to bed.

When Maggie awoke and came down the stairs, hoping that Rory had come home and everything was now set to rights, the women's faces appeared, pitying and sorrowful. The women patted Maggie's shoulder and belly. Maggie felt as if she was split in two: one part saw, and heard, and felt touches; the other was terrified to surface, wholly unable to speak what it heard now dinning inside—Rory was dead, they had buried him that afternoon without her, she knew he would be lonely and cold so far beneath the ground. Mrs. Kernan put on her shawl, preparing to go.

Don't leave me, don't leave me alone! Maggie thought, then gasped out the words. The old woman hastened to her as the other women clucked in sympathy.

"They'll be stayin' dearie, don't you worry, good Lord bless you!" Mrs. Kernan said.

Bridget squeezed her hand. "I'm here. I won't leave you," she said.

"You ought to be in bed, Maggie," Rose said, but Maggie shook her head emphatically. She clutched her belly and said wildly: "Is Baby still alive?"

"To be sure!" Rose answered, "Mrs. Moore came and said it was fine. Baby is still with you."

"Rory," Maggie whispered, "How will you see your baby, how will you see your boy?" Bridget wiped her eyes and nose with the back of her hand, and when her hand seized Maggie's again it was wet and warm.

"Will they come?" the seeing-hearing part of Maggie spoke for her, "Do we have enough to feed them?" Bridget told her again that they had all come after the funeral and there was more than enough for them all to eat. It was while you was sleeping, don't you know, so of course you did not remember it all. She described how everyone praised Rory, and mourned him again, as they ate, and drank to him; and Mr. Dooley said that everyone had put maple leaves and evergreen branches on the coffin and Father Kelly had said so many fine things at the grave.

"Are you hungry?" Bridget asked Maggie, who startled.

"I ain't. I'll never be again," Maggie said.

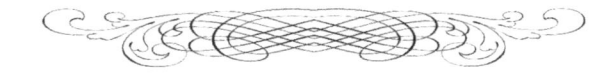

Three men came through the front door, without knocking, and entered the front room where the women sat.

"You!" Mrs. Leary said, and leaped from her chair, standing in front of the first man, shouted at him: "The man is dead and buried, as if you care, for you did not wake him nor show your face at the Mass. You're not welcome here."

Maggie realized dully that the man was Brian Harrigan, followed by hound Hurley and a big man she did not know. Harrigan smirked and commanded the big man to look to the rooms upstairs, and stifled Mrs. Leary's protests.

"Shut your gob, you old witch! I own this house, and will Corcoran—dead and buried—be paying me so much as a penny in rent from here on? Don't be telling me I've no right when I am master of the place."

Rose came out from the kitchen, leading Maggie's mother.

"Get out, get out of here!" Mrs. O'Shaughnessy screamed.

Harrigan cursed at her then smiled a nasty smile, saying: "Mary, Mary. Have you forgotten all I done for you? You're well rid of that lying son of a bitch, as your stupid girl is of Rory Corcoran. And you know why I am here. Rory has something of mine, something he owed me, so I've come to get it." He told Hurley to search the kitchen and then pulled out a side chair (*that's Rory's chair,* Maggie thought, *that's where he always sits*) and sat down.

"Who are you?" he said to Bridget.

"Mrs. Dooley," Bridget managed to say.

"Ah," Harrigan responded, "He works at Rock Mill, don't he? And a word from me could have him fired."

Mrs. Leary said something under her breath, but Bridget was speechless.

"Go to the kitchen and get me what's left of the food and drink," he said. Bridget shook her head but at a nod from Mrs. Leary, she got up, weeping with frustration, and left the room.

"Now," Harrigan said to Maggie, "Where did Rory keep all his things?" Maggie simply stared at her lap. There was no man here to help her or any of them. She felt the dark wave of his power; Baby kicked hard inside her.

"I don't know," she said aloud, unable to stop the tears that slid from her eyes.

"You don't know?" he replied softly, "didn't you hear me, dearie, I own this house and I could put you out of it this very night. Now, think on it."

Maggie heard a crash in the kitchen, and the heavy feet of the man upstairs, the sound of furniture being moved, a drawer striking the floor, splintering wood. He smiled at her. "Out with not a stick of furniture to your name. You're not wanting that, now, are you? You'll need to sell it soon, won't you, being a widow, and who'd be about buying a broken piece? So tell me where he kept his things."

"Mother of God," Maggie murmured. All at once, as if she was possessed by something other than her own soul, Maggie felt a power in the room, pouring all that it had into her. Rory here, right here now, she could feel him: his energy, his strength, his bright mind. She took out her handkerchief, wiped her face, looked long at Mrs. Leary, then said to Harrigan: "Tell them to stop breaking everything, and give me some quiet to think on it. Would Rory Corcoran hide something valuable in a chest of drawers or inside a crock? You know better than that."

Harrigan's smile slithered away.

"What is it that he may have had that you're needing?" Maggie asked, "large, small, coin, paper?"

"Look inside the books," Harrigan yelled, as Hurley went up the stairs.

"Well, Mrs. Corcoran," Harrigan said, "Did Rory ever tell you what the English did to him when he was just a boy? Did he tell you about the churchmen—the charity men! shrilling at him to turn Prot then and there in order to take their charity soup, and when he would not they turned him away starving? Did he tell you that when I found him in Boston only two weeks off the boat he was thin as a bone and barely able to stand, and that pretty face beaten bloody by the thieves who owned him? And yet he had no gratitude to show me."

Although the man opposite her was a liar, Maggie sensed that this tirade was more true than not. In her mind, she wrapped her love around the boy Rory, held him to her heart. She said: "I know he loves Ireland and hates the English for all they did."

As Bridget came out of the kitchen with a plate and a mug of beer and set it down on a chair, Maggie thought, *I hope you spat in it, Bridey.* She said aloud: "Go home, Bridget. Mam and Rose and Mrs. Leary will stay. And I'm sure Mr. Harrigan has no need of you." Bridget protested feebly, but after a nod from Mrs. Leary, took her leave.

Harrigan drank deeply and began to eat the meat with his fingers. After a time, he said: "They killed all his family, the English. Starved them out, like so many others. If you hate what they did to him, to all of us, think on it: where might Rory have hidden something, something that might help us all?"

Trying to slip under the door, came Rory's voice in Maggie's ear. A black rat sniffed and bared its teeth in her imagination. She had gone upstairs to their bedchamber one evening and seen Rory poking at the rafters. "I thought I saw a rat," he had said to her. *If I tell him,* her mind whispered to Rory's, *he will go away and leave us be.* Maggie's first unbidden thought slid from her mouth: "Why do you hate us all so?"

He blinked and said: "What the devil?" *Get him out,* Rory's voice said to her.

Maggie went on: "I think I may know where 'tis, what Rory had. Rosie, take Mam home with you."

As Rose and Mrs. O'Shaughnessy roared in the negative, Harrigan said: "No. They stay."

Rose helped Maggie out of the chair, and they all labored slowly up the stairs, followed by the muttering Harrigan. In the bedchamber, Maggie told the big man to poke a stick deep into the rafters. After a short time, he pulled out a dusty roll of paper, tied with red string. Harrigan crowed with glee, and seized the roll, opened it. It contained a dozen or more large pencil drawings of landscapes, each labeled with the name of a place in Ireland.

He shook the bundle, turned each sheet over, examined the wrapping, growing more furious by the moment. "What in hell are these?"

Maggie now sensed her own father smiling at her. She said: "Look at the edges of the drawing, look sharp. Here." She walked to the top drawing, touched it gently. "My Da always put messages in when he drew things for me. D'you see how the lines form a letter there, the letter P, and up here a number, seven."

Harrigan uttered a short humorless laugh and said "Pen O'Shaughnessy, you bastard." He re-rolled the bundle and tied the red string again. Thrusting the bundle at the big man, he commanded the men to take it away. Harrigan stood still for a moment, shaking his head in grim relief.

Mrs. O'Shaughnessy said: "Ye got what ye came for, now get out."

He turned upon her. "Mary," he said, making it sound like a threat. Maggie's Mam covered her mouth. "All this trouble you've caused." She dropped her hands, held them out in supplication. "I din't know, I swear I din't," she said. *Look out,* Rory said in Maggie's mind, and she felt a storm gathering.

Harrigan said, "No, mayhap you didn't, Mary. You haven't the sense God gave a goose. But this one," he pointed at Maggie, "is her father's girl—thinks she's clever, don't she."

"Sit down," he said to Maggie, and motioned to the other women, "Gather around. I have a story for you, to answer her question."

Mrs. Leary said, "Leave her be, you blackguard, you got what you came for. For mercy's sake, she just lost her man, leave her be."

He ignored her and said to Maggie: "Or stand there with your feet hurtin'. Why do I hate you so? Indeed, you have your father to thank for that. And your mother needs to hear the whole truth about him, and so, surely do you."

He leaned against the wall, took out his clay pipe, filled it with tobacco, lit it, puffed at it with satisfaction. "Did you know, Mary," he said conversationally, "when you squawked and carried on to get your precious Pen to marry you because you had that tart in your oven," he gestured at Maggie, "did you know he was itching to skedaddle? Och, you must have guessed. The fact is, that's all he ever did, run away. I knew that and I tried to tell you, but you'd not hear a single word against him—your handsome little man." Her mother responded by cursing Harrigan to hell. He laughed. "For all your ways, and how he complained of them! But for all your drunken ways, Mary, you had better luck in keeping him nearby than his first wife, the one he left in Ireland. And she was a sweet child: carryin' his baby when he lit out. Left them behind, he did, just as he did you, and this girl."

Mrs. O'Shaughnessy's face held all her grief. He said to Maggie: "He left you, in the night—just as he did to his baby girl back in Ireland. Left her to die at her mother's breast."

Maggie thought of her dream of the starving child. *A sister,* she thought, *instantly come and instantly gone?* "How do you know?" she asked him. *You liar,* she thought, *you're a liar, he had to leave us.*

"Don't believe a word of it," Rose cried.

Harrigan chortled, pointed at Mrs. Leary. "Ask this old witch, she knows." As all the women looked at her; she glared red at Harrigan but kept silent. He happily puffed at his pipe: "But Pen O'Shaughnessy, damn him! he had to go, and quickly, didn't he? When you've murdered a man in cold blood, you cannot linger to wait for your wife to birth your child. No, certainly, you must run like a rabbit to save your own skin."

No, Maggie thought, *'tisn't true. I'm cold, I will never be warm again.* She put her hands on her belly, willing the child not to believe. It could not be: there was no way to reconcile the gentle father she had known with this wicked story.

"NO!" Mary O'Shaughnessy shrieked. She crumpled in Rose's arms, down, down to the floor.

Maggie let go of her belly and her rage sent her feet toward the liar. "You'll kill my Mam with your talk!" she shouted, surprised to hear herself, but the words would come out no matter what. "God has twisted your soul," she said to Harrigan, "And it will never come right for you."

Harrigan stared at her: Maggie could feel his hatred, ice and dark and death it was.

Mrs. Leary went to Mrs. O'Shaughnessy's side, patted her

friend's body which shook with sobs, and said to Harrigan: "You've told your tale, you've done your harm. Leave us be."

Harrigan said triumphantly. "You be out of this house in two days, Mrs. fucking Corcoran, and the lot of you. Hurley found some money Rory had hidden away, quite a bit, so there's the rent he owed me paid! I'll be glad to see the back of you." Now, the flowing hatred had come to Mrs. Leary too, and came from her, as she said to him: "You'd take a widow's last bit of money."

He laughed. "Corcoran's widow I would indeed. He gave me nothing but trouble, the ungrateful bastard."

There were winds swirling in the room that Maggie could see like pale hands, then a cloud bigger than them all, pressing them in its dark center. She saw a man gasping—shocked and gray—the order upset. Shivering, she walked right up to Harrigan, took the pipe from his hand, and dashed it to the floor. A red ash fell from it and she ground it under her heel.

"Whatever you put your hand to, what is most a part of your heart: that will fail," she told Harrigan, "From that time, nothing will ever come right for you. Never again. And so says Rory's stupid girl who sometimes sees things others cannot."

He struck her across the face. As the women surrounded her, he spat on the floor, grabbed his pipe and left.

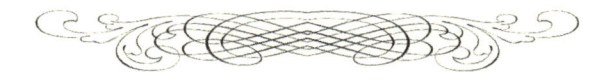

As he approached the house for supper, Ned saw Mrs. Moore's chaise in the drive. He hastened inside, hearing Eleanor in the back parlor, crying in a panicked way. He steeled his stomach and went to her. She sobbed harder at his approach.

Mrs. Moore said: "Edward, Maggie's husband was killed in an accident at the Rock Mill two days ago. I saw her today..." she stopped.

His mother murmured: "Seven months along. What will she do?"

He ought to feel something. There were certainly any number of emotions to choose from, any normal fellow would come out with the decent thing: surprise, concern, somber head-shaking. Ned felt nothing, simply counted backwards mentally. Seven months along; March, perhaps. Had conceiving the child been her birthday gift from the handsome fellow, now dead? He shivered. *Dead. I beat you on that anyway,* he thought, *you sorry devil. If she'd waited for me, she wouldn't be a widow today.*

Widow. Widow with child. All the widows whose men were harvested by the sickle of war, all the widows of the Bible, all the aged widows tottering along in windrows of black crepe, all the widows he had tutted over while reading probate law—yet he could not imagine Maggie as a widow. His Maggie laughed and twiddled her hair and went off into daydream land when she was not telling stories or listening, whole-souled, to his. He thought to ask Mrs. Moore if Maggie was all right, but hesitated, how could she be, with such a shocking loss? He could not marshal his thoughts; they ran on in a disorderly rout.

"The poor thing," Mrs. Whitfield said, and this cry from the heart shamed him.

"What can I do to help?" he asked the women, looking at none of them. No-one answered him.

Chapter 44

Zek held a negative up to the light. "He was a good lookin' fellow; he don't sit a bad picture. I guess Maggie, um, Miss Shaw, I don't know as I heard her other name—she's mighty sad, 'course she must be."

Ned took the negative from Zek, held it up, and ruminated. "I thought she might like a picture of the man," he observed, "but I don't know which one to print up. I don't know which one she'd like."

Zek said: "Well, that's mighty good of you, considerin' all that truck that went on."

When Ned did not respond, Zek continued: "When I saw you up here in the window, I was hopin' you might be back for good." Ned shook his head. "Even if Alonzo wants to re-open the gallery, I can have no part in it."

Zek swung his arms. "That's an all-fired shame!"

"I did put in a good word for you with Alonzo," Ned added.

"Yep, I bet you did, thank you...Morton ain't so bad, I guess... even if he just can't stop yarning with the customers about how he saved your skin. If I'd have been there, I'd have beat that crazy man into the dirt."

Ned nodded and placed the negative back on the table. It tasked his temper to look any longer than necessary at Corcoran.

Zek pulled on his lower lip. "If you ain't the boss, any more, nor Mr. Alonzo, then I am, ain't I? So, I say print up all them plates, every last one, and let Maggie pick out what she fancies, or keep the whole lot. Free of charge."

"A capital idea!" Ned said.

" 'course it is, " Zek replied, "I'll fetch the printing frames. We got to catch that sun while it's still shining."

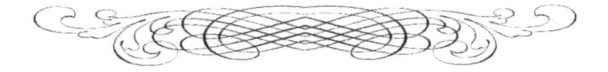

"Oh, I made sure that I gave them to her directly," Mrs. Whitfield said to her son, then went on: "She... she... oh heavens, the poor little thing... I hardly knew what to say to her. It was such a sudden death, such a young man." She dropped her gaze, paused to compose her voice, then murmured: "She clutched them as if they were a lifeline. She said she never drew his picture: he was the only one she never drew. I sat with her for a while, but that was all she ever got out. It was the best thing for her, those pictures." They sat in perfect quiet at the kitchen table; Mrs. Whitfield blinked away tears while tracing the grain of the wood with her fingers. Ned was as still as deep water, trying to push aside the vision his mother had conjured.

Finally, she said: "Are you...?" Escape was imperative.

"Yes," he said automatically, getting up, "Yes. Fine."

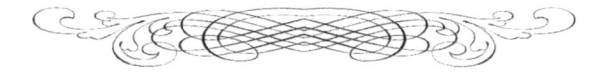

Maggie took the photograph of Rory from where it rested beneath her bodice and showed it to Bridget. Bridey said that she'd already seen it and the other pictures, but she praised it again and Maggie returned it to its nest near her heart. They sat together, but every word Bridget said fell to the floor. Maggie's mind was wrapped in cotton wool; she had no way to take up the fallen words and no words to return to her old friend. When Bridget wished for a child of her own, Maggie shrugged. Eleanor had written her, every week— one of the letters said that sister Kate was expecting a baby too. *Take mine instead,* Maggie thought, *good luck to you. I want to shed my burden.*

As Bridget took her leave, Maggie overheard Rose complaining to Bridey in a whisper, "She has no mind of her own, she's like a child herself."

I've lost my husband, Maggie thought angrily; a*nd Mam, and my father **again**!* Since that black day when Mrs. Leary confirmed that she had heard from other lips the same tale about Pen

O'Shaughnessy, Mam was an erratic shadow, drinking more than eating, weeping more than speaking. Maggie struggled out of the chair and went to the window. Thin frost webbed the windowpane, and there was a carnage of dead flies inside the sill.

"Come away from the winder," Rose said, "ye'll take a chill."

Maggie was not cold, she was too hot, the blood within her beating hot because of the baby. Last spring, when Rory was alive, there had been a flood that damaged the mill and closed it for three days. She had seen the power of the shouting water carrying away the wrecks of trees. She thought now of how good it would be to gaze down at the rushing force and then close her eyes and step into it. Surely it would be a quick death, and there was no reason for her to be alive any more. Except baby, as Bridey had today reminded her in a scolding tone, as Rose said every day and Mam repeated. When Frank said it too, last night, at supper, Maggie had screamed in frustration.

If she could speak to the Blessed Virgin, she'd tell her, I don't want to hurt the baby, but I can't bear to live another day! "If I want to die, is that a sin too? I'd best go to Confession again, don't you think?" she asked Rose.

Rose scowled: "None of that, Maggie. You just went to Confession not a week ago. Yer holy enough altogether."

"I want to go to heaven when Baby's born," Maggie said.

"And leave ME with the work?" Rose said.

'Tis a joke, Maggie told herself after a few minutes of dudgeon. She saw the loss of her own humor as further proof that she was cleaving closer to heaven. Little Mary came in and ducked behind a chair.

'What are ye about?" Rose said.

"Whissht Mam I'm hiding," Mary whispered.

"In plain sight," Rose muttered indulgently.

Maggie's baby kicked and turned. "Baby likes that," Maggie murmured.

Rose heard her, saying: "A year from now yer own little one will be playing hide and peep with ye."

Baby kicked again. *T'wouldn't be fair to leave a little one with no father or Mam of its own,* Maggie thought. Have I truly lost a sister, did Da leave that baby behind to die? She pushed the thought away. *Dear God,* she prayed, lightly touching her belly, *either both of us live or both die.*

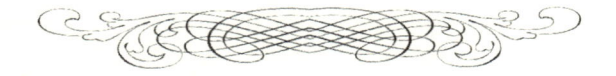

Ned charged through the barber shop door. "You're back, you're home!" he said, pumping Joe Creasey's hand. "You got home, when was it, the last week of November? I'm sorry I didn't meet your train when it came in."

"Minnie and her pa met me at the train—I never was gladder to see anyone in all my days."

"Ah," Ned said, "I guess there will be a wedding soon?"

"No doubt about it," Joe replied, "As soon as we can." Creasey went on, tutting in mock disgust: "Say, you look like a haystack again, Mr. Whitfield. Ain't that Yardley taking care of you?"

"What do you think?" Ned responded.

"I guess it's mowing time," Joe said, waving Ned toward the chair.

Over the snicking of the scissors, Joe said: "I got your letters: it took near a month, longer sometimes, for them to come through. I sent you one too; in August? I can't recollect. And I want you to pass my thank you on to your mother and ladies of the church who tried to send us those supplies."

"Tried? Didn't they reach you?" Ned asked.

Creasey said: "Some of them did, finally. You know, when our regiment was doing duty in the trenches in front of Petersburg, our uniforms turned into rags right quick, our shoes wore right down to nothin' and I spent considerable time a-thinking about those barrels the good ladies sent, all but a few tore apart by some sutler or thieves or Secesh...."

"That's a shame. The 14th was at Petersburg earlier," Ned put in, remembering what George Dunn had written about the battle at the mine crater.

"We relieved the 18th Corps end of August last year and got posted there for a month. We had a little to eat and drink, but nothin' to wash with. It sure was bad, I never have been so hungry, and scratching head to toe from those nasty little graybacks."

Ned sighed. "They're not much of a joke, are they."

"No sir," Joe said, "The secesh folks, the women and such in

Petersburg, I hear they were starvin'... at least we had hardtack." They were silent for a time as Joe trimmed Ned's beard.

Ned said, "Did you say that your regiment was in the 18th Corps?"

"No sir," Joe said, "We relieved them at Petersburg but we were part of the 10th Corps until after we fought at Fort Harrison. That's pretty near Richmond. That was a hot fight. I remembered later on, you told me that the 14th was pinned down for a day, in that field at Sharpsburg, you said. Near Richmond it happened to us. The rebs got entrenched and we were out in an open field for a night and a day."

He stopped trimming. Ned finally craned his neck back to look at the barber, who was staring fixedly at the floor. "That sounds like a bad one," he muttered.

Creasey made a sound. "We ran out of bullets and powder, so we took some from our boys that...that weren't a-going to use them no more...they're so many of us dead and wounded, everywhere, like a man dumped a barrel of trash, all spread around, and the boys that got hurt, we... could hear them calling out for water... for their mamas..." He stopped speaking, cleared his throat, and went on in a thinned voice: "We wanted to help them, we couldn't do a single thing."

"When you're pinned down," Ned began.

"Hope I never see such a sight again!" Creasey suddenly cried out.

For months the war had sat at the back of Ned's mind: dimly seen hills at the edge of the horizon. Yet memories still lit down like a hawk on a mouse—soundless the sudden hit, catch and fly. He had no control over how and when—in the time it took to blink, he was cold skinned, gut clenched—there again. Sometimes the taste of whiskey threw him back into uniform, hiding away from the tents on a dim and drizzling night, idly scratching at the damned lice, passing the bottle to a morose messmate who had joined him. "I'm for it," Lieutenant Forrest had said before Sharpsburg. He had lasted through that battle, though not through the next.

Hope I never see such a sight again, he thought. How long would these recollections swoop, and hold fast? Was this how men who had lived through war went on until death, with the same sordid memories disabling them as unexpectedly as neuralgia did him? Or did time make all mercifully distant and golden-hazed: the men more heroic, the officers bold and wise, the sharp screaming turned to low, graveling pain and finally gentle regret?

"Yes, by God," he said fervently, "By God! I hope we never see such sights again."

Creasey stepped back and put the scissors down on the table, rubbing his hands together. "I'll start on you again in a minute," he muttered. He walked to the window, looked out, one hand on the glass. When he came back to the chair, he said: "Well. Well sir, I'm sorry."

Ned looked at him. "I see them too. I see them again—all we went through. I can't seem to get them out of my mind."

Joe nodded, wiped his hands on his apron, picked up the scissors. "You know I have steady hands. I, it was just that I was thinking about those poor fellows."

Ned nodded.

"If they heard I was shaky, folks would say I drink, and I don't at all. Just a little in the Army…" the barber went on.

Ned replied: "We've all taken too much 'oil of gladness' at one time or another. Too much Tanglefoot, as we called it." He wondered if Billy Vickers had told Joe about the judge's son riding in the baggage car.

Joe said: "Tanglehands is what it'd be for me, and I don't need nothing like that." He held up the scissors. "See there? straight as an arrow. I'm going to work on that thatch under your nose and see if I can get it back to looking like a mustache."

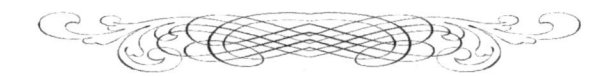

Once again, the Vinton land records thwarted Mr. Putnam in his attempt to advance the interests of his client to flood another man's property.

"That's what the deed said," Ned repeated, "66 rods to the stone wall, and…"

"I can read it!" Putnam interrupted. There was a soft knock at the office door.

"Come," Mr. Mix said.

Davis put his head in. "A Mr. Flynn here to see Mr. Whitfield."

"About what?" Putnam said.

"He said about starting a benevolent provident society," Davis reported and closed the door.

"Is there such a creature as Irish benevolence?" Putnam commented. "I declare, **there's** something for Barnum's menagerie, a provident Irishman!"

Mr. Mix smiled at this and motioned for Ned to go.

"Sergeant Flynn," Ned said, shaking the big man's hand. "Pardon me, Mr. Flynn."

"I was about to call you Lieutenant, sure as you're born," Flynn replied with a smile.

"Come and have a seat here," Ned gestured to the work table, removing a stack of statute books from a chair, and pushing a tower of case digests aside. He pulled the step stool over and sat down.

"How are you?" Ned asked.

"Fine," Flynn replied, "And look at you! 'tis a wonder to me how you made it alive through all that shellin'. When I hauled you out, you were chokin' on your broken teeth, and I was thinkin' this one won't last the hour. I'm glad I was wrong."

The scratch of Davis' and young Morton's pens stopped. As Ned glanced up they dropped their eyes back to their work.

"I'm glad you were wrong, as well," Ned murmured, disturbed by Flynn's description, "And I thank you for hauling me out. Now, I understand that you want to start a benevolent society? Tell me about it and how I can assist you."

"Some of the men get hurt when they're working, and some killed. Did you hear about the fellow died at the Rock mill back in October?" Flynn asked.

Ned's scalp prickled. "Yes," he replied, "and left a widow. Ah, according to the probate papers."

Flynn went on: "And so he did, and that got some of us thinkin'. Us soldiers get a pension, as little as 'tis, but these fellows get nothin' for their family if they can't work or if they die. We heard about an Irish provident society in Hartford: the men in it all give a bit of their wages to the society and if one gets hurt or sick and can't work, the pot of money helps them out. So that's what we'd like to have for ours here. There's some papers you file in the law to start one, so we heard, so they sent me to you."

"The members sent you? And how many prospective members are there?" Ned asked.

"No, Sullivan and Cohan sent me. They said you're working

on their case against Adams, that lyin' scrap of potato peel!" Flynn responded.

"An appeal against the potato peel is under consideration," Ned affirmed.

Flynn laughed. "Cohan's got cold feet, but Adams don't know what he's in for: Sullivan'd sooner be bucked and gagged than give a inch: he'll pay to take it to the highest court. He wants justice." *Hearsay,* Ned thought, but it answered Mix's question about whether the defendants had the means to pay legal fees going forward.

Ned asked Flynn more about the aims of the proposed society; then discussed defining who could be a member, writing and amending bylaws, and finally the procedure for filing documents with the Connecticut Secretary of the State. Mr. Putnam came out of Mix's office and stood close by the worktable, as he made a show of examining a case book.

Flynn looked at him and then at Ned. Ned said coolly: "Is there something you need, sir?"

"Are we starting a benevolent society?" Putnam said to Ned.

"Yes," Ned said through his teeth.

"How laudable," Putnam said, his tone like a scrape from a dull blade, "When you've completed your benevolence, come to my office."

Flynn leaned over the table and spoke quietly after Putnam had left. "Captain Biggars, do you remember that pig-headed lump? This boss—I'm wonderin' if they're any relation one to the other?"

Ned snorted a laugh.

When Flynn said: "Sweep the streets!" and mimed a salute at Putnam's back, Ned busied himself with making notes.

"Well," he said, "I have another question for you. Regarding the man who died at the Rock Mill, do you know if the owner made any provision for the widow?"

Good humor fled from Flynn's face. He growled, "No! No, they never do. "

"So how is his widow to survive?" Ned said, and added: "I mean, perhaps that is an additional purpose your society might consider: aid a widow or family in certain circumstances, even if the husband was not a member. If the funds permit, a more general charitable activity beyond the membership's needs."

"We might, we might," Flynn said, " 'twould be a good thing

to do, if we have the means. I'll ask the fellows who'll be joinin'. And these bylaws, would we be writin' them up, or would we tell you what we want and you can write them?"

"Either way, as you wish," Ned said distractedly, "It's... it's good work you are planning, Mr. Flynn."

"'tis laudable?" Flynn said, his eyebrows raised.

Ned smothered a laugh and said softly: "It appears that the army did not march the rascal out of your hide."

"No sir!" Flynn said.

Chapter 45

The Whitfields' kitchen was smaller than most and crowded now with his mother and Martha contending within it. Ned stayed in the corner, pushing the pestle around in the mortar in preparation for mincemeat pies. Dance weaved in and out among the women, begging for scraps.

"It don't take that long to stone raisins," Martha complained, "You ought to be done! We'll have no time to finish the pies if you dawdle so."

He shrugged. She had scolded him when he was a youth and would not quit it no matter what age he, and she, attained.

"Judge Whitfield will want his supper, and how can I make it up for him, there ain't room to heat it if there are pies in the oven," Martha said.

Mrs. Whitfield made a placating response, moving aside as Martha grabbed the chopper and began to pulverize the meat. A bit of meat flew over and landed on Ned's hand, and the dog shot past the women and to his side. Ned slipped him the scrap, but not quickly enough to elude Martha's notice.

"Stop feeding that dog! We have little enough to make two pies! Get him out of here," Martha commanded.

"Do you want the raisins stoned or the dog out first?" Ned asked his mother.

"The dog..." she began, but Martha interrupted.

"We need those raisins. Shut him in the sitting room."

"The dog needs to go outside," Mrs. Whitfield said firmly.

Ned got up. "I will take him out, and then I'll be back to finish these." He seized Dance's collar.

"I'll join you," his mother said, and at Martha's outrage, she replied: "Ned and I are in your way. You work much faster than I do. I will return as soon as I can, and you can take a rest. You've been run off your feet, and we will all be the better for a recess."

Martha said: "Eleanor is no help at all today, with her...aches and pains or whatever's ailing her. There is no rest for me, ma'am." She chopped the meat more vigorously, muttering additional complaints as Ned hauled the dog out into the hall and tied on the leash. He donned his overcoat, woolen hat, and old boots, as his mother did the same. Defying custom, they left through the front door. Dance "did his business" in the snow, then leapt ahead pulling Ned with him. After a while, the excited dog tired and Ned circled back to his mother who was walking at a slower pace. She smiled at him as he approached.

"Shame on you," she said, "I'd have thought a law student would be an expert at stoning raisins!"

"Phew," he said, "She fancies she could command an army..." His mother seemed so pleased to be away from the kitchen that he said no more. They walked companionably. Ned said: "I hope Katie appreciates our advocacy for her pies."

His mother nodded. "Her appetite is so poor for these first few months; mincemeat pie was the only food that she said appealed to her; and it IS her birthday tomorrow."

In a cold parlor, surrounded by her grieving husband and family, Ned had photographed a young woman who had died in childbirth, with her still, cold infant. "Katie will be all right, won't she?" he said.

"I expect so," Mrs. Whitfield said quietly. After a time, she stopped to pet the dog. "I have you to thank for my escape," she told Dance, who wagged his tail in response.

"Am I walking too fast for you?" Ned asked.

"Heavens, no! It is so good to get out of doors. I've always liked to walk outside, so I could think," she said.

"You don't tighten your stays as much as Katie does...or used to. Not now, of course," he remarked. "I like to walk outdoors too, so I **don't** think."

She nodded. Plucking a tall, dry stalk of weed from the roadside, she trailed it along the snowbank, making an odd pattern in the snow. "Are the nightmares troubling you?" she asked. Ned waved his hand in dismissal.

"Baby is due around the first of May," she went on, "that is Mrs. Moore's guess, but babies follow their own timetable, as you and Dan did. You were expected in October and came in the first week of September. And of course, *you* were not expected at all, since I did not know I was carrying twins. I was astonished, but no more than your father. He was the one who sat with you by the stove to keep you warm."

He had heard the story before. "Before I fell out of favor," he added.

"Before we all fell out of favor," Mrs. Whitfield replied, "And I doubt that any one of us will ever please him."

He looked at her in surprise: she was rarely this frank. On an impulse, he said: "How did father's mother die? Grandmother Whitfield said that she drowned."

Mrs. Whitfield plodded on, not meeting his eyes. She said: "That is all I know."

"By flood? Or accident? Or suspicious accident? Or by her own choice?" Ned asked.

She kept her eyes turned away and said: "I truly do not know. I have always hoped that it was accidental, despite my own disgust at how badly she acted. From what I have heard, she cared not at all for her boy. And despite what Mother Whitfield says, his father was nearly the same. He had charming manners, but I never knew what to think of him." She pulled her hood tighter around her head. "Two selfish people, I'm afraid. Your father made me promise..."

"Promise what?" Ned put in anxiously. She shivered a little.

"Before we married, that I would be a good mother, and would always be faithful and tied to home."

"And you are a good mother!" Ned asserted.

"And tied to home," his mother added wryly.

"Which is not to your liking," Ned announced.

Mrs. Whitfield did not answer. So, he told her about the appeal, about Attorney Lang's comments, about Mr. Flynn's visit and the proposed Millville Irish Brotherhood and Mutual Benefit Provident Society.

"What a wonderful idea!" his mother exclaimed, "what did you advise?"

He wiped ice off his mustache with his mitten. "To shorten the society's name." At his mother's chuckle, he continued: "And to consider assisting widows of Irish lineage even if the husband was not a member."

"Do you think that they will? Will they help Maggie?" she asked.

"I don't know," he said, "I wonder if she is...if she will be all right."

Mrs. Whitfield said: "Her baby is due quite soon. Mrs. Moore is looking in on her whenever she is able."

He slowed his pace, the snow squeaking under his boots in place of conversation. "Will you... Tell me when it happens, if you please." His mother nodded, shivered again, and he said: "Shall we go back?"

"I suppose we must," she said reluctantly. She dropped the weed, and picked up the dog, who snuggled against her.

When the house came into sight, he said suddenly, "Maggie was not like the others. She far excelled Harriet, despite her social station." He kept walking.

"I know that," his mother said, behind him.

He went on rashly: "Father mocks the Seeleys because they are farmers—as if that was not respectable—as if it was not honest work! I've heard him hold it over your head, even now."

His mother said: "Yes, he does, but I pay no attention."

Ned stopped: "He's the worst of hypocrites: he blames them for their lack of social standing, when it's clear to me now that he came from so little himself. And the other Whitfields never came to his aid when he was a boy, did they?" His mother shook her head. After a time, he muttered, "There's more of a Dickens story there than I would have imagined."

At the front gate, she said: "Eddy, hear me, because you know that I do believe that one's social class can rise or fall and is not a measure of one's character, I have certainly witnessed that in my life. My only objection to Maggie is her Papism, and, to be fair, that is nothing she chose for herself any more than her station of birth. She has done wonders for Elly."

Surprised joy shafted through him. "Yes," he said, ready to go on, but thought better of it, and shut his mouth. Instead he announced: "When I have completed my law studies, Mama, and am a lawyer, I intend to go to San Francisco to join Uncle Benjamin. And I'll take you with me, and Elly too: we'll give her enough laudanum to sleep all the way. We'll find a place to live where Elly can have her garden year 'round, and we'll call at will on Uncle

Benjamin and the California Seeleys, and leave Father and Martha here to rule their kingdom of vexation!"

Mother laughed. "I should be delighted to see the rest of our country!" she said, "What a glorious dream! Do keep that ambition for yourself, my dear. And I shall bring it to mind to comfort me when I am blue. But my duty will…

"Tie you to home? **Bind** you to home!" Ned said. His mother did not answer.

As they tracked through the fresh snow to the back door, she said: "Mind your wet boots. Martha cleaned the floor this morning and…"

Ned interrupted her: "Martha can go hang."

"Tch, tch," Mrs. Whitfield clucked her tongue, sounding like Kate. Dance yipped and wagged his tail.

"Dreaming of more mincemeat, are you old boy?" Ned said. He said to his mother: "Are you saying the dog has more chance of getting what pleases him, than you or I ever will?"

Mrs. Whitfield sighed: "I'm sure there is ample work in San Francisco for an attorney. Have you written to Benjamin about this?" They opened the back door, and Martha trundled into the kitchen looking as if she had quaffed liquid brimstone.

"No, but I will," Ned said.

"Do," his mother said, with a defiant smile as she dutifully wiped her boots on the mat.

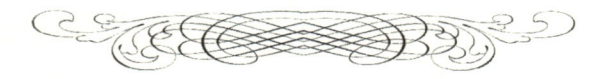

"Mary, save a bit of cake for yer Aunt Maggie," Rose scolded. The child turned her back and downed the last piece of fruitcake that Mrs. Whitfield and the other church lady had delivered in a Christmas basket. "For shame," Rose said to her without much conviction, "What if Maggie is hungry too?"

"She's fat," Mary said.

"She's about to have a new baby, and she's not fat enough, in truth. Tell her you're sorry and run and fetch me some kindling," Rose replied.

"Sorry," Mary mumbled and wandered off to take her cloak from the peg by the back door.

Maggie kept her tongue. She had not slept much for several

nights, with weight of the baby pressing on her bladder, and Paddy snoring, and Mam sprawled across their shared bed. Today she had a griping pain deep inside. Like an over-ripe apple ready to be crushed in the press for cider, she wished to peel her own skin and jump out of it into freedom. *You test us,* she thought, then took it back for 'twas surely a sin to find fault with God's ways. If God took Eve from Adam's rib why couldn't a baby come from there too, and then the hole sealed up as good as new? She took up the pile of mending and started on Denny's trousers. After a moment, she looked up at Rose in confusion.

"It hurts," she said.

Rose put down the paring knife and came to her. "Where?"

Maggie shook her head, sweating. When the pain passed, she pointed down and said: "'tis like a bad monthly!" Rose nodded.

"Well, 'tis about time, I'm thinkin'. Baby is on the way. Tell me when the next comes."

"Call Mrs. Moore!" Maggie wailed.

"Never you mind her, dearie," Rose said kindly, "You've a long road to go before Mrs. Moore comes."

"It hurts too much. I can't do it!" Maggie said, wiping her eyes on the trousers. Rose shrugged, and patted Maggie's shoulder. "Och, but you must. We all do somehow."

At breakfast, Martha reported that preparations were complete for the New Year's Day callers.

"Edward," the judge said, "with this ague in my shoulder, you must drive the sleigh while we make our evening calls." Ned broke up a piece of toast and buttered it, then said: "I have an obligation to call on my friends in the late afternoon. In fact, I've been invited to a wedding supper."

"Who?" the judge demanded, "I have not heard of any weddings."

Ned replied: "Mr. Creasey and Minnie Park."

The judge put down his cup with a loud clank. The dark liquid slopped onto the tablecloth. "Moses Park's girl?" he snarled, "and **Mister** Creasey—you mean that barber who's as black as the ace of spades? Are you mad? What foolishness: you will NOT go!"

"I will go," Ned replied hotly, "I have already accepted the invitation: they are both respectable, so I do not understand why you…"

"Oh no, on the contrary," the judge said, "You do understand, but you choose to ignore me. It is fine to do business with a colored fellow such as Moses Park, as we do for our butter and eggs and sundries, or to have them cut your hair, or to show them charity, as Kate did in Washington, but it is not acceptable to call upon them!"

Ned had learned at Mix's knee that, given a space of silence in the presence of an attorney, some clients provided their own answers, revealing much about themselves. Whether they were right or wrong, it was often unwise to disabuse them of their notions. He knew as well that sometimes delivering a well-crafted answer with only a portion of the truth sufficed to satisfy men: it was useful knowledge, yet he wondered why this and other legal artifices sometimes felt like a sharp pebble in his shoe.

He said: "I attended Phin Shackelford's wedding because he was in my regiment. Joe Creasey served honorably in the 21st colored troops. I saw nothing in the newspaper about Phin's wedding, and as you pointed out, presumably correctly, that was because he married a Fish; so, I doubt that Mr. Creasey and Miss Parks' wedding supper will be reported."

"You cannot be sure of that," his father rejoined.

"If it is reported, and I am one of the guests named, I will point to the fact that I have attended the weddings of each and every Millville veteran to which I've been invited," Ned said.

"Now you sound like a lawyer," his father replied, as Ned grimaced. "This fellow and Minnie will like as not be expecting quite a pretty gift from the judge's son. Ha! Wait 'till they see you've come empty handed. You are up to your ears in debt."

Better to amuse or confuse the enemy, Ned thought. He said: "Father, I will endeavor to return early so I that I can drive you for our evening calls."

The judge said: "Get that sleigh back here by 5:00 or there WILL be hell to pay."

The race of New Year's Day visitors began in the late morning. Miss Minton and her wealthy father were the first out of the gate, much to Eleanor's delight and the judge's satisfaction. Ned was cornered by Mrs. Carpington Highnostril Eller and her large but lamblike husband, Justice Eller's brother. Mrs. Eller questioned Ned minutely about the George Dunn incident, and lavished praise upon George's father and stepmother—how bravely they were standing up to the scandal—and then excoriated both the father and dead mother for raising a criminal. Mr. Eller put in his two cents with vigorous nods and frequent utterances of: "Indeed!"

Ned saw Mrs. Moore arrive but could not make his way to her. She spoke briefly to Mrs. Whitfield and Eleanor, stiffly delivered New Year's wishes to the judge, then nodded to Ned with a meaningful look, and took her leave. An hour later, Mrs. Whitfield motioned to her son. When he followed her into the kitchen, she said: "Maggie had a baby boy the day after Christmas, and both of them are well." He nodded, not bothering to hide his relief. "Go a little early to the Parks," she added, "so you'll have more time to visit—and give them my best wishes."

Part Three

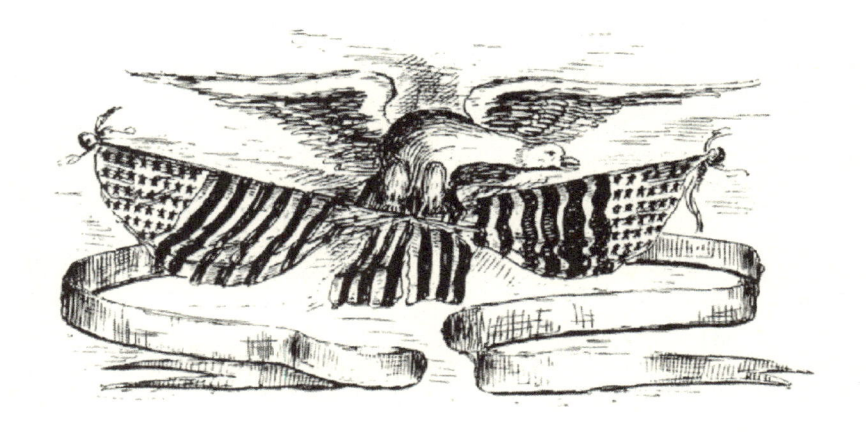

1866 - 1867

Chapter 46

The manufactory's morning bell woke Maggie, who stumbled out of bed, stepping around the trundle bed where little Mary slept. She used the chamber pot behind the curtain; her breasts tight, she peeked into Baby's cradle: he was sleeping soundly and had done so since the midnight feed—now for the third night. She grinned at him; surely he was the best child who'd ever been born, her little James. She got back into the bed, trying not to wake her Mam, her niece or the boys.

As Rose grumbled and got up in the adjoining room to poke at the stove and at her husband, Maggie enjoyed the moment of waking peace. It seemed forever to her since she'd had a moment of real sleep. Before Baby came, there were the days of weeping for Rory and the terrors in the dark about dying in childbed. Since Jem was born, there were all of the nights she had gritted her teeth at the discomfort of her own innards—turned inside out and wrung like wet laundry—beginning to take their proper place again. Every evening, she had longed for her narrow solitary bed at Mr. Merritt's or Mrs. Ives' where if someone cried it was not her job to see to them. During Baby's first month she had taken him into bed with her and Mam, drowsed while he nursed, then awakened with terror that she had smothered him. She was afraid to leave him in his cradle near the stove and got up every hour to make sure that he had not frozen in the night. Rose told her this would pass.

Through the dirty window Maggie could see the slanting pink light. In her mind, she was painting it, clear and triumphant. *I am back! My own self*, she thought with surprise, sitting up straight in bed—as ready to dash into the day as if she had drunk a strong cup of tea. *I been gone such a long time, in the wild.*

Two days later, she was at the dish tub, staring out the window. The buds on the trees were starting to soften and would open soon.

Rose said to her: "Och, our Jem just said a word. His first word."

Maggie turned from the tub. "Pooh, I heard nothing. He's too little to be talking." Her sister-in-law and niece were smiling widely. Jem was in his grandmother's arms.

Maggie stroked his hand and said: "Truly? What did he say?"

Little Mary giggled. "It's a joke!" She had left her disdain for the baby cousin behind once he had begun to smile at her.

Mam said: "He don't say much yet, but ain't he the best little boy in seventeen counties?"

"And I'm the best little girl," Mary asserted.

There was a knock at the back door and Mrs. Moore came in.

"Baby and I are well," Maggie said to her in surprise.

"Maggie, I need you. As soon as you are able to come!" Mrs. Moore said. "Mrs. Fariday had her baby nearly two days ago but she is very ill and cannot feed him. Would you come with me and see if you can get him to eat? He's early, and such a tiny thing, and I am afraid he won't last long without nourishment."

"Mother of Mercy," Maggie said, "I will. Surely I... I'll do anything I can."

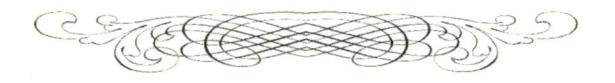

Turned away again from Katie's bedchamber, Ned staggered down the stairs and sat heavily on the bottom step. He sat without moving, hoping that if he was still enough, life would turn like the earth and right itself. Through the closed door upstairs, he could hear his sister moaning. He got up and dashed into the back parlor to escape the sound. But someone was there in the dark room: an unknown woman dressed in black except for her white collar and cuffs, with a black ribbon tying her hair. No, by God! It was Maggie. Night after night he had imagined her again with him, and the things that he would tell her! But she now looked at him with the cold eyes of a stranger.

"What are you doing here?" he said, stepping back. She patted the bundle at her bosom. "Feeding your nephew—trying to…" she said, and there was the familiar, rather odd little voice he had loved. All of his reactions slowed; he found it difficult to form any words.

He said: "It's alive?"

"He," Maggie said, "I don't know his name, perhaps he ain't been named yet."

Ned shook his head. "Nameless heir to the Whitfield name," he muttered, "No. Fariday. Fariday of course." Something grizzled in the basket. Edward swung around. "What's that?"

"My son," Maggie said.

"It sounded like a squirrel," he said. He moved gingerly around her, edged toward the basket, peered into it. "Well," he said, "Yes, I… I heard that you had a baby. That you had a boy. Mrs. Moore told me. After Christmas."

Then he was silent. The house was very quiet. Maggie nervously checked the infant in her arms to reassure herself that he was still breathing. She and Edward listened for any sign from the sick room upstairs "How is…" she began.

"Christ almighty, they won't let me in," he groaned, "I'm afraid… What am I to do?" He rubbed his blind eye beneath the patch.

"I'm sorry," Maggie said, "I'm so sorry! But I…" she stopped, uncertain whether it was wise to tell him what she had seen not half an hour before: a vision of Kate wearing a black dress and a large veiled hat, standing at the pier table in this room, removing her veil and weeping.

Edward pulled out his handkerchief. He covered his face with it for a moment. *Like they covered Rory's poor broken head,* Maggie thought. She shivered. Kate was alive in her vision, but who was she mourning?

"You must fetch Eleanor," she said, "She ought to be here."

He dropped his handkerchief and advanced on her, almost grabbed her arm. "Why?"

"She ought to be here with her sister," Maggie said again.

"Did you have a vision?" He gazed at her with horror. Maggie's skin prickled. ***Now he believes I have the sixth sense,*** she thought, *'though sure enough, I don't. I never saw Rory's leaving.* She said: "She has healing hands, so you said. I just know she must come."

"You did see something! Dear God, what? No, don't tell me." He closed his good eye and covered his mouth with his hand.

"Mercy! I don't know what will happen. 'tis in God's hands," she said hastily. Then: "Do go and bring her here."

He said from behind his hand: "She won't come. You know that."

Maggie replied: "Did anyone think to tell her she's <u>needed</u> here? Tell her that and she will come."

He nodded slowly, then wandered out of the room, out of her presence, as if he had lost his way.

She went to Jem's basket—her child had dropped back into sleep. *A squirrel, he said!* she thought, annoyed. *My own dear baby boy.*

She cupped her hands around the un-named newborn's head. He grimaced and whimpered. "You must live," she whispered fiercely, "there must be something good come of this! Now you drink." She sat down and tried everything she could think of to stimulate the child to suckle. Her milk was coming too fast. The baby coughed and cried weakly.

Maggie wept with frustration, and then with grief for all the lives she could not mend. The tears and milk flowed, salt and sweet mixed, and she wiped her face with the wet blanket, rubbed the baby's cheeks with her thumbs, wet a finger with milk and put it in the baby's mouth. There was a feeble suction. She repeated the action, taking a drop from breast to finger to the infant's mouth. Baby swallowed. With more going onto the blanket and her bodice than into the child, yet Maggie crooned to him, and he began to awkwardly suckle.

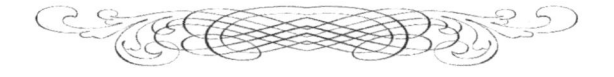

Ned walked slowly around the Fariday house as the sun was setting. *She has healing hands*, he repeated to himself like a marching cadence. The Whitfields' gray horse, still hitched to the chaise, had pulled the reins from the hitching post and was cropping at a small tuft of new grass. With no conscious thought, Ned checked the harness, then climbed into the judge's chaise, and found himself on the road to the Whitfield house.

Dance's barking ceased as he came in the back door. Martha met him there. "No news," he told her. "Where is Eleanor?"

"Up in her chamber," she said, "I expect she's asleep."

"It's not time to sleep," he replied. He took Dance's leash from its hook by the back door, then shouted Eleanor's name.

Eleanor cried in panic from the second floor and clattered down the stairs. "It can't be!"

"No news," he replied. She slumped onto the kitchen chair, white-faced. Her dress was creased and crumpled. Dance looked at his mistress as Ned fastened the lead on the dog's collar.

"Get your shawl," he commanded his sister, "I'm taking you to see Kate."

"I can't, you know how much I want to! Don't be cruel, you sound like Papa."

"Maggie said you have healing hands. Katie needs you there," he went on.

Eleanor gaped at him. "Maggie? Maggie is there?"

"She's there to nurse the baby. She had a vision about Kate. She said you must come."

"I can't!" his sister shrieked.

He was not prepared to cajole her or repeat years' worth of arguments. Over the dog's whine, he said: "By God, Eleanor, if you ever do it, you must do it now."

Eleanor moaned and began to cry hysterically. Dance yipped and strained at the leash; Ned let go and the dog went to her.

Martha said: "Come, Elly, you'll have to go the funeral service when she passes. Go and see her now and say your goodbye."

He watched his sister shake and wail, but was not affected by her distress, only single-minded in his purpose. He said calmly: "You have healing hands. Maggie said you are needed there. I have the chaise outside. I'll light a lantern, and Dance can ride with you. You'll be safe with me."

He grasped the leash. Dance resisted, hovering near his mistress. "Do I have to carry you?" Ned asked the dog, who looked at him mournfully.

Eleanor sobbed out: "No. Wait".

He fetched the lantern, returned, and lit it. They waited. Eleanor had not moved.

"It's time," he said. Slowly his sister stood and picked up the dog.

When they reached the Fariday house, Ned lifted her down and supported her as she crept toward the door like an old woman expecting a blow. The dog ran back and forth, barking in confusion. Mrs. Carruthers opened the back door, captured the dog's leash and pulled him into the kitchen: all the while calling for Mrs. Whitfield. After sweeping her daughter into an astonished embrace, with tears and exclamations, mother ushered her up the stairs to Kate's bedchamber.

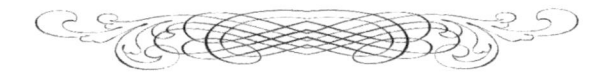

"No news," Ned muttered, setting the lantern in the middle of the floor, as his father paced in the unfinished tack room of the new stable, an unsmoked pipe in his hand.

"Well, some news," he amended, "Eleanor is here."

"Are you drunk?" the judge said in a monotone.

"I wish I was," Ned said. "No. Eleanor is here."

"Don't try to joke with me, boy. I won't have it," his father said.

Ned replied: "I'm not joking. She's up in Kate's room."

"Great God in heaven! How…?"

"I put her in the chaise and here we are. Go and see for yourself." The judge dropped his pipe and ran toward the house.

Ned stared at the wall across from him, at the thin lath clenched to the uprights, the horsehair poking through like gristle between bones. He slid to the floor, covered his face with his hands and wept.

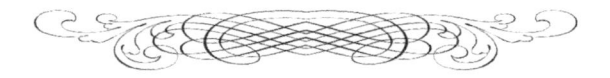

The sun had set, and the room was dim. As Maggie's thirst grew and her stomach growled for supper, Mrs. Carruthers, the cook, and the hired girl, Kathleen Sullivan, came into the sitting room to usher her and the two infants into the warm kitchen. Maggie bathed the babies and wrapped them in clean toweling and blankets as Mrs. Carruthers set out a meal of hot stew, good bread, cheese, and cider.

While they ate, Kathleen told Maggie that Mrs. Leary had

been there yesterday with her crew to do the laundry again for there was lots of bloody mess from the Missus, poor thing, she was still hoped to live; and there was a laundry room in the basement with running water and a boiler and even a water closet! Mrs. Carruthers added that the nursery on the third floor was unfinished since baby had come early. She and Kathleen discussed where to put Maggie and the boys, deciding on the family sitting room where Maggie had been thrust earlier that day. The two women gathered supplies from around the house: a basket for Baby Fariday, a basin, pitcher, and chamber pot for Maggie. Mrs. Carruthers donated her footstool, an extra pillow, blanket, and her own rocking chair. They piled these supplies in the sitting room. As Maggie settled little boy Fariday and began to feed Jem, Mrs. Carruthers demonstrated how to work the gas light, then both women disappeared.

Rocking, comforting, and dozing by turns, Maggie heard a man speaking in the hall: it sounded like the judge, but it could have been his like-sounding son. *No matter which of the two,* Maggie thought, *I must leave this place, the sooner the better. But I'll not go while anyone still needs me.* Baby boy Fariday had surprised her by taking a second feeding - however brief.

Making a nest of blankets for herself, she curled her body onto the parlor sofa. She was awakened just before dawn, not by a squalling baby but by a dog's cold nose and friendly whuff. She patted Dance and smiled sleepily in the dark.

Chapter 47

Ned savored the fine cigar as he watched his brother-in-law struggling to let down his guard. Dr. Green (three days later than Mrs. Moore) had proclaimed Kate "on the mend". Yet Fariday stood by the door of the unfinished guest room, a lit but unsmoked cigar in his fingers, and listened for his wife.

"Sit down," Ned said, "She'll be all right."

Fariday made his way to a chair, balanced the cigar on its arm, and rubbed at his prosthetic leg. "This blasted thing!" he snarled, "It will never fit right."

"If you want to go to bed, I'll be on my way," Ned replied, "When is the last time you had any sleep?"

"No, stay awhile," Fariday said. He lit the cigar, dragged on it, coughed, wearily brushed ash from his waistcoat. "When is Mother Whitfield coming back? She's been talking to the help for me. I ought to get back to the manufactory soon."

Before Ned could answer, Fariday went on: "He has not come to see Katie in days, and now he's keeping her mother away from her! What on earth is he thinking?"

"He was elected state representative just before Kate took ill," Ned put in, "And he would tell you Mother is needed to prepare him for the journey to New Haven to be sworn in and begin his hobnobbing."

Fariday grunted. Ned went on sarcastically: "Come now, Fariday, this is the pinnacle of his success!"

"Don't tell me she is going to New Haven with him," Fariday said.

"In a pig's eye!" Ned retorted, "She'll stay here, and frankly, I can't speak for her, but I'll be glad to see him go." They smoked in silence for a time.

Fariday said: "I suppose I ought to speak to the help about their wages, and so on. They seem to be competent."

"I've been acquainted with Mrs. Carruthers for a while," Ned said, "and Mrs. Corcoran." Fariday looked blank. "The nursemaid," Ned added.

"Yes. Yes, Mrs. Moore says she does a good job," Fariday remarked, "And your little sister has been helping all around. I'm glad she's here. I expect she's still afraid of me, though. She always ducks out of sight when I pass by." He stubbed out the cigar on the bottom of his shoe. Groaning a little, he poked at his leg. "I guess I ought to look in on the baby. I... just don't... it's... I forget he is here. It's all been such a... a..."

A Fredericksburg, Ned thought. He said: "You're played out." He stood up and grabbed Fariday's crutch. "Here, take this. I can't order you because you outrank me."

"Not anymore," Fariday said.

"True, so take off that leg and go to bed." Ned replied.

Fariday sighed and reached for the crutch.

Maggie awoke before the babies, as first light came through the nursery window. She rolled over, and admired the handsome wainscoting, the delicate new wallpaper, Jem's sturdy crib and Baby Fariday's ornate cradle. *Better than that,* she thought, *what happened yesterday!* Mr. Fariday had called her into one of the guest chambers, and asked how she was faring. She was a bit afraid at first that he would tell her they had found a replacement nurse, then stunned to silence by the generous wage he offered for her continued employment. Seeing her open-mouthed surprise, he had upped the number, at which Maggie had stammered out a grateful yes. *How much higher might the number have gone, if I'd bargained a little,* she wondered now, *Well, too late for that... och, you'd think my brains were leaking out with my milk.* Jem made waking noises in his cot. *But 'tis also like a dream,* she told herself—such a pleasant place and so much money coming in for her labors.

She liked reading novels where a young man made his fortune, and a young woman found her love; wasn't it queer that the books never told the story the other way around? The men and girls in the books made their way in the world by wit, courage, talent, a good marriage, or good luck. *I've made my fortune, oh ho, I have,* she thought, *but with my breasts, and no one would ever put that in a book.* She got up to greet her son.

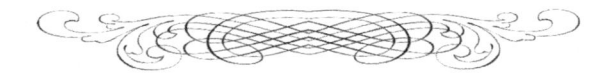

"Mr. Fariday was awfully glad to see you at table for dinner," Eleanor said to her sister.

Kate shrugged as she sagged upon the sofa in the back parlor. "I can't seem to wake up anymore," she said.

I'm the one that Baby's keeping up at night, Maggie thought. As instructed, she spent more time in the sitting room, kitchen, or veranda than in the nursery; Mrs. Whitfield wanted Baby to be part of his mother and father's daily life and become used to household noise and activity.

"Baby is a month old today," Eleanor said.

Kate remained quiet. Finally, she said, "Mrs. Moore says he's feeding well."

"Yes," Maggie replied. She was nursing Baby Fariday now. Jem rolled over on his blanket spread on the carpet and squawked at this accomplishment. Eleanor took him into the rocking chair with her, the chair squeaking as she rocked.

"Does that bother you?" Eleanor asked her sister, slowing the chair.

"Elly, for heaven's sake! I'm not a piece of porcelain!" Kate shouted. Baby Fariday stopped suckling and frowned. Jem's face puckered, ready to cry.

"Hush, hush," Eleanor said, putting him on her shoulder and going to the window so he could look out. "I know what that is like, Katie," she said. Then: "Oh, here comes Ned."

"I'll go up to the nursery," Maggie said.

"No," Kate said, "Stay. Here's my shawl." She arranged it over Maggie's shoulder for modesty, looking at the infant for just a moment. Edward breezed into the room, greeted the women, announced that he had eaten dinner on the march, and sat in the rocking chair.

"This thing needs a good oiling," he said.

"You did not ask how I am feeling," Kate said. He said: "You're right, I didn't. How are you feeling?"

"I'm glad you didn't," she replied.

"Ah," he said, "I'm off the hook."

"How do I look to you?" she asked.

"Beautiful," he said earnestly, then: "I hope that was not a trick question."

"A beautiful hothouse flower," Kate mumbled angrily. "Oh, pardon me, I guess it is polite only to speak of the weather."

He scratched his beard. "Windy and chilly and bright. What is this game?"

Kate stared at him and then said: "It must be glorious to be out of doors. I expect I will be trapped in here forever."

"You had better be out of doors soon. You promised to teach me the game of croquet," he put in. Kate shook her head. Eleanor sat on the sofa opposite Edward and put Jem in her lap facing the guest.

"Good day, Master James," Edward said to him. Jem was unsure what to make of this creature in front of him. He turned his face into Eleanor's chest. Edward quietly sang a bit of nursery rhyme. Jem turned back and stared.

"When have you ever seen such a queer looking fellow, heigh?" Edward asked him. "I remember when cousin Julia was as little as you, she used to look at me just that way, and I had no scars then. So. What do you have to say for yourself, James?"

Eleanor kissed Jem's head. "We call him Jem. He's just a baby, he's much too young to be talking."

"Tell me something I don't know," Edward said equably. He went on, mimicking Eleanor's voice, "Just a baby. Are you going to stand for that slur, Jem? Since you can't stand yet, I guess you'll have to let it pass. You'll have to wait until you're bigger to have your revenge: then you and your comrade over there will cut some capers. But you'll have to watch out, with young Albert. I should warn you that his mother's a renowned mischief-maker. "

"Not any longer," Kate said weakly. Edward's face lost its light. He frowned at the floor, and then at Jem, who frowned back, chewing on the fingers of his left hand. Maggie did not like the silence. She prayed once again for Mrs. Fariday.

Whitfield broke the quiet, addressing the child: "You intend to stare me down, I see. Two can play that game." They did for a minute or two; Maggie was mildly diverted. "This is the most solemn baby I have ever met," he pronounced.

"He's had reason to be, poor little fellow," Eleanor said, wiping drool from his chin.

"No offense intended," Edward said, "I was just trying to see if I could make him smile. I know what your problem is, old man. Your teeth hurt and you don't like living with a wet chin."

"He hasn't any teeth yet, Ned, he's too little," Eleanor retorted.

"Oh," Maggie said, "No, it could be he's cutting his first. I cut my teeth early, so Mam says."

"That's it." Edward seemed pleased at this successful guess. He took out his pocket watch to check the time, then, noticing the baby's interest, he said: "Say, do you like this?" He stood and bent closer to the baby, twirling the watch. Its silver rim caught the shine of the light from the window. Jem made a sound, popped his hand out from between his gums, and reached eagerly for the watch.

"Ned! He can't have that, it's dirty." Eleanor seized it and held it away, as Jem screeched a protest.

"Nothing I own is dirty. He likes it," he replied. Jem had three slippery fingers on the watch where it was closed in Eleanor's grasp. "Let him have it. Unless his mother objects?"

"I don't want him to ruin it," Maggie said.

"It's sealed pretty well. It's been through a rain storm or two," was the response.

Maggie thought suddenly of the thunderstorm, their soaked clothes in the barn, how he had shaken the watch after… and smiled at its steady ticking. "He may have it for a moment, then, seeing as how you don't mind," she said, with her head down, not wanting to know if he meant the comment for her alone.

"Not at all. There you are, Jem, an award for being the most solemn baby in the county," he cooed, then grinned at the child. *Och, there's more to come,* Maggie thought, eyeing Edward, *for he's happy now.* Baby Fariday had finished feeding, so she rearranged her bodice, removed the shawl and held him on her shoulder to burp him. Baby responded with a loud belch.

Edward swung his attention to his nephew. "Albert Worthington Fariday, Junior," he said as he walked to the back of the nursing chair, "That's a long handle for such a short fellow.

Phew, look at that vast and intelligent forehead. You are Albert Worthington Fariday, Senior writ small: a perfect abbreviation in the flesh. A ditto, in fact. Say! There's a name. Ditto! A.W. Ditto Fariday."

Kate stifled a laugh and scowled at her brother. "Ha. Ha. Ha," she said.

Edward played the lawyer. "Come, what is a ditto but the same word or phrase abbreviated to avoid unnecessary repetition?" Baby Fariday squealed and grimaced at gas in his belly. "Ho, you object, Master Ditto?" his uncle said, "Don't fret, soon enough you'll grow to be an ampersand, and if you set your type rightly you can aspire to be, ha! an entire parenthetical expression like your worthy Pa." Eleanor giggled and Kate smothered a snicker.

She said: "You dog! Or a hyperbole like your uncle."

He smiled and countered: "Or perhaps a sardonic exclamation like your sweet Mama." Baby Fariday belched again and made a satisfied sound.

Edward continued: "And your nickname goes in perfect tandem with young Master James'. It sounds like a partnership from Dickens. Jem & Ditto: Purveyors of precious stones and fine duplicative goods, specializing in rubber stamps and repeating rifles..." He stopped to laugh.

Eleanor exclaimed in delight. "It's perfect!"

"Little Nell has spoken, well and truly," Ned said. Hearing a giggle from the corner, he turned to look at Maggie, who smiled slightly. *She does not hate me,* he thought, *she does not hate me!*

"I call him Bertie," Maggie said, patting the baby's back.

"Much better," Kate remarked, settling the matter. Ned bowed to his sister. His long walk from downtown had turned out far better than he could have hoped.

Chapter 48

"I believe you are acquainted with Mr. Lang," Mr. Mix said to Ned, who nodded and shook the attorney's hand. Mix continued: "He prepared an appeal to the state Supreme Court of Errors; when was it? A year or two ago?"

"Three years this fall," Lang said.

"You don't say! Was it that long ago? Tempus fugit. He has agreed to assist us in preparing Adams versus Sullivan and Cohan for appeal; and I would like you to work with him on it, Edward, as Mr. Putnam is far too occupied."

"I'd be glad to," Ned replied. He and Attorney Lang sat at the work table, and Ned opened the first of the case digests he had pulled out at Mix's request.

Lang put his hand out and closed it, saying: "Mix gave me your notes on that patent case—very thorough. He's referring that one to me in exchange for my advice on this tavern case appeal. Do you recall that old yellow dog I told you about last summer?"

"Yes," Ned responded, surprised that Lang would bring up his sister's divorce case against her husband. The passionate affair between Lang's young wife and his sister's older husband had been the primary topic of gossip at the rest cure.

"Well, that yellow mutt has come back home with his tail between his legs," Lang went on, "and that other little pet is home too." Ned glanced at Lang, but the attorney's face gave no clue regarding how he felt about this development.

"Is that so?" Ned prevaricated, aware that young Morton and Davis were listening, as usual.

Judge Whitfield came into the office, breezing past the two

clerks, and calling out for Mr. Mix. He stopped upon seeing Lang. "Mr. Lang, Good day. Did you hear that I was elected to the state house?"

"I did," Lang answered, then after a short silence, he added: "I suppose congratulations are in order."

The judge said: "Perhaps congratulations are in order for you as well? I hear that you have withdrawn your petition for divorce."

Lang grimaced. Morton kept at his copy work, but Davis stopped writing and looked up.

"Took her back, did you," the judge said. When he had no response, he went on: "Well, you're a forbearing fellow. I'm not sure I'd have done the same."

Lang regarded the Judge with open distaste. After a moment, he said: "The quality of mercy is not strained; it droppeth as the gentle rain from heaven, and on the just and unjust alike." *Shakespeare,* Ned thought, *and the Gospel of Matthew.*

The judge scowled at this and said to Lang: "Well, I suppose we ought to heed the Gospel. I would not tolerate such behavior as hers. You're a better man than I am to do so."

"You have said it," Lang responded quietly.

Matthew again, Ned thought, keeping his face as blank as a new slate. "Is this the reporter that you needed, Mr. Lang?" he said, sliding the book toward the attorney.

"Yes," Lang said, "Pardon us, Judge."

As the judge entered Mix's office and closed the door, Lang shook his head, very slightly, glanced at Ned, and opened the volume before him. "Another proverb exploded," he mumbled, "Sometimes the apple falls far from the tree."

Maggie sat in the corner of the kitchen, with Bertie in his basket, and Jem seated on the floor propped up with pillows, near her feet. In between Dance's mournful howls from the stable, she could hear all the Whitfields and Faridays in the dining room at Sunday dinner. The judge spoke loudly above them all about his meeting with Governor Buckingham, and his introduction to the newly elected Joseph Hawley. *Ain't you grand,* Maggie thought crossly.

She hoped that Edward would not leave through the kitchen;

she would be ashamed to see him. A few days before, in the sitting room, he had offered to fetch her some paper and a pencil so that she could draw. "When do I ever have time to breathe!" she had instantly, irritably muttered. He had heard her and retreated across the room.

Well, 'tis true enough! she thought now, *but I oughn't to have snapped at the man.* She got up to right Jem, who had tipped over onto the blanket. As she rearranged the pillows and moved the spool toy closer to him, last night's bad dream still crouched in her mind: she had left her son in the laundry basket and Mrs. Leary had carried him away with the dirty clothes. Maggie was charged with the crime of abandonment and was bound and brought before a large dark door for the prince to judge her. Mother of God, when Baby cries, you'll hear him and find him! she had protested. She was sure the prince was Rory, but instead it was Edward Whitfield, perfectly unscarred, and dressed in a golden suit, but cold-mannered. 'You had your chance,' he said, but then he commanded: 'Untie her hands.'

For mercy's sake, it ought to have been Rory chiding her: she had not dreamt of him since his child was born. That dangling thread, once stepped upon, unraveled her resolve: what would Rory think to see her here among the kin of her former beau? If he could see from heaven, surely he would be mad with anger. She shivered. Somebody's walking over your grave, Mam always said when someone was a-shiver. Maggie picked up Jem, kicked the pillows under the chair, grabbed Bertie's basket and climbed the back stairs to the nursery.

After the two boys went to sleep, she sat still in the upholstered nursing chair. *I must make a living, to care for our boy,* she told Rory in her mind, *certainly that's the right thing to do.*

Someone with a heavy tread was climbing the front stairs to the third floor. Maggie checked her bodice to make sure it was fastened, and stood up, ready to speak to Mr. Fariday.

Judge Whitfield entered, alone. He peered around in the dim light, located his grandson's cradle, and gazed down at him. "He looks puny," the judge said, "Are you feeding him properly?"

"Yes, sir," Maggie said. "Mrs. Moore is pleased."

The judge advanced upon her. "And you, undoubtedly, are pleased to be drinking porter and sitting in the lap of luxury. The little stray cat has lapped up all the cream."

Maggie stepped back towards Jem's crib. *Porter?* she thought scornfully, *it tastes like dirt.*

He went on: "This temporary good fortune is all due to circumstances, you know."

Maggie shrugged.

"Speak up!" he said, "I asked you a question, so you must speak up."

"Yes, sir," she said.

He stared at her for a moment, then said: "You've been very fortunate in your acquaintance with my daughter—although that will soon pass, now that she has the right sort of friends. Miss Minton, you have heard of her, I'm sure. You must abandon any notion that my daughter will keep up any friendship with you. Eleanor merely pities you."

You don't know her at all, Maggie thought, pushing away a pinprick of doubt. Since it was what he seemed to be expecting, she said aloud: "Yes, sir."

He moved closer, only a foot or so away. Maggie did not step back. He said: "As soon as my daughter's boy is old enough to take food and tinned milk, you'll no longer have a position here. In the meantime, you will have nothing to do with my foolish son. If you have any notions in your head about him, quench them now, or I'll ensure you lose your position immediately."

You blackguard, Maggie thought, *you hateful puffed-up blockhead.* She answered: "Yes sir," but after she thought a moment, she added: "whatever *Mr. Fariday* says."

"I'm telling you!" he shouted, "You conniving Biddy, if you think you'll set your cap to lure my son, I will…"

Feeling Rory shouting in her heart, Maggie interrupted: "That again—stop your talk!" She rushed to the bedside table, snatched Rory's picture and nearly thrust it in his face. "This! This is the man I love! Don't you dare to tell me of any other man. I lost the one I love!"

"Don't you dare to raise your voice to me," the judge admonished, but it was half-hearted, and he stepped back.

Angry tears stopped Maggie's voice. She held the photograph to her chest, wiped her nose with the back of her hand. Bertie was crying with little mews.

The judge said, "I intended to come up here to see my grandson, and now you've got him crying."

As his nurse and his grandfather faced each other, Bertie's cries wound down. Maggie pulled a handkerchief from her sleeve and mopped her eyes.

The judge put his fingers in his vest pocket, saying: "My wife trusts Mrs. Moore, so I suppose you may remain for now. And of course I am aware you are a widow; I am the judge of probate, for heaven's sake. My wife wished you to have a little token of her appreciation." He took a coin from the pocket and held it out to her.

Maggie glared at it. "No need for that, I'd do anything to help. Mrs. Whitfield was kind to offer it, and I thank her, but Mr. Fariday pays me well," she said.

He made an exasperated sound. "Remember who you are!" he admonished. Jem began to cry, and Maggie looked over toward his cot. "Take it, take it for your boy," he went on, "If not in gratitude to my wife."

It looked to be a gold coin. Maggie inched forward. "For my boy, I will; and in thanks to Mrs. Whitfield." She took the coin; it was hot in her hand. She put it on the table, anxious to get it out of her fingers.

The judge said: "You don't rule the roost here. If you are saucy to me or any of my family, you will be out the door. I intend to come and see my grandson whenever I wish. You had better not show him even a particle of that bad temper of yours..."

Maggie said, "I'd never!" He shook his head at her in disgust, stared into his grandson's bed, then left.

Chapter 49

"It's Miss Minton come to see you again," Kathleen said, handing the calling card on a tray to Eleanor, who replied, "Oh! She's early for the party."

"I'll go up to the nursery," Maggie said.

"No, stay, Maggie. I'd like you to meet Rebecca. My two friends!" Eleanor said, then asked Kathleen to show the visitor in.

Bless your heart, Elly, Maggie thought, *your Father don't know you one bit. I hope I look proper; I hope I smell decent!* Bertie had just brought up a little milk with his burp, and it had landed on Maggie's apron.

Miss Minton came in and Eleanor made the introductions. *How tall she is, such deep brown eyes,* Maggie thought, *I'd like to paint her; yes, as a pirate or adventurer from long ago.*

Miss Minton paid little attention to her, but Maggie was pleased to see the woman's smile bloom as she turned to Eleanor. "I came early, Elly, to let you know that I will unfortunately be late to your birthday party this afternoon. My father needs me to accompany him to a business meeting. Do you remember me mentioning Mr. Schwarzkopf from New York? The fellow who has a new turbine patent?"

"Oh, yes," Eleanor said.

"I studied the patent designs when we were in New York and am more familiar with them than Papa is, so I must attend. But I will be here as soon as I can be," Miss Minton went on, as she sat down on the sofa opposite Maggie's rocking chair. "I would not miss it for the world."

"I'm so glad!" Eleanor said, with delight, "And you will get to meet Mr. Barton. I'm sure he will be so interested to talk to you."

Miss Minton closed her eyes for an instant. "Mr. Barton?" she said, quietly. "One of your brother's friends, I think you said," then the slender hope in her expression snapped dead like a mouse in a trap, as Eleanor replied.

"He's a wonderful gentleman! I played the piano for him at our last visit. He's been away in Europe ever so long. Do you remember, Maggie, I read his letters to you, about the ruins he saw in Rome?"

"Yes," Maggie peeped, suddenly saddened by Miss Minton, but not sure why. There was a short silence. "Oh, I must go," Maggie said, "I've got to get this little one up to bed."

Miss Minton made a polite reply as Maggie got up from the rocking chair and put Bertie against her shoulder and Jem on her hip.

Maggie stopped and said lightly: "Eleanor talks about you so much, how smart you are, and how you both go out for such grand rides, and what a good friend you are to her, so I'm glad to meet you."

Miss Minton glanced at Eleanor, as if her head had a will of its own.

"Oh, yes I do," Eleanor agreed earnestly.

"It was nice to make your acquaintance, Maggie," Miss Minton then said. *Well, a little less cool to me, anyhow,* Maggie thought, and took her leave.

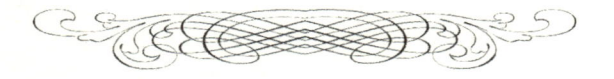

Ned liked croquet better than he had expected to, and more so after he sent Katie's croquet ball with a sharp whack into the flower bed. Henry made a joke which made Kate raise her eyebrows and two of the Misses Topliff giggle loudly. Ned ambled over to his friend and the two misses, as Kate went to retrieve her ball. "What witticisms of yours did I miss, Henry?" he asked.

"Countless gems," Henry replied.

The middle Topliff daughter said gleefully: "He said that he's glad the little dog was locked away, or he'd have sent it flying with his mallet!"

"Is that so," Ned said, disturbed by the image. It was true that Dance had been a nuisance during the beginning of the croquet game. "He's a good dog, most of the time," he added. "Don't let Eleanor hear that joke: she is very fond of him."

Henry twirled the mallet between his hands. "Don't insult my intelligence. I've seen how fond she is of the little creature. You know I don't like dogs. The only pet I want a lady to have is me." He grinned at the two Topliffs, who twittered appreciatively. They moved on with the game. Ned saw the middle sister go to the youngest and Eleanor and say something, as the youngest sent Eleanor's ball off the course. Ned prepared to hit his own ball, but a glimpse of Maggie at the sitting room window spoiled his aim and his shot missed the wicket.

As Eleanor and Miss Minton approached, he saw the youngest Topliff whisper something to Henry, clinging just a little too long to his arm; the two shared a laugh. Ned hastened over to greet Miss Minton, and it was he who steered her toward Henry, and he who made the introductions.

"Mr. Barton has just returned from the grand tour of Europe, Miss Minton. Henry, Miss Minton has traveled widely there with her father, who is owner of the Lockett Mill here in town."

"Eleanor has mentioned your interesting letters from Rome, Mr. Barton," Miss Minton said coolly. She was exactly the same height as Henry Barton.

"Yes," Henry said, "I find it difficult to adjust to life in Hartford, after all that I have had the privilege to see overseas. Miss Minton, I understand that your father has a particular interest in the improvement of power turbines." He did not react as the youngest Topliff stifled a giggle.

"He does," Miss Minton said, unruffled, "And I do, as well."

Henry smiled, as if she had been joking. When she continued to stare at him, he said: "How remarkable."

Miss Minton matched his challenging gaze, and it was he who finally shrugged and said, "Join our game, won't you?" and handed her his croquet mallet. "I need some tobacco; pardon us, ladies." He poked Ned's shoulder, "Don't you owe me a cigar, old man?"

The two men sat on the veranda. Ned handed his friend a cigar, lit his own, and waited. "It's a trial, a sore trial," Henry said, "to return to this damned cultural backwater. You have no idea what I've left behind: I attended the opera every week while in Italy."

"Yes, you wrote to me about the opera. What a privilege to hear that!" Ned said.

"Immensely," Henry agreed, "Had things been different I would have studied opera—started in the chorus if need be, but you know that. Instead, here I am back in the desert: no music, no art, no fine wines, no stimulating society, no passionate grown women always ready for something beyond flirting—just a clutch of silly, giggling virgins and a poker-faced Amazon who studies power turbines."

Ned coughed. "Miss Minton is a very intelligent..." he began.

"Come now, Ned. An intelligent woman is an entirely useless article to me," Henry replied, "you know that. Where the devil did you come up with her?"

"I didn't come up with her. She's a friend of Eleanor's from school," Ned replied.

"Girls and their school friends," Henry erupted, "Girls and their little dogs." Ned shrugged.

Barton lowered his voice and recounted the details of a passionate tryst with a French woman.

So many orifices in so many ways, Ned marveled, then remarked aloud, "That's a thumping good story!"

Eleanor and Kate looked over at them. Henry laughed and ceased his story telling. The men smoked a while in silence, watching Miss Minton and the youngest Topliff battling to win the croquet match.

Henry stood up. "I must eat something before I dash off. Say, who is that pretty thing looking out the window? Why isn't she invited to the party?"

"Mrs. Corcoran," Ned said, "Well, you might know her as Miss Shaw. She worked at the photograph gallery."

"Yes, I remember," Henry said, "So some hod carrier did carry her off, eh? What's she doing here?"

"She's a recent widow. She's here as nursemaid to my nephew," Ned answered.

Henry frowned, then said: "Is this all we have to look forward to, puttering at business and marrying some respectable girl and siring brats? No passion, nothing to stir us and all the while listening to nothing better than amateur chamber trios or German brass bands: my God, deliver me!"

The way his friend described this future was decidedly unappealing. Ned shook his head, saying: "You must go to New York as soon as you can. In the meantime, I suggest we forage in the kitchen."

"Capital," Henry replied. He got up and ground his cigar butt under his shoe.

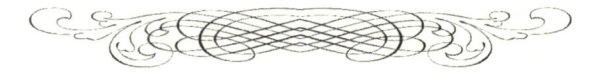

Maggie watched the guests leave from the nursery window. Both boys were napping, so she sat down for a moment herself and began to drowse. Someone knocked softly at the nursery door.

"Maggie?" Eleanor said. Maggie opened the door to her. "I'm sorry that you could not come to the party," Eleanor said. She moved her handkerchief from hand to hand, and her eyes were red.

"I watched from the window," Maggie replied.

"Oh," Eleanor said, "I so wish that those Topliff girls hadn't come. It would have been much better with you and Rebecca. Do you like her? I hope you do."

"I like her, as much as I saw," Maggie said, "And all you've told me of her, she's a grand friend."

"Yes," Eleanor said, "Yes, she is." Now her eyes were wet. "Oh, Maggie."

"You look dreadful tired," Maggie said. She sat on her bed. "What's wrong?"

Eleanor sat, still wringing the handkerchief. "Everything is wrong," she said, "I did it all wrong: I must have. Mr. Barton barely spoke to me all day, and he left early and did not ask me to play the piano, even though he said he would love to hear it. I must not play it as well as I think."

"You play it better than anyone," Maggie said.

Eleanor said passionately, "No, no, I'm sure I do not. Mr. Barton's been to Europe and heard all the orchestras and the opera too, in Italy. Everything has gone wrong, and I'm afraid he does not care for me at all!"

"Mercy, Elly…" Maggie began.

Eleanor interrupted, nervously pulling at her hair. "Dance was very naughty, he was chasing the croquet balls and barking at everyone and mussing their skirts. I knew I ought to have tied him up earlier, but I was so busy getting dressed. Laura Topliff said that Mr. Barton told them if I had not taken Dance away, he would have struck him with the mallet. But I'm SURE he never said such a thing, he would never say such a horrid thing! Would he?" Eleanor said, then answered her own question. "No, he would not."

Maggie recalled the man's scrutiny of her at the photograph gallery. She said uncertainly: "I'm thinking 'twas a joke. Good looking fellows like him, they like to have the girls all around them and making them laugh."

Eleanor thought about this for a while, then dabbed at her eyes. "And they said he...that he...did not like Rebecca, and he called her a giantess, and a...a...man in woman's clothing. But they must be lying, he would not say such a thing." *Men don't tell the truth,* Maggie thought, *they break your heart, and they don't hear you, and they leave you behind.*

Through the ache in her own throat she said, "Faith, most fellows just want what they want. I'm sorry that those girls came, and Mr. Barton wasn't pleasant."

"He was before," Eleanor whispered, staring at the floor. "I must have done something wrong."

Maggie said, "You did nothing wrong. Those bad girls did something wrong, surely, telling you tales just to make you sad - and on your birthday! And Mr. Barton ought to have left them alone."

"Did he say it?" Eleanor wondered aloud, her voice mournful. "Do you think he did?" Bertie began complaining with little cries in his crib.

Maggie bit her lip. "Och, those girls... they just want him for themselves, I'm thinking."

Eleanor covered her mouth. "Oh," she said, "Of course. Oh laws, why am I so stupid?"

Maggie touched her friend's arm. "No, no, you're good, you're too good to think of such a mean trick is all. Not stupid."

"But why did he spend so much time with them? Why'd he leave so quickly?" Eleanor went on.

Maggie said: "Do ask your brother. 'tis his friend." She felt little regret at shifting the burden to Edward, where it rightly belonged. Bertie was now crying in earnest. She took him out of his bed. "He's hungry," she said in apology to Eleanor, but her friend had already left the nursery.

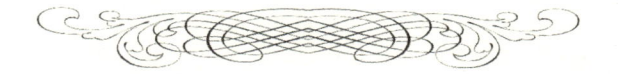

Mrs. Eller was dead, dead as a doornail—as Dickens had written of Marley—and unexpectedly so; it was she who had turned Ned's life topsy turvy. Temporarily installed very early this morning as manager of Mix and Putnam's Law Office while the partners plodded through the deceased's lengthy will and organized her funeral, he blinked like a mole coming out of the earth. In addition to the normal work of the office, five clients were slated to come in today, only to be told (respectfully, graciously! Mr. Putnam had cautioned) that their affairs must take a back seat to Mrs. Eller. Innumerable probate documents were stacked to be copied, some to be certified and all sure to be scrutinized minutely by Judge Whitfield and his clerk. Davis' hand had already cramped, and Morton, Junior fumed at his own ink blots and missing words. Ned raced through the day's mail, making docket notes on each envelope. He tied the bundle with string and placed it in the center of Mr. Mix's desk.

"If you have something short to copy, give it to me," he said to Davis, who handed over a draft letter without a word. Seated again at the work table, he shoved the inkwell next to him, slapped his ruler down on the draft letter and began to make a clean copy on good paper.

Mr. Mix would be pleased, et cetera, to meet with Mr. Jarvis on such and such a date to discuss a breach of promise case in re Miss Jarvis. Ned paused: breach of promise to marry: generally brought by a lady against a gentleman. But just who had broken his own engagement? Though it had been a boon in the long run, it amused him to imagine bringing a breach of promise suit against Hattie Caldwell. He completed the copy, proofread it, blotted it.

Holding the dog in her arms, Eleanor had come to him in tears at breakfast; the tears were nothing new and he had put her off to get to the office early. She had mentioned Barton, but how could Henry have been the cause of her weeping? Merely because he had not stayed to hear her music? Something—presumably the combination of the three Topliffs and Miss Minton—had shaken his aplomb. That remark about Dance was quite a poor choice for a joke. Ned was glad that Eleanor had not heard it. As he wiped the pen's tip, his stomach dropped.

She must have heard of Henry's joke; that, or his remarks about Miss Minton. Through the triple Topliffs' telegraph, no doubt, drat them! But Eleanor was much too sensitive: if she did not like what Barton said, she ought not to be so all-fired eager in future to invite him to everything under the sun and dress up like a fashion plate. She did not do that for anyone else.

He signed the breach of promise letter as secretary. *Hell's bells, I'm an idiot,* he thought, *she must believe that Henry cares for her. Does she think he is a suitor? Impossible!* The idea paralyzed him for a moment. *No, Eleanor, not him. You are as unlike each other as night and day.*

"Can you copy another one, Mr. Whitfield?" young Morton inquired.

"Yes," Ned replied, taking the draft. He sat down. "Tarnation. Now I've lost the ruler."

"It's on the floor," Davis said. Ned retrieved the ruler, scowling at Eleanor from under the table. Kate would have to talk sense into her sister. *Better her, than me,* he thought, vowing to ask Katie soon: as soon as Mrs. Eller was laid to rest.

Chapter 50

The Independence Day firecrackers and Dance's barking from the stables had gone on all day; neither baby boy had napped well. Eleanor normally would have lent a hand, but she had retreated to the guest chamber after a heated exchange with her sister and brother that morning. *I wonder,* Maggie thought, *what was that about?* She had never heard them shout at each other before. Jem was rubbing his eyes again, so she laid him down, then sat in her chair and listened, praying that they would sleep. The air was still, warm, damp, and a clot of flies rattled and buzzed in the flycatcher.

  At twilight, she went down the back stairs to the kitchen for a drink of water. She heard voices through the open window, boys' laughter, and then, loudly, more crackers set off near to the house. As the crackling ended, she heard a scream. She dashed toward the back stairs, thinking it was one of the babies, but the shrieking continued from the back parlor. The door was sticky from the damp, Maggie pulled at it, as the cries continued. It was Eleanor, keening from beneath the sofa, flailing her arms at her sister, brother, mother. Her sounds tumbled out in a horrified babble, but Maggie heard "Wolf".

  Then Eleanor wailed clearly: "Mama! He's biting me!" Mrs. Whitfield called frantically to her son: "Fetch Mrs. Moore! Run!"

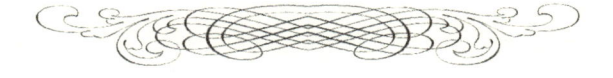

Ned sat in the darkened back parlor, lit by a single gas light. The fireworks and the firecrackers had finally stopped. He stared numbly at the table: a ladies magazine lay there, opened to an engraved illustration of a small boy and girl and their kitten. *They will grow up to know dissembling, dissension and evil,* he thought, *and the cat will grow old and die.*

"Just you, eh? Where is everybody?" The judge said as he came into the parlor, "It's not that late."

"Yes. It is. Eleanor remembered," Ned replied.

His father did not bluster. "The wolf?" he whispered.

Ned shivered. "Everything," he said. *Facts. Facts,* he reminded himself. He said aloud: "They are all upstairs with her. She could not stop screaming until Mrs. Moore gave her laudanum."

The judge made a tiny sound, a shuffle of breath in a dry throat. He held his hands up then clasped one within the other helplessly. Ned was glad to see him suffer, but not so glad that he would linger to watch.

How many hundreds of steps to the Whitfield house? He began to count them. *She will be all right,* he thought. *It is like cutting out a rotten piece of skin, like pulling the broken teeth in my mouth, so they wouldn't cut me further. Some pain needs to be borne so that a soul can heal. She's a woman now not a baby girl. She'll understand the fear and overcome it, as I have. Have I indeed? Where was I? One hundred and fourteen, one hundred and fifteen. Fifteen men on a dead man's chest, Yo ho ho, and a bottle of rum.* He watched the bobbing lantern on a carriage coming toward him and stepped off the road into the deep dark. There were no street lights on this stretch. '*Ripe for an accident. Someone might get hurt.*'

'Is she hurt, is she drowned?' he had screeched to the woman who held him tight, forced his head away from its turn toward the lake. She pressed his skull against the hard bones of her bodice, his eyes seeing only calico fabric, maroon and black flowers. But he had heard his father's bellow, and the extremity of pain. And below the woman's muffling arm he could hear Katie screaming and the woman's sobs. "Katie!" he said.

'No, no,' the woman said.

'Is she dead?' He'd asked, unsure that anyone heard him.

'No, no,' the woman said again and he took that for his answer.

'Take the boy away,' a man said. And they did, for he had not dared to struggle against them.

"*I've lost count.*' He was now at Falls Avenue. Arriving at the judge's house, Ned drank from the pump in the kitchen sink, until he felt sick at his stomach. Then he fetched a pail from the shed, pumped it full of water and hauled it to his chamber. He lit the lamp. Stripping off his sweat-sodden clothes, he threw a towel on the floor and began to scrub himself.

The water was too cold: that was the cause of his shakes. Pushing the pillows and bolster aside, furiously tearing at the blanket, he peeled a sheet from his bed and wrapped his lower half. He rolled up the wet towel with his feet and kicked it into the corner and sat rocking in his side chair: a moth pinioned half-way out of its cocoon, hanging in the sultry night.

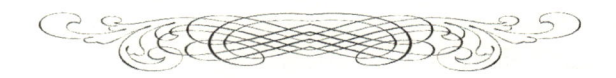

After two full days when the Fariday household was noisy with turmoil, Maggie blessed the quiet, as she lay Bertie in his bed, relieved to see him finally asleep. As she adjusted her dress and left the nursery to have a cup of tea with Mrs. Carruthers, she heard Eleanor calling from the guest bedroom one floor below the nursery. *Whissht, I blessed too soon!*

"Eddie! Eddie come here," Eleanor said. She was in the hallway, out of bed for the first time in two days, wearing only her chemise.

Maggie said: "Elly, where's your wrapper?"

Mrs. Fariday and Edward Whitfield appeared at the bottom of the staircase. "Do you want me Elly, I'll come up," Mrs. Fariday said.

"No," Eleanor said, "I want Eddie. Come here, Eddie, please."

"Why do you want me?" Edward asked.

"Go back to bed, mouse, do!" Mrs. Fariday said, beginning to climb the stairs. "Mama! We need you."

"Not Mama," Eleanor said, "Not you, Katie. Just Eddie and Maggie. I'll get back in bed."

Mrs. Fariday went back down the stairs and poked her brother in the arm. "Well, go!"

"Where's your wrapper?" Maggie asked again as she ushered Eleanor back into the guest bedroom and onto the bed. She found the garment thrown over a chair, and helped Eleanor put it on.

"I had a dream," Eleanor said, as her brother came into the room. She said this every time Maggie saw her. Edward grimaced, stepped backward into the doorway.

"Tell me what happened," Eleanor urged him.

"What happened?" he said. Eleanor nodded.

"But you know what happened..." he said.

"No, I do not. I want you to tell me what happened when the baby got hurt."

"What? What baby? The babies are well," he said.

"The little girl who was hurt by the wolf," Eleanor said impatiently.

He replied with deep reluctance: "Dash it, Eleanor, this is absurd. You know what happened."

She mumbled: "I have the dream. But Kate and Mama told me about her, and she truly did get hurt, so it is not only a dream, I must have seen it somehow. It was horrid and it frightened me. But you were there, too, Katie said so. So if you tell me what you saw, then I can understand what happened to her, because you know I am so worried about her!"

"Her?" Edward said, "Do you mean Katie?"

"No, the little girl that got hurt," Eleanor said.

Edward pulled on his beard. "I'll get Mama." He turned to go.

"No, Eddie, come back. You must tell me. Mama says she wasn't there, but you were."

"Kate was too. Ask her," he said.

Eleanor went on: "Please, Eddie. You tell me and Maggie will hear it too and if I forget she will tell me again what you said." Edward stared at the ceiling, ran his finger under his collar.

"Come in, for mercy's sake," Maggie hissed.

He did so, saying: "I was seven years old, what can I tell you."

"You're good at remembering things. You always have been," his sister said. "Tell me what happened to her and afterward, too."

"Her," Edward repeated, "why do you keep saying that?" Maggie made an exasperated noise. He looked at her for the first time, briefly, then said in a monotone: "It was the Fourth of July. We were living in New York state then. There was an Independence Day celebration, and a picnic, at the lake. Reading of the Declaration and fireworks et cetera. And we all went except Mama. I suppose she was ill or something, I don't know, but she didn't go with us."

"We all went: so I was there too!" Eleanor said, "That's what Kate told me, that I was there. So, I saw the little girl."

"You didn't see *her*. It was you," Edward said, clutching the facts to his breast as a shield.

"I was there. I saw her and the wolf!" Eleanor whimpered.

"There was no wolf," he said. He stared straight ahead.

"There was too! I saw it! You didn't see it!" Edward remained silent. "I saw it," Eleanor insisted.

"You saw..." he struggled to control his voice. "You...I th-thought two days ago, I thought you remembered it. It happened to you, you remembered it! It, it, I don't know, maybe it seems like a dream where you saw another little girl, that's all. Like the shelling. Ah, I, I was thinking about the shelling: when I came home I had dreams about it, no, not dreams, I was awake, but it was happening again, I mean it seemed as if I was there again, it was happening all again."

She said: "Poor Eddie."

He went on: "But it wasn't real, it was in my, my mind, that's all. We ought not to remember those things, but we do, I don't know why. And f-for you, it did happen too but it's over now and you're safe, it's just that the picture stays in your mind."

"Mama says I remembered that the wolf bit me, but I don't! I saw the wolf biting the girl and that's what made me so sick and afraid. It was dreadful." Edward was unable to answer.

"I did not mean to make you sad, Eddie. I'm sorry, I know it was dreadful what he did to her, maybe you did see it too," Eleanor moaned.

He shook his head repeatedly, took a gasping breath, one hand shading his eye as if the light bothered it. When he finally spoke, his voice was unnaturally high, strained: "No wolf. A man. Hurt you. You have the...the...those...on your arms..."

"Oh, those are because I got hurt when I was a baby. Mama told me that a long time ago. See, these too." She opened her wrapper and pulled down the neck of her chemise, nearly exposing her breasts.

"Cover her up! For the love of God," Edward said in anguish. He covered his eye. Maggie saw, for the first time, on the top curve of Eleanor's breasts the scattering of pale, paired half-moons. She reached to pull up the covers but could not take her eyes from the marks: there were so many. There was a break in the line of each upper half-circle, a crooked tooth. It was this that made Maggie's throat close with horror. These wounds came not from shredded metal belching from a gun, but from the mouth of one human being upon another's flesh with the mingled intent to consume and harm.

She saw hairy knuckles and blunt fingers curved to the task of tearing at the child's dress. She heard the sheer cambric ripping, all of Mother's careful little stitches rent; and the child's screams as the yellowed teeth sank in, cut, and tasted flesh so intimately. The man, so big, so hairy, so tall he must have seemed to fill the sky, had seized the baby, crushing her (like Rory did, that heavy body pressing you down, shoulders sharp against your chest, whiskers a briar on your cheek, arms a vise, so you couldn't breathe.)

Maggie cried out, flung herself onto the bed, scrambling to cover Eleanor's body with her own in futile comfort, futile protection. "The wolf!" she wailed, "'twas a man. That man, he did it! 'twas a man w-worse than a beast."

Beneath her, Maggie felt Eleanor stir and murmur. Maggie sat up, put her cheek to Eleanor's as she would to Jem's or Bertie's, and kissed her and rocked her. "Poor baby," she said over and over. Then they rocked in the silence.

"Yes," Edward said, startling them. Maggie had forgotten him. He now stood in the corner of the room opposite Eleanor's bed, like a reprimanded child.

"Why?" Eleanor said from behind Maggie's sheltering arm. There was no answer.

"Why?" she asked Maggie. Maggie felt heavy and cold. She shook her head, wiped her nose on her wrist. Eleanor sat up. "Why?" There was stridency in her tone.

"Eddie, you know, you saw him. Why did the man bite her?" Edward whirled, reeled forward, crashing into the dresser on his way to the door. A china jar there tipped over, rolled off the edge of the chest of drawers, and broke as it struck the floor. He stopped and stared at it.

"You broke it," Eleanor said in a tiny voice.

"Didn't mean to," he said, and began to pick up the larger shards. He stacked these on the dresser. Maggie waited to hear the steps on the stairs, the query from the people on the first floor, but no one called out or came up. *'tis a mad-house here,* she thought, longing to be back in Mr. Merritt's kitchen with dour Mrs. Wilkin, with no thought beyond the next chore, with no responsibility save washing up, with no power over babies, and no thought of the doings of evil men. She waited for Edward to regain command of himself and of the situation; he pushed the china fragments under the dresser with his foot, evidently finding it difficult to make his way back from boyhood.

"Wicked, wicked, evil, horrible man," Maggie said, "Blackguard! He was a devil. He had no call to bite a child!"

"I wanted to go," Edward said in a tight voice, "That's why it all happened. I begged Mama to go because Kate and Father were going, and I didn't want to be left behind. So, she said I might, but then you begged to go too. We didn't know he was there, Elly, the man, I swear it, we didn't know. I would have stayed home with you and played in the yard. But *I didn't know.*"

"I was naughty," Eleanor said, "I didn't stay with Papa. I was a naughty girl."

He went on: "It wasn't your fault, El. It was mine, I guess, f-for begging to go, and Father's for not watching you."

Eleanor thought about this. "Father ought to have watched out for the baby. Because there was a wolf."

"There was no wolf, it was a man!" Edward yelled.

"Oh, stop shouting," Maggie said frantically, "You'll make it worse."

He turned to her. "What the devil? How could it get any worse?"

"Please don't quarrel," Eleanor said.

"He must have looked like a wolf to you, dearie," Maggie said to her friend, "big and hairy and you thought he was because he...." she stopped.

Eleanor rubbed her temples, gazing at her brother with great concentration. Finally, she said: "But if it was not a wolf, why did he bite?"

Edward made a strangled sound.

"No one knows why," Maggie said, and then, to Edward, "She ought to sleep now. Where's the medicine she takes?" He turned a piece of the china jar in his fingers, frowned at it, held it up.

"Isn't there something your Mama had to dose her with?" Maggie asked, disappointed that he had done nothing to help his sister, although he was so clearly distressed. She watched him studying the bit of porcelain.

"Say," he put in loudly, "I think I know why he bit you! I think you bit him first. You must have bit him when he caught at you or tried to carry you away. You didn't like to be hurried along and you used to bite me or Katie when we tried to pick you up and you didn't want to go. You took a chunk out of me one time, although it didn't scar up. You must have bit him when you tried to get away."

Maggie instantly sensed that this was true. She closed her eyes, imagining the man's outrage that his effort to lure and despoil had met with any opposition, any small opposition from a female, and from such a tiny girl. Spewing his fury, in revenge he had turned his huge, crooked teeth against her. Maggie prayed urgently to the Holy Mother that the little girl had fainted early on, had felt no pain, had remembered nothing save the sight of the wolf.

"If I bit a man, that was naughty," said Eleanor. There was a question in her voice.

"No!" Maggie spat out, "You were trying to get away!"

Edward smiled as saliva collected unheeded at the left side of his mouth. "Ha! You bit him: bit the bastard good and proper. That's it! He expected you to go with him like a lamb to slaughter. He probably meant to take you away or smother you or drown you there at the lake. But you fought him! Good Lord in heaven, I'll bet it saved you."

"She was just trying to get away," Eleanor said, tasting revelation.

"You were. Yes, what a brave little one," Maggie answered.

Edward spoke over them: "Bravest baby in the world!"

Eleanor shook her head. "I'm not brave, Eddie."

He said: "Don't Eddie me, Eleanor. You're not a baby any more. Can't you see what you did? You fought the wolf. You made him drop his prey. The demon in wolf's clothing, I mean. Animals are meant to hunt and take prey, men are not!" He hesitated, then wiped his face and went on: "No matter, you fought back, that's the important thing. That's bravery, in anyone's dictionary. Especially at the tender age and size you were."

Eleanor was entranced.

"Believe me," he urged, "Believe me for once, not Father: not all that wrong-headed bunkum he pours out like gospel truth. What does he know about any of us? Nothing, he knows nothing!"

Eleanor shivered in Maggie's embrace. "Don't say that. He'll be angry." Edward snorted. "He will be angry at me," his sister said, "Promise you won't start a quarrel with him, Eddie."

"No, I won't promise! Angry at you, at you? What are you thinking? How can he be angry at you, when he has no one to blame for your condition but himself!"

Eleanor's face crumpled. "Don't shout, don't shout at me. He hasn't come, he hasn't come to see me, he must be angry at me for being so afraid. Don't make it worse, Eddie, or he'll send me away!"

He said through his teeth: "Send you away, I'll be hanged if he'll send you away, when this is all his fault, for not watching you, for sending Kate and me away to play while he tickled you to make you laugh and showed you off to his friends. There's nothing like a pretty little girl to beguile the voters, by heaven, when I…"

Eleanor interrupted this tirade with an astonished comment: "Papa showed me off?"

"Yes of course," Edward responded impatiently, "Don't you remember? No, I guess you don't. You were a pretty thing, with those golden curls, and you used to sing and dance and recite the story of Goldilocks and the Three Bears. You had it by heart as your party piece. Huh. You were as charming as the dickens."

"Papa was proud of me?"

Maggie felt tears return as the wild longing of Eleanor's words pierced her. Edward covered his face with his arm. As Maggie wiped her nose on her apron, he suddenly took off his eye patch, swiping at his eye.

"Good Lord almighty," he murmured. It was a prayer, Maggie knew that. Then he breathed deeply, tugged on his nose, snorted again like a war-horse. "Yes. Yes," he said, "He was. I don't know why he does not remember that, why he…How much he sees of, of anything, of any of us: it makes no sense to me."

"He was proud of me," Eleanor repeated sadly.

Her brother came to her bedside. "Put him out of your mind. I'm proud of you, by heaven. You bit the wolf himself and tried to get away. And then you… you've seen it again and again. It's the living with that after you think it's over, that's the hardest task."

Eleanor stared at him. "You had bad dreams too when you came home. You were glad when I brought you the slate to write on. I could tell from your hands." She put out her tongue, like a child, to lick in the tears.

"You saved my sanity," he replied, "I had no way to talk until then. A fate worse than death."

She said: "I thought of it. Nobody else did. And the very first thing you wrote on it was 'Thank you.' I remember."

Edward bowed his head.

She went on: "It was because you gave me Tabby Cat. You hid her in your jacket and brought her to me when she was a kitten and that's when my remembering starts, when you brought my first friend when I was... how old was I then?"

"Five, I think," he responded. Eleanor nodded. "I remember that."

"Remember Tabby and go to sleep now," Edward said.

"I can't sleep. I can never sleep. You know, Eddie. You know how it is at night. It's because it's so dark that I could not see if someone came. And it comes into my mind, the dream, like you said, even when I'm awake, and it pushes out all the good things. Oh, Maggie! If you had seen her, what the wolf did..."

"No!" Edward exploded, "Let it go!"

Eleanor startled. "You scared me."

"There was no wolf, you remembered just now, it was a man, but it was long ago, and he's gone..." her brother said.

"But we, we don't know where he is now," Eleanor said in a tiny voice, "I'm tired, so awfully tired. I know there is something horribly wrong with me, but Doctor won't tell me what it is. Mama says I won't die from it..."

"You remembered," Edward pleaded, "You remember, don't you, Elly?"

Trying to please him, his sister replied: "I do remember how I saw the wolf...?"

Mother of God, will she ever come out of there? Maggie thought.

"I cannot go through this again," Edward whispered, desperation fraying his voice.

Maggie was desolated. Deep truths offered in good faith washed nothing away, changed nothing, moved no one. Even this man with all the answers had none. "You tried," she said to him.

"I'm so tired," Eleanor said. Maggie told her to sleep. "I'm afraid to. Stay with me, Eddie."

He said dully. "I'm too big now. Maggie will stay with you."

He left them alone. Eleanor burrowed her head into the

pillows. Weeping now, she clutched at Maggie, who held her tightly as, one by one, her friend's sobs undid the pins fastening all of her own sorrow.

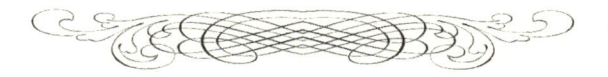

"Eleanor's canary is dead," Ned announced to the judge, "She asked me to see how it was, and look at this!" He held up the cage with its desiccated contents and shook it angrily. An orange feather floated to the floor. "Didn't anyone think to feed and water it, while she is gone?"

The judge said: "It's been ailing for a while."

Ned said: "She will be most unhappy to think that it died of neglect."

His father closed the ledger but did not look up. "Is she improving?"

"You've been neglecting her, too. Why don't you visit and see for yourself?" Ned retorted.

"I have been occupied," the judge said. "My work does not stop just because my daughter is ill and fretful..." Seeing Ned's expression, he added: "Surely, she understands *that*. And I do not believe that my visiting would benefit her; she cannot put two sensible words together when she gets into this mad state of mind." Ned thumped the cage onto the table.

"I have nothing to say to her," his father responded, "What could I say... Good Lord, I turned away for just a little time and off she went. It could not have been more than five minutes. That devil! I did not know he was there."

"She is still afraid he is out there, looking for her," Ned replied harshly.

The judge made an unearthly sound: the Minotaur, bellowing, lost in his maze. He scraped at his eyes with his fingers. "I wish to God he was! I would string him up by his thumbs, the bastard! I would cut off his balls and make him eat them!" His hands knotted together.

Ned said: "Wh... When I was a boy I th...thought he would come back. I hid the knives, all the knives, all around the house so I could stab him and cut his throat if he came to get her." With shaking hands, he grabbed a chair next to the table and sat down.

The judge muttered: "I thought you were rid of that childish stammer." He looked up: "Your mother wondered where all the table knives had gone to. We will never find him. He has done his evil and is long gone. It was not my fault, Edward! I don't know what to tell her."

"Tell her anything!" Ned shouted, "that... that you are sorry for what happened—that she's still your girl!"

His father kept his gaze down on the table and neither moved nor spoke. Ned rubbed his hands together to stop their tingling, breathed deeply then stood up.

"Go to see her," he commanded. "Just... go and see her," he pleaded.

The judge fumbled in his suit pocket and drew out a ten dollar banknote. "Here," he muttered, "Get her a new canary. Bring it to her so she can hear it sing."

"No!" Ned replied, "You bring it to her."

The judge rose with surprising speed and stuffed the note into Ned's pocket. As Ned reached to remove it, the judge's hand clamped down hard, and his face moved close to Ned's. "Do this," the judge said, "Do this for me."

He wrenched away from his father's grasp, hissing "Go to the devil. I will do it for HER." As he moved toward the door, a metallic crash stopped him. The bird cage rolled against his feet.

"Get rid of that god-damned thing," the judge said.

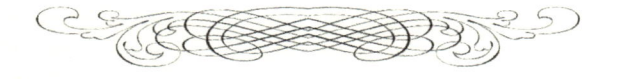

Ned stopped on his way downtown to quiet his breath. He dumped the little bundle of orange behind a large bush near the St. James Church. "Requiesce in pace," he muttered, staring at the cage. He longed to throw it back at his father's face; but perhaps it was better for Eleanor to have a new canary, no matter who purchased it. He put the cage on the grass and stared at the church. The building had been an object of debate and distaste in town when he was in his teens and its construction was completed. Someone had broken the windows shortly after they were installed, but the Catholics (joined by a few Protestant natives in town who thought the vandalism a scandal) had raised money to repair them.

Perhaps he could tack the judge's money on the church's

door, as Martin Luther had tacked up his Ninety-Five Theses. At the least he would be rid of the money and its odor of guilt. Tack it up, with what? He might instead slip it under the door. The gate of the wrought iron fence surrounding the church was open. A door at the side was unlocked, so he stepped into the darkness. Dozens of candles were flickering in a metal stand by the door, with a sign saying "For the repose of the souls."

Superstitious nonsense, he thought. There was a faint spicy smell in the air, like patchouli, like his mother's paisley shawl. He fingered the money in his pocket, looked up and was startled by a face in the shadows. He cleared his throat, but it was a statue: almost life size, St. James in plaster. And there was Mary, patient and mournful, frozen in blue and white. His eye traveled to the painted Christ on the cross over the altar, gruesome, the wounds on the hands and feet and the side garish red. *Nothing else about the unclothed human body is so bright a color,* he thought. *Who could bear to look at such a thing at every service?* Yet it did arouse pity for the man suffering there, and perhaps that was the point.

He startled at a sound from the vicinity of the painting. A fleshy (and fleshly) white face above black shoulders appeared indistinct in the shadows.

"Who's there?" the man said.

"You gave me a start," Ned said. The man, a priest, clean-shaven, with the look of a "son of Erin," advanced to peer at him. The man was in turn as startled as Ned had been. The priest took in the scars and Ned's good suit expeditiously, then said: "Take off your hat." Ned did so.

The priest said: "If you're here for confession, it begins at 7:00 tonight; but the church is open for prayer now, if you've need of it."

"No!" Ned exclaimed. Anxious to leave, he said simply: "I was looking for the poor box. Do you have one here?" The priest looked confused and slightly suspicious. "You're not a member of the parish, then," he said. "Even a visitor ought to know his manners. I'm Father Gerrity."

"Yes. Father," Ned said, "H-how do you do? I would like to make a contribution," he held up the bank note, "for the poor."

The priest's countenance changed. "We do have one, 'tis back by the confessionals. Or I can take it for you."

"Yes," Ned replied and handed it over. Upon seeing the

note's face value, the priest said: "Well, God bless you, sir."

Ned started to back away. "It's not from me, it's from my sister. She's ill. I saw the church, so…"

"Does she need the sacrament?" the priest asked. Ned was alarmed. "No. I just came to give that."

The priest nodded. "We'll say a prayer for her then, and you can light a candle for her, if you like. What's the name?"

"No. No name! That's not necessary," Ned said firmly. The priest stared at him, frowned. "Prayer is necessary, indeed it is! And surely she'll want some thanks for her generous gift."

"No. She wouldn't. She would like to remain anonymous," Ned said, inching backward.

"Very well." The pastor shrugged. "The good Lord knows His children, knows us each by name, and all our needs. We'll pray for her healing, if that's God's will."

"Thank you, sir. Uh, Father," Ned said, "Pardon me. I must go. Good day."

Sweating like a laborer, he hastened away with visions of the priest pointing him out in a crowd, there is our mysterious donor! He laughed shortly: in punishing the father, he had benefited the Father. Well, it would make a good story to tell Eleanor; or maybe not, there was no way to know.

If only lighting a candle and saying prayers would help her, if it was only that simple. They could pray all they wanted for their anonymous benefactress, what good would it do; if you carried the enemy with you always, you could never turn your back, not even to mourn the child who'd been brutalized. If the grievous damage showed like a missing limb, she could learn to live in spite of it, with crutches, false leg, a wheeled chair; and there would be no end to the sympathy the world would pour upon her. But this un-seeable wound had no balm and had to be borne by all in shame and silence.

The good Lord knows us each by name, and all our needs, repeated in Ned's mind. S*he could get better,* he thought. *I'll buy her a new canary, spend my own money, and tell her that it was my idea, but that Father wanted her to have a bird to sing to her.* That last was true. He picked up the bird cage. Heading toward Morton's store, he recognized Miss Minton and her father approaching. He tipped his hat and greeted them.

"I do hope Miss Whitfield is well," Miss Minton said with a shade of concern in her face, "we have just returned from a holiday at the shore."

Ned hesitated long enough that her concern deepened. He said: "In fact, she has been ill."

She said, with detectable anxiety: "I am so sorry to hear that. When I did not receive a response to my letters..."

"To the shore, you said," Ned put in, suddenly inspired, "I do believe that fresh air might help her. Can you recommend a resort or rest cure there? A quiet place. She, as you know, is not seeking a fashionable venue."

"Yes!" Miss Minton said immediately, "I know just the place!"

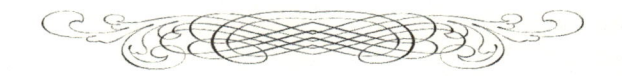

"It's a marvelous resort, very quiet, Miss Minton told me, and just a short walk to the beach." Ned said enthusiastically, "You know how Elly has always wanted to go to the beach. They've done excellent work with nervous cases. You and Elly could go and stay together, Mama. We could even go in a private coach, if that was easier for Elly, although she said a while ago, one time, that she'd like to go on a train someday." Eleanor had no outward reaction beyond a sad shake of her head.

"I'm sure it's costly; I'm not sure that your father would agree to pay for such a thing." Mrs. Whitfield said.

Ned scowled. "Hogwash. He's feeling so guilty about Elly that if she asked for all of Barnum's zoo, he'd pay for it." His sister grimaced in pain. Ned talked over his own embarrassment. "I'll ask him for the money. He'll do it. Look Mama, it's like an equation: you lay out the problem, what are the parameters, what are possible solutions, then try whatever you know won't harm, and may help. She'll have to try something."

Eleanor said: "Don't talk about me as if I'm not even here! I'm here. I wish I wasn't. I wish I was dead."

Mrs. Whitfield said with distress: "Oh, Elly, don't say that. Don't say that again."

Kate watched them all for a moment, then said: "Elly, would you allow Miss Minton to call and tell you about this place? It's a pity that you haven't seen her in weeks, I know you got on so well this Spring."

"It's not her," Eleanor said, "I like her very much, you know that. But she would not understand **this**. You know I can't go anywhere. I'm trying, I am, you don't understand how hard I've tried."

Ned said: "But Elly, the chances that he is still alive and out there…"

"Stop it!" Kate interrupted. The dog whined, then got up and went to Eleanor. Ned subsided, rubbing his forehead.

"Do you have a headache, Eddy?" Eleanor said, "Ask Mrs. Carruthers to make you some sage tea."

"Sage tea" he said bitterly, "The perfect remedy for a fool! I'll have her brew me a gallon."

Kate burst out: "Oh, don't be so dramatic, Ned, and put it all back on yourself."

"I am trying, Ned," Eleanor said, "I am."

"I know that," he said.

"Come along to the kitchen," Mrs. Whitfield said to her son, "I'll brew some for you and some for me."

After they left, Bertie started to cry. Maggie was feeding Jem. He had popped his mouth from her breast and grimaced as the adults shouted, returning to nursing when they quieted down. "Elly, could you take Bertie until Jem's done?" Maggie asked.

"He's hungry," Eleanor said, "I can't help him."

"I suppose I must," Kate said, with no pleasure. She scooped him up and sat holding him as she would a sack of dry goods. He cried. "I don't know what to do with him."

"Just rock him a bit and talk to him," Maggie said. Bertie wailed. "Or, or, sing to him," Maggie said louder, "Do sing to him, Mrs. Fariday, for you have a lovely voice, and he even likes to hear me singing what I can."

"Anything to quiet him," Mrs. Fariday said. She sang *Oh Susanna* and the baby gradually calmed. Jem did not resume nursing, apparently more interested in the sound of Mrs. Fariday.

"I used to sing to Worth when he was in the hospital," Mrs. Fariday said, "He says that's when he fell in love with me." She sang another chorus. "Now we have a trick up our sleeves, Elly, singing quiets them down," she said, pleased at her success.

"I don't sing," Eleanor said flatly.

"You used to," her sister replied, "You'd always sing for us, and we…"

"Ned told me," Eleanor cut in, "Just because I did then does not mean I will now. I sang before it happened. That's how he found me." The room was horribly quiet. Jem resumed nursing.

"Oh, mouse," Kate said painfully.

Chapter 51

Maggie stood on the Faridays' front porch with Jem to watch the sun rise. A man on horseback neared the house, and Jem bounced as if he too was riding.

A deep voice greeted her with "Good morning."

Maggie called out: "'twas decided yesterday: they're going to Watch Hill in Rhode Island. All of them, Eleanor too! I thought you ought to know." She grinned at his surprise. Edward dismounted from his horse, held the reins.

"Miss Minton told them all about it." Maggie went on. "And then Mr. Fariday said Mrs. Fariday must go because she needed a rest, and he told Elly that she must either go home and stay with her Papa while Mrs. Fariday was gone or go to the shore."

He tied the reins to the hitching post. "Miss Minton, the voice of reason. And Worth, the voice of authority. It was a very unpopular idea when I introduced it a week ago."

Maggie shrugged. "I always thought 'twas a grand idea."

"It will do you all a world of good," he commented.

Maggie murmured to the horse, gently patting his flank. His ears flicked forward. "I'm sure 'twill be grand for them," she said, "The babies and I are to stay here with Kathleen and Mrs. C."

"Huh," he muttered, frowning. Maggie patted the horse's neck as he moved his head to snuffle at the sleeve of her dress. "Where did you find this friendly fellow?"

"He's mine. I just bought him. Jacob took a look at him and said he was sound, although his owner wasn't feeding him right."

Maggie cooed at the horse. "Yes. The poor thing is so thin."

Ned shrugged. "I'll soon fatten him up. I admit he's not

much to look at now, but he's good-tempered and a steady goer."

"Like his master," Maggie said without thinking.

"I'll take that as a compliment," he replied immediately, and smiled wider at Maggie's embarrassment.

Best to make a joke of it, Maggie thought. She said: "Since you're like Adam who named all the animals, what do call this fellow?"

"I haven't named him yet. His prior owner called him Jack—a name I'm inclined to avoid." He looked the horse over. "He's as bony as a shad."

The horse snorted. Maggie laughed. "Now you've hurt his pride, he's sure to act up."

"I've made up my mind. Shad is his name."

Maggie made a face. "Och, no. He needs a name he can wear when he's not so thin as he is now. Like..." It came to her abruptly. "Shadrach. 'Tis an Irish name, though."

"No indeed," he said, "It's aptly Biblical. Don't you recall Shadrach, Meshach and Abednego, who went into the fiery furnace?" She shook her head.

"Oh," Edward said, "I forgot to bring you the newspaper story I saved for you back in June. I meant to give it to you at Eleanor's party. It was about the Fenian Brotherhood - they got up an army and invaded Canada."

"You're joking!" Maggie said.

"No. Their army occupied a town or two, so the President sent General Grant and General Meade up north to our border to sort it out and arrest any suspected Fenians. The Fenian army battled with the Canadians and then surrendered to them."

Rory, they did it! she thought, *they raised an army.* "Mercy, was anyone killed?" she asked.

"I don't know, I think some of the Canadian defenders died. The Fenian general, a man named Sweeney, was arrested," he replied.

"Nobody else?" she asked, "Harrigan?"

He replied: "Ah, was that the fellow who plagued your father? I don't know. His name was not in the newspaper."

He plagued me too, she thought, glad that Harrigan's mission had failed, that this would break him! But more likely, he'd simply hide until he could skitter out again, like a roach, to surprise and frighten those around him.

Maggie wiped Jem's wet chin with her apron and nodded. "I have to see to Bertie," she said.

"Good day, then," he responded.

"Good day, Shadrach. Come again soon," Maggie said.

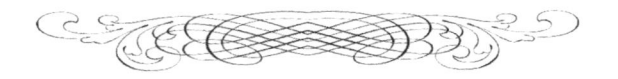

'tis as bad as winter, Maggie thought, *these closed in days, just hot in place of cold.* The babies' routines did not vary: feed one then the other, bathe them, play a bit, put them to nap, feed again and so round and round. Thank heaven for my friend Mrs. C., Maggie thought, for Kathleen don't lift a finger with the little ones: it's not **my** job," she always said - miss saucy-face.

After supper, she and Mrs. C. fanned themselves on the back porch, as Bertie fussed in his basket, and Jem crawled on the grass nearby, then plopped down to examine twigs. A wagon came slowly up the drive, its cowbell clanking. Mrs. Carruthers looked at Maggie.

"Go, then," Maggie said. Mrs. C. walked to the drive to meet Mr. Schmidt, the butcher. Their visits had become more than a matter of dinner selection and sales.

As the sun was setting in a hectic sky, a knock at the back door was most unexpected. Maggie was closest to it and opened the door to Edward Whitfield. He was sunburned and smelled fresh and salty. *Perhaps he's come to take us there,* Maggie thought for an instant, and was glad to see him. He told them that Mr. Fariday had arrived and decided that he and the three women would be staying another week at the shore because they were having such a marvelous time. Maggie fidgeted and suddenly longed to retreat to the airless nursery.

"Kate has begun to look well again," he said, "she and Worth are mighty fond of sea bathing."

"How is Eleanor?" Maggie asked.

"Well enough," he said. "Miss Minton took her into the bathing machine at low tide, so that was a first."

"I'm glad to hear it. I haven't had a letter from her in two weeks," Maggie broke in. He stared at the kitchen range and drummed his fingers on the table. There was a little silence. "But, but, I wonder, is she better?" Maggie said. Edward shrugged. "What does Mrs. Fariday say?" Maggie kept on.

"She ventured no opinion," he said.

"Mrs. Fariday ventured no opinion?" Maggie said skeptically. There it was, at last, a sidelong glance at her, and a twitch of his lips perhaps meant as a smile.

"Neither ventured an opinion to me," he said, looking troubled. "Why aren't you all out on the porch, it's hot as blazes in here."

"I must listen for the babies," Maggie said, "I can't hear them out there. That porch is on the wrong side of the house entirely."

"Where are my manners?" Mrs. Carruthers put in, "Would you like something to eat or drink, Mr. Whitfield? "

"No, thank you. I was hungry and made the mistake of buying something from a runner at the first station in New London. Worth asked me to look in on you."

Mrs. Carruthers looked at Maggie, then replied: "The little ones keep us busy, sir, but other than that it's been quiet. It's awful hot here."

Edward said: "There's a spanking breeze down at the shore. It is ten degrees cooler there than here. I wish that I could take you both, babies and all, to see it."

Mrs. Carruthers nodded in agreement. Just a few days before, Maggie had told her it was Rory's birthday, and had run away to hide her own tears. When she returned, Mrs. C. was holding Jem and had Bertie beside her in his basket, and she gave Maggie a cup of tea and a piece of gingerbread.

He stood up and unloaded from his pockets a handful of sea shells, and rounded stones, saying: "These are for you… if I cannot bring you to the beach, at least I brought some of the beach to you." He picked among the stones and identified each one: "This one's granite, this is sandstone; hmmm… gneiss, I believe."

Maggie took a smooth white stone. It fit her palm perfectly. "This one looks like moonlight," she said.

Edward smiled at her. "It's not a moonstone, I think it is quartz, but it does look like moonlight captured, now that you say it. Since you like it, that's my gift to you. Mrs. Carruthers, I'll hope you'll take one of these too, for a keepsake."

"Oh yes sir, "she said, "I like that black one with the white stripe."

"Then you shall have it," he responded, "That one is volcanic in origin."

"And what are these shells?" Mrs. Carruthers asked. He said: "These blue ones you'll recognize as mussels, and the raggedy ones oysters, and this is a scallop shell. The small ones are periwinkles. This lacy one I expect housed a crab at one time. You ought to see the crabs walk sideways and they go like an express train! Dance has a fine time chasing them."

Maggie watched his fingers, they were active, as always: touching the shells, smoothing along the table top, mere inches away from her own hand still cradling the white stone. His long, clean fingers picked up the curly shell, and twiddled it, then thumbed the pointed tip. A small shower of sand fell from its interior.

"Oops, I guess I didn't rinse them as well as I thought," he said. Then his middle fingers worked in unison, rather delicately, to push the small pile of sand into a line. *Those hands,* Maggie thought, *touched me in that most private place and made me... No, I can't think of that.*

She stood up. "I hear Bertie," she said.

Escaping into the back staircase, she climbed to the second floor and stood at the bottom of the stairs, listening. No baby was crying to save her from the man in the kitchen. She longed to go back there and tell him just how it was to stay here while others were having a holiday, and how awful to feel as if Eleanor was slipping away from them all, and to feel the agony down to her toes knowing that Rory was gone. She would not see his hands again, his broad shoulders, his grin, and that bright hair that had given him his nickname.

How you twist my heart, Edward! If she could speak to him true, she'd tell him all she was thinking: how she knew she would not escape his presence because where Eleanor was, he would always turn up, until Miss Minton replaced Maggie in Eleanor's affection. The white stone fell from her hand as she tried to swallow away the strangling in her throat. She retrieved it, brought it to her mouth and brushed it against her lips. It was cool, so smooth, and smelled of the sea. She wanted to lick it to taste the salt. Instead, she returned resolutely to the kitchen.

"Nary a peep from the both of them," she said, placing the stone on the table. *Look at him straight,* she told herself, *remember what he did to you, and what he refused to do.* "Here," she said.

"That's for you to keep," he said.

" 'twouldn't be right for me to take it," Maggie announced,

folding her arms across her chest.

He said: "Mrs. Carruthers has taken one. I meant them for both of you." Maggie shook her head, while Mrs. C. looked down nervously.

"Well," he said. "I'll just leave it here... and take my leave." He stood up, turned his hat around in his hands several times, then added: "I... ah... I thought I might hire a rig tomorrow morning and take you ladies and the boys out for an airing if the weather holds fine."

"Oh yes!" Mrs. Carruthers clapped her hands. Maggie let her breath out and smiled in spite of herself.

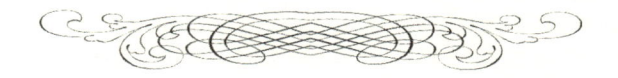

As Maggie brought the two babies out to the hired carriage, Mr. Schmidt came by to keep company with Mrs. Carruthers. Flustered, the cook explained the sudden outing invitation. Edward spoke a few words in German to the butcher and asked him to join them. Mr. Schmidt protested weakly, before agreeing to be "the fourth wheel." He helped the ladies into the carriage and sat up front next to Edward. Mrs. Carruthers, red-cheeked and smiling, took Jem in her lap while Maggie dealt with the agitated Bertie.

The ride to the lake was scenic, but Maggie enjoyed it only in little glimpses. When the party arrived at the lake, the scope and size of the deep blue water, shading to green in the shallows, took her breath. There was a scramble to unpack the babies and their things, and then the talk stopped. Edward said there was a short walk around the promontory, with a fine view of the lake. Mrs. Carruthers and Mr. Schmidt wandered off together. By the time Maggie looked up from retrieving the rapidly crawling Jem, Edward too was nowhere to be seen.

Jem bawled when the sand he had just eaten was not to his taste. She washed his hands in the shallow water, stripped off his clothing, and bounced his feet into the ripples at the shore. This turned out to be his favorite game, and they played it for a while, with Maggie looking over her shoulder every minute or so to make sure that Bertie did not roll off the blanket.

Wouldn't Rory have loved this, she thought. He savored his leisure, the golden air, the light, "the smell of the green earth," as he put it that last summer they had together. How he would have doted on his boy—so handsome, and healthy. She fed Bertie, then Jem and put them down on the blankets in the shade of a tree. She stared at her sleepy son, his damp red curls. Rory, can you see this boy? she wondered. *Och, I'd like to sleep right here,* she thought. *But there's no one to watch, and what if Jem crawled into the water and drowned?* She got up and splashed a little water on her face, glad for the cool trickle down her neck.

"How are you enjoying your outing?" Edward said from behind her.

"Mother of God," Maggie said, "how you sneak up on a body. How can I enjoy it, 'tisn't much of an outing, for here I am left alone again with two babies and daren't close my eyes or stray far - 'twouldn't be safe, and then one would need a feeding and then the other. I'm a hobbled cow."

Edward blinked at her, and then had the grace to appear embarrassed. "I ought to have thought of that," he said.

"You're the one who told them to go for a walk," Maggie said, "and off you went."

"I'm sorry," he said, "you're right. I just thought of that while I was exploring, and so I came back."

I won't cry, she thought, *I will not cry.* His arrival had sliced into her internal conversation with Rory, who'd have loved their boy but hated her being here with this man, the traitor. What would have been her sweetest dream just two years ago—alone with Edward Whitfield—was now hard to bear.

He said: "I wasn't sure whether you wanted me for company, I mean whether you wanted me to stay, but I ought to have known you'd need help."

"I didn't want you to stay," Maggie broke in. It came out far sharper than she intended.

Edward stepped back, rubbed the bridge of his nose, then said: "Well. I… actually, so I surmised. I guess that's why I lit out when we arrived here." His voice was dulled by disappointment, which fueled her anger.

She said: "I knew you'd light out anyhow, I knew it! Besides, haven't I bin taking charge of these two well enough for months. Surely I can do the same for one afternoon. But so close to the lake: 'tisn't safe, I'm thinking. You go for your walk, you needn't stay, since you don't want to."

She did not look at him, but when he spoke, confusion overtook the hurt in his tone: "First you... I thought... but you're right, perhaps it isn't safe? Or fair to you. Shall I stay or go?"

Maggie scrambled to her feet. "Faith, there's the question! The right question at the wrongest time entirely! Just do as you please: you will anyway, you always do."

He scowled. "What do you ..."

She interrupted. "Do whatever you want!"

"I only wanted to... please you... I promised an outing," he began.

Maggie said: "You promised: so NOW you're paying heed to your promises?"

She saw that look of recognition; yes, he now knew they were back on the same well-trodden and shaky ground. To her dismay, he gave her a look similar to the one Rory used when facing an unreasonable woman. He cursed soundlessly, but Maggie knew the word.

He said: "I presume you're referring to what you perceived..."

"Perceived, what a twist of words!" Maggie hissed, "And don't you dare to define it for me, I know what it means, I surely do. Maybe I'd ought to have listened harder to your careful words then. But I wasn't thinking—oh ho, pardon me—the worst sin in your book. I heard you with my heart, I heard a promise to love me as I loved you always. Then you told me none of it was ever there, I just never heard your lawyer words..."

Edward held up his hands in frustration. "That's not true."

Maggie went on unheeding: "I'd have done anything for you, save murder. Left my home and my family, lost my church - all on your promise, but you broke it and turned your face from me!"

"No!" he said, "I did not, I just needed time to sort matters out. But then you married Corcoran so soon, it was just a few months..."

Her scorn tasted hot and clean in her mouth. "Did you mean for me to pine away for years while you made up your mind! I found a man who did not tarry, who knew what he wanted: who wanted me."

"I wanted you!" he shouted, startling her, and causing her son to wake and cry. "I wanted you! By God, do you know what it was like, what I... when I heard you were married. My life was gone."

Maggie was riveted by the desolation in him. Pushing back tears, she said: "I didn't know. I had no word from you."

Like a man in a nightmare, he held out his hands, as if in pleading, as if in prayer. His voice a thread, he said: "I wrote... I tried to write you... I made a dozen drafts. I... I... did not know what to do, what to say... I could not say it right."

"Jesus, Mary and Joseph!" Maggie said, "'twouldn't have mattered to me what you said nor how you said it. All I needed was a single word, Come! And I'd have come."

He looked straight at her, in his face the full measure of realization, and core-deep pain.

Maggie panicked at this, and blurted: "And he came for me, Rory. And you did not."

He shuddered as if she had struck him, then reeled away from her, staggering a little and walked back into the woods, shoulders bent. The tears hit Maggie like a cloudburst. She dropped to her knees under the tree where the babies were whimpering. Pulling the both of them into her arms, she rocked them, weeping and crooning as much to comfort herself as them.

Ned surfaced from the dream at dawn, pausing at the edge of waking to turn back, longing to re-join that left-behind world. The voice of the judge had been chiding him for bringing shame to the family and had forbidden him to go into the lake lest he drown. In that fluid way of dreams, he was suddenly naked and diving deep into the green water. The voices of mermaids surrounded him and sang him welcome. Although he feared drowning, he dove. The drowning did not come: as he took in water and realized, in surprise, that he could breathe, he could breathe there.

That dream-born peace still cradled his mind as he awoke - far different than the shame that had driven him to bed early the day before. His battering headache had lessened, but not the memory of the day: his refusal to look at her, his rude silence with Mrs. Carruthers and Mr. Schmidt, his continuous internal volley of self-loathing and the damning repetition of all of the "might-have-beens."

He swung out of bed and moved the baseboard to retrieve the box. He took out the last draft of the letter, crouched with it in his hand. *When you fall off the horse, you must get right back on,* he thought. Running from her would not suffice, nor would running to her. If she hated him, or if she had not, but hated him now—he must bear it. Somehow. He decided when the day broke (it promised to be as hot as yesterday) that she would have this letter; he would bring it to her. And then he would return to the lake alone, in the bright day, and go into the water.

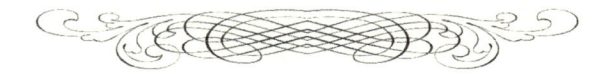

"Is that you, Ned?" Mrs. Moore called out.

He turned his horse. "Good morning."

"I just had a letter from your mother," she said, halting her chaise, "I guess Rhode Island suits her nicely. I'm glad she got away for a rest."

"Yes, it suits her fine," he replied, "I made a short visit a few days ago, and I would have liked to stay longer."

"I wish I could join her," she said, "I just delivered Betsy Greenhill's fourth, another boy. Her husband fetched me just after daybreak and Baby arrived in an hour. They're not often so prompt. I expect I'll have a nice nap this afternoon if I can sleep with this heat."

"I'm headed up to the lake soon," Ned said, "It's cooler there."

Mrs. Moore fanned herself. "I haven't been up there in years."

"Why don't you come with me?" Ned asked, not sure why he'd spoken up except that he liked her. "There's bound to be a bathing spot that you can have all to yourself."

"Well, bless you! I'd like that," she said.

"I have an errand and then I'll come by to fetch you," he replied.

If I take one lady I may as well take them all, Ned thought, sure that Maggie would refuse. He knocked at the Faridays' back door.

"Oh! Are you feeling better, Mr. Whitfield?" Mrs. Carruthers said as she opened the door to him. She scooped Jem into her arms so that Ned would not trip.

Maggie was in the corner. Ned took a large breath and

readied to dive. "Since I was ill yesterday, I thought you all might like to try again for an outing. To the lake," he said, looking at the cook stove. He spoke again into the resulting puddle of silence. "I promised you one, then cut it too short. I like to… I try to be a man of my word. Mrs. Moore wanted to go, I invited her too, so if anyone would like to get out of this hot house, just say the word. Is Kathleen here?"

"There's no one here but us," Mrs. Carruthers said, "her mother ain't well so she's gone home to help. Until Mr. Fariday comes back."

Ned nodded, wiping his hands on his handkerchief. *And now to face the jury of one,* he thought. "Mrs. Corcoran," he said, taking the now-damp letter from his pocket, "here is the… here is something I spoke of, which I neglected to deliver to you earlier." He advanced upon her and held out the letter, taking care not to look at her nor step on the child sitting at her feet. Jem smiled at him and babbled a set of incomprehensible words. She took the letter. Jem let go of his mother's skirt and seized Ned's leg, babbling two sounds. The little boy raised his arms, and Ned picked him up.

Mrs. Carruthers said: "I must wait for the meat wagon and the ice man, so I cannot go, though I thank you for asking me again. You're awful good to us." Ned made a polite reply. Jem whined.

In that narrow voice that failed to hide tears, Maggie said: "I'm thinkin' he wants your watch." *Don't make it more difficult, Maggie,* he pleaded without words. He took out his pocket watch, as the boy babbled delightedly. Maggie put Bertie on her shoulder and wiped her eyes with the back of her hand.

"Shiny watch," Ned said abruptly, for he could not bear to see her hurt. "I think that babble is his way of saying how much he covets the thing."

"I expect you're right, sir," Mrs. Carruthers said with a chuckle. Maggie made a sound that in better times would have been a laugh. "I'll go," she said, "I'd like to go back there."

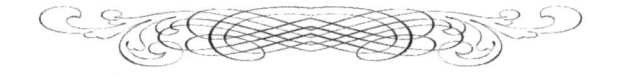

"What a good idea," Maggie said, peeling off her damp clothing until she was down to her chemise. Mrs. Moore was already in the same state of undress. After a quick look at the slumbering babies, she seized Maggie's hand and ran with her into the water. They both whooped at the unexpected chill, then Mrs. Moore showed Maggie how to float on her back. Maggie had a little difficulty.

"Large people are more buoyant," Mrs. Moore asserted.

Maggie's giggling caused her bottom to sink, so she stood up in the water. If she stood still, she could see the water grasses, the pebbles, and her own feet in the clear water. Nearby, Mrs. Moore's chemise flowed out around her, arrayed on the water like a cloud.

"I'm so glad you came," Maggie said to Mrs. Moore. *I wish you were my Mam,* she thought.

"Isn't this heavenly?" Mrs. Moore said. Surging back to her feet, she pinched her nose and ducked under the water, then jumped upwards and ducked again. When she surfaced, her laughter roared out. "Lovely," she said, "Try it!"

Maggie ducked, opening her eyes to see how things looked underwater, and came up. "I never bin so wet all over since I was born," she said.

"I declare, there's a breeze. We haven't had one in days," Mrs. Moore replied. She tipped backward into a float and sighed.

"Hello," a male voice called out from a distance. Mrs. Moore got to her feet and shouted, "Go away! We're not decent."

"Retreating," the voice said. The two women listened for fully a minute but there was no further sound.

Mrs. Moore ducked under the water again. "I suppose," she said, when she surfaced, "that we ought to get dried and dressed so the beast in the woods may have some dinner."

Maggie snickered, "It sounds like you're telling a fairy tale." Mrs. Moore smoothed back her wet hair and grinned. Dried and dressed, Maggie rummaged through the basket Mrs. Carruthers had packed, and found some bread crusts for Jem to gnaw upon. Now almost nine months old, he was cutting teeth as fast as a puppy. She seized him just as he crawled to the edge of the blanket.

A song came on the breeze from beyond the woods, in a baritone voice:

> *I seek for ones as fair and gay*
> *But find none to remind me*
> *Of how sweet the hours did pass away*
> *With the girls I left behind me.*

"Hello," Mrs. Moore yelled, "We are eating all your dinner, so you'd better hurry." He did, and helped Mrs. Moore unload the basket, tasting food as he unpacked.

"I will eat quickly, Maggie," Mrs. Moore said, "then take that little rascal off your hands, so you can have some dinner."

"Och, I'm used to eating however I can, with these two," she replied. Edward retrieved three bottles of ginger beer from where they had been soaking in the shaded water and handed her one. Bertie began to wail at the same moment.

"Is he hungry?" Edward asked.

Maggie shook her head. "I fed him not an hour ago."

Edward picked up his nephew and clucked to him, then walked to the edge of the shore.

"Do you want me to take him?" Mrs. Moore called.

"Go ahead and eat," he answered.

"I was thinking," Maggie said to Mrs. Moore, "I oughtn't to wean Jem 'till he's closer to two; for then I can keep him by me longer."

Mrs. Moore said: "Is he eating table foods already?"

Maggie nodded reluctantly. "A bit…"

Mrs. Moore said: "I always say they do better at the breast until they've reached 18 months. And that's what I'd recommend to any mother, Mrs. Fariday as well." Maggie smiled her gratitude.

They watched Edward swinging Bertie in his arms. The baby continued to fuss.

"Sing to him," Maggie suggested.

Edward plopped onto the sand and began to sing to the boy:

Amazing grace how sweet the sound
That saved a wretch like me.
I once was lost but now I'm found.
Was blind but now I see.

Maggie was struck to the heart. "What is that song?" she murmured.

"You have never heard it? A beautiful hymn," Mrs. Moore answered.

He sang a repeat of the last line: "Was half-blind but now I see," and glanced back at the women with a smile.

"Hush your nonsense," Mrs. Moore said pleasantly. Bertie

seconded her comment with a loud sucking noise as he popped his fingers out of his mouth.

Edward sang slowly:

> *Through many dangers, toils and snares*
> *I have already come,*
> *'Tis grace has brought me safe thus far*
> *And grace will lead me home.*

Could it be so? he wondered, meditating upon the words of the song; glad at least for these hours of peace. Bertie seemed sufficiently lulled, but the ladies were silent behind him.

He toted the child to Mrs. Moore. "Shall we trade?" he asked her, "this handsome child for that roasted chicken leg and some cornbread?"

She laughed and took the little boy. Maggie giggled too and he dared to look at her. *This is how it ought to be,* he thought, *let's just be easy with each other.*

As if she had heard him, she nodded and said: "Thank you." Not trusting his own voice, he nodded in return.

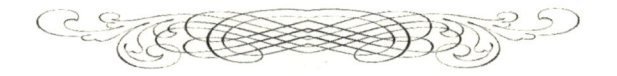

"Maggie, I should like to speak with you," Miss Minton said. Behind her friend's shoulder, Eleanor nodded, wet-eyed.

"The babies…" Maggie began.

"I'll watch them," Eleanor replied and sat on the floor next to Jem. Maggie followed Miss Minton out doors and toward the stable where Dance was barking.

"It is time to walk," Miss Minton said as she took the dog's leash. They followed a path behind the new houses, staying away from the street. Maggie silently fought her curiosity, for Miss Minton kept herself straight backed and contained. Misery seemed to encase her. *Something's a-boiling there,* Maggie worried.

They walked along the ridge, so far that the downtown was nearly in sight. Dance was panting.

"May we rest a bit?" Maggie asked. Miss Minton startled, and then agreed. They went into the shade beneath a spreading tree. Miss Minton stood still, staring at the ground.

"I'll take Dance," Maggie said, picking up the dog and sitting under the tree.

Finally, Maggie said: "She's... she's not..." Better, she meant to say, but did not finish her words.

To her horror, Miss Minton sobbed and turned her back. As the dog whined, Miss Minton said brokenly: "She said you would tell me what happened."

Maggie repeated faintly: "What happened?"

"To the little girl who was bitten by a wolf; that... horror... that has made her so ill," Miss Minton got out.

"I can't!" Maggie wailed, "I can't!"

The other woman finally faced her. "You must, she said that you would. I need to know! What did she see? What happened? You must tell me."

Maggie covered her face. Dance nosed her hands.

"Tell me, Maggie, you must! Or I fear that she will never recover," Miss Minton begged, and the agony there broke Maggie's resolve.

"Sit down," Maggie said, gathering her wits and gulping for breath. As Miss Minton sat near her, Maggie kept her hands over her eyes. Then she told the story of destruction, fighting to keep it short, to keep her voice going, not to falter when she got to the bites. She stared at her own fingers: how the prints whorled, how red the scab on her thumb.

"It couldn't be," Miss Minton said in a frayed voice, "It... such a thing... it can't be: she dreamed it."

Behind her hands, Maggie simply shook her head. Then it was far worse than she had expected, for Miss Minton howled and tore at her own hair like a madwoman. It came loose and flew wildly around her. The dog scrabbled from Maggie's lap, scratching her arm as she grabbed to keep hold of the leash. He stood near the tall woman, barking at her. Maggie did not mean to watch but her eyes did as they would. She had seen her Mam wild like this, shrieking like a banshee; but she had never seen a rich lady act so mad. She put her hands up again, in defense, to stop her ears.

It took a long time for Miss Minton to quiet down to deep sighs and a mumbled forlorn plea that all those who loved Eleanor had repeated: "It can't be." Maggie thumbed the moisture from her eyes, called to Dance, who had wandered. The dog returned, stood on her lap and tried to lick her face.

After waiting several minutes, Maggie said tentatively: "I'm so awful sorry. Don't turn away from her, she thinks 'twas her fault! But she was just a baby."

Miss Minton moaned as if her stomach pained her. Maggie stood up and let the dog go to the end of his lead. Soon she would have to be back at Faridays, to feed Bertie.

She said: "You know so many things, and you been all over the world, so they say." Miss Minton sat up abruptly making no effort to repair her ravaged face. *And you love her still,* Maggie thought with relief.

"So, you must help her, if you can," she said, as she inched toward the other woman and offered her handkerchief. "Here, take it. 'tisn't ironed, but 'tis clean."

Chapter 52

At the Supreme Court of Errors special session in Norwich, Adams v. Cohan and Sullivan, (being the last case heard that day) was rapidly remanded to Superior Court for re-hearing, due to the justice court's errors of law. After Attorney Lang had duly congratulated Charles Mix and Isaac Putnam and been thanked for his help on the appeal, Lang held his hand out to Ned.

"Congratulations, Mr. Whitfield. Now all that evidence you collected will finally be heard."

Ned balanced the pile of books and documents on his left side, shook Lang's hand, and thanked him. "I hear that you took the photographs that Justice Eller would not allow as evidence," Lang continued.

"Yes sir, I did," Ned replied.

As Mr. Putnam hurried past them, Lang commented: "Those pictures are sure to be a thorn in Adams' side. I shall have to pay a visit to Superior Court for the hearing. I'd like to see that: Tolliver Adams, for the first time compelled to pay, rather than collect."

"Here now, Mr. Lang," Mr. Mix put in, "Don't count our chickens before they're hatched. I try to keep my law student away from speculation." Lang smiled and bowed slightly: "Even a fool, when he holdeth his peace, is considered wise."

"Proverbs," Ned said, "from the Book of Wisdom."

Mix said: "A good proverb indeed. Good day, Mr. Lang. Come along Whitfield, it's a long journey home from here."

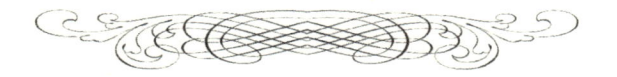

"You appear to have civil torts well in hand," Mr. Mix said to Ned, "but be sure to review Negotiable Instruments, you are lacking somewhat on that topic."

"Yes, I will." Ned stretched and closed the statute book, glad that his weekly seminar and examination with Mr. Mix had gone well. Mix continued quietly: "I hope that your sister Eleanor's visit to Hartford will be beneficial. Your mother confided to my wife, and I am glad she did so," Mix said, "I remember Eleanor as a baby, before your father moved to New York. And I recall... in short, I wish her well."

"Thank you," he said to Mr. Mix. "Time will tell, I guess."

He did not mention his own unsettling meeting with Eleanor, Rebecca Minton, and his mother.

"She will never be far from me," Miss Minton had said, "and her dog is welcome, too." Her voice taut, her hands wrestling on her lap, she had described the private home rented in a respectable area not far from the Retreat for the Insane; the care that a doctor at the Retreat would provide, the Retreat's beautiful natural setting, the opportunity for rest.

Miss Minton finished by saying: "We shall drive out in the carriage every day." At this Eleanor had made a small sound, like a child just awakening from sleep.

He had asked his customary factual questions, receiving controlled responses from Miss Minton, then had asked Eleanor "is this what you want to do?" She shrugged, and he repeated his question.

"I can't go on this way," she finally replied. Only his mother had wept at this; he believed he had no space left in him for pain, but he was wrong.

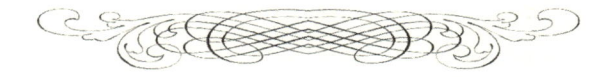

Maggie carried Bertie and Jem into the sitting room, at Mrs. Whitfield's request. Mrs. Whitfield took her grandson and cooed to him, as Jem crawled to the ottoman and pulled on the tassels, with a victorious chortle.

"So, the great debate continues?" Edward remarked to Kate. "What was the resolution?"

Kate answered, "Worth has won that dispute. I'm just as glad, I don't care a fig either way."

"Good," Edward commented; at Maggie's questioning look, he went on: "It was a matter of disagreement between grandfather and father whether Bertie's christening would happen at Christ Church or the Second Church of Christ."

Maggie said in confusion. "Ain't they the same? They sound the same."

He said: "Christ Church is Anglican, and Mr. Fariday was raised in the Anglican church and prefers to have the boy baptized there. The Second Church of Christ is Congregational and is our church." He glanced at Kate. "Well, the Judge is a nominal member, and he's fit to be tied."

"And I'm a member," his mother reminded.

"You don't look as if you're fit to be tied," Edward commented.

Mrs. Whitfield shrugged. "I have stepped out of the middle of this. I just want to see the little fellow christened."

"Will would likely not have agreed with Worth," Kate said, looking out the window.

"I expect you're right," Edward said, "But I do recall that he tolerated me well enough, even when my thinking strayed far from his orthodoxy."

Mrs. Whitfield said, "Will was a good friend. He had a very good effect on you."

"He did," Ned went on, "He put a stop to my transcendentalist leanings, took away my books of German philosophy and ordered me onto an improving diet of new Calvinism, which I carried in my haversack into the war, and promptly lost—along with my good watch and everything else of value."

"In my opinion, you've always been a Deist," Kate said. Mrs. Whitfield frowned at this.

"What's that?" Maggie blurted.

"Deists believe in God," Edward replied, "but in no special creed other than working for the common good of mankind. Of course, I simplify…"

"How a child is raised is of vital importance," Mrs. Whitfield said unhappily.

"I suppose so," Edward said to his mother.

"'tis important!" Maggie murmured.

Edward turned to her as Mrs. Whitfield nodded. "Go on," he said.

Maggie stammered, "Well, certainly 'tis important how you start a baby in the church. I mean... some do decide for themselves when they're grown, I'm thinkin' that may be so, but with your own baby, yes, Jem's baptized Catholic, same as I was. If you don't mind my saying so, 'tis sacred, 'tis an important thing." Edward got up and went to the window, closing the shutter. Jem crawled to his mother and grabbed her skirt.

Maggie's skin was hot. She picked up her boy and hugged him. "'twas my sacred duty," she said. *All this to a room of Protestants,* she thought, *and I've no way to explain about Rory and my own heart.* The only one she had meant the words for had turned his back to her.

Mrs. Fariday said: "Bertie will be christened, so which of the two churches does not matter much to me, although I'm glad Worth has made a decision, since it means so much to him."

Kathleen knocked at the door, opened it and said: "There's a card here from two ladies from a church, will you see them?"

Mrs. Whitfield glanced at the calling card, then said: "They're from the Freedman's Relief Society, Katie, we had better see them. "

Kate smiled: "Yes, I'd be glad to. Show them into the parlor, Kathleen. Tell them we'll be there shortly."

"I'll be going," Edward said, "Can you bring my hat, Kathleen?" He stood in the doorway after his mother and sister had left and said "I hope I have not shocked you. I believe in God, but I'm sorry to say I do not do what I do for God's glory or under His command, as good Christians ought."

"You're a good man, for all that," Maggie said, unable to hold her tongue. He looked at his shoes then at her. "I'm glad that you think so." *Och, that sweet smile of his,* Maggie thought. There was no way to mend her words now.

He went on: "They say that God's hand is present in our lives. I don't know if that is so. I have been unable to detect any pattern or plan, although presumably that is a failure on my part and not His."

Maggie shook her head: "He saved your life. And mine, because you were there on the hill."

Back and forth went his fingers on the bridge of his nose. "I had not thought of that! I suppose we are a family of narrow escapes." He cleared his throat. "I guess that merits some pondering. At any rate, if he saved me solely to save you, that's enough. But why bring us together only to force us apart?"

"'tisn't His doing," she said, "Please can't you see…'tis my sacred duty to my boy! If Rory… if it… if I could change it…"

He said: "Now that I think of it, it must have seemed to you when we were…when I first spoke of it, like those men who forced the 'soupers' to convert in order to eat and live. Would I have taken the soup? I like to think I would not: but I guess, Maggie, I want you to know that I'd be more of a Quaker than…"

Kathleen returned, and he took his hat, said "Good day," and took his leave.

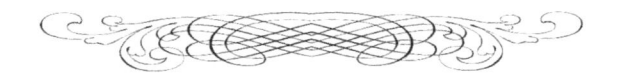

Things come in threes, Ned thought, staring at the train's rain-smudged window. Within a fortnight, Sullivan and Cohan had triumphed over Tolliver Adams in the Superior Court, he had achieved a workable knowledge of Negotiable Instruments law, and Maggie with her trembling voice and "sacred duty" had broken his resolve and his heart. So, two hills climbed and conquered: while his dearest wish (or had it always been folly?) had slipped into the abyss.

"Oh!" his mother said abruptly. "I forgot to tell you, I've been so absent minded, thinking of Elly. I got a letter from your uncle Benjamin. He says there are more lawyers than you can shake a stick at in San Francisco but few of them are worth their salt, and he expects if you come, you'll do very well."

Ned sat up, glad for the distraction. "First rate! Did he recommend any law firm or say where to board, or recommend the best way to get there?"

"You know, I can't recall. I'll fetch the letter as soon as we get home," she replied.

His mind was full of all that he had read about San Francisco and the interior territories of America. "I guess I'd travel cross-country rather than go sailing around Cape Horn," he said, "at least there are trains for part of the way overland."

His mother looked into the basket by her side and tucked the cloth more closely around the pie she had baked for Eleanor, as she said: "It might be the best thing for you. But... then the nest will be empty."

It took a moment for him to realize she spoke of home. *More like a nest of vipers,* he thought, then quickly exempted her: a nest with the king viper, and one still-breathing but subdued prey. "I think it's worse for you when I'm there," he said quietly.

She answered in a low voice, although the train made enough noise to cover their words, "It's not you: he will find any ready target. As you know."

He looked at her. "Can't you—you're all right, I mean you manage...and Elly will be back," he said. "I expect you'll be all right, both of you, won't you? now that he's down in New Haven most of the time. And Katie's nearby."

She blinked rapidly and pulled her wrap up to her neck. "Yes," she said. "I expect so."

He wiped the window with his sleeve, there was still nothing to see. But soon, two years or less, he would leave all that was familiar behind. Despite his worries, a devilish tickle of glee wriggled inside him: he did not welcome it but would not smother it in its cradle. He proclaimed to his mother. "By heaven, there's a task worthy of every atom of our efforts—the Judge's perennial re-election to the Connecticut House!"

He always gets his way, Maggie thought, as the judge debated something with the minister, who was dressed just like a priest. She swayed Bertie in her arms and prayed again that he would not scream as he had during the service.

"I'd cry," she whispered to him, "if I'd such a bunch of fuss around me." Upon Mrs. Whitfield's advice, the baby's legs were swaddled thickly with layers of cloth so that he would not mess through to the white and heavily starched christening gown.

Bertie's parents and the few guests had already duly admired the baby, and Maggie was impatient to take him home. *Just as well,* she thought, *to stay away from his uncle,* who had greeted her politely, but with a stiff smile that she recognized as pain. I'm sore too, she wanted to tell him, just as much as you.

She wished she could speak to Miss Minton who was here at the ceremony, at Eleanor's request and in her place. Eleanor wrote to her every week: there was the struggle, the scarring sadness, Maggie told herself—this distance between her brother and me, 'tis nothing in comparison. His animation when he spoke now of California was not new: there'd been a time she welcomed it, for she'd be joining him on that journey. Now she was the silent listener, 'though wanting to shout "Don't go!"; and she would never be his partner.

Bertie grimaced and farted, then grunted. Och, here it comes. She signaled to Mrs. Whitfield, then left the sanctuary, grabbed the bundle of cloths she had left in the entry, and took the stairs down to the basement. When she had cleaned the child, bundled up the messy diapers so they would not leak, and re-dressed him, he ended his fussing and smiled at her.

"You're a rascal," she told him.

With the messy bundle in one hand, and Bertie on her hip, she started back up the stairs, but was met by a man coming down.

"Oh. Pardon me," Edward said, stepping aside.

"No, 'tis my fault, go ahead," Maggie replied. He took his nephew in his arms. "I'll see to this fellow. Or would you like me to take that," he pointed at the diapers and wrinkled his nose, "out to the carriage?"

"Och, you mustn't!" she said.

"It's no worse than a camp hospital full of men with dysentery," he replied.

"No, I'll take it, you mustn't," she said, then: "I'm so sorry." For the first time in weeks he looked at her full on, until she dropped her gaze.

"It's all right," he said.

"I'm sorry," she repeated, "about… about the whole of it…"

"Don't fret," he said, as he had so often to her in the past. He turned and carried the baby up the stairs. Maggie scrambled up behind him and out to the carriage, to dispose of the odorous bundle and her own distress.

"Good day, Joe," Ned said, as Creasey came down the stairs from

Mix's office, "What brings you here?

Joe shook his head unhappily. Brushing past Ned, he muttered, "They told me I've got to see Mr. Peasley. Good day."

Ned heard Putnam expostulating in Mix's office and knocked at that door. "I have the deed copies from South Lancaster," he said to Putnam, adding: "I just saw Mr. Creasey on his way to Peasley's?"

Putnam grimaced. "He came for some fellow named Park with a complaint about cutting down a tree on his land, and I would not hear it."

"What kind of complaint, was there any legal basis for it?" Ned asked.

"Whether there was or not makes no difference. I sent him to Peasley," Putnam said irritably.

"I'd just like to hear the facts of Mr. Creasey's complaint. He's a good barber," Ned said.

"Yardley is far better," Putnam growled, "It's out of the question. Our reputation has already suffered damage from all of the Irish coming by! You opened that gate and now we are flooded."

Ned looked at Mix but was favored by a grim frown. "The success in Sullivan and Cohan surely..." Ned began.

"I was just telling Charles," Putnam interrupted, "we have a serious problem. I saw Mr. Topliff today, and he asked me if we intended to open a Pigtown branch." He slapped his hand on the desk. "Clients like that will destroy the fine reputation that Charles has built over the years!"

"Mr. Mix," Ned said, "You have known Moses Park for years; he is a respectable man. And Mr. Creasey is married to his daughter Minnie, and he is just as..."

Mix held up his hands. "We can't do it. Such minor matters must go to Peasley. What I may think of Park does not matter."

"Precisely!" Putnam said in exasperation.

"But we do not know if this a minor matter..." Ned began. At Putnam's outraged snort and Mix's disapproving look, he said: "But it is your decision, of course."

"Let him try his luck with Peasley," Putnam said, "Perhaps you could too."

"What do you mean by that?" Ned replied, staring at the man until Putnam looked down.

"Here now," Mix put in hurriedly, "We've settled the matter, and we've got more important things to address. Give me those title copies."

Chapter 53

"Mikey, 'tis good to see you," Maggie said, "And Aggie, how are you getting on?" She gave her sister-in-law a hug, and patted Agnes' pregnant belly for good measure. Jem giggled as his cousin Mary whirled about singing a tuneless song.

Mike said: "Where's Mam?"

"Out the back," Rose said, then: "Mikey don't start a row, I'm watchin' her, she hasn't had a drop." He went out the back door anyway. Agnes shook her head. "He takes it hard when she's ailing," she said.

"Never you mind," Rose replied, "We're keeping an eye on her."

Agnes eased down into a chair next to Maggie. "I'm glad you got leave to come on a day we're here."

Maggie answered: "I'm here for just an hour or so, Oh, here's Mam." She embraced her mother and kissed her cheek, so glad to see her.

Her mother grinned. "Your boy's grown so, I'd hardly know 'twas him."

Desmond Dooley and Bridget arrived, and Maggie ran to her friend. "How are you feeling Bridey? Congratulations! Mrs. Leary told me Baby is due in November. It seems most everyone is expecting a little one."

"Except me, thank the Lord," Rose put in.

"And me," Maggie said. Bridey hugged her. "Och, don't be sad Maggie. We all miss Rory, but you have his son right here—a little Rory he is, to be sure."

"He's his own self. Jem," Mrs. O'Shaughnessy said coolly,

"And there won't be another like him, so I hear. More's the pity for holy Annie."

"What are you talking about, Mam?" Maggie said in confusion, as Bridey rolled her eyes and frowned.

Rose said: "'tis nothing."

"'tis something," Maggie went on, troubled, "Mam, what do you hear?" Mrs. O'Shaughnessy shrugged.

Bridey looked at Mr. Dooley; at his nod, she said: "Well, we heard from Mrs. Leary that Annie Mulrooney means to join the Sisters of Mercy over to Hartford."

"Annie?" Maggie exclaimed, "She ain't holy at all. Why would she do such a thing?"

Rose suddenly left the stove and took her young daughter by the hand. "We'll go out and find some flowers for the table. Come along now."

"She had good reason!" Agnes sniffed, when the two were safely out the back door. "Aint you heard?"

Maggie said: "Heard what?"

Bridget and Agnes spoke at once, then Agnes ceded to Bridget. "Annie had a baby in May, Maggie. But the poor little thing died the same day. We don't even know if he got baptized, dear little soul. I'm thinkin' he didn't, by the way she took on. Not that I blame her a bit; to lose your baby is a terrible thing."

Agnes proclaimed: "And before you start askin', no, she ain't married, and we none of us know who the father is; she won't tell. She won't say a word about it."

It serves her right, Maggie thought for an instant, then felt ashamed as she glanced at her healthy (and lawfully baptized) child on his uncle's lap. "Oh," she said, "I'm sorry to hear that. But she oughn't to have done what she did."

Something else was wrong, Maggie felt, from the way the women were looking at her, from the men's silence and averted eyes. "'twas no man here, at any rate," she said.

"Not here!" Mikey said firmly, "Not a soul here. Where's Rose? Ain't it time for dinner?"

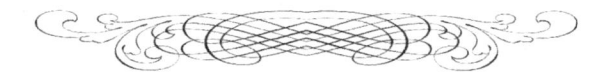

"No, everyone here treats me kindly," Eleanor said, stroking Dance's ears, "But... I'm afraid I'll say something wrong; I don't know what they want me to do. I want to be good! But I'm not sure what they want."

Kate replied with a frown: "You ARE good. What makes you think you are not?"

Eleanor shrugged.

"If the doctor or the folks here want something of you, they must tell you," Ned put in.

"They want you to get well," Kate said, "all of us do. It is just so sad to see you this way—so blue."

"I know they want me to get well," Eleanor said, "But I don't know *how*. And I'm awfully sorry, Katie, to make you sad, and Mama too."

"Don't worry about us," Katie said, "We just think of you. Have you ever thought not of what they want, but what **you** want to do, or what pleases you, or what makes you feel peaceful?"

Dance rolled over and Eleanor rubbed his belly. "I... I can't say it."

"You can say it, Elly," Katie urged.

Eleanor straightened in her chair, then hunched her shoulders. "But I do things wrong,"

"Such as?" Ned asked. The dog got up and put his chin on Eleanor's knee. She held herself tightly and shook her head. Ned felt in his pocket for his notebook and pencil. He took them both to Eleanor. "Here," he said, "sometimes I don't know what I'm thinking until I write it down. Write down the first thing you are thinking of." He returned to his seat. She sat still for a long time. "Do you want us to leave, so you can have some quiet?" he asked.

"NO!" Eleanor shouted, as Dance barked. "Stay, do stay," she went on in a shaky voice. She wrote something in the notebook, then tore the page out and placed it on her lap, pushing down on it with her fingers. "Oh, I tore your book, Ned, I'm sorry."

He snorted. "I don't care about the book. Feed it to Dance if you like."

She dropped her shoulders a little. "He likes bacon better," she said, "and you'd be angry if he ate your book."

"No, "Kate said.

"The blasted book," Ned repeated, "it means nothing. I wouldn't be angry at you."

Eleanor glanced at him, then folded the notebook page neatly into a small square. "Do I have to tell what I wrote?"

Kate looked at Ned. "No, you do not," she said, "and even if you wrote bad things about anyone on that paper, I, we, would not be angry. So there."

Eleanor stared at her. "But... do you think I'm doing things right: to be here anyhow. I'm trying hard. Aren't I?"

"Yes," Kate said, "My dear mouse."

Eleanor smiled slightly. "Sister mouse? Rebecca says that we are like sisters, she says that no matter what I do or say, she is my friend."

"She's a true friend," Kate said, "and so are we. No matter what."

"Yes," Eleanor said, "like the three musketeers." She unfolded the page, tucked the pencil into the notebook and stood up. Dance wagged his tail. She went to Ned and handed them to him. "You can read it, my secret message." He did so and smiled thinly. "Out loud," she said.

"*I'm afraid to go home, I don't want to go home,*" he read, adding, "Well, why in heaven's name would you?"

Kate got up and put her arms around her sister. "You don't have to go home unless you wish to, Elly. And when you do, you can stay with Worth and me, and Maggie and Mrs. C. and the boys."

"But Mama," Eleanor said in agitation, "Mama will need me."

Ned put in: "I had the same worry when I began to plan for California. I talked about it with her, and she insisted that I must go when I can. You know Mama, Elly. She told me that she wants us to be safe and well - she wants the best for us."

"But she'll be all alone!" Eleanor said.

Kate shook her head. "Elly, she's at my house every day or so when Father's not here! Do you think that I'd leave her there if there was a... a problem? Although I expect she can fend for herself; she has for so many years."

"But I was there to... to help her, I always tried to help," Eleanor said.

Kate added wryly, "She told me that she sings a little hymn inside her mind whenever Father is angry at her, so that she doesn't answer back or get too fretty."

"That must be one almighty powerful hymn!" Ned commented.

Eleanor smiled for a moment. The mantel clock chimed. "Oh!" she said, "It's time for you to talk to the doctor. All that he does is ask questions! Don't... I know you won't say anything bad about me: I am trying very hard to not say the wrong things."

"We would never say anything bad about you, how can you think that?" Kate said.

Ned put in: "What wrong things do you mean?" Eleanor was silent.

Kate said: "I expect you need to tell the doctor the truth, even if that's a difficult thing."

Eleanor shook her head. "I can't. No words come out. I'm not brave enough."

"Yes, you are," Kate asserted.

Ned said, "I wouldn't cross her if I were you, Elly. She still thinks she's Miss Boss."

"Rebecca is Miss Boss," Eleanor said with a faint smile, "So there."

"Why did he insist on seeing us separately, and why you first? Did he suppose I'd be too emotional? Slow down, Ned!" Kate huffed.

"Perhaps he was trying to see if our answers aligned," Ned responded, as he held his handkerchief to his mouth to dam the saliva.

"He's not an attorney, for heaven's sake. What did he ask you about?" she demanded.

"We must catch that horse-car," Ned said, "That's the one that goes to the train station. He asked me about Father, and was he kind to her, as Eleanor apparently has said. I disabused him of the notion."

"I had the same questions and said the same. Why would she say he was kind?" Kate said quickly, as Ned helped her up the stair. They sat down hard on the benches and grabbed for balance as the car jolted forwarded.

Kate said in a low voice: "I'm surprised that Elly did not tell some of the things that occurred when Father...is in a temper. No, Ned, don't answer now, your voice is too loud, just nod or shake your head."

"Yes, Miss Boss," he said quietly, but poked his knuckle into her side. "Ow."

"The corset's revenge," she whispered. "You won't try that again. It sounds as if she did not tell him **anything** about Papa. Where did she get the notion that she was…" She dropped her voice so far that he could barely hear her next word: "bad."

Ned scowled and shook his head. "Utter nonsense," he said.

"What are we to do?" his sister said. He had no answer.

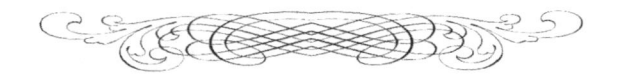

Maggie peeked into the sitting room. "Mrs. Fariday, Bertie's much better tonight, and he's sleeping now." Seeing Edward in the corner, she kept her eyes down.

"Well, that's a relief," Mrs. Fariday said.

"What was wrong?" Edward asked.

"He ran a fever," Mrs. Fariday said, then looked at Maggie.

"He was warm, and off his feed. They get the sniffles when they're cutting teeth," Maggie said to the floor.

"If they're both asleep, you can join us," Edward said, "It's a windy night, so I was just about to read a rattling good story by Edgar Allen Poe."

"Sit down, Maggie. Ned reads very well, and you'd like to hear it," said Mrs. Fariday. Maggie thanked her and sat down as far from Edward as she could.

"And so it begins," Edward said, and began the story.

Let me call myself, for the present, William Wilson. That is not my real name. That name has already been the cause of the horror—of the anger of my family. Have not the winds carried my name, with my loss of honor, to the ends of the earth? Am I not forever dead to the world? to its honors, to its flowers, to its golden hopes? And a cloud, heavy and endless—does it not hang forever between my hopes and heaven?

As Edward continued the narrative of the boy who was shadowed by a fellow who resembled him and bore the same name, Maggie wondered again if she was dishonoring Rory by sitting with these people. *They're kind to me,* she told him in her mind. *You're* the servant, Rory said back to her, that ugly Yank just wants to bed you; you sit among them like that little dog does. He'll be going off soon, West like Da, she countered to Rory, and shivered. Ned had told her when he loved her that the West could be their salvation and means of escape: no one would know them there.

He read on of the coincidental meetings between the two William Wilsons, as the second tried to stem the excesses of the first. Maggie thought he looked a bit dissolute himself, and pale in the gaslight. He paused to look at his sister.

"What do you think, Katie?"

"Mysterious," she replied.

"Not so mysterious, if you listen to the clues," he teased.

His sister made a disparaging noise. "I don't care for Poe. He's overwrought and deliberately muddy."

"What do you think, Mrs. Corcoran?" he asked. Although she enjoyed his reading, and how he had spun the tale out like a delicious conundrum, the gist of the story was plain to her. She shrugged.

"I've heard that he was an opium-eater," Kate put in, then snickered at his glee. "Read on."

He continued, and the tale of the first Wilson's bad behavior became darker. Before the climax of the story, he paused again: "So who is this mysterious additional William Wilson, and who will prevail?"

"Oh, stop that," Kate said, "Just read it."

"Mrs. Corcoran?" he said.

"I'm thinkin' 'tis he himself, his own conscience, but he's a stranger to it," Maggie said.

"Yes!" Mrs. Fariday said, "Of course. And since this is Poe, there will be a grim ending, no doubt."

Edward looked at Maggie. "Remarkably astute, Mrs. Corcoran, as usual." Maggie repeated the compliment to herself with pleasure, then mentally shook herself. Pretty words meant little. "Let's see if you've spoiled the story," he said.

The other Wilson finally arrived late at night, masked, and with a sword, which the narrator Wilson seized and stabbed through the intruder's heart. The narrator then saw Wilson in a mirror,

'As I walked toward it in terror I saw my own form, all spotted with blood, its face white, advancing to meet me with a weak and

uncertain step. It was Wilson; but now it was my own voice I heard, as he said: 'I have lost. Yet from now on you are also dead...dead to Heaven, dead to Hope! In me you lived—and in my death—see by this face, which is your own, how wholly, how completely, you have killed... yourself!'

"The End," Edward said dramatically.

Mrs. Fariday snorted. "Overwrought."

Maggie suddenly thought of Annie. Overwrought Annie, and now wanting to be a nun. Why would she lay with a man when she wasn't married? Maggie counted all the nights Rory had rolled onto her in their bed—so ardent a husband. Though she missed him she did not miss that. What a relief it had been those few nights when she had a head cold and he had slipped into bed late and not disturbed her at all from head to toe, just said how sorry he was, and held her lightly and kissed her forehead. See, that was good of him; he did think of her and care for her. It made her all the more willing that last night when he was so tender to her. *Just what did you do, Rory,* she thought, *that I never knew, that would make you a friend to Brian Harrigan? All those nights you came in late from seeing him...*

The idea came like a drenching of ice water: he could not have, not lain with Annie after he was a married man! It couldn't be. But what had caused that embrace of remorse? She got up, excused herself, and fled.

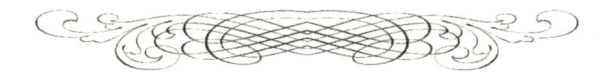

With Jem on her right hip and Bertie on her left, Maggie raced down the basement stairs. "Is Mrs. Leary here today?" she asked Aggie's sister, who paused to take a breath while wringing out a wet sheet.

"She's about here somewhere, may be in the water closet," Maura replied. Maggie gripped the babies tighter, carefully skirting the boiling vat, and stood by the water closet door.

"Och, Mrs. Leary, I need to see you, just for a bit. Please!" Maggie said to the old woman as she came out.

"What's wrong, dearie. Is it your Mam?" Mrs. Leary asked.

"Come outside with me, you must! I've something important to ask you. 'twon't take but a minute, truly," Maggie said. Once they were well outside the kitchen door, Maggie put Jem down on the grass, but kept Bertie in her arms.

"'tisn't Mam, nor the family," she said, trying to blink away tears, "I... I'm... you must tell me, who's the father of Annie Mulrooney's baby, the one that died. Frank says she won't tell it, but you must know, you must have heard from Mrs. Kernan, you must have heard what folks are sayin'."

"Don't take on so, Maggie. Why are ye askin' me about this... 'tisn't any of your concern," Mrs. Leary said, watching Jem as he examined a clump of yellow grass in his hand.

Maggie wiped her nose on the back of her hand. "Is it Rory? Are they sayin' 'tis Rory? You must tell me!"

"Whissht," Mrs. Leary said, still gazing at the boy, "Who's been sayin' such things to ye?"

Maggie shouted, "Why'd he come to bed so late sometimes? Was it to do Harrigan's business? Was it for the Fenian Brotherhood, or... oh, mercy! Something worse..." She sobbed at Mrs. Leary's grim expression, and Bertie began to whine.

Mrs. Leary said: "Aw, mavourneen, ye mustn't cry. Nobody knows for certain the poor babe's father."

"What... are they... sayin?'" Maggie gasped.

Mrs. Leary looked at her with sympathy. "Poor colleen. What do ye think?"

Maggie cried out. Mrs. Leary came to her, took the child from her arms, and patted her back. When Maggie's sobs slowed, she wiped Maggie's face gently with a corner of her own apron.

"I have to know, for certain," Maggie whispered.

"And why is that?" Mrs. Leary said, "Some men will stray - 'tis naught to do with their good wives. Rory was proud to marry you, you were a good wife to him. Put your chin up now and dry your tears. You've a fine son. Rory would be proud of him." *I'm broken in two,* Maggie thought, *can't you see that?* Bertie was roaring in Mrs. Leary's arms, but Maggie picked up her son, who wrinkled his brow at her expression.

She pressed him against her heart, kissed his wild curls, murmuring "How could he, how could he do that?" Jem put a grimy hand against her cheek: the dirt and grass mixing with the wet.

Chapter 54

Portions of what Father Foley was saying, with many serious nods, Maggie recognized from her old catechism, yet his words still confused her. What he seemed to be saying was not, not at all, what she had hoped to hear, but what she had feared. Indeed, Mrs. Corcoran, if your late husband had died without mortal sin on his soul then he would be in purgatory, and God would hear your prayers and the prayers of the faithful on the poor fellow's behalf. But if he had, God forbid, died with a mortal sin on his soul and without final penance or extreme unction then he had no hope of ever seeing heaven.

"Forever?" Maggie interrupted in horror, "For one mistake?"

"And better you should ask," Father said, "why does a man raised in the true faith ever sin? Because it is in our sinful nature to do so. Some men, in the exercise of the free will God gave us in His wisdom, choose to turn their faces from God and gravely sin." He took his gaze, at last, away from the picture on the wall and looked at her. "Do you know when your husband had last been to confession before he died?"

"He went sometimes," Maggie said, "It counts for something. It must. For if he didn't mean to do anything bad, if he didn't know it, that something he did was a mortal sin, then God wouldn't shut the door!"

Father Foley's brow creased. He wasn't much older than Rory had been when he died, yet the priest looked as ancient as the trees to Maggie. He said: "I'll say it again, Mrs. Corcoran. A man who dies with a mortal sin on his soul, will not see heaven. You don't seem to know when his last confession was, and I was not here at St. James when he died so only God knows Mr. Corcoran's fate."

"No!" Maggie cried at him, "It can't be. God wouldn't punish forever... not for a mistake!"

"Mrs. Corcoran!" Father Foley broke in, "D'you think for a moment that any one of us can say what our Lord would or wouldn't do! That's blasphemy. I'll excuse it, for I see you're distressed, but you must pray for strength and humility and remember that God's ways are not our ways."

She wasn't aware of how much longer she sat in his presence, of how much more he said, only that she pulled out her handkerchief, knowing that her face would be wet as soon as she finally felt it: this fact that Rory was left behind as he had been when a boy, still suffering; he might be alone, in torture forever—beyond her aid and perhaps beyond her prayers. She did not want to be in the church when the horror came. Wasn't it blasphemy too for a woman to turn her face from God's anointed priest, and to hate the sight of him?

"I will, Father, thank you," she replied to whatever he was saying, "I must go."

Then she was out on the street, for a moment empty and purposeless as a blowing leaf. She knew the scythe of pain was nearby, swinging out to catch her and take its harvest: she wanted to meet it alone, away from the road. She walked stiff-legged across the street, until she heard the sound of water.

At the lip of the road, she looked down a low hill to a brook. As if the scythe had cut off her feet, Maggie suddenly collapsed and slid down the incline. She stayed flat on the ground, breathless, waiting, hiding her face in the crook of her arm. *Take me,* she prayed. *Take all my hurt. Let me die, only give him rest!* As if heaven had heeded only her first words, her sobs ripped through her, tearing like the pain of childbirth. She pressed her face into the earth, anxious for oblivion. *God's ways are not our ways.* Like sharp hail dropping on her head, the phrase repeated in her mind. It was hard to get a breath now. 'Don't carry on so,' her father used to tell her. A stone was under her ribcage. She sat up, scooted away from the stone, and curled up again in a different spot, wishing her father near. He, at least, was still alive, though far away. She wiped her nose on her sleeve. Ah, what was the use of life, what a cruel thing God had made it.

She heard a soft sound, and looked up to see movement in

the brush close by. A bird, the color of smoke, stood an arm's reach away from her. *God's ways are not our ways,* she heard again in her head, this time as quietly as the bird stood watching her. She looked her fill at the bird, which did not fly away from her gaze.

"Mercy..." she whispered. The bird seemed to bow to her, then took wing, alighting for a moment in the big elm. As she sat up to watch it, it flew away and was lost to her sight. Her breathing returned. She got to her feet as uncertainly as an infant learning to stand and began a slow journey up to the level of the road.

There she is, Ned pulled the horse to a stop, *What the devil?* Her face and clothing were spotted with dirt, her hair was straggling beneath the crushed hat. He threw down the carriage weight, hopped out.

"Maggie, are you all right?" Seeing her dazed reaction, he said: "You've hurt yourself. Here, get in, I'll take you home." She moved so slowly and stiffly that he lifted her into the vehicle, placing her on the front seat. As he climbed in, he asked: "Did you fall?"

She looked at him, blinking like a child called forward in the classroom to recite a lesson that she has not studied. She looked at her lap, murmured: "We all of us fell, so he says, so the Bible says, when Adam sinned. But then how can we **any** of us know, just hope?"

He waited but she did not continue. He said: "What are you talking about? Who is he, who said this? Did someone hurt you?" She did not appear to hear him. His concern increased. "Maggie, listen to me. Did you hit your head when you fell?"

She clutched his wrist, her muddy fingers staining the white cuff. "Was it a sign, then? That I'm not meant to know, only hope?"

Ned wondered what possessed her to go to church on a weekday, and what sort of a church conducted services on weekdays anyhow; and what sort of a service would reduce a woman to such a state that she would wander off thoughtlessly away from the road leading home? Perhaps someone had accosted her.

"Maggie. Pay attention. Did someone hurt you? Should I take you to Mrs. Moore?"

"No," she replied calmly. She appeared to be in that deep

meditative state that Ned had witnessed once or twice.

Suddenly she raised her eyebrows, squeezed his wrist, looked directly at him. "Agnus Dei!" she whispered. It was as if she had shouted, "Eureka!"

"Agnes who?" Ned said in frustration, "Did she knock you down?" She didn't answer.

Incomprehensible: it wasn't like Maggie to brawl. Who the devil was Agnes Day-ee? Some Irish girl? But it sounded like Latin—ah, 'Dei', of course. Catholic services were in Latin.

"Agnus Dei," he repeated aloud, automatically correcting her pronunciation. "Lamb of God."

She favored him with a slight smile. She said: "Qui tollis peccata mundi," then frowned, as if she was trying to remember something. Her hand slipped from his wrist and fell limply on the seat.

"Who takes away the world's sins," Ned said, relieved to have found some reasonable explanation for her babbling. "Um. It's clear you had some sort of... experience at church, but now you're injured. I'm taking you home." He hauled in the carriage weight, then clucked to his horse, giving it a touch of the whip when it did not move fast enough for his taste. *Haven't I had enough of this business—more than any man's fair share!* he thought, *Crisis at every corner.* She said something that he could not hear over the sound of the carriage wheels. "I beg your pardon?"

"Miserere nobis." He glanced at her: she looked at him expectantly. "Forgive us," he translated, as she seemed to want.

"And the last is, Dona nobis pacem."

He could not hear her sigh, but saw her chest and shoulders rise and then fall with it. "Grant us peace," he said gruffly, touched by the words and her demeanor. After a few moments, he said: "Amen." Maggie smiled at him sadly.

He said: "I'm afraid it's in short supply, at least at Kate's. I came by to give Eleanor a new piece of music I bought for her and found them all in a flurry because you'd disappeared and the babies were with Mrs. Carruthers."

"The babies!" Maggie said in horror, "Ah, the poor things. I forgot them entirely. They'll be roaring. Mother of God! I'm a selfish, forgetful wretch, wandering about in a fog, and can't even keep one foot free of tangling with the other. That's what happened, Ned, I tripped and went headlong down the ditch at the side of the road."

"Everyone stumbles at one time or another." He had noted her verbal slip too and liked the sound of his nickname in her mouth. "At least you weren't injured."

She shook her head, biting at her lip. "Not so's you'd notice. 'twould serve me right if I was. And yet you came along again and picked me up and sorted me out. I hardly deserved it then, and now, my garters! even less."

"It seemed to me it was out of character for you to leave Jem and Bertie for so long, so I... guess I was worried."

"Yes," she said warmly and gave his comment a moment's respectful silence, "You came along like the Good Samaritan. Thank you." He looked at her and she back at him. "I'm so glad that it was you."

Ned felt better than he had in weeks. "You're welcome," he said. When they were a block or two from the Faridays, she suddenly gasped, then giggled. "Share the joke," Ned said.

"Agnes, you said, *Agnes who*!?"

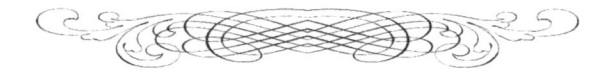

"Ow!" Eleanor said, "Bertie, no! stop pulling my hair." She disengaged the boy's hand.

Maggie said: "Elly, he's happy to see your pretty curls again. And I'm just SO glad to see you! Oh, Jemmy must've spilled his cup on my shoe, look at how Dance is licking it. I'm thinkin' 'tis a good life to be a dog. They have no worries."

"I should like that very much, to have no worries," Eleanor said ardently, "You know, I missed you all terribly. Even though Rebecca and Mr. Minton were so kind. He asked me to play their piano every night and I was glad to... I wish I could be... Oh, bother, I don't know. It just seems as if I can't find myself anymore." Maggie looked at her. "I say a lot of silly things," Eleanor went on.

"No, you don't," Maggie answered, "I feel the same! After I married Rory, everything was so different, I didn't know what to do, I hardly knew who I was either. And he wasn't who I thought."

Eleanor put Bertie on her shoulder and patted his back. "Neither was Mr. Barton. I don't think Mr. Corcoran treated you very well, I'm sorry to say."

"He did not!" Maggie hissed, "You're right—and he's torturing me still—thinking of him."

"Oh." Eleanor said tentatively, "I'm sorry. You miss him so? and I said a bad thing…"

"No," Maggie said, "HE did a bad thing! You've nothing to be sorry for."

"What did he do?" Eleanor asked, then said: "Maggie, you don't have to tell me, not if you don't want to. But I wish you would."

"He…" Maggie began, sure it would all come out—every word of the harm—if she went on speaking: so she did.

After the torrent, the shocked responses, the comforting embraces, Eleanor rubbed her forehead and said: "Men are so queer. I don't believe I'll ever understand them."

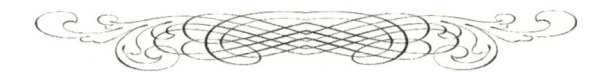

"Ah, Mr. Whitfield," Mr. Lang said, as he made his way down the aisle, "May I join you?" Lang fell into the seat as the train rounded a bend. "Studying for the bar?" he asked, pointing to the case book Ned was reading.

"Continuously," Ned answered, "and deeply mired in Landlord and Tenant."

"That's a common examination topic, so you are wise to give it attention," Lang said, "Well met, actually. You've saved me a trip to Millville. I have a thorny pension case. I'd like your help with it if Charles is amenable."

"He's likely to agree," Ned said, "and I'm glad to help. Is it a documentation issue?"

Lang shook his head. "His documents were as sound as a dollar, with the local surgeon in agreement. The Pension board turned him down because the ink was the wrong color, or the weather was rainy, or the reviewer was bilious: who knows? And now this fellow says he won't beg for something that he's owed. Of course, that's his choice to make, but he's lost the use of his arm and a leg, can't work, and has a family. They will all be turned out of their lodging if he cannot find a source of income."

"How can I help you?" Ned asked. Lang replied: "He may

listen more readily to a fellow veteran than to me. You ought to know, however, that he lives just outside of Hebron. I hope that you don't mind a short journey."

"Not at all. The further from Millville the better, in fact."

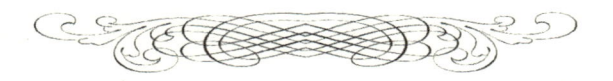

"What are you reading?" Edward asked.

Maggie looked up from the book. "*Elsie Venner* by Oliver Holmes. Eleanor gave it to me."

"I've read it," he commented, "That one is full of twists and turns, and fear, oddities, and snakes. I'm surprised she recommended it to you."

Maggie glanced across the garden where Eleanor sat with Bertie under Miss Minton's happy gaze. "She didn't. She only read a bit of it and hated it." She set the book down on the bench as Jem crawled to her and pulled himself to a stand. "Jemmy," she said, "Look at you, up like a big boy."

"I didn't know he was standing yet," Edward said.

"He hasn't done it before," she replied, with a pleased smile. "What's that in your hand, Jem?"

The baby opened his hand, lost his balance and plopped to his bottom, then crawled to Edward. He pulled on Edward's trousers and stood. "Ga," he said triumphantly.

"Who is this little man?" Edward said to him. Jem overbalanced, fell again, and crawled to a drift of fallen leaves. Edward squatted next to him, as the boy flourished the remains of a leaf.

"Leaf," Ned said, "Maple. Red."

Jem pushed the leaf into Ned's hand, then said, "Ga da." He crawled away and grabbed another and showed it to Ned.

"You're a single-minded fellow. You like this pretty red thing, don't you? Not every pretty thing must be 'Ga', how about 'yee' for a change?"

Jem waved his arms. "Ga dah." He put a leaf in his mouth experimentally then spat it out, and grabbed another, crumpling it in his hands, chortling.

Maggie said. "Everything goes into his mouth. Do you think leaves will hurt him?"

Ned smiled. "No harm."

Jem crawled to steal the leaf from Edward's palm, causing Edward to observe: "Ah ha. You want total possession, I see. What is the definition of 'ga', James? A certain indefinable longing? Or are there several measurable qualities that limn the boundaries of 'ga'?" The baby looked at him for several moments, then let the leaf drift to the ground.

"What's in a name?" Edward went on, "That which we call a 'ga' by any other name would be as red. Wherefore art thou Romeo? Deny thy father and refuse thy name, or if thou wilt not, be but sworn my love, and I'll no longer be a Capulet."

Maggie made a small noise of protest, but Jem stared on in silence. Ned picked up the leaf, frowning, and gave it to Jem.

"Dah," the child said in a soft tone, "dah."

"I never liked that Italian play," Ned muttered.

Maggie refused to ever go back to that exciting and terrible roundelay of loving and wanting and being unable to have. Yet there was something she was compelled to say: "'twasn't your fault, nor mine."

Chapter 55

"Catch me if you can," Kate yelled at her brother as she brought her horse from a trot to a canter.

"Hey!" Ned hollered in return, "I thought this was a Sunday pleasure ride."

"MY pleasure!" she called with a laugh and swept past him. He tapped Shadrach and said: "Go." Shadrach began to trot. With his ears pointed forward toward Kate's bay mare, he lumbered into full speed. Ned reached up to jam his hat on tighter. The wind of their movement slapped lightly at his face and hands. They rushed past a field full of angled shapes, cornstalks bent against each other like fighters in a circle. An edge of sunrise lit the tips of the horse's ears, and his grunts kept time with his hooves; he seemed as eager as his rider to run.

This early in the day, the road belonged solely to his sister and him. She was at least a dozen yards ahead of him, but he could see the scarf twined around her hat flipping a salute to him.

"Can you see our colors?" one of the men in his company would shout to him. On his belly in the field where he dared not raise his head; or squatted near the pontoon bridges below the heights in Fredericksburg, he would look for the flag.

He leaned low on his horse's neck and yelled, "Come on!" By the time he reached Kate, she had pulled her mare into a slow trot. Ned slowed Shadrach's pace, and the two horses trotted together: the mare barely winded, the gelding puffing.

"I'll race you on the way back," Ned said, "And I'll win. You took me by surprise."

"Pooh," Kate scoffed, "Maybelle can run circles around

Shad."

"She does like a good run," Ned said, "better than pulling a carriage. Karl told me she sets up a ruckus when there's any traffic."

"Oh, she may be a little hard to handle," Kate replied, "I like them that way."

He kept better time on the run back toward the Faridays' home, just a few lengths behind Kate. She looked over her shoulder at him at the same moment that a chaise turned in front of her to enter the Fariday drive.

"Look out!" he yelled, and his sister kicked the mare faster, crossing just in front of the startled gray horse pulling the chaise. Ned slowed his unhappy horse and turned him sharply. They just missed the still-moving chaise, then safely crossed behind it. He pulled Shad into a trot.

Both had recognized the horse and its driver: Greylock and Judge Whitfield. Ned settled Shad out of the trot into a slower gait and then turned him at a walk up the driveway. It had been a close call. He came alongside the chaise. Karl was leading Maybelle away. The judge had exited his vehicle and was remonstrating with Kate, who stood with hands on her hips: mulish, stubborn. And here came Eleanor (always wakeful) out the back door, equally curious and alarmed.

Ned dismounted and reached for Shad's bridle to walk him to the stable for a cool-down. There was a snapping noise behind him; he felt a sharp pain in his side. His horse shied and sidled a few steps away.

The judge shouted: "You! You reckless fool! You could have killed her." Something slapped at Ned's jacket, what the devil was stinging him so, a thousand hornets? He reached to the source of the pain. Eleanor went to Shad and grabbed his reins.

"Stop it, stop it!" Kate shrieked.

The judge still brandished the large carriage whip. Ned charged: his shoulder and fists meeting flesh and wool. For an instant he savored his father's shock, then his own momentum nearly took them both down. Ned kept his feet.

"That's enough!" he yelled, seizing the whip, "What in hell is wrong with you?"

The judge took a moment to catch his breath. "You knocked me down," he said. He pulled away from Ned's grasp, just as Kate advanced upon him.

"It was an accident," the judge stated, "You ought to have known better, racing your sister when she is still in a weak condition."

Kate turned on her father: "Get out!"

Fariday appeared. "What's going on here?" he said, adding "Keep cool, Katie," as he took her arm. His wife disobeyed him immediately, commencing a topper of a rant, which briefly distracted Ned from the pain in his side. As Fariday listened with patience, leaning on his crutch, Ned resisted Eleanor's attempt to guide him back to the house.

When Kate stopped for a breather, Fariday said to the Judge: "What possessed you, sir! To attack your son, with no provocation."

The Judge gathered himself. "It was an accident. Purely an accident."

"Bunkum!" Ned put in.

Fariday contemplated the Judge for a moment. "It was an accident," the judge repeated.

"I think not," Fariday said. "It is time for you to go." At this, Ned allowed Eleanor to lead him away.

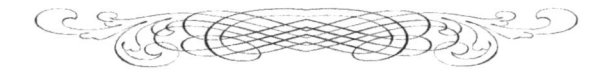

Ah good, no one was home. Ned went to his chamber and methodically gathered all his necessary belongings: the wooden box under the floorboards, his books, and Maggie's sketch bundled into a few changes of clothing. He loaded them into a carpetbag and a few empty feed sacks, tying them behind Shadrach's saddle.

Re-entering the house, he went quickly to the judge's study, and rifled through the desk drawers in pursuit of the reckoning of his debt that his father had always insisted was diligently kept. The family ledger revealed none of his own payments; and there was nothing applicable among the judge's other papers. This particular lie irked Ned as fully as the whip cuts had. He took his ceremonial sword down from its bracket on the study's wall. It glittered as he pulled it out of the scabbard: someone besides him had kept it well shined. This weapon had never seen battle: the shorter infantry blade he'd carried had been left behind on Fredericksburg's slippery ground.

He waved the sword just as he used to wave a stick when

playing war as a boy. Yet he was not the Spartan his father had wished for: he had not come home with his shield but upon it, half-dead. He put the scabbard on his father's chair and laid the ceremonial sword on the desk, its tip pointing at the chair. Taking a piece of his father's good stationery from the drawer, he scrawled a bitter note stating that he'd paid the debt with his pound of flesh; then crumpled it and threw it in the basket: it would mean nothing to the man. Suddenly tired, he took another piece of paper, writing only *'My debt is paid.'* Like a good law clerk, he initialed it, dated it and laid it on the desk blotter where his father could not miss it. Then, with no small measure of glee, he seized the Judge's penknife and drove it through the felt hard enough to enter the wood of the desk.

Ned flipped through the state statutes to review the criminal law and refresh his memory about the less frequently used writs. Mandamus? Latin for "we command." Quo Warranto? What on earth was that? He got up from his seat to consult the law dictionary.

"Who's here? Are they all out to dinner?" the judge said as he pushed through the door. He paused to look through Mix's open office door; knocked on Putnam's door, then opened it. He glanced at the closed windows. With a satisfied grunt, he faced his son. "What did you tell them?"

Ned opened the dictionary to the letter Q, then said: "Writ for quo warranto," and read the definition aloud: *a writ requiring the person to whom it is directed to show what authority they have for exercising a right, or power or franchise they claim to hold.*

"I don't have time for your nonsense!" the judge growled, "What did you tell them?"

Ned flipped to the letter R in the dictionary and remained silent.

The judge went on: "I was concerned about Kate. You know her health is delicate. I lost my temper. And that's the end of it; but you're your mother's son and had to blow the thing up beyond all reason."

"Beyond all reason? You cut me, ruined my coat—an unprovoked…" Ned began.

"Pah. What did you tell them?" the Judge interrupted. *Just relent,* Ned told himself, *what is it to you to satisfy him and send him away a contented (if never a happy) man?* "Come now," he responded, "what do you think I said?"

"What did you say to them? Spit it out now, or I'll wring your neck."

"Keep your voice down, for God's sake," Ned said quietly, "I hear Davis at the back door." He picked up the statute book as Davis came into the main room.

"Good day, Davis," the judge said.

"Good day, sir," Davis said, "Did you want Mr. Mix? He's at dinner but he'll be back soon."

Ned cleared his throat, and said: "No, he came by to counsel me on what to study for the bar examination," Ned said. "We were just discussing Title 19, Prevention of Frauds and Perjuries." He looked at his father, who took his meaning and scowled.

The judge said to Davis: "Moving nearer to the office has given him more time to study for the bar. We miss him at home, of course, but his duty comes first. I must go. Give my regards to Mr. Mix."

I am in an iron box, Ned thought, *I can see out but you cannot see in. One good word from you, and you would have had your answer: I told them nothing and no one asked. And in fact, if you'd listen and hear me rightly, I'd say that a few cuts are a small price to pay for escape.*

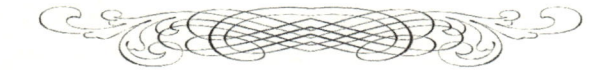

As Ned read aloud from the index of the Atlantic Monthly magazine, Kate and Eleanor could not agree which article to hear first. "The one about the veteran," Kate insisted.

"But it will be so sad," Eleanor protested, "Like the song that…"

"I'd like to hear it," Kate interrupted. So, he began to read aloud, soon proving his younger sister correct: the soldier had multiple amputations. Ned consciously steadied his voice as he read the sentence: " *'This set me to thinking how much a man might lose - and yet live.'"*

"The poor devil," Worth muttered.

"Have you had enough?" Ned asked Kate, as he scanned the

succeeding pages quickly. Kate sighed. "Now I want to hear what became of him, for well or ill."

Ned snickered as he read.

"Don't read ahead! Don't keep us in suspense," Kate commanded.

"Very well, but I give you fair warning," he replied. The story ended with the soldier at a spiritualist meeting. When the spirits were summoned, what rapped on the table and then materialized were the soldier's two missing legs, which carried him across the room. Ned was taken with a fit of laughter and Worth joined him. Ned gasped: "So that's what'll greet us in heaven - a litter of missing parts harvested in the war? Ha, ha! Will my eye see and know me, or will I search through a pile of them to find mine!"

He kicked his brother-in-law. "Hallo, Worth, look sharp, don't you know me? I'm your leg!"

"How can you?" Eleanor said. "How can you make fun of the poor man?" But the two veterans, helpless with laughter, did not answer, and Kate giggled with them.

Eleanor repeated: "The poor fellow!" Ned wiped his mouth with his handkerchief. "Come now, El, it's a joke, the whole story - look at the title: *Deadlock*, well, of course you would be with no limbs. It's totally absurd."

"But it's in the magazine," Eleanor said faintly, "so it must have happened."

He went on: "No, the author's just pulling your leg; though in fact you're right, he couldn't pull it for he has no hand to pull anything with!" Worth let out a loud haw, which made Kate giggle louder.

Eleanor relented and smiled slightly. "But," she said, "the first part may have happened to some poor solder. There's so many horrid things in war. Maggie sang me a song about that; it's to the tune of When Johnny Comes Marching Home. She says it was an Irish tune first, called Johnny I Hardly Knew Ye. It is much sadder than our song. It's just like this story."

The two men quieted. "Will you sing it for us?" Ned asked, hoping that she would.

"I'll say the words I remember," Eleanor said solemnly, and in the steady, soft cadence of the tune she did not sing, she recited:

With your drums and guns and guns and drums, hurroo, hurroo

With your drums and guns and guns and drums, hurroo, hurroo
With your drums and guns and guns and drums
The enemy nearly slew ye
Oh darling dear, ye look so queer
Johnny I hardly knew ye

Ye haven't an arm, ye haven't a leg, hurroo, hurroo
Ye haven't an arm, ye haven't a leg, hurroo, hurroo
Ye haven't an arm, ye haven't a leg
Ye're an armless, boneless, chickenless egg
You'll have to be left with a bowl out to beg
Oh Johnny I hardly knew ye

Ned prided himself on being a top-notch mimic, but as his sister spoke, he could hear the roll of Maggie's words and almost see her in the shadows. When Eleanor stopped, there was a long, musing silence.

"Heavens," Kate said.

"Some of the soldiers with amputations in the city have to beg," Eleanor said. "They beg on the street corners. In New York. Rebecca told me." Ned nodded in agreement.

Finally, Kate said: "And some get a pension, even that client of Mr. Lang's who turned Ned out three times before he'd accept any help. So, some do have a roof over their heads and food on the table. Elly, the story made me laugh, and I'd rather do that than cry."

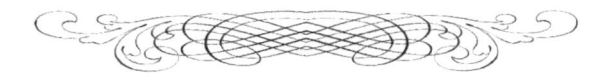

Since the bar examination date had been set in February—two months to go—Hannibal was at the gates of Rome! Ned's brain was a heavy cask near to overflowing, so much so that he hesitated tonight to lay it down. His good eye itched like the dickens, so he closed it and the Contracts textbook at the same time. He put his writing desk aside, and splashed water on his face.

The books he had rescued from the judge's house still slumped against the wall in the grain sacks. He turned up the gas light and began to pull the volumes out: wasn't there a book or two of poetry at the bottom, something to make him believe that he was more than a cistern for facts? He tossed the rejects onto the bed, setting Wordsworth aside on the floor, then at the bottom of the sack he found Aesop's Fables, and smiled at it. The book's spine was worn: a pity, since its leather binding had once been quite fine. The engraved illustrations were first rate as well; ah, there is the Tortoise and the Hare. And further on, some lady had placed a flower to dry as a bookmark. No, it was a pretty little sketch of a rose drawn in the margin by an unknown hand.

He flipped the pages to find the Grasshopper and the Ant, one of his father's favorites. At the age of 13, he had debated the merits of this fable with the judge, insisting that some grasshoppers could be ant-ish and store up for winter, or some ants could have moments to enjoy the sound of a fiddle.

"The moral is as plain as the nose on your face," the judge had shouted, "Just wait until you must work for a living!"

The illustrated plate for the fable in this book had an instructively dutiful ant and a starving grasshopper. Behind the plate there was a page with the top edge bent over. Ned turned to it to smooth the corner: smiling at him from the top margin of the page was a sketched likeness of Homer Merritt. Ned smiled back.

He sat and held the book gently for a time, leaning against the bed, lost and at peace.

Ned handed Eleanor the book and watched her smile. "Oh! Aesop. He's one of my favorites."

"Look inside where the pages are marked," he said. She opened to the first bookmark. "That's Mrs. Wilkin - I met her when she came to the house. Is this Maggie's book?" she said in surprise.

He answered, "I expect she has not seen it since Mr. Merritt died: I bought it at his estate sale. It's full of her sketches."

"Oh, this picture of the clouds, isn't it lovely!" Eleanor said, "You don't mean to keep it, do you? She'd be ever so happy to have it back!"

"I'd like to keep it," he said, "but it's hers, she must have it back; and you must give it to her. Do you remember how Mother used to leave a new book on our beds early on New Year's Day? Perhaps you could leave it on her bed at Christmas. "

"She will be so surprised!" Eleanor said, "But don't you want to give it to her yourself?"

Ned shook his head.

"Well, I can do it, of course," she said with a frown, "but…is there a quarrel? Are you angry at her?"

"No, in fact, I mean to protect her and her position here."

"Oh, my, did Worth say something to you?" Eleanor asked apprehensively.

"No, indeed, can't you guess who's the problem? Didn't Maggie ever tell you how the judge cornered her at…"

"Oh, what is wrong with me," Eleanor interrupted, "Yes, she did, when he came to the nursery to see Bertie, she told me all about it!" *Another confrontation?* Ned thought, *Damn his hide.*

"But Maggie told Father that Worth was her master, and he was to decide if she'd go or stay," Eleanor giggled nervously, "I'd have never dared! I don't think Father's gone up to the nursery since, thank heaven; or she'd have told me."

"Yes. Well, that's why; hence my caution. I can't be seen giving her a gift."

Eleanor was clearly hesitant. "You will give it to her, won't you?" he asked. She said: "I… for a long time, since you… it seemed to me as if you did not care any longer or… perhaps just as friends?"

"I don't want to discuss it," he said.

"Do you want to write it down? Just as you told me to do?" Eleanor said slyly. *It's never wise to underestimate her,* he thought. "Come now, don't you think I've looked at every possibility?" he said, frustrated, "There was never a way for us. And in any event, I don't want to put either of you in trouble. I'm trapped between the devil and the deep blue sea!"

"Oh, I didn't know, Ned. I thought you both were… done courting." The sympathy in her voice annoyed him.

"She's still grieving her husband!" he said irritably.

Eleanor shook her head: "I'm not so sure."

"Why do you say that?" he asked, too eagerly. Her lips thinned.

"He wasn't very kind to her."

"In what way? What happened?"

Eleanor grimaced. "That's all I can say, she told me in confidence. But I wish that… oh bother, I'm so sorry! that you can't, I don't know, be good friends or…"

He rolled over her words. "In any case, the less you know, the better. You do see that?"

"Yes, I do," she said, "To protect me, and Maggie, and Mother, too, I know." She shivered.

"Well," Ned croaked, then cleared his throat, "wrap up the book nicely, if you please, and give it to Maggie, and tell her the story of its journeying. And... and that I'm glad it found its way home."

Chapter 56

On their way to Mrs. Fariday's chamber, the women wondered aloud why all three of them had been beckoned. Kathleen knocked on the door, and Mrs. Fariday threw it open. "Come in! I have a surprise for you."

Maggie glanced around the chamber, which was hung with handsome paintings: landscapes, children on a farm, a pretty dog. The table was strewn with books; the bed was heaped with dresses, at which Kathleen made the slightest of sneers. She often complained that the mistress was untidy.

"My birthday is coming soon," Mrs. Fariday said, "so I'll need you to serve a tea, but when the serving's complete, I'd like you all to come to the entertainment afterward and have an hour to watch it, without lifting a finger!"

With a quick smile at their reaction, she went on: "I've far too many frocks, and I've lost weight, and I don't want all of these cluttering my wardrobe," she gestured toward the bed, "so I would like each of you to take one to wear to the party! My dressmaker will alter them to fit you." Over their sounds of pleasure and thanks, Mrs. Fariday said: "Who's first?"

With the look of a slavering dog, Kathleen dashed to the bed, taking up the best dress: of fine wool the color of goldenrod with gray silk velvet facings and trim. Mrs. Carruthers held back uncertainly, and Maggie waited for her. Mrs. Fariday held up the blue figured one with the lace collar that Maggie liked best, and put it up against Mrs. C.

"That's the one for you, Mrs. C," Mrs. Fariday exclaimed. Mrs. C. held it gingerly, but her blush was pronounced and complemented the frock's color.

"Your year of mourning dress has ended, hasn't it, Maggie?" Mrs. Fariday asked. Maggie nodded, thinking that the aftereffects of that year still trailed behind her like a torn hem. She came forward and patiently submitted as Mrs. Fariday held up a mustard colored dress. "My stars, no! That's a dreadful color on you."

The next was a gray twill dress. "This one looks ill on everyone, why on earth did I ever have her make it out of such a piece of drab," said Mrs. Fariday. She threw them both back on the bed in a tangle, her delight ebbing, then went to the wardrobe, and shuffled through a drawer. A dark red sleeve trimmed in black slid over the edge of the drawer.

"Och, that's a pretty red," Maggie peeped.

Mrs. Fariday took the garment out of the wardrobe and stood next to the looking glass with the bodice held against her chest. "Hmm," she said, "I like the color, but I think it wars with my complexion. " She placed the bodice near Maggie, who had to fight herself not to stroke the silk velvet, glowing like a garnet. "Yes, indeed!" Mrs. Fariday said jubilantly, "that's just the perfect shade for you." She hesitated for a moment then said: "Pooh, it doesn't suit me, so you shall have it."

Maggie helped Mrs. Carruthers slice and plate the pie and add its contents to the serving tray. Mrs. C. raced it out of the kitchen to the dining room, as Maggie put the pan in the sink. On the remaining tray, she laid out the tiny silver spoons and the ice cream dishes - when you held one up you could see the light right through it! Then she made yet another trip up the first flight of back stairs, listening for the boys, but heard nothing except the thrum of conversation and a man's laughter below her. Back in the kitchen, she pumped water to soak the pan, spitefully happy that Mr. and Mrs. Fariday had not invited the elder Mr. Whitfield.

She opened the back door for a moment and stuck her head and shoulders out into the freezing air. "Are they ready for the ice creams?" Kathleen asked Mrs. C. behind her. "Yes! Maggie, can you fetch them?" said Mrs. Carruthers, so Maggie clumped out into the snow and lifted the two cans from the back walk. The three women bustled to spoon out the portions and Kathleen loaded them onto the trays.

"This is the last," Mrs. C. told Maggie, who was warming her hands and toes near the stove.

Will I have time to dress? Maggie wondered. She attacked the dirty pans and dishes, hoping to carve as much time as she could for a quick sponge bath. She heard laughing approval from the dining room.

As Mrs. C. and Kathleen re-entered the kitchen, Kathleen sighed with annoyance. "They're slow as molasses! I'll never have time to dress."

"Do go ahead, Kathleen," Mrs. C. said, "I'll gather the dishes when they're done." Kathleen plopped the tray down and dashed up the back stairs.

"Without so much as a thank you or by your leave," Maggie commented, "You're too good to her."

"She's been awful helpful with all the serving," Mrs. C. said, "and you with the cleaning. Why don't you go on up to dress and I will once I've finished the last clearing off."

" 'tisn't right to leave it all to you," Maggie replied, longing to do up her hair and don the bright dress, "I'll wash this lot up and then I'll go. Eleanor will be playing the piano and I'm sure she won't let the music start without us."

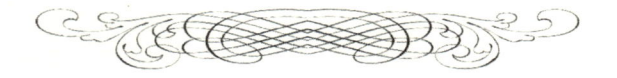

Ned tested the rope for the third time and with Eleanor's help, pulled forward the curtain to hide the piano and the corner where he'd be enacting riddles. The party filed into the drawing room: Rebecca and Mr. Minton, Kate and Worth, Kate's school friend Joanna and her new husband, Mr. Brand; Mrs. Whitfield, Mrs. Moore, Kathleen the maid.

All were now seated, but there was no sign of Maggie or Mrs. Carruthers. He greeted the guests with a jest or two, then peeked around the curtain. Mrs. Carruthers entered the parlor, and... was it Maggie, could that be her, glowing in dark red? By God, so beautiful!

Maggie's heart was jumping from the race down the stairs (the front stairs!), from being late, from how he looked at her.

Edward began with complimentary remarks about his eldest sister in honor of her birthday, then pulled the large curtain back a bit to reveal Eleanor at the pianoforte.

"*I Know a Pair of Hazel Eyes*," he said then sang the song.

I know a pair of hazel eyes,
So tender and so bright;
That I could sit a live-long day,
And gaze upon their light,
And gaze upon their light.

His voice is like drinking hot chocolate, Maggie thought. She stared at her hands so as not to look at him, nor smile too big.

And would my heart impulsive beat?
If, when on mine they rove,
Those hazel eyes should give to me
A sister's look of love.
Those hazel eyes should give to me
A sister's look of love,
*A **single** look of love.*

Och, he changed the words, she thought, watching Mrs. Moore snicker, and Mrs. Whitfield cover her smile with her hand.

Mrs. Fariday and Mrs. Whitfield next sang a Negro spiritual. *Faith, she can sing too,* Maggie thought, as Mrs. Whitfield carried the lower part of the hymn's tune, her voice twining softly but truly with her daughter's soprano. When the song was completed, Edward went behind the curtain. Eleanor announced: "A historical event."

The opened curtain revealed Edward holding a plaster bust of Caesar and miming its descent to the floor.

"Too easy," Mr. Fariday said, "The Fall of Rome."

The next two riddles were also quickly solved. Then Edward announced: "A tableaux: The Four Seasons." When the curtain was pulled, there sat a caster set with salt, pepper, mustard, and vinegar.

Mrs. Moore groaned: "That one's as old as the hills," and the assembled party joined her merrily in the catcalls.

The curtain drew again. Thumping was heard behind the drape.

Eleanor came forward and announced: "A Literary Work."

The opened curtain revealed Edward standing at the top of a ladder. He held a set of scales and placed weights on each plate until the scale balanced. The party was silent.

"Justice?" Miss Minton said, "The scales of Justice?"

"The weight of the world?" Mr. Minton said.

"Wait? Wait upon the Lord?" Mrs. Brand said.

"Why the ladder," Mr. Brand said, "It must have something to do with the ladder."

Edward took each weight off and then replaced them, rebalancing the scales. Finally, he said, "Do you give up?"

"Never!" Mrs. Fariday said.

"I'll give you two more minutes. Elly, you watch the clock," he said. Mrs. Whitfield got up from her seat and peered at her son. "Is that quite safe?"

"Is that your answer?" he replied. She smiled and sat down. *He's up so high,* Maggie thought, and said the word aloud.

"I know, I know! The Highwayman!" Mrs. Whitfield shouted triumphantly.

"What?" Mrs. Moore said, "Another dreadful pun?"

"I thought it exceptionally clever," he said, as he climbed down, "and I nearly stumped you. And now a game—Going to Jerusalem. Only Eleanor is exempt from this one. The first one out pays a penalty."

He rearranged the chairs in a circle, while explaining to Kathleen that the game was also known as Musical Chairs. When Eleanor stopped playing the piano, everyone must find a seat, and there was always one less chair than the number of players.

He was the first one out when Mrs. C skittered with surprising speed in front of him and flopped into the last chair as the music stopped. Maggie lasted through two more rounds, losing to Mr. Brand. Mrs. Fariday and Mr. Minton were the final two players, and he yielded the last seat to his hostess.

"I win!" Mrs. Fariday crowed, "And how lovely to make the master of entertainment pay the penalty. Ah, I've got it," she replied after a few minutes thought, "Put ALL the chairs in a circle, except for one. Ned, you'll stand for this one."

"Perhaps I **won't** stand for it," he joked. The men rearranged the chairs, and the party sat down, except for Edward. "Your penalty is to Make a Perfect Woman," his sister commanded. To the guests, she went on: "Breathe a sigh of relief, gentlemen. Ned is the beggar who must ask each lady if she will give him a necessary attribute to make a perfect woman. Each lady may say yes or no. If yes, he goes on to the next lady; if no, he must ask for something different until she grants his request."

Mr. Fariday clapped loudly and said: "Hear, hear!" Edward appeared cool, but Maggie saw his left hand go to the bridge of his nose, as if the motion would help him think. He stood in the center, tapping his forehead for some time.

"You took the wind out of his sails, Katie," Mrs. Moore said.

"No," Edward said, "I am just awaiting the next breeze."

He cleared his throat and approached Mrs. Brand. "My dear Mrs. Brand, to make a perfect woman, I seek your voice - not simply melodious and charming, but honest, unselfish and just. Will you give it?"

His sister made a sound, but Mr. Fariday put a hand on her knee and quieted her.

"I thought it was supposed to be beautiful hair, or a lovely face, or some such thing," Mr. Brand commented, "Isn't that part of the rules?"

"I don't think so," Kate said, glowering at her brother, "I'm sure Ned would never break the rules."

Mrs. Brand smiled at her friend, then announced: "I will."

Edward bowed to her in thanks and moved to Miss Minton. Maggie saw her stiffen and could feel her discomfort across the room. "Miss Minton," he said, "I must ask two things of you which are vital to make a perfect woman. First, an intelligent and flexible mind, capable of seeking the good for all. Second, a warm and steadfast heart. Will you give them?" Miss Minton stared him down, looked at her father, who nodded. "I don't know," she replied, "are you serious?"

"It's a game," Mr. Brand said.

"Never more serious," Edward responded, his hands at his sides.

"He is," Eleanor asserted.

"Then I will," Miss Minton said, her face pink.

He thanked her and turned to Mrs. Fariday, who unconsciously touched her vibrant hair. "Katie, Katie," he said, "Ah, what shall I ask of you? Methinks a sense of humor, without which man, woman and child cannot survive. Will you give it?"

Mrs. Fariday's hand dropped into her lap. "You rogue," she

said, "No, I won't."

Her husband laughed, "Oh play nicely, Katie".

"Oh, very well. I will give it," she said to her brother.

Edward flexed his shoulders. "And two things I ask of you, Mother. First, a pair of able and willing hands, to comfort a child, hold a book, and prepare all things that a busy mind can imagine. Will you give them?" Mrs. Whitfield agreed, and he went on: "Second, a pair of sturdy feet, to trot to each task and to stand their ground when that is needed,"

"Ah," his mother said, "indeed."

"Will you give them?" he asked.

"I will," she said.

"Isn't that four things?" Mr. Brand commented, but no one paid him any attention.

"Mind your manners now," Mrs. Moore said as Edward approached her. "To make a perfect woman, a beautiful and genuine smile is needed," he said, "Will you give it?"

Mrs. Moore laughed: "You have your attributes out of order. You ought to ask me for the hands and feet and your mother for the smile."

"Have mercy," Edward answered lightly.

"I will give it, and with thanks for the compliment," she said.

Next was Eleanor. "Her hair," Mr. Brand suggested in a stage whisper. Eleanor anxiously twisted a curl around her forefinger.

"Elly," Edward said, "No perfect woman is without this quality, and you have much of it, so I ask it of you: courage. The courage to travel life's twisted pathways and not lose heart." Maggie held her breath, as Eleanor sat silent, staring at her lap. There was a small "ahem" from Mr. Brand. Miss Minton shifted forward in her chair.

"Will you give it?" Edward asked, easing his handkerchief from his pocket and dabbing at his mouth. Eleanor nodded, and he moved on to Kathleen.

"Well," he said, "Miss Sullivan. Confidence! The belief in one's worth is vital, and I cannot make a perfect woman without it. Will you give it?"

"Yes, sir," Kathleen said, sounding very pleased with herself.

"Mrs. Carruthers," Edward said with a smile, "Two things I ask of you." Mrs. C. grabbed Maggie's hand anxiously. "Ingenuity is the first: the talent to take what is at hand and make nearly a miracle from it. And kindness toward others is the second. You have them in abundance, and I cannot make a perfect woman without these."

"Whatever you need, sir," Mrs. C said with a nervous laugh.

He thanked her and came at last to Maggie, who did not dare to look at him. "And last, Mrs. Corcoran, to make a perfect woman I need a set of bright eyes, to take in the beauty of the world and watch over the little ones in her care. Will you give them?" *Holy Mother of God, what kind of thing to ask,* Maggie thought, scorched with disappointment. She fingered the fine braid at the bottom of her bodice and muttered. "Yes, I will."

Edward turned from her to his sister and said: "I have made a perfect woman."

"Hurrah," Mr. Brand said, "That was quite a mysterious game. I suggest a game of The Minister's Cat." The men began to re-arrange the chairs. By the clock on the mantel, it was past the hour that Maggie had been granted. She reluctantly slipped through the door and trudged toward the kitchen.

"Maggie," a low voice from the back hall.

"Och, you gave me a start!" she said to Edward.

"Come," he answered, and took her arm, drawing her into the alcove under the stairs. "You must hear the truth," he said in a whisper, "What I wanted to say to you and to all of them: to make a perfect woman I needed your beautiful eyes, the blue I could happily drown in, because..." His face came closer to hers as he tightened his hold on her arm. "I love you, and I always have," he said and took her two hands in his, gently turning them over, kissing her right wrist and then her left.

Maggie closed her eyes. *Kiss me, kiss me,* she thought. Although he had freed her hands from his, she thought she could still feel his lips on her expectant skin.

"I love you," she said in a croaky voice like she had just awakened, "And I always will." She kissed his right cheek. "I must fly." And she left him there, barely feeling the stuffy air of the back hall, the door knob in her hand, the heat of the kitchen, the climbing stairs on which she soared.

Ned let her go. For a moment, even the swing of the kitchen door, the faint cadence of her footsteps on the stairs were to be savored. Then he, too, went through the kitchen, to open the back door—needing the expanse of black sky, slivered moon, white branches, and the stunning air—not to quell but to build the fire within him.

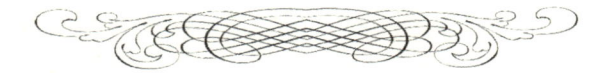

"They'll be having a chamber concert; violins, and a cello, and piano too! And Rebecca said I might sit in the back parlor and listen there if I, if I'm too shy to sit with the guests," Eleanor said, "and I can help them to trim their Christmas tree; I do like that."

"Your sister has lots of candles to set on the tree here; I hope it don't burn down. You'll be missing the babies seeing all the lights and the pretty toys for... for Bertie," Maggie said, "But all that music; you can't miss that, 'twill be like heaven."

"You do not mind if I go?" Eleanor asked.

"Whissht," Maggie said, "Not a bit. You must. Then come back and tell me all about it."

Eleanor gave her friend a hug. "I'll be back for Jem's first birthday. I have a little gift for him, and we'll have such fun."

"Thank you for that! He'll be a happy boy. Will your mother... and all the family be here for Christmas dinner?" Maggie asked.

"I don't know," Eleanor said, "since Father's no longer welc... ah, may not come; Ned will not. He told me he'll be in Hartford to hear the orchestra there and the Messiah chorus."

"Oh," Maggie kept her voice neutral.

"With Mr. Barton," Eleanor added.

"That one!" Maggie rolled her eyes.

Eleanor said, with a grin, "I am not half as stupid as I used to be. Fool me once, shame on you; fool me twice, shame on me! Oh! Maggie, I have a gift for you; let me fetch it now, since I won't be back till late on Christmas Day."

Maggie set Bertie on the floor and opened the chest of drawers, scrabbling for a bit of ribbon to bind up her sketch of Eleanor reading, but all she had were black and gray ones. She ignored Bertie's wails and Jem's "Mama" and pulled out all the drawers, finally spying a scrap of twine. Eleanor returned with a book under her arm. "I did not have time to wrap it, but I can't wait for you to have it. Close your eyes and don't peek!"

Maggie felt the book in her hands and opened her eyes before her friend gave her leave to: the world she knew shifted away—Mr.

Merritt's warmth was there in the drafty, scoured house; the chickens clucking outside; the smell of porridge and wood smoke.

"Aren't you surprised?" Eleanor said, clapping her hands. Maggie touched the cover in wonder. "This is my book," she said, "My own book. How?"

"Ned found it!" Eleanor said, then told Maggie the story of the inveterate book buyer browsing at the estate sale, the lonely room and the search within the flour sacks, and his instant recognition of the art within the book. Maggie picked up and patted the unhappy Bertie to hide her tears.

Eleanor said: "He wanted to give it to you himself, but he could not."

"It changes everything," Maggie said when she was able to speak. She thought to tell Eleanor of the kisses under the staircase, but then thought better of it.

"I… it…" she began.

"You love him," Eleanor said sadly, "I know."

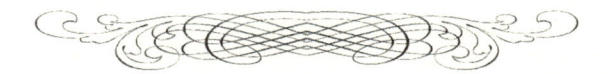

"Is your wife cooking for New Year's Day?" Ned asked.

"She's putting up a considerable spread," Joe Creasy answered. He began trimming Ned's beard. As Joe paused in the clipping, Ned smiled. "Did you know she was such a good cook when you met her?"

"No sir," Joe said, "She was just a little girl then and I was a boy. She came by with Mr. Park when my grandmother died. All the Parks were friends with my grandma and grandpa. But I liked her even then." He nodded and went on: "Then when her Mama passed on, I came by to pay my respects. Her mother was ailing for quite a time, and Minnie took care of her. I told her it was good of her, nursing her Mama all that time; and she looked at me straight and says: 'It was a privilege.' Just like that. I guess that's when I knew she was one of a kind."

"A remarkable woman," Ned agreed.

"Yes sir, I knew she was the girl for me."

Ned was silent for a time, then put in as Joe began to trim his hair: "So you chased her here to Millville, then she waited for you while you were in the army. I guess some things are worth waiting for."

"Some women are worth waiting for," Joe amended. Ned had much on his mind regarding this topic: surely Joe would not gossip, but was not prudence always the best choice? He said: "You're right."

"Can you look at me straight on?" Joe said. "I don't want this to be lopsided. I expect you'll be calling on lots of folks tomorrow. Maybe some young ladies too?"

At the end of his New Year's Day rounds, Ned intended to end up at Kate and Worth's home; perhaps to see Maggie, and surely to avoid further drinking. Christmas at Henry Barton's had been rough enough already on Ned's resolutions: he had broken all save one.

"There is one I would like to see," he replied rashly.

"You don't say…" Joe said with interest, pausing his cutting.

Ah, how do I explain this, he thought. "But it has no future."

Joe frowned. "That's too bad. She must be a fine girl if you like her. You told me before about that other one who broke the engagement, and it was lucky for you that she did."

"Fortunate beyond belief," Ned muttered, brushing hair off the drape.

"You know, Mr. Park he said no one was good enough for his Minnie. But she wanted me, and we wore him down. It took a while," Joe commented. He clicked the scissors in his hand a few times. "I'm just about done, except for a trim on the back of your neck."

Ned bent his head, as Joe said: "Some of the gents and some of the ladies who take the train, they point their noses up and complain to Billy Vickers now that he's conductor. Billy asked one fellow to sit down because no one could get by him in the aisle, and the fellow said 'you ain't the boss, you ain't driving the train'. Billy says to him: I'm **conducting** this train: the engineer can't start on this track 'till I give the order, so if you want to ride, take your seat."

"First rate!" Ned said.

Joe smiled as he removed the drape. "I've got an invitation for you." He pulled a small envelope out of his apron. "Open it now, if you please."

Ned did so, and said: "New Year's Day supper? I'll be there."

"May I ask you a question, ma'am?" Maggie said to Mrs. Fariday, "Can a woman put money in a bank, her own money, or does a man have to do it for her? And what if she has no man to do it?"

Mrs. Fariday replied, "I believe that a widow can open an account in her name. If she's of age, you're not twenty-one, are you?"

"No, ma'am, not 'till March."

"Well, it's too bad that Ned is not here to give us all of the particulars, but I can ask him, and let you know."

Maggie nodded her thanks. "I'd like to save a bit of money for a headstone for my husband's grave. I bin thinking on it for a while."

"Ah," said Mrs. Fariday, "Just a word of advice, Maggie, do save some of your wages for yourself and your son. I know that you give some to your family, to help your mother. You needn't always put others before yourself, despite what the world says."

"I guess I could," Maggie said, "but he... there's nothing now to mark his grave. He was proud. He'd... I'd like to have a stone for it."

Vowing that Rory would have the best headstone in the graveyard (folks would come just to see it, and he'd be glad of her vision), she had looked through a book of medieval art in the Faridays' library and drawn a grand picture of St. George piercing the dragon. The dragon got bigger, more fierce, and then St. George's face was just too hard to picture, so she had scribbled them both into oblivion, frustration fueling her hand. As she crumpled the paper, she recalled Rory throwing her pictures into the stove, all the while telling her she had no rights. You never loved me, she heard him whisper, as his child made a soft sound turning in the crib. With tears, in expiation, she drew a cross, and surrounded it with lettering like the old script her Da was so good at creating. But maybe such things could not be worked in stone.

"I could save half for the marker, and half for us," she said.

"Or get a smaller stone," the mistress responded, "I understand, truly I do, why you want to mark his grave, but your husband is past caring about the size or style of a stone."

Maggie sighed. "That's so."

Chapter 57

"Your examination must have been so difficult!" Eleanor exclaimed.

Ned nodded vigorously: "I was ripping along at full gallop, picking off Contracts, Conveyances, Negotiable Instruments, Torts, ad infinitum…" He mimed repeating rifle shots, "and then Justice Eller flanked me with a ridiculous question about dower and curtesy and I gibbered like an idiot."

"What the dickens are those?" Worth asked.

"I know what they are: a spouse's right to claim a share of a deceased's estate," Ned sputtered, "but when I told him I would go to the statutes regarding his question, having no ready answer otherwise, he chided me for not memorizing a case of his that had gone to the Appeals Court on the matter!"

"You had enough to memorize," Eleanor said.

"I'm glad to be in business," Worth said, "and not at law."

Kate said: "And I am glad you're done with it, Ned."

"Indubitably," he replied.

"You studied for so long, even when you were tired out: you are just like the persistent crow in *Aesop's Fables*," Eleanor said, smiling at her brother.

"I don't recollect that story," Worth commented, "But then, I was a dismal scholar."

"Maggie has a book of them that Mr. Merritt gave her," Eleanor said, "It's her favorite one: about a crow who was terribly thirsty but the only water he could find was at the bottom of a pitcher, and he could not fit his head in to reach it. So, he picked up a pebble with his beak and dropped it into the pitcher, putting in pebble after pebble, until the water was high enough for him to drink."

"That's a clever bird," Worth said.

Pebble after pebble, Maggie, yes I can! Ned thought.

"I remember that one," Kate said, "And Elly's favorite - the Lion and the Mouse."

"The lion ate the mouse, so that's a short story," Worth said.

"He did not," Eleanor replied with a laugh, "The mouse was caught, and pled for mercy, telling the lion that such a tiny prey was not worthy of capture, so the Lion let him go. A while later, the lion was caught in a hunter's net, and the mouse came and gnawed through the rope and set the lion free. A favor given and a favor returned."

"I see that there's a moral to each one," Worth said, "They may have been in my readers in grammar school."

"They are not just for children," Ned commented, "Buy a copy of the book, and read The Farmer and the Viper, or The Fox and the Grapes—it may remind you of folks you know."

"Sour grapes!" Kate said, then giggled at her husband's sudden look of comprehension.

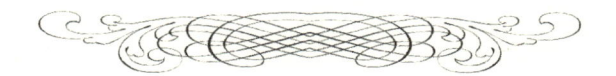

The judge gusted through Mix's front door, stomping snow from his boots. He approached Ned at the work table and tapped his son's arm. "Well, well," he said, "You made it through after all. Congratulations are in order." Glancing at Mix's and Putnam's closed doors, he took Ned's elbow, "I'd like to have a word with you."

"May I take your coat, sir?" young Morton put in.

"No, I must be on my way soon," the judge replied, as he guided Ned into the far corner of the room with their backs to Davis and Morton.

"It's time that you got your own office here," he said to his son, just above a whisper. "Keep your voice down, I don't want those two to know any of our business."

"There's not enough space," Ned replied in the same tone. The judge waved his hand. "They must put you in with Putnam for the time being, then look to moving to a larger place."

"I'm not sure that I…" Ned began.

"I'll talk to Mix," the judge went on, over Ned's protest. "You can't stay out here with the clerks; that don't set well with me. You made a big mistake with Justice Eller. If I had been there, I'd have advised you to study his case. You never remember the important things."

His father took off his gloves and flexed his hands. He went on: "It's just as well that I wasn't there: I'd have seen your brother in your place, succeeding far better than you could hope to. Did you know that your examination was on the day he died? That very day so many years ago. Don't think I've forgotten." *What if my brother had died in the war,* Ned wondered, *what if he was blasted in battle, what if I was living a quiet life as a teacher without the burden of your ambition. What if Dan loved me?*

"I miss him too," he said. His father gave him an empty look, blinked and slowly removed his hat. Snow spattered the floor.

After a moment the judge said: "You cannot. You can't remember him - you were too young when he left us."

The two boys had slept in the same bed, like puppies. Ned remembered only the warm body, a baby's muttered words in his ear. "I miss his possibilities," he said.

His father graced him with a look of surprise, an instant of grief. And then: "Don't be a sentimental fool. You could never have topped him."

"Come to dinner on Sunday," he said loudly, clapping Ned on the back, "We must celebrate." He turned and smiled for the benefit of the clerks and took his leave.

Ned reined in Shadrach near the judge's stable. "Good morning, Jacob," he said. The old neighbor held the plodding horse's halter. "What's wrong with Grey?"

"Say your prayers it ain't bloat," Jacob threw back, "Stint on good feed and buy bad hay and that's what you get. I warned him but he don't heed me."

Ned dismounted. "I take it Father's not here?"

Jacob grunted in the affirmative. "He knocked at my door at the crack of dawn, told me Grey was sick and he'd have to borrow my horse and my sleigh, by hook or crook. He was in a almighty hurry. You can help me. Fetch that bottle of horse physic back in with the old harness."

Ned found the bottle and took off his coat and jacket. He rolled up his sleeves and held the slavering horse's mouth open as Jacob poured the medicine down. He took a rag from Jacob's pocket, wiping his own hands, as he walked with horse and neighbor.

"Is the pony out at pasture?" Ned asked.

"Nope. Sold," Jacob said.

"Why?"

"Don't know. Guess he's short on money. Sold him to the knackers, for all I know," Jacob answered.

"I hope not," Ned said, thinking of Eleanor.

Jacob snorted. "I guess a-feeding all them important folks over to Lancaster is worth more than feeding his horse right."

Ned said, "So he... but he never hired you back? But you're here to..."

Jacob walked faster with the horse. "I ain't goin' to let a good horse die, no matter if his master's a fool."

Ned rolled the rag in his hands. "By God, Jacob, I know you won't. I've got some coin, and I can..."

"No, boy, get your hand out of your pocket. This's a good horse, always has been. Get along into the house and tell your mother I'm doin' what I can." The horse blew out some gas. Ned stepped away, coughing, and pinched his nose, as Jacob grunted in approval. "Keep a-walkin' Grey," he said.

"Ned!" his mother said urgently, "I saw you out in the yard. Greylock is ill?"

"Good day, Mother. It could be bloat. Jacob's doing what he can."

"Bless him for that." She sat down in a kitchen chair. She was dressed in her nightgown and wrapper, hair still braided for bedtime. "Dear Lord, what will we do if our Grey dies—your father will be fit to be tied. Where is he? I don't see him out there."

"Don't you know?" Ned said, "He borrowed Jacob's horse at dawn. You must have been sleeping."

"At eleven last night he was still in his study," she said, "I...

have had trouble sleeping, so I've taken Elly and Kate's chamber." She rushed on: "But he must have had some urgent errand."

Ned scrubbed his hands and forearms in the kitchen sink. "And... and... well I'm glad to see you," she went on, "But I wasn't expecting you. Are you hungry? I must get you some breakfast."

He shrugged. "Father came to Mix's yesterday and invited me to dinner today. To celebrate my passing the bar, he said."

"He did? I did not know!" she said. "He said we were going to meeting this morning."

"I assumed he said it for the clerks to hear," Ned replied, rolling down his sleeves, and re-donning his suit jacket. "So, I thought I'd surprise you, and call his bluff, that's all. At any rate, I haven't seen you in a month or more, so, surprise!"

She smiled for a moment. "Yes. A good surprise! It's just that he told me nothing, as usual. I haven't even got a proper breakfast here ready to eat." She got up and took the bean pot out of the oven. Her hands were shaking.

"Let me take that," he said, "What's going on here?" At her hesitation, he went on: "Jacob said Father's been stinting Grey on the proper feed, and Malabar's been sold."

Mrs. Whitfield sat down at the table. "Yes. Poor Elly." He fetched two dishes and forks, found some ham in the pantry and sliced it.

"Has Father run out of money?" he asked. She pressed her lips together and did not answer. He served a portion of beans and ham into each dish and said: "Go ahead and eat. An army can't march far without victuals."

She picked up her fork and took a bite. "I'm sorry, I wish that I had more to give you, I think I've got some eggs in the cupboard."

"Don't fret, Mama, it's my fault for coming by so early."

"Well, no, I'm glad to see you. I'm so proud of you, passing the bar. And I will make you a nice supper! someday, soon, when... whenever we can."

"Thank you," Ned replied, "I am glad that examination is over."

His mother looked at him sadly. "I hope that...I hope that he congratulated you, at least."

He shrugged again, refusing to add the judge's words to her burden.

"I'm sorry," she said, then: "You are cleverer than he. I

believe you'll do very well."

Ned said: "You know, he did say that Dan... he said my examination was the very day that Dan died."

Mrs. Whitfield blinked, then sighed deeply. "Yes. That's so."

"What was Dan like, Mama, did we get along? Do you think we'd be friends now if he lived?" Ned asked.

She sat back, her cheeks red. "Of course, you would! There's no question of that, you were two peas in a pod. You played together, you had your own language between the two of you before you learnt to speak to us."

He nodded and they sat in silence, Ned poking his fork at his dish of beans.

"He liked when I read you both stories, but he'd often push you out of my lap," she went on, "and you'd sit on Katie's."

"Did you sing us fiddle tunes, as you did for Elly?" he asked, "Did I ever push him out of your lap? I'll bet that he liked your apple pie too."

"I did sing for you both, and you gave as good as you got to your brother," she replied, rubbing her eyes, "I recollect that you always quarreled over pie—who'd get the bigger portion."

Ned smiled at her and got up to look out the kitchen window. "Grey's head is up, and he looks better to me."

"Oh, thank heaven! It's been such a dreadful morning. He said we... we were supposed to go to meeting."

"Ah. What kind of urgent matter would take him off at dawn on a Sunday forenoon," Ned put in.

Mrs. Whitfield scrubbed at a mark on the table. "Something at the probate court, I think," she said.

"On a Sunday?" he repeated. At his mother's tight shrug, he said again: "What's been going on here?"

Her reply came in a torrent: "He's been traveling all over the county drumming support for the Party, at the Governor's request he says. Election Day's coming up soon, and the House in Washington is still pursuing its impeachment inquiry of President Johnson. Yes, the Republicans here support that inquiry, as well they ought, but then your father convinced the election registrars here to register a colored man to vote. My, what a stir!"

"I didn't hear that," Ned responded, "Who is it?"

"Mr. Vickers the train conductor."

"Vickers is well liked," Ned put in.

She said: "Mr. Vickers is well liked—he is not the problem. The party believes that Connecticut will ratify Congress' amendment to enfranchise the Negroes; but your father charged ahead of that, to make a political point, and Mr. Mix says that some folks here don't like to be first at anything new."

She shivered. "I am sure the amendment will pass at our State House, it MUST! Those Black Codes in the Southern states are as near slavery as can be, and after all, folks believe that the war must... that something good must come from all the suffering."

"Indeed," he said bleakly.

His mother pushed her dish aside, then got up and went to the sink, saying: "Mr. Quint's been hearing that folks don't take kindly to your father's absence from Probate Court. Mr. Mix said the same."

"He's been Judge of Probate for years, I presume that is a sinecure," Ned said dismissively.

"I'm afraid that he won't be re-elected," she said quietly, her back to him.

"That election's a year away, Mother, so don't fret," he responded. "If he's as smart as he says he is, he'll spend more time after April at Probate Court than on party business and can still mend the situation."

His mother turned from the sink and looked at him. "If he was as smart as he says. Too many cases have not been seen to, and he rushes to get them done. He wants to kill two birds with one stone; he wants to court favor with the local voters now for his re-election next year. And he insists... he told me that I, just Martha and I, must cook and host a tea here for folks from around the entire county—twenty or more he said!"

"That's mad," Ned exclaimed.

"We can't do it!" she said, "Not without paying some help to cook and serve, and he gives me nothing extra for the cost of the food. And where would we seat all the guests in our little dining room?"

"Tell him to go hang." Ned put in.

Mrs. Whitfield rubbed her forehead. "He asked Katie if we might gather them all at their house. She refused, as well she ought!"

Ned pushed his dish away and said: "We know why."

"Yes," his mother said, so softly he could barely hear her, "I can't tell you how glad I am that you're away from him, all of you. I rest easier."

"Amen," he replied, then added: "He'll just have to give up this pet notion of his. One fancy 'do' is not going to re-elect him."

She said: "Perhaps he is as afraid as I am. Mr. Mix says your father's burned bridges with many voters, so perhaps he thinks a windstorm of favors will repair them. I don't know."

"Ah," he answered, "that's another kettle of fish." Mrs. Whitfield dropped a knife and muttered as she bent to clean up the spill. He joined her at the sink, wishing that he could help her with more than drying the dishes.

"Be careful with that one. It's Daniel's favorite," she said absently as he dried a drinking glass. He mimed dropping it, then showed her it was unharmed, saying: "How many things has he broken?"

She looked at him and simply nodded.

"Mama, leave the dishes in the sink. Go and get dressed. I'll harness Shad to the sleigh and get you to meeting," he said.

"Oh, how might that look..." she began, then threw the wash cloth into the sink, "I don't care. He's not here. We'll go! Thank you, Eddy. I'll only need ten minutes to spruce up. Or maybe a quarter hour."

"Take your time," he said.

"You're the best little boy in seventeen counties, Bertie," Maggie said as soon as they reached the nursery. He had smiled for his Mama and Papa in front of the guests and reached for his grandmother Whitfield, who grasped him as an answering smile passed over her anxious face. It was only the sudden appearance of several loud men that had set the baby wailing.

She sat Jem on her bed and told him: "That judge. Inviting all those people, who surely won't even have a place to sit and making Mrs. C. and Kathleen and Aileen, and that Martha, and Gertie Schmidt run their feet off. Mrs. Whitfield wanted to help, I could tell, but he wouldn't let her, oh no, not him!"

Bertie tugged at his fancy Scotch bonnet with a frown. She removed the hat and the baby's ornate dress and bundled him into his sleep clothes, then picked Jem up as he toddled toward the window.

Below, Karl Schmidt and his father, joined by Ned, were meeting the sleighs and taking charge of the horses. Maggie watched him as long as he was in sight. Jem pointed out the window, as she sighed.

"Yes, snowing hard, and 'tis time to go to bed," she replied, calculating how soon the boys might fall asleep so that she could go down to the kitchen. The thrum of noise from the guests crowding into the house reached as far as the top floor.

"Three quarters of an hour, if I'm lucky," she muttered as she opened her bodice for Bertie to nurse.

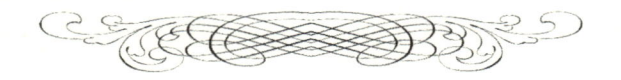

After all, Ned thought, *I cannot keep all their names straight.* How fortunate it had been, in that respect, to be a lieutenant: he could address everyone simply by rank. The knowledge that Maggie was here, in this house, just two floors away, had distracted him since his first glimpse of her at the window.

Well aware of the judge's eyes upon him, Ned said. "I beg your pardon," to the short fellow in front of him, adding "It's quite loud in here, and I did not catch your name."

"Parley," the man responded, spitting a bit of bread in Ned's direction. *How apt,* Ned thought, saying: "Ah, yes, from Hebron? I believe you have a fine bay horse," and that lead was good enough to set the fellow off in praise of the animal. Maintaining an interested expression, Ned glanced at his mother, who was playing a similar game with a more vociferous gentleman.

"There's no reason to linger," Kate said to her brother as they sat in the back parlor later with their feet up. "Don't ring for Kathleen, fetch your own coat and go home and get some sleep."

"Stand not upon the order of your going, but go at once," Ned replied. She swatted his arm wearily and left. As he headed down the back hall, Maggie came out the door. Her grin delighted him.

"Mrs. C. saved some cake for you to take home with you," she said, holding it forward to him as if she had just offered her heart.

"I'd like to take **you** home with me," he said in a low voice, "a far sweeter companion."

"Mercy, what I'd do if you could!" she said.

"Just to sit with me," he went on, almost at a whisper, looking into her eyes. "To talk a little, to hold my hand."

Suddenly she pleaded: "Och, what will they say if they saw I'd been crying? Come into the kitchen with me, do!" She handed him the cake, and took his other hand in hers, holding it tightly until she turned the knob on the kitchen door.

Chapter 58

Two days after the state elections—won primarily by Republican candidates, with the exception of the Governor—Ned ambled toward the law office door. He considered the wins good, not the least because it appeared that the Judge had, like a hookworm, wriggled his way back into the favor of the wealthiest probate clients.

"Mr. Whitfield, come here," Mr. Mix called from his office. He looked as if his breakfast had disagreed with him. "Sit down," he said. After signing several of the stack of letters on his desk, he looked up. "Your father spoke to me about an office for you. And I've been meaning to talk to you about that, but matters here have been occupying me, as you know. The facts are that we do not have space for an additional office."

"I did not expect to have an office at first," Ned responded, "That was the judge's de... request, but I am in no hurry for that."

Mix studied his inkwell, then splayed his hands upon the desk. "Although your father may think otherwise, the office space is not the important issue. To be perfectly frank, Edward, I have reviewed our finances and our client list in detail and most carefully... I believe that the business' income will not support an additional partner: office or no office."

"I beg your pardon," Ned said, then continued in protest: "I apologized to Mr. Putnam for laughing at the Eller Fountain—but seeing Mrs. Eller in full bronze with the water dripping off her dress! Well, at any rate, I understand that I stepped out of line. But he and I have been working together well lately."

"You have," Mix agreed, "Nevertheless, I do not believe we will ever manage to afford an additional partner."

"Ever," Ned repeated. The word was a stone in his gut. Mix nodded unhappily.

"Have I done something wrong?" Ned blurted.

Mix said: "This decision has nothing to do with your work. It is my misfortune not to be able to offer you partnership, and I believe it's…"

"You're not letting me go!" Ned interrupted.

"No," his employer replied, "We need you here, but I cannot raise your current wage; and that is the crux of the matter. I recall that you spoke of your desire to go to California at some time in the next few years. I think it's an adventurous choice, although probably a good one for a young man, but it will cost a pretty penny. It's only fair that I let you know now, so that if an opportunity arises for a position at a better wage, you will be able to take it. And I will give you a letter of recommendation in that event, of course."

"Mr. Putnam said I ought to go to Peasley," Ned muttered.

"He did not mean that," Mix said. His discomfort was evident.

"I have brought in clients," Ned went on.

"You would have to bring in many wealthier clients," Mix replied neutrally.

What in hell am I to do, Ned thought. "This is sudden! I had no idea," he mumbled, "I had assumed, I had thought… otherwise."

An unwelcome silence answered him. Mix finally spoke: "I regret the circumstances."

Ned looked up, hearing the man's impatience, the finality of decision. He stood up with an effort. "Since I cannot change your mind," he said, "blast it! that's that, I guess." He left the room, considering whether to walk away from this place, from his own stunned dismay. *How many times must I change horses in the middle of a race?*

As he stared at the litter of books and files overflowing the work table and scattered on the floor beneath, young Morton offered: "I can help you with that, if you like."

"He has no need to tear up the place," Davis added acerbically. *I have better reasons to damn that partner,* Ned thought.

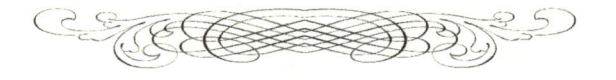

There, that pile of dirt, it was a grave, Maggie knew, and in this dark green place she could not see a gravestone. This corpse had no name, though it was someone she knew. With a rush of wings a buzzard landed upon the pile, and as if in triumph, flapped its wings.

She awoke with the frights in her own bed, as storm-driven rain blew against the nursery window. The dead one—Rory, it must be, he had no name on his grave. "I'm saving the money right now, I'm doing it as fast as I can," she said in a whisper. She heard only the wind. She got up and felt her way to the nursing chair.

"I'm sorry," she murmured aloud to Rory. Are you, then, dearie? she heard his voice (scissor sharp) in her mind, or are you looking to put another in my place? Maggie folded over in the chair and covered her eyes with her hands, hot with guilt.

A soft woof startled her. The nursery door creaked with a sigh as a nose poked through. Maggie followed the dog into the hall.

"Och, Elly! Are you all right?" she said, "No, you ain't, surely, I can tell, I had a nightmare too, of someone dead."

Eleanor seized Maggie's arm but said nothing. At the dog's whine, she picked him up. "Is everyone safe?" she asked, "is everyone still here?"

Maggie shivered. "Yes."

Eleanor put Dance back on his feet, then felt her wrapper all over: sleeves, chest, waist, pockets. "I don't have a knife," she said, "I thought I did, I dreamt I did." Talking over Maggie's response, she said: "He was coming for me, but it was here in this house, but it didn't look like this house. He came in and I shouted at him to stay away, but he kept coming. And... and... he grabbed at me, I had a knife and I pushed it right into him, right into his belly. I tried to warn him, I told him to stay away, but he didn't heed me. So, I, I put the knife in, it must have killed him."

"That was an awful bad nightmare," Maggie replied.

Eleanor said, "It went right in. I just wanted him to run away. But he wouldn't stop."

"He ought to have listened to you, then; twas his own fault he got stabbed," Maggie said.

Eleanor was silent for a time. "I'm afraid," she said. "I'm afraid the dream will go on... and he wouldn't stop, and he might have the knife then. He would take it from me."

"No, he won't take it, you'll have it again if you need it, and you'll fight him if need be, and you'll live," Maggie retorted, "I'm sure of it."

"Will I?" her friend said in a quavery voice.

"You will, certainly! And he deserved what he got - the blackguard," Maggie said.

"I didn't mean to, to kill him," Eleanor murmured.

"Ow, my feet are cold as ice. Come down to the kitchen with me, Elly, and have a cup of milk."

When Maggie returned to the nursery, she lingered at Jem's cot for moment, then sat shivering on her bed. *I can't do all that you want: on and on and on, no end in sight,* she told Rory, *you must leave me be.*

A block away from the marble grandeur of the law offices of Hawthorne, Shaftoe, and Stack, Ned relaxed his shoulders and pulled a cigar out of his pocket. He had expected scrutiny during the interview, but never had he met such an inscrutable trio as the senior partner and junior partners he had faced for an hour or more. More uncomfortable there than he had been when first faced by a company of soldiers under his newborn command, he had delivered all his rehearsed answers in a monotone and discarded any response that breathed of levity. In short, (he would report to Henry) *I sounded like a schoolboy at examinations.* It would be a comical story to relate to his friend, who had arranged the meeting but often mocked the law firm.

Ned returned the cigar to his pocket. There was a tavern near State Street; he told himself that a beer would not be harmful. Absorbed by the debate between his nerves and his better nature, he stumbled off the curb. Thereby convinced that the mis-step was an augury, he turned down a side street and entered the library of the Connecticut Historical Society, giving the librarian his name and Henry Barton's.

"Ah, yes, sir. Mr. Barton is a member of the Society, and I can assist you. What are you researching?' asked the librarian.

"A... some sort of history of the Protestant Reformation," Ned replied. It was the first thing that had come to mind. The man led him to a small table in the reading room. Ned sat in the hard chair, an old-fashioned Windsor like the ones at his grandfather's farm; he savored the room's womb-like quiet, and the smell of old books. "This is the most comprehensive history," the librarian said.

Ned opened volume one and glanced at the table of contents: Luther, John Calvin, Melanchthon, John Knox. Yes, he was already acquainted with the names and their histories. He opened the volume at random, read briefly of the Thirty Years' War, then flipped to the back of the second volume to scan the index, beginning with Catholic. No, far too many references, of course. He decided to look up Marriage.

"Mr. Whitfield, I beg your pardon," said a voice. Ned looked up and greeted Mr. Lang.

"I don't mean to disturb your research," Lang continued, "but well-met. I have a letter in my pocket for Mr. Mix asking for your help in another patent application, so perhaps you'd be good enough to pass it on to him." He fumbled in his suit pocket and retrieved a packet of letters.

"Of course," Ned said, "it will save you a stamp."

"It will save me time assuredly. The client is convinced she will make her fortune from the matter and wants to proceed in haste."

"She?" Ned said. Lang smiled. "Yes, this proposed easy needle threader is one of her many inventions. None has succeeded yet, but I admire her persistence."

"Well, that's an admirable quality. I'll take it," Ned said, accepting the letter.

"If Mr. Mix has you too occupied, he can let me know," Lang said. Ned replied without thinking: "I will likely be able to see to it, I'll be there for a while, I expect."

"Do you have some travel planned?" Lang asked. "Are you off to the West soon?"

"No," Ned said, "If I had the money to go, I'd already be a-journeying. It's a different matter actually. Mr. Mix has told me he, the business cannot pay another partner; and he was good enough to let me know, so, in fact I just had an interview here with another firm."

"You don't say," Mr. Lang remarked.

"It was not... Mr. Mix made it clear that it had nothing to do with my work; it was a business decision, assuredly." Ned said, "In any event, if you've heard of any lawyer looking for help, I'd be glad to hear of it as well."

Lang re-pocketed the letters and sat down at the table opposite Ned. "I am sure you will have an excellent reference from him. Are you looking for a small establishment or one of the larger firms? May I ask with whom you have interviewed?"

Ned paused and smiled thinly. "Hawthorne, Shaftoe, and Stack."

Lang had caught the smile. "And do you hope to be hired there?"

Ned shrugged. "It has a good reputation of course."

"Of course," Lang said, "An old firm with many wealthy clients; and many junior partners." Ned nodded, as Lang went on: "And a great deal of experience with estates, banking, real estate, railroad interests; but not much with other probate matters, or pension applications or patent applications, for that matter. But if you intend to work there for a while and then travel to California, it may suit you."

"I have not had an offer of employment there yet. When I mentioned that my father is a state representative, one of the partners said, yes, from one of the *country* districts," Ned remarked.

After a moment, Lang said: "Out in the country, I have more work than I am able to handle and more clients than I can successfully assist. My wife has complained that my single week at the rest cure was not curative. I have considered taking on a partner, but I'd need a man who could stay for more than a year."

Ned replied eagerly, "I have no particular time table for going West, that is to say, I believe I'd have opportunity there, but I am not in a hurry. First, I'd like to find a place—here, I suppose, in the state where I could do good work for a decent wage, and to learn considerably more than I already know."

Lang regarded him, and said: "But would you prefer Hartford? Or might you be bold enough to venture further out into the country to Pelham County?"

"Well, I happen to know a lawyer from Pocantic Mills who travels three counties, and it is no wonder he is a busy fellow," Ned answered with relief. "I would go to Pelham County to work with the right man. Indubitably."

Lang smiled. "Could you come by later this week or next for a visit? I could put you up overnight."

"I've been to Maryland and Virginia, but I can't say I've ever visited Pocantic Mills and that's a shame," Ned said, without concealing his joy.

"Ah, but that will be soon and easily mended," Lang said.

"And here's Mrs. Corcoran! And the boys," Ned said as she opened the sitting room door. He went to her and took Bertie from her arms. One strong fast gaze was all she got, though she saw how he tried with his smile to show how impatiently he had waited and how glad he was to see her. Maggie smiled back; but knowing her nerves weren't far from breaking, she ducked her head and fussed with Jem's collar. As always, the room was full of others. She could not be free with her smiles or frowns, her many questions. The longing must be stoppered up, no matter how hard it pushed at her.

He sat down with Bertie on his knees and sang "Trot, trot to Boston," slipping his nephew down and up again at the words "look out little boy, you'll fall in."

"I'll be at a boarding house about half a mile away from Mr. Lang's office," Ned commented to his mother, over Bertie's giggles. "I'm told she's a good cook, although she could never match you."

Mrs. Whitfield smiled at Bertie's glee, and said, "Mrs. Mix says that Charles thinks well of Mr. Lang, although your father disagrees."

"Consider the source," Ned replied.

With a glance at Maggie, Eleanor said: "You'll come to visit us, every week if you can, won't you?"

"I'll come as often as I am able to," he replied, "I can stay at the hotel if Katie and Worth won't have me."

As the Mister said that he'd like to have another man around any time, and the Missus joked about joining them to smoke cigars on the porch, Maggie looked her fill at her man. *I can do that,* she thought, *at least for now! Why are you going so far away? I know you must make a living but why can't you do it here? The photograph gallery is still for sale.*

"You'll write to us, won't you?" Eleanor said.

He nodded, then said: "Say, do you remember how we used to talk backwards, Mama, until Father forbade it?"

Mrs. Whitfield smiled. "And then you moved on to

rebuses—and other puzzles."

"Oh, Maggie would be good at rebuses because she draws so nicely," Eleanor said, "Our pictures were not very good. Remember, Katie, when I drew an eye, and you thought it was a marble!"

"deedni I od," Mrs. Fariday replied.

Ned went on: "I've just finished reading a book about codes. I believe it would be fun if I wrote to you all sometimes in code." Maggie looked up with interest.

"Did you work with codes in the army?" Mr. Fariday said.

"No, but I have always been interested in them," he answered, "The simplest codes are some combination where numbers substitute for letters or vice-versa. Everyone knows the basic A=1, B=2, but those are instantly broken. The ones I was reading about are the most interesting; they're based on a key which only the writer and his reader know."

Oh, mother of mercy, yes! My smart fellow! Maggie thought.

"What kind of a key?" Mrs. Whitfield said.

"It is usually a piece of writing such as a poem, but it could be anything: a newspaper article, a recipe, or a piece from any book, in combination with a short set of numbers known only to the key maker and his correspondent," he said.

"A recipe? For mischief?" Mrs. Fariday commented.

"Why not?" he said, his voice jiggling as he jigged Bertie in another round of Trot, trot.

"Oh, I should like that!" Eleanor said.

"I like it too," Mrs. Whitfield said, "It's a good way to exercise the mind. All work and no play makes Jack a dull boy."

"I'll send out the keys," he answered, "and each of you can send me the numbers chosen. You can choose as many as you want, but any series eventually has to add or subtract to single or double digits not exceeding 26." Mrs. Whitfield nodded.

"Unless you add in the Greek alphabet," he added, "which will give you a few more. So, say if the first letter in the key is N, and your key number is 11, you would have Y. So N=Y, and so on; unless I count backwards in the alphabet - then you will have to be on your toes. Worth, would you like a key too?"

Fariday shook his head. "I'd rather play cards."

"Send mine in care of Katie," Mrs. Whitfield said, "We can work on them together if I am flummoxed."

"I won't be flummoxed," Mrs. Fariday asserted. Jem whined

and struggled to get out of Maggie's arms.

"Young James wants his shiny watch," Ned said, setting his nephew back on the floor. Taking Jem, he fished the watch out of his vest and tutted at the boy's victory cry. "Would that all our pleasures were so simple and easily attained."

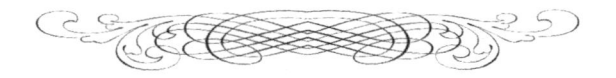

On his way to Creasey's barber shop, Ned glanced at the upper window of the photograph gallery: a florid sign, **Superior Photograph Rooms**, had replaced the For Rent card. Had the premises expanded? He climbed the stairs and was met at the door by Zek Fish. Zek pumped Ned's hand enthusiastically. "Come and have a look!"

"It's good to see you, Zek. The sign says Rooms, but it looks the same size as before."

"Yep. But rooms sounds fancy. Say, I hear you're going out of town to lawyer. Mr. Morton told me. He's letting me work here a few days a week with Mr. Dunn."

"Excellent, you belong here," Ned replied, "Is Alonzo here? I'd like to say good day."

"Nope. It's the other Mr. Dunn," Zek said in a low voice, "old Georgie's father."

"He knows very little about photography," Ned said in the same tone.

Zek looked over his shoulder, then shrugged and shook his head. "I do most of the camera work and all the printing, and he keeps the books. It's a good thing you taught me all that, or he'd be up the creek. Say, why don't you have your picture taken?" Seeing Ned's expression, he went on: "Or we got one of those old glass plates when you were teaching me the camera—you're at the side. Right profile too. Maybe your folks'd like a carte-de-visite since you'll be over east."

"I remember those," Ned said. He thought of Maggie: she might like a picture of him, and Elly could slip it to her somehow. But he had no picture of her, nor of his little sister. He scratched his beard. "I'd like to look through them first. If I see something I fancy, I'll have you print one."

"There's a whole lot of 'em," Zek said, "Have a seat and I'll fetch the box."

The velvet chair had not been properly dusted. Ned ran his fingers over the wood and wiped them on his handkerchief, hoping that John Dunn would not emerge from the office.

Zek set the wooden box on the small table. Ned joined him there as Zek flipped through the negatives. "They're back here with the ones that nobody paid for," Zek said. He slipped each glass plate out of the envelope and squinted at it in the window light. "Nope. Nope. No. Oh, here's Miss Shaw." Ned kept his expression disinterested but took the glass and held it up to the light.

"That's a good one," Zek said, "It ain't too dark. I did a good job on that one."

Ned nodded. He slipped the negative back into its envelope and placed it on the table.

"Here it is," Zek said, "You're over in the corner, but it's pretty dark."

Ned saw himself next to the curtain, frowning at the camera, in shadow, as Zek captured a picture of a bouquet that Maggie had put together. He grimaced as he replaced the negative in its envelope.

Zek said: "If you don't like that one, why don't you sit for me now. I'll take your right side, so your mother can have your picture."

"You're still a good salesman," Ned commented, "What's your price?"

"Well, Mr. Dunn put it up a little."

Ned picked up the negative of Maggie, hovered it over the wooden box then replaced it on the table. "I'll print that one up for you too, if you like," Zek said, "For old times sake. We had a good time here - you and me and Miss Shaw. I'll do it at the old price for you."

"I'll tell you what, Zek, I was just on my way to the barber. Print that one up for me and I'll have you take my picture after I get my hair cut."

Her bright eyes haunt me still, Ned thought. Wasn't it odd how a negative image couldn't reverse a woman's beauty, but made you see her differently; made you desire more deeply to see the blue of her eyes, the dark hair.

"There you are," the judge said, not five steps ahead in the road.

"I have an appointment," Ned replied and kept walking. The judge stood in his way and said: "I see that you were back at your old haunt. Superior Photograph Rooms, ha! Alonzo Dunn has some gall to open that place again! With his do-nothing brother in charge and that criminal of a nephew running wild and free out west."

"I was curious to see what it looked like," Ned said, "and I must get to my appointment."

His father demanded to know who he was seeing, and Ned answered.

"That negro must wait for you," the judge said, "You need to hear what folks here say when I tell them you've leaving to work with Lang. WHO? they say. And I already see them wondering if you were not good enough for Mix, or if he turned you out. You ought to have fought to stay, not shown them your belly like a groveling dog. You have always been afraid of a challenge."

"As evidenced by my enlistment and service in the army?" Ned retorted loudly, "As to Mr. Lang, I have a good possibility for partnership with him which Mr. Mix could not offer."

The judge abruptly tacked to leeward. "Mix told me that your work has been sufficient. He ought to have taken you as partner. It's an insult to me that he did not. He still holds that old grudge against me."

"For what?" Ned asked, seeking ammunition.

"That is none of your business," his father said, "I'll no longer look the other way when one of his cases is sloppily prepared, no, indeed."

"That sounds as splendidly fair and impartial as a judge ought to be," Ned commented.

The judge stepped closer. "You're twisting my words again. I'll wager that you won't set well with Mr. Methodist tee-totaling Lang once he finds out what you're like. You won't get the sort of reputation with Lang that you would with Hawthorne, Shaftoe, and Stack. I'll call upon Mr. Stack this week and put in a good word for you so that you're sure to have an offer from him."

"No," Ned said, "I have engaged to work for Mr. Lang, and I will keep that promise, and that's the end of it."

"It's not the end of it!" the judge growled.

Seeing a couple approaching, Ned said quietly: "This is not your court, and I am not a petitioner."

"Good day, Mrs. Bascom, Miss Bascom," he said. The judge turned around as Ned tipped his hat to both women, then said with a smile, "Please forgive me, ladies, but I am late for an appointment."

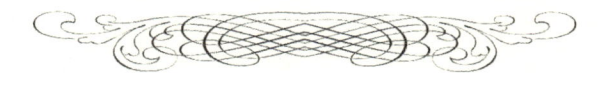

"You look tired, Joe. Is that little girl of yours keeping you up at night?"

Creasey stood in front of Ned, contemplating the problematical half-mustache. He said: "Oh. Sometimes she calls out, but her Mama sees to her. Maybe I'll take off some on the right there, try to even it out a little."

He did not cut, just went on: "No, it ain't Mariah, just… nightmares, you know. Some mighty bad ones. There was a fellow I knew for a long time, since I was a boy. A friend. A good one. He was in the army. He went up to Massachusetts early on to join up."

"Yes, I remember that," Ned said. "Apparently he didn't make it home?"

Joe shook his head. "He's in them dreams I have though. But not dead, in my dream he's like he was when we were boys. That don't make much sense, I guess. But dreams are queer like that, sometimes they can keep you a-thinkin' about them."

Ned replied: "I lost my friend Rob McKay, he died at Belle Plaine. I don't see him while I'm sleeping, but other times when something reminds me."

Joe clicked the scissors absently. "Luke always made us laugh. There wasn't ever a time he couldn't cheer us up. I wonder, what would the world be like if they were all still here—all those fellows."

"What would the world be like…" Ned repeated. "When I speak of Rob, I always say he died at Belle Plaine. Why do I do that?"

"It sticks in your mind, I expect," Joe said.

"Yes! But hell's bells, Rob was… it makes little of him to say only where he died. He didn't talk much, but he could take an old piece of wood and whittle it into a fine looking horse or a duck with whirligig wings. He never got tired when we'd climb Knott's Hill. He loved to hear a good story." Ned stopped to clear his throat, then added: "That's what I ought to tell about him." *Not unceasing rain,* he thought, *the shit everywhere blackening the cot, Rob's feeble apology for a thing he could not control, my own gut twisted, my brain lost, my heart was bursting: I had no comfort for him.*

Joe answered with a slight smile, looking toward the shop's window for a time, then said "In that dream, Luke, he says to me: Why so blue, Joe? He used to call me sober-sides. Huh."

"I ought to speak of Robbie alive," Ned said finally. "I think we ought to tell that about the ones we knew. And, perhaps, live— live well. As much as we are able to."

Joe nodded. "Yep, that may be. It makes sense to me. I guess Luke'd say the same."

"And not be so blue," Ned went on as Joe huffed a laugh: "I don't even mean that as a joke, just a word of advice to myself."

"Well, maybe a little blue because you're heading off to another county and you won't be in this chair again," Joe replied, "You won't get as good a cut out there, as you do here, not by a long shot."

"That's true," Ned said, "But I will be in this chair again. I'll write to you, and let you know when I'm coming back for a visit."

"I'll be mighty sore at you if you don't," Joe said.

Chapter 59

Mr. Putnam rendered his words of farewell concisely and passed Ned on to Mr. Mix.

"It was a pleasure to read law with you and have you as a teacher," Ned professed.

"And a pleasure for me," Mix said with an audible sigh, "I hope that we will see you again if we refer a pension or patent matter to Mr. Lang."

"I wish you could stay," Morton the clerk said, tapping his pen on the desk top.

Davis added in a vehement whisper to Ned: "You're a sight handier than Mr. Putnam will ever be. He'll never lift a finger to help us." *It's all old news,* Ned thought. He wished them good luck and once they had returned the wish, he readily took his leave to join his mother at dinner.

He had not expected to see Kate's mare Maybelle hitched to the chaise in the yard, nor to hear Dance barking a welcome from inside the house. Martha surprised him at the front door by announcing that she had baked his favorite pie, and his mother surprised him further when she clapped her hands and Eleanor and the dog popped through the dining room door. He smiled at them all. "Where's..." he said and stopped. Maggie was never far from his thoughts, and he had almost revealed his heart by saying her name.

"Where's Worth?" he went on, "at the factory? He's missing out on a good dinner."

As he ate the meal with them, he thought that the room had not heard such pleasant chatter since the last time they were all together with the judge in absentia. He confirmed with a glance that his mother shared his sentiment.

"I'll be selling Shad soon," he announced, "I can't take him to Pocantic Mills."

"I'll buy him, Ned," Kate said, "Maybelle is fond of him, and he'd go well in harness with her, although he's not the handsomest horseflesh I've ever seen."

"You must!" Eleanor said with relief, "And he'll be gentle with Bertie."

"Ow," Kate said, as her son pulled her hair, "I doubt Bertie will be gentle with him!"

After downing two pieces of pie, Ned produced the packet of photographs and passed them out to his family. Kate smiled widely. Mrs. Whitfield stared at his photograph as if she meant to memorize it.

"I am so glad to have this," she said. Eleanor saw that she had two wrapped in paper, dropped them in her lap and raised her eyebrows at him from across the table.

He lingered at the back door. *Sentimental fool,* he silently chided himself. His mother stepped around her daughters and held him for a moment in a fierce embrace. "Come back when you can," she said.

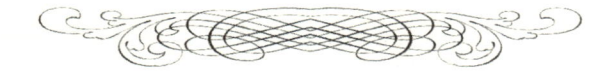

Maggie cuddled her son and nursed him briefly. She planned to wean him soon and was not looking forward to their separation. "Jemmy," she said aloud, "It's a cloudy day, and your Mam's so sad." Ned was leaving today to take his new position and she would be separated from even the sight of him for a long time, who knew how long? A noise rattled the nursery window. Jem climbed down from her lap and raised both arms.

"Uh!" he insisted.

Maggie lifted him up and carried him so that he could see out the window. "Look at the trees moving," she said, "It's a windy, windy day."

"Dee," Jem repeated soberly, then, pointed his finger as a horse and rider came up the driveway.

"What's that?" Maggie said. This game was his favorite. "It's a horse. It looks like Shadrach and..." Her voice creaked to a stop.

Mother of God, here he is! How can I get downstairs, 'tisn't time for breakfast yet.

Mrs. Fariday appeared in the driveway in her calico wrapper and a shawl. As Maggie watched, Ned dismounted, and pointed to the saddle, all while conversing with his sister. *Look up here,* Maggie urged him, *look up.* Now he pulled a paper from his coat. It almost flew away and he pushed it back into a pocket. Mrs. Fariday gestured toward the stable, and he led the horse in that direction, as she followed.

"Och, don't go!" Maggie said. Disappointment slapped down her hope. She set Jem on his feet and hugged herself instead. "Don't cry, don't you dare to cry," she muttered, not to her boy but to her own ragged soul. *If he does come in and you get downstairs, he can't be seeing you weepy.*

Kate and Ned watched as Karl examined Shadrach from head to tail, then nodded his approval. Kate agreed to her brother's price, and asked Karl to harness the horse to the chaise.

"Thank you," Ned said as he walked her back toward the house, "I feel easier knowing Shad will be with you, and everyone is taken care of while I am gone."

Kate mused on this, then said: "Father seems manageable. At the moment."

"And what if he is not?" Ned asked hurriedly, "If he has one of his wild tempers? We're not there now to help Mother."

Kate fiddled with the fringe on her shawl. "The truth, Ned?" she said, "Elly told me when you were away in the army and I was in Washington, she and Mama would talk every night about a plan to stay safe: what they would do if Father got too angry. It made Elly calmer and Mama too, I'm sure. They hid clothing and money, and they knew where to run to."

"No! Tell me you're joking," he responded.

Kate shook her head. "Mother has always walked a tightrope. You must have known **that**. When you were at home, you were the primary target. And then sometimes, it was me, you remember. Why do you think Mama sent you and me away to uncles and aunts or to Grandfather's, and to Hartford for school? But Elly could never go anywhere."

"But now she has you and Rebecca Minton," Ned said.

"Thank the Lord for Rebecca!" Kate interrupted, "And Worth."

Ned brushed dust from his trousers, scratched his beard. "I wonder if I ought to go to Pelham County. If I stayed here maybe I could—"

"No," Kate interrupted, "you'd be miserable and..."

"And what?" he challenged, ready to cross-examine her if she implied that he would go back to drinking.

"Oh hush," she said, putting a calming hand on his arm, "and who knows? But you would be miserable, don't deny it."

"There must be something I can do to help," he went on.

"Go. And do a good job and stay on the straight and narrow. The biggest threat to Mother is if any of us causes shame, or harm to Father's reputation."

"Blast him and his blasted reputation—it's all for show! No one knows the facts," Ned shouted.

"And no one ever will. Didn't you hear a word I just said?" Kate said in a warning tone.

He rushed on: "He can be a whited sepulcher for all I care. Aren't we all grown now and able to follow our own paths?" Kate made a face at this pronouncement. "I just want to...I want everyone to be all right," he added.

Now his sister took pity on him. "Worth and I will keep an eye on Mama. Don't fret! Karl's getting the chaise ready, and you must go and catch your train." She grabbed him in a rough hug, then ran into the house.

At dawn he'd been afire to leave town; now he looked toward the stables uncertainly. He clamped his hand on his head, as the wind almost took his hat. Katie had given him fair warning together with his marching orders, and he must follow them. He looked up to the nursery window. Maggie was there, watching for him, as he had hoped she'd be. Could a look—at this distance—tell her sufficiently how he loved her? He kept his gaze on her; placing his hand on the left side of his chest, he held it there until Karl rumbled up to take him away.

You are right, Mother, Ned wrote in his draft, *I am finding my way and navigating the current. Mr. Lang is sometimes exacting and sometimes lax - but regardless, is still correct 99% of the time, which far exceeds my own rate. Fortunately, he favors the Socratic method and is likely to answer a question with a question, so I am learning far more than I did as Mr. Putnam's over-educated scrivener.*

He scratched through his notes on Thomas, the competent (although overly fussy) clerk, and on Mrs. Lang's melancholy behavior. Beyond the usual polite talk of the weather, she had said little until he mentioned that he'd like to attend the Methodists' Sunday night service to hear their fine choir. Then she had said (nearly whispered) that she used to sing there.

"Perhaps you may again," he had replied. "There is nothing like music to salve the soul."

"There is a balm in Gilead," her husband had added, and she had seemed to hear him.

When he and Maggie married—he now refused to countenance the word "if"—he would take her to every concert he could find. He had not heard from her by way of Eleanor, who wrote that they were still intent on breaking their respective codes. When Maggie broke it open, as she would soon, would she understand that his reference to the canny habits of the crow and its thirst was not a code within a code for folly's sake, but the means to say he had laid his heart in her hands? If he had her here, he'd tell her that in no uncertain terms and show her with every inch of his body. He'd tour her around the small city, introduce her to his colleagues (few as they were at present), and recount how pleased he'd been with Lang's words: "I am well satisfied with your work."

Would he also confess that he'd envisioned those words as a stick with which to beat his father? And then, at her disappointment (or laughter?), how sorry he was to have dragged that old burden with him to this new place?

"I'll be putting the lights out soon, Mr. Whitfield," his landlady said.

"Very well," he said, capping the inkwell and wiping the pen, gathering the paper into a pocket, and steeling himself for his roommate's snores.

"There 'tis," Maggie said, "I thank you for the ride." Mr. Schmidt shouted, pulling his horse up short as a child ran into the road, followed by a little girl who caught him up and carried him back toward the front dooryard.

"Mother of God!" Maggie said, as she clambered off the meat wagon and ran to them. Jem wailed for her as Mary handed him over.

"Where's your Gran?" Maggie said, "Why ain't you in school?"

"Mam went to work with Mrs. Leary. I don't wanna go to school. Gran's here."

"Faith, you stopped him from running into the road, bless your heart! Jemmie, you're choking me," Maggie said, as she shifted him to her other hip. He was filthy from head to toe and had a sore just under his nose.

"He's been crying all the time since he came here," Mary commented.

"Where is your Gran? Maggie repeated acerbically.

Mary shrugged. "She told me to watch him and leave her be."

"Is she ill?" Maggie asked.

Mary made a face. "She smells bad, she's been drinking all the beer!"

As Mary pointed to the back yard, Maggie added: "Well, I'm glad you were watching him, Mary. You're a good girl."

Her mother was lolling in the back yard, half asleep in a sunny corner.

"Mam!" Maggie yelled, over the continued whining of her child, "Wake up. Jem almost got run down by a wagon! You're supposed to be watching him."

Mrs. O'Shaughnessy roused and mumbled: "Och, he'll be all right. Mary's keeping an eye on him. You used to wander off with never a care."

"He could have been hurt! Like the time I went off and fell in the mill pond, and Da was fit to be tied! Mam, what have you been drinking?"

"Naught but a little to wet my throat. I told you to stay away from the water, you knew better than to go there. A great girl almost going to school, you knew better."

Immaterial, Ned would have said if he was here, Maggie thought. She said: "You were supposed to be looking after him."

"And haven't I bin doing just that for a week or more while you were weaning," her mother retorted.

As if he understood the conversation, Jem whined: "Mama, tee, tee!" as he pulled at her dress bodice.

As she pushed his hands away and said "No tee" he placed his mouth on her chest and soaked it with saliva and tears. "No tee, ducky," Maggie said again and took him into the kitchen. He cried harder when she sat him down in a chair, so she picked him up again and rummaged in the cupboard. A cup of weak tea with a wink of sugar mollified her boy as he sat on her lap at the table.

When Mrs. O'Shaughnessy came in, Maggie persisted: "Mam, you ought to have watched him. Mary's too little to do that,"

"You never come to see us," her mother responded, "and here you are, coming at me so hard!"

"I do come when I can," Maggie said, "and 'twas good luck I fell in the shallow end of the pond when I was little. Da was awfully angry."

"We never see you, 'tis so—don't go on so, dearie," Mrs. O'Shaughnessy said mournfully, "and don't tell me about your father. He's the one who ought to be here next to me so's he could see his grandbaby."

Not that again, Maggie thought. "Jem's got a sore on his lip," she said.

" 'twill mend. My heart never will!" Mam said hotly, "Don't be thinkin' I forgot what he did: left us behind like he did that other woman and his own babe!"

"What's this?" said Mrs. Leary as she came in the door with Rose, "What's this, Mary, what's got you weeping?"

"The same thing as always," Maggie said. Rose pulled a chair out from the table and eased into it. "How are you, Rose," Maggie asked, "now that baby's almost due?"

"I've got her ironing," Mrs. Leary said, " But she won't be working much longer." As Jem still clung to her like a burr, Maggie fetched them both a cup of tea.

"Go take a nap, Rose," Maggie urged, "I'll be here awhile, 'til Mr. Schmidt takes us back when he finishes his rounds." Rose nodded and went to bed.

"Och, Mary," Mrs. Leary said to her friend, "you've had a bit too much today, certainly. Dry your eyes." Mrs. O'Shaughnessy blew her nose in her apron and got up to visit the privy.

"How'd you get a ride with that butcher?" Mrs. Leary said to Maggie. "I see him in church sometimes, sitting at the back with all the Germans."

"He comes to the Faridays every day: he's sweet on Mrs. C, my friend, the cook, she's a widow too. From the war," Maggie replied.

"Yes, I know her. She's a good soul." Mrs. Leary said, "She always brings Rosie a bit of cake when we're there for the laundry."

"She is, surely. I don't know if he's courting her or not, but I'm thinkin' he'd like to. She's a Protestant though, and a Catholic can't marry a Protestant," Maggie said, a little too sadly. She added a shrug for Mrs. Leary's benefit.

"Awhile back," Mrs. Leary said, "when you were just finishing school, there was a widow from here—her man fell off a horse and died a week later—he was one of the Connor boys. I'm thinkin' she was a cousin to the Donnellys afore she married. She went a little mad when he died and got herself with child by some Prot from Lancaster who was working on the mill-race."

Maggie said, "Mrs. C. ain't with child. But she may want to marry him, since she's a bit lonely; she's got no other family since her husband passed."

"That's just as well for her, did ye hear about Fee Sullivan, she laid with a Frenchman and had his baby and Johnny's turned her out and won't pay a penny to keep her?" Mrs. Leary said.

"Poor thing," Maggie mumbled, remembering the pretty gloves and hoopskirt, and how gay and generous Mrs. Sullivan had been.

"She made her bed and now she must lie in it," Mrs. Leary retorted.

"What happened to the Donnelly cousin?" Maggie said, thinking instead of Annie and the death of Rory's other boy.

"Ah, her. She went to see an old priest in Hartford, and he married them, her and her Protestant, so she got the butter to her bread," Mrs. Leary said.

"She did! He did?" Maggie exclaimed, "They can do that?" As Mrs. Leary nodded, and Jem banged his tin cup on the table for fun, Maggie said in a rush: "Who was he, that priest? What's his name? What church was he head of?"

"It's bin such a long time, I don't know," said Mrs. Leary.

"But, for Mrs. C., you must remember! Maybe she'd be courting him, Mr. Schmidt, maybe there'd be a way," Maggie said in agitation. "Don't fret for your friend. I'll ask Celie Donnelly, she may know about it," Mrs. Leary said, unknowingly throwing a lifeline to Maggie.

"Oh, please do, Mrs. Leary, and tell me what you hear," Maggie said, her thoughts spinning askew like a loose wheel.

"Are **you** lonely, dear?" Mrs. Leary said. Maggie looked up, and seeing her mother looking at her as well, she managed an indifferent shrug.

"There's a man or two I know of who'd court you, once that Fariday baby is weaned and you're back home. Kevin Foran still ain't married," Mrs. Leary went on.

"I ain't a bit lonely," Maggie said, scorning poor Kevin in her mind, "The Faridays treat me awfully nice, and I'm making good money."

Mrs. Leary nodded. "When you're ready, we'll find you a good one, one who won't make you pull the plow all on your own, like Himself did, God rest his soul." She made the Sign of the Cross. "When you're ready. The good is never late."

How did it all work? Would Ned consider such a thing? Maggie wondered. A Protestant and a Catholic COULD marry - it was as unlikely as snow in August. Yet one summer out of three she'd seen a hailstorm. "I hope that priest that married them would do it for Mrs. Carruthers, and Mr. Schmidt," she said.

"He was older than the hills ten years ago and likin' his whiskey too well even then. He could be under the sod now, for all I know," Mrs. Leary said. Maggie did not, could not, hide her disappointment. Mrs. Leary tutted at her, and said: "But I'll ask, dearie, don't you worry."

I'm going to need another notebook, Ned thought, as he scribbled a task list during his morning meeting with Mr. Lang. "Next," Lang said, but paused when he heard a woman's voice in the outer office, and the clerk's louder than usual response. Ned caught the words "must see him," followed by Mr. Thomas' knock at the door.

"Come," Lang said. The clerk entered, closing the door behind him. "It's Miss Solomon, sir. I'm sorry. She's insisting on seeing you."

"Again," Lang replied, "I saw her a week ago, and she had no legal matter."

"She says this is a different matter," Thomas answered apologetically.

"No," Lang said, "We've too much to do today. I can't waste my time with her." To Ned, he added: "She had a probate matter that was resolved years ago. Since then, complaining is her sole occupation."

"Ah, this Solomon has no wisdom?" Ned said.

Lang quirked a smile. "Mr. Thomas, tell Miss Solomon that Mr. Whitfield will see her, but is limited to thirty minutes, since she has no appointment."

"Hoist on my own petard," Ned said with a groan.

At thirty-five minutes, he escaped from Miss Solomon. Lang looked meaningfully at the wall clock.

"Miss Solomon is a woman of many opinions," Ned began.

"As I am too well aware. Give me a summary," Lang said, "A one minute summary."

"Ah. A neighbor of hers has been telling all and sundry that the butter and eggs she sells for a living are dirty and not fit to eat. She wants to sue him, and…"

"Of course she does," Lang interrupted, then waved at Ned to continue.

"However, she said she has not lost a customer, and nobody believes the fellow, who is in her opinion shiftless and good for nothing and never has been. She said he was so poor he hadn't a pot to you-know-what in. I told her that since her business had suffered no harm, we had no sufficient basis to sue. She disagreed, loudly. I also tried to tell her that you can't get blood from a stone, and finally got her to agree with Ben Franklin, and she left."

"Ben Franklin?" Lang looked pained.

"I told her she was an intelligent and sensible woman who must understand that 'a penny saved is a penny earned': in this instance, she could pay us to sue and get nothing in return," Ned said.

"I ought to have known you'd come up with a proverb," Lang said with a slight smile. Ned nodded, as he thought: *No criticism, no further questions, no second-guessing?*

"The next item is Mrs. Barry's action to quiet title," he said aloud, "I've begun a review of the facts."

"Two letters for you, Mr. Whitfield," the postmaster said. Ned thanked him, stepped away from the counter and opened the one that Eleanor had marked "Read first." Enclosed was a Shakespearean sonnet and her note: "Keep this." He slit the second envelope with his penknife and confirmed that this letter was in code: a new one.

Leaning against the wall of the post offer, and using the sonnet and Eleanor's birthday as keys, he quickly deciphered the letter. Although he could hardly credit the notion, apparently Catholics could and did marry Protestants. The old Irish laundress with the long memory had told Maggie this, and thus it must be so.

At Eleanor's phrase "could be good news," he nodded and at the end of line "for Mrs. Carruthers," he laughed aloud. "I expect that's a comical letter," the postmaster commented, "or good news."

"Both," Ned replied.

Chapter 60

"No, she drowned," Mr. Lang said, "just beyond mill number 3. It's presumed to be accidental."

"That's a shame," Ned said, "Who is she?"

"I don't know. The constable has the shawl she was wearing at her waist, and the boarding house keeper recognized it. She says the woman came into town early yesterday and gave her name as Mrs. White."

Ned replied: "Ah. The constable ought to inquire at the railroad office. The conductor may have a ticket record for her."

Lang grimaced. "Yes, the constable ought to; but you haven't met Mr. Foster. The man is tolerably honest, but lazy."

"Isn't one of the selectmen named Foster?" Ned asked. As Lang nodded, Ned went on: "I take it that if no-one can establish where she came from, or locate any of her relatives to… to claim her, the town would be responsible for burial costs."

Lang nodded again. "And there is not much space left in the Pelham Poor Farm's graveyard."

"The poor woman," Ned said, thinking of his father's mother.

"God rest her soul," added Mr. Lang, as he closed the statute book.

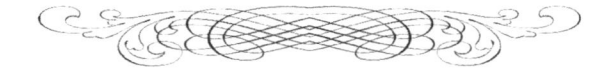

There was a swollen body in the water, and they dragged it up. Soaked calico and a bit of bright shawl drenched the ground. Go and identify the body, a man said. *I can't, I can't look at it, and I have a*

bad eye, he answered, as if in excuse. Do you know her, the man asked. *No, it had nothing to do with me!* What is her name? someone said. A face with red eyes and mouth round in a howl said: Her name is True.

He awoke as his hand hit the bedside. What a crazed dream. He adjusted the towel on the bolster and turned on his left side. Evidently something he'd eaten at supper had unsettled his stomach, and the dream was due to indigestion—just a bit of bad beef or a blot of mustard, as Scrooge had said to his spectral partner.

What happened to my grandmother, Ned thought, *I don't even know her Christian name.* He knew every Seeley of his grandfather's generation by name, if not by personal acquaintance or story, but nothing of his Whitfield grandmother beyond the fact of her death. Accident? Or suicide? No one spoke her name; perhaps only family shame would cause that omission.

His mother had told him that the judge (not a judge then of course, but a mere boy) ran away afterward: in horror? In mourning? In guilt? Grandfather Whitfield had easily shaken off the loss of the woman, the flight of the son, and married within six months the now bitter lady who insisted on believing the best of her husband—that man who had undoubtedly lied about his own faults and debts! That man who had ignored his first son to favor his second. *This is not your doing, you weren't even born yet,* Ned told himself. *Go to sleep, you must be up early. Think of something else.*

So, a Catholic can marry a Protestant. Excellent news, but only one link in the chain. Daily he pondered how to get Maggie to Pocantic Mills without harm to any party. A solution eluded him, as every avenue ended in the same circle. At least the judge could not cause any further trouble for Maggie. Unless, by chance, the man eluded his daughter and son-in-law's objections and made one of his surprise attacks, disguised as a visit to Kate's progeny.

Ah, that was to be avoided at all costs. If the man cornered Maggie this time, might he warn her again against his son, spewing that excoriation he'd learned at his own father's knee? She had been hurt enough by all the judge had said to her on his first and second forays. Ned squirmed to remember her distress: all those teary questions about Betsy Dunn! Well, that was long ago. And so was Keller's tavern, of which she was (thank God) ignorant, as well as of all that came before it. Kate's unspoken implication still stung him.

He recalled when the judge had accused him of dipsomania,

after that problem in Hartford. Dipsomania? That was not only insulting, but ridiculous. *That behavior is behind me.* After some contemplation, he admitted that he had been a heavy drinker. He had not been able to govern himself properly in the Army after Rob died, and then when Maggie left. *Soldier's heart, Mrs. Moore called it.*

By the almighty, if the mention of Betsy Dunn had troubled Maggie: what of his visits to Mrs. Campbell's? Those skirted the bounds of decency and crossed the line of legality. She must never know of that! As in the law, one must endeavor to keep secrets yet try not to lie, particularly under oath. It was not lying if one did not discuss past mistakes. *Unless they were material to the matter at hand. Too many secrets,* he thought, *just like my father, brought up as a secret-keeper. God damn it, I can't live that way! I want to tell you, Maggie, but I can't risk it. There is too much at stake.*

There was that cold whisper in his ears. He rolled over, and shook his head, touching his left cheek. No, it was not neuralgia, thank God, yet the sound continued as the dark became a heavy dead horse upon him, stifling his breathing, his belly sore and twisting. He flung off his coverlet, fisted his shaking fingers, then fumbled for his trousers and fled barefoot down the stairs, through the back door and into the night air.

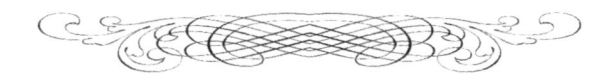

Maggie carried the mystified babies up the back stairs at such a rate of speed that she ran out of breath halfway to the nursery. She stopped short and leaned against the staircase wall, gasping. Bertie made griping sounds and Jem whimpered.

"I can't bear it!" Maggie said, as if they could understand her. "He ain't coming, he ain't coming after all. All that waiting, when I was so sure that he'd come! Just for a minute, 'tis all I wanted!" Jem was struggling to get down. "No!" Maggie said, "you'll tumble and crack your head." At that, her boy began crying in earnest. She grabbed him tighter, shifting Bertie on her hip, and began the climb again.

Once in the nursery, she put them both on the floor, shut the door and slid down it to sit and moan, ignoring Bertie's wail and Jem's attempt to sit on her lap. She pulled a damp handkerchief from her sleeve and wiped her face. Where was Ned when she needed him—with his pockets full of clean handkerchiefs, with his comforting embrace, with his own grand self? Jem sat on the floor with his head against her side, sniffling and sucking his thumb.

Maggie went on: "'tis bad enough that I can't go to Eleanor's birthday at Miss Rebecca's, oh no, 'twouldn't do to have a nurse maid there! Why'd she ever have to give that party so late in the afternoon? He even has to take the last train back to horrid Pocantic stupid Mills. And I miss Elly, she's so busy now, I hardly see her, and I want to hear the music too!"

"Poo," Jem said, as Bertie did so - not in his potty but on the floor. She grabbed the odorous child. "Jesus, Mary and Joseph!" she said.

It was good to talk with his mother as Mr. Minton thanked the cellist and violinist and they took their leave; but soon Miss Minton announced a special encore and asked for quiet. Eleanor walked to the pianoforte and sat, with her back to the small party that had gathered for her birthday. She began to play a piece; after the first five hushed yet confident chords, Ned unclenched his hands. She was magnificent; she was transformed, oblivious to all others.

When I hear music, I fear no danger, Ned thought, who had said that, Emerson perhaps? Or the poet Longfellow? His sister was borne aloft on the sounds she was making. He closed his eye and let the music empty him of thought. As the music grew triumphant, he looked over to see his mother blinking rapidly, her face joyful. Eleanor surprised them by adding mournful, minor notes, then ended the piece with several arpeggios and a final quiet major chord.

She stood and bowed to the applause, went and clasped Rebecca's hand, then came straight to her family.

Kate wrapped her in a hug. "I knew you could do it! You play so much better than I ever could!"

"Come here," Mrs. Whitfield said, and embraced her, then wiped her eyes. "I was transported," she said.

"Remarkable! Masterful!" Ned put in, "and not a hint of nerves."

Eleanor said: "No, I wanted to play it for you, all of you. And I practiced it for weeks."

Miss Minton had joined them, smiling.

"I did not see any music on the stand," Ned added. "Who composed that beautiful piece, was it Schumann?"

Rebecca laughed and said: "Tell them."

Eleanor replied "I did. I wrote it."

"I thought so!" Mrs. Whitfield crowed, "You said you had a surprise."

Mr. Minton and Mrs. Moore overhead this and entered the conversation, until Eleanor seemed surfeited with compliments, and said: "Is it time to have tea?"

"Ask him," Kate urged her sister.

"But he'll miss the food," Eleanor said, "he has to take the early train."

"Then talk quickly," Kate said, "You know what you want to say."

Eleanor took Ned's arm and led him into the back parlor. "Oh, I wish Maggie could have heard me, too," she said.

"You took the words out of my mouth," he replied, as he closed the door.

"Are you happy about Catholics marrying, what Mrs. Leary said? You never told me," she asked.

"I didn't want to put it in a letter, but, yes, of course. There's still much to be done, however."

"They're in code, so he couldn't know anyway," she retorted.

Ned shrugged. "I am glad he wasn't invited."

"He was. I don't want him here," Eleanor said, "It's just so much simpler when he's away and Mama doesn't have to worry."

Ned sighed. "What did you want to ask me?"

"I am twenty-one now, and I wondered what rights do I have? Don't make a face at me. I need to know what rights a grown woman has. He cannot make me go anywhere now, can he?"

"Since you're no longer a minor, no one can make you go anywhere unless you commit a crime," he replied lightly.

"I can't go back home! I want to help mother, you know that!" she said in a rush, "But he's there sometimes, sometimes Mama doesn't know when he's coming back from the legislature or the court. Becca and Mr. Minton have been so kind to let me stay here, and Worth too, at Katie's, but I don't want to live off others' charity for the rest of my life, like a useless limb!" At his nod, she plowed on: "And don't say until I marry. I won't do it."

"That is your choice," he said, after a moment.

"It is! Yes, it is. I loved Will, everyone thinks I was too young and too much a baby; but I loved him with all my heart, and if I had not been so, so, ill and afraid, and then the war came, and he was promised to Katie...but there will never be a man like him in the whole world, nor marrying for me."

"Everyone loved Will," Ned replied.

"Yes," she said in frustration, "but you don't understand! We love who we love and cannot help it. Becca did all of this for me, this wonderful party, and she has always believed me, even those nights in Hartford when I thought...when I was lost. Whether she lived here or in a garret, I love her."

He shifted uncomfortably, but nodded.

"And she loves me," Eleanor said quietly, the anguish ebbing from her face, "She and her papa say that I am always welcome here. Becca said it'd never be charity, never. It makes her angry when I use that word. But I want to help, to be busy, to, to occupy myself—Becca knows me so well! She says I could give piano lessons; I could teach music to young ladies and to children. Could I? do you think I could?"

"That's a capital idea. I have no doubt that you could," he said, "But, my beard and trousers do not, ipso facto, make me a blockhead. I understand that we love who we love and cannot help it."

"Maggie! oh yes," Eleanor said. "I'm sorry, Eddy." He consulted his pocket watch. "You have to go," she said, "Do come into the kitchen and eat something." He shook his head and smiled. "I will take what I can carry. And Happy Birthday!"

Chapter 61

There's some word for it, surely, Maggie thought, *being wet to the skin.* Ned would know. She looked at him, just as he had been looking at her for the last hour: both trying to keep their faces smooth and proper as smiles crept on. He too, like the baby boys, like Elly, was sweating, rumpled and drooping as the sun moved higher and cut away at their patch of shade. Well, not her, Maggie thought, with admiration and a bit of envy, Miss Rebecca never droops. The woman was fanning herself with unflagging energy.

"I expect the trains were quite crowded, with everyone going here and there for the 4th," Miss Minton said to Ned, "Even the early train that you took?"

"The early trains," he replied, "indubitably." *He came just for me,* Maggie thought.

"The train to Hartford was the worst," he continued, "Some rowdy fellows were standing in the aisles and nearly fell into my lap whenever the train took a curve. And the conductor was nowhere to be seen. The line to Millville was tolerable because Mr. Vickers had the passengers under control."

"That first conductor ought to have been reprimanded. Don't you find," Miss Rebecca said, "that there are many incompetent men who do not deserve to hold their positions?"

"Would I quibble over the word 'many'?" he said, "Yes. Many men are competent in their work, and some excel. Nevertheless, if you'd asked me the same question when I was in the army, I'd have heartily affirmed that many officers were not competent to lead a herd of sheep, much less men."

"Ah!" she said, "Well, I have a tale to tell you. I toured

Father's mill in April and observed that the power belts running the machinery were worn and a hazard."

"That's dangerous," Eleanor put in.

Rebecca nodded. "I told Father, and he suggested that I attend the managers' meeting and report this hazard to them. I did so, just a week ago, but one of the men addressed his questions only to Father. Father told the fellow to address the questions to me. Well, that little worm nearly fell over himself apologizing. The very next day, when I gave him the names of manufacturers for good replacement belts, he said to me that he would only speak to the owners. When I reminded him that I am a part owner and about his assurances the day before, he finally came out with the pronouncement that women knew nothing of these matters!"

`Maggie blurted: "He's a liar then! He oughtn't to have lied." Eleanor's "Yes!" and Miss Minton's "Exactly!" twined together, and each smiled at the other.

"You can't ever trust that fellow now," Maggie added, "Even if he acts as nice as pie." She looked at Ned for affirmation, but he was looking down at his feet with a scowl. Bertie pulled on Dance's ear and was answered by a yelp as the dog scrambled to get away. Jem chose that moment to snatch Bertie's toy horse. Master Fariday screamed as if he had been impaled while Jem escaped at a run.

"No, Jem! Naughty!" Maggie captured him and wrested the toy away, to the sound of Jem's protests.

Ned stood up. "Clearly, it's time to divide and conquer. Maggie, why don't you take Jim into the house? Eleanor can watch Bertie for a while."

"I'm thinking Jem's in need of a nap," Maggie replied.

"Dance is panting, Elly," he said, "He's not as young as he used to be, and this heat is perishing. I'll take him up to the house for a bowl of water and see if there's any lemonade left in the ice box." He clucked to Dance, who regarded him skeptically. "Come," he said, then picked the dog up.

"You'll get your suit dirty," Eleanor cautioned.

"It doesn't matter," he said, and set off for the house.

Maggie hastened behind him, struggling to hold onto her squirming son." 'tis so hot, we're all cross," she remarked loudly over her baby's cries. When he did not answer, she asked: "What's wrong?"

And now he would not look at her. "Jim, hush!" he said, and

to her: "Wait until we get to the house."

Once inside the kitchen, he shed his jacket and loosened his necktie, then filled Dance's dish with water.

"What's wrong?" Maggie repeated.

"Jim has messed all over his dress," he said, "wash him up and fetch a clean one. I'll wait here for you, and then…"

"And then?" Maggie asked anxiously. "Did I say something wrong?"

"You?" he said incredulously, "No. No indeed. It's not… go and take of care of him. I'll wait for you here." Maggie made short work of those tasks. When she reached the kitchen again, Ned had walled off the cookstove with chairs. He removed his pocket watch from his vest and handed it to Jem, who plopped happily upon the floor to study it.

"What's…" Maggie began, but he stepped over the child and took her in his arms, and stopped her question with a kiss, which turned into another. She could feel his desire matching hers, and the two halves making a whole. When he finally broke the kiss, she moaned, and he buried his face in her neck, mumbling something that she only heard as "leave" and "missed you."

"I won't leave," she said aloud, "I've missed you too."

At this, his hands tightened on her back, he made a muffled sound and stepped away from her. "Out," he cleared his throat and tried again, "Out to the veranda. Come, Dance."

Dance found a spot of shade, and after a moment in his mother's arms, Jem joined the dog on the veranda floor, gazing at the coveted watch.

"Sit there," Ned directed, so she sat on the bench facing away from Eleanor and Miss Minton, with only her feet left in the sun. "Tell me!" she pleaded, as he turned his left side toward her, "Tell me what's wrong."

"What's wrong," he said. "Yes. I have a friend, who I know quite well. He's courting a young lady. An extraordinary girl, in fact, who he dearly loves." *Och, he's got his handkerchief out,* Maggie thought. He dabbed his mouth. "But he has, he had, some troubling incidents in his past and is… hesitant at any rate, to tell his sweetheart because, what if she turns him away? He could not bear that loss."

"Who is it?" she said. He did not answer. "Does she love him, do you know?" Maggie asked.

He said: "I have no doubt that she does."

"Does he love her the same?

"I have no doubt that he does," he answered.

"What did he do? Is he the sort of fellow who'd slap a woman when he was angry, or call her bad names?"

He raised his head but did not favor Maggie with his right side. "No."

"Was he cruel to someone like your...like the judge is?" Maggie went on.

"No," he repeated.

Maggie thought for a while, as she waited for him to tell the rest of the story. When he did not, she said: "So he's a good fellow who did some bad things." He nodded. She pondered again, wanting to poke him to go on. His earlier smiles had disappeared when she called the mill manager a liar. She said: "Would he ever lie to her; and say he was going one place and then go another, and tell her to keep her gob shut and never ask him?"

He looked at her briefly then replied in a ragged voice: "No. In fact, as to lying, he wants to tell her the truth now and going forward, but he's... afraid she will not want him."

"Faith," Maggie said softly, "He must've done bad things, or he'd know that she loves him and wouldn't turn him away. 'tisn't any crime he's done, surely?"

"No crime. No assault or battery, or theft." After a pause, he went on: "Ah, misdemeanors, if anything, such as a youthful caper disturbing the peace. He drank liquor...umm, quite a quantity, unfortunately, when in school, and in the army."

"Oh, 'twasn't Mr. Barton, then," Maggie interrupted, "for he wasn't in the army."

At his nod, she added: "Well, she oughn't to marry a fellow like Mr. Barton anyhow who don't like women."

His voice was surprised. "Henry likes women: he always has a cluster of admirers around him."

Maggie made a face, since he couldn't see her. *Och, there's too much there to explain,* she thought. "Well, lots of folks drink a bit too much," she said, "As long he don't let it get away from him all the time, and he keeps a job and can, will be good to her, she oughn't to turn him away just for that."

"He intends not to let it get away from him," Ned said tightly. *What is happening,* Maggie wondered again. *He's loyal to this fellow, certainly.*

Not sure if she had offended him, she blurted: "My Mam drinks. Sometimes she drinks too much. But she's my Mam, so I love her."

Rather than pick her apart, as she had feared, he simply rubbed the bridge of his nose as if he had discovered a new fact, and muttered: "Hm."

He said: "Regardless of past behavior, he truly loves his sweetheart for all that she is. Uh, this friend of mine." It was that unnecessary disclaimer that puzzled her. *How do you know?* Maggie thought. *How do you know him so well?* A heartbeat later, she knew it was Ned himself. Oh, mercy, it was hard to breathe! She'd never seen him drunk. He said it was over. Some drinking, she could accept that then, surely? Rory she had seen in his cups, many a time, home from the tavern but not ready for bed, before he went out… to lay with Annie. Mother of God!

"This fellow," she choked out, "if he loves her, if he does, he wouldn't, he couldn't (if he loved her truly) he'd not bed another woman. Would he?"

Ned made a strangling sound. He began to pluck wilted blossoms from the wisteria vine at the edge of the veranda railing, still with his back turned to her. *No, no, no!* Maggie thought.

After too long, he said: "Well, not NOW, if he had—it was in the past—before her, when he thought…it was before her, but never since."

I will not cry, Maggie told herself, *I will not. This is too important.* Each word a knot that she was desperate to untie, she said: "She wouldn't like to hear that! Some say it'll happen because a girl was too forward!" *That Betsy Dunn,* she thought, *but didn't I kiss him too before he ever touched me.* Her voice now a-squeak, she kept on: "They blame the girl always but sometimes it ain't entirely their fault, for the fellow did wrong too, surely he did!"

Ned's entire body sagged. He tossed a blossom onto the dirt. *You're breaking my heart,* Maggie thought.

"When a fellow is going off to war," he said, "things that one ought not to do can fall by the wayside." *He did it, he did it,* she thought, wanting to demand that he take the words back, that he'd let her hold on to hope.

He stood up straighter. "Mitigating circumstances… but that does not excuse the behavior."

Gripping the words in his last sentence, she said: "This friend, he don't drink too much now, certainly. He don't bed other girls now, because he loves only her, and he's sorry for what he did!"

He turned to face her. "Sorry? Yes! No bad behavior now, no, indeed," he said vehemently, "He loves only her."

Maggie stared at her lap, not fully comforted, but calmer. After a few minutes, she thought *'tis time.* Taking a shaky breath, she said: "This friend of yours, he's like that William Wilson in the story, ain't he? But if he'd listened to his conscience." He made an anguished sound. *Don't look at him,* she told herself.

His voice was quiet and raw: "I always want to be honest with you. I always want to tell you the truth and hear the truth from you. But I can't, I can't lose you again!"

Don't look. She said to her lap: " 'twasn't Hattie. Was it Betsy Dunn?"

"No!" he shouted. She pressed her hands against her thighs. "Some friend of Mr. Barton's?"

"Dear God!" he said, "Christ almighty." His laugh was a sound like a wrench on a rusted bolt, like a sob. "You could put it that way." Maggie glanced up quickly. His face was red, and the tips of both of his ears—the good one and the battered one—were red as well. She looked down.

Loose women, she thought, *like Mrs. Sullivan, a Mrs. and a Sullivan no longer. Or women who sold their bodies—soiled doves some folks called them*—she did not want to think of that, how horrid to be a woman like that with no other way to live. Certainly, a hussy would be Barton's perfect woman: for use and then tossed in the rubbish heap. She wrapped her hands, one around the other. It hurt her to think of her Ned with such women, when she had been denied him for so long.

"But you didn't love them," she muttered, and at his negative sound, she added, "They were strangers to you." His "yes" was despairing. "When you went to war? "she mumbled. He must have nodded, though she wasn't looking at him.

He said: "And when I lost you."

This tore at her. Gratified, wounded, appalled, she cried " 'tis still a horrid thing!" Now he turned away from her. She heard him breathing as if he had run a race.

"I... I don't expect..." he began but said no more. Though he had not moved from the veranda, Maggie felt him retreat. She waited for him to rally, to try again, to argue his case. He was too quiet. But just so, 'though loud and teary and all out in a heap, did her Mam say "don't be coming hard at me," with the downcast eyes and her hands raised helplessly.

"What?" she urged. "Say it, what you want to say!"

"Can you forgive me," he said, in a dulled voice, as formally as asking a lady to dance. His shame came toward her, a fast-rising puddle in a hard rain. *He's giving up,* she thought, *so quick? Giving up again? And I want to tell you the truth too: my father is said to be a murderer, but I won't ever believe it and I can't tell you, for then you would not have me!*

"What's in the past," she said anxiously, "I don't care about that, but what we do now, how we mend our ways for good and start new!"

He sagged with relief. She waited until he found his voice. "Thank God," he mumbled. His handkerchief was busy on his face. He wheeled around and shook the wisteria, waving away the bees that tumbled out. "I thought… I was so… I had no right to hope." He tried a smile. "I'm spent. It's been on my mind, worse than anything. I couldn't think of anything else. To lose you…"

"No," Maggie said, wanting to run to him, tug on his beard, box his ears and kiss him. *If you don't want to lose me, don't you ever lay with another woman, don't you ever lie to me,* she thought. She stood up and went to her child, who was sleeping on top of the snoring dog. She pried the watch from her son's hands. It was slimy and smelled of dog and baby. She wiped it on her apron, angry still, and uncertain what to do next.

He's told me everything, she thought, *he's confessed, Rory did not; and Da ran in the night and left me behind.* She opened her mouth to tell all this, but instead kissed the smudged watch and held it out to him. "I'm sad," she said, "that you ain't perfect, for there was a time I thought you were."

"My sweet girl," he said, "I love you. I'm sad too, that I'm far from perfect and ever will be."

"But so well-spoken!" Maggie added slyly, sure he would laugh at this, and he did.

"As further proof—were ANY needed—of my imperfection," he said, "If we did not have the eyes of others upon us, I would kiss you!"

"You already did," she said, "very nicely, and I'm thinkin' there'll be time for that." He flung out his arms as if thanking the heavens, as if giving her the world. "All I want is to have you on my arm, to have you with me always, with no need to hide!"

"Amen," she said, "'tis all I want."

"I'm spent," he said again.

"Me too," she replied. He looked at her for a time. "Bless you for your tender heart, Mary Margaret."

"Bless you for the truth, Edward Seeley," Maggie said earnestly.

"Phew," he said.

"You nearly picked the flowers clean," Maggie said, pointing at the empty wisteria branches. At his barking laugh, she giggled in relief and said: "They're looking over here and wondering what's so funny."

"Or more likely, where's that lemonade," he replied.

"Who's that woman in the kitchen with Mrs. C?" Eleanor whispered, as Maggie guided her out the back door.

"Och, that's Maura, she hurt her arm when she was doing the wash at the house; the doctor took care of it, but now she's out of work. I asked her to mind the boys until your mama comes so's we could visit. Let's walk—I never get to without a baby hanging on me."

"I'm so glad to see you!" Eleanor said. She laughed and seized Maggie's hand. They reached the side of the stables and stood in the shade.

" 'tis grand to see you!" Maggie said, "How are you, how was going to the ocean side, did you like it? Wasn't it cold and too salty? Did you go out sea bathing?"

"Oh, oh my, I don't even know how to tell you; I SO wish you could have seen it. It's just… vast. I thought I'd be afraid of it. But I came to love it, to see something so… wild and ancient, I suppose, and so much bigger than any of us!"

"I wish I could see it," Maggie said.

"I did go sea bathing," Eleanor went on, "and it was cold and salty, and the waves push you, and after the first time with Rebecca,

I could not wait to go into the water again. I never thought I'd like it so. And it was lovely to be with Becca, she's never afraid, and it was just us two, and …"

Maggie said: Miss Rebecca is such a grand friend." Eleanor's cheeks went pink and she put her head down and smoothed her skirt. She nodded several times.

"That's the biggest smile I've seen in a long time," Maggie said fondly.

"Yes," Eleanor said, "We only went to the beach, no sight seeing, I didn't want to, I just had such a fine, quiet time…nothing happened, and…"

" 'twas a good nothing, then," Maggie said.

"Yes! And everything!" Eleanor giggled nervously. "I'm not making any sense, am I? Oh! Heavens! I completely forgot! I have a surprise for you, but we have to go in to the parlor."

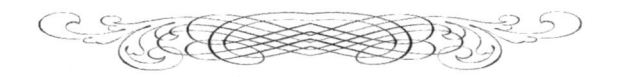

As Eleanor played the last chord, she looked up from the piano at Maggie, and said tentatively: "Did you like it?"

Maggie stood up and blotted her eyes with her sleeve. "Very much," she said, "'twas like I was in a dream. How can you play it so well? Not even a piece of paper to look at!"

Eleanor grinned. "It was easy enough to do."

"Easy? My garters, that must be a joke."

"No. It was easy to remember because I wrote it," Eleanor said.

"YOU wrote it? You made it up, all on your own like you said to me a long time ago—such a beautiful thing?" Maggie whooped and wrapped her friend in a hug.

Eleanor went on: "And, I intend to give piano lessons to children." She laughed at Maggie's astonishment.

"How?" Maggie asked, "Where?" After hearing all the details of Eleanor's plan, Maggie shook her head and proclaimed: "I never!"

"That's what you said when I wore that hoop skirt the first time," Eleanor said, "I would not wear one now, they're so out of fashion."

"So Kathleen told me. What you have on today is pretty, is

that the fashion now?" Maggie asked.

"No, silly, Becca and I don't care for fashion! I was joking," Eleanor said, "Clothes are just a guise for the world to see and judge one by."

Maggie nodded. "Ah, but don't you like to see a pretty piece of goods sometimes, and think how it might look on you, and how nice it feels in your hand?"

Eleanor contemplated this, then said: "Well, actually, sometimes, I do. But hoop skirts, Maggie? Dreadfully impractical. Oh, Katie told me they bought a new pony. I can't wait to see him, Let's go out to the stable, and this time I'll name him."

Ned arrived at the Faridays and rang the bell at the front door; at no answer, he went to the kitchen door and surprised Mrs. Carruthers and a homely woman wearing a sling on her arm. After he had greeted them and been introduced to the woman, who could not refrain from staring, he said: "Has my mother arrived yet?"

"Yes, she went out to the stable to see the pony," Mrs. C. answered. He could hear Bertie whining and opened the kitchen door, not to Maggie, but to Mrs. Whitfield.

"Mother!" He gave her a one-armed hug, as Bertie peevishly pushed him away. "I take it the pony did not meet Bertie's expectations?"

"It's a pretty little fellow, but Bertie's teething, so nothing pleases him now," Mrs. Whitfield replied, putting her grandson in his high chair. "He might like a cracker, Mrs. C., and a small cup of milk. I'll leave him with you, Maura."

"It's good to see you," Ned said as they stood in the shade at the side of the house, "How are you faring?"

"Not too badly, your father is very busy," she said.

"Good. And is Martha behaving herself?"

At his snicker, his mother replied: "She is more of an ally than you know."

"You're joking," he scoffed.

"No, she takes your father seriously, all his desires and unspoken needs and sees to them, or makes sure that I do, and then my days are easier."

He said, "I was not aware that Father had any unspoken needs."

"As changeable as the weather," she replied, "The speaker of the House will be going to New London and he would like to catch his ear, so I may have a little time to rest, if we go to the shore."

"I should choose the seaside," Ned put in.

"And so should I, were I not on duty," and at his surprise, she continued: "Being sociable from breakfast into the evening with ladies with whom I am not acquainted, inquiring to discover whatever I can about their husbands' opinions in order to report to him. I cannot even walk the beach alone. He says it does not look right to do so, as if there is distance between us." She laughed without humor, "I am better off here."

"If only life with him was not such a..." she began.

"Burden," Ned supplied.

"A game of chess," she finished.

"You ought to come to Pocantic Mills on your own some time, or with Katie," he said. "It's not in his district, so he's unlikely to want to visit. I admit that it isn't as nice as the shore, but I'd meet you at the train, and find a good place for you to stay and I believe you'd enjoy meeting Mr. and Mrs. Lang."

"I'd like that," she said.

He was glad to see her smile. "Shall we?" he said, as he moved out of the shade, his eyes on the stable.

"You seem happy," she said, "And eager to see… the *pony*."

She still has her eagle's eye, he thought. "Well, why not?" he bluffed, "It's good to be here. I promised Mrs. Corcoran I'd take her to the graveyard to see that man's, her husband's stone, the one she paid for, so I'd like to get on the road soon. Elly will be joining us, and Jim. You're welcome to come too."

She said: "No thank you, I haven't been sleeping well, so I expect I'll stay here and take a nap."

"Capital! I'll tell them to get ready," he said, already striding ahead of his mother.

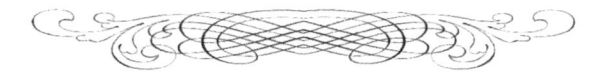

The graveyard was bigger than Maggie had guessed. Ned drove the carriage down each narrow roadway, as she and Eleanor looked for the gravestone: Maggie longed for it to be one of the large clean white ones capped with scrolls or crosses, but none had the right name. The final section had only a short path to an overgrown area with wildflowers and weeds a-mix and the tips of stones showing through. He stopped the horse.

"I guess we'll walk from here," he said.

Maggie was anxious to find Rory, so she thrust Jem into Eleanor's arms and hopped down from the carriage by herself and walked quickly from stone to stone. At the edge, the far edge, under a patch of old evergreens, as in her dream, was the stone. It was not the smallest, but so plain—though his name was clear; *here he is, down there,* she thought. She knelt down, not daring to touch it.

Ned and Eleanor looked at each other, then nodded almost simultaneously. He helped Eleanor out of the carriage.

"Mama," Jem said.

"Mama's resting," Eleanor said in a shaky voice, "Ned, none of these graves have any flowers. I'll get some."

"Are you," he began, "are you afraid of," he waved at the place.

She gave a wondering laugh. "Oh, silly! I'm not afraid of the dead." She let go of Jem's hand and walked with purpose toward the weedy border. He watched as Eleanor plucked blooms among the tall grass, and went from grave to grave, dropping a blossom on each. *It is a peaceful place,* he thought. He tried not to think of Robbie. Jem had picked up a stick and was whacking the ground.

"Do you want to pick some flowers?" Ned asked, then took the boy's hand and led him to the overgrown edge. He picked a few while Jem pulled fistfuls of grass. As Ned squatted to place a flower on the first stone, only ankle high, he said: "A flower for you." There was no name on the marker, only initials, so he said: "S. R. Known only to God."

He did the same at the next marker, and the next, and the boy followed him, dropping grass on the markers, and muttering: "Fow, you, fow, you."

Maggie had slumped onto the ground and appeared to be talking but he could not hear her. He hoped she would be all right. *Poor devil,* he thought to the absent Corcoran, *you have a good boy here. I'll take care of them both. I'll make sure they never want for anything.* He resolved to buy life insurance, and perhaps some railroad stock as soon as he could afford it.

I'm here, Rory, Maggie said in her mind, *'tisn't a big stone but it's carved deep.* She murmured aloud: "If I go somewhere else, when I go, I'll bring your James back, I swear it, to see this and remember you." She finally touched the rough surface, which was blood warm. "'tis all I can do," she told him. She got to her feet slowly, uncertain if she would ever forgive him.

Eleanor approached her, holding a bouquet of wildflowers. "Would you, do you want these, for him?" her friend asked in a whisper.

"There's no need to be so quiet," Maggie said, feeling stronger.

"I put a sprig of evergreen in with these," Eleanor said, holding the bouquet out to her.

Maggie wiped her nose. "No, you put them on for him, so's he can see that some Yankees have a good heart," she said.

Eleanor looked at her for a moment. "Are you all right?"

When Maggie nodded, Eleanor placed the flowers against the stone. Maggie made the sign of the Cross. They both looked down for a moment.

"You must be thirsty. May I get you a drink from the basket?" Eleanor said.

Maggie burst out: "I'm thinkin' Bertie will be weaning soon, by November at any rate, and I been thinkin' your sister would likely keep me on, but if I'm going to Pocantic Mills SOME time, I'd have to tell her why, and that won't do, to tell the truth, but I don't want to lie to her. She's been so good to me."

Eleanor nodded. "I've been thinking about it too. Becca always says to look at a problem from all the different sides, and then turn it on its head and look again. What are some other reasons that would cause you to leave?"

"If my Mam was sick, but she ain't and I hope she stays well," Maggie said hesitantly, "Or if I was marrying, but I can't say who!"

"That's true," Eleanor said, "and you oughn't to lie."

"If it weren't for going away, I'd stay at your sister's as long as I could, for then I can keep my boy with me: most women who hired help surely wouldn't let me do that, as she has done. My mam can't mind him while I'd be working, and I just want him with me." She was ashamed to tell Eleanor (who had such a good and watchful mother) why her Mam couldn't be trusted to care for a child.

Eleanor said: "Oh, Maggie, Ned is looking here, so wipe your eyes again, and he'll stay away for a little while."

Maggie did so but whispered "I don't want him to stay away."

"I know," Eleanor said, "but let me tell you what I was just puzzling out. It's most important that you have Jem with you, and Kate would understand that, and perhaps if you found a position in another town and that employer let Jem stay with you…"

"I wish I could just tell her the truth!" Maggie countered.

Eleanor sighed. "If wishes were horses, then beggars would ride, as Mama always says. There, he's gone to get the picnic basket. I am hungry, too."

"Two heads are better than one, so they say, maybe three is best," Maggie said, and smiled wanly at Eleanor's giggle.

Maggie swigged down the ginger beer, took a sandwich from the basket and sat her son in her lap, feeding him bites of food and water from his cup. Eleanor looked at Maggie questioningly, and at her nod, said: "Ned, are there lots of jobs in Pocantic Mills, do all the girls work at the mills, or are some of them domestic help?"

"Some of them work in the mills, but I don't know the particulars about how many work as help," he said, "I guess I could find out if I had to. Why do you ask?"

"For Maggie," Eleanor said, "If she found a position in Pocantic Mills, she'd be able to leave Katie when Bertie's weaned and she needn't tell her an untruth about leaving."

He put his sandwich down and turned to Maggie. "Would you do that?"

"Yes, so long as I could have Jemmy with me there, at that position, then I'd do it," she said.

"Now?" he asked, with a smile.

"As soon as Bertie's weaned," she said.

"First rate!" he crowed, "Clever girl!"

Maggie grinned. "**Two** clever girls," she said.

Ned shrugged out of his coat and folded into a chair opposite Lang's desk.

"A brief summary, if you please," Lang said, "I've been late to supper for weeks."

"It will brief, but not satisfactory. It's barely a fortnight since Mr. Huber died, and the third woman has left her position," Ned replied.

Lang sighed. "The condition of the house again?"

"Not this time. This woman lasted four days and I expected her to stay. However, I went to the house to get a glass of water and saw Miss McMahon leaving Mrs. Huber's with a large carpetbag."

At Lang's expression, Ned went on: "I asked where she was going so soon after dinner and why she had a carpetbag. She made quite a show of innocence at first: said it was hers, that she carried her dinner in it. Remarkable, I said, half a week's dinner would fit it, may I see what you have to eat? She eyed me for a while, then gave up when I told her to put the bag on the doorstep. Such a clanking." Lang muttered an imprecation. "I opened the bag: two silver candelabra, two Britannia candlesticks, and a parcel of silver flatware. She insisted she was taking them home to polish! I fired her on the spot."

"Three days of carpetbags," Lang said.

Ned nodded, "Mr. Grimes and I completed our inventory of the contents of the barn and most of the outbuildings, but we haven't yet begun the house. With the Mount Etna of stuff in there, it's probably impossible to know what else she pilfered. I will make a note of the incident for the record."

Lang rubbed the back of his neck. "I'll pursue the matter with the constable tomorrow. You will make a complaint to the intelligence office regarding our carpetbagger. We will not interview anyone else they offer for employment. And how is Mrs. Huber?"

"The kitchen is the most habitable room," Ned said, "It is now furnished with a light bedstead and bedding, a commode, an armchair, and Mrs. Huber has been supplied with crutches. I spoke to the doctor, he expects the fracture will heal with time."

"Nevertheless she will need help for some time," Lang said.

"I've had no word yet from her daughters in Kansas." Ned replied.

"Did you inquire at the Catholic church they attended?" Lang asked, "Several of the ladies came to the funeral."

Ned loosened his tie. "I called on the pastor. He said the Hubers had not attended church since their son died at Gettysburg. I believe their lives were something of a mystery to their neighbors. One or two of the ladies have called informally, bringing food for her: whether from a sense of Christian duty or curiosity about the state of the Hubers' house, I can't say."

"You must go farther afield. Make an inquiry to an

employment office in Lancaster," Lang said.

"I will," Ned agreed, "There may be a woman who is seeking a place to live, perhaps a widow herself."

Like Maggie, he thought, but pushed the thought away. He couldn't ask her to deal with this grim, injured woman engulfed in the clutter her lost husband had deposited in every room, hall, stair well, chamber, ell and corner. He and Mr. Grimes had created paths through most of it, but an errant step or elbow out of place could topple tinware, bed curtains, or cracked crockery down upon one's head. To bring Maggie to such a problematical place would do her a disservice. He knew only a little of Mrs. Huber: so far, he had seen her in a condition of shock from her husband's sudden death, and pain from her fractured leg. When addressed, she shook her head angrily and spoke not at all.

Ultimately wasn't it Maggie's decision to make, and not his? He said: "I know a widow in Millville who is honest and capable and has mentioned the difficulty of finding a position which allows her to keep her young child with her. He's not yet two years old, and she has no one else to care for him. It's unlikely, but possible, that she may be interested. Mrs. Huber permitted that first woman, who stayed only a day, to bring her child, as you'll recall."

"It's worth a letter of inquiry to her," Lang said.

"Umm. Yes. Currently she works for my sister as a nursemaid, but my nephew's being weaned now. My sister may intend to keep Mrs. Corcoran on in the nursery, so I'd rather step out of the middle. It's better for you to sign the letter, if you don't mind."

"Draft it, and I will. I trust that you'll make the advantages and disadvantages clear without scaring her away," Lang replied. "It's suppertime."

Chapter 62

Is Bertie missing me? Maggie wondered, and why'd he take so well to Maura? She handed a potato peel to the waiting Jem, who took it to the chickens in the yard and dropped it among them, laughing as they pecked at it. Through the window, she heard Rose chiding baby Tom for not having a proper feed. The small infant was slow to eat, with a useless right arm to boot, yet when he nestled in Maggie's lap she petted and cooed to him, her heart hurting for his parents. *I do what I can to help out,* she thought. While that quiet routine in and about the Fariday's nursery had allowed her mind to wander lonely as a cloud, none of that would do here.

Maggie scowled, still disgusted at what she'd said to Eleanor, when Elly had proudly told her stories of traveling to Hartford with Miss Rebecca.

"If I went away would you come to visit me?"

"I would certainly try to," Eleanor had said. 'Twas a good thing altogether that Elly was too kind to make fun of her. When Ned finally became her own (openly) would she ever see any other Whitfield again? Only the loss of the judge would be a boon.

Two years now since Rory left us. Everything is changing, she thought, *October's the month for leaving. Mercy, wouldn't Ned make a pun of that?*

Jem came to her with a handful of leaves and dumped them in the pot with the peeled potatoes. "No!" She picked them out, shaking her head. "Come in with me, I have a new dolly for you." She sat him at the table and gave him the little man she had made of empty spools strung together with sturdy twine, with an inked face and small broken bobbin for a hat. Maggie rinsed the potatoes, filled the cooking pot, and started them boiling. Jem reviewed his doll, turning each spool, and pulling at the bobbin hat. She watched his examination: just so had Rory looked when he read the newspaper. She turned back to the sink. "Can you make him dance?" she said.

"This one's not having any of it," Rose said, dispirited, "You take him." She spread butter sparingly on the bread, and ladled soup into bowls, muttering to herself. The boys clattered through the back yard, disputing loudly. Maggie swayed the baby in her arms, looking out the window for Mary. As usual, the girl was dawdling behind.

"Have you been picking on her?" she said to Paddy, as Dennis seized Jem's doll. Her boy screeched and reached for it as his cousin held it away.

"Give it back," Rose said. Maggie grabbed for the toy, but Denny ran away.

"Lemme see it," Mary said as she came in, "I want it!"

Patrick plopped in a chair. Around the bread in his mouth, he said: "That boy screams like a banshee."

Maggie said, "Och, Denny, if you want a new dolly that much, I'll make one for you.

Patrick laughed, as Rose said: "For shame, Denny."

At this, Dennis sat down and began to eat. Mary had temporary possession of the doll; she held it out of Jem's reach as he whined.

"Give it to him," Rose commanded.

Mary pouted as she handed the doll over, then said to Maggie: "Make one for me."

"I'll show you how," Maggie replied. She crumbled a half-slice of bread into Jem's bowl of soup. Rose rapped Dennis' hand with the ladle: "That meat's for yer father, leave it be."

Frank came in with a container of beer and sat down to eat.

"Yer mam just went to get a growler," Rose said.

"I saw her in the line," Frank concurred.

"Why'd you let her stay then, when you had yours already?" Rose asked.

" 'twasn't worth making a stir," Frank answered, then busied himself with downing the corned beef.

"Now she'll be drinking the whole lot of it her own self, and sleeping the day away," Rose went on in irritation.

Patrick muttered something. His father looked at him, then said to Rose: "Weren't you saying you needed a little peace and quiet? Now you'll have it if she's asleep." Maggie saw Dennis sneak another slice of bread and hide it in his shirt. He got up and went toward the front room.

"Put Tom in his cradle, Maggie," Rose said, "Eat your dinner."

"The mill's hiring," Frank said.

Patrick sat up straight.

"No," Rose said, "he's going to finish school."

"I want..." Patrick began.

Frank said: "No, Paddy, yer mam says to wait." Maggie didn't like the silence that ensued, broken only when Jem clacketed his dolly on the table.

"I could do it," Patrick said.

" 'twould help to pay the bills," Frank said. Rose glared at them.

"I'll be going back to Faridays soon and then we'll have more," Maggie put in. "Only a few days now, and Bertie will be weaned."

"The postman's coming here," Dennis announced from the front room. He opened the front door, then ran back to the kitchen. "It's for Ant Maggie."

"I don't get my mail here," Maggie said, as she took the envelope from him. It was addressed to her, and postmarked Pocantic Mills, but the handwriting was not her Ned's. She opened it and scanned it.

"An invite from yer Yankee friend?" Rose commented sourly.

Maggie shook her head. "From Mr. Lang."

"Who's that," Frank asked.

"The lawyer that Ned, Mr. Whitfield works for," she replied, too surprised by the contents to do much more than give the barest answer. "He's asking if I'd take a position helping an old German lady there, her husband just died, and she broke her leg not a day after."

"What about your boy? And them Faridays? Whyn't they find some girl who lived there? If no one there will help her, she must be a bad one," Rose said.

"What'll it pay?" Frank added.

"It says that the lady would welcome Jem too and let me have him with me all the time," Maggie said.

"You ain't a nurse," Rose's protest was halted by Mrs. O'Shaughnessy's arrival at the back door, singing tunelessly and waving the growler.

During the ensuing argument between mother-in-law and daughter-in-law, Maggie wiped Jem's face and toted him into the back yard. The letter was too much, come too suddenly. She stood in the shade, shivering, indecisive. Frank escaped through the back door and approached her.

Although he had never been her confidant, Maggie blurted: "What am I to do? How can I leave the Faridays, what'll they think of me if I do! I'm thinkin' the pay will be good, but I don't know a soul there, except one, but I could have Jem with me. And that'd be best for him. Mother of God, I don't know!"

Frank said: "If it's best for you and Jimmy, then you ought to go."

Maggie tried to think straight but failed. "Won't you keep Paddy in school, Frank? Just till the Spring. He's done well, he's a smart fellow," she said. Her brother shrugged unhappily.

"I'll be back at Faridays next week. Or... if I take this position, I'll send you money every week," she said, then instantly regretted the promise.

"I know you will," he replied with a sad smile, and headed back to work.

Excited, juggling Jem, luggage, train schedules and her nerves, Maggie fared well for the first half hour of the ride south from Vinton Center. In the second half hour, now heading east to Pelham on the swaying train, she reviewed all that had happened so unexpectedly. It had been the right thing, as Eleanor had suggested, to show Mrs. Fariday the letter from Lang, to let it speak for itself, and to say to her employer, what would you do if you were me. Mrs. Fariday had asked the same questions Rose had, fancy that. But then, once given leave to go with Mrs. Fariday's blessing, Maggie was undone by her own tears.

What kindnesses they gave her freely: Mrs. C., Mrs. Fariday, and Eleanor. And Mother of Mercy, the goodbyes were the worst, especially to part with Eleanor and to sob like an infant, shamefully, in front of Miss Rebecca. When they'd gone away, out West, Da, and Mikey and Aggie and baby Jennie, surely they didn't have this fear she had, or this jagged pain to have all the people that she knew now behind her and perhaps not to be seen soon again.

Her boy mumbled drowsily. The note Ned had written with her final stop was tucked in her sleeve, wrinkled and rough on her wrist. *Think of the one waiting for you,* she told herself, *the train won't turn around just for you.*

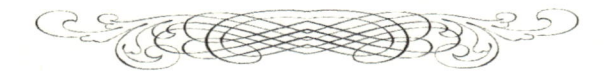

Approximately 38 steps, Ned thought, *proportionately fewer if I lengthened my stride. For a county seat, it certainly has a small station. Blast these train delays, if Billy Vickers was conductor on this one, it would more likely be on time. How much shall I tell her about Mrs. Huber? I ought to have written her. Everyone needs time to contemplate such a queer situation.*

He went again to the side of the platform and checked on the nag that the livery stable had supplied, its sole remaining horse today. The animal was not only slow, it looked barely able to pull the small chaise he had rented. Back toward the ticket office, ignoring the sleepy attendant on the bench and the ticket keeper who spat tobacco every 5 minutes into the spittoon, Ned consulted his pocket watch, then nodded with a grimace to the attendant's comment: "It'll come along soon." After another 20 minutes of waiting and pacing and questioning the definition of "soon" as well as the efficacy of schedules that never delivered what they promised, he heard the sound of the train.

She looks so frightened, he thought, as she came down the steps carrying a large bag and her unhappy boy. He fought the urge to run to her, put aside boy and baggage, and take her in his arms—breast to chest, hip to hip, and kiss her. He advanced and began the performance expected by the ticket office, the attendant and the few people on the platform.

"Mrs. Corcoran, let me take that bag for you. Do you have any other luggage?"

"A trunk, a little one," she said, but with a small smile. Jem made a cranky sound.

"I'll fetch that for you, I have a carriage waiting," Ned added,

"Have a seat on the bench, if you please."

Trunk fetched, baggage and passengers packed into the chaise, and Jem occupied with a treat of gingerbread, Ned got the horse on the road, now glad that it was a plodding beast. "Thank God you're here," he said to Maggie, "You're finally here."

"I'm truly here," she said, in a wondering tone, "It don't…it feels like I'm dreaming. And I'll wake later tonight and be back where I came from."

"I felt the same way the first few nights in the army, and when I came here," he replied. There was no one else on the road. He took her hand and smiled at her. "Thank you for coming here. Thank you for your bravery," he said.

"Bravery?" she said.

He nodded. "To go to a new place and take this challenge."

"D'you mean to care for Mrs. Huber? She's not mean, is she?" This she said with apprehension.

"Um. Her circumstances are very difficult, and her husband had… outlandish habits. The challenge is the state of their house," Ned answered, then delivered a short summary.

"I ain't tidy, but I'd never let my house get to such a state!" she said, when he stopped to take breath. "But where are Jim and I to sleep?"

He sighed, then said: "Mr. Grimes and I cleared out part of a chamber on the second floor. It will be habitable and safe, if not clean; but you have no obligation to clean for Mrs. Huber, at least until we have finished further clearing and completed our inventory." He began to explain the purposes and method of an estate inventory but halted when she pulled her hand away from his.

"No, Jim, 'tis all gone. You'll have to wait till we get there. Do you want to see what else Ned, Mr. Whitfield brought for you? A new book!" She took it out of a pocket in her short coat and gave it to her son, then went on: "I know about that from when Rory passed. They had to come around and take things to sell for our debts. Mr. Flynn was the one who took care of all the papers."

"Matthew Flynn?"

"D'you know him?".

"He was my sergeant in our company. You couldn't find a better man," he said.

She took his hand again. "I'm awfully glad to be here; with you, anyhow."

"No gladder than I am!" he replied emphatically, at which the horse's ears twitched.

"I know," she said, "that last letter you sent me, with all the things you said you wanted to do… 'tis a good thing you put it in code." She blushed but also grinned at him.

"Yes. But I recall that you recently urged me to be honest."

"Mama! Wha dis," Jem pointed to a page in the book.

"That's Jack," she said, "Jack be nimble, Jack be quick, Jack jump over the candlestick."

"Wha dis!" the boy said, pointing at Ned, then answered his own question, "Mitter Wiffa."

"What did he say?" Ned asked.

"That's his name for Mr. Whitfield," she said with mock politeness, "I hope it don't offend you."

"I like it," he said.

"No nap for you, rascal, and no rest for me," Maggie said as Jim called for Mama and climbed up into her bed. He slid next to her and sucked his thumb.

"What are we to do about Mrs. H?" she asked him. Mrs. Huber's broken limb was the least of her problems, for she had learned to use the crutches and get herself from bed to chair to table and on and off the commode tucked behind a folding screen. Ned had told her that the lady did understand and speak English, yet every word Maggie said to her: questions, kind expressions, the stories of how she herself could barely move for months after Rory died, made no mark on the woman's lowered gaze and silences. Maggie had never seen her weep. *Well, you can't get wool from a goat, so they say.*

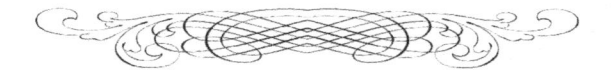

Mr. Lang patted his pockets, pulling out notes. "Summary," he said. "An exceptionally long list in an exceptionally long day." He read aloud his list of the day's matters which were completed or pending, ending with the Huber estate. "I met Mrs. Corcoran," he said, "she seems a resourceful woman. I asked her whether there was anything she needed to fulfill her duties, and she said: 'A cat who's a good mouser.'"

"Oh, yes," Ned said, with a slight smile matching Lang's. He wrote Mouser in his notes.

Lang went on: "Mrs. Corcoran asked if there was a man who was hired to survey the grounds, for one such fellow had come through the back fields past the dump, not a beggar nor a farmer, she said, but a decently dressed fellow on horseback. She said that she'd seen him at least twice, on Tuesday forenoon and three days ago before sunset, and that someone came with a lantern to the same place yesterday evening at dusk."

"That makes no sense," Ned said.

Lang opened one of the folded papers. "When I asked her to describe him, she handed me this sketch."

Ned took it, then said, "I don't recognize the man. Do you?"

"He does not resemble any of the creditors or neighbors that I have met, nor is he the surveyor that I generally hire," Lang replied, "She said the first time she went forward to tell him to come to us, but he rode away as she approached. The second time he kept his distance and rode off as she watched."

"I don't like the sound of that," Ned muttered.

"He may be a creditor," Lang continued, "they still have considerable time to file claims with the court. I trust that Judge Butler will approve the sale of the outbuilding contents within the next few weeks. Until it is time for the vendue, I am considering posting No Trespassing signs on the property."

"A capital idea," Ned replied after a moment.

Lang stared at him. "Since it appears your speculation is already well underway, tell me what you think."

"If you wish," Ned said with surprise, "First, if the man is a burglar, he is a stupid one. Any thief worth his salt would stay out of sight. If he was a scout for a partner, the same applies. Fortunately, the outbuildings are well secured now." He glanced at the sketch again. "Second, as the fellow is clearly not a youth, we may rule out visits intended to answer a dare, or start a prank."

Lang said: "I had not considered either of those as possibilities."

"I have no experience with burglary, but I do, I did, with youthful pranks," Ned answered, then continued: "Third, it's unlikely that he was a curious resident or neighbor; such a curiosity seeker may or may not make periodic visits, but not at night."

Lang added: "We have ruled out burglar, prankster, and set aside curious neighbor and creditor. Yes, I can see you have more. Proceed."

"Last, perhaps it is someone who held a grudge against Mr. Huber?" Ned threw in, trying to stifle his unease: the appearance of this man coincided with Maggie's arrival. He wondered if it was some outlaw associated with Harrigan.

"Mr. Huber evidently did not have many friends," Lang admitted. "I instructed her to keep the doors locked, and to allow on the property only those known to Mrs. Huber, such as the laundry women, meat deliveryman, as well as the appraiser and anyone who arrives in our company."

Ned deliberately put on a grumbly tone: "Good. But I hope this fellow does not frighten her off."

Lang shrugged: "Since Mrs. Huber and the disorder of the house have not yet frightened off Mrs. Corcoran, I doubt that a stranger who keeps his distance will do so."

Once in the bed that he had coveted during supper, Ned experienced no rest. Utilizing the principle of Occam's Razor: what would explain the facts with the fewest assumptions? Simply, that the stranger was no more than a rude or confused creditor, and his visits after Maggie's arrival mere coincidence. But why the night visit? He strove to remember the face in Maggie's sketch. Although he did not recognize it, he had a niggling sense that he had seen it before, here in Pocantic Mills, perhaps at the post office, or maybe during that short walk along the river early one morning or passing by in the busy streets.

Three times that stranger watched: two in the day, one in the night. As a knight moves in chess. He rolled onto his back, recalling a chess game between the judge and Katie just before the war began. When she put the judge's king in check, he had flipped the board angrily, spilling all of the pieces into his daughter's lap.

Outside the tavern, that's where I saw the man, he went in and out of the hotel tavern within minutes. Not to drink, maybe he was looking for someone. Ned scratched at the scars on his shoulder, then smoothed his nightshirt.

Not me, at any rate. I've no time for the tavern. Father's not here to scrutinize me, thank heaven. Even if he were, he'd see nothing amiss. Who was the stranger looking for? Did he think to find what he sought at the tavern, and at the Huber's? What's the connection? It couldn't be someone Maggie knew by sight; she would not have asked Lang about him. The man's acting like a Pinkerton's agent; albeit a sloppy one.

Wait, not sloppy, if the man expected to be seen, if the appearances at the Huber house were deliberate, to intimidate Mrs. Huber? Or Maggie? Ah, or me. Maggie's here now: likely Father heard it from Mother or Kate, so he is sure to be more suspicious—I ought to have predicted that. He wants to send me a warning, or he's hoping to hear a report of, of what, an assignation with Maggie?

By God, this is madness! What would folks say about the judge, a pillar of the community, if they found out that he had paid or pressured someone to spy on his own son? Outrage. Disgust. Or... nothing. Millville already knows his temper and grudges and tolerate them. My, my, he'd say, Edward's imagining all of this. I simply asked a friend to look in on him.

Oh, he likes this, he likes it too well—this reminder to me of his continuing power—an insulting slap in the face, yet rebuttable! There is no crime here, he'd say, no civil tort, no harm meant. And in each of those, save the last, he'd be correct.

Damn the man.

Chapter 63

Maggie looked at the letter from Lang's office, a copy of the state statutes regarding probate inventories in the clerk's neat handwriting. *A new key. Ned is a step ahead of me.* She frowned at the statutes. *Once I break the code, what will I write, what can I write, when I just want to talk to you, to someone? I'm lonesome; only a baby, a cat, and a mad woman for company.*

Mrs. Huber had got some starch back in her spine yesterday, insisting repeatedly that she must go upstairs. One crutch had clattered to the floor, as she almost fell. Maggie spent a good half an hour cajoling the woman to try going up one step at a time bottom-first, pushing with her arms and good leg. And so they had, half the way anyhow: Maggie carrying the crutches, watching Jim with one eye and the Mrs. with the other, as the boy climbed up and stepped or slid down happily.

"I miss you," Maggie whispered to Ned. *And all of them too: there's no Eleanor here, no Mrs. C., nor Mrs. Fariday to chat with, to watch the boy so's I have time even for a bath. Mother of Mercy, yes, in a nice warm spot, clean clothes right at hand, and time to put up my hair. Here, 'tis a race out of bed, wrap up in layers to stop the shivers, run down the stairs to stoke up the kitchen stove and fetch hot water for Mrs. Huber, all the while hoping Jimmy will stay in bed and out of mischief. And there ain't a single English book here to read, save a Farmer's Almanac. As if I even had time for that. And how long will I be wedged here?*

I wasted the day, there's barely half an hour left of daylight, Ned thought as he locked the office door. He was angry at himself for bumbling through most of the afternoon, making errors on his drafts, causing additional work for Mr. Thomas. *What a mistake, to break the code after dinner and read her letter. I was too eager.* No one was in his path, so he stopped. He took out the letter, sternly scolded his nerves, and read it again. It had the same effect upon re-reading: her cries of longing and confusion hurt him. Worse was her clear-eyed view—the paragraph that had occupied his thoughts half the day.

'*I know why you want to go to California. You believe you won't be free until you are so far away from him that he can't get to you. But if we think of the judge always and are afraid of what he can do, don't we carry him with us wherever we might go?*'

Will I never be free of the man and his constant scrutiny? he wondered. *Will he thwart me forever from having all that means the most to me?* He folded the letter. All of the words in all of the world's dictionaries could not have expressed the problems (the truth) more accurately than she had. Scenes unspooled in his imagination: happiness with her but a loss of his livelihood, living in boardinghouses as he travelled with a photograph gallery in a wagon, his wife rejected by the father, but welcomed by the mother and sisters, or rejected by all. *One may strategize intensively, and the battle still end in a costly defeat.* Like pictures in a zoetrope his thoughts moved as the circle spun, beginning and ending, only to repeat.

If the stranger is my father's scout, I must act soon, but attack or retreat? Does Fortune indeed favor the bold? He stuffed the letter into a pocket and trudged toward the boarding house.

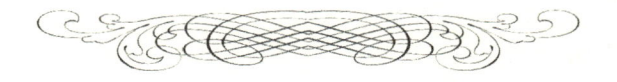

The snowfall had ended in a timely fashion, and Ned was glad to see the weather had not dampened the crowd's appetite for the vendue. About three dozen men and a woman or two threaded their way through the barn and sheds. He turned around abruptly as he recognized Miss Solomon, and nearly ran into a man.

"Pardon..." The man was the stranger in Maggie's sketch.

"Pardon me, sir," Ned said, "Say, you look familiar, I've met you before, I'd wager, but I've forgotten your name, Mr. ...?"

"I don't think so," the man said.

Forcing a smile, Ned said: "I'm sure I have. What is your name?"

The man hesitated, grimaced. "Smith," he said.

Weak answer, Ned thought. He waited for the man to ask his name in return, but it did not happen. *He knows my name.* "Are you here to buy for yourself, or on behalf of someone else?" he pressed, dropping all pretense.

"Just wanted to see what there is," the man mumbled.

"I'll wager you don't need much of a preview," Ned growled, and left the man behind.

Mr. Lang said, "I see your canteen and haversack are out. We've caught up on most matters. There's no need for you to work through your dinner hour."

"I wasn't hungry," Ned replied. Lang sat down. "That's the first time I've heard you say that."

Ned drained the canteen and stowed it away with the haversack. "I guess there's a first time for everything," he said, forcing a light tone, which fell flat. He rolled the pencil beneath his fingers, feeling Lang's gaze.

"We've had an uphill road in the past month," Lang remarked.

"A quick march," Ned agreed.

"Perhaps it's time for a rest," Lang went on, "At ease, I believe, is the military term."

"Or stand down," Ned added, thinking *I cannot.* He placed the pencil carefully in the center of his notebook, then folded his arms across his chest. *It's time to fish or cut bait.*

"I do have a question," he said.

"Proceed," Lang answered.

"Three questions, in fact. The first is material, quite so. And, and the others, reliant upon the first." Ned clamped his arms tighter.

"A hypothetical, if you please. If a fellow in your employment was contemplating marriage to a woman who was a domestic servant, and... not a Protestant, would that be considered a sufficient reason to let him go? In terms of damaging the reputation of the law firm."

"A pure hypothetical?" Lang said quietly, too much so for Ned's taste. The left side of his mouth began to leak, and he unclenched his arms and grabbed for a handkerchief. Before he could reply, Lang went on: "You're not considering leaving your employment here, I trust?"

"What? No," Ned said behind the handkerchief, "not at all, I should like to stay!"

"Ah," Lang said, "You gave me quite a turn." He steepled his fingers and stared at the bookshelf, then went on: "As to your hypothetical, this business of mine has survived a far greater scandal, as you know."

"But if the woman was Irish?" Ned blurted.

Lang paused again, then said: "That has no legal import, nor effect on my business, presuming the man and woman are of legal age and status to marry."

"Yes," Ned muttered, sagging in the chair. His audible sigh puffed the handkerchief slightly. He glanced at his employer but could not read his expression.

"May I ask you a hypothetical in return?" Lang said, and continued without Ned's assent. "Might the female in question be a resourceful young woman with whom the suitor has been acquainted for several years?"

Ned nodded, aware that the handkerchief did not cover his relief. He waited until Lang continued the game.

"And the gentleman has evidence to assume the proposed bride will accept his offer? If not, I would be able to testify that she has praised him to high heaven in my presence."

Ned felt the color rise in his face—a happy embarrassment. "I shall call upon you if needed," he said.

"Pray do so," Lang said, "I predict that your second and third reliant questions have mainly to do with When and How."

"Just so," Ned replied, "When. As soon as possible. Before the week is out."

"Ah," Lang said, then went on: "That is a short time in which to organize a wedding."

"I assure you that there is no... immoral or, or dishonorable reason to act quickly," Ned said.

"The thought never entered my mind," Lang responded.

"It's just that, we have both waited such a long time," Ned put in. Lang nodded at this. "You have readily answered When and perhaps How is none of my business."

"But it is in part," Ned responded. "Mrs. Huber is still dependent on someone to take care of her needs, and who the devil could we find on short notice to do that if Mrs. Corcoran was living elsewhere? Here is your How: I have searched for a nearby house in which to board, but there are none. If Mrs. Corcoran, ah, as my wife, and I were to room at Mrs. Huber's for a while, paying the estate a suitable amount for that, while covering our own board, would Judge Butler consider that a conflict of interest or an acceptable situation?"

"I believe he might consider that acceptable. I will inquire," Lang said.

"If Judge Butler approves, here is the final question. In the short term, Mrs. Corcoran, uh, my wife, would still be keeping house for Mrs. Huber. At present, she sends much of her current wage to Millville to support her mother. And I'm not currently able to take on that added expense. In summary, I should like Judge Butler to advise whether a continued wage to her, ah, of course through me, once we're married, might conflict with my duties as an administrator of the estate."

"Haven't you researched it, Mr. Whitfield?" Lang said, playing the game again.

"What do you think?" Ned scoffed.

"Very well, I will inquire. But you have missed an entry in the When column: I expect you'll need time to inform your family?"

"No," Ned said emphatically, "But I could use an afternoon off to get a marriage license."

Lang raised both eyebrows. "Isn't a proposal to your intended in order first?"

"Good point: two afternoons off," Ned agreed.

"Today is Thursday. Go now and I will not expect you back until Monday morning," Lang said.

"I…thank you. You don't know what this means to me," Ned said slowly.

"On Monday I shall expect to hear all pertinent details, as you see fit," Lang countered, "Go!"

Chapter 64

"Stand still, Jim, just another minute." Maggie held the wool garment up to her son's shoulders, but he squirmed away. "Nothing fits you," she said, "I wish we were home, I'd have use of Mrs. Fariday's sewing machine." As she pawed through the trunk to see if there was any other warm fabric of use, a flash of dark red velvet stopped her hand: the dress she had worn to Mrs. Fariday's birthday party. What a grand color!

Perhaps she'd wear it again – someday - it was fine enough for a wedding. *My garters, no, not for that! Married in red, you'll wish yourself dead, so they say. It may not be so, but I don't want to test it.* Feeling cross, she re-folded the red dress, and dug to the trunk's bottom. *Oh good, there's my blue frock that never saw a hoop skirt; I always liked that one.* She pulled it out. *I'll make it over.*

Jim followed the cat who had jumped into the washtub. "I had my bath last night," Maggie commented to her son, "Tonight you'll have your turn, dirty boy." The doorbell rang. Jim scooted out of the room and his mother ran after him and scooped him up. As always, Maggie peered out the side window to see if the visitor was friend or foe.

"Och, it's you," she said, and unlocked the door to let Ned in. "The front door? Who's with you?"

"No one, it's just me," Ned said. He was grinning.

"Are you up to mischief, or did you hear some good news?" she said. "Both," he answered, and took her hand, and Jim's and pulled them along the narrow path to the kitchen. He tossed his overcoat and scarf on a chair, and his hat on the table.

"Good day, Mrs. Huber, I have need of Mag... Mrs. Corcoran's help in the dining room; we shall be starting the inventory of the house soon, as I'm sure you'll be glad to hear. The dining room is first on our list. Would you mind watching the boy for a short time here in the kitchen?"

"You start soon?" Mrs. Huber said, "and then a sale here?"

"Yes, ma'am."

"I will watch him."

"I'm glad you'll be starting soon. How can I help?" Maggie said to him as they wove their way back to the dining room. Each squeezed separately through the door. Maggie saw a carved lion's head behind a heap of tin milk-pans and hill of rolled carpet and pointed it out to Ned.

He smiled. "Nothing surprises me here," he said, "and in answer to your question, you can help first by listening."

"Then so I will."

"Indulge me as I propose a hypothetical, as to religious beliefs," he said, "yes, humor me for a moment, I've been thinking a lot about the matter."

He took a deep breath. "I concede that here I grossly simplify: the Catholics say that Protestants will go to perdition. Protestants assert that Catholics are on the wrong path and headed to the same place. The Bible says that the Jews are God's chosen people, but no Christian will believe it. And how many of the members of those three religions presume that God factors out all the Hindoos, Muslims, pagans, et cetera—who are also his creations."

She squinted anxiously at him, as if she was threading a needle.

"You must think me very odd," he blurted.

She sighed. "Must I? I been acquainted with all sorts of queer types."

"Ah. A point in my favor!" he said with a nervous laugh and went on: "Greater minds than mine have pondered such matters, I have no answer; yet, since there is a sole Creator, I wonder if perhaps our lives are just a million channels cut into soil, all born from the same source and headed to the same sea." Maggie looked puzzled, but after a moment she nodded.

"Well, enough speculation," he said with a grimace: "to summarize: I would not bar anyone from seeking God in the way they believed was right, with their efforts fruitful for mankind. I do draw the line at human sacrifice and other particularly gruesome habits of worship." He laughed a little, then said: "Forgive me. I do not mean to border on the profane."

"You joke about the things that bother you most," Maggie said.

"Right on point," he replied, "Dulce est desipere in loco."

She smiled at him. "I don't know that Latin."

"It is sweet on occasion to play the fool," he said.

"Och," she said in response, "On occasion?"

"Now you sound like Katie," he said.

He pulled a small Bible from his pocket. *What next?* Maggie thought, *and not a word about the dining room?*

"*The kingdom of heaven,*" he read to her, "*is like unto a merchant man, seeking goodly pearls: who, when he had found one pearl of great price, went and sold all that he had, and bought it.*" Held rapt by the expression of his voice, Maggie did not guess his meaning, until he seized her hand and said: "Where your treasure is, there your heart lies also."

Astonished, joyful, she could not think straight or speak. Then the enormity of this choice kept her voice away: all that he had? How could she do that to him? She shook her head several times, staring past his shoulder. She finally said with her voice thinned to a whisper, "What if the pearl ain't worthy of a man *giving all he had* to have it?"

"But it is worthy, it would be, by definition," she heard him say with alarm.

"But if the harm to the other was dreadful…" She trembled with distress.

He dropped the Bible and took hold of her hand. "Maggie, the harm is in not having you with me, all of the time. The rest is dross."

She closed her eyes tightly, overcome, and tear-blind. When she got her breath back, she gasped, "thank you!" then wiped her eyes and nose on her sleeve. As she had expected, he produced a clean handkerchief and gave it to her.

"'tisn't blarney!" she said, giggling and sniffling.

"Nor tomfoolery! Nor malarkey," he said, with relief. She blew her nose. "Say what you'd like to say then: it don't have to be just the right words."

"Will you…" he began.

"Yes!" she said.

He pulled her into a tight embrace, then lifted her off her feet. "I don't want to let you go," he said in her ear, sneaking in kisses between breaths.

"Don't ever!" she said.

"But we must go now," he went on.

She was bewildered. "Go where?"

"To the Catholic church," he answered, smiling.

"NOW?" Maggie said, "This minute?"

"In an hour," he said, "when I've been hanging fire for so long, now is the time."

"But the priest won't do it without notice," she stammered.

"He has already grilled me no end. We have an appointment with him, an hour from now," he replied, "I hoped you'd say yes."

"What?" Maggie squeaked, grabbing his jacket lapels and almost shouting in his face. "Now? Right now? I've nothing to wear! What about Jim?"

He cleared his throat, re-adjusted his eye patch and fumbled in his pocket. "Don't you want to see your new ring first? If you don't like it, we'll exchange it for another. Jim will come with us. I have a plan."

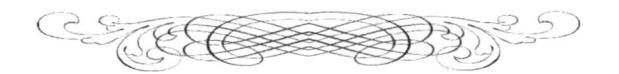

Maggie had been nervous and uncertain at the clerk's office, and her hand had quivered while signing the marriage license. Ned was proud of her now, and glad that her awe of the priest (or the occasion?) had lessened and that her shivers had ceased. He took her hand, and leaned against her, as Father Moriarty laid out documents, ready to begin the ceremony in the rectory's office.

I've no flowers to hold, Maggie thought. *Rory's hands were damp when we married, though Ned's are not.* She watched as he looked intently at the document on the table, all in Latin, his eye scanning the page, as the priest read from it. She squeezed his hand and smiled at him. After all the Latin, all the official and particular words, the counseling from the priest, the signing of this and that, Ned shook a little as he slipped the ring onto her finger. It only fit her pinky, but she wanted no other, as she had affirmed to him in the Hubers' dining room. *Such a shy kiss,* she thought, as the ceremony finally ended.

"Factum est," her Ned said, as if it was a delicious jest, grinning at her, the priest, and the rectory housekeeper who had kept Jim plied with crackers and milk.

The rest of his plan unfolded, as he had told her it would: a stop at the general store for the makings of some sort of wedding supper, a stop at a bakery for a small wedding cake, a stop at the post office, and to send a telegram. "Mrs. C and I married," Ned enunciated slowly to the telegraph operator, "Keep Mother safe. Letter to follow." The operator repeated the message and the Faridays' address.

"Correct. Thank you," Ned said as he paid.

"She'll be all right, your mother, she'll be all right, surely?" Maggie said as they left the telegraph office.

"I... believe she will. That is my sincere hope," he replied, unhappy for the first time that day.

"Mother of God, I hope they don't hate me!" she said.

"They won't," he said, striving for calm, "Mother won't, she's not that sort. Elly won't, she loves you. Katie will take some time to get used to it, then she'll come around, I expect. So, put it out of your mind."

"I wish Elly was here today," Maggie said longingly. Jim had been quiet most of the day, but now crumbled into a whine. He pushed against Ned's arms and reached out for his mother. Ned handed him over and said: "He's tuckered out."

"It's time to go home," Maggie said, taking the boy and hugging him.

"Such as it is," Ned put in sarcastically, "I assure you that we'll find better lodging as soon as we can."

Maggie shrugged. "Home is being with you."

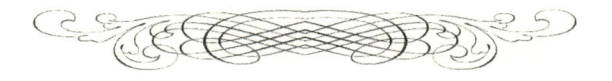

"Is that the last on your list?" Maggie asked as she laid down the sheets and coverlet on the two single beds they had pushed together in the sparse back chamber.

He stared at the tintype of a soldier which was placed on the mantel, then turned to her. "Supper, Jim's had his bath and is asleep, and we've got a bed. There's only two more to go," he said.

"Ain't you tired?" she asked as she shook out an old quilt. They both sneezed.

He wiped his nose and replied: "That's last on the list."

Maggie poked the bolsters. "There's only one that has any stuffing left."

"I don't care," he said, flopping across the joined beds. He seized her and pulled her down beside him. *This is what I must remember,* she thought, as her husband squirmed his head in next to her shoulder and tucked his body comfortably against hers, with a sigh of satisfaction.

"You're like a puppy," she said.

"Ah, shall I lick your face?" he got up on one elbow.

"No!" Maggie covered her face with her hands, giggling.

"Very well, later then," he said.

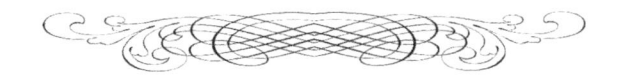

Warm and aroused from his bath, Ned watched Maggie take the pins from her hair, ready to braid it. "Leave it down," he said. "Come over here and sit on my lap." She obeyed him. He stroked her through the nightgown, so happy that the corset and layers of clothing were gone. He looked at her bare feet, and smiled, perversely glad that they were ugly, nearly as ugly as his own. Finding this small flaw made him even more confident in pursuing the evening's pleasant goal.

Maggie enjoyed the kissing and the stroking. She relaxed for a moment, then remembered what would happen later, for she could feel his excitement growing. He broke off a kiss: "Are you cold? You're shivering." His hands paused. "Am I hurting you?"

Not yet, Maggie thought. She giggled nervously. "What a thing to say. It's some different, than before, that's all."

"What do you mean?"

"It was all so fast, and, and I'd had a drop to drink, and he too... and you're not drunk."

"I expect you wouldn't want me to be, and I don't want to be," he said, displeased.

"No! Mercy. No indeed."

"Is something wrong?"

Maggie sighed. When he chose to pay attention, that

attention was acute. "Nothing," she answered. His hands tightened slightly on her shoulders. She could almost feel him thinking. The worry grew in her.

"That is patently untrue."

The hurt in his voice launched her into apology: "I'm sorry. It's nothing. Truly. I'm just tired, and it's been such a long day, and... oh, so many things like that." He contemplated this. "Truly," Maggie said in agitation: a mistake.

"I see." He removed his hands from her shoulders. "You seem... fretty tonight. I should like to know why?"

He'll stay, Maggie told herself, *he'll listen, surely. Even to the truth?* "I'm afraid," she said.

"Of what?" Maggie didn't know how to answer. "Surely not of me?" He sounded astonished.

"No. Not of you. Mother of God, never of you." She hugged him tightly. "Of," she adjusted the collar of his nightshirt, stroked the soft hair at the back of his head. "Of... of... it."

"Oh." That stopped him for only a moment. "Maggie, that makes no sense. I am aware that young ladies who have never been married might approach their wedding night with some... trepidation, I would suppose. But you've been married."

"I know, I know," she said.

"And the culprit that was tenting my night shirt earlier has beat a retreat, for the time being. So, there is no need for you to be afraid of that now. There is no need for you to be afraid of me, ever. Good Lord! I would never hurt you."

"I know. I do believe that. I do. I'm sorry to be so weak. I'll be fine, first-rate, as you say. I love you."

"There's nothing to be afraid of. Not after the first time, and that's behind you now," he said.

Maggie didn't trust her voice. She simply nodded her head where it pressed close to his shoulder. He was silent. *Don't think about it,* Maggie commanded him internally.

"He was drunk?"

Maggie did not answer.

"Did he hurt you?" Ned asked. His voice was cool and distant.

Maggie stiffened. Finally, she murmured. "It can happen." Because she did not like the sound of his silence, she murmured on: "But I'll be fine. I'll get used to it every night again. I know I will.

And I like all the rest, you know I do."

"Every night," he said it quietly.

"I know that is how 'tis, I do indeed," Maggie said in a like tone. "I don't mind. It's just getting used to it again."

"When you were expecting your child? When you had your... monthly flow?" he said in disbelief.

Maggie remembered her faltering questions to Bridey on the same topic, and Bridget's mortified, cryptic comment: don't be giving Mr. Dooley any ideas. Like a child, not knowing what else to do now, Maggie told the truth by nodding her head. It was all in his hands: she felt better having passed the burden to another.

"It will be... grand with you, because not being drunk and all, I know you don't mean to hurt me," she said. She still wanted to believe that Rory had not deliberately hurt her. "I trust you with my life," she said, "You gave me my life, on the hill, surely, and when you loved me, you gave me my life again. I'm a little fool, like a child with a fright."

His crushing embrace surprised her, and so did the whirlwind of kisses he swept upon her head, her brow, her cheek. His breathing was rough. *Well, sometimes the desire takes a man fast...*she was ready now. "If he wasn't already dead, I'd kill him," he whispered in a terrible voice.

"*Now* you're frightening me. Let it go," she begged.

He uttered a sound like the thrash of branches on a windy night, then placed her on her feet, and strode to the window, cursing under his breath.

"Whissht, you'll wake Jim." She went to him and placed her fingers on his mouth. "No. 'Twill do no good to think of it, it's over and done."

He moved her fingers aside, cursed several times, quietly but succinctly.

Hysterical laughter bubbled out of her. "Such a lot of Army words!" She heard his deep breath, then a grumbling sound. "Now you've said your piece," she went on, "so let it be. 'tisn't the time now to think of anyone but us."

"However..." he began.

She snickered suddenly and crowed: "I ain't ever known such a fellow as you!"

He welcomed the laughter that overtook him, as he felt the universe shifting back to its proper course. He towed his wife to the armchair and sat down. "Come and sit with me. Then we'll be off to bed, the two of us, to sleep, perchance to dream."

She sat on his lap and hugged him, talking of little of consequence, telling him how glad she was and hearing him answer the same, stroking his hair and he stroking hers.

"Another pretty calf has escaped its mistress." He caressed her bare leg.

"I was dreaming that day, that day you said first said that. I used to dream..." she stopped.

"What? The truth now, that's what you always direct me to do," he responded.

"I used to dream that you were Irish."

He blinked. "Good heaven. Guess I should be flattered?"

"And that you were my own dear Eddy McWhitt," she continued, hiding a laugh behind her hand.

"Tarnation! I don't begrudge you the dream, not a bit, but the name! Why would you want to saddle me with such an opprobrious moniker. That means..."

"Och, I know what it means! I can tell from all the words around it," Maggie said.

"The context," Ned put in.

"...indeed, that you don't care for my pet name, more's the pity," she continued.

"Context is most important," Ned said, and kissed her. "And what did I do when I was your Irishman?"

"Just what you're doing now," Maggie replied.

"I see, a happy fellow under either name," he said, kissing her again, more intently, then broke it off to gauge her reaction. She made no protest.

He said: "I had a dream too, after I lost you, that you had come back and were my wife. But I didn't know it was you at first, you know how queer dreams can be. I was looking through a cloudy glass into a darkened room, a lamp was on the dresser in front of a beautiful lady. She was wearing only the skin she was born in, all glowing, and she was brushing her long dark hair. I wanted so much to touch her. She turned her head to see who had come. The lady was you."

Maggie was hypnotized. "What did you do?" she breathed. She could feel a hard throb in his lap under her thigh. The culprit had returned, but she was more intrigued than fearful.

"Stand up, I'll show you," he said. She did and he guided her to the bedpost and positioned her hands upon it a little higher than her head.

He stood behind her. "I came nearer. She turned so I could see half of her, part of her bosom in silhouette. I didn't want to frighten her, so I whispered that her love was here. I put my hands on her," he did so, one on Maggie's hip and the other moving her hair aside with gentle fingers. He kissed her neck in just the way that had undone her so long ago, creating that wonderful lassitude and warm urgency that made her fingers run out of control then to unfasten the hooks on her bodice and the strings on her stays. She relaxed into him, and he pressed against her in response. The culprit had definitely rejoined the fray.

"And then what," she whispered. She could almost feel his smile in the dark.

"And then..." a soft bass rumble of laugher near her ear. He crushed her nightgown in both hands and inched it up and slid his hands beneath it, caressing her bare flank, cupping one of her buttocks. She felt the same jolly and sickening swoop of her stomach as when her father tossed her in the air, and the fall before he caught her as she squealed in delight. It was a lovely dizzy teetering now; still with an edge of indecision. Ned had not hurt her then in the hayloft. His worst injury was his leaving and now that was mended. His mouth had stilled but his hands were busy: one lingered at the top of her thigh. *Oh my yes,* she thought.

"Then?" she said. He moved his other hand up to her breast, creating havoc within her with what it did there. The culprit pressed hard against her buttocks but did not insist upon its rights. And the culprit's owner, (if no longer its master), moaned her name.

"What then?" she said.

He lifted his lips from the curve of her neck where they had been doing delicious things. It took him a moment to find voice. "I woke up," he said, a remarkable sound of humor and lust.

"Och, no!" Maggie said, turning her body within his embrace. "I'm here," she said. She put her arms around him and opened her mouth to his.

Epilogue, Millville

Ah, another evening of play-acting done. I ought to be used to the dreary chitter-chatter. Tonight, there seemed to be little that Daniel might benefit from, though I spoke with Representative Dowling for at least ten minutes. It was pleasant speaking with Senator Purnell and Mrs. Purnell, who are newly married. She kept her hand on his arm the entire time and he smiled at her often as if he couldn't help himself. Then Daniel came to horn in and as we were taking our leave, he put his hand on my back, perhaps to impress the lovebirds. I drew away and shuddered, I could not help it. He dropped his hand, and I made a silly excuse about being chilled and tired. I cannot bear his touch, there are too many vile memories that rise up in an instant on their own accord!

I received a letter from Katie asking us BOTH to come on Thursday evening "to share some news." I pray that she is not pregnant. Drat, I hear him on the stairs.

She tore the page out and thrust it into the stove.

Epilogue, New York City

He took off his forage cap and scratched at his head, his chest, the crotch of his trousers. "Fecking bugs," he muttered. He did not often speak with the old accent, especially when asking for a penny from a gent; but there was here no man to beg from, so why not speak as you please? This cellar corner was neither damp nor cold; perhaps there'd be a tap to drink from nearby. Sunday morning it must be, for someone had fed the furnace and had it roaring high to warm the churchgoers soon to gather above.

He rubbed his stiff hands, then gathered some soft char from beneath the coal. He filled his palm with it, dipped his fingers and drew a picture on the wall: not of the things he most desired (bread, meat, beer), but of a cross filigreed with thorns.

The End

About the Author

Rocelia Kinsman, formerly a historical society assistant curator, paralegal, and archivist in New England, now lives in upstate New York where she enjoys writing, hiking, music of all kinds, volunteering for non-profit organizations and being a book nerd. **A Turning** is her first novel, inspired by her story-telling family. Its creation over several years has been a joyful experience and has sustained her during hard times. She looks forward to publishing her next novels in the series, ***Unexpected Journeys.***

Dedicated to my beloved storytellers:
Don, Milt, Jeanne, Harry, and my dear brothers.

Special thanks go to Jetty, who fostered my writing
and wouldn't let me quit; and to authors Esmerelda
Little Flame and Sadie Blackburn who made the way
forward a clear path - not the labyrinth I'd feared.

And last, but certainly not least, the Connecticut Historical Society
and the Connecticut State Library, for sharing their marvelous
collections and archives during my years of research.

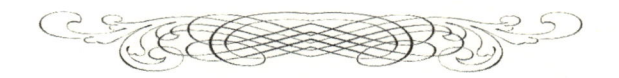

Made in United States
North Haven, CT
13 July 2023